I0762106

Black Leather and Blue Denim

A '50s Novel

By

Jay Dubya

Black Leather and Blue Denim
A ‘50s Novel

By
Jay Dubya

Published by
Bookstand Publishing
Pasadena, CA 91101
1556_21

ISBN 978-1-58909-131-3

For all those who like or love the 1950s

But especially for all those who had actually lived them.

Other Books by Jay Dubya

Adult Fiction

The Great Teen Fruit War, A 1960 Novel
Frat' Brats, A '60s Novel
Ron Coyote, Man of La Mangia
Pieces of Eight
Pieces of Eight, Part II
Pieces of Eight, Part III
Pieces of Eight, Part IV
The Wholly Book of Genesis
The Wholly Book of Exodus
The Wholly Book of Doo-Doo-Rot-on-Me
Thirteen Sick Tasteless Classics
Thirteen Sick Tasteless Classics, Part II
Thirteen Sick Tasteless Classics, Part III
Thirteen Sick Tasteless Classics, Part IV
Thirteen Sick Tasteless Classics, Part V
So Ya' Wanna' Be A Teacher!
Mauled Maimed Mangled Mutilated Mythology
Fractured Frazzled Folk Fables & Fairy Farces
FFFF & FF, Part II
Nine New Novellas
Nine New Novellas, Part II
Nine New Novellas, Part III
Nine New Novellas, Part IV
One Baker's Dozen
Two Baker's Dozen
RAM: Random Articles and Manuscripts
Time Travel Tales
Modern Mythology
UFO: Utterly Fantastic Occurrences
Prime-Time Crime Time
Snake Eyes and Boxcars
Snake Eyes and Boxcars, Part II
The Psychic Dimension
The Psychic Dimension, Part II
Shakespeare: Slammed, Smeared, Savaged and Slaughtered
Shakespeare: S, S, S & S, Part II
First Person Stories
The Arcane Arcade

Thirteen Tantalizing Tales
PLOTS
PLOTS, Part II
THEMES
Hawthorne: Hacked, Shakespeare: Sacked, & Thurber: Thwacked
Hawthorne: Hazed, Hooked, Hammered and Hijacked
Suite 16
The FBI Inspector
Poe: Pelted, Pounded, Pummeled and Pulverized
Twain: Tattered, Trounced, Tortured and Traumatized
London: Lashed, Lacerated, Lampooned and Lambasted
O. Henry: Obscenely and Outrageously Obliterated
Homer's Odd Sea Odyssey
HOMER'S ILL ILIAD
Homer's Ill Iliad and Odd Sea Odyssey
The Timeless Time Machine
War of the Worlds
The Invisible Man
Parody Paradise
Parody Paradise, Part II
Parody Paradise, Part III
Parody Paradise, Part IV
A Christmas Carol
Bee 17, Short Stories
Bee 17, Part II, Short Stories
Bee 17, Part III, Short Stories
Bee 17, Part IV, Short Stories
Bee 17, Part V, Short Stories
Bee 17, Part VI, Short Stories

Young Adult Fantasy Novels and Stories

Pot of Gold
Enchanta
Space Bugs, Earth Invasion
The Eighteen Story Gingerbread House

Contents

Preface

Black Leather and Blue Denim, A '50s Novel is a work of pure fiction. If any story character or characters resemble any real person or people on planet Earth, dead, alive, unborn, or reincarnated, then that similarity is strictly coincidental.

The author remembers living at 50 Daffodil Lane in the Dogwood Hollow section of Levittown, Pennsylvania between 1954-'59. The author admits suffering from severe fugues of amnesia and from perpetual hallucinations. He often has difficulty distinguishing reality from fantasy. Sometimes, the writer thinks that fiction is fact, and also that fact is fiction, so this makes him no different than the average American who watches television, or who reads the daily newspapers. The writer has always enjoyed escapism, preferring that phenomenon to the monotonous rigors of everyday life, and this, he believes, is his vital link to the remainder of his species.

Black Leather and Blue Denim, A '50s Novel is the sister book of *The Great Teen Fruit War, A 1960 Novel.* In the *Fruit War* novel, J.W.'s family moves from Levittown back to Hammonton, NJ, an agricultural community famous for its blueberry and peach crops. The high school senior becomes a member of the Reds, a gang of peach farmers' sons that have continual conflict with the Blues, the sons of wealthy blueberry growers.

Frat' Brats', A '60s Novel completes the "coming of age" trilogy. In *Frat' Brats* J.W. attends a South Jersey teachers' college and joins a non-sanctioned, off-campus fraternity, Lambda Phi Sigma, which has ongoing conflict with two rival fraternities that have the support of the college deans.

Chapter 1
"Forty-one Years Later"

It seems like it all never happened, but over forty-one-years-ago, it did. I had moved from Levittown, Pennsylvania to Hammonton, New Jersey on December 29, 1959. My greaser gang's brain trust had had our farewell meeting the night before, inside our Levittown hangout, the Feed Bag.

On July 1, 2000, over four-decades later, I found myself heading north on New Jersey *Route 206* to honor a rendezvous *we* six gang members had arranged on December 28, 1959. As I proceeded past peach orchards and blueberry fields on opposite sides of the two-lane highway, I wondered what had happened to Quinn, to Bo Jalonec, to Carnie, to Robbie Wilkinson, and to that rotten, vitriolic skunk, Tinker.

As for myself, financially I had done very well in the four-decade span between the Golden Age of Rock & Roll and the Madonna and Rap eras. I own a nice house; have three intelligent sons; drive a new car, and have a wonderful Italian wife. I am content with my station in life, but I was completely happy growing-up in a time when I had little money and no "wheels". I lived most of the '50s in a very average home at 50 Daffodil Lane with my parents and younger sister and brother. Back then, I had few serious responsibilities. I also had the great companionship of my loyal Levittown friends to protect me from the Ks and the Rs, the area's most ruthless greaser gangs.

Forty-one-years-later, I sincerely hoped that my former Levittown pals had done as well, if not better, than I had. Come to think of it, the reunion idea was actually mine. At least, *that* conclusion was what the other five members of my gang's executive committee thought.

Well, maybe not Bo Jalonec, who had always understood me as if I was an elementary school reading textbook. Jokes perceived my every motivation and my every flaw. Quinn, our gang leader, had delegated me "official thinker" for the group, and only Bo Jalonec knew that almost every idea I claimed to be original had been stolen from some literature plot I had read in school. My personality was really a collection of themes from William Shakespeare, Sir Arthur Conan Doyle, Jack London, O. Henry, H.G. Wells, Alexandre Dumas, Washington Irving, Edgar Allan Poe, Mark Twain, Nathaniel Hawthorne, and other great authors.

This is how the reunion idea developed on the evening of December 28, 1959. In high school, I had read an O. Henry surprise-ending story about two friends that lived in New York City. One pal was going out west to seek his fortune, while his good buddy wanted to remain in Manhattan. In *their* favorite restaurant, the men agreed to meet in that very same place exactly twenty-years later.

I ingeniously proposed to my five gang members that we six should meet again several decades in the future. Then, we could compare how our lives had changed since December of '59. Like the men in the O. Henry story, *we* would celebrate our nostalgic reunion in a restaurant, our favorite restaurant, the Feed Bag.

"Damn it J.W. That was a great idea," Carnie concluded and expressed. My buddy had always been borderline neurotic. "Ya' sure have the brains to come-up with some real gems."

"Let's make it twice as long," Bo Jalonec suggested. "Instead of twenty-years, let's make it forty."

"Twice as long is too easy!" Carnie objected, exhibiting my alter-ego's contrary nature.

But then Quinn showed his leadership by taking command of the contentious discussion. "Okay, then, J.W. How old are you?"

"I'll be seventeen," I proudly replied with fake maturity.

"And J.W.," Quinn continued, "how many guys are sitting at this table?"

"Six," I firmly answered.

"I mean without me and you," Quinn clarified.

"Four," I determined.

"Great," Quinn declared. "Twenty-years plus seventeen-years plus four-years adds up to forty-one. We'll meet again right here in the Feed Bag at seven p.m. on December 28, 2000."

"Yeah, that ought to make it all the more challengin'," replied Carnie, who was trying to conceal his dissatisfaction at being overruled and outsmarted by Quinn. Carnie had always reminded me of Mark Twain's Tom Sawyer. The guy only enjoyed matters when situations were more complicated than they really had to be.

The six of us knew quite well that most reunions occurred after only five or ten years of separation, as opposed to a ridiculous number like forty-one years.

Forty-one years was nearly half a century. A lot of unexpected factors could worm their way into Quinn's bizarre mathematical equation. "But what if the Feed Bag is no longer here forty-one years from now?" Tinker interrupted. "What if it burns-down, or is destroyed by lightning? What if it is washed away in a flood if the *Delaware* overflows its banks?"

Quinn was ready with a good explanation. Our leader had a post office box, number 2000 in Bristol, a neighboring community. Prepared for any problem, Quinn then distributed five keys to Box 2000. Bo Jalonec had found the time to illegally duplicate the five forgeries in the back room at Harley's Hardware, his former place of occasional employment.

Quinn then made us promise to write him at Box 2000 if any of us would have a future change of address. "If the Bristol Post Office should ever change locks on my mailbox, I'll have new keys made-up and sent to you," Quinn promised us. "If any of ya' have a change in address, write me at Box 2000. My final instructions will be placed in it. If the Feed Bag no longer exists, then check out Box 2000 on July 1, 2000 for further instructions. I see no problem. Everything's gonna' be cool, ya' dig?"

That commentary was one of the longest speeches I had ever heard Quinn make. Normally, our gang leader was a shy, laconic greaser. Public speaking was out of character for him. But when he had something to say, it was said, and each of us heeded the gravity of his words. Our Diablos' leader commanded respect and authority, qualities the rest of us were still attempting to refine.

As I drove north on *206,* My brain was still in shock from the relationship between Bristol Post Office Box 2000 and the scheduled reunion of December 28, 2000, but I lacked the courage to challenge Quinn on that strange coincidence. Any statement *he* ever made I had always regarded as a prime directive. As far as I was concerned, the year' 2000 seemed like a distant fantasy time zone belonging to Flash Gordon and Buck Rogers. Y2K was then a crazy millennium removed from the all too real '50s greaser era.

I had changed addresses five-times in the last forty-one years, and obediently, I had forwarded each new one to Quinn's Bristol Post Office Box.

"Sounds bitchin' to me," Tinker injected. The poor excuse for a human being almost enjoyed cursing as much as the pugnacious punk liked fighting and destroying an enemy's property.

"My *sediments* exactly," echoed Jokes Jalonec, who had an unquenchable fancy for toying with language, making play on words and puns at every opportunity.

And that's how it all began; the proposed Feed Bag meeting of December 28, 2000; my automobile odyssey of July 1, 2000, and my duplicate of Quinn's Postal Key, Number 2000, still attached to my ignition key chain. Either the Feed Bag, or the key, held the clues to a number of questions that had been fostered by over four-decades of separation. Were we all still alive?

On July 1, 2000, I journeyed north to honor my reunion commitment. As I passed by Atsion Lake on New Jersey *Route 206,* I clicked on the radio dial to Philadelphia's *WOGL-FM* to listen to some "golden oldies". I figured the music would set the mood for my trip, which was actually a nostalgic mental journey back into the glory of my youth.

I mechanically nodded my head to the rhythm of "Forty Miles of Bad Road" played by Duane Eddy's guitar. Ironically, forty-miles was the exact distance between Hammonton and Levittown. I had often selected that tune for Quinn on the Feed Bag jukebox way back in the '50s. Our Diablo commander had a definite preference for lively instrumental numbers. The unique guitar fret made my mind flash-back to my teenage years, when I had lived on the other side of the *Delaware River* in Pennsylvania.

I recalled that I never intended to have enemies in Levittown, but certain individuals made it their passion to target me as a personal adversary. That fact complicated my life, and *their* lives, and by 1959, eventually had made all of us virtual mental cases. Many people in Levittown really resented me. To be honest, I don't believe I ever detested or loathed anyone there, but instinctively, a small cluster despised my existence and my guts.

Sal Palermo was paranoid about me having any romantic relationship with his Italian princess daughter, Angie. Bubbles Messina (Angie's cousin) hated my immaturity and my silliness, and Popeye Messina (Bubbles' brother) had a crusade against any kid who was not a member of his greaser car gang, the Kenwood Kamikazes. And then there was Father Malcolm, the rigid disciplinarian at Cardinal Reagan High School, who happened to favor brainy eggheads and brawny jocks over punk greasers.

Salvatore Palermo was my neighbor who lived at 66 Daffodil Lane in the Dogwood Hollow section of Levittown. Sal Palermo believed that I was hot to trot for his daughter, Angela. Several times, Mr. Palermo threatened to make me a "soprano in the world-famous Castrati Boys Choir". The Mafia boss's disdain for me started in the mid-fifties. Palermo verbally crucified me whenever our paths crossed.

"But Mr. Palermo, I'm really a nice kid once you get to know me," I said, right after my folks and I had moved into our new Levittown home in the early spring of '54. "I come from a decent family, and I get good grades in school. All I'm doing is walkin' by your house."

Suspicious Sal Palermo became very belligerent and thought that his antagonism would intimidate me. "Listen carefully, you delinquent punk. If ya' once lay a fingernail on my daughter, I'm gonna' get a stick of dynamite, shove it up your ass; light it, and watch you explode into a million pieces!"

Ever since Salvatore Palermo made that prediction, I had scads of nightmares where I would dream that a fuse was sizzling up my hindquarters, and I would then wake-up in a sweat before I was blown to smithereens. My father thought Sal Palermo was an underground criminal figure. Dad often warned me to stay away from "the Mafia", but I swore to myself that I would not be bullied by any lunatic adult Sicilian. I knew that Angie's nutcase father was very emotional and demonstrative, but what alarmed me most was that Palermo talked and behaved in a more hostile demeanor than Tinker did, the craziest of my teen friends. And I knew that Dante Messina, Sal's brother-in-law, and Messina's son, Popeye, possessed very similar dysfunctional, volatile temperaments.

Popeye's sister Bubbles Messina was a knockout. I would see her around from time to time in public places. From 1956 to '59, I observed her breasts grow progressively larger as the sultry chick advanced through the various stages of puberty. Even when I was sixteen, I still viewed The *Mickey Mouse Club* hosted by Jimmie Dodd on TV, and sure enough, Annette and Doreen, two of the *Mouseketeers,* like Bubbles, started to sprout cleavage.

But Bubbles never stopped! The doll developed torpedoes that rivaled those of centerfolds Jayne Mansfield and Marilyn Monroe. And Bubbles, who always shuddered when I called her *that* nickname, had breasts that weren't just huge; they were solid and hard, and her chest projected-outward as if it contained a pair of female erections.

One night at a Bristol, Pennsylvania record hop, Bubbles lost her patience with me. The hot babe saw me staring at her bosom, so she walked over. Naturally, I thought she was going to ask me to dance, but instead, she snarled several malicious comments in my direction.

"Why don't ya' go lick a pound of dry ice!"

"Would ya' mind repeating that?" I requested in total amazement, for honestly, I desired to prolong the exchange of small talk with the luscious babe.

"I said why don't ya' go lick a pound of dry ice, and after enjoyin' that, I'll make ya' thread your pickle through the metal rings of a *Slinky,"* Bubbles clarified. "Then, I'll have the pleasure of squeezing the *Slinky* so tight that you'll think your dingle was caught in an automatic vegetable dicer!"

After Bubbles' caustic testimony, I had severe nightmares of meat grinders, sink garbage disposals, and electric potato peelers ravaging my sensitive rooster. But Bubbles and her cousin Angie Palermo both appealed to me. The Sicilian girls had good looks, hot bodies, and quite frankly, their wild tempers were exciting departures from the standard female politeness that other girls exhibited. The two Italian dolls were more like male greasers in the "tuff" way they talked and acted. Their harsh language fascinated the heck out of me, mostly because Dad and Mom rarely screamed at other family members at home, and I was seldom exposed to wild fits of rage. The girls' outrageous language appealed to the primitive instincts of my youthful soul.

Just as the *Garden of Eden* apple tree must have enticed Adam, I found Bubbles and Angie alluring. The swarthy-skinned beauties were irresistible forbidden fruit, and their fascinating temptation I found too powerful to ignore.

Besides my major '50s Levittown foes, I had a few minor ones, too, like Spits, Worm, Stanley Tezeeker, Cummings, and Brother Timothy. Spits and Worm moved into the Kenwood section of Levittown, and the thugs soon became friends with Bruno "Popeye" Messina. The pair quickly joined Cummings's ruthless greaser gang, the Kamikazes.

Stanley Tezeeker was an egghead, a genuine '50s nerd. The walking encyclopedia possessed a peculiar squeaky voice, wore thick-rimmed eyeglasses, and had tooth-pick arms and legs. Stanley was a goody-goody-two-shoes, who often wore red and black, or green and yellow diamond-designed argyle socks with matching sweaters. I fixed his wagon on several occasions for squealing on me about the eighth-grade "inkwell incident", when I deliberately ruined his immaculate white shirt.

Of all my minor enemies, I feared Cummings the most. The brute looked and was vicious. The future criminal was over twenty-years-old, had tattoos and scars, and flexed biceps the size of pumpkins. Cummings was a definite enemy; a cruel redneck; a vile racist, and a vindictive greaser. The other redneck Kamikazes usually imitated his offensive, anti-social behavior.

Brother Timothy was Father Malcolm's understudy at Cardinal Reagan High. The academic assistant sometimes helped Malcolm when the disciplinarian's log of recalcitrant students became overbooked. Brother Timothy, who Carnie and I called "Tiny Tim", thought *he* was as tough as nails, but *we* believed he was as weak as pinky fingernails. After catching me trying to touch the tip of my nose with my tongue in study hall, Brother Timothy criticized my endeavor. The religious zealot emphatically stated to the class, "J.W.'s cerebellum is smarter than his cerebrum." Brother Timothy then gave me one of his patented "lobotomies", where the Franciscan would yank a kid's earlobes until they nearly separated from the victim's skull tissue. The entire fourth-floor study hall at Cardinal Reagan High School burst-out in a roar. I sullenly sat there and suffered through the very painful physical and public embarrassment.

I promised myself I would never be subjected to such public humiliation again. Carnie sympathized with my plight, and we made a pact that we would rise above the school's unjust discipline system, frustrate its enforcers, and avoid future punishments at all costs. We vowed to become so furtive, so stealthy, so clandestine, and so surreptitious in all our misdemeanors that Father Malcolm, Brother Timothy, Sal Palermo, Popeye Messina, Cummings, and the police would never get Carnie or me in trouble with adult authority again.

As my July 1st, year 2,000 mind resurrected '50s memories, I believed that my antagonists' animosity had made me stronger, more daring, more cunning, and more devious than my adversaries ever imagined I could be. I had learned to counter their enmity with military precision. I soon mastered retaliation with deftness and slyness. I began to cherish their general repugnance. And when 1959 came to a close, I basked in the knowledge that my greaser gang' friends and I had become some of the slyest, most surreptitious, most clever teens in the Eastern United States.

The reality of my July 1, 2000 driving excursion to Levittown again sentimentally focused my mind as the car radio played "You Send Me" by Sam Cooke. That melodic tune reminded me of the mailbox key for compartment 2000 at the Bristol Post Office, that had been jangling against my other keys, which were hanging next to my red Buick *Park Avenue's* ignition.

'I'll bet Bo Jalonec had put Quinn up to the 2000 reunion idea,' I mused. 'Only Jokes could have been clever enough to connect the 2000 Post Office Box with the 2000 reunion scheme.' I then recollected the setting for most of my teenage years.

The '50s Levittown gangs weren't street smart; we were lane smart and drive smart. The place wasn't really a town, but rather a small city divided into various sections, with eventually about seventeen-thousand spanking new houses, and upon completion, a population of around sixty-thousand newly transplanted people.

Levittown, Pennsylvania was modeled after Levittown, New York on Long Island, which had preceded it by five-years. Each section had as its theme a letter of the alphabet. For example, I lived in the somnolent Dogwood Hollow section of several hundred homes. To avoid monotony, there were four different house styles. The newly constructed homes were either situated on a drive or a lane, and each lane began with the same letter as the drive of the section.

Quinn lived at 318 Dogwood Drive with his cousins, Chuckie and Jimmy Callahan. Robbie Wilkinson resided at 164 Dogwood Drive. The drive was elliptical in shape, the circumference being about one mile in length. All of the interior streets of Dogwood Hollow had to begin with the letter D.

I lived with my parents and younger brother and sister at 50 Daffodil Lane, just four houses away from Salvatore Palermo, who lived at 66 Daffodil Lane, which intersected with Deepgreen Lane.

Carnie lived on Darkleaf Lane, and Tinker, my most lethal buddy, lived on Dewberry Lane. Ace Roberts resided on Disk Lane, Slip Carson on Dahlia Lane, and Fritz Feldcamp on Deerfield Lane. Some other fellas' in our gang, the Diablos, were Gabby Spencer, Spear Bauers, Slim Jennings, and Toby Chandler. All in all, we totaled two-dozen fun loving guys looking for any feud, folly, frolic, or festivity that might "turn-up like a turnip", as Bo would often joke.

Bo Jalonec lived at 95 Jonquil Lane in Junewood, which is a section just adjacent to Dogwood Hollow. A grassy field behind Robbie Wilkinson's house served as a division between the two housing developments. Since Junewood had no gang, Bo Jalonec was a welcome member to the Diablos.

Our gang had gotten the designation "Diablos" in the summer of '57. Quinn, Bo, Carnie, Tinker, Robbie Wilkinson, and I were sitting at our favorite table inside the Feed Bag, a greasy spoon eatery we regarded as "home away from home". Giving our gang a name came rather easily, because most of the guys in our group already had nicknames.

Bo Jalonec had dubbed me "Words", and I had appointed him "Jokes" to account for his happy-go-lucky personality. And then Carnie's dad was a carnival barker who had abandoned his family in late 1954, and Tinker could fix or break anything that had a motor or that operated mechanically. Tink walked with a slight limp, and we often called him "Chester", a character on the western TV show *Gunsmoke* starring James Arness as Marshal Matt Dillon. Dennis Weaver played Chester Goode, a lame deputy notorious for his salutation, "Mister Dillon, Mister Dillon!"

When Quinn was around, we all acted more mature, more civilized. We respected and feared him. He was our leader. The guys didn't have any election or vote to establish that fact. At six foot-two, weighing one hundred-ninety pounds of taut muscle, Quinn was my hero, a true greaser in the strictest sense of the word. My buddy owned and repaired his black '42 Ford coupe with its chrome flat-head engine, which featured three gleaming two-barrel carburetors. Quinn had dropped-out of Delhaas High his junior year; worked in the shipping department of a small department store on Mill Street in Bristol, and spent four nights a week with his pretty blonde chick, Patty Van Arsdale, who resented and was jealous of Quinn, when our leader hung-out with the Diablos.

Quinn was a genuine greaser; I was a greaser wannabe'. My idol was the only guy I knew in Dogwood Hollow who was self-sufficient, being virtually independent of adult supervision. My hero was strong and fair. Those were the traits I most admired in my greaser champion.

In retrospect, I believe that Quinn, Bo, and Carnie had thought-up the Bristol Post Office duplicate keys idea, whether or not I had mentioned to the gang the futuristic Feed Bag reunion.

Angie Palermo, Sal's dark-complexioned daughter, worked as a part-time waitress at the Feed Bag four evenings a week. If Palermo had known that the Diablos were interacting four nights a week with his precious offspring, the Mafia kingpin would have put Angie in a chastity belt and secluded her to the dungeon of a Catholic convent.

I had always had a certain weakness for Italian girls having olive skin, and so Angie Palermo and Bubbles Messina appealed to my adolescent fancy of beauty. And if it hadn't been for Angie, Bubbles, Popeye Messina, Cummings, and the other nefarious Kamikazes, then I would have had a boring, nondescript teenage existence. I pondered all of those considerations as I drove north on New Jersey *Highway 206* on my pleasurable excursion to Levittown.

Chapter 2
"The Diablos"

As I drove north on *Highway 206,* I recalled late July of '57. Carl Perkins' "Blue Suede Shoes" had just finished blasting through the Feed Bag's jukebox speakers. Jokes Jalonec dropped a quarter into the slot, and the joker played the next two songs for Quinn, "Honky Tonk, Part I" and "Honky Tonk, Part II" by Bill Doggett. Quinn had a definite preference for lively instrumental tunes. Bo then selected his final song for me, because I loved the melody and would always listen to the record on my *RCA* 45-rpm player at home, Gogi Grant's "The Wayward Wind".

Angie Palermo reluctantly ambled-over to my gang's favorite table to take our orders, only because Luigi, a co-owner of the Feed Bag had insisted on it. Luigi knew quite well that my friends and I blew most of our money patronizing his greasy spoon establishment.

"Okay, what does the Peanut Gallery want?" Angie requested as the Sicilian doll applied her pencil to the order slip.

"Well, if it isn't *Winky Dink and You!"* Carnie sarcastically responded. "Say, Honey, where's your crayons so that ya' can draw and color on the plastic ya' stick on your television screen?"

Tinker gave Carnie a quick elbow to the ribs to remind him that we were in the company of Quinn, who frowned upon excessive verbal abuse directed toward the opposite sex.

"I'll have a *snake* sandwich with *marijuana* sauce," Jokes demanded. "And go easy on my onions!"

"You mean a steak sandwich with marinara sauce and onions," Angie eloquently clarified.

"I'll have a cheese furburger with brunette pubes," emphasized Carnie, whose demented mind had a certain obsession with perverted sexual associations.

Tinker gave Carnie another jolt to the ribs, increasing the diameter of his recently received black and blue mark. Quinn stared at Carnie menacingly while the neurotic greaser avoided eye contact with "my hero" as *he* silently contemplated Angie's huge, solid breasts. We were all aware that Quinn would only tolerate a small degree more of Carnie's adolescent stupidity.

Quinn ordered two slices of pizza, Robbie ordered a "veal perm' sandwich", and Tinker insisted on a Mexicali chiliburger because the repulsive thug claimed he hadn't had a bowel movement in two weeks. I said I wanted a meatball sandwich deluxe, and we all agreed on large *Pepsi Colas* to wash-down the fast food.

"If we have a gang, we're going to have to have a real cool name," began Jokes, who was anxious to become organized and kick some Kenwood Kamikaze butts.

"Yeah, the Dogwood Daffodils just doesn't cut it," agreed Tinker, who was afraid of D flower names that suggested a lack of toughness.

"That's pretty 'gear'," observed and stated Bo, who was always up on the latest teenage slang. "Almost boss."

"Whatever it is, it has to begin with a D," Quinn asserted.

"What about the Dogwood Dumb Dicks?" Robbie inquired, trying to inject a bit of humor into our serious conversation.

Everyone listening shook our heads in disgust while we all realized deep-down inside that Robbie's remark might have actually contained an element of truth.

"Words. You're always great with creative ideas. What do ya' think?" Carnie asked, putting me on the spot.

I pensively rubbed my chin, feeling that I had to defend my Dogwood Hollow reputation for inventiveness. A Feed Bag patron then played Bobby Helms's "My Special Angel" on the jukebox, and *that* record selection activated my brain. Angel=Devil. Devil means demon or diabolical. The Spanish word for devil is Diablo! It was a choice between "Demons or Diablos".

"Listen-up guys. I like Diablos," I announced. "It's the Spanish word for Devils, and its meaning is secret enough that only a few kids will know what it stands for until Jokes paints cute, little devils with pitchforks on the back of our black leather jackets."

Everybody pondered for a minute. The guys knew we needed to come-up with something strong to send a clear message to Cummings and his Kenwood Kamikazes. The Ks had become notorious for harassing kids from Dogwood Hollow. Then, Quinn rendered his imperial opinion. Everyone at the table knew that *his* decision would be final and absolute.

"I like Words' idea. I say Diablos it is!" our gang's boss approved.

"Solid, Ted, enough said," concurred Bo Jalonec, the lieutenant of the newly-formed pack.

The Diablos sitting at the Feed Bag table extended our left hands towards the center napkin dispenser, each straight arm like a spoke in a wheel. And then, I borrowed a phrase from *The Three Musketeers* by Alexandre Dumas, which I had read for an oral report in ninth-grade. "All for one; one for all!" I exclaimed.

The five other Diablos at the table reflected upon the import of my comment, and then my merry colleagues lustily acknowledged in unison, "All for one; one for all!"

"I dig it, Words. Ya' really have a lot of great ideas!" Tinker said as the dirty rat mistook mediocrity for brilliance.

Bo Jalonec, who was just as academically gifted as I was, knew all along that almost every idea I ever presented was really a glorious plagiarism of some plot I had read in literature. But the true greaser element of the Diablos: Quinn, Carnie, Robbie, and Tinker, who never saw any benefit in studying literary classics, believed that I was an authentic genius.

Again, we joined our hands in July of '57 across the table in the far-right corner of Luigi and Domenick's Feed Bag, and we proudly proclaimed, "All for one; one for all!"

"What does that really mean?" Tinker seriously asked.

"J.W. will tell ya', if you promise to take at least one bath a month," Bo laughed and mocked.

Gorgeous Angie Palermo returned with our orders. As the doll placed the platters onto the plastic tablecloth, which had a red and white checkerboard pattern, Jokes addressed the well-built waitress. "Hey Angie, do ya' know who the tallest President is?"

"No," the harried waitress replied.

"Eisen*tower.* He's *Nick's son!"* Bo clarified.

We all laughed at Jokes' remarkable timing. Angie became a trifle confused by all of the raucous commotion and got several of the orders mixed- up.

"I'm really sorry, Guys," the Sicilian beauty apologized, feigning sincerity. "I got a little confused."

"That's, okay, Angie. I've pulled a few boners in my time, too," Jokes responded as he made a naughty jerking gesture with his right hand, much to *our* amusement.

Everyone again laughed, even Angie and Quinn.

"You're so adorable!" Angie answered, as she gave Jokes a pinch on his rosy cheek with her thumb and forefinger.

Bo Jalonec was the most popular Diablo with the area Levittown girls. My pal's great looks, golden blond hair, and cheerful disposition enchanted all the chicks with whom the Casanova flirted. If Jalonec had lived in ancient Greece, his magic could have lured the girdle off of Helen of Troy, and if he had resided in the land of the pyramids, Bo would have charmed the nipples off of Cleopatra. That's how powerful his animal magnetism worked with the opposite gender.

I must admit I did have more than a minor crush on Angie back in 1957, and I had become a tad jealous of Jokes hitting it off with her so naturally. But then, I realized that I admired Bo Jalonec much more than I envied him. I also knew that if Tinker, Carnie, Robbie, or myself had been as aggressively flirtatious with Angie as Jokes had been, then

Quinn would have beaten the living daylights out of us. But Bo could successfully pull it off, and we couldn't; it was all so simple, and yet all so mysterious.

The Dogwood Hollow greasers finally had achieved unity, and now we were organized. The Diablos had to gain the respect of the Ridgewood Renegades, led by Langford, and the Thornridge Tornadoes, headed by Jensen. But most of all, the Diablos wanted honor and respect from the Kenwood Kamikazes, governed by Cummings. That dangerous posse featured punks like Bruno "Popeye" Messina, Jake Mullins, and Dave Evans. The Kamikazes were our chief rivals, no doubt about it, but now we had Quinn, who never liked Cummings, and with Bo Jalonec also in our Diablos' gang, the Kamikazes had some serious, direct turf opposition. We believed that our new fraternity would protect the Dogwood Hollow guys from Kamikaze aggression and intimidation.

The Levittown gangs had a certain code of ethics, which every area greaser understood. We were allowed to pass through each other's territory en route to any given destination, but the Diablos weren't allowed to hang-out in Kenwood, and the Kamikazes weren't permitted to loiter in Dogwood Hollow.

There was also a common understanding of safety zones, just like *Go* and *No Parking* on the *Monopoly* game board. The Feed Bag, the Dairy DeLite, and all other hangouts were labeled "neutral" territory, as were shopping malls, schools, community swimming pools, basketball courts, and sports fields. These were unwritten rules, and the Kamikazes, the Renegades, the Tornadoes, and the Diablos understood those unwritten rules perfectly.

Some sections of Levittown, such as Birchwood, Violetwood, Junewood, Lakeside Park, Crabtree Hollow, Stonybrook, Farmbrook, Greenbrook, Holly Hill, and Magnolia Hill didn't have any organized greasers. There were gangs like the Willowwood Warriors and the Northside Nomads, but those rivals were geographically distant from Dogwood Hollow. The Diablos definitely regarded Cummings and the Kenwood Kamikazes as our main adversaries. The Ks had caused Tinker, Carnie, and me great grief before the Diablos had been officially organized. Our new unification would cause the Kamikazes to back-off.

During the daytime, the gangs didn't bother too much with each other, but just like Dracula turning into a vampire after dark, we all thirsted for nighttime adventure, havoc, and excitement.

What separated greasers from jocks and eggheads was our code of ethics. We believed kids should never squeal or rat on fellow teenagers, regardless of the circumstances. Jocks would rat on jocks; and jocks would rat on eggheads; and jocks would rat on greasers, and eggheads would do likewise, but greasers would never rat on anybody, greaser, jock, or egghead. This was our "Diablo Code First Commandment". We might get other kids in trouble with the police, with their parents, or with other gangs, as a result of pranks we would play, but we would never deliberately squeal on any other teen. That is the way I remember it as a Diablo in the late '50s.

I had idolized Quinn ever since I was thirteen. He was sixteen, dropping-out of Delhaas High School. Quinn was tough, cool, and collected; brave, rebellious, but not wild, and in total command of his non-visible emotions.

In '50s Levittown, being "cool" meant being in charge of one's emotions, and not displaying either fear or affection in public, but most importantly, not taking any crap from anyone. Tough guys were known only by their last names, like Quinn, Cummings, Langford, and Jensen. So, it was a compliment of the highest degree to call someone by his last name. This gave the gang leaders their status, and it insulated their identities from their wannabe' followers.

Simply study the heroes of history and mythology to analyze figures like Geronimo, Hercules, Lafayette, Odysseus, and Attila to fully get the message. Being called by only one name meant only one thing: You could kick ass, and all those suckers running-around with two names understood that reality perfectly. Even though I knew Quinn's first name, I never uttered it in his presence. I felt that calling him "Jack" would be an egregious insult to his integrity.

Several formidable motorcycle gangs, the Barbarians and the War Lords, "cruised" the area. Quinn was very skeptical of the bikers and advised the Diablos to "Stay clear!" The Harley brutes were into chains, knives, heavy drugs, murder, life-in-the-fast-lane, handguns, and switchblades. The Diablos were more into mischief, pranks, and practical jokes. For the Diablos, *Halloween* was a three-hundred-sixty-five-day continuous activity, and my gang would only fight skin on skin and knuckles against jaw should a rumble develop.

The Diablos (except Tinker) would only "mix-it-up" as a last resort, after exhausting all other alternatives and means of escape. But if cornered, like desperate rats bent on survival, we would fight according to the greaser code, to the death.

The Diablos did not have to worry about being publicly designated as "egotistical sexists", "male chauvinist pigs," "politically incorrect iconoclasts," "horny perverts", or "gay and lesbian bashers". Those critical terms didn't exist back then. Even our victims comprehended that we were only silly kids dealing with our overactive hormones.

Everyone back then knew all about Darwinian "survival of the fittest", and that "only the strong survive".

The 1950s had been a decade that abounded in male chauvinism, racism, and sexism, and the Diablos were products of that era. Most '50s tough guys regarded sensitivity and empathy as signs of weakness, and to camouflage our fragile, insecure egos, we would badger anyone we perceived as an enemy, or anyone who we suspected might be an ally of an enemy. Every Diablo, except Bo, felt awkward publicly expressing our genuine feelings.

Greasers were compelled by a "tuff guy" image to hide their tenderness under hard, thick shells. We were selfish and predatory, and looking-back to my chaotic youth, there was no justification for the Diablos' mimicking the Kamikazes' practice of blatant teenage anarchy. Social Darwinism belonged to the prehistoric age, but *we* were too into "defending our fragile reputation" to comprehend *that* moral principle.

Chapter 3
"Déjà Vu"

A red traffic signal in Burlington brought my mind back to July 1, 2000. As my Buick approached the collector's booth for the two-lane *Burlington-Bristol Bridge,* I noticed that the toll had been increased to two-dollars for a two-way transit. I chuckled when I handed-over eight quarters to the affable bridge attendant. I recalled my father driving his green and cream '55 Chevy Bel Air across the span and had honestly complained to the family how abominable it was that the crossing fee had risen from a nickel to a dime.

Everything today is nearly ten-times as expensive as it had been in the '50s. Burgers were fifteen-cents; *TastyKake* pies and cupcakes were ten-cents; new automobiles were two-thousand-dollars, and gasoline was less than a quarter a gallon. Every time Bo Jalonec pulled into my driveway at 50 Daffodil Lane, Jokes would automatically extend his hand and say, "Fifty-cents for gas." That was equivalent to two-gallons of fuel, and if Carnie, Tinker, and Robbie Wilkinson were also picked-up to go cruisin', we could "gallivant around" all night on two-dollars-and-fifty-cents.

As I drove toward Pennsylvania, I noticed that even the structure of the ancient bridge had changed. I hadn't crossed the *Burlington-Bristol* for nearly twenty-years. I ordinarily traverse the *Delaware* via the *Walt Whitman,* the *Ben Franklin,* the *Betsy Ross,* the *Tacony-Palmyra,* the *Commodore Barry,* and the *Delaware Memorial Bridge*. Back in the '50s, the ramps onto and off of the *Burlington-Bristol* had been curved but apparently, modern engineering has alleviated those particular unique characteristics.

Midway up the all-too-familiar bridge, the red-flashing signals lit up, and railroad-like gates descended, indicating that the metal draw in the span's center would be lifted to allow a large cargo ship to safely sail underneath.

I relaxed in my cherry *Buick Park Avenue* and listened to "Personality" by Lloyd Price, and then to "Stagger Lee" by the same artist. I was in a rather jovial frame of mind, and was buoyed by a cute thought. 'If I had displayed just a trifle more personality back in '59, I could've landed either Angie Palermo or Bubbles Messina.'

It has always been a tradition for local motorists to leave their cars to watch a large ship with its high mast travel the channel under the drawbridge. However, I was unprepared for the shocking surprise I was about to witness.

My eyes observed a vessel heading north up the *Delaware* with a full hull of raw materials to be processed at a refinery or factory along the river. As the immense black ship slipped past the center of the bridge, heading in the direction of Bristol, my pupils widened. I first noticed the vessel's waterline, showing ever so slightly as the waves receded from the ship's stern. When the red line is visible, then the boat is empty, but when it isn't, the marking is submerged in the river, signifying that the cargo ship is fully laden. Shortly thereafter, I almost fainted when I viewed and read the ship's name, *Caracas*. An elderly gentleman standing next to me noticed my alarm.

"Are you alright, young man?" the old gent asked. "I'm a retired doctor if you need medical help!"

"No thanks, I'm okay," I replied as I felt my heart palpitating wildly inside my chest cavity. I suddenly grabbed the railing on the bridge to achieve more stability.

I had seen that same ship gliding-along on the *Delaware* in my youth. I was only eleven-years-old in 1954, and my family had just recently moved from Hammonton, New Jersey to Levittown. I had transferred into Bristol's St. Mark School on Radcliffe Street, which parallels *the Delaware*.

In mid-spring of 1954, the Fairless Hills Steel Mill had completed construction, and the *Caracas* was bringing the first shipment of iron ore from Venezuela past Bristol to the new processing facility. Since *this* was a voyage of monumental proportion for the area, economics, nationalism, patriotism, religion, education, and Americana were all amalgamated into one major event. Students from schools all over Bucks County had been transported to Bristol to participate in history in the making. We were all there on the waterfront as patriotic Americans happy to greet the arriving iron ore from Venezuela.

I had been a sixth-grader at St. Mark's for only a few months. My class had to march across Radcliffe Street to witness the historic passing. Carnie, my first real friend in Levittown, also attended St. Mark's, so we proceeded toward the riverbank together. The several thousand students assembled were given small, linen, American flags on wooden sticks. We were instructed to wave the flags at the crew of the *Caracas* as the vessel drifted north up the scenic *Delaware*. The kids were reminded that we could keep our flags as mementos of the historic day.

As it turned out, the day was more hysterical than historical. The importance of the event paled in comparison to the chaos that soon ensued. Carnie and I were standing directly behind several classes from Levittown's James Buchanan and John Fitch schools. My buddy and I recognized some of the kids because those from Dogwood Hollow attended James Buchanan, and those from Kenwood and Farmbrook sections went to John Fitch, where I later discovered that Bubbles

Messina had been a student. I saw the doll conversing with Angie Palermo, whom I knew had attended James Buchanan on Haines Road, because she was a new Dogwood Hollow neighbor of mine.

My heart raced when I noticed Bubbles, but after I saw her talking to Angie, I thought it was going to explode. Carnie and I somehow squeezed through the thick humanity to the vicinity directly behind Angie and Bubbles.

A boisterous roar rose from the crowd as the *Caracas* passed-by. Some students behind us, anxious to capture a closer glimpse, started to push forward from the rear. When push came to shove, mayhem broke-loose, and then six humans in the front line of spectators plunged over the bulkhead into the murky *Delaware,* which was excessively polluted in '54 from tons of industrial waste.

The embarrassed casualties turned-out to be Sister Bernadette, Sister Veronica, who doubled as Mother Superior of St. Mark's; two students from the Immaculate Conception School, and also Angie and Bubbles.

Carnie and I made it our duty to exclusively rescue Angie and Bubbles from drowning in toxic water. We tried pulling the girls from the river by their arms and blouses, but that technique didn't work because their bra straps ripped from too much weight. The Italian chicks again plummeted from the bulkhead back into the grimy water.

Finally, with the aid of two teachers from James Buchanan, Carnie and I managed to salvage Angie and Bubbles, who were thoroughly angered from experiencing their terrible ordeal. The Sicilian chicks became even more furious when the babes discovered that their magnificent bosoms were fully exposed to the amazed assemblage of students, teachers, nuns, priests, and government officials.

In our haste (and inspired by the general pandemonium), Carnie and I had accidentally ripped the girls' blouses and had desperately tugged their bras right off their torsos, much to the delight of the appreciative boys, and much to the mortification of everyone else in the multitude.

"We were only tryin' to save ya'," Carnie pleaded.

"Save this, ya' dumb-ass jerk!" Bubbles shouted, giving Carnie such a stout clout to the jaw, sending my friend tumbling backward over the bulkhead into the dirty *Delaware.* Those crazy proceedings took precedence over the passing of the *Caracas,* which blew its loud horns repeatedly, only to the indifference of the preoccupied audience assembled on the river bank.

That afternoon, a still wet Carnie and I sat in Mother Veronica's office on the third-floor of St. Mark's School. The stern, elderly nun was not too elated about her unexpected encounter with the *Delaware River.* As Mother Veronica sat there staring and glaring at us, the nun reminded me of a ferocious bulldog attired in a black and white two-toned igloo. Her wicked frown would have been enough to scare the living communism out of Nikita S. Khrushchev. Mother Veronica's hearing aids must have shorted-out from her recent river splash, because the school administrator kept adjusting the devices during her brief conference with her two "vile creatures".

"Do you two geniuses realize you've damaged, if not ruined the reputation of this school?" Mother Veronica yelled. "I've devoted my whole life to giving St. Mark's an admirable name, and in a matter of less than a minute, you two demented morons have destroyed what it took me forty-years to build! The newspapers will have a picnic with this abominable story," the chief nun elaborated. "You clowns both better bring along a ton of marshmallows when you die, because you're going to spend a good deal of eternity doing Penance in Purgatory. Do you understand, Penance?"

Carnie felt obligated to reply. "Yes m'am. The *Phillies* won one in 1950, but the *Yankees* beat them four games to zip in the *World Series*. That Joe DiMaggio was too...."

"You're both disgraces! You're both agents of Lucifer. You're both retarded, not only mentally, but spiritually as well!" the chief nun very distinctly screamed. "You're insolent; you simpletons are lunatics; you delinquents are little demons; you're outrageous; you're obnoxious; you're intolerable, and it's my pleasure to inform you two stooges that you're both outa' here, suspended for a full week!"

It was a long school bus ride from Bristol back to Levittown. The thought of staying home for one solid week, isolated in my room, was a real bummer. Carnie's parents were a lot more liberal than Mom and Dad were. My close friend's dad was still living at home on Darkleaf Lane, but his parents were having severe marital problems, so I guess it was good for him to have the freedom to get-out of the house and escape the perpetual wrangling and arguing.

"That's the last time I'm ever going to save somebody from dying J.W," Carnie confided. My pal felt angry about being punished for his honorable intentions.

I also had trouble understanding the benefit of aiding people who were in danger of drowning. "I know what you mean. It just doesn't pay," I agreed. "Ya' try to rescue somebody, and the next thing ya' know, you're suspended from school. There ain't no justice in being a Good *Sumerian*."

"Geez J.W., ya' really know your *Bible*. I can't see why Mother Veronica gave you the ax," Carnie sympathized and related. "Maybe if she had learned to swim better, or even float better, maybe she would've gone a little easier on us!"

Carnie and I commiserated some more as the school bus turned off of Haines Road into Dogwood Hollow. We believed that we had been innocent victims of circumstance. Although the entire *Caracas* fiasco was an accident, the irate St. Mark's Principal held us accountable.

"Now ya' know why everyone calls her 'a mother', Carnie," I related. "But the old battle-ax goes against science. Sister Bernadette taught us that penguins were one of the few birds that could swim. They'd better rewrite those science books, Carnie. There're too many false facts in 'em."

"Not only that," Carnie added. "Angie, Bubbles and their crazy Mafia families will blame us for that river incident. We might've made more lethal enemies today than we can count."

I was afraid of confronting my parents about the bad school news. The thoughts of suspension and parental disapproval were new, ugly experiences for me, and I didn't quite know how to handle them. I suspected that Dad would accuse me of being on a collision course with juvenile delinquency.

"I might as well stick my fingers between two live wires," I sighed.

"Why?" Carnie asked with a look of concern on his face.

"Because I'm grounded for at least a month," I regretfully replied. "My father believes in old fashioned punishment."

Carnie, who was rebelling against his parents' constant bickering, suggested that he would climb through my bedroom window to play *Monopoly* and *Chinese Checkers*. The instigator stated that he would also bring along some of his father's girlie picture magazines and show me what Mother Veronica, Sister Bernadette, and Sister Justine were supposed to look like underneath all of their heavy black cloth and white cardboard.

"That's cool. See ya' later alligator," I replied.

"After while, crocodile!" answered my loyal pal, as the care-free kid departed the yellow school bus.

If it hadn't been for Carnie, I think I might have dropped-out of school at age sixteen. Tinker was actually a bad influence on Carnie and me, since the deranged greaser did quit Delhaas High when the delinquent turned sixteen. Carnie professed that he wanted to emulate Tinker, so my job was to keep Carnie interested in irrelevant academics, and his job was to remain in school to keep me from being expelled, which might sabotage any chance of me receiving a decent Catholic High School education.

"I'll do the pains because you got the brains," my alter-ego often told me. I'll never forget Carnie's memorable words.

The *Burlington-Bristol* drawbridge was about to close, so I stepped back to my cherry sedan, wondering if any of the other motorists or their passengers had any fond recollections of the *Caracas*. If it had not been for South American iron ore, then there wouldn't be any sensational '50s story to relate. The *Caracas* event was the genesis of a series of totally-bizarre, imminent adventures.

On December 29, 1959, Jokes Jalonec visited 50 Daffodil Lane at 9:15 a.m. Quinn had instructed Bo to remind me about the Bristol Post Office on July 1, 2000; that is, if the Feed Bag no longer existed. According to Jokes, this would give Quinn enough time to make arrangements to meet the other five Diablos at a designated location on December 28, *Y2K*. I had spoken on the phone with Bo several times after his last visit to 50 Daffodil Lane, but then his family moved away to Pittsburgh, and we then lost contact.

The mystery of everyone's fate was getting near. I still had some time to kill before my scheduled July 1, 2000 rendezvous with either the Feed Bag or the Bristol Post Office. I wanted to see if some of the Diablos' old hangouts were still in existence. Forty-one years was more than half a human lifetime.

Chapter 4
"The Feed Bag and the Dairy DeLite"

My cherry Park Avenue descended from the *Burlington Bristol Bridge* onto *Route 413*. I passed a familiar chemical plant that was still around. When Dad used to pass the treatment facility in the '50s, a terrible stench usually accompanied our transit. Little odor is apparent nowadays, thanks to the existence of strict environmental laws. 'At least that's one improvement over the Golden Oldies decade of James Dean, Elvis Presley, and Chuck Berry,' I thought.

My recollection of '50s Levittown made me recall something Brother Timothy had taught in his Ancient History class at Cardinal Reagan High. The pretentious Franciscan informed his students that the bard Homer had organized the *Iliad* and the *Odyssey* legends to glorify the ancestors of the ancient Greeks. The noble conquest of Troy and the thrilling adventures of Odysseus were really designed to disguise the fact that the Achaeans of 1184 BC were pirates and marauders. As I bypassed Bristol on *Route 413,* I wondered if I also had been guilty of attaching too much dignity to past misdeeds. Was I attempting to justify '50s teenage rebellion? Was I trying to dignify Diablos' juvenile delinquency?

My eyes glanced into the rear-view mirror and I thought to my reflection, 'Brother Timothy nearly yanked my earlobes off several times. The sadist, along with Father Malcolm, were fanatics, just as the Greeks and the Trojans were 1184 BC ancient barbarians,' I imagined. 'The Diablos and the Kamikazes were aggressively trying to define *our* places within the '50s social pecking order.'

As I entered Pennsylvania on that sunny July 1st morning, I mentally tried defending what my pals and I had done in the name of Diablos' honor, but I enjoyed little success. Besides harassing wimpy eggheads, my gang also retaliated against those who threatened or harmed us, but in hindsight, not even our misconduct against Popeye and Cummings could be righteously justified. The Dogwood Diablos were nothing more than young barbarians embroiled in a brutal greaser war with the savage Kenwood Kamikazes.

My imagination focused again upon my next objective, The Feed Bag near the intersection of Pennsylvania's *Route 13* and Haines Road. I drove under the old rusty Pennsylvania Railroad Bridge, which hadn't changed nearly as much as I had since late 1959; turned right, and motored north on 'Pennsy *Route 13*. I passed by what used to be *Robert Hall Clothing,* but now it's a business titled Dimensions III, a bridal apparel store.

Dad and Mom often took me to *Robert Hall's* to be fitted for sport jackets and trousers, required male dress at Cardinal Reagan High. When a kid attended Catholic school, at least in 1954 through '59, that garb was the standard male uniform. Around *Christmas* of '55, I was having my wardrobe refurbished. The *Robert Hall* tailor adjusted his tape and stated, "Now son, I want to measure your crotch."

I stared at the salesman in complete astonishment and asked, "In public?" The tailor looked at my parents and all erupted in a burst of laughter. My juvenile perception of the '50s haberdashery world as it related to the onset of puberty had been accurately revealed.

Now, I realize how hard Dad had to labor just to feed, clothe, and shelter his family on a welder's $85.00 weekly salary. Pop was proud of his wages. The average working man's pay in '54 was $75.00 per week, and minimum wage was $1.00 an hour. We weren't the Rockefellers or the Vanderbilts, and although Dad was a quiet, modest man, he did provide well for us, and our needs always preceded his. I remember him saying how he felt sorry for those poor devils that had to support families on only $75.00 a week.

I stopped at a red light and checked-out *Lower Bucks County Hospital* on my left, where I had once received a rabies-shot for a vicious dog bite on my right hand.

I next noticed Silver Lake on the left, the scene of several splendid Diablos' exploits. Behind the lake was Snake Road, a favorite '50s "passion pit". My cherry sedan soon traveled under the Turnpike Bridge, which crosses the *Delaware* and connects the '*Pennsy Turnpike* with its New Jersey counterpart. The construction of that span had been finished right after the nightmare *Caracas* incident, and on a clear night, the Diablos could see the blinking red lights atop its highest towers, all the way from Dogwood Hollow, a full two-miles to the north.

Before I knew it, I had passed Green Lane, and soon I was stopped at the Edgely Road and *Route 13* traffic signal. The dual highway had been widened to three lanes in both directions. I realized my location was only a half-mile from the Feed Bag. What would it look like? Was it still there? What had happened to its likeable owners, Luigi and Domenick?

When the Edgely Road light switched to green, I hit the accelerator harder than usual. In my haste, I had passed The Dairy DeLite, which much to my joy, was still there after over forty-years of wear and tear, recessions, and wars. I veered into the next entrance, which should have been the old Feed Bag. The building looked almost identical in size and shape, a little smaller than I remembered, but instead of the familiar neon sign in the form of a bag, a large shingle read: 'Under the Pier Sea Food House, 600 *Route 13'*. More information was provided in smaller lettering: 'Crabs and Lobsters: Cold Draught Beer: Open 1 P.M. to Midnight'. I then remembered that the Diablos' former hangout had still been there in 1986, the last time I had been in the vicinity.

My eyes became misty and soon several tears rolled-down my cheeks as Little Caesar and the Romans reached a crescendo on the car stereo, "Those Oldies but Goodies, Remind Me of You!" All I could do was sit in my vehicle and stare blankly at the edifice situated before me. My mind was temporarily paralyzed, and so was my body. My former high spirits had also been instantly traumatized.

The Feed Bag had become extinct just like the dinosaur', the saber-toothed tiger, and the *Robert Hall* discount clothing chain. I sat there for several minutes in a stupor. The Feed Bag was not only the main hangout of the Diablos, but the restaurant was also our military staging area where Carnie, Jokes, and I planned our sophisticated strategy, our elaborate pranks, and our extravagant war games to be implemented against the pernicious Kamikazes. It was our personal retreat, our corporate office, and our special asylum from the rigors of adult society. The Feed Bag was also the Diablos' gazette where we exchanged the latest local and world news, teenage gossip, sports' page information, and music scoops with area girls.

I did not have the guts to put my feet to the asphalt of the seafood restaurant's parking lot. My eyes glanced to the left, to where a strip mall was still standing, but all of the stores I remembered from 1959 had new identities. In '59 I had maintained a part-time job three-nights a week at the middle store, Hal's Talk of the Town Delicatessen, where I had peeled enough spuds for potato salad to feed a small army. I also specialized in preparing corned beef sandwiches and roast beef orders "to go". The space formerly occupied by my place of employment is now the premises of Claude and Bob's Eagle Nest Tavern. The Golden Arches of a large *McDonald's* is now situated at the intersection of Haines Road and *Route 13,* which back in late '59 was a spacious, grassy field. That new fast-food competition had probably contributed to the demise of Hal's Delicatessen and the venerable Feed Bag.

As I stared out the windshield of my Park Avenue at exactly 11 a.m., my mind recreated an interesting anecdote from the spring of '59. Carnie, Jokes, Tinker, and I were sitting at our familiar Feed Bag table. Jokes was in a jovial mood, while Carnie and Tinker were debating which New York baseball team was more formidable, the *Brooklyn Dodgers* or the *New York Yankees*. Since the *Dodgers* were in the *National League* with the *Phillies,* I backed-up Carnie by arguing that the "Bums from Flatbush Avenue" were the superior squad.

"Remember in '55 Brooklyn beat the Bronx Bombers in the *Series,"* Carnie nervously lectured. "Ya' can't beat a lineup that has Duke Snider, Gil Hodges, Roy Campanella, and Jackie Robinson. And I think Don Newcombe is the fastest pitcher in the majors," Carnie maintained, noticing that for once he had a captive audience, so the junior Cicero continued bombarding us with his predictable, mundane propaganda. "The Bums from Flatbush rule!" Carnie was both loquacious and emphatic. Baseball was as much a major interest in his life as it had been in mine.

When Bo heard the noun "Flatbush", Jokes became inspired to utter, "I've seen a flat bush from time to time, and believe me, Guys, they're much easier to get to than fluffy ones. Flat bushes are much better than flat chests. I know that fact from actual experience. A flat bush makes it a lot easier to pull-down a girl's panties!"

As usual, whenever Carnie and I were engaged in serious forensics, we simply ignored Jalonec's drivel and continued pursuing our excellent repartee.

"Words, I'm tellin' ya' man," Tinker argued. "The Bombers are the greatest. They have the best pitcher in Whitey Ford; the best outfielder in Mickey Mantle, and up to '56, the finest shortstop ever in Phil Rizzuto. The *Yanks* even have the best announcer in Mel Allen."

Tempers were getting hot. Baseball was all right to debate, but the sport was not important enough to quarrel and fight over. But whenever the mercurial Diablos weren't brawling with the Kamikazes, we were especially notorious for vehemently arguing and debating amongst ourselves.

"Tinker, you're all wrong. Pee Wee Reese can field and hit better than Rizzuto ever could in his prime," I stubbornly answered. "You're just prejudice against the *National League* because you were born in the Bronx."

"Yeah, the Bronx Zoo," Jokes sarcastically added. "In the gorilla cage with King Kong's favorite niece."

As usual, Tinker was wearing his greasy Davy Crockett coonskin hat and a pair of plastic 3-D movie glasses. Those items were Tinker's trademarks, and the brawler would challenge anyone to a black eye if the doomed critic dared stare at him for more than three-seconds. Sometimes, I thought that my gimpy pal wore the strange accessories simply to instigate an altercation with an unsuspecting stranger.

Tinker was the one Diablo who was cruel and crazy enough to be a Kamikaze. Even the Ks were afraid of his prowess. The auto mechanic loved hand-to-hand combat, and the teen warrior derived pleasure from pummeling and hurting greasers or jocks with his clenched fists. I feared Tinker more than Popeye and Cummings put together, and I was always glad to have the "car guru" at my side whenever any nasty Ks were around. Tink was my personal bodyguard, and thanks to simple geography, his fate was to live in Dogwood Hollow, and his destiny was to become "a D". But in truth, Tink had the mean heart, the brutal spirit, and the black soul of a diehard Kamikaze. Looking back in time, Tinker had to be the most dangerous kid I have ever known.

Angie Palermo came-over to take our orders, and her splendid female appearance put an abrupt cessation to the mild baseball exchange between Carnie, Tink, and me being discussed.

"Well, if it isn't Alvin, Simon, and Theodore," Angie sarcastically began her nasty greeting. "How are the Chipmunks doin' tonight? Say, where's David Seville?"

"He's bein' consumed by the Purple People Eater," Jokes explained, deftly alluding to a popular Sheb Wooley '50s novelty song.

"Ya' know doll, ya' oughta' go on *Ed Sullivan*. Now, what do you' four imbeciles want to order? Perhaps you vampires would like to order some zombie fruit juices?" the Sicilian waitress impolitely asked. Angie closely studied Bo's bright blue eyes and his wide smile. His charm made her momentarily forget her allegiance to the Kamikazes.

"Do ya' have any sweet dough?" Jokes asked.

"No, we're all out tonight," Angie' answered as the Italian broad aggressively chewed on a thick wad of bubble gum.

Bo pondered for a few seconds. "Well, do ya' have any dill dough?" the comedy machine inquired.

"Dill dough? How would ya' swallow it?" Angie shrieked.

A shrill burst of laughter erupted from other Feed Bag patrons after Angie had screamed the word "dildo" at the top of her lungs. Extremely embarrassed, the Sicilian doll ran into the Feed Bag's back room to recompose her self-esteem. Maggie, another waitress on duty, was assigned by Luigi to finish taking our obnoxious orders. She noticed Carnie's shiny black '49 Merc' parked outside the big-paned window and asked, "Whose black Mercury is that?"

"It's Carnie's boss machine," Bo instantly responded. "And it's a nice car, but my dear friend has trouble parking it inside a thermometer every night. It's a tight fit, but the genius eventually manages to get the Mercury job done."

Maggie finally figured-out the explicit relationship of "Mercury automobile" to the liquid found inside a thermometer. "Ha, ha, ha. Very funny, Handsome," the waitress admitted. "But your car, it looks just like James Dean's in *Rebel without a Cause.* I really loved that movie. And Natalie Wood, she's the ultimate. Now Blondie, what could I get ya' before Luigi fires me?"

Bo suddenly remembered why he was there. "I have a date tonight with Susie Parker, my steady. She'll be meetin' me here in about ten-minutes," Jokes revealed in a rather serious tone. "Get my friends three psychiatrists and three exorcists, and then please quickly come back with two one-way tickets to paradise for just you and me."

After regaining her senses, flustered Maggie asked Bo what he really wanted.

"A small *Pepsi,"* he replied. "And go easy on the Arctic ice."

Unfortunately, for the Diablos, the Feed Bag was also the principal hangout for the Kamikazes, a band of hedonistic delinquents who often accosted black kids in the restaurant's parking lot, harassing them until the "rug-heads" left the establishment. If the black kids did not cooperate, Cummings, Popeye, and their cruel henchmen kidnapped, intimidated, and psychologically tortured their victims.

After Bo left the Feed Bag for his date with gorgeous Susie Parker, Carnie told Tinker and me that he had overheard Cummings and Popeye bragging over at the Dairy DeLite about how the callous Ks had abducted two black guys who had stopped at "the Bag" for directions. Five Kenwood thugs (pretending to be helpful) escorted the innocent black kids' car to the Edgely Bridge, which was an overpass of the Pennsy' Railroad.

After getting out of their trademark black '52 Fords, the Ks roughed-up their captives, and then tied-up the Negro boys back-to-back, using the ends of a fifty-foot-long rope. The Kamikazes dangled the black victims from the bridge, suspending their petrified hostages just above the railroad tracks. When the next freight train approached the Edgely bridge at around fifty-miles an hour, Cummings, Popeye, and the other three Ks yanked the rope, lifting the hysterical black teens above the speeding locomotive.

"What happened next?" asked Tinker, who, like the repulsive Ks, also didn't like black people.

"It ain't pretty," Carnie confided.

Carnie disclosed that the Ks commandeered the black kids' car, and then followed Cummings' black Ford. The autos' were driven five miles north to Morrisville. The three cars stopped at the foot of the 'Pennsy Railroad Bridge that connects Trenton with Morrisville.

Everyone exited the three vehicles, and using two fifty-foot-long ropes, Cummings and Popeye tethered the ends around the black kids' waists. Then, the contemptible Ks haphazardly tied the two ropes together and pushed the "colored kids" off opposite sides of the railroad bridge. The screaming hostages were suspended midway between the bridge and the *Delaware River* below.

"Did a train come?" I asked with great curiosity.

"Stop buttin' in Asshole, and just let Carnie finish the friggin' story," Tink insisted and threatened.

"When the express train from New York to 'Philly came flyin' by," Carnie continued, "its wheels sliced the ropes laying across the tracks. The two black kids plunged into the river. The scared-to-death "shines" were yellin' like maniacs."

I felt sorry for the two black kids, but Tinker thought that the gruesome story was extremely amusing. After Dr. Destructo stopped laughing, I asked Carnie what had happened next.

"The black dudes were scared out of their minds. When the duo wildly swam towards the riverbank on the Morrisville side, the Ks punctured all four of the black kids' tires with switchblades," Carnie revealed. "Cummings then warned the wet "trespassers" to stay away from Levittown and the Feed Bag, or else the encroachers would not live to tell about their next meeting with the Ks," Carnie finished.

"The Kamikazes are even cooler than I thought," Tinker declared.

"Ks describes them exactly," I observed and stated, "because the word Ks should stand for Ku Klux Klan."

The desperate plight of the two black kids jolted my mind back to the morning of July 1, 2000. I started my *Park Avenue's* engine and slowly backed-up. I put the gearshift into drive and rotated the steering wheel in the direction of the Dairy DeLite. The place looked exactly as it had back in the '50s, a well-maintained building with ample parking on three sides.

I slowly exited my vehicle, stepped up to the counter, and ordered a medium vanilla custard cone. It was eleven-thirty a.m. and the Dairy DeLite had just opened for business. I asked the young man waiting on me if he knew what had happened to the Feed Bag.

"Mister, that place has been called Under the Pier for as long as I can remember. I've never known it by any other name."

"Could ya' ask somebody about it?" I insisted. "That joint used to be a pretty hot spot when I was a teenager." At first, I thought that the young employee standing behind the counter's sliding screen would be helpful, but then I detected in his personality the exact same sarcasm that I had possessed and exhibited when I was his age back in '59.

"Are ya' some kind of historian, or are you a *Civil War* veteran?" the kid wisely asked.

"Neither," I adamantly replied. "The last *Civil War* veteran was named Walter Williams. He died at age 117 on December 19, 1959."

The teenager behind the counter was not thoroughly impressed with my historical knowledge. "Do ya' read encyclopedias all night long, or is your last name *Guinness?"* the callow attendant sneered.

I detested the kid's general nastiness. I soon realized I really was resenting the way I too used to act. 'It's a good thing this churlish punk wasn't around in the late '50s, or he'd be cruisin' for a bruisin',' I thought. "You see, son," I candidly answered. "December 19, 1959 was just ten-days before I moved-away from the area. My buddies and I were discussing Walter Williams' death over there in what used to be the Feed Bag on the evening of December 28, 1959."

I felt like telling the wise-ass that I remembered things by association. Since I connected Walter Williams' death with my own departure from Levittown, I mentally joined those two events with the eventual demise of the Feed Bag. The kid should then understand that Walter Williams' passing was relevant to my current needs and purposes. Rather than bore my listener with more past and present trivia, I figured I would pursue a different line of questioning. I was still trying my best to be sincere, although I was rapidly losing patience with the bad-attitude adolescent. "Has anyone else come here and inquired about the Feed Bag?"

"Not to my knowledge," the cocky kid confessed. "Now, Sir, I hate to be rude, but I was a little late for work today, and since the new manager is a real bitchin' bastard, I have to clean-up the back room, and wipe down the machinery before noon."

My frustration with the insolent jerk was mounting, and I wondered how adults ever tolerated the flippant remarks of the Diablos back in the '50s. At that moment, I felt like a frustrated District Attorney trying to interrogate a complete idiot.

"Well then," I persisted. "Answer me just one more thing. What ever happened to the phone booth that used to be to the left of this building facing the Feed Bag, er, I mean Under the Pier?"

"Hey Mister, are ya' Clark Kent or somebody? There hasn't been a phone booth at the Dairy DeLite for the last seven-years or so. Just the phone you see on that stand over there is all I can remember. But," the young rogue continued, "if ya' want to change into your other costume right now, I promise you I won't look!"

'Smart ass' punk,' I thought. 'I could've gotten more information from a polite deaf mute.'

I paid the arrogant kid for my vanilla custard and then thanked the jerk for his lack of cooperation. I mumbled to myself all the way back to my cherry *Park Avenue* how the world's future was in danger because of disrespectful, impertinent, brazen, snot-nosed youth.

As I sat in my car licking my delicious custard, I considered that if the kid had been around in the late '50s, I would have made a point of beating the living feces out of him. 'Unless that smart aleck would've had Cummings, Langford, or Quinn around to protect his rear-end, then that young punk would've been dead meat, road kill, if the Diablos were still haunting the area,' I thought.

I felt like getting out of my car and telling the kid that if he were a trifle prettier, he would look half as good as Lois Lane, or that he couldn't even carry Jimmy Olson's jockstrap, or Perry White's enema bag. 'How could I ever communicate with a ridiculous moron of his ilk?' I concluded. 'The only links between his era and my generation are George Reeves and Christopher Reeve, separate '50s and '80s *Superman* actors.'

Then, my mind produced a very scary thought. 'That wise-ass at the custard counter would've probably made an excellent Diablo.' I finished eating my tasty cone, started my motor, raised the power windows, blasted the air-conditioner, and then flicked on the stereo.

I stared at the spot where the Dairy DeLite phone booth once had been located back in the '50s, and then my head twisted to the left to view the building that had once housed my other hangout. 'The Feed Bag and the Dairy DeLite were settings for numerous Diablos' adventures,' I recollected.

I finally decided to motor into Bristol to locate Post Office Box 2000. I hoped that the postal key held the answers to the many puzzles still occupying my addled mind. 'Have Quinn, Bo, Carnie, Tinker, and Robbie also remembered our 1959 reunion pledge? Did anybody else remember, or even care?'

Chapter 5
"The Letter"

I fondly recalled the 1950s on my pleasant drive from *Route 13* to the Bristol Post Office. The *Korean War* had ended, prosperity was flourishing, Suburbia was expanding, and with the *G.I. Bill,* war veterans like my father were able to obtain low interest loans to purchase homes.

White families had evacuated the crowded cities in pursuit of a higher standard of living, cleaner air, better shopping centers, escape from urban crime, and most particularly, a brighter future for the ever-proliferating baby-boomer generation.

The early '50s decade was a less complicated era than the present computer age. Interaction between human beings was direct and personal. There were no ATM Machines, no *Xerox* machines, no fax machines, no telephone answering devices, no cellular phones, no compact discs, no video games, no personal computers, no databases, no *911,* and no cable television. Strangely enough, the Diablos lived perfectly well without *McDonald's, Burger Kings, Pizza Huts, Denny's, Taco Bells, I-Hops* or *Boston Markets*. All we needed was a place like the Feed Bag to satisfy our lust for food.

Most stores and restaurants were mom and pop operations, or were family run, like Luigi and Domenick managing the Feed Bag, and Hal Irving overseeing Hal's Talk of the Town Delicatessen. The '50s decade was a much simpler and less chaotic period before the deluge of giant franchises, corporate conglomerates, and the perils of an impersonal Megalopolis. And we got along pretty well with only one public telephone company serving our communications' needs.

As I traveled south on River Drive, which paralleled the *Delaware,* I cherished that time before Rap Music, before the Eagles, before Fleetwood Mac, before the Doors, before the Beach Boys, before ABBA, before the Rolling Stones, before the Supremes, before the Temptations, and yes, even before The Beatles.

Roller blades and skateboards were unheard of in Levittown, Pennsylvania in the '50s era. Hula-hoops, Davy Crockett coonskin hats, poodle skirts, saddle shoes, and black and white sneakers were regarded as being "cool". Pegged pants, hangouts, saddle-stitching, *Edsels,* white bucks, penny loafers, pedal pushers, sock hops, and *American Bandstand* were "boss". Passion pits, "submarine races", DA haircuts, and multi-zipper black leather jackets were "not square". And finally, 3-D glasses, the jitterbug, and "cruisin" around the main drag in a sleek convertible were the "in things" for teens to do.

There were friendly greetings like "Boogety-boogety-boogety-shoo" and "Ootie-ootie". There were fifteen-cent hamburgers, the Salk Vaccine had been developed, roll-on deodorant had been invented, *Disneyland* had opened in California, and the *Hand Jive* had become a new dance sensation. And '50s teenagers were not haunted by the twin specters of drugs and AIDS. The '50s decade was a very special time for guys and gals to grow-up; to share friendships; to fall in love, and to experience life. The only real perils to such Utopian joy were criminal greasers like the Kenwood Kamikazes.

The AM dial dominated the radio waves, and in the Philadelphia metropolitan area, the "in" station was WIBG, Wibbage Radio 99. The biggest name DJ was Joe Niagara, whose "Niagara Calls in Philly" was a battle cry for great rhythm and lyrics about to be spun. Later, there was Hy Lit, another popular WIBG disc jockey, whose immortal refrain "Hyski-O-Roonie-McVouty-O-Zoot" captivated the hearts of millions of teen fans. Other great radio personalities like Jerry Blavat, the "Geator with the Heater", also known as "The Boss with the Hot Sauce", soon would also appear.

Every once in a while, Bo Jalonec, Tinker, Carnie, or Quinn would tune-in Cousin Brucie out of New York, or Alan Freed, a DJ transplant from Cleveland to Manhattan. Freed had coined the term "Rock and Roll" as a code name for "black rhythm and blues". But for the most part, Philly' was where it was at, and Wibbage gave us our daily diet of Bill Haley and the Comets, Buddy Holly and the Crickets, and Jerry Lee Lewis.

The Diablos despised "cover versions" of black rhythm and blues performed by such lily-white artists as Pat Boone. The Diablos didn't mind Pat Boone's original "white" melodies like "Love Letters In the Sand" and "April Love", but when the artist did "white cover versions" of Fats Domino's "Ain't That A Shame" and Little Richard's "Tutti-Frutti," the nice guy with the "white bucks" turned us off from the first vocal note.

As I entered Bristol from Edgely, my car stereo picked-up the familiar baritone of a Philly' DJ, "Let's take a walk down Memory Lane." "Born Too Late" by the Poni-Tails was played, and I felt a degree of remorse for all of those twenty-first century kids who were not interacting with their peers; who were sitting in their bedrooms playing video games on their computers, and living a lonely, isolated existence, having electronic machines as their best friends.

Today, "virtual reality" allows kids to function in an artificial computer-generated environment, but back in the '50s, we had "actual reality", where we experienced firsthand thrills and chills, not adventures simulated through a machine or floppy disk, but through minute-to-minute, face-to-face contact with other human beings.

I managed to locate a parking space a half-block away from the Bristol Post Office. I locked my car, something the Diablos had seldom done in '50s Levittown, and I briskly ascended the flagstone steps. In my rush, I nearly ran into a middle-aged woman and a young girl I presumed was *her* granddaughter, as the pair exited the building.

After scanning the boxes during several seconds of confusion, I discovered compartment 2000. I anxiously inserted the key, turned the lock, and to my satisfaction, a small tug opened the door. Inside were two envelopes. One was addressed "Words", and the second was designated "Carnie".

I removed my property and then quickly locked the box. I scurried out of the building, descending the stone steps in a hurry. I almost knocked over a short, fat, bald-headed man that was also in a rush, and we both instinctively said, "Excuse me".

When I reentered my vehicle, I fumbled with the envelope for a second, wanting to rip it open to learn its contents. But then, I said to myself, "If you could wait over forty-years for this information, why not another hour or two?"

So, I placed the letter next to the driver's seat for further examination, when I would feel good and ready to analyze and comprehend its instructions. I headed north again, planning to see if the Edgely Fire Company had also become extinct as had the Feed Bag and Hal's Talk of the Town Delicatessen.

I was somewhat surprised to find two Edgely Fire Department buildings. I quickly recognized the Edgely Hall, which had been the tan, stucco firehouse I remembered from late 1959. The newer structure had a brick facade. The more recent edifice was the current location of the Edgely Fire Department. The former firehouse I had frequently observed in my youth has been converted to its new appearance. It is now used in 2000 as a hall to raise money with Bingo games, dances, civic club fundraisers, and private rentals.

As I stared at the tan stucco building, I recalled my fifteenth birthday. Tinker, Carnie, and I had volunteered to become junior firemen, and we were assigned to work the fire hall's Bingo games every other Thursday night. My chief responsibility was to sell paper Bingo sheets at a quarter per card to supplement the cards already held by the players. We three Diablos sometimes created our own social morality system. Just like Robin Hood often stole from the rich to give to the poor, we sometimes imaginatively rigged the games to redistribute winnings in order to assist certain deserving, have-not Bingo patrons.

Carnie's mom wasn't too well off financially after her deadbeat husband had stopped paying the family bills in 1954, so the three of us manipulated events so she would win at least one game a visit. After getting four legitimate numbers, Carnie's mom would write-down a fifth number that had been recently called to fraudulently complete a Bingo column or row.

Tinker, Carnie, and I worked the floor, so when Carnie's mother yelled out "Bingo", one of us would bolt-over to her table and read-off the five numbers (four of which were authentic). Then, one of us would dash to the stage, collect the prize money from the cashier, and deliver it to the grateful lady.

I almost had a cardiac arrest one Thursday night when Carnie's mom screamed out "Bingo!" Lieutenant Collins instructed me to analyze the card of another lady, who had also called-out "Bingo!", and he himself hustled over to scrutinize Carnie's mom's card. Much to my relief, the woman to whom I was assigned had placed a red plastic marker on a wrong space. But I was trembling to think that the Diablos' little scam would be discovered by the Edgely Fire Hall officers.

Lieutenant "Bingo" Collins read-out the five-numbers on Carnie's mom's card, and the fire department's ball announcer confirmed Carnie's mom's winning column numbers as being valid. The woman had finally achieved an honest "Bingo!" just when she had needed it most.

Driving north to Levittown, I compared the '50s behavior of the Diablos to a pride of lions on a *National Geographic* television special. The male lions are dominant in the pride, and the females take subordinate roles' as did the girlfriends of the Diablos, the Kamikazes, the Renegades, and the other Levittown gangs. And there was a definite pecking order prevalent within *our* gang.

Although I never saw my hero Quinn in a complete fight from beginning to end, he was our leader, and just like a dominant male lion, our 'general' always held his head high. Submissive lions lower their heads to confirm who rules the pack, and Carnie, Tinker, and I often lowered ours in deference to Quinn's eminent presence.

After Bo Jalonec, I wound-up being third in the pecking order, not because of my strength, looks, or mean appearance, but simply because of my brains and my love of literature. Tinker, Carnie, and Robbie were at the bottom of the Diablos' brain trust, because those gang members needed guidance, reassurance, and leadership. Tinker was an ill-tempered follower; Carnie was a confused fool; Robbie lacked confidence; I was a shy wordsmith; Jokes was a confident stud stallion, and Quinn had an awesome silent power that made the rest of us (except Tinker) revere and worship his presence.

Lion behavior also applied to the interaction of the Levittown gangs. On animal TV specials, lion prides often battle each other for territory and superiority, just like the Diablos would predictably challenge the Kamikazes and the Renegades. But then, lion clans often join together in alliance by necessity when threatened by marauding hyena packs, for I have seen hyenas on *National Geographic* jump lions in groups of three or more, and knock the living stuffing out of the kings of beasts, sending them scurrying up trees for safety. In that respect, the greaser gangs would sometimes unite to thwart joint adversaries like the jocks and the police.

The Diablos always regarded the police as just another gang, wearing peculiar blue uniforms, and it was a triumph to outwit the fuzz and to also annoy and frustrate their existence. It would have been regarded as a shame and dishonor to ever be apprehended by the cops, for being caught and arrested was tantamount to being caught nude with Stanley Tezeeker in the third-floor Men's Room at Cardinal Reagan High by Father Malcolm. So, if Carnie, Tinker, Jokes, and I were ever stopped and arrested by a policeman, then that embarrassment would be analogous to four proud lions being victimized by one stupid hyena.

The Diablos "liked" people, but we absolutely "loved" things. To screw-around with our cherished street machines was viewed by Quinn's Dogwood Hollow gang as a grave and unforgiving declaration of war. Our hotrods were our freedom mobiles, yes, our escape mechanisms. The autos got us away from parents, adults, duties, chores, responsibilities, high school, drudgery, and the mediocrity of middle-class values.

I observed a mint-condition '58 Ford at the intersection of Levittown Parkway and *Route 13,* and that treasure from the past made me remember the neat cars the Diablos used to pilot around southeastern Pennsylvania. I would occasionally ride around with Quinn all night long and be perfectly happy not saying a word. I loved his black '42 Ford coupe, with its wide white-walled tires, even more than I enjoyed Jokes' enviable green and cream '57 Chevy. The '42 coupe was souped-up, had class, and the boss wheels had a wicked rep for being fast off the line. And when I had the honor of sitting in Quinn's impeccable chariot, I felt like a happy lark about to soar to new heights.

But at least four nights per week, Quinn was out gallivanting-around with Patty Van Arsdale. Romantic relationships often complicated the lives of the Diablos, because when one of the guys did find a girlfriend, he spent more time with her than with his buddies. His friends often got pissed-off, and simultaneously, her friends got pissed-off at her, so everyone else went-out to meet new companions of the opposite sex, causing more and more people to become extremely pissed-off. That jealousy pattern would perpetuate the monotonous cycle, and that's why the dating ritual made life crazier and more hazardous in Levittown.

When Quinn wasn't with Patty, we still had to scout him down because our leader was a recluse, staying within himself, grooming the mystery of his introverted personality. Once Jokes and I were riding in Quinn's '42 Ford coupe, speeding down Haines Road and Jalonec innocently expressed, "Slow down Quinn, or you'll be stopped for *recluse* drivin'!"

Quinn got madder than hell with Bo and answered in a very firm and stern tone, "Grow a second rectum *BO*zo, since you're so full of crap that you need two anuses." It wasn't so much what Quinn had stated, but the authoritative manner in which he had expressed it. Bo shut-up right there and then, and I instantly knew the difference between the two. Jokes Jalonec was a spouter of words, and Quinn was a man of decisive action.

Bo had the second neatest car in the Diablos. His dad drove-around in a blue and white '53 Chevy just so his son could be spoiled rotten by the green and cream '57 Chevy, which was the "braggin-wagon" of the gang. In 1959, Bo's dad wanted to purchase a new Chevy for Jokes, but Jalonec loved the design and style of his "green and cream" two-door so much that my pal declined his pop's offer.

Jokes' employment at Harley's Hardware was merely a token gesture to convince the world that the blond Adonis was seriously preparing for the monotonous routines of adult life. I had asked both Quinn and Jokes if I could drive their cars around, but each was smart enough to ask me if I possessed a valid Pennsylvania driver's license, and after I answered "yes" to their questions, each guy insisted on seeing it with *their* own eyes. As a result, I never had the opportunity to pilot either terrific vehicle.

Carnie's black '49 Mercury had to be my third choice of Diablos' transportation, followed by Slip Carson's '54 green Chevy convertible, and then Ace Roberts' blue and white 1955 '88 Oldsmobile.

Tinker's black '49 Plymouth would have to be at the bottom of the gang's hot-rod totem pole, because like its owner, it was unkempt and filthy. Tinker was the only Diablo who daily wore his dirty laundry, and his car was always cluttered with wrenches and pliers on the greasy seats, and the tin pig had motor oil cans and *Coke* and *Pepsi* bottles littering the floor. But the jalopy did transport us around Bucks County pretty well, and despite its hideous, musty appearance, the raunchy vehicle was always reliable.

Once I had asked Carnie and Tinker if I could drive their cars around Levittown. Each inquired if I had a license, and each believed me when I responded "yes". That difference had to be a major distinction between Quinn and Bo Jalonec on one hand, and Carnie and Tinker on the other. Carnie and Tinker believed my prevarications and the too trustful, gullible fools never worried about me smashing-up their precious automobiles.

My affirmative answer to Carnie and Tinker was really a little white lie, since I did own a legitimate Pennsylvania Fishing License, but Carnie and Tinker had neglected to specify what kind of license I had acquired and owned.

"How come your old man doesn't let you drive his green and white '55 Chevy?" Carnie asked.

I had to ponder hard for a moment to create a plausible explanation. "Because Pop thinks I'll either crack it up, or bust the engine block doing 110. He says he'd feel more comfortable knowin' I'm bustin' up your car rather than his."

Carnie must have found some merit in my inferior logic. "Okay, J.W., take the wheel while I pick my nose, fart, scratch my balls, jerk-off, or do something else even less constructive."

I drove my *Park Avenue* around the Levittown Shopping Center, and I became depressed while noticing the "Shop-A-Rama's" poor appearance. I remembered how all the buildings were brand-new, thriving businesses back in the '50s, and my memory recalled how the expansive outdoor mall was a genuine showplace for area people and tourists to visit.

I next passed the old baseball field where I had played organized sports as a teen. My heart sank when I observed the dense growth of yellow and purple weeds in the outfield. The overall ruinous condition of the place greatly distressed me. It contradicted the pretty setting I had known in my youth.

My mind gradually returned to the reality of July 1, 2000. I made a turn onto Mill Creek Parkway, coming from the direction of Fairless Hills, and my next objective was Dogwood Hollow. I pulled into the familiar entrance off of Haines Road, which I had passed through so many times during my youth.

I glanced into the rear-view mirror and studied my fat, middle-aged face with its double chin. The only youthful features that still appeared the same were my pale blue eyes. 'I didn't always look this way,' I imagined. 'There was a special time when I didn't have this hideous widow's peak. I once possessed a full head of hair, combed neatly along the sides with thick *Vaseline Petroleum Jelly*, culminating in a neat duck's ass (DA) with a razor cut straight across the nape of my neck, done in tribute to my teen hero, Quinn, the epitome of '50s Levittown bad-ass greasers.'

I stopped outside 318 Dogwood Drive, the former residence of Quinn and his cousins, Chuckie and Jimmy Callahan. Over the years, the home had been radically changed in its exterior appearance. Who knows how many families had occupied the house since 1959? My curiosity got the better of me, and I decided to slit-open the envelope from the Bristol Post Office box. I squinted my eyes to read the following typed letter.

> Words,
>
> How ya' doin'? Hope you're still alive to read these sentences. The reunion of the Diablos was established in the Feed Bag (which you probably discovered, no longer exists) on December 28, 1959. After exactly forty-one years of suspense, please meet me at Corvette's Diner, between University and Fifth Avenues, in the Hillcrest section of San Diego, California.
>
> My new address is 1028 Brookes Avenue, Mission Hills' section of the same city. Looking forward to seeing you and the guys at 7 p.m. sharp on the evening of December 28, 2000. I hope that God and fate have been good to you!
>
> Thanks for the memories,
>
> Quinn

One last item needed to be investigated before my return trip to Hammonton. I drove through Kenwood, turned right onto Haines Road, and casually guided my sedan into Junewood. My pilgrimage followed the exact path of my old *Philadelphia Bulletin* Junewood paper route, and I recalled every one of my 124 former customers' houses as I nostalgically repeated the familiar itinerary.

I started my nostalgic pilgrimage at the corner of Junewood Drive and Jewel Lane, just across the grassy meadow behind Robbie Wilkinson's house on Dogwood Drive. The high-tension electric power towers still bisected the field, exactly as the imposing structures had back in '59.

I then proceeded east on Jewel Lane; hit Junewood Drive again, angled left to Jolly Lane, and finally arrived at Jonquil Lane, stopping dead in front of Bo Jalonec's old abode. I wondered what ever happened to the slickest and most handsome of the Diablos? A tear trickled-down my right cheek, and I recalled trekking up and down those streets a thousand times on my paper route as I heard Jimmy McCracklin sing "The Walk" over oldies station *WOGL-FM, 98.1.*

While finally motoring south on *Route 206,* I stopped to gaze at a familiar landmark. I contemplated the ripples on cedar-watered Atsion Lake, which rekindled an unsavory memory from March of 1960. In Pennsy', a kid could obtain a driver's license at age sixteen. While in Levittown, Dad did not allow me to drive, claiming I was too irresponsible. I took offense to his inflexible edict, but in the final analysis, his wisdom was correct. After my family moved back to Jersey in late December of '59, I gladly received my driving credentials after turning seventeen.

In early March of '60, I had been invited to a Levittown birthday party given by a pretty girl I had dated, Carol Zella. As I traveled *Route 206* south towards Hammonton, I noticed that the highway was dark, quiet and deserted. I buried the speedometer on Dad's '55 Chevy all the way from Atsion Lake to Hammonton, a distance of seven straight, monotonous miles. Everything seemed copasetic until I approached the light at the intersection of *206* and *Route 30,* the *White Horse Pike.*

As I waited for the green signal to appear, I noticed a large cloud of hot steam billowing from the Chevy's exhaust pipe. In my exuberance to experience intense speed, I had broken the six cylinder's head gasket, and water had leaked into the crankcase, causing a dense jet of white vapor to be emitted. My stupidity had cracked the motor block and had damaged the engine's camshaft. My wild joyride had resulted in a considerable, unexpected expense for Pop.

Although Dad was not Robert Young, Pop often had to show me that *Father Knows Best.* My father was a good judge of character, who believed in punishment for misdeeds, and who also had me easily figured-out as if I was a primary school addition problem. I was forbidden to drive his fixed '55 Chevy out of Hammonton for a year.

My stupid fascination with speed had cost me the privilege of visiting my old Diablos' pals. Soon, Carnie and Robbie also moved out of Dogwood Hollow; Bo's family moved to Pittsburgh, The only ones left there were Quinn and Tinker. I was always in awe of Quinn, and strongly desired to remember him as a superhuman legend. As for Tinker, I honestly never wanted to see the miserable maniac's evil face ever again.

Chapter 6
"Dogwood Hollow" (1954-'55)

New schools, changing environments, new towns, and different friends can all be traumatic experiences for any kid struggling through maturation. From fifth-grade through high school graduation, I had attended six different schools, and so, like a Darwinian chameleon, I had learned to adapt to new situations as second nature. I had discovered plenty about human "social survival", which can be just as treacherous as battling for physical dominance in the animal kingdom.

I remember my folks getting their first black and white television early in 1953, and I had to sit-down with them in Hammonton and watch the Queen Elizabeth Coronation. The formal ceremony went on for hours and hours. I thought to myself that the mere act of putting a crown on somebody's head should take no more than fifteen-seconds. So, even at ten-years of age, I had already been showing symptoms of cynicism with the artificiality of adult traditions.

Before 1954, my early youth was rather nondescript. At age ten, I recall helping-out with chores at my grandparents' farm market on *Route 30* in Hammonton; playing *Little League* baseball for DiDonato's Bowling, and being very sad leaving childhood friends at St. Joseph School.

I had just turned eleven in 1954 when my family moved-out of New Jersey to 50 Daffodil Lane in the Dogwood Hollow section of Levittown, Pennsylvania. My sister Annie was six, and my younger brother Skip was an infant. My parents had nicknamed my younger sibling Skip because he was addicted to *Skippy Peanut Butter.*

My parents became friendly with Jack and Stella Burns, who looked almost identical to Fred and Ethel Mertz on the popular *I Love Lucy Show*. The Burns' lived next door to Sal Palermo, his wife Carmella, and their beautiful daughter, Angie. Mom and Dad would return home from the Burns's in the spring of '54 and report tales of yelling, cursing, bullying, and general mayhem originating at 66 Daffodil Lane, the Palermo domicile, where Dad thought "the local Mafia" resided.

Levittown was designed to be a "middle-class community", but more specifically, the place was a "white middle-class community". Caucasian families moved there in quest of a better way of life, free from the rampant social disorganization that existed in eastern U.S. cities. Levittown was an innovative experiment in suburban living where shopping centers, houses, highways, schools, and recreation areas were engineered to mix together like a kitchen recipe to form a tranquil, harmonious, physical environment. All in all, my first impression was that it seemed like a great place to live.

In 1954, human interaction was stratified and compartmentalized in Levittown. The new city was exclusively "white". I would come in contact with some black kids at St. Mark School over in Bristol, but most of them lived several miles away in *that* town, and few blacks belonged to my Catholic faith. Blacks mostly interacted with blacks, and whites stayed mostly with whites, and that brand of racial segregation was conveniently explained to young people as "separate but equal" by their parents.

"Ethnic and religious segregation", as well as racial separation was quite evident. The Kalens, who were Jewish, lived across the street from us on Daffodil Lane, and their neighbors, who were Irish and Scottish, wouldn't allow their kids to play with "the Hebrew children". To avert neighborhood conflict, Dad allowed my sister Annie to play with the Kalen children on Monday, Wednesday and Friday, and she was permitted to interact with the Irish and Scottish kids on the other four days of the week.

Divisions along nationality and Christian religious lines also existed. Protestants did not marry Catholics, and Irish Catholics did not marry Italian Catholics, and Baptists did not marry Presbyterians, and Christians did not marry Jews, and Occidentals did not marry Orientals.

So, to me, looking back, Levittown, Pennsylvania was like a giant Bingo card with horizontal and vertical lines drawn in orderly rows to demarcate race, religion, culture, nationality, and a person's economic status. Levittown reflected the rigid norms and standards of America that had been established by the predominance of White Anglo-Saxon Protestantism.

Before I could even talk about a girl, the elders wanted to know about her family's economic level, their religion, their nationality, her father's employment, and the ancestral tree. People were imprisoned in rigid general classifications. At least, that is the way I recollect American society as being constructed in the 1950s.

I don't remember too much about 1954, except that Mom would faithfully watch the *Arthur Godfrey Show,* and Betty Furness would always say, "You can be sure if it's *Westinghouse".* And if I was well-behaved, I was allowed to stay-up and watch *The Tonight Show* with Steve Allen. Everyone was afraid of someone calling him or her "a Communist". And an American adult's greatest dread was to be called a "Communist" or "a Communist Sympathizer" on national TV by Republican Senator Joseph McCarthy of Wisconsin.

Twenty-nine million American households had television sets in the mid-fifties, or about sixty-percent of the national population. The new medium was already anchoring itself as a powerful force in the marketing of products and in the forging of a new set of contemporary values to challenge the practices supported by ultra-traditional WASP America.

In 1954, the Cold War was mounting between the United States and Russia, and on the domestic scene, racial segregation in public schools was being challenged in the judicial system, with rulings outlawing the practice of "separate but equal schools" in certain parts of the United States southland.

Jackie Robinson had recently broken the color barrier with the *Brooklyn Dodgers,* and Little Richard, Fats Domino, and Chuck Berry were about to do the same thing in the music world. The stage was set for massive and sweeping social changes, and Levittown was like a vast social test tube, ready to undergo cultural experimentation, upheaval, and evolution.

In '54, at age eleven, like most starry-eyed boys, my aspiration was to become a professional baseball player. I loved athletics: baseball, football, basketball, and running. In *Little League* I played second base for Meenan Oil, and the coach was grooming me to be a pitcher for the team in 1955.

I was thrilled with Willie Mays' over-the-head catch off the bat of Cleveland's Vic Wertz at the Polo Grounds, and being a National League fan, I was elated when the *New York Giants* beat the *Indians* four games to zip in the '54 *World Series.* That was done in spite of Cleveland's awesome pitching staff that included Bob Lemon, Bob Feller, Mike Garcia, and Early Wynn.

I was greatly influenced by long distance runner Roger Bannister, who had broken the four-minute-mile with a time of 3:58.8. The circumference of Dogwood Drive was approximately a mile long, so I would imitate Roger Bannister's feat by dashing and sprinting as fast as my legs would carry me. If I could have improved my training methods and my-conditioning, I might have been able to shave some time off of eight-minutes and fifty-three seconds, my fastest lap.

It was on one of my running expeditions that I first met Tinker. The psycho was selling lemonade at a nickel a glass out in front of Robbie Wilkinson's house at 164 Dogwood Drive. Tink told me that Robbie was inside "takin' a dump" in the toilet, and so I paused from my cross-country exercise to enjoy some liquid refreshment. Although I did not know Tinker formally, I had known of him, for the slippery weasel had the reputation of being the most uncivilized student at the James Buchanan School.

"What's your name?" I amiably inquired.

"I go by Tinker but my close pals call me Tink," the unkempt-looking kid snottily replied.

"I *Tink* I get the message," I joked.

My new acquaintance was hardly amused with my sense of humor. "Not only are you a wise ass, but you're also a stupid ass!" the argumentative kid deliberately chided.

I was totally astonished with Tinker's crass, uncouth personality. Seldom would a new comrade address me with such lack of manners.

"I don't follow you," I replied. I was still stunned that a guy would call me a name without really knowing me. The rambunctious bully seemed to violate all the rules of proper breeding, and that's precisely why I found his attitude fascinating.

"Ya' run around Dogwood Drive every night tryin' to show everybody you're Roger Bannister, or somebody," the nasty kid sneered. "That's shit-ass stupid! If ya' used as much energy doin' other stuff, ya' could learn how to fix cars; get a girl pregnant, or even have your first orgasm. Ya' probably don't even know how to work your stick, do ya'?"

Before I could answer Tinker's crude insults, Robbie Wilkinson came out of his house. He formally introduced me to Tinker, whose real name was Jeremy Foster. After shooting the bull, the two amigos and I shut-down the makeshift lemonade stand for the afternoon, and next, we trekked-over to Tinker's house at 87 Dewberry Lane, just a few doors down from Susie Parker, the cutest twelve-year-old girl in Dogwood Hollow.

Tinker escorted Robbie and me into his bedroom, which looked like a marriage between a dump and a cesspool. Wrenches, screwdrivers, hammers, nuts and bolts, and jars with living and dead creatures, ranging from insects to frogs, were everywhere.

"I love all sorts of animals," Tinker declared, opening the door to his bedroom closet. "In fact, I like animals better than I like people!"

"Ahhhhhh! What the heck is that?" I shrieked. I had never expected to see such a bizarre sight inside somebody's house.

"It's only Herman. He's my pet boa constrictor. He's pretty old now. I expect he'll die in the next year or so. I haven't fed him since last Saturday, so in a way you're lucky. You'll get to see Herman eat a healthy meal."

Tinker winked at Robbie, and I didn't know what to expect, since I was still in shock from seeing a twelve-foot-long snake. My new friend reached-up to a high shelf and gripped a glass jar with a large brown rat inside. The nutcase unscrewed the top, and casually dropped the doomed rat into Herman's cage, which was really a six-foot-long and three-foot-high empty aquarium, having a hinged lid attached to a wooden frame.

My eyes saw the petrified look in the rat's eyes as the boa constrictor uncoiled and stretched its scaly neck in its victim's direction. In a matter of thirty-seconds, the snake had wrapped itself around the helpless rodent, squeezing it to death. Then, just as skillfully, the boa opened its huge jaws, chomped-down several times on the luscious vermin, and proceeded to devour its prey with morbid efficiency.

"Pretty damned cool, eh?" Tinker asked me.

"So cool that I feel like pukin'," I honestly answered. I had never before seen such graphic animalistic behavior in person. It was the most horrible thing I had witnessed in my young life.

"It ain't so dramatic after ya' see it five or six times," Robbie admitted. "It loses its effect."

"Do ya' have any *Alka-Seltzer?"* I asked. "I think I need to gulp-down about a gallon a water!"

"Sure, no problem," Tinker replied. "I'll get ya' some after I show ya' something else."

Tinker reached-up and grabbed a second jar with an airtight lid from the closet shelf. Honestly, his unpredictable behavior fascinated me. Tink then unzipped his shabby dungarees, turned his back to Robbie and me, pulled-down his dirty jockey shorts, which were more gray than white, and quickly farted quite loudly into the glass jar. Hastily, the sociopath screwed the lid back on, and I had trouble fathoming his modus operandi.

"What the heck was that all about?" I inquisitively asked.

"I just farted in the damned jar," Tinker declared.

"I know that, but why?" I challenged. Tinker wasn't like any kid I had known in rural New Jersey. Every friend I had known would never flash his rear end to a new acquaintance.

"Ya' really have a low IQ, don't ya'," Tinker scolded. "Because if I screw the lid on right away, the fart's odor is preserved. If I want to gross somebody out, I simply unscrew and remove the lid and ask the person to smell inside. Isn't it a gas?"

I did not know whether Tinker was bluffing or if the nutcase had been serious. I had to dig a little deeper into his cerebral dynamics. "Does it work?"

"Yes, it does," Tinker verified. "Because just two weeks ago, I took a portable fart to school and grossed-out Angie Palermo."

"What did she say?" I wanted to know.

"Nothin', 'cause the Bitch nearly choked to death. She had to go to the nurse's office, vomit for a minute, gargle with *Listerine,* blow her nose, and then puke a second time," Tink proudly disclosed. "I gotta' admit; it was really pretty cool!"

"That's pretty neat. I really like your style, Tink," I instinctively answered like an eleven-year-old submitting to peer pressure.

Even when Tink was only eleven, his beleaguered mom, who worked as a cashier at the *Grants Department Store* in the Levittown Shop-A-Rama, was afraid of his misconduct. But I respected the young rebel because even a year before the Davy Crockett coonskin hat became popular, Tinker would trap and catch his own animals in the woods adjacent to Robbie's house, and so to me, the young maverick was a contemporary, 1950s-style frontiersman.

Several months later, I was cleaning-out and washing an empty jar of peanut butter at 50 Daffodil Lane. Mom asked me, "J. W., what are you doing?"

"Oh, nothin' major, Ma. I'm gonna' start collectin' some of those Japanese beetles out on the side rose bushes," I falsely stated. "I figure I'll need a glass jar to keep them in."

"Sounds like a rather interesting hobby," Mom evaluated and commented. "Don't forget to puncture some air holes in the lid so they can breathe!"

And then a rather interesting scenario entered my brain. 'Could a serious fart kill a colony of Japanese beetles trapped inside an air-tight lidded glass jar?' I wondered. I never suspected that Tinker's negative influence was already adversely corrupting my innocence.

The modest home at 50 Daffodil Lane cost Dad $10,000, a considerable sum in 1954. As a rule, I use the "ten times principle" because most goods, items, products, and services are at least ten times as expensive today in 2000 as they were in the 1950s.

Delivery-men were always actively prowling the Daffodil Lane neighborhood. Milk was mostly brought to the door in glass bottles. We got ours from *Harbison's Dairies,* which competed with *Abbotts Dairy* for residential customers. I remember what a change it was when *Harbison's* orange juice was suddenly packaged in a waxed carton, as opposed to the standard glass bottle, and how reluctant Mom was to try the new product.

And then there was the *Bond Bread* man, and the fruit and vegetable hucksters, and the three ice cream trucks that competed for area business, *O'Doyle's, Jack and Jill,* and *Good Humor*, all claiming to sell the best flavors in their brand's mixtures.

When I think of the year 1955, my memory suddenly becomes more acute. I began to really enjoy music, and when "Rock around the Clock" hit the airwaves, that terrific song by Bill Haley and the Comets became the new national anthem for young people. The lyrics said it all, a new generation with boundless energy, capable of partying all night, and going far beyond the normal limits of fun. There was also a trace of rebellion in the song's lyrics that was more than rhythm; that in fact, was a statement of youth exploding out of *our* David Nelson stereotype and proudly revealing to the world, "This is what we're really made of!"

"Rock Around the Clock" was my generation's version of Patrick Henry's famous "Give me liberty or give me death!" speech. It was also my generation's *Declaration of Independence* to the adult world, saying, "We the Teens of the United States", and my generation's *Bill of Rights* and *United States Constitution* all compacted into one refrain, "We're gonna' rock, rock, rock 'til the broad daylight." Bill Haley and the Comets, a little-known Country and Western band from Chester, Pennsylvania, performed summer gigs down at the Jersey Shore. But the group had accomplished something magical when the band bridged the gap between white country and western music and black rhythm and blues. Their hit song really gained national attention in '55 when it was used as the theme for the motion picture *Blackboard Jungle,* and the pop tune soon opened the floodgates for Elvis, Chuck Berry, Buddy Holly, Little Richard, and the other founding fathers of rock and roll.

In the summer of '55, dances for teens in our area of Levittown were held in the outdoor basketball court, which was located in back of the Olympic-sized Brooke Swimming Pool in the recreation area between the Farmbrook, Stonybrook, and Greenbrook sections. I wore my standard attire of pegged pants with saddle-stitching down each side, and of course, flaps on the back pockets were in vogue. A plain cotton short-sleeved shirt was worn, and penny loafers and white socks completed the ensemble.

In 1955, I had a flattop haircut that was symbolic of being a jock, as opposed to the James Dean greaser look of sideburns, long hair smeared with *Vaseline,* and engineer boots with rolled-up dungarees. And tough guys wore either a white or a black tee shirt, depending on whether one was a "good tuff greaser" like Quinn, or a "bad-ass greaser" like Cummings.

Other songs in 1955 were played on the radio like: "Moments To Remember" by the Four Lads; "The Yellow Rose of Texas" by Mitch Miller and his orchestra; "Love is a Many Splendored Thing" by the Four Aces; "Mr. Sandman" by the Chordettes, and "Autumn Leaves" by Roger Williams. Although I spent time listening to those other artists, "Rock around the Clock" was the song that fully captured my imagination, stirred my soul, activated my spirits, and made me think about evolving into a greaser.

What Bill Haley had done to my ears, James Dean and *Rebel without a Cause* had done to my eyes, and it was the synthesis of those two magnificent cultural forces that affected my choice to "switch" from an avid jock into a prospective greaser. I finally found my comfort zone two-years later with my new pals: Quinn, Carnie, Bo, Robbie, and Tinker.

When I was twelve, Mom took me to see *The Wizard of Oz,* and a month later, I painfully struggled through her favorite movie, *Gone with the Wind,* because Mom had almost memorized Margaret Mitchell's lengthy novel, which she had read so many times. And after I became really friendly with Carnie, we saw Walt Disney's *Twenty Thousand Leagues under the Sea* seven times, which was five less than we had seen *Rebel without a Cause*. Almost my entire allowance was spent on movies and theater popcorn.

Smoking was regarded as a glamorous activity in '55. Mom and Dad each smoked over a pack of cigarettes a day. Dad smoked *Pall Mall,* and Mom puffed on the shorter *Lucky Strikes*. It's amazing that I don't presently have lung cancer from all of the passive smoking I had experienced.

One time, Dad drove us down to Baltimore to visit relatives, and when we stopped at a traffic light on *Route 40,* the *Pulaski Highway,* I looked-over to another kid, just like myself, traveling with *his* parents. The guy was enveloped in smoke, and I was trapped in a thick cloud of tar and nicotine, and I truly sympathized with my unidentified colleague as we both endured our dense environments. I waved to the anonymous, poor kid, and he waved back, in tacit acknowledgment of our mutual confined situations.

On the return trip from Baltimore, I tried an experiment. I lit up a cigarette in the back seat, and I signaled to Annie to remain quiet. I smoked the entire *Chesterfield* down to the bottom without my parents ever knowing, because the '55 Chevy was so saturated with fumes that my additional puffs spiraling upward went completely undetected. It was then that I seriously contemplated becoming a greaser. Of course, the peer influence of Carnie, Tinker, Quinn, Robbie, and Bo Jalonec eventually had a lot to do with my final decision two-years later.

The *Philadelphia Athletics* had left Connie Mack Stadium, moving to Kansas City, Missouri in 1955. Tinker liked the *A's,* and he and I got into countless arguments as to which was the better team, the *A's* or the *Phillies*, and which major league was better, the *American* or the *National.*

Tink thought that Bobby Shantz was a better pitcher than Robin Roberts, and that Gus Zernial was a better clean-up hitter than Del Ennis, and that Ferris Fain was a better first baseman for the *A's* than

Eddie Waitkus had been on the 1950 *Whiz Kids*. Tink did make a concession when it came to centerfielders. The *Phillies'* Richie Ashburn was easily the winner, hands down. Richie Ashburn was my baseball idol and hero.

During a particular *Little League* game, I imitated Richie Ashburn's batting style. I surprised the opposition by making a perfect bunt down the third base line. The count was one ball and two strikes, and if I had failed, my audacity would have resulted in an embarrassing out. Luckily, my daring effort was successful.

While on first base, I glanced over to the stands behind the boisterous visiting dugout and my eyes saw Bubbles Messina, a well-endowed girl sitting in the bleachers, cheering with a familiar young lady, Angela Palermo. The Sicilian dolls were both yelling mild criticisms in my direction: nasty derogatory words like "jerk," "creep," "freak," "punk", and "moron".

It was a tie game with my team, Meenan Oil, and our opposition, O'Connor Sanitary Disposal, each having two runs. I peered-over at the opposing shortstop, Popeye Messina, who had huge forearms. His hairy arms bulged-out from his uniform's sleeves.

Carnie came to bat and hit a slow chopper to the second baseman, who then flipped the ball to Bruno Messina at second. I slid very aggressively into the bag, but instead of making the relay throw to first base, Messina came-down hard with his elbow, and his hard bones intentionally caught me between my mouth and nose. I leaped-up; a trickle of crimson was flowing-out from my right nostril.

"What the heck did you do that for?"

"That's for pushing my sister into the *Delaware River,* you lousy chicken-shit!" Popeye was fully demonstrating that his family blood was thicker than mine was.

"You know Connie?" I angrily asked.

"Connie Who?" inquired Popeye, who was ready to bloody my other nostril.

"Connie Lingus; you can smell her all over your breath, ya' dago dirt bag!"

I had no idea what cunnilingus meant at age twelve, but I had once heard Tinker use the Connie Lingus insult before cruelly beating-up a jock, so it was the first invective that my devious mind could produce.

Before Popeye and I could begin brawling, the three umpires acted as referees and broke-up the ensuing skirmish. Our managers and the other players got into it pretty good, too, and several reserve policemen on duty had to come onto the field to separate the combatants.

In the bottom of the eighth inning tied game, I really aggravated Popeye. I won the game in true "Richie Ashburn style" by sprinting home after a passed ball. Popeye gave me the royal finger for my daring exploit, and then the muscular creep told Carnie after the game that the bully was on the lookout to get me for "intentionally pushing" his sister and his cousin into the *Delaware River*.

'Why am I always attracted to conflicts with the worst people in the worst families?' I kept repeating to myself as I looked into the stands and saw Sal Palermo and Dante Messina also yelling a litany of insults at me, alongside their beautiful daughters.

In June of '55, Carnie and I were walking home from Levittown's St. Michelle's School. As part of our daily ritual, we would take a shortcut through the field behind Robbie Wilkinson's house, separating Dogwood Hollow from Junewood. Every day, a mongrel dog would bark at us from behind a six-foot-high pen, and every day my pal Carnie would taunt that feisty mutt until the canine positively hated our guts. The nasty brute belonged to a patrolman for the local township police department.

On that particular afternoon, the cop's canine leaped over the fence and came like a rabid animal after Carnie, who faced the wild barking beast and shouted, "Don't bite me! Bite him!" I was around fifty-feet away, and the ferocious mutt abandoned its principal tormentor, and then obeying Carnie's command, snarled-up to me and administered a savage bite between my right hand's knuckles and wrist.

The dog's owner, still in uniform, came running on the double. Upon seeing my swollen, bleeding hand, the cop apologized for his animal's hostility and offered to take me to *Lower Bucks County Hospital* for a rabies shot. The officer captured his ill-tempered dog, returned it to its area of confinement, and then drove me to the emergency room where I was given the appropriate medical treatment.

Mom had to be notified, for even in those days, parental consent had to be obtained. The officer again apologized for his pet's aggressiveness. The cop let us off in front of Carnie's house, and after exiting the patrol car, my pal and I promised each other that *that* was the last time either of us ever wanted to ride in a police cruiser.

"Don't worry, J.W. I'll get even with that cop," my chum predicted.

"For what Carnie?"

"For havin' his dog bite your hand!"

"It wasn't *his* fault. And besides, it's just a dumb animal that lost its temper," I suggested in an attempt to quell my buddy's apparent inexplicable, vindictive anger. 'Why does Carnie hate that patrolman for helping me?' I wondered

"But J.W. I'll get even with that cop, and some other lousy cops, too," Carnie repeated in an almost obsessed tone of voice.

I could not identify the basis for my friend's great resentment. "It doesn't make sense. The dog bit me, not you!" I argued. "It's like killin' somebody for stealin' an apple, or something stupid like that. What do ya' have against that cop?"

Carnie then revealed something quite personal. I listened intently to his disclosure. "That jerk and two other cops are hittin' on my mom. He thinks I don't know what's goin' on, but they're all gonna' pay. Tinker knows about it, and they're foolin' around with his mom, too," my friend sobbed. "Getting' bit by that dog was the straw that broke the camel's back. Ya' in with Tink and me?"

"Well, I, I don't know! Is that what they call *cop*ulation?" I joked, trying to make Carnie laugh. I did not realize at the time that I had inadvertently formulated a silly play-on-words. The only reason that I knew what copulation meant was because Tinker had once made me make a list of dictionary synonyms for the word "sex".

"Decide now J.W., or you're gonna' have two less good friends and two more damned dangerous enemies," loudly threatened my totally disgruntled companion.

I was extremely frightened of Tinker and dared not make *him* my immediate enemy. "Okay, Carnie, you're the big boss," I reluctantly answered. "So, tell Tink I'm in."

I remember receiving one other needle in '55. A kid I had known at St. Mark School had contracted polio. The Salk Vaccine had just been developed, but at that time, the injection had not been available for local distribution. I had to get a gamma-globulin needle in the right cheek of my butt. It hurt like hell, but I endured the excruciation, and quickly realized that pain was an intricate part of life as was happiness, music, friendship, enemies, wild dogs, immoral cops, and baseball.

'50s kids were very inventive when it came to sports and games. Carnie would often visit me with his green hula-hoop. We created a game where one of us would flip the hula-hoop backwards with a sharp wrist snap onto the four empty lines of mom's clothesline, and the object would spin on the cords for maybe ten to fifteen seconds. I would keep time for Carnie, and he would keep time for me, and we would amuse and occupy ourselves for hours watching the hula-hoop skim and hop upon the clotheslines, as if the practice were some intense event in *Olympic* competition.

In the fall of '55, Carnie and I were playing a variation of football that we had improvised on Daffodil Lane. Metal light standards were situated every two-hundred-feet or so apart, and the playing field was six-hundred-feet, or three streetlights long.

Carnie and I would take our positions a hundred-feet or so to the left and right of the center streetlight, and punt a football back and forth for long distances. Whoever could kick the football past the opposing punter's goal (streetlight) would be deemed the winner. We never suspected that being inventive with an ordinary football would ever antagonize anyone in the neighborhood.

Carnie really put some foot into one particular punt, and the pigskin sailed onto Sal Palermo's front lawn. Sal must have perceived us as sinister characters, because the fanatic dashed-out of his house with a baseball bat, ranting and raving like a maniac.

"Eunuch; eunuch!" the crazed loon vehemently shouted, menacingly brandishing his *Louisville Slugger* baseball bat.

"No, my name's J.W., not Nick," I innocently answered.

"You junior jerk-off; *eunuch* means to cut your balls off. That's what I'm gonna fuckin' do if ya' trespass on my property one more time," Salvatore Palermo vehemently warned. "Do it again and you'll become a eunuch!"

"Mr. Palermo, we're only playing a game!" I replied in defense of my pristine integrity.

"Don't give me that shit, you little crotch breath! Ya' know my daughter's built like a brick shit-house, and you're lookin' for lavatory privileges!" screamed the livid bully, who was trying to intimidate me with his adult rage.

I attempted to maintain my natural, pleasant demeanor. "Mr. Palermo, we're only playing a game of kick football," I pointed-out. "I'm sorry the ball landed on your grass."

"You're gonna' be a hundred-dollar a week flunky, just like your old man. I want my daughter hangin' around with *Wall Street* material, ya' hear!" the enraged Sicilian shouted.

I did not think that my dad was a failure, despite Sal Palermo's arrogant claim. I remained as calm as I could. I did not wish to trade insults with the father of the girl I keenly desired. "I promise, it won't happen again," I courteously pledged.

"I know what ya' really want," Palermo claimed. "Ya' want to get into Angie's panties, don't ya'?"

"I think her hips are too wide. They'll never fit. Besides, I prefer jockey shorts," I objectively responded.

Mr. Palermo did not appreciate my zany reply. The gruff Italian bully had the sense of humor of an irritated grizzly bear. "Just remember, retard, stay away from Angie, or I'll bend this bat around your throat! Ya' aren't gonna' get your tiny noodle wet in my daughter's soup hole!"

I cleverly pointed to my head. "Mr. Palermo, this is the only noodle I ever use."

"Go lick a dozen hairy roosters, ya' obnoxious little cock-sucker," my maniacal neighbor ranted.

Outside of those minor events, 1955 was a rather bland year. Families watched a lot of television back then. The novelty of the new media was still having a hypnotic effect upon the American public.

On Saturday nights, Mom and Pop watched the *Jackie Gleason Show,* and on Tuesday evenings, it was the *Milton Berle Texaco Star Theater*. Mom and Dad would argue about what news to watch. Mom preferred Douglas Edwards, while Pop would tune into *John Cameron Swayse and the Camel News Caravan.* Both agreed upon Bishop Fulton J. Sheen as an entertaining religious philosopher, and I personally developed a special fondness for *Alfred Hitchcock Presents*. I looked forward to seeing his weekly chubby silhouette. But there was one thing on television that scared the living daylights out of me.

Rocky Marciano was the world heavy-weight-boxing-champion. Whenever the Italian fighter would pound his opponents on TV with wicked body jolts and uppercuts to the solar plexus, his grim face would remind me of Sal Palermo, and I would cowardly shrink-down into the living room sofa, vicariously being pulverized to death by a flurry of vicious Sicilian punches.

It was widely publicized in the newspapers that *Peter Pan* starring Mary Martin was opening on *Broadway,* and I made the mistake at the Feed Bag of teasing Tinker about the play's debut.

"If ya' refer to me as Tinker Bell one more time, your parents will have to notify the undertaker to haul away your damned skinny carcass," my paranoid pal warned.

I then realized that Tinker might even be a bit more formidable than Sal Palermo was. "Gee, I was only tryin' to be funny! Say Tink, why do ya' walk with that limp? Ya' got only two toes on your left foot, or what?"

Tinker perceived my innocent humor as a direct abuse of his credibility. "No, my right leg is two inches shorter than my left. I don't mind though, because that means it's my third shortest leg," the detestable sub-human emphasized, making an absurd statement that revealed his own fragile sense of insecurity.

"Right, Donkey-dick," I replied, gambling that Tink might actually value my friendship over heinously decapitating or slaughtering me, right then and there.

Chapter 7
"Signs of Trouble" (1956)

In January of '56, Carnie and I took-up playing ice hockey. We were inspired when the *Detroit Red Wings* had defeated the *Montreal Canadiens* in the '55 *Stanley Cup Playoffs*, four games to three. But we had to wait for another winter to arrive, in order for the ice to freeze on the Delaware Canal.

Carnie had found an old hockey puck in a Dogwood Drive storm sewer grate. We constructed a makeshift goal out of available lumber scraps, along with an old fishing net, and my pal and I alternated being goalie and puck shooter.

Cummings was a mean-ass greaser who terrorized almost every area kid that lived outside of Kenwood. The brute had just obtained his driver's license, and he and Popeye Messina wildly pulled into the dirt road that paralleled the Delaware Canal, just off of Haines Road.

As Carnie helplessly watched, Cummings and Popeye stepped onto the ice, picked me up, and tossed my body headfirst toward the dam going under Haines Road. I skidded along the frozen surface like a runaway Eskimo sled, and when I stopped, the ice began to crack. Before I knew it, I was under the surface, heavy clothes, ice skates, and all. I recall seeing everything appearing in emerald green. I must have experienced hypothermia, because the underwater canal reeds and algae even seemed enchanting in appearance.

Fortunately, Robbie Wilkinson happened to be walking by the Delaware Canal on his way to the Feed Bag. I surfaced from the same frigid hole into which my body had plunged, and remarkably, I noticed that Robbie and Carnie were bravely lying flat on the ice. After several desperate attempts, the brave rescuers managed to pull my nearly frozen form out of the frigid canal. I was lucky, having a near-death experience and surviving. I felt dizzy, cold and disoriented.

But then, four other Kenwood punks showed-up while Cummings was still laughing incessantly. The despicable Ks threatened Robbie when the reprehensible punks bragged that the roughnecks had a worse fate in store for him'. Cummings told Robbie, "Get the hell outa' here before we chain two cinder blocks to your legs, and throw your ass into the same damned canal hole!" Robbie swiftly high-tailed it across *Route 13* to the Feed Bag, to see if he could find Quinn.

The diabolical Kamikaze thugs were accommodating enough to have some old dirty towels and greasy rags inside the trunk of Cummings' '52 Ford. The temperature was in the high twenties. The Ks stripped me down to my jockey shorts, and then the scoundrels roughly dried me off. Then, the sadists also made Carnie strip-down into his jockey shorts, even though his clothes were dry. Before the ice incident had happened, my buddy and I had ridden to the Delaware Canal on our English Racer bicycles.

Popeye Messina picked-up my English Racer; slammed it over my head, and soon my weak arms and cold chest were trapped between the pedals and the triangular metal frame. Cummings did the same punishment to Carnie, and we both had the horrible ordeal of having to trek down Haines Road toward Dogwood Hollow in our underwear and socks. The distance to my Daffodil Lane home was over half a mile. Our arms were wedged down at our sides, encompassed by the English Racer frames.

Cummings, Popeye and the four other fiendish Ks nearly coughed their larynxes out in response to our futile dual predicaments. Several motorists stopped their cars to gawk at us trudging along Haines Road, but then Sal Palermo came by in his red pick-up truck. Sal's crude and obnoxious brother-in-law, Dante Messina was accompanying him.

Palermo's pick-up skidded to a halt, and the two laughing Sicilians jumped-out and lowered the tailgate. Sal and Dante first lifted-up Carnie and next me, and then deposited our limp bodies in the flatbed of the red half-ton pick-up. After covering the attached bikes and us up with an old tarpaulin, the jolly Sicilians elevated the tailgate. Laughing like two hyenas, the pair leaped back into the cab. Sal then sped-off in the direction of Dogwood Hollow.

My neighbor's red '54 Ford entered the driveway at 50 Daffodil Lane. The bigmouth blew his horn five times to announce our presence, and Sal Palermo and Dante Messina removed the tarpaulin and then roughly tugged Carnie and me from the rear tailgate to the driveway. My buddy and I still had the English Racer bikes wrapped around our arms and chests. My father came darting-out of the house with a stunned expression on his face. Dad stared at Carnie and me, standing there in our jockey shorts.

"Here's your juvenile delinquent kid and his pus-faced friend," said Sal, who actually believed that Carnie and I had once tried to drown his precious daughter in the *Delaware River*.

"What in the hell is going on here?" Dad nervously asked.

"We just found these two demented perverts on Haines Road down near the Delaware Canal," Salvatore Palermo meanly articulated. "Apparently, the weirdos got tired of bein' normal kids; took their clothes off; put these bikes over their shoulders, and started howlin' at the moon in broad daylight."

Dad was not at all amused by Sal's descriptive narrative. Pop knew there were two sides to every controversy.

"Has your kid been tested for mental illness lately?" asked Dante Messina, who also thought that Carnie and I had tried to drown *his* voluptuous daughter "Bubbles" in the *Delaware River*.

"No, he hasn't. Who did this to you, Son?"

I remembered the greaser code: never squeal or rat on another kid, which Carnie once had called "the greatest truth ever". But more importantly, I was afraid that Cummings and Popeye would torture and then execute me should I get them in trouble with anyone, so zippering my mouth seemed to be the best practical solution to my wholly uncomfortable dilemma.

"Nobody, Pop," I lied. "Carnie and I were just foolin' around and then Mr. Palermo showed-up and generously offered to take us home."

"Get inside, son," Pop insisted. "You and Carnie hop into the shower right away before you both freeze to death or catch pneumonia. First though, I'll have to dislodge you boys from those bicycles. Thank you, Mr. Palermo, for taking my son home. I'm very sorry if it caused you any inconvenience."

Sal was deeply amused. "I would give my right arm to see it all again. Let me tell you, your kid is an asshole with a capital A," Angie's father haughtily stated. "If your punk kid was twice as bright, he'd advance to the level of imbecile. Ha, ha, ha, ha!"

Carnie and I talked it over in the hot shower. We suspected that Palermo and Dante Messina were after more than simple revenge; the men wanted to humiliate my friend and me for an alleged brutal event that we had not deliberately done to their daughters.

From that moment on, my Dogwood Hollow friends and I believed that Sal Palermo was putting Popeye and Cummings up to busting on us every time the main Ks had the opportunity. Even though we were only thirteen-years-old, Carnie, Tinker, and I knew that we had to protect ourselves from "the local Mafia", as Tink *also* referred to the fearsome trio of Sal Palermo, along with Dante and Popeye Messina.

The "D boys" surmised that it was more than a mere coincidence for Sal and Dante to appear and humiliate us only moments after Cummings and Popeye had committed their dual Delaware Canal deviltry. To add insult like that to injury like that could only have been strategically planned in advance. The Ks were Sal and Dante's surrogates, we had conjectured and suspected.

That frigid afternoon in January of 1956, Carnie and I made a holy alliance under the showerhead to battle "the Sidgees" with everything we had in our arsenal of tricks.

"Those lousy Italians want to kill us, J.W.," my paranoid companion theorized and insisted. "They think we pushed Angie and Bubbles into the river on purpose."

"You're right, Carnie. We were shoved from behind," I concurred. "And I only hope our flimsy bows and arrows will stand-up to their Mafia machine guns."

In March of '56, I was dared by Carnie at St. Michelle's School to pour an entire bottle of black ink down an egghead's white shirt. Stanley Tezeeker sat in front of me in Sister Marian's eighth-grade mathematics' class; earned all A's on his report card, and was the perfect teachers' pet, who brown-nosed his way through every academic subject. I was caught during the climax of the "inkwell incident" by Sister Marian and was given a week of detentions.

That night, Stanley Tezeeker's father brought his son's ink-damaged shirt to 50 Daffodil Lane. This upset me because Stanley had violated the "sacred code" that no kid should ever rat on another kid, regardless of the circumstances.

My judicious father asked if I had committed the misdemeanor, and I reluctantly acknowledged my guilt. Pop then gave Mr. Tezeeker (who was almost identical in dress to his weakling offspring, except that the man wore yellow and green diamonded argyle socks with matching sweater vest instead of red and black ones like Stanley had on that day) seven-dollars for a new white shirt.

"I promise you, Mr. Tezeeker, my son's not a hooligan," Dad apologized. "Some of his delinquent friends probably put him up to doing it. I assure you that it won't happen again."

A week after the Tezeeker inkbottle incident, I needed a serious haircut, but I decided to let my waves grow long. I did not want to be like Stanley Tezeeker in any way, shape, or form. Almost overnight, I had abandoned the rigorous world of jock-hood to become a full-fledged greaser wannabe'. I figured I no longer could excel at my favorite sport, baseball.

When I had played *Babe Ruth League* for Window Mart, the longer pitching distance to the plate had inhibited my proficiency from the mound, and the greater thirty-feet distance from home to first base stymied my bunting and fleetness of foot. I relinquished the larger playing field to the likes of Richie Ashburn, Willie Mays, Ted Williams, and Duke Snider, and I joyfully buddied-up full time with Carnie and Tinker. I surrendered my baseball glove to the top shelf of my bedroom closet. And to look like a true greaser, I started addictively smoking cigarettes.

A month later, Dad had discovered a cigarette butt in my bedroom bureau and intensively interrogated me about the evidence. I was very defensive from the outset, but Pop had certain methods that he employed to get the truth out of me. Back in the '50s, a kid had to tolerate his parents' disciplinary action, or be thrown out of the house to sleep in the dog pen, or in the utility room. Parents had more say and more control because *DYFS* was not around to shield kids from stern discipline that today could be construed by the state as "child abuse".

"Son, is this your cigarette?"

"Where did you find it?" I answered defensively.

"In your bureau, middle drawer."

"What are you doin' snoopin' around in my room?" I was worried and apprehensive of my father's sudden anger and disenchantment. I was beginning to fear the consequences of my actions.

"Your room happens to be in *my* house!"

"What are you gonna' do about it?" I wanted to know.

"Come into the kitchen. You'll see."

Pop instructed me to sit-down at the table. My parent reached into a cigarette carton and pulled-out a pack of *Pall Mall.* He obtained a sharp scissors and neatly trimmed an inch off of the pack's top, and then another inch off of the packaged product's bottom's perimeter.

Dad then directed me to put the twenty cigarettes into my mouth. He lit a match and demanded that I puff as hard as I could for twenty-seconds until all twenty cancer sticks had been thoroughly lit. Then, Pop told me to inhale deeply and to take additional drags every fifteen-seconds or so. I was soon turning green in the face after the first five puffs, and after the ninth, I felt compelled to run to the sink and puke my guts out.

From that decisive moment on, I promised myself I would never again be caught with cigarettes in my room. I also made another pledge to myself that day. If I were ever to misbehave in school again, my furtive actions would be so covert that no one in authority would be able to detect the culprit's identity.

I locked myself in my room and turned on 'Philly D.J. Joe Niagara, since I couldn't listen to records because the needle on my phonograph had to be replaced. I sobbed through "Heartbreak Hotel" by Elvis, "Ivory Tower" by Cathy Carr, and "Chain Gang" by Bobby Scott to express my eclectic sad, idealistic, and punished moods. Then, I flicked-off the radio and voyaged into deep slumber-land.

In May of '56, I was visiting Robbie Wilkinson when the yellow *O'Doyle's* ice cream truck came rumbling around the corner. The driver hit a small mallet against a gong four times. His method contrasted to the *Jack and Jill* vendor, who jingled a set of bells, and to the friendly *Good Humor* man, whose loud chimes made four distinct tones.

Robbie introduced me to Teddy, the affable *O'Doyle's* driver, who would stop his truck, walk to freezers directly behind the cab, and then enthusiastically sell popsicles, dipped cones, and bulk ice cream to

Levittown residents. Robbie and I rode around with Teddy, and I got to know *him* pretty well. The ice cream huckster was a sex fanatic, always trying to hustle older girls and young women along his route.

As spring turned into summer, I would always observe Teddy driving around Dogwood or Junewood Drive, and at every opportunity, I would flag him down for a ride. The vendor would often brag about all his philandering and about all his female conquests, and I was a captive audience, simply because a fascinated thirteen-year-old kid can't learn enough about sex, and I would absorb everything the horny guy said as if my mind were a hungry sponge.

Teddy was thirty-three years old, about five-foot-ten; had Elvis-like sideburns, a long nose, and a vivid-but-perverted imagination. The self-proclaimed Don Juan often invited good-looking females onto his truck, and allowed them to dip their own cones. The ice cream vendor taught me how to check-out their rear ends, as the ladies in skimpy bathing-suits scooped deeply into the freezers for their favorite flavors.

One day, Teddy saved my ass from Popeye's wrath. Four Kenwood punks were chasing me from Farmbrook into Dogwood Hollow, and Bruno "Popeye" Messina was leading the hot pursuit. Teddy spotted my dilemma and sped-up his truck, picking me up just two-hundred feet or so in front of the hostile pursuing posse.

"Where ya' goin'?" I panted.

"I'm gonna' hit Kenwood, and then circle back down Haines Road into Dogwood Hollow. Care to come along?" Teddy offered, knowing that my answer would be a gasping "yes". "I could use a little help today." Anything seemed better than to be captured by the band of ruthless enemy greasers.

"Fine with me," I agreed, still out of breath. "And thanks for saving me from those insane crazies," I gratefully replied as Teddy drove-off. "The fanatics said they were gonna' stick three broom handles up my ass, and I think the villains would've done just that if they caught me."

Teddy later drove-around Kenwood Drive. We made some big sales and saw some nice butts of pretty chicks scooping ice cream flavors. Teddy stopped in front of the Messina residence, and Popeye's sister Bubbles came running-out barefooted. The Sicilian babe was wearing black shorts and a tight-fitting red halter top. My brain almost exploded out of my skull when I noticed her massive hooters jiggling-around inside her taut top. Teddy had the radio blasting Elvis Presley's "Heartbreak Hotel" over Wibbage Radio 99.

Bubbles approached the truck's counter and ordered a double scoop of vanilla fudge. Teddy was busy selling a half-gallon of butter pecan to a comely lady in a white bikini bathing suit, so the driver delegated the cone detail to me. While handing the huge cone to

Bubbles, I was a trifle nervous, and as my right-hand shook, the top scoop of vanilla fudge toppled-off and landed squarely inside her red halter top, right between her luscious breasts.

"Ya' stupid dip-shit! Just look what you've done!" the Italian doll yelled. Do you have some nervous medical condition, or something?"

"I'm sorry! I didn't mean to do that!" I honestly replied.

"Yeah! Just like ya' didn't mean to push Angie and me into the goddamned *Delaware River!"*

Bubbles then stuck her hand into her halter, removed the cold scoop of vanilla fudge, and squashed the cold lump squarely into the center of my face. The blob splattered pretty well all over my features.

Teddy handed me a towel to wipe-off the gook, and as a gesture of friendship, the sex-addict driver invited Bubbles onto the truck to dip her own second scoop. That assignment the doll merrily did, and I got to enjoy seeing her leaning over into the freezer, her shorts rising up to the firm cheeks of her magnificent ass. When the Messina chick was through completing her sensational endeavor, Bubbles gave Teddy a little kiss on his cheek, and then the broad deftly exited the truck, ignoring me as if I had never existed.

Teddy didn't like the competition he was receiving from the *Jack and Jill* and from the *Good Humor* ice cream vendors, so I told the O'Doyle's vendor that Tinker, Carnie, and I would think of something imaginative to take care of *his* business problem.

Herman the snake had just passed-away. Tinker brought the animal's carcass over to Robbie Wilkinson's house in a burlap potato sack. Carnie and I were visiting R.W., and we all agreed that it would be fun to creatively honor the memory of the deceased boa constrictor. I hailed-down the *Jack and Jill* truck, and strolled-over to the driver before he could get out of the cab. I then deliberately asked him if he had any half-gallons of cherry vanilla.

"No, Son. I only carry popsicles, ice cream sandwiches, and Dixie cups," the vendor responded in a disappointed tone of voice.

I knew I had to stall the man some more to allow Tinker and Carnie additional time to complete their vital mischievous mission. "Well, do ya' have any butter almond coated popsicles?"

"No, Son. You're thinkin' of the *Good Humor* man."

"Do ya' have any butter pecan cones?"

"Sorry, Son. Now you're thinkin' of the *O'Doyle's* guy."

"Well, Sir, thanks for your valuable time," I graciously added. "Maybe tomorrow I'll be hungry for a chocolate covered ice cream bar, or a cherry ice pop."

Even as thirteen-year-old kids, Tinker, Carnie, Robbie, and I would help those we thought were our friends, and we would often assist our friends in defeating *their* enemies or competitors. While I was busy distracting the gullible *Jack and Jill* man, Tinker and Carnie had opened the truck's back freezer compartment, and then placed Herman's limp body inside. The three of us merrily trailed the vendor down Dewberry Lane where he eventually made another stop.

Two little kids wanted purple icicles. The *Jack and Jill* salesman nonchalantly reached into the freezer; felt Herman's cold scaly form; pulled-out the snake; let out a shriek that would have frightened Boris Karloff; ran to his truck; opened the door, and peeled-out like he was at the *Indianapolis 500* starting line. Upon seeing the twelve-foot-long dead snake lying in the street, the two little tykes let-out simultaneous screams, and dashed up the lane to their mother's waiting arms. Tinker picked-up Herman, returned the limp boa to the burlap bag, and pondered what to do next.

"What's that bonging noise over on Darkleaf Lane?" Tink asked.

"Sounds like the *Good Humor* man to me," Carnie answered.

"Let's do it again," Tinker snickered.

Everything was cool for a while. Teddy's business multiplied with the absence of the *Jack and Jill* driver and the *Good Humor* man from Dogwood Hollow for the balance of the summer of '56. The *Good Humor* man returned one other time, but after he stepped into his cab and sat on Tinker's stuffed alligator "Ollie", the spooked salesman wisely removed Dogwood Hollow from his daily itinerary.

One sultry afternoon in August of '56, Teddy picked me up in Junewood after I had walked to the Windsor Pharmacy to buy Mom a carton of *Lucky Strike* for $2.50. It was a good deal because the pharmacy would give ten free packs of matches with the cigarette carton purchase. Teddy asked me where I was going and I told him, "Home to Dogwood Hollow."

"What street do ya' live on?" Teddy asked. "I've never taken you home before."

"Daffodil Lane, number 50," I promptly answered.

"Do ya' know a pleasant, good-lookin', red-haired woman on Daffodil Lane? I'd like to get a date with her," the ice cream Casanova requested.

I was completely staggered by Teddy's imprudent description of a very familiar female. "There's only one red-haired woman on Daffodil Lane," I angrily replied.

"Do ya' know her then?"

I was very perturbed by Teddy's over-aggressive reference. "Yes, I do!" I exclaimed. "And ya' can stop the truck right here and let me off. You're talkin' about my mom!"

When it personally hit home, all of a sudden Teddy's perversion about sex didn't seem interesting any more. I gave Mom her cigarettes and change; went straight to my room, and listened to "The Wayward Wind" by Gogi Grant; "Long Tall Sally" by Little Richard, and "Be-Bop-A-Lula" by Gene Vincent twenty-times each until my new needle broke on my *RCA* record player.

Things got tough in late summer of '56. Dad was laid-off from his welding job after his company had finished manufacturing the last of the tollbooths for the *Pennsylvania Turnpike*. Money was scarce, so I asked around and picked-up a *Philadelphia Bulletin* paper route in Junewood. I built the route up from fifty-three customers to one-hundred-and-twenty-three subscribers, and I had more pocket money than I ever had before, even though my weekly allowance had been curtailed because of Dad's unexpected unemployment.

I thought that I was an average kid growing-up in an average middle-class family in suburban Philadelphia, but after I decided to become a greaser, my life soon was to change from boring tranquility to one of dangerous conflict.

Chapter 8
"Black and Blue" (1957)

In early March of '57, Tinker's mom drove him and me to the giant Bristol Farmers Market on *Route 413,* and it was there that I purchased my multi-zipper black leather motorcycle jacket that would constitute the bulk of my official greaser uniform. While I was being fitted, Jeremy Foster quietly ambled-over to another stall to make several valuable acquisitions, but the secretive creep kept the items inside a brown paper bag, and later refused to show me what he had purchased.

It was also in mid-March of 1957 that I first met Bo Jalonec at the Feed Bag, where Jokes immediately impressed me with his jovial nature. Since Bo was a strong-looking guy, I figured that his personal company might protect me from the likes of Cummings and Popeye Messina, and also get me properly introduced to some decent-looking, available females.

"Hi. I'm J.W. What's your name?" I cheerfully asked.

"Beau," he suspiciously replied.

"Bow? Like in tie, or arrow-shooter?"

"No, Dorkface! It's spelled B-E-A-U!"

"Like in Bozo?" I asserted, again, trying to be funny.

"Like in the name Beauregard, you freakin' jerk-weed," my new acquaintance answered in a very peeved tone of voice, as if he were ashamed of his real first name. "You'd be almost cool if you didn't have shit and worms for brains."

"Beauregard sounds like a rich kid's name. Are ya' rich?" I curiously asked.

"No, but I will be when I get older."

I was impressed from our initial conversation, because Bo (Beau) appeared to be more facetious and clever than the average teenagers I knew. I just had to probe the depth of his sense of humor.

"Could I call ya' Bo Beau?"

"Quit the damned clownin' around, J.W. That would be a serious boo-boo! Just call me, Beau!"

It was clear that I had aggravated Jalonec, and I was greatly savoring my effectiveness. "Okay, Bo."

"Look J.W.," Bo sneered. "If ya' don't give me respect I'll havta' kick you in your third knee."

"What third knee?"

"Your high knee, Stupid!" Bo then checked-out my apparel and had a few critical remarks to convey. I diligently listened to his words of teen wisdom, as I studied the accommodating smile being shown on his handsome face.

"J.W., that's a pretty swift-lookin' leather jacket you're wearin', but you're not gonna' ever be a full-fledged greaser until you're black and blue."

I could not fully discern the meaning of my new pal's statement, so I requested clarification. "What do ya' mean? Do I have to get beaten up by some Kamikazes and get cuts and bruises all over my face?"

Bo laughed at my naivete. Every idea to Jalonec seemed to have a double meaning. Jokes often thought and talked in silly-but-pert riddles, and it was as if his mind existed in two separate realities at the same time. I found his individuality, along with his fascinating rhetoric, both puzzling and intriguing.

"Did ya' just get off the immigrant boat or what?" Bo chastised. "Just look at your shoes. Ya' never wear penny loafers with a black leather jacket. You're supposed to wear engineer boots like I have on. And just take a gander at your brown pegged pants," Jokes continued his critique. "Ya' gotta' have on blue denim jeans, just like James Dean did in that *Rebel without a Cause* flick." Bo further explained that I was only "half cool" until I went all the way "black and blue", with black leather and blue denim all the time. "You're just a damned 'tweener until ya' junk those silly-lookin' shoes and trousers."

I saw plenty of merit in Jalonec's keen observations. Suddenly, my perception of the greaser universe had dramatically changed. In addition to his erudite intelligence about greaser ways, I admired Bo's comical nature, and I must confess that much of my teen personality I later owed to mimicking his stellar example.

"Bo, some of the Dogwood Hollow guys wanta' start a gang. The Kamikazes are givin' us a lot of grief, and we gotta' defend ourselves," I maintained. "You're invited to join my pals as long as ya' don't live in Kenwood."

"Great J.W. I just moved to town into Junewood," Bo informed me. "Confidentially, I could use some new buds, even though I'm not a freakin' flower."

"Terrific," I told my new friend. "I'll introduce ya' to the guys. We hope to have a gang goin' by mid-summer."

In the spring of '57, Cardinal Reagan High School was still under construction, and so Jokes was attending West Catholic High in Philadelphia as a sophomore while Carnie and I were attending Immaculate Conception School in Levittown as freshmen. Bo's dad dropped him off at the Philly' school and picked him up on *his* way back from work. Right from the outset, Jalonec bombarded me with stupid drivel, punning his way through virtually every conversation. One such exchange occurred at the Dairy DeLite.

"J.W., when you wipe your ass, do ya' use your left hand or your right hand?"

"My left hand," I answered a little too sincerely.

"Well, J.W. I happen to use toilet paper," Jokes cackled. "Ya' know J.W., you're the only half-decent guy I know."

"Thanks, Bo."

"All the rest are decent," Jalonec concluded in one of his classic put-downs.

From my initial contacts with Bo Jalonec, I knew that I would prefer indulging in Jokes' company; pattern my personality after his demeanor, and hang with the handsome guy whenever feasible. On Saturday afternoons, besides driving the shoppers at *Pomeroy's Department Store* crazy, Carnie, Bo and I conducted a rather slick extortion scheme.

Carnie and I would accost an egghead (a geek or nerd in today's vernacular) walking alone in the giant outdoor shopping center. An egghead was easy prey for our predatory mischief because the brainiac would seldom retaliate against feigned aggression. We would demand all his money as protection for "insurance purposes", or if he didn't cooperate by paying us extortion money, we would threaten to beat-up the wimp and remove his trousers in public.

Right when Carnie and I were about to start puncturing the prodigy's rib cage with our fists, Bo would happen to saunter by; chase us away in a contrived rescue, and then console the thankful egghead about the dangers of roving bands of juvenile delinquents.

"How could I possibly ever repay you?" Stanley Tezeeker gratefully asked.

"How much money do ya' have on you?" asked Jokes, indicating that he would graciously accept a cash reward for his effective rescue and protection services.

"Six dollars," replied the thankful kid.

"Just give me five and I'll call it even," Bo negotiated. "If those snot-nose punks ever bother ya' again, just let me know, and I'll beat the total crap out of them!"

Predictably the vulnerable sissy willfully coughed over "bonus bucks" to Jokes, being totally grateful for *his* essential intercession. The extorted money that Carnie and I would have "stolen" from Tezeeker was voluntarily "donated" to Jalonec as a prompt reward for his vigilance and good citizenship.

Then, Bo would later meet Carnie and me at the Delaware Canal, and we would hike the mile or so down the familiar dirt road from the Levittown Shop-A-Rama to Haines Road, where we would cross *Route*

13 to the Feed Bag's friendly confines. We must have earned at least a dozen "free pizzas" using the effective "egghead extortion scam".

In the early summer of '57, Tinker and I were hitchhiking on Haines Road outside of Dogwood Hollow, looking for a ride to *Route 13* and our hangout, the Feed Bag. A black '52 Ford stopped around a hundred-feet ahead, and we anxiously ran to catch our ride.

The car quickly sped-off, and soon the black Ford abruptly stopped two-hundred-feet down the road. Tink and I again sprinted toward the stationary vehicle. Again, the rod zoomed-off with loud mufflers, halting several hundred more feet down the two-lane highway.

Tinker and I thought that the occupants were playing teasing games, and so we simply resumed hitchhiking. The black Ford sped in reverse, squealing its tires until it halted directly opposite us. Much to our distaste and displeasure, the occupants inside were Cummings and Popeye, two dye-in-the-wool, despicable, pugnacious adversaries, who always valued malice over mischief.

"Hop in turd-heads," Cummings suggested. "We were just havin' a little fun with you guys, that's all. Where ya' goin'?"

"To the Feed Bag," I genuinely responded.

"Get in. We're headin' in that direction," Popeye directed in an inordinate, courteous tone. "Actually, we like helpin' disadvantaged and handicapped pedestrians like you two wimps."

I could not fully believe that Cummings and Popeye would ever be so amiable and kind. Their all-too-polite behavior seemed very inconsistent with their mean reputations.

Tinker and I climbed into the back seat, which I must admit, was rather clean and comfortable.

"You guys getting any?" Cummings asked.

I knew that Bubbles's brother was sitting in the front seat, and I dared not answer "yes", or Popeye might have mendaciously cremated me, right there and then.

"Naw, we're puttin' it on automatic," I answered.

"I knew these Dogwood pecker-heads were *boner*-fide jerk-offs," Cummings laughed, regressing into his true nasty personality.

"Yeah, there's a fungus among us," Popeye curtly replied. "J.W., have ya' recently gone swimmin' in the height of winter in the Delaware Canal?"

I was scared to the max' because Cummings and Popeye had reportedly hospitalized several black kids from Bristol just the week before. My throat gulped, since I could not speak a viable reply.

"J.W., do ya' still fit inside your English Racer?" inquired Cummings, who was bent on ridiculing and mocking my dignity.

"Wait a minute! You've passed the Feed Bag. Let us out!" Tink noticed and demanded.

"We'll let you two dorks out when we're good and ready. Until then, we'll give you ungrateful piss ants an educational tour of the area," Popeye finished.

Tinker and I then had to listen to Cummings and Messina brag about how the delinquents had kidnapped two black kids in north Philly' back in April. The demonic Ks boasted how the molesters had tied-up their victims; gagged their mouths with handkerchiefs, and then deposited the "spooks" in a freight train at a railroad yard. Cummings finished the story by elaborating that the freight train was headed for Boston.

'We've traveled south along *Route 13* and passed *Route 413.* At least we weren't going across the *Burlington-Bristol Bridge* into New Jersey,' I thought. The black Ford continued motoring south through the towns of Croydon, Eddington, and Cornwell Heights. About that time, Tinker, who was a little slow at making a realization, leaned over to me. "I think we're bein' kidnapped," my unstable friend observed and softly whispered.

I nodded my head, having recognized that we had been hostages when we had passed the Feed Bag twenty-minutes earlier. Every time Cummings saw a phone booth the tormentor would slow-down and say, "You fucked-up guys want to call home?" And then the ball-breaker would mash his right foot upon the accelerator before either of us could answer a word.

The fearsome driver zipped through Andalusia, the site of a popular drive-in movie, and then proceeded across Pennypack Creek into North Philadelphia. We next journeyed through the Mayfair and Frankford sections of the city. Finally, Cummings hit Erie Avenue and followed the trolley tracks to Broad and Erie.

"Here's your stop. Nice knowin' you two pathetic jerk-offs," Popeye giggled, pretending to be a fancy hotel doorman, bowing and politely opening the door. "Hope ya' dumb fucks are enjoyin' your new stompin' grounds!"

Tink and I exited without saying a word, fully comprehending that we could have been dead in a ditch or inside a storm sewer, or tied-up inside a tractor-trailer, bound for Chicago or Los Angeles. Cummings sped-off, turning north on Broad in the direction of Levittown.

"How we gonna' get home?" I asked.

"Don't worry. Have any change on you?"

"Yeah," I answered as I searched and removed five nickels from my pants' pocket.

"I'll call my Uncle Jerry," Tink replied. "He lives about five blocks from here at Eighteenth and Lehigh. Are the *Phillies* playin' tonight?"

I was very surprised that Tinker would ever want to see *National League* teams in a baseball game. The *Phillies* and the *Cardinals* were against his loyal allegiance to the *American League*. "Yeah Tink. The Phils' are goin' up against St. Louis."

"Great. And good old Uncle Jerry lives just two blocks away from *Shibe Park,* or is it *Connie Mack Stadium*. He's a great guy. I'll call him and see if he would like to take you and me out to the ballpark."

Thank goodness, Uncle Jerry was home, and yes, the adult proved to be an admirable human being. Tinker's relative called my mom and told her not to worry and that he would drive Jeremy and me back to Dogwood Hollow after the baseball game. Jerry bought us box seats, and I got to see Richie Ashburn go three for three with a walk, and had the pleasure to witness the *Phils'* left fielder Del Ennis smash a tape measure home run onto the left field stands' roof.

Three things impressed me about that evening. First of all, Richie Ashburn had made a spectacular catch in centerfield, climbing the wall to haul in a Stan Musial line drive. Second, Tinker was unruffled by Cummings and Popeye Messina kidnapping us. The psychopath kept his cool while I had hit the panic button after being left off at Broad and Erie; third, Uncle Jerry had a limp very similar to Tinker's, and so I learned the importance of good genetics in a family tree.

Most of all, Tink had demonstrated that the young villain had guts and street savvy, and I then knew that "the holy terror" would be a powerful ally against all future enemies who might harass me. In late July of '57, the Diablos were officially formed at the Feed Bag.

One day that I'll never forget was October 4, 1957. I was a sophomore at the newly opened Cardinal Reagan High up on the Levittown Parkway, across from the largest outdoor shopping center in the country. The whole "free world" had been stunned when the Russians had launched the first *Sputnik* satellite, communicating to the rest of the Earth that the Soviets had effectively established technological supremacy over the United States.

I observed the grim countenances of the entire religious and secular faculty after the astonishing news had been released and reported. The grim-faced instructors had been staggered by how a godless, sadistic, economically inferior nation could achieve such a major scientific breakthrough. It was like evil had triumphed-over and defeated good at the first battle of Armageddon.

The faculty's general consensus was that American civilization had to have more science and math' courses incorporated into its high schools' academic diet in order to surpass the ruthless Marxist pagans, who according to Father Malcolm, "Are being aided by Satan's evil genius." The somber and solemn expressions upon the priests and nuns' faces reflected a determined dedication to protect our proud Christian-American culture from the hostile perils of the wicked Bolshevik menace.

I was not quite as upset as the Cardinal Reagan clerics were. Carnie and I walked home from school after we had learned about the Russian's monumental scientific accomplishment.

"J.W., how about those freakin' Russians?" Carnie marveled and emphasized. "And most of them are either Stalin*grads* or Lenin*grads* without ever goin' to colleges or universities!"

"What good is it to have space satellites in orbit when their impoverished citizens don't even have enough toilet paper to wipe their ugly rear ends?" I generalized.

"Do ya' think they're gonna' invade us?"

"If they do, you and me are goin' to have to protect ourselves," I quite seriously replied. "Those jealous, greedy Russians are more dangerous than Cummings and his punk Kamikazes are." But in actuality, I viewed the Kenwood gang as being a more immediate threat to Carnie and me than the formidable Russian Communists were.

"Yeah J.W., maybe those shit-heads will kidnap us, take us hostage, fly us to Moscow, and drop us off at Lenin's Tomb."

"I could live with bein' their political prisoner," I added. "But if those Russian men start kissin' me three times on the cheeks and the fourth time on the mouth, I'm gonna' find some arsenic to put into their vodka." I feigned toughness because I knew that true greasers hated public affection, especially between males. No "tuff" greaser wanted to be labeled "a queer or a faggot".

"I know exactly what ya' mean," Carnie agreed. "I'd rather die than have Khrushchev or some other Commie slobber all over my face. Bo told me last week that the average person has more germs under their tongue than the entire population of *Germ*any. Jalonec would probably tell those Russians to kiss-off. What's playin' on TV tonight, *Ozzie and Harriet* and *Lawrence Welk?"* my mercurial Diablo' chum asked.

"Come over to my place right now," I offered. "We'll watch *Ramar of the Jungle* and *The Life of Riley*. At least Chester Riley only kisses his wife, and Ramar only smooches a wild animal, now and then."

"Okay, I really dig that William Bendix guy," Carnie opined. "He's a lot funnier than John Daly on *What's My Line?* Say J.W. Does Bendix fix washing-machines?"

Later that week, Carnie and I watched the movie *Bridge on the River Kwai* at the Towne Theater, and the film only accentuated our paranoia about the ravages of a cruel dictatorship. The Oriental imperialists were ruthless and savage, but Carnie and I found some consolation in the fact that the Chinese didn't kiss their captives like the "faggot Russians" would probably do.

"Who wants to be a prisoner of war of a bunch of homosexuals?" I lamented and verbally shared.

"I know exactly what ya' mean," Carnie declared. "The Commies start kissin' us on the cheeks and lips, and the next thing ya' know, they'll probably want us to give 'em lengthy blow-jobs, J.W., or us prisoners suckin' them off while being blindfolded. If all the Russian men are homos, how do their damned women have children?"

"Don't know, Carnie," I confessed. "But I hope we never have to find-out *that* mystery! Carnie, that Alec Guinness character was pretty smart in that movie."

"You know it, J.W. And he was smart enough to be captured by Orientals and not by faggot Russians. And Orientals are smart enough not to kiss everyone and everything. That's why there's less sex disease in China than in Russia or in Arabia. The damned Russians are all gonna' eventually die from bacteria-infections, just like those freakin' Martians did in that *War of the Worlds* movie we saw last month over in Bristol."

"Those Russians sound like the *Real McCoys,"* I remarked.

"Yeah, just like that zombie-lookin' Walter Brennan, with billions and billions of nasty sex germs all in and out of his ancient body," Carnie aptly and preposterously concluded.

Chapter 9
"Greaser Pranks" (1958)

1958 was a tremendous year for rock and roll. Great melodies, lyrics, harmonies, and rhythms literally exploded onto the music scene. Carnie and I had tons of fun socializing at the summer pool dances at the Stonybrook-Greenbrook-Farmbrook recreation area. My pal and I also played "Spin the Bottle" and "Post Office" with girls at parties around Dogwood Hollow and Junewood, which further solidified *our* friendship. Our introduction to "Post Office" corresponded with the increased postage of mailed letters from three cents to four cents, and I remember how angry Pop was over the significant rise in mail tariff.

In '58, Sugar Ray Robinson had won the middleweight boxing crown by out-pointing Carmen Basilio, and blacks were making impressive headway in boxing, baseball, football, basketball, and music. "Rockin' Robin" by Bobby Day, "Sweet Little Sixteen" by Chuck Berry, "Johnny B. Goode" by that same artist, "Yakety-Yak" by the Coasters, and "Western Movies" by the Olympics served as testimony to the rise in popularity of "black rhythm and blues" as an alternative to pure "white country and western". But even though my greaser friends and I loved Chuck Berry and Little Richard's music, we never discussed why only white people lived in Dogwood Hollow, or for that matter anywhere in Levittown.

One afternoon, my father heard me listening to "Get A Job" by the Silhouettes on the radio. Pop seemed rather peeved that I found fascination with "Negro music". My parent reprimanded me for wanting to spend ninety-eight cents for a record that espoused laziness and a poor "un-American" work ethic. I knew indirectly that Dad wanted me to only buy records performed by white artists.

"What the hell are you listening to that ghetto trash for?" Pop criticized. "Only lazy people need to daily look in the Want Ads for a minimum wage job!"

"Maybe it's hard for dark people to find work because of their skin color," I idealistically suggested and retorted.

"J.W., I want you to imitate white people. I have nothin' against Negroes. There are plenty of nice colored people livin' in this world," Pop clarified. "But I would prefer that your cultural heroes were white, like Richie Ashburn used to be with you!"

"Sure, Pop. But it's only a song. I like the beat, that's all," I returned. "I don't pay too much attention to the lyrics."

Dad tried explaining that the song "Get A Job" was a form of indoctrination into laziness and that his desire was for me to go to college and be the first educated person in our family. "Son, I want you to have goals and to enjoy things that I could never afford. I honestly want you to have a good job, and to keep a good job!"

"But I already have a paper route. I'm earnin' my own money right now," I defensively argued.

"I want you to have a profession J.W. A job won't be good enough in the future," Dad maintained. "The definition of job is *j.o.b.* Those three letters stand for *J*ust *O*ver *B*roke. That's what you'll be if you only have a job and not a profession or a good career."

Dad then took issue with my black leather jacket with the small devil painted on the back, and with my teen DA haircut. He had heard and known from neighbors about the Diablos being formed, and about the vile fear tactics being employed by the Kamikazes.

"Now, J.W. I know what *DA* means."

"It stands for District Attorney, Pop!" I awkwardly exclaimed.

"It stands for duck's ass! I know all about it. If you no longer want to play baseball, that's okay with me," Pop stubbornly stated. "And if you want to look like a punk greaser, then you got to keep that paper route, because at least you have a good work habit despite your juvenile delinquent appearance. And watch the company you keep. I don't want to see you becomin' a teenage Al Capone!"

I respected Pop all the way from the WW II tattoos on his forearms to his ambivalence about smoking. Dad was concerned about my well-being, and Carnie would often tell me how lucky I was to have parents who stayed together, and a father who gave me direction, and Tinker would begrudgingly say that the young hoodlum wished that *his* pop had given him more guidance while growing up.

When I reconsidered that dad had gone-up against the Germans in France and at the Rhine, fighting for numskulls like Sal Palermo, Dante Messina, Bruno "Popeye" Messina, and Cummings, then my family pride swelled-up inside my chest.

One afternoon in July of '58, Carnie and I were at the Olympic-sized Brooke Pool that then serviced Farmbrook, Stonybrook, Greenbrook, Junewood, Kenwood and Dogwood Hollow. We had been planning a shenanigan for several weeks, and at last, the occasion presented itself.

Angie Palermo and Bubbles Messina were wearing black bathing suits while sunbathing on reclining beach chaise longues. The C Man and I noticed a pattern where the two *Cinderellas* would take-off their white tee shirts, fold them up neatly, and then place the apparel under their tilted chairs almost every sunny day, while relaxing alongside the pool's dry cement perimeter.

Carnie and I had furtively purchased two identical large white tee shirts the day before, and we exchanged them with the pair the Italian dolls had tucked under their pool recliners (when the girls weren't paying attention). The only difference in the exchanged apparel was that Carnie had Bo Jalonec draw a pair of big brown nipples and exaggerated cleavage lines on the new white shirts, which we had carefully folded, face-in. The two voluptuous lovelies exited the pool, entered the new white tee shirts, and then pulled them down over their swimsuits.

Immediately, a roar of laughter rose from all those assembled, particularly the young bucks. Bubbles and Angie glanced-down and before they could gather their wits and verbally react, Carnie and I pushed the Sicilian dolls into the deep end of the Olympic-sized swimming pool. In spite of the refreshing water, the painted brown nipples on the soaking-wet tee shirts looked as good as new.

"You shit-face dunces! Ya' dumb puny punks!" coughed Bubbles, while spitting-out about a liter of water.

"Ya' perverted deviates," Angie choked-out. "You're the same two disgustin' horny twerps who pushed us into the *Delaware River!*"

Angie and Bubbles possessed volatile tempers similar to their fathers' erratic dispositions. Carnie and I reveled in pushing the girls' buttons and pulling their chains, just to make the Italian babes go nuts and lose their "cool", which according to the greaser conduct code, was the most "un-cool" thing that could happen to a '50s teenager.

If Mr. C and I could goad Angie and Bubbles into exploding into scornful tirades, then that reaction translated into the belief that *we* were in control of their predicament. We would pester the "broads" until our objective of disintegrating their normal "cool" had been expertly accomplished. Since we couldn't get their attention for what we were, Carnie and I frequently contrived situations where the girls would have to recognize our childish presence.

Boy, Popeye sure got even with me for harassing his sister at the community swimming pool. In early August of '58, I was sitting in the Feed Bag expecting to meet Tinker. Apparently, my depraved friend had been delayed for some reason, and I was later to discover the cause of his absence. Suddenly, three Ks pulled into the restaurant's parking area in Cummings' notorious souped-up black '52 Ford. The two Kamikazes in the front seat leaped-out and then frantically rushed into the teen-oriented establishment.

"Are ya' friends with that weird-lookin' dude who wears the Davy Crockett coonskin hat and the 3-D glasses?" Cummings asked with a rather serious expression on his crater face.

There was an unusual sense of urgency in the brute's dreaded voice. I was a little alarmed at the Ks presence, and very concerned for Tinker's well-being. "Yes, what's up?" I cautiously asked.

"I think your psycho buddy was just in a serious accident," Popeye added. "There's an ambulance team lookin' at him over near Kenwood Drive. Come blow this scene with us and we'll take ya' there."

Cummings, Popeye Messina, and I darted-out of the Feed Bag. Jake Mullins, a big tough Kamikaze, was sitting in the back seat of Cummings' car. The black '52 peeled-out of the restaurant's parking lot, made a quick left from *Route 13* onto Haines Road, and the vehicle quickly barreled past the Delaware Canal and the Windsor Pharmacy. Moments later, Cummings hit the brakes and skidded to a halt behind some evergreen bushes, just before we reached the main entrance into Kenwood. I should have known that the diabolical Ks were not driven by sincere humanitarian goals.

"Okay, Punk, the official tour's over. Take your shirt and pants off," Cummings snorted. "And don't forget your goddamned shoes and socks, too."

"What the hell is goin' on? Where's Tinker?" I demanded.

"You'll see in a minute," Cummings insisted. "Do what we say or we'll tie ya' up, gag your raunchy mouth, piss and shit on your face, and then stuff ya' head first into a sewer to leave ya' to die alone without honor."

I cooperatively did as I had been ordered, stripping-down to my shorts. I then handed my clothes to Mullins, who shoved me back ito the black Ford. Cummings left his '52's cover behind the high evergreen bushes, and then swiftly peeled-out into Kenwood.

As we approached Dante Messina's house, my pupils perceived Tink standing bent-over in his gray jockey shorts. His coonskin hat, 3-D glasses and other assorted articles of clothing were strewn all over the ground. His head had been shoved into Dante Messina's concrete reinforced mailbox, and my encumbered buddy was hitting the metal sides of the container with clenched fists, trying to gain someone's attention.

Although I was extremely scared of Cummings, I was at that moment angry that the chief K and Popeye were exploiting my friendship with Tinker, were harassing Tinker, and were persecuting my lame buddy to the extreme.

"Ya' oughta' go on *Ted Mack's Original Amateur Hour* as a novelty act!" Popeye loudly chuckled in Tink's direction.

"What about *Candid Camera* with Allen Funt?" Cummings suggested and indulgently laughed. "He likes featurin' jerk-offs like you fucked-up Dogwood Hollow dunces!"

Moments later, the black Ford (with me as a hostage) squealed-out onto Haines Road. The mean machine soon veered right in the direction of Dogwood Hollow. The hotrod stopped in front of

Salvatore Palermo's residence, where a heavy, wrought-iron mailbox, a twin to Dante Messina's, was situated between the residence's lawn and Daffodil Lane.

Cummings, Popeye, and Jake Mullins escorted me out of the car; threw my clothes onto Sal's lawn; dragged me over to Palermo's atomic bomb-proof mailbox; opened the hatch, and violently pushed my head inside, nearly breaking my windpipe and voice-box with the forceful forward thrust.

"Maybe ya' can star on *The Naked City,"* Popeye cackled. "But I can't picture eight-million asshole stories like this one, though."

"Ya' look a little like Eddie Arcaro in those jockey shorts," Cummings screamed right before I heard his '52 Ford coupe jerk forward in first gear.

I made quite a racket attempting to summon assistance, banging my hands against the sides of the metal mailbox in a similar manner to which I had seen Tinker doing over in Kenwood. Soon, the entire neighborhood was congregated around the box to witness the extraordinary in-progress spectacle. Salvatore Palermo came-out to personally inspect the crisis. Even Mom and Dad heard the turmoil and bolted-over to evaluate the source of the hullabaloo.

I ceased my intense struggle, worrying inside the dark enclosure that I might sever an artery or major vein in my neck. I felt stupid, embarrassed, and helpless. Soon, I recognized the sounds of several sirens coming from emergency vehicles, and then the familiar strong voice of Chief Bradley of the Edgely Fire Department was very distinguishable.

It required around fifteen-minutes of surgical cutting, but finally, my cranium had been gently liberated from its stubborn snare. Chief Bradley instructed me to slowly twist my chin to my left shoulder and then to my right, while he loosely held my neck to ascertain whether or not I had sustained any broken vertebrae behind my throat. At last, the Fire Chief gave me his stamp of approval, and the neighbors let out a loud round of applause.

"Your kid's idiotic stunt will cost you twenty-three bucks," Palermo informed Dad. "This bizarre stunt is almost as good as the English bicycle fiasco."

"My son's life is worth every penny," Pop intelligently replied.

Palermo was not amused. "Next time ya' take your kid to *Robert Hall's,* have him fitted for a straight-jacket," Sal shouted, much to the appreciation of most of the neighborhood audience.

At that particular moment, the Edgely dispatcher contacted Chief Bradley, who shook his head in disbelief at the nature of the message. The fire official announced to Pop and Sal Palermo the startling news.

"Another kid over in Kenwood has his head stuck in somebody's mailbox," the Chief divulged. "Monkey see, monkey do! Is there a full moon out tonight, or what?"

Chief Bradley, his police escort, and an accompanying fire engine activated their sirens and cut a course to rescue Tinker over in Kenwood. Sal Palermo pointed his left index finger in my chest.

"I only tolerate you, you little twerp, because I feel sorry for mentally retarded people. Next time ya' wanna' destroy someone's mailbox, then choose somebody else's."

I nodded my aching head in tacit agreement. All the while, I believed that there was some weird connection between the dual mailbox incidents and the coincidental presence of Popeye Messina, Cummings, and Salvatore Palermo. I didn't give a damn whether Dante and Sal were Mafia or not. Tinker was pissed-off; I was pissed-off, and Carnie would be aggravated, too, at our joint adversaries, and when the time was right, we would get our retribution in triplicate.

In the spring of 1958, Elvis Presley had been drafted into the *United States Army*. In late August, Carnie and I had just returned from the Towne Theater where we had viewed Marilyn Monroe in the western classic, *River of No Return*. We met Tinker that night in the Sweet Snack and Sundae Shop situated in the Levittown Shop-A-Rama. The abusive crap that had been happening to us was not the type of humor a person would see on the *George Burns and Gracie Allen Show*. The beleaguered Diablos needed to organize an action plan to counter the persistent threat and treachery of Cummings, Popeye, Dante Messina, and Sal Palermo.

Soon, Elvis's voice came over the speakers singing, "Wear My Ring around Your Neck", and the guys began discussing "the King's" recent drafting into the military.

"It's a damned government plot," Carnie asserted.

"What the hell do ya' mean?" asked Tink.

"He's goin' in the *Army* against his will," Carnie argued. "Elvis says in the papers that he doesn't mind doin' service for Uncle Sam, but I know he'd rather cut records and continue his career than do lousy boot camp."

I was confused about the entire conversation. I could not decipher how Elvis was associated with any government conspiracy. "Why do ya' say it's a plot?"

"Because the government is tryin' to destroy rock and roll," Carnie replied. "And *that* J. Edgar Hoover guy doesn't like the new music and thinks it's causin' juvenile delinquency. And besides, lots of black singers are getting rich, and powerful white people in the country don't like that happenin'."

I had no idea that Carnie could be so philosophical and erudite outside of school. It all did make sense, though. Eliminate “the King”, and his rock and roll empire would soon disintegrate. Carnie’s conspiracy theory had definite merit. The U. S. government was out to destroy rock and roll.

“If ya’ can’t trust the government, then who can we trust?” I assertively asked.

“Each other,” answered Tinker as the Quinn wannabe’ pointed to the three of us, emphatically rotating his right hand in a complete circle. “It’s the Diablos against the rest of the friggin’ world.”

“Rock and roll isn’t responsible for juvenile delinquency in Levittown,” I answered. “The Kamikazes and the Renegades are.”

Tinker and Carnie laughed at my general assessment. All three of us lifted our *Pepsi* bottles and saluted the validity of my impeccable remark. Before our delicious banana splits arrived at our table, we discussed what we would do if the Ks persisted in enacting their ruthless aggression against innocent fun-loving Diablos. The evolving rivalry was the classic match-up of mischief versus malice.

Chapter 10
"Pomeroy's"

In late August, Bo, Carnie, and I were strolling through the state-of-the-art Levittown Shopping Center. *Pomeroy's,* a popular two-level department paradise was the Mall's main anchor store. The emporium had the most modern escalators in Bucks County, along with a pair of better than average elevators. The three of us constant visitors thought we were wild and reckless guys, just like "Charlie Brown" in the Coasters' popular hit tune.

The Diablos' trio was descending on the *Pomeroy*'s escalator when Jokes spotted an egghead directly behind us. Eggheads were brainy '50s nerds who were often targeted for greaser abuse.

"Hey Kid," Jokes began. "Do ya' own any land?"

The befuddled wimp inspected the serious grimace on Carnie's face; studied the inflexible frown on my mug; noticed the sneer on Jalonec's countenance, and then submissively shook his head in a negative twist.

Carnie and Bo quickly administered two swift jabs to the geek's nuggets. and then all three Diablos yelled in unison, "Well egghead, now ya' own two acres!"

The tortured kid immediately slumped-over in pain, and upon reaching the first-floor, tumbled off the escalator in extreme agony. The fruitcake academic wizard howled worse than a werewolf would have, rolling on the floor, holding his tender testicles, and spinning in rapid circles like Curly of the *Three Stooges*.

"Wub, wub, wub, wub!" we laughed while imitating Curly.

That particular molestation was more than a random act of egghead bashing. We knew precisely who Mortimer Ralston was. He had squealed on Carnie in Sister Mary Alice's class at Cardinal Reagan High. Carnie had placed a huge wad of chewing gum in Karen Crosley's brunette ponytail, and the gorgeous chick refused to rat on my buddy, but Mortimer did after class. My pal had his fanny paddled by feared disciplinarian Father Malcolm, and the ornery Diablo was suspended for three days.

Mortimer was a good chum of my longtime enemy Stanley Tezeeker, so Ralston's negative *Pomeroy's* experience with the Diablos was an indirect warning that I still remembered *his* grammar school tattling to Sister Marian. Greasers regarded "squealin" as the most-ugly of social offenses, and worthy of swift retribution.

The Diablos despised eggheads because the arrogant scholars were proud of getting all A's in school. The "Einsteins" were the perennial teachers' pets; were involved in "corny" and "faggot" activities like the Latin Club, the Drama Club, the Chess Club, and the Forensics' Club, and we resented the pompous weaklings because the finks would have bright futures in both the college and corporate worlds. The brainy eggheads' only real crime in life was being more academically motivated and more dedicated to learning than the jealous greasers were.

The Diablos were rather insecure about ourselves, so we had to act like a wolf pack rather than behave as discreet individuals. As Jokes aptly stated, *we* had to make Mortimer feel "real swell" about his lowly position in the Levittown teen pecking order of dominant greasers, tough jocks, and finally recessive eggheads, occupying the bottom of the teen power matrix.

I wasn't really excessively proud of the misdeed that Bo, Carnie and I had done to Mortimer. Like his goofball friends, the obnoxious egghead was an easy target for our bullying. Tezeeker and Ralston had great intellectual potential, and *we* instinctively sensed and feared *that* mental factor. Someday, their kind would be our gutless bosses in business and industry, and subconsciously, the Diablos knew and dreaded *that* grotesque notion, even though we never extensively talked about it. So, we had to demonstrate our 1950s physical prowess to compensate for the eggheads' assumed mental supremacy. But in retrospect, Stanley and Mortimer deserved our sincerest apologies for our sadistic, barbaric, perpetual greaser terrorism.

After Jokes, Carnie and I had enacted our "fun caper" with Mortimer, the *Three Musketeers* headed for another section of *Pomeroy's* to search-out another prospective prey. We moved swiftly through the store's sporting goods section. In the camping and picnic department we encountered Bubbles. The Messina chick had a part-time job as a salesgirl, and the well-stacked doll fascinated the heck out of me, regardless of the setting.

Earlier in the day, Jokes had purchased a new camera at Photo City and wanted a chance to practice with his new device. Jalonec was a respectable six-foot-tall, had wavy blond hair, and possessed a sleek one hundred-seventy-pound frame. Girls drooled when his bright blue eyes flashed in their direction.

"Pardon me, Miss," Bo prefaced quite genially. "But I just bought this new camera and I want to test it out. Would it be askin' too much of ya' to pose for my first picture?"

The well-built beauty admirably studied Bo's smile, pearly white teeth, and captivating eyes. "Why, not at all! Ya' look perfectly harmless Tiger," the knockout babe said with a grin. "And besides, I might even get to know your real name."

It really bothered me that the only reason Bubbles tolerated my presence inside *Pomeroy's* was because Bo was there, charming her mesmerized eyes and mind.

"One more thing, Doll. Could ya' just pick-up and hold those two picnic coolers on that table. I need to adjust the camera's lens to allow for scale and balance."

"Sure. Anything ya' say, Cutie-pie," agreed the totally vivacious chick. "Ya' might even have to return me the favor someday."

Bo then announced that his focus had become plain and clear. Right before he pressed the button, the handsome Diablo bartered some more banter with the attractive young lady. "Say, did ya' know that ya' have a nice set of jugs there?" Jalonec quipped.

"What did ya' say?" Bubbles asked.

Carnie felt obligated to interrupt and aggravate the situation. "My good friend just said you're wearin' your SCUBA gear backwards. Those firm oxygen tanks you're sportin' should be on your back."

Before Bubbles could readily reply, Jokes told her that she could do heavy local charity work for the "Community Chest", and then the infuriated girl associated Carnie and me with some former swimming pool tee-shirt mischief along with serious *Delaware River* splashing.

"Ya' sleazy Dogwood Hollow creeps. I'm gonna' call the cops."

"Call the *National Guard*, the *IRS,* and the *FBI,* too, if ya' want," Carnie snottily answered.

And with the C Man's boastful remark, all three Diablos whipped-out miniature water guns, and we effectively drenched Bubbles' white blouse pretty good, until her thin bra exposed some massive cleavage.

"You're all gonna' pay for this, you dumb-ass cockroaches!" the Italian babe shouted at the top of her spectacular lungs. "I'd rather go out with Stanley Tezeeker than with any of you jerks!"

In short time, we three greasers scampered out of *Pomeroy's*. Bo, Carnie, and I leaped-over low display counters and hopped-around merchandise tables that temporarily impeded our rapid exit. Shocked shoppers shook their heads in dismay as we made our hasty escape. A male sales clerk yelled, "Hey you delinquents! Come back here!"

Much to our relief, we successfully exited the crowded department store, thinking about more havoc we could instigate elsewhere.

Bubbles Messina had been an object of Diablos' deviltry ever since Angie and she had accused Carnie and me of pushing the cousins into the *Delaware River*. Their indictive testimonies in Bristol were the clinchers that had convinced Mother Veronica that Carnie and I were the chief culprits who had caused a scene of wild pandemonium.

Popeye Messina and Cummings had almost gotten me drowned using a semi-frozen canal attack, and also, "Bruno" almost got Tinker and me killed using twin metal mailboxes. On the other side of the coin, I did have a major crush on Bubbles all along, but being an immature teenager, I didn't quite know how to get her attention other than by embarrassing her in public. The Diablos felt we had to harass the Messina and Palermo girls to send a distinct message to the toxic Ks that we weren't afraid to play hardball.

Sometimes, greaser persecution happened in reverse. Carnie saw his cousin from Fairless Hills pushing her baby carriage through the vast outdoor Shop-A-Rama. Bo and I decided to play a little pinball in a nearby amusement arcade, while Carnie and his cousin Dolores were chatting and gossiping about distant relatives. A half-hour later, the C Man rushed into the arcade, all out of breath.

"Guys, it was really horrible. Cummings, Popeye, and Jake Mullins approached us and started insulting Dolores's infant bambino. The three Ks had recognized me, and decided to ridicule my cousin's kid, lying in the baby carriage. I really felt helpless and intimidated."

"What did the Kenwood punks say?" I asked.

"Popeye said that little Jimmy looked like a cross between Frankenstein and the Werewolf, but only much uglier. And Cummings then said that little Jimmy looked more like a groundhog, or an otter, than a human baby. And next, Mullins contributed to the verbal abuse, stating that crying little Jimmy already-needed full facial and complete body plastic surgery!"

"What did your cousin Dolores say?" Jokes interrupted.

"She was horrified and petrified, and so was I," Carnies revealed. "Luckily, several mall security guards began walking-over in the direction of the verbal abuse, and the three thugs casually meandered-away from the scene as if nothing ever happened."

After leaving *Pomeroy's,* we three itinerant Diablos stepped across the outdoor shopping center in the direction of Jokes' sparkling green and cream '57 Chevy Bel Air. Forgetting about Carnie and Dolores being accosted in public, Jokes and I were howling lustily as we relived our most recent successes at social disorganization inside *Pomeroy's.*

Suddenly, a police siren was heard blaring in the distance. When two cruisers instantly converged in the nearby Levittown Shop-A-Rama's parking lot, we didn't have time to bolt to Jokes' car. The three of us instantly moved into the alcove of a family shoe store, pretending to be interested in purchasing black and white sneakers.

Four officers with nightsticks raced by and then darted into the Levittown Tavern where a nasty fistfight was in progress. Although we had created a good deal of aggravation to Mortimer and Bubbles, we had done our retaliations in the name of Diablos' justice. We weren't into felonies and brutal violence as were the maniacal

Kamikazes. We preferred performing well-orchestrated mischief rather than sending suspected enemies to the hospital emergency room. But felonies and pranks go together like a match and gasoline. It was just a matter of time for matters to escalate and get much worse between the treacherous Ks and the obstinate Ds.

Chapter 11
"The Phone Booth"

It was a Tuesday night in late August of '58. As usual, Quinn was absent from the gang. He had taken Patty Van Arsdale to a North 'Philly theater to see two Marilyn Monroe reruns, *Bus Stop* and *Niagara.* Earlier in the day, Bo had told me he planned to escort Susie Parker that night to the Levittown Shop-A-Rama's Towne Theater.

Carnie, Tinker, Robbie, and I were assembled at our favorite Feed Bag table facing the Dairy DeLite. As we sipped our traditional *Pepsi's,* Bo entered the teen hangout and disappointed the guys by announcing that Susie would be pulling into the parking lot in about a half-hour. So, we only had about thirty-minutes to "shoot the bull" and enjoy his exquisite company.

"Susie and me are headed to the Levittown Towne Theater to see *The Seventh Voyage of Sindbad,* followed by that new sci-fi flick *The Mummy,*" Bo informatively related. "After that boredom, my chick and me will merrily attend and participate the nightly submarine races down at Snake Road."

"Tell us how you *make out,*" Carnie snottily interrupted, "and make sure ya' don't make Susie into a *mummy.*"

Bo did not like or savor any humorous competition originating from anyone else in the gang. As was Jokes' unique style, Jalonec had to invent some silly jargon to show everyone his wit was much more-clever than Carnie's could ever be.

"Well guys," added Bo as the blond-hair Adonis briefly pulled a chair up to our table. "In about five-hours, I'll be very busy feedin' the cat."

"But ya' don't have a damned cat," observed Tinker, who valued animals over human beings.

"I most certainly do," Bo countered. "J.W., please explain to these jive turkeys what I mean." Jalonec gave me a wink; rose from his creaky chair; walked through the front entrance doors, and ambled in the direction of the Dairy DeLite's frequently used phone booth.

I seriously pondered Bo's cryptic riddle for several moments, while the other three Diablos impatiently waited for *my* thorough deciphered explanation. I surmised that the term "to feed the cat" had to have some profound sexual connotation. I almost vomited my tonsils laughing when I finally determined the cute comment's true interpretation. Then, I revealed its humorous relevance to the other fellas'.

No sooner had Bo left the premises that the Feed Bag jukebox pumped-out the instrumental "Tequila" by the Champs. Most of the assembled regulars would always join together at the end of the tune and in unison yell out the word "Tequila". The next song, "School Day" by Chuck Berry, also received participation from nearly everyone seated or standing in the place. When Berry's lyrics came to "Hail, Hail Rock and Roll, Long Live Rock and Roll" all the teens, Kamikazes and Renegades included, boisterously chanted-out the dynamic words. Some kids even hopped-up on their chairs and waved their arms to give the powerful verses more significant impact.

Jenny, a very capable waitress, approached our standard table to take our regular orders. The broad was a well-stacked babe whose tough body would have been enough to make *Superman* swallow kryptonite just to see more of her thighs and bust. The only thing Jenny lacked was missing between her ears, but her curvaceous figure seemed to generally compensate her male audience.

The platinum blonde bombshell was taking the night shift with Maggie. But whenever Bo was inside the restaurant, Jenny would continuously stare at him as if he were a cross between Clarke Gable and Rudolph Valentino.

I watched Bo through the pane-glass window pick up the receiver in the Dairy DeLite phone booth. I thought about how lucky he and Susie Parker were to have each other. I wondered if I would ever be fortunate enough to have such a beautiful girlfriend.

But then, I was surprised to see Angie Palermo enter the main part of the restaurant from the kitchen area. It was her night off, but Luigi had asked the Sicilian babe to come in to cover for a sick waitress. The Palermo doll pretended ignoring Carnie and me after what we recently had done to her cousin Bubbles with water pistols inside *Pomeroy's*. Angie's contempt for us was interrupted by a phone call. The Sicilian broad quickly answered the ring.

"Ya' say you want a medium pizza with lots of pepperoni. What's your name?" Angie asked. "Jack Inhoff! How do you spell your last name? Okay, Sir, your pizza will be ready in about a half-hour."

Tinker broke the momentary table silence to hide the essential fact that the Diablos were up to something. "I wanna' get a copy of that *Lady Chatterley's Lover* book by that D.H. Lawrence dude," the academic dolt falsely uttered, feigning intellectual literacy. "I heard on the radio that the government wants to ban *that* pulp fiction because of pornographic language."

We all knew quite well that Tinker never read books, magazines, or newspapers, but since the Diablos were always very interested in any conversation about sex, we tuned right into Tinker's remarks about D.H. Lawrence, and ignored the obvious truth that the avid Neanderthal never read anything written by anyone.

"Who needs to read?" Carnie dramatically criticized. "Come over to my place and you can look at all the dirty pictures ya' want. I got a stack of girlie magazines four-feet-high."

Although the assembled Diablos' inside the Feed Bag imagined that we were indisputable experts on the topic of sex, most of our distorted information had been disseminated by Bo. The trouble with *that* bad habit was we never knew when Jokes was being facetious, or when the frivolous jester was being honest. And so, even though Carnie and I were authorities on the complex subject in theory, we were only rank amateurs in actual practice.

Jokes returned from the Feed Bag/Dairy DeLite connection, and the other Diablos were anxiously awaiting the outcome of his pizza-order Dairy DeLite phone call. Bo detoured into the Men's Room, and about three-minutes later, sauntered-over to our table to await the fruits of his cute labor.

As my eyes stared at Jalonec, I kept thinking about Susie Parker, undoubtedly the cutest girl in Dogwood Hollow. Susie lived on Dewberry Lane, only a few doors down from Tinker. I guiltily recollected that when I was fourteen, Tinker, Carnie, Robbie, and I were acne-faced voyeurs. We hid outside Susie's bathroom window, hoping she would forget to close the shade before entering the shower. This was all before Bo ever lived in Levittown, because according to Diablos' morality, it would be grossly unethical for any of us to do a little "body spying" on another guy's chick, no matter how exotic her figure might be.

I noticed that the Feed Bag was exceptionally crowded and busy for a Tuesday night, so the waitresses were in a perpetual frenzy trying to keep-up with their grueling work demands. The pizza order was finally ready and Angie bellowed out from the oven area, "Pizza for Jack Inhoff. Anyone here named Jack Inhoff?"

The Diablos bowed our heads and held our hands up to our mouths, attempting to conceal our snickers. Angie was a little perturbed from the lack of a response, so the Italian knockout bellowed-out, "Who's Jack Inhoff in here?"

A roar of laughter immediately filled the restaurant. At least twenty male hands wildly waved in the air. Angie was appalled by all the greaser bravado and finally fully realized her embarrassing utterance.

The humiliated Sicilian beauty hustled back into the kitchen, overwhelmed by her stressful work responsibilities, and emotionally hurt by the Diablos' appetite for dark comedy, which sometimes was ridicule in disguise. At that moment, the gang thought we were only having a little fun at Angie's expense. We were too preoccupied making a mockery of her pride to even think of how cruel and vulgar our actions actually were.

Since the mysterious Jack Inhoff never showed-up for his pizza, the Diablos coughed-up three-dollars and together bought it for our own consumption. Angie recovered from her mortification in the back room, and upon hearing of our generous purchase, the Mafia knockout came-out and thanked us for our charitable benevolence.

"I might've been docked three-dollars if you guys wouldn't have bought the pizza. Ya' guys aren't so damned bad after all."

"Glad we could help out," Bo replied with a straight face. "In math' we were taught that *pi* r square, but if ya' study most pizzas, ya' know that most pies are really round."

Angie gave Bo a huge smooch on the cheek. If the doll had known that Jokes had been the elusive phantom Jack Inhoff, she might have reacted differently to the Diablos' altruistic act. The gang was very crafty at manipulating people and situations, but we were completely wrong in thinking that money was a viable cure for our high-jinks.

Susie Parker pulled-up in her powder blue and white '55 Ford Crown Victoria. Jokes jumped-out of his chair, checked his face in the slanted paned window, and then wiped all traces of Angie's lipstick from his cheek. Bo, who was a little parsimonious, gave me a whole quarter to cover the expense of his large *Pepsi*. I followed him out to his '57 Chevy, and admired the handsome skirts over the back wheels. Bo opened the passenger door, and Susie gracefully slid into the extraordinary pussy-wagon.

"Hi Susie," I shyly greeted. "I've been doin' my best keepin' Bo out of trouble."

"It's hard keepin' me out of trouble when *I am* trouble," admitted Jalonec with rare honesty. "J.W. keeps me honest, but Susie here keeps me *straight,"* Bo chuckled, making another one of his deft sexual allusions.

"Bo," Susie laughed. "Why can't you be normal like J.W. instead of acting goofy and nutty all the time?"

"Because, normal guys like J.W. have to mercilessly suffer watchin' weird eccentric guys like me get all the chicks."

I felt a trifle insecure at not having a permanent girlfriend, so I awkwardly changed the discussion's subject matter. "Are ya' guys still goin' to the movies?"

"Naa, no way!" Jokes replied. "Susie and me are certified upholstery inspectors. We'll have to check the back seat for defects before we begin the submarine races out at Snake Road."

Susie and Jokes laughed. Bo backed out, hit the gas pedal, and then adroitly peeled-out onto busy *Route 13.* The beautiful green and cream machine fishtailed north into denser traffic. I peered at Susie's immaculate *Crown Victoria,* and wished I could own such a boss set of wheels. Then, my vivid imagination pondered for a second. I also jealously wished that I could have Susie Parker, along with her magnificent powder blue and cream '55 Ford, all to myself.

Chapter 12
"Carnie's Frustration"

Carnie had always been envious of Bo Jalonec's unrivaled success at handling the opposite gender. On Thursday night, Carnie joined Tinker, Robbie Wilkinson, and me inside the Feed Bag. Bo was out again somewhere, cavorting-around with Susie Parker, and Quinn was driving-around Atlantic City with Patty Van Arsdale. The absence of Jokes and Quinn deeply disturbed Carnie and Tinker. Both resentful guys wanted more power and prestige within the Diablos.

"It just ain't fair," Tinker opined. "Bo and Quinn are never around. They'd rather be with their women than with their true friends."

"I agree with Tink," Carnie despondently admitted. "We have no leadership. If the mean-assed Ks walk through that door right now, and challenge us to a rumble, we're basically doomed."

Robbie was a little more objective in his observations. I always liked R.W. because unlike Tinker, he'd rather help people than hurt them. Also, I remembered Robbie saving me from drowning in the Delaware Canal and felt deeply indebted to him. But R.W. was about to start arguing with Carnie, who had also significantly helped in my rescue, so I figured I had to play the role of peacemaker.

"You two knuckleheads are jealous because Bo and Quinn have women and you monkey faces have *nada,"* Robbie indicted, trying to show us he had passed Spanish I. "Senor Roberto" usually made good sense when he wasn't drunk or fooling-around.

"Hombres, calm down por favor," I pleaded. "If ya' two guys are unhappy with Bo and Quinn, then tell them, not me."

Jenny came-over to take our predictable orders before the escalating debate could become more heated. Her physical presence seemed to relax the tension among the guys.

"Say, whose boss Mercury is that out there?" asked the waitress. "It looks like the one James Dean drove around in *Rebel without a Cause.*"

"It's mine," Carnie proudly confessed. "And I just got it a few months ago. You're the third waitress who remembers it from that James Dean movie. I'm glad I had lent it to the Hollywood film studio." Then, Carnie recalled one of Bo's witty quips about *his* black '49 Merc'. "It's a nice car, but I have a little trouble parkin' it in a thermos bottle every damned night."

Jenny peered at Carnie with a strange look on her face. "Are ya' high on marijuana, or opium, or something? Why would ya' put Mercury in a thermos bottle?" the waitress admonished. "You're liable to get ptomaine poisoning, or the gout, or something!"

Carnie had a strong desire to date Jenny, but she was a couple of years older, and a couple of decades more experienced than he was. Mr. Mercury instinctively tried to cover for his stupid remarks. Sometimes, I thought the C Man would have a better chance of landing a pretty babe if he were simply a blind deaf mute. "Well, Jenny," my pal awkwardly and pathetically stammered. "How would ya' like to go on a bowlin' date up at Thornridge Alleys?"

"Don't do it, Jenny," Robbie cautioned. "Carnie's not a good bowler. His mind is always in the gutter, and that's where the ball winds-up almost every time."

Carnie resented Robbie's brazen interference in what the amateur lover considered making some goodwill progress with the stacked waitress. "Speak for yourself, Slime-ball. Jenny, if ya' go bowlin' with me, I'll definitely teach ya' how to score." Carnie was using a line he once heard Bo say. The only difference was it had worked for Jalonec.

"I already know how to score, Dimwit. But I do it with the right guys," the waitress chastised. "I wouldn't go-out with you if ya' were James Dean, and that black Mercury out there was really *his* friggin' wheels parked outside instead of your pig wagon."

"I've scored with a lot of girls," Carnie self-consciously claimed, bragged, and prevaricated.

"Yeah, probably kindergarten chicks, ya' stupid child molester!" Robbie laughed.

"Ya' couldn't score if you had five testicles," Jenny viciously admonished. "On second thought, make *that* lucky magic number seven instead of five."

"We call Carnie Mr. *C Man,"* Robbie contributed. "But Bo calls Carnie Mr. See-Man, as in semen."

I tried to appeal to Jenny's better judgment. I thought the waitress might show some genuine sympathy for Carnie. "Ya' know, Jenny. My pal Carnie here has a big-time crush on you."

"Well, really now. Please tell him to enter puberty, and then there's maybe a one in a millionth chance I might be remotely interested!"

Mr. Se-man's sperm count instantly shot-down to zero. I wished the relentless guy would just learn to keep his big trap shut. The nasty remarks ended when Bo Jalonec pulled-up to the Feed Bag in his boss '57 Chevy. Susie waited in the car, while Jokes entered to buy some chewing gum and some antacid tablets from a dispensing machine. Noticing us seated at our favorite table, Jalonec came over to say "hi". As soon as Jenny saw Bo, her demeanor automatically oscillated from antagonistic to cheerful on the attitude scale.

"Hi there, dreamboat," Jenny greeted her idol. "I see you quite often. Are ya' a regular here?"

"Yes, I am a regular," Jalonec responded. "But right now, I'm sufferin' from irregularity. That's why I need some damned antacid tablets. Tonight, I feel like a toilet and need to flush myself out."

Jenny desired to prolong the table conversation when minutes before she didn't want to have anything to do with the Diablos. "That's really clever, ya' intelligent, gorgeous, dimple-faced, blond-haired angel," the waitress praised. "Angie tells me ya' have a special lady friend. That's too bad. It would give me great pleasure to have some of your personal action."

Jokes stood beside our table and blushed. His brain was thoroughly enjoying his own magnificence, while Carnie sat alongside me and seethed. Carnie, Tink, Robbie, and I figured we'd let Bo dominate our side of the talking, so that we could study and perfect his splendid magic with girls.

"Tell me, Sir Lancelot," Jenny inquired. "Who are your four obnoxious friends? Let me guess now. You're Bucky Beaver; you're Markie with the cereal ad; you're Mr. Clean, and you're Choo-Choo Charlie from the silly television commercials."

Jenny's associations afforded the four-seated Diablos to act like perfect idiots in an imperfect world. "Brusha, Brusha, Brusha, here's the new *Ipana,"* Carnie inanely chanted. "I want my *Maypo,"* I dramatically cried. "I'll get rid of dirt and grime," Robbie predicted as he flexed his muscular biceps. And then Tinker kept obnoxiously repeating "Choo-Choo Charlie is an engineer, *Good and Plenty*, *Good and Plenty,"* making the repetitive sound of a runaway locomotive.

Jenny was not impressed with our lunacy, wishing that we would refrain from our juvenile refrains. "Ya' four jerks are born losers. Come to think of it, you're born morons. Ya' freaks probably weren't even born. I'll bet ya' were hatched like those giant killing ants in that scary movie *Them*."

The tough-talking, buxom waitress then wiggled into the kitchen area to transfer our orders to Luigi and 'Nick'. Jokes looked-out at his car and saw Susie putting on lipstick while gazing into the rear-view mirror. Bo knew he only had a few minutes to reveal some special secrets he knew about females.

"Do any of you unworthy nitwits think Jenny's a true blonde?" Bo esoterically asked.

"I can't really tell," Carnie answered. "She has platinum blonde hair, but I can't tell for damned sure."

Even I knew that no girl was ever born with platinum blonde hair, but I was very much aware that Carnie and I knew as much about the opposite sex as we did about Advanced Calculus and Latin IV.

"The true *lint-mist* (litmus) test," lectured Bo, "is whether or not the hair on her head is the same color as the hair on her bush. In other words, does it match the patch? That's the friggin' $64,000.00 question!"

"How can ya' know for sure?" asked bewildered-but-curious Carnie. "I need to record this new information in my skull!"

I was equally as intrigued as the other seated Diablos, for we all thought that Bo Jalonec knew more about women than women actually knew about themselves.

"Very simple, Retards," Bo preached like a flustered and frustrated minister addressing his mediocre congregation. "Ya' simply check-out the broad's eyebrows. If the hair on her head matches the hair on the brow, then the hair or her head matches the fuzz on her bush. I hope ya' dumb ass-lappers are payin' strict attention."

"I'm a ready-teddy," Robbie declared.

"Meanwhile, back in the states," I chuckled as I quoted some of the lyrics to "Stranded in the Jungle" by the Cadets. "I wonder if that group ever graduated from *West Point?"* I asked.

"Who?" Tinker inquired.

"The Cadets," I knowledgeably replied.

Tinker, Carnie, and Robbie thought I had made a stupid remark. The trio crumpled-up their paper napkins and spontaneously chucked the balls in my face.

"Get bent, Words," Carnie rankled as everyone else at the table smiled and nodded their heads. Only Jokes found some merit in my corny comment, calling me "a rank freshman who just made his first big step on the path to getting laid".

Jokes again glanced out the window. His brain figured Susie was becoming restless waiting in his car, so Bo bid us "farewell" for the evening, and then nonchalantly strolled-out of the establishment. I saw him give Susie a peck on the cheek before he activated his engine.

When I glanced out again, I saw Jokes again kissing Susie, and that seemed to contradict the greaser code which stated a Diablo had to be in control of his emotions at all times, and also, that one should always act "cool" in public, and not express affectionate feelings outwardly.

Everything 'except bravado' had to be internalized. Laughter was okay, even though it involved emotion. Our humor was usually derived from ridiculing or making fun of others. But public kissing and affection did upset us, mostly because it was usually passively done at home with family or relatives, and the greasers were rebelling against adult authority, trying to establish each other as family substitutes. 'And besides,' I thought. 'Only Arabs, Mafia, Russians, faggots, and women kissed each other.'

In the glorious '50s, greasers didn't *love* people. We *liked* people. The '50s were an age for liking. When Elvis Presley's movie *Love Me Tender* opened in New York, the girls wore buttons that read *I Like Elvis,* and when Dwight D. Eisenhower ran for president, the political banners read *I Like Ike.*

The Diablos were a product of the "age of liking". We believed that *things* were what really should be loved in the '50s. Teens loved sharp cars, shiny new motorcycles, pinball machines, sock hops, drive-ins, ice cream parlors, and terrific hangouts like the Feed Bag and the Dairy DeLite. Tinker, on the other hand, disliked people in general, and since Carnie, Robbie, and I liked most folks, the three of us were really '50s Don Quixotes seeking distant relationships with females, while pretending to be searching for close contact with cooperative and accommodating whores.

Robbie started talking about the Russians going completely bonkers with their devastating atomic and hydrogen bombs. "I'll tell you circus clowns the truth; nuclear war scares the hell out of me," R.W. admitted. "I heard where that rich kid Phil Jackson's family is havin' a well-equipped bomb shelter built underground in back of his house!"

Tinker, who greatly valued conflict and violence, saw the world a little differently. "Those freaky Russians are a bunch of faggot homos!" Tink rudely exclaimed and exaggerated. "I saw Khrushchev kissin' his chief advisers last night on TV. That fat queer asshole really grossed me out!"

"As long as the faggots stay in Russia," I maintained, "who really cares what the Commies do?"

Tinker was not so compassionate about international politics. "If those freakin' Russians ever come into Dogwood Hollow, I'll fix their sorry asses' good. "I'll steal their vodka; shit in their babushkas, and piss on their sputniks." The T Man looked at the rest of us with fire seemingly coming-out of his eyes, and then the demolition expert proceeded with his haughty rhetoric. "And if any Russian asshole tries kissin' me, I'll cut off his lips and sow them on his old lady's crotch, so that she'll think she has two vaginas instead of one."

Tinker was crazy, and was worthy asylum material. We just sat there and listened to his venomous remarks. We all feared the mental defect because he was, without a doubt, the most vengeful and vindictive Diablo. If someone crossed him, then that person would be double-crossed a thousand-fold. And when Tink lost his temper, the maniac would also lose his sanity and turn into a sadistic animal, lusting for blood and carnage.

So, when the T Man stated that he absolutely hated someone, then man the torpedoes. Tink had a wild mean streak bred into his *genes,* as well as brass testicles inside his *jeans.* And if adequately motivated, the vindictive delinquent would feel no guilt or remorse about destroying someone's car, or sending someone to the hospital, or to the morgue. Basically, the awesome kid had no conscience.

Jenny finally delivered our orders and we voraciously ate our daily diet of pizza, French fries, and steak sandwiches. Everything seemed to be tranquil until I told Carnie to clean-up the excess ketchup on his face, which had been smeared from his mouth to his right ear. That innocuous suggestion seemed to ruffle his feathers. Jenny cautiously returned to our table to deliver the check.

Carnie was extremely envious of Bo. In fact, so obviously envious that the insecure bozo imitated Jalonec whenever Jokes was not present. Mercury Man never quite knew when to quit. The clown tried laying on Jenny some rhetoric he once heard Bo Jalonec successfully give to a waitress at the Carousel Grille over in Bensalem.

"Hey, Jenny," the greenhorn Don Juan prefaced. "What's your favorite record?"

Jenny figured she would be polite and earn a decent tip. "I like 'At the Hop' by Danny and the Juniors. What's yours?" the waitress asked, while momentarily tolerating Carnie's excessive immaturity.

"I really like 'The Happy Organ' by Dave 'Baby' Cortez!" And after making that very un-sensational remark, Carnie stood-up and pointed to the area of his pants where his miniature sausage would be found under the material. The absolute fool really never sufficiently comprehended that only Bo Jalonec could be Bo Jalonec, and that only Carnie could be Carnie.

The basic problem was that Carnie and Tinker never fully fathomed who they themselves were, and as far as Bo Jalonec was concerned, Jokes was a marvelous fake, a skilled con-artist. Jokes could get away with just about anything, and being the impressionable chameleon of the Diablos, I would often foolishly imitate him, too. We all tried to assimilate *his* behavioral traits into our personalities, thinking we would enjoy similar triumphs with hot-looking girls. Even though we all knew Jokes was a phony, a notorious hoax, we always admired the noteworthy results the suave guy always obtained with members of the opposite sex.

But Jenny was not-too-thrilled with Carnie's stupid persistence, which was really Carnie impersonating Bo, which was truly counterproductive and detrimental to Carnie.

"Say, Jenny," Carnie stupidly continued his obnoxious oratory. "How would ya' like goin' miniature golfin' with me tomorrow? I'll even let you rub my balls for good luck!"

"You're totally disgustin', and a disgrace to humanity, ya' know that!" Jenny boisterously yelled. "If ya' had a higher IQ, you'd still be too dumb to play Goofy on the *Mickey Mouse Club,* or Flub-A-Dub on *Howdy Doody."*

"Lay off of her, Carnie," I pleaded to my enraged, embarrassed pal. "Cool it, Man!"

Jenny was not through with her antagonism for my pretentious buddy. "If ya' was the last guy on earth, I'd still avoid ya' like the *Blue Bonnet* plague," she belittled. "Ya' could never be as cool as a ghoul in a swimmin' pool!"

Carnie was so angry about being put-down in public that the insulted kid stormed-out of the Feed Bag. I looked at Tinker, and all the junior mechanic could do was shrug his shoulders, nearly tipping his coonskin hat down onto his 3-D glasses. Mr. C Man rapidly trekked over to the Dairy DeLite phone booth. The obsessed teen put a coin into the slot and courageously dialed the Feed Bag.

Jenny was so upset about her encounter with Carnie that she had rushed into the Ladies Room to powder her nose. As the phone rang, Angie Palermo, who had arrived at the restaurant to visit Jenny, exited the kitchen to answer the call.

"Hello. Feed Bag here," Angie acknowledged.

"I'd like a medium-size pizza with lots of pepperoni," ordered Carnie.

"What's your name?"

"Jack Inhoff," the C Man said in imitation of Bo. Carnie was under a lot of duress, and actually, all the while, thought he had been speaking with Jenny.

"Well, Dip-shit," Angie replied. "If you're *jackin' off* in a phone booth, you' dumb-ass jerk-off, you'd better come quick, because I'm gonna' call the cops and have ya' arrested for indecent public exposure!" Click.

I peered out the pane-glass window and observed Carnie slam-down the phone inside the Dairy DeLite's booth. The defeated kid had been frustrated for the second time in less than an hour. First, Jenny had verbally brutalized Carnie inside the Feed Bag. And then, Angie Palermo had masterfully vanquished my insecure pal via *Ma Bell,* while *he* had believed he had been conversing with Jenny. It certainly wasn't Carnie's best day, or night, living on the planet.

Chapter 13
"Labor Day Humiliation"

Labor Day evening, 1958, was a night I'll never forget. I was wearing my black leather jacket with the Diablos' name and insignia on the back. Bo had drawn those symbols and painted them red, accompanied with white lettering. All of the local greasers, no matter their gang affiliation, wore their black leather jackets at all times, whether it be snow, rain, sleet, hail, cyclone, monsoon, or hurricane. It didn't matter whether it was winter, spring, fall, or a 105-degree July day. The Diablos' leather jackets were our uniforms, our pride and joy, and to hell with any narrow-minded adult who thought we were foolish, or impractical-looking punks.

That September night, Quinn had again been absent from the gang. Our leader and Patty had double-dated with Bo and Susie, which caused more dissension within the Diablos' lower echelon.

Around 7:30, the usual nucleus of buddies was assembled inside the Feed Bag: Carnie, Tinker, Robbie, and myself. Chuckie Callahan, Jimmy Callahan, and Ace Roberts were huddled-around one of the two pinball machines, and Slip Carson and Fritz Feldcamp, two other Diablos, were busy blasting-away targets on the Skeet-Shoot Machine. As we sipped our *Pepsi's,* I listened to chronic-complainers Carnie and Tinker vent their dissatisfactions about how Bo and Quinn had again abandoned their buddies for the opposite sex.

"Instead of yappin' about Quinn and Bo," Robbie answered, "would you two knuckleheads rather talk about the Dairy DeLite phone booth embarrassment, or about heads getting stuck in Sicilians' mailboxes." Robbie's critical comments accurately hit home with Carnie, Tink, and me, so I figured it was time to be the great mediator before Tinker decided to demolish both of us, and destroy the Feed Bag, too.

"Speakin' of Bo and Quinn," I said. "Jokes told me a strange story about our fearless leader. Ya' guys interested in hearin' the hairy details?" All three listeners apathetically shook their heads in unison.

"According to Bo," I continued, "Quinn told him that people have seven times as many germs in their mouths as they have in their ass-holes. Seven times as many!" I emphasized. "So, every time ya' kiss someone on the lips like those dumb-shit Russians do, it's just like one of us stickin' our tongue way up a person's rear end seven freakin' times in a row."

"Where did Quinn read that dumb-shit information?" Tinker questioned. "In the Encyclopedia Stupidity?"

"What weird name does Jalonec call this new asinine theory?" Robbie perceptively asked.

"The 'Seven Asshole Principle'," I aptly and succinctly replied.

I knew Bo Jalonec better than I knew the *Pledge of Allegiance,* and I fathomed that the jokester had invented that peculiar story about Quinn, who never would have made such a preposterous statement. Quinn had a value system very akin to that of a Mormon or an Amishman. Since Bo had little credibility when it came to anything other than tantalizing sexy girls, we all agreed that the whole tale was nothing more than sheer fiction.

I was still laughing about Bo's extravagant story when I happened to glance out the large pane-glass window. Stanley Tezeeker, resident egghead, was pulling into the Feed Bag parking lot in his miniature Nash Rambler. Waldo Hunsburger, Melvin Speigleman, and Mortimer Ralston were accompanying craven Tezeeker. The four were giggling incessantly, probably being giddy over a minor error in a quadratic equation, or chuckling over a technical miscalculation in a geometric theorem. Just the thought of more than one egghead academic wizard in our presence instantly turned our stomachs sour.

Stanley parked his wimpy-looking vehicle close to our side of the restaurant, where the nerd immediately noticed our three faces staring menacingly him down. The coward and his feckless entourage quickly leaped back inside the Nash, and in a matter of ten-seconds, the brown-nosers were speeding off the premises.

The Feed Bag was neutral territory for greasers and jocks, but the Diablos, the Kamikazes, and the Renegades regarded it as off-limits to finks, faggots, and eggheads. We always discouraged brainiacs from desecrating our valued sanctuary.

I again glanced-out the large window and was alarmed to see Cummings pull-up in the parking spot recently vacated by Tezeeker. An identical black '52 Ford pulled into the next space. Cummings and Popeye exited their awesome autos.

"What do those criminals want?" Robbie wondered and asked. "They seem to be on-a-mission without standin' on top of the Alamo!"

"Maybe they're gonna' invite us to the annual Kamikaze *Labor Day* barbecue and drug fest," I quipped.

"If the Ks wanta' rumble, then where the hell are those missing bums Quinn and Bo?" Tinker angrily demanded.

Since the Feed Bag was "safe turf" to area gangs, I felt no cause for panic. Cummings and Popeye approached our table in a cheerful holiday mood, which was contrary to their ordinary uncivil dispositions. Cummings held a copy of *Life Magazine* in his right hand, and the awesome gorilla opened the periodical to a featured article about carefree college students. The King K smashed the story's photo' against the red and white checked plastic tablecloth. All activity within the crowded building seemed to suddenly stop.

"Who here is in charge of the Diablos?" Cummings thundered.

I looked around the room, trying to act unaffected by the bully's vociferous demand. "I reckon I am," I returned.

I nervously smiled and evaluated Cummings' overall savage appearance. The brute had cold, metallic blue eyes, and his moon-shaped face was pocked with acne craters and blackheads. The brute's tattooed biceps were bulging-out of the cut-off sleeves of his cut-off Kamikaze leather jacket. Cummings' first lieutenant, Popeye Messina, stood directly behind his boss, and behind Bruno were seven more smiling, criminal-looking, Kenwood creeps.

Although I was petrified half-to-death, I felt it was my duty to Carnie, Tinker, Robbie, to Chuckie and Jimmy Callahan, and to Ace Roberts to represent them with honor. I picked-up the magazine article and orally read its headline.

"Look here, Amigo," Cummings stressed. "These college campus punks have this crazy fad. Check-out the picture. The asshole finks see how many fraternity brothers the dumb-shits can stuff into a phone booth. What do ya' think?"

"I think thoughts," I boldly answered the frightening King K. "What do you think?"

My heart was wildly palpitating, and I was stalling for more time to organize my disheveled mind. My mouth was awkwardly attempting to talk like Bo Jalonec to try and impress my very imposing rival. I gulped several times to catch my elusive breath. The burden of leadership in *that* time of imminent crisis was quite overwhelming.

"Ya' asked me what I think," growled Cummings. "I think you're a dumb dip-shit, but that's beside the point on top of your head. Right here and right now, the Kamikazes challenge the Diablos to a little holiday competition. What do ya' think, Popeye?"

"I think we're wastin' our time dealin' with a bunch of kiddy wimps. The Diablos are no better or tougher than a gang of sissy eggheads," berated Messina. "The Dogwood jerks need to take that Charles Atlas muscle-building course advertised in all the cheap magazines. Too bad we aren't at the beach, or I would kick a ton of sand in their faces!"

"Look, Jerk," Cummings continued, staring me directly in the eyes. "Here's a bet of twenty-dollars," the King K boomed, smacking a new crisp *Andrew Jackson* against the tablecloth. The Kamikaze chieftain then raised the bill above his head for all in the establishment to see. "I bet the Ks can fit more men into a phone booth than the Diablos can. What do ya' say about that wild bull-shit, Daddio?"

Before I could adequately respond, Popeye quickly chimed-in. "Whichever gang can squeeze the most dudes into the huge Dairy DeLite booth wins twenty-buckaroos."

"And whoever wins the contest is the coolest gang in Levittown," Cummings clearly indicated.

I was momentarily at a loss for words. Carnie and Tinker coaxed me to accept the challenge, so reluctantly, I walked-around the Feed Bag and managed to collect twenty-dollars from the worried Diablos who were in attendance. The deal was sealed when Cummings extended his King Kong-sized hand.

"Give me some skin, Brother," the human beast commanded. Cummings squeezed my right hand with his vice-like grip, nearly disintegrating my finger and wrist bones into pure powder.

I dispatched Chuckie Callahan and Robbie out to scout-up other Diablos in the vicinity. Three were found in Hal's Delicatessen playing the Snafu pinball machine, and two more guys were already over at the Dairy DeLite, munching on Polar Bars.

Cummings and I led a company of fifty or so greasers over to the aforementioned Dairy DeLite phone booth. The Kamikaze had his right arm wrapped around my bony shoulder, pretending that I was one of his best chums since kindergarten. I felt beads of perspiration rolling-down my scrawny chest and back. I never had felt so inferior or frail in my life.

"I figure these college punks are no better than us greasers," Cummings effectively emphasized. "Do ya' agree?"

"Yeah," I mechanically concurred, nodding my head. "They're nothin' but a lot of lazy rich kids with hours and hours of free time to burn. All that the college eggheads do is sit-around and scheme-up stupid pranks and contests."

Finally, we all reached our destination. Popeye counted seventeen Ks outside the Dairy DeLite phone booth, and Tinker added-up sixteen Diablos. Some Renegades were also present in the crowd of fifty or so, mostly male spectators looking for entertainment.

"Let Popeye hold your twenty-dollars," Cummings suggested. "You Dogwood gumdrops can go first. After ya' give it a go, we'll have Tinker Bell over there hold our *Andrew Jackson* when the Ks pile-in."

The idea of indirectly being called "a fairy" made Tinker's normally pallid face turn crimson. "That bastard will pay for that remark," Tink mumbled to Carnie. The possessed maverick had his fists clenched, and the lowlife Kamikazes didn't realize it, but Tinker had just made what represented a death sentence declaration.

I handed our twenty-dollars in smaller denominations over to Popeye, and then signaled for Robbie to squat-down inside the phone booth. Chuckie and Jimmy entered next, followed by Carnie and Tinker. Ace, Slip, and I squeezed inside, and I managed to nestle snugly into a space between Robbie and Chuckie. The last to be sandwiched inside was Fritz Feldcamp. The Diablos thought we had enacted a great accomplishment, fitting eleven guys inside the extra-large metal and glass case.

"Not bad, not bad at all," Cummings marveled and uttered, as the insolent harasser meticulously inspected *our* great achievement.

"Not too shabby for a pack of friggin' pussies," Popeye vindictively and characteristically belittled.

I saw Cummings' ugly face while peering through the glass door. His features were grotesque, even when the brute smiled or laughed. The King K was an unscrupulous animal who was out to annihilate anyone or anything that stood in his way. Fun to Cummings meant the same thing it did to Tinker: the injury and humiliation of teens who opposed *his* destructive goals.

Without warning, Cummings and Popeye pulled the phone booth's glass door shut. Lots of screaming, cursing, and swearing were happening inside the booth. No one trapped inside could budge an inch. The pay phone was out of reach, because nobody could even move an arm or finger to dial a number. And even if one of us could, finding a coin, placing it into the slot, and picking-up the receiver would have been a futile series of impossible tasks.

"Suckers," "Assholes," "Marys!" "Dumb-dick Dogwood Dipshits" the totally amused Kamikazes shouted.

Those names really angered the entrapped Ds awkwardly wedged inside the booth, especially the term "Marys", a '50s code word for "fairies", "neuters", or "effeminates".

I was being crushed somewhere near the center of the bizarre chaos. My left nostril was crammed against Tinker's Davy Crockett hat, and my right nostril was pressing against my pal's filthy, stained-underwear, which smelled like a full septic tank through his *dung*arees.

The Kamikazes gleefully returned to the Feed Bag parking lot, clambered into their black Fords and Pontiacs, and the entourage then buzzed the Dairy DeLite. I heard Popeye yell-out, "Thanks for the twenty-bucks, you stupid-ass, neuter, faggot cootie-munchers!"

Langford and several other ruthless Renegades tried prying-open the phone booth door, but their efforts were to no avail. The Dairy DeLite manager hit the panic button and nervously called the Edgely Fire and Rescue Squad.

Ten long minutes elapsed before Chief Bradley arrived with his reliable crew of seven skilled rescuers. As the men discussed the best way to extricate the phone booth victims, I was fearful of some Diablos suffocating inside the vertical glass sardine can. 'The booth might topple over,' I thought, 'and the guys sandwiched inside might suffer multiple cuts and lacerations.'

Chief Bradley peered inside the vertical enclosure. Sirens were blaring and red flashing lights from a dozen emergency vehicles were rotating. Firemen galore were standing-around, ready to use their axes and hatchets as a last resort. I noticed that some of the Edgely rescuers were frantic and hysterical, while others were laughing, and a few astounded and bewildered fire company members just stood there with their mouths agape. Lieutenant "Bingo" Collins used a crowbar to gradually rip the hinges off the door. Slowly but surely, the humiliated prank victims were rescued one by one from our metal and glass temporary prison.

Chief Bradley recognized Carnie, Tink, and me from the Edgely Fire House Bingo games. "You three lads look familiar. Aren't you three boys Edgely Junior firemen?"

"Yes, Sir," I admitted in a shy, weak tone of voice.

"Well, let me congratulate you," the Chief commended. "This phone booth crisis was a fine emergency practice drill, yes indeed, it was. Lieutenant Collins and I couldn't have thought of a better emergency practice session if we spent a week of planning."

"Of course," added the ball-breaking lieutenant, "the phone booth door will cost you fellas' about fifty bucks to replace."

"We'll come-up with the money," I promised. "Honest men always pay their debts," I proudly declared, remembering a line from Plato's *Republic* I had read for a book report at Cardinal Reagan.

The firemen and other onlookers gave-out a loud cheer. A Bristol Township policeman walked-over holding his report pad and pen. "Okay boys, who did this nonsense to you?"

I remembered the greaser code of silence, "Never squeal on another kid, especially another greaser."

"No one, Sir. We saw an article in *Life Magazine* about college kids stuffin' themselves inside phone booths," I maintained. I became a bit flustered by the pressure of the moment. Carnie stepped forward to help me out of my momentary mental block.

"We thought we could get out as easily as we got in," the C Man proficiently lied. "But then, something went wrong; the door accidentally closed, and the next thing we knew, we were seriously trapped inside."

"We apologize, Officer, if we've caused you any trouble," Robbie orally contributed. "It was just a dumb prank that got out of control!"

The somewhat-puzzled cop closed his notepad and shook his head. "As long as you boys are gonna' pay for the broken door, I guess this is a case of no harm no foul. Fortunately, nobody got either hurt or hospitalized!"

Fifty-bucks was a lot of money back in 1958, not to mention the twenty-dollars the Ks had shrewdly conned and swindled us out of. Seventy-dollars represented an awful lot of hamburgers, custards, French fries, pizza, hot fudge sundaes, and gasoline, but the money expense was nothing compared to the loss of pride and reputation the Diablos had experienced and suffered. Carnie was very devious; Tinker was extremely treacherous, and I was provoked to take action. Insufferable Cummings and Popeye Messina had no idea what the Kamikazes' imaginative phone booth prank was about to generate.

Chapter 14
"Spits, Worm and Phil Jackson"

Carnie, Tinker. and I were still licking our wounds after the embarrassing *Labor Day* Dairy DeLite phone booth debacle. Several weeks later, Tink and I were seated inside the Feed Bag, chewing the fat. The jukebox blared-out Elvis Presley's "Don't Be Cruel", and the lyrics symbolically reminded me of the totally incredible phone booth misadventure. I thought that maybe the Diablos should not seek retribution against the Ks, and should just pretend that nothing at all had ever happened.

"Well, Tink," I began my evaluation. "I guess you're still fuming from that nasty trick the Ks played on us at the Dairy DeLite."

"Damn straight, J.W. If I get a chance, I'm gonna' get my *sour* revenge," Tink predicted. "The next Kenwood creep who walks through that door, I'm gonna' kick his ass good."

"Even if it's Cummings?" I asked.

"Even if it's the Pope, or even goddamned General MacArthur. Anyone who's wearin' a black leather K jacket," my crazy colleague promised. "Even if he's the chief Catholic, or the main General, that doomed guy's goin' down if he's a K."

Luigi and Nick had just gotten a brand-new pinball machine with a baseball theme, so I thought I'd cool Tink down a bit before he had a colossal French hemorrhage. The conversation instantly switched to Quinn and Jalonec.

"Tink, I talked to Quinn and Bo yesterday about the Dairy Delite disaster," I disclosed.

"Big fuckin' deal! Who the hell cares? Those guys don't show me nothin'. And the two no-shows don't give a crap about you and me. All they care about is feedin' their freakin' cats."

"Well, Tink," I orally proceeded with caution. "Those guys do care. Quinn says he wants to be more active in the gang, and Bo says even Susie is gonna' support the Diablos."

"That's just great, J.W. Real friggin' super-great," the moody T Man observed and commented. "Football teams are the ones who have and need cheerleaders. Not tough greaser gangs. Tell Bo I said thanks, but no thanks about havin' *his* favorite hungry cat as our chief mascot."

I stopped talking because sometimes having a discussion with Tink was like going back in time and conversing with Genghis Khan about the ten easiest ways to commit random genocide.

I was immensely enjoying the Feed Bag's new gaming apparatus. Before Tinker could even get a chance to play, I had already racked-up fifteen free games while scoring an unbelievable eighty-seven runs with only one out in the first inning. Tinker was really getting more pissed-off with the phenomenal success I was enjoying as the "Visiting Team". I could not make an out, even when I made a serious attempt. While trying to appease Tink and make some subsequent outs, I was smashing singles, doubles, triples, and up-the-ramps home runs with the flipper bat blasting pinballs all over the playing surface, and much to my companion's mounting chagrin, my lucky, amazing score kept accumulating.

Two new Kamikazes who recently moved into Kenwood cockily entered the Feed Bag. After checking-out the place, the gruesome-looking dregs strolled-over to our vicinity, scraping the heels of their engineer boots against the black and white checkered tile floor. The ferocious-looking punks wore new leather jackets that read "Kamikazes" on the back. A drawing of a Japanese Zero was pictured crashing into an U.S. naval destroyer. The un-American artwork immediately offended me, because Dad had fought in *WWII* against the Germans, and Japan had been a staunch ally of Hitler.

The two pugnacious characters soon arrived at the restaurant's pinball area. The newcomers definitely looked like the thugs belonged in Cummings' gang. The Ks didn't believe in harmless mischief. The sinister rogues believed in calculated and deliberate violence.

"Hey, where you' duds, er' I mean dudes from?" I asked, trying to be indirectly friendly and funny, but still acting "tuff".

"North 'Philly," the taller punk answered. "I'm known as Worm, and this here is Spits. We just moved into town. Looks pretty dead around here to me. What do ya' greasers do for fun? Eat crabgrass, or chew and swallow weeds?"

I closely inspected the duo's physical appearances. Spits had a large gap between his front teeth. I theorized the separation would allow him to spit large quantities of saliva whenever and wherever the weirdo wanted. Worn was tall and skinny, and his gaunt red face looked as if it had been suffering from a bad case of diaper rash.

Worm caught me staring at his strange-looking physique and didn't seem to appreciate my scrutiny. "Hey Man, ya' got a problem?"

"I wish I only had *one* problem, but I really have hundreds of issues," I smartly replied, trying to exhibit the suavity and coolness of Bo Jalonec. "And we eat lobster grass in addition to crab grass!"

"You raunchy fuckheads are crashin' for a damned thrashin'," Tinker belligerently warned our current adversaries.

Spits stuck his left hand into his dungaree pocket, pulled out two quarters, and then rolled the coins onto the pinball machine's glass cover. "We got next rights here," Spits claimed. "After you creeps finish playin' this game, it's Worm's and my turn to enjoy operatin' this challengin' baseball machine."

I became almost livid. I had never before experienced so much success on any pinball machine, and now those two antagonistic Ks demanded that I surrender the flippers.

Before Tinker would belt both punks right through the Feed Bag's slanted paned window, I figured I would give reason a try. I estimated it would take a whole month's savings just to pay my five-dollar share for the Dairy DeLite's telephone booth door, and I wasn't quite in the mood to make another major contribution to cover half of a giant commercial window.

"Look, Spits," I bravely argued. "Be a gentleman. I've got fifteen games already racked-up on this baby. Ya' can have your dibs when Tink and I finish playin' them off."

The two Kamikaze recruits had no regard for standard pinball protocol. "That's what the hell *you* think, Jerk-off," Spits replied. "Worm and me are gonna' have to kick your butts good for showin' us a lack of respect. Whatta' ya' think of them apples?"

"Look, fellas'!" I objected. "The Feed Bag has greaser rules. No fightin' inside the premises."

"You tryin' to threaten us with stupid bullshit?" Worm nastily asked. "Rules and laws are for assholes like you!"

"Blow me, tornado lips!" Tink snapped back.

I tried my best to remain calm, but then the Ks verbally attacked the Diablos' native turf. "Ya' creeps live in Dogwood Hollow, don't ya'?" Worm sneered. And then, the sleazy instigator pointed his index finger at me and boomed, "You totally ugly freak of nature. I'll bet ya' probably happily live on Dingle Drive." And then Worm turned toward Tink snd opined. "And you, Tinker Bell; ya' more than likely live on Dip-shit Lane. Ain't I right Spits?"

"Yeah, Worm. Your accurate descriptions match their fucked-up personalities perfectly."

Tinker and I were expertly aware of standard greaser tactics. Insults always preceded fisticuffs. The temperature of our heated exchange with the new Ks was rapidly ascending to a kindling point.

"If ya' guys wanna' fight, you'll have to wait until Tink and I finish off these here fifteen-games," I insisted.

"We'll meet ya' jerk-offs out-back in an hour," my fellow Diablo clarified. "Your faces look like they need to be readjusted!"

"Gladly, zit tits. We'll be ready," Spits promised.

"That'll give us just enough time to down a couple bottles of cheap wine," Worm gleefully stated.

After the two vitriolic cavemen exited the Feed Bag's main portals, a funny thought occurred to me. "Tink, ya' said you was gonna' clobber the first K that walked into the building."

"That's right, J.W., I did. But," my slightly warped friend qualified, "you've noticed that *two* Ks entered the place. I always keep my word, J.W. If it was only one punk, he'd be either unconscious or dead by now."

"What would Carnie do if he was here?" I asked.

"That dumb asshole failed first-grade," Tink revealed. "That's why he's old enough to drive, and you and me ain't. Carnie barely made it through kindergarten. Since the dumb fuck failed first-grade, ya' shouldn't care a shit about his lame advice, because the imbecile is definitely more stupid than either you or me are. What ya' think of Worm and Spits?"

I thought deeply for a second and I remembered Mom's favorite book and movie. "Those two jerks look like they have V.D. The clowns look like they could star in the movie "Gonorrhea with the Wind", I said, seriously trying to mimic Bo.

"You're finally right about something, J.W. And Spits and Worm oughta' have car jacks put under their chins. The retarded freaks both need face lifts pretty fuckin' bad."

The next hour passed by all-too-slowly. Time stood still as I kept thinking about the two dreaded Kenwood punks getting intoxicated while laying for us outside, cunningly waiting for Tink and me to leave the restaurant. Did Spits and Worm have criminal records? The ground rules for the confrontation had not yet been established. 'Would they fight Diablos' style, fist on jaw?' I wondered.

I wasn't afraid of getting beaten-up. That regrettable result had already happened three times in the past two years. But I was totally frightened about the prospect of being brutally killed and sent to the cemetery by '50s American teen barbarians.

The fifteen free pinball games were finally played. Tink and I exited the front entrance of "the Bag" at 11 p.m. We cautiously turned the corner on the Dairy DeLite side. In a matter of ten-seconds, T Man and I were standing in the vacant lot behind the eatery, face to face with our new-found rivals.

"Are ya' wick-dicked apes ready to rumble?" Tinker challenged.

"We're ready, Dogwood dung heads," Worm slurred and answered in a drunken stupor.

'The fight should be a fair one,' I thought. Tink, Spits and I were about the same height, five-foot-nine. Worm was about six-foot-three; had a body that resembled that of an ostrich; had a neck like that of a giraffe, and had the trust factor of a rattlesnake. I suspected that Tinker was comfortable being in his dog-eat-dog element. My dangerous friend stood there, ready for violent action. Jeremy held his head up high with clenched fists raised in front of his chest.

I still wasn't too keen on being maimed or murdered. I figured I'd try the more sophisticated diplomatic route one more time. "Look Spits," I pointed-out. "Isn't it kinda' dumb to be fightin' over the use of a silly pinball machine?"

"What's your shitty name again?" inquired Spits, whose breath reeked of cheap wine.

"It's J.W.," I nervously answered.

"Now looky here, J.W.," Spits declared between loud burps. "If you and Tinker Bell say you're sorry, ya' miserable turds might not have to fight Worm and me after all."

"No way, Jose," responded Tinker, who wanted to mash and bash each of their skulls to a pulp. Tink's comment inspired Worm to advance some more threatening innuendo. "You'd better count your goddamned teeth so that ya' know how many are supposed to be in your disfigured, fucked-up, bleeding mouths!"

"We'd have more competition Spits, if we was to fight those TV hand puppets Beanie and Cecil, or a couple of Disney cartoon characters," Worm chided, sounding just as inebriated as his nut-case colleague.

'How would *Dragnet's* Detective Joe Friday handle this mess?' I wondered. "Let's keep the facts straight and drop the personal insults," I suggested. "All Tink and I want are the facts."

"J.W.," Tink remarked. "Worm and Spits oughta' grow large ears in the center of their faces. Their looks would then improve greatly."

By the tone of Tink's voice, the craziest Diablo was reverting into his sadistic animal state. My comrade snarled like a wild rabid beast, nearly foaming at the mouth. I sensed that the first greaser to run out of offensive derogatory remarks would be the one that would throw the first punch.

"Your fathers are pimps and your mothers are hookers," Spits belched and insulted with mounting fury.

"Your mother wears gingerbread combat boots and plastic underwear," I countered.

"Oh yeah, Spits. Your faggot father has a clitoris instead of a dick," Tink asserted, "and that's why the best part of you never left his limp pecker."

The Kamikaze creeps reached-down into some high weeds, picked up two empty wine bottles, shattered them against the Feed Bag's back wall, and held the jagged remains in front of their chests. I was stunned by the sudden appearance of weapons.

"Look, fellas'," I shakily addressed Spits and Worm. "Around here, we fight skin against skin. No chains, knives, guns, or glass! Ya' dig?"

"In 'Philly," Worm replied, "anything goes, Asshole. The rules are there ain't no rules; just life or death. Now let's stop yappin' and begin playin' scissors with glass."

I was petrified. My knees were knocking against one another, and my lungs could not suck in enough oxygen. I imagined my fate: *Lower Bucks County Hospital,* or the nearest Catholic cemetery. I finally realized I preferred living to dying.

"I thought only punks fought with glass," I answered, paraphrasing a famous James Dean line. Just when I thought it would be final curtains for Tinker and me, my dependable pal whipped-out a switchblade from inside his leather jacket. Tink pointed the closed knife at our two dastardly enemies. "If either of ya' move an inch, no butcher's gonna' know what the hell kind of meat he's lookin' at!"

Despite their excessive intoxication, Spits and Worm seemed to totally digest the significance of Tinker's threatening words. The two belligerent Ks suddenly had blank expressions appear upon their pallid faces. Our appalled foes then looked at each other, dropped their shattered bottles, clumsily sprinted to *Route 13,* and then scurried south past the Dairy DeLite like startled jack rabbits.

I smiled at Tinker, who gave me the *Ballantine Beer* three ring sign, his forefinger touching his thumb. I reckoned we had won the first battle of our greaser war against the reprehensible Ks. I was amazed at what Tinker had so easily accomplished. That was the first time I had ever seen any Diablo wield a lethal weapon.

"That stand-off was tremendous Tink," I conceded. "But where did ya' get that really cool switchblade?"

"Remember that night when ya' bought your black leather motorcycle jacket," Tink recalled and reminded. "We was at the Bristol Farmers' Market over on *Route 413,"*

I informed Tink that six-weeks later, Jokes had painted the nifty artwork on the back of our black leather jackets.

My conflict-oriented amigo paused for a moment, apparently savoring his surprising disclosure. "Well, J.W., while ya' was getting measured for your black leather threads, I was at another stall buyin' this here switchblade."

I still couldn't fully comprehend exactly what my unpredictable grease-monkey buddy truly meant. "But they don't sell switchblade knives in the Bristol Farmers' Market!" I exclaimed. "It's illegal!"

Tink laughed at my naivete. "Who the hell says it's a goddamned switchblade?" And with that extraordinary remark, my audacious pal pushed a side button, and the teeth of a hair comb sprung-out. "J.W., ya' wanna' groom up a bit before we hit the trail?"

"*Les b*e friends and go homo," I awkwardly declared, employing one of Bo Jalonec's favorite lines. I felt I needed to swallow a half-dozen aspirins to relieve the enormous headache that was pounding-away between my ears.

"I really bluffed the livin' crap out of those scumbags, didn't I Words?" Tink questioned.

"Ya' could include me in *that* 'being afraid category', too," I sighed and laughed.

* * * * * * * * * * * * *

In late September, Carnie pulled into the driveway at 50 Daffodil Lane. I was surprised when the novice mechanic asked if I wanted to help him work on a prominent jock's car. "Who is it?" I asked.

"Phil Jackson," Carnie answered. "Tink and me hate his guts, but he's gonna' pay me twenty-bucks to replace the sparkplugs and fan belt in his 'Vette. Jackson has already bought the replacement parts, so we're talkin' about twenty-bucks clear."

I hopped into "the James Dean Special", and five-minutes later Carnie drove his black Mercury off of Haines Road over the Edgely Bridge, and then took River Drive south in the direction of Bristol.

At the time, Carnie and I were sophomores at Cardinal Reagan High. Phil Jackson was a junior who possessed extraordinary athletic ability. The jock was the first-string football quarterback, and scouts from *Penn State* and *Notre Dame* were keeping an eye on his gridiron statistics. While Quinn was the quintessential greaser, Jackson was the consummate jock.

The muscle-bound athlete lived in a large, opulent mansion overlooking the *Delaware* between Edgely and Bristol. Obviously, Phil Jackson was born with a silver spoon in his mouth. His dad was a wealthy business tycoon who owned three grocery stores, two taverns, a pharmacy, and three blocks of commercial real estate in the downtown Bristol shopping district.

Carnie and I eagerly arrived at the sprawling riverfront estate. After greeting us outside, Phil informed that he had some important chores to do for his folks, so the rich kid dismissed himself, leaving Carnie and me freedom to work on his immaculate white '55 'Vette without any major interruptions.

Three hours later, my loyal buddy and I finished the designated project. Jackson came-out of his manor house, gladly paid Carnie a crisp *Andrew Jackson,* and as a gesture of gratitude, took my buddy and me for a wild ride on the *Delaware* in the family speedboat.

After tearing-up the historic river between Bristol and Burlington on the Jersey side, Phil docked his expensive boat and invited us inside for *Pepsi's* and pretzels.

Jackson's mom came home toward the end of our visit. The aristocratic woman summoned Phil into the library, and Carnie and I surreptitiously eavesdropped on their private conservation. I was shocked at the nature of their discussion, which centered on *her* son's poor choice of friends.

"But Mom, those guys aren't really my friends," Phil claimed. "They only came over to work on my 'Vette's engine."

"Really now, Phillip," Mrs. Jackson sternly answered. "You know your father and I want the best for you. Best education, best wife, best career, and the best success in business."

"Yes, Mom. I understand," the star athlete responded.

"You should know, Phillip, your father is considering sending you to a private prep school. He feels your choice of companions will be limited to boys and girls of your own social status. Do you follow what I am saying?"

"Sure, Mom. You want me to be happy and successful," the rich jock acknowledged. "You don't want me coming under any bad teen influences."

As Mrs. Jackson lectured her son on the merits of only socializing with those in the highest socio-economic strata, Carnie and I became aware of the ugly existence of American class prejudice. We listened intently as Jackson's mother lectured about how Levittown kids were really decent boys who were economically destined to suffer mediocre adulthoods; and destined to become lowly garage mechanics and factory workers in their later lives. Mrs. Jackson emphasized that Phil would be enjoying a bright future with the flourishing family businesses to oversee. His loyal cooperation would guarantee the college graduate a fabulous inheritance.

"That's bribery," Carnie whispered.

"That's how high society works," I softly replied.

By then, Mrs. Jackson was terminating her parental-advice speech. "In the future, Phillip, your father and I would prefer if you didn't associate with the middle-class riff-raff from Levittown. Stick to your own kind. Can you do us that big favor? We don't think we're asking too much."

I realized that the mother and son discussion was about to terminate, so I tacitly motioned my hand to Carnie for us to tiptoe into the wood-paneled game room. When Jackson and his pompous mom finally discovered our whereabouts, my buddy and I were pretending to be enjoying a friendly billiards' match.

On the familiar drive back to Dogwood Hollow, Carnie and I talked about how Mrs. Jackson's recommendations to her son had penetrated our vulnerable hearts like sharp, double-edged swords. We became aware of something we hadn't much thought about until then. Class bias was a definite 1950s reality, and snobbish high society WASPish whites nonchalantly practiced it against the "have not" white, middle-class, proletarian, Levittown residents.

Phil Jackson was true to his vow. After that day in late September, the jock avoided Carnie and me as if we were infected with both the black and the bubonic plagues.

Chapter 15
"Cardinal Reagan High" (1959)

Many Diablos and Kamikazes attended Cardinal Reagan High. The four-story school was situated on the Levittown Parkway across from the landmark Shop-A-Rama. Student life at Cardinal Reagan was a big contrast to what we generally experienced in the outside world. The priests were of the Franciscan Order, and "the padres" wore long, dull, light-brown robes with ropes tied around their waists. The priests proudly proclaimed they belonged to the "Mendicant Order of Gray Friars", founded by St. Francis of Assisi in 1209. I could never understand how or why twentieth century people would want to dress and look like thirteenth century religious peasants. The male faculty seemed like a tribe of walking anachronisms, lost and meandering-around inside a time vacuum.

The Cardinal Reagan nuns belonged to the Sisters of the Sacred Heart Order, and they too seemed out-of-sync with the dynamic '50s era. "Poverty, chastity, and obedience" were not the immediate honorable goals of the Diablos, Kamikazes, and Renegades.

Student behavior was governed by a strictly enforced dress code. Boys either wore a suit, or masqueraded in a sport jacket and dress slacks. Pegged pants were forbidden, and black leather jackets, engineer boots, and sneakers were not allowed in the building (except sneakers for gym class).

Girls had to wear uniforms, but the guys could still tell which chicks carried "the blimps" and which ones toted "the molehills" on their chests. Father Malcolm futilely tried to indoctrinate us with the phrase "Temptation is the tool of Satan". Although the cranberry-colored girls' uniforms were designed to camouflage Lucifer's sinful work, the lustful boys had a devil of a time distinguishing heaven from hell, when visually evaluating the dolls' breasts, buttocks, knees and hips.

The strict separation of the sexes was evident in that most academic classes were either all boys or all girls, and the boys had their own two stairwells to use during the change of classes, and the girls had their own two sets of steps to use to go from one subject class to the next on a different floor. Only cafeteria time and assemblies saw mixed sections of male and female students sitting in the same room. But in the cafeteria, it was either all boys' tables or all girls.

Carnie and I had dual personalities, mostly because we were forced to live in two separate worlds. When in school, we acted mature and civilized while the priests and nuns were ambling around. Sometimes, we were even falsely virtuous, humble, respectful, and subordinate.

While we were pretending to display those obedient qualities externally, internally, we still thought and schemed like the "outside world" Diablos. Carnie was a master of *that* clandestine technique.

Mr. C found high school to be a definite sacrifice. The remote abstract world of academics was completely irrelevant to the cruel abnormal family environment that *he* all-too-well knew. It was a sadistic act for Father Malcolm to force Carnie to study the *Seven Wonders,* ancient Greeks, and right triangles when all my friend really understood and valued were scams, cons, shills, and freak shows. Still, I always liked Carnie. I hurt, laughed, and sympathized with him, and I would fight for him because I knew in my heart that he would reciprocate if the tables were reversed.

Carnie understood me better than the rest of the guys, and in some respects, even better than Bo had. Jokes Jalonec was slick and smooth, but when Carnie and I were alone, Mr. C was genuine, open, and sincere. Bo, who still attended West Catholic High in "Philly, like myself, tolerated the rigors associated with academics. We actually loved history and literature. Carnie hated history, but he loved histrionics. The "Mercury kid" also loathed eggheads, even more than he abhorred trigonometry, Latin III, and physics.

The school dress code could not completely disguise greasers from jocks and eggheads. Styles and lengths of hair were sure giveaways. Greasers maintained long hair, slicked-down with *Vaseline Petroleum Jelly*. Most Diablos, Kamikazes, and Renegades had high ridges of greasy waves on both sides of our heads, and we sported razor cuts straight across the napes of our necks.

Jocks usually had short flattops, or crew cuts. 'Tweeners' were guys who liked both the greaser and jock looks. 'Tweeners had short hair on top that was complemented by long greasy sides. Bo once told me, "A 'tweener is a wiener with a t in front of it." Tweeners were often active in baseball or football, but at night, the dual-look kids preferred the more dangerous greaser lifestyle.

Eggheads wore their hair short and slicked-down close to the scalp, having a part on either side. The finks also wore corny checkered or diamond patterned socks with matching vests. Most eggheads talked in high-pitched voices, sounding somewhat like comedian Arnold Stang. Their almost falsetto-pitched vocal cords made the greasers theorize that the eggheads suffered from testosterone deficiencies that traveled all the way from their testicles up to their throats.

And so, although the Cardinal Reagan Administration's dress code attempted to thwart individual expression in terms of student appearance, certain external characteristics and visible styles still distinguished haughty-naughty greasers from jocks, from 'tweeners', and from eggheads.

The Diablos sometimes fraternized with certain Kamikazes and Renegades who attended the high school. We also had some 'tweener' friends, but generally, the Diablos considered jocks and eggheads as outsiders. Our biased philosophy matched perfectly with the latticed pattern of social separations that were prevalent in the '50s. Just as religion, race, ethnic origin, and economic status rigidly defined social boundaries, in the Diablos' world, physical appearance and overt behavior categorized and stereotyped kids. Even though the Diablos, Kamikazes, and Renegades might be adversaries outside the school, the greasers all knew we were more akin to each other than we were to either jocks or eggheads in the student body.

Greasers were masters at concealing true feelings in public. If a gang member liked a particular girl, that individual wouldn't tell anyone out of fear of being humiliated to death. When we saw a Diablo in the Feed Bag or at the Dairy DeLite with that "particular girl", we would leave him alone to tend to his own business.

Carnie and I were deft at substituting artificial, phony behavior for sincere communication. Tough greasers would never cry in public; would never sing in any chorus or choir, and would never say "uncle" in a fistfight.

Carnie and I invented "candy code language", and we would use brand name comparisons to describe girls shuffling around the corridors. If a young lady walked by with small tubes on her chest, the unfortunate female would be called "*Milk Duds,"* suggesting a degree of lactose deficiency. A suspected virgin would generate a "Hi Men (hymen) *Peanut Chews*" response. A nice firm set of knockers would result in a *Good and Plenty* salutation, and a large hard bust would merit a *Mounds* and *Almond Joy* greeting. Decent udders were described as *Juicy Fruit,* and dolls like Susie Parker would rate our highest honor, a chorus of "*Milky Way, Milky Way"*, because upon initial eye contact, the vixen had just the right equipment to produce an instant erection with the possibility of premature ejaculation.

The thoroughly confused Cardinal Reagan girls often thought that a weird confectionary war was occurring inside the school. And when the 'tweeners' caught-on and conveyed our candy codes to the other greasers and jocks, the chicks became even more confused. The boys sounded like residents of the *Tower of Babel,* and Robbie aptly called us *Babbleonians*. Many girls would shake their heads in sheer disillusionment after being exposed to a cacophony of *Good and Plenty*, Hi Men *Peanut Chews*, *Juicy Fruit, Milk Duds, Mounds* and *Almond Joy,* and *Milky Way*.

"The guys in this school are really strange," one girl noted and claimed in the third-floor corridor between classes.

"The sugar addicts must all be super chocolate freaks," added another. "No wonder why there's so much male acne."

"Don't they know what dentists are sayin' about chewing too many sweets," indicated a third bewildered babe.

"No wonder they have so many pimples," answered the first female. "You'd think those idiots would be more interested in girls. Talkin' about silly candy all the time is so juvenile! Haven't the dumb shits discovered tits and ass yet?"

Father Malcolm thought himself a stern captain running a tight ship. The school disciplinarian tried reflecting the persona of being a cruel taskmaster and a no-nonsense martinet. Although Malcolm was a bona fide Franciscan priest, the Diablos merely tolerated his antics and semantics, but we certainly didn't admire or respect *his* mean character. Carnie, Robbie, and I viewed the Reagan head honcho as just another talking head transmitting authoritarian commands in our direction. However, when Malcolm's mortal words transformed into actual physical punishment, then that was the precise moment the Diablos decided to show the demented friar who the real bosses were in *his* parochial high school.

It all started in early January with Carnie. Father Malcolm called my neurotic pal down to his first-floor office over the intercom. Carnie had been caught cheating on his Western Civilization mid-term exam', and after a brief conference with the austere disciplinarian, my dear friend was directed by Malcolm to pull-down his pants, to bend over, and to suffer some severe ass-paddling.

Such corporal punishment was commonplace in '50s Catholic schools, even though the *Dark Ages* had ended around 1000 BC (*B*efore *C*arnie as Jokes once described it to me). Malcolm had also paddled Robbie Wilkinson that same week because R.W. had been caught simulating farting sounds in religion class. Robbie was adept at putting his left hand under his right armpit, causing a suction-pocket when the Diablo flagrantly flapped his chicken wing. Ace Roberts was another victim of Malcolm's sadistic abuse. The 'King of Spades' was caught pouring a beaker of urine into Sister Anna's botany plants, and according to Robbie, "Sister Anna was pissed-off because her plants were pissed on."

In '59, Father Malcolm was lord of his castle, and Cardinal Reagan High was his twentieth century feudal estate. Catholic schools were under no legal obligation to honor educational psychology or the normal 'checks and balances' representative of American democratic environments. The school disciplinarian had absolute power, and

Malcolm was the executive, legislative, and judicial branches of religious education, all wrapped into one neat package. Father Malcolm's opinion was both assumed and regarded as being final and supreme. He was Zeus, and his high school was *Mt. Olympus*.

Every eighth-period Carnie, Robbie, and I had Father Malcolm for study hall in Room 406. The nasty friar prided himself in being a self-appointed 'greaser torture machine'. The vengeful priest would march up and down the aisles like a band major, hitting each greaser on the head with his fisted knuckle, which was accentuated by a very huge college ring. By the third week of January, the abundant greaser abuse was happening every single day. My scalp felt like a big bag of large marbles. Carnie, Robbie, and I were bitterly angry because Malcolm never clobbered jocks or eggheads. The sadist was conducting an ongoing vendetta specifically against victimized greasers.

Finally, Carnie had the audacity to question Malcolm in study hall about the friar's medieval practices. The disciplinarian didn't like being challenged by a mere student in front of the class.

"Father Malcolm," Carnie said after receiving a patented "knuckle sandwich" for doing nothing. "Why do ya' gotta' hit me and my friends on the head every day? We're only just sittin' here studyin', and not botherin' anybody."

"I hit you nice boys on your heads with my knuckles," related Malcolm, "to demonstrate to the rest of the class that you greasers are nothing more than a bunch of lazy, good-for-nothing knuckleheads."

After the class stopped roaring at the priest's degrading comments, Carnie, who never quite knew when to shut-up, pursued the matter further. "But we haven't done nothin' wrong. It just ain't fair!"

"I do it," Malcolm replied softly and curtly, "because you boys might do bad things when I'm not around to officially observe them happening." The class let out another burst of laughter.

"But, but," the C Man stammered.

Father Malcolm was savoring Carnie's very obvious insecurity and nervousness. The cagey, egotistical, mean-spirited Franciscan enjoyed the persecution of greasers even more than he relished his daily prosecution of them.

"And in fact," continued the spiteful disciplinarian, "when you go to Washington next year on your senior class trip, I'm goin' to make ya' walk up and down the *Senate* steps fifty-times, just to show you the true meaning of *Capitol* punishment."

Again, the non-greasers in the study hall let-out waves of laughter to further acknowledge Malcolm's mockery of Carnie and the Diablos.

Carnie Robbie, and I thought it was the appropriate time to obtain some serious vengeance. But before we took any real action, I figured

I should pay Father Malcolm a personal visit. I believed that if I used discretion by not directly challenging "the Dictator" in front of other students, the priest would treat me more benignly in his office than the enforcer had treated Carnie in the study hall. And so, as a loyal friend embarking on a delicate mercy mission, I stepped into Malcolm's private office on Carnie's behalf.

"Father Malcolm," I cordially began my appeal. "You have no idea how harmful your punishments have been to Carnie. He's so upset he's thinkin' about droppin' outa' school."

"Listen, J.W.," Malcolm sternly warned. "I've heard hundreds of students threaten to do that exact same thing, just because the losers feel sorry for themselves. The self-pitying victims think they're gonna' skirt the rules and get special treatment from the faculty. Your friend wants to be judged by a double standard," 'Malo Malcolm' explained. "Your conniving friend wants a special privilege that the most hard-working Reagan A students don't even have."

Although I completely understood the priest's position, I could not agree with the injustice of *his* discriminate, Draconian practices. I further pleaded Carnie's case. "But what about the athletes? What about the eggheads?" I inquired.

"What about them?" the disciplinarian promptly interrupted.

"Ya' never hit *them* on their crown or paddle their fannies."

Father Malcolm grimly stared into my pupils. "They're all good boys, J.W. They have direction," Malcolm pointed-out. The priest proceeded to lecture that the jocks and the eggheads were going to attend quality colleges, graduate, and then *those* students would make valuable contributions to American civilization. "They have honorable goals, J.W. They don't cause grief or trouble like you' greasy hair types perpetually do," Malcolm concluded and articulated.

I realized right then and there that our conversation wouldn't yield any favorable results for Carnie. The closed-minded priest was biased for jocks and eggheads, and yet at the other end of the discrimination spectrum, he was prejudiced against greasers. That, in essence, was the alpha and the omega of Malcolm's inflexible disciplinary philosophy.

"But Father, Carnie's even threatened to commit suicide," I futilely countered. "You wouldn't want something drastic like that tragedy on your conscience, would ya'?"

I thought that moral responsibility would weigh heavily in the priest's judgment, since Father Malcolm was a high-ranking religious personage believing in the Ten Commandments. My logical scheming quickly backfired.

"Look here, J.W. The major difference between me and your friend is that I have a conscience and he doesn't," the chief friar asserted. "Now stop trying to utilize that phony psychology crap on me!"

Malcolm paused to see if his comment had any significant impact. Then, the 'absolute power cleric' cleared his throat. "Carnie's nothing more than an avowed agent of Satan, and a listless slave to Lucifer's relentless demonic commands."

I was stunned by the priest's narrow-minded opinion of my innocent pal. "That's not true, Father!" I argued. "Carnie's a good kid once ya' get to know his character."

My mind was ninety-nine percent convinced that Father Malcolm was an ally of Stanley Tezeeker and of Popeye Messina, and an avowed foe of what the disciplinarian considerd the diabolical Diablos.

"J.W., I understand you and your buddy belong to a gang," Malcolm reminded me. "First, you boys showed deviation by growin' that long, filthy hair, and now you're bypassing purgatory and speeding right down the chute to hell. What's the name of your gang?"

Malcolm knew our name, but the ball-breaker wanted to hear it straight from my lips. The interrogating priest was searching for guilt by association, a confession outside the confessional.

"Diablos," I softly answered with my head crestfallen.

"The Diablos!" Malcolm sternly snapped. "Do you have any idea what that despicable word means translated into plain English?" Malcolm rhetorically asked. "It means 'Devil'! If you and your deadbeat greaser chums don't correct your wayward ways pretty soon, you're all gonna' be doomed to eternal damnation. Don't you wish to go to heaven?"

I sensed that Malcolm was attempting to trap me in some sort of philosophical spider's web. "Who's gonna' be there?" I asked.

"For starters, all the good people like well, me of course; Brother Timothy, and Sister Mary Alice."

Well, that particular comment really annoyed me. All my mind could picture was Father Malcolm smacking me on the head with his gargantuan college ring, and Brother Timothy ripping-off my precious earlobes over and over again for all eternity. I also envisioned Sister Mary Alice yanking-off my sideburns just like she had done to Carnie when he had screamed, choked, and vomited in her class after accidentally inhaling a yellow jacket that had drifted into his open mouth while my innocent friend was merely sleeping inside his desk.

My theory about the afterlife was quite simple. If Father Malcolm, Brother Timothy, and Sister Mary Alice were destined to become favored saints in heaven, then I wanted to take my chances with the Devil, because I didn't want to be knuckled, lobotomized, or ripped-off for all eternity by those three crazy religious zealots. Robbie believed that all three had "dropped their transmissions". If the greaser violators were ticketed for heaven, I certainly wanted a passport to a more tranquil, warm destination.

And besides, to be perfectly honest, what I saw of temptation, sex, gluttony, and sin didn't appear as bad as Father Malcolm and his sanctimonious colleagues made those singular faults out to be. So, mortal sin now, and immortal sinning in the next world, seemed to be credible alternatives to an excruciating infinity with Father Malcolm, Brother Timothy, and Sister Mary Alice perpetually abusing my physical well-being.

And if Lucifer gave the Diablos any grief in hell, Carnie, Robbie, Ace, and I would tie his red tail into knots, and then prod his ugly rear with *his* stupid pronged pitchfork.

"And now, J.W.," Malcolm concluded with a cruel smile. "Since you've shown me' your true colors, kindly drop your trousers and pull down your shorts. I'm gonna' beat the Devil out of you right this instant. Someday, you'll thank me for doing this beneficial act of penance. Look at this process as a form of modern-day exorcism!"

Well, the welts on my buttocks throbbed for three whole days. I was certain Malcolm always used the aegis of Catholic morality to facilitate student mind-control and behavior control, and when those measures failed to work, the disciplinarian practiced flesh mutilation. I called for an executive meeting of the Diablos at the Feed Bag, but only Carnie, Tinker, and Robbie showed-up. As usual, Quinn and Bo were out "feeding their cats".

It took the four of us thirty-short-seconds to declare war on Father Malcolm. But it required five long hours of hard thinking to devise a well-conceived scheme to implement. Finally, my taxed brain came-up with a tremendous plan that involved Tinker.

"Of course, Tink," I reminded the grimy degenerate. "Ya' gotta' be at the school Thursday at exactly 2:30 right before dismissal."

"You bet," the most insane Diablo who attended Delhaas High agreed. "That Latin speakin' jerk is gonna' wish he was never born."

Tinker hated authority figures even more than the rebel deplored authority. Jeremy always despised teachers, guidance counselors, vice-principals, principals, and superintendents. Tink even had contempt for school janitors, secretaries, and cafeteria line brunhildas, simply because *those employees* happened to work inside a school building that *he* found repugnant.

Thursday afternoon finally arrived. At the end of seventh-period at precisely 2:28, Carnie obtained a lavatory pass from Father Anselm, his U.S. History instructor. Father Malcolm entered his eighth-period study hall in Room 406. Robbie Wilkinson was leaning over and looking down from the classroom's fourth-floor windows.

"Father Malcolm!" R.W yelled. "Come quick. Look down there. Someone's jumped! The kid looks like he's dead!"

Everyone in the room raced to the side windows to investigate the incident. Father Malcolm's face instantly turned ashen when the instructor assessed the dilemma.

"Father Malcolm!" Ace hollered. "I think it's Carnie lyin' down there. He's dropped outa' school!"

"Oh my God!" Malcolm worriedly screamed. "The lad's lyin' on the pavement face-down. Robbie! Run down to the Main Office. Tell them it's an emergency. They gotta' call an ambulance right away!"

"Father Malcolm," I again called-out. "Don't ya' remember I told you Carnie was thinkin' about committin' suicide, but ya' thought he was fakin'. Carnie never fakes anything. This might really be a homicide case!"

"Good heavens!" the alarmed priest exclaimed. "The fool really did attempt it! The confused lad has literally dropped-out of high school! J.W., notify the nurse over the intercom. I've gotta' get down there this instant and give the boy his last rites."

Father Malcolm didn't know the main piece of our little puzzle. The boy lying face down on the pavement was not Carnie; it was Tinker. After the friar shot out of the room like a rocket, I yelled our secret word "nur" ("run" backwards) down to Tink, who then leaped-up; turned; looked-up to Room 406, and promptly gave all of us the royal middle finger. Then, Tink dashed so fast that he nearly sprinted his butt off, bum leg and all. I saw his vague form zooming through a distant field of high weeds. Within seconds, the accomplished instigator was behind the wheel of his '49 Plymouth and completing his stellar getaway.

I next noticed Carnie enter the room with Father Anselm's lavatory pass. My pal quickly hustled-over to the side windows. We gleefully watched Father Malcolm desperately searching the yew bushes for a non-existent corpse. Carnie shouted-down to Malcolm, who twisted his enormous body to look-up to the fourth floor. The pedagogue's eyes quickly recognized the suspected suicide victim shouting and waving down to him from the study hall's window. Malcolm's heart and lungs couldn't take the immense strain. The priest collapsed into the yew bushes, and then his massive anatomy rolled-down an incline onto the sidewalk. The mammoth Franciscan's body occupied almost the same space that Tinker had just vacated.

The dependable Tullytown Rescue Squad arrived on the scene. The driver and his assistant administered some first aid to the unconscious cleric. The very capable paramedics next plopped the limp priest onto a stretcher. Within a minute, the ambulance's siren howled, and the emergency vehicle screeched-off and then sped down *Route 13,* heading in the direction of *Lower Bucks County Hospital.*

A week later, the protector of the faith was listed in "satisfactory condition". The student body faithfully participated in get-well prayers recited during the morning and afternoon announcements. Doctors insisted on keeping Malcolm in their hospital custody another week to comprehensively evaluate the extent of his brain concussion and also, of his persistent shortness of breath.

With Father Malcolm on the sidelines, it was time for the Diablos to focus on Brother Timothy, the practitioner of the "dual lobotomy method" of physical discipline.

Brother Timothy, like most of the male clerics on the faculty, was a heavy smoker. Carnie often said Timothy was a heavy smoker because the corpulent, poor-visioned brother weighed over three-hundred pounds. Mimicking his idol Father Malcolm, Timothy would light-up a weed toward the end of study hall. The male instructors often smoked in study hall, or when the students were taking tests, to deliberately tantalize and frustrate the greasers who, by the eighth-period, would be craving nicotine.

An amber ashtray was situated upon the teacher's desk in Room 406. Like his mentor, Timothy was a creature of habit. After polishing-off most of his cigarette, the stocky brother would predictably rise from his chair. Next, 'Tiny Tim' would amble-over to the side windows, stare out at God's good earth for fifteen or more seconds, flick his butt to the ground, watch it hit the sidewalk, and then slowly return to the instructor's desk.

A week after Father Malcolm's massive hallucination involving co-conspirators Tinker and Carnie, Brother Timothy was confidently taking the disciplinarian's place in eighth-period study hall. Timothy was doing some heavy-duty meditation as the ponderer held his cancer stick and gazed out the window, again evaluating the splendor of God's magnificent planet.

Ace Roberts, who sat in the first desk of the middle row directly in front of the amber ashtray, lit-up a cigarette and took five quick, deep puffs. Fifteen-seconds later, Timothy flicked his *Lucky Strike* outside and watched the butt float to the ground.

The good brother returned to his front desk and sat-down, thinking that his mind was playing tricks on him. Not wanting to look stupid in front of his students, the junior friar picked-up the lit weed from the amber ashtray, which the corpulent instructor believed he had recently chucked outside. The addled teacher lifted the cancer stick to his lips, and greedily inhaled a deep drag. Enjoying the rich aroma, the enchanted fellow inhaled six more times. A broad smile beamed from Timothy's normally grumpy fat face. The friar was in a state of ecstasy.

Carnie, Robbie, Ace and I had doctored-up the cigarette with a strong blend of Mexican Red, a powerful marijuana concentrate that Tinker had obtained from a Renegade, who had bought "the stuff" from a Kamikaze. After Brother Tim had taken twenty-seven intense drags, the happy cleric's mind was voyaging to distant exotic places. The pedagogue's eyes began rolling-around in their sockets, and the cleric started mumbling oddball gibberish to no one in particular, since Brother Timothy was then residing on Weird Street. Soon, the psycho's random articulations became more discernible.

Timothy initiated a rather peculiar litany of dumb jokes, beginning with corny blather, and then escalating to more graphic terminology. The mixed study hall class, especially the astonished girls, sat stunned in their desks. None quite knew how to interpret Timothy's bizarre conduct, all of which appeared unbecoming of a man of the cloth. Of course, the Diablos considered Tim's strange antics quite entertaining.

The junior friar asked himself a rhetorical question, which the rogue then answered in inane verbalizations, all the while giving the distinct impression of conducting an idiotic conversation with himself. "Who was Noah's wife?" Tim asked his alter ego. "Mrs. Noah," Brother Timothy replied to himself.

"What's the best day to have your fortune read?" After a three-second pause, "Palm Sunday, ha, ha, ha," Timothy chuckled.

"Priests are always horny because they get nun in the morning and nun at night, ha, ha, ha," the drugged fool stated, without any other part of his multiple personality conversing with the speaker.

"What's the Pope's private phone number?" Tim asked himself between his final drags. "Et cum Spiri : tu tu o, ha, ha, ha. What did heaven say to the Lord on the first *Easter Sunday?"* Brother Timothy asked himself in a giddy mood. "Rise and shine!"

The bell rang and all the non-Diablo students, fearing that crazy language would soon convert into crazy behavior, exited that peculiar study hall in a hurry. Ace, Carnie, Robbie, and I stared at Timothy, who sat there smiling in his fantasy stupor, oblivious to the bell's ringing and to the rapid student exodus. As the amused Diablos left the fourth-floor room, we turned and heard Brother Tim continuing his comedy routine of sacrilegious puns and utter nonsense.

* * * * * * * * * * * * *

In January of '59, Carnie, Robbie, and I were juniors. The four of us delighted in confronting and teasing eggheads, especially Stanley Tezeeker. Greasers stereotyped eggheads with '50s jargon such as "sissies", "finks" (Carnie once said *they* guarded the pyramids), "faggots", "Marys", "fairies", "fruits", and "queers". We all knew we didn't want to be anything like Stanley Tezeeker or Mortimer Ralston. The Diablos detested the eggheads, even more than we despised jocks, adults, and the police.

Carnie, Robbie, Ace, and I daily enjoyed accosting Stanley on the stairwell situated between the high school's third and fourth floors. Dense student stairs' traffic had to detour around the four stationary greaser bodies. Tezeeker somehow miraculously endured his perpetual daily nightmare.

"Hi Stanley," Carnie deviously began. "That's a pretty neat diamond vest ya' got there. How do ya' manage to keep it dry?"

"What do ya' mean?" asked Tezeeker, who always took our words literally and not figuratively. We knew in our hearts that Stanley was just as afraid of the Diablos as we were of the Kamikazes.

"Stanley," Ace greeted. "How can ya' keep your vest dry when that freakin' tie you're wearing is a real pisser!"

"Can't you four guys find a 'tweener or jock to pick on?" our targeted victim stated in near-perfect articulation. "Please let me pass!"

"Well, Stan the Man, and I don't mean Musial," Ace continued. "If ya' put a patch of bubble gum on your boner, ya' probably could get your *Wads*worth on your Longfellow."

Stanley became increasingly flustered and apprehensive. The abused kid would have preferred chewing and swallowing his whole thick physics textbook rather than fearfully enduring our incessant harassments three times each day.

"Stanley," Carnie pestered. "Who invented the laser beam?"

"I really don't know or care!"

"Cardinal Ray-gun!"

Stanley really never appreciated our highlights of his day. "Guys, I really like your company, honest I do," Tezeeker pleaded. "But I now must go to Father Gregory's very difficult 'Advanced Poetry' class. I don't want to spoil my perfect attendance and never tardy records."

Just then a priest's booming voice originated from the fourth-floor. "Tezeeker," bellowed-down the familiar *Gregorian Chant*. "I'm disappointed in you even talking to those reprehensible greasers! Come to class immediately, or I'll mark you late."

During the third week of January, Carnie, Ace, Robbie, and I strolled into the third-floor boys' lavatory. Ace detected a pair of yellow and black diamond argyle socks clearly visible beneath the center stall. Immediately, we all perceived and knew that Stanley was "takin' a dump".

Carnie perceptively spotted a janitor's bucket. Ace and I held the large pail under an opened sink spigot; filled the metal container as much as we could, and then Robbie grabbed the object's handle and tossed the liquid contents over the top of the stall. Right before the dramatic water heave, Ace naughtily had lit two firecrackers. The instigator quickly handed me one, and we tossed the miniature bombs into the two stalls on either side of Stanley's middle compartment, creating loud stereo explosions at the exact time Tezeeker was being deluged with the bucket of water.

"Ahhhhhhhhh! What the fudge!" Stanley hollered, for it was against *his* rigid morality code to ever utter any obscenity.

"School's a blast, isn't it Stanley?" Robbie very appropriately yelled. "Lavatory is really a dynamite subject!"

"Yeah," Ace laughed. "Stanley should now release more crap than the Diarrhea of Anne Frank."

The Diablos bolted-out of the Boys Room like four colts fleeing a burning barn. We knew that our treatment of Stanley had been cruel and vicious, '50s discrimination at its worst. It was as Carnie always put it, "Survival of the fittest."

American culture and Cardinal Reagan High had failed to teach us the vital difference between the animal world and the world of human rights. And besides, we had thought, if the Diablos eased-up on the eggheads, the Ks and Rs might think we were becoming soft, and ripe for experiencing harassment ourselves. We had to bug the hell out of Stanley, Mortimer, and their effeminate friends to keep the other cantankerous greasers off our backs.

The following morning, I visited the Reagan "Main Office" under the pretense of borrowing lunch money. While I was patiently waiting at the counter, my keen eyes detected that the secretaries were very busy performing their daily administrivia. I glanced to my left and noticed no one inside the teacher mailbox room.

Vertical and horizontal slats neatly separated office forms into various cubicles for the convenience of the teaching staff. Pass slips, lesson plan forms, field trip forms, personal day request sheets, class attendance forms, chaperone sheets, student discipline forms, and "Official School Announcement" forms were readily available. 'Do I have the guts to do it?' I wondered.

I felt blood rush-up to my ears as I excitedly pilfered two office announcement forms. I furtively slid the pilfered documents into my ringed notebook, and stealthily left the "Main Office" undetected by the overworked secretaries. While being bored to death in Father

Ignatius's sixth-period Latin III class, where we were translating Caesar's strategic campaigns against the Gauls into English, I found the time to neatly write-up several creative announcements.

Between seventh and eighth-periods, I surreptitiously re-entered the "Main Office". My eyes observed that the secretaries were still preoccupied with their deluge of afternoon adminis*trivia.* I slipped the pair of newly-composed forms into the announcement folder located on the office's side counter. I was prepared to ask a secretary for a "Parent Permission Slip" for a scheduled junior class trip to *Pennsbury Manor* if one of the office personnel had noticed and acknowledged my student presence.

Mary Ellen Jensen, a holier than thou brown-noser from the word "go", read the daily announcements that afternoon. Her style was to focus on each word's exact pronunciation without heeding or comprehending the boring scripts she was reading. Mary Ellen always mechanically went about her responsibility, not paying too much attention to the import of her read messages. I nervously listened to Mary Ellen's all-too-perfect, nauseating voice being transmitted over the high school intercom. 'Would my first unilateral mischief be successful?' I wondered and speculated.

"There will be a very important candy sale in Room 107," read the ditsy senior prom queen. "The sale will benefit the *National Honor Society. Milk Duds* and *Peanut Chews* will be sold. Hurry before we run out of *Three Musketeers."*

"Booooooooo!" jeered the majority of male listeners in their individual classrooms.

"We'll be selling *Good and Plenty* and *Juicy Fruit,* too," Mary Ellen informed. The greasers, 'tweeners, and jocks all wildly cheered, while the girls and the eggheads throughout the school shook their heads in absolute disgust. The objectors were condemning what they honestly believed to be disrespectful barbarian behavior.

"And for you real chocolate lovers out there," Mary Ellen proceeded, "*Mounds* and *Almond Joy,* along with *Milky Way,* can also be purchased in Room 107."

"Hoorayyyyyyy! Woeeeeeeeee!" hooted most of the delirious and attentive greasers in the listening audience.

"The scheduled junior class field trip," articulated Mary Ellen, "to *Pennsbury Manor* has been cancelled due to student apathy. In its place, Father Adrian, class adviser, is considering a more exciting field trip to the *Jezebel Lounge on Route 13*."

There was a pause of about five-seconds. Then, the afternoon announcements continued over the intercom. "Can Stanley Tezeeker please report to the Reagan Gynecologist's Office for your scheduled castration session?"

I sat high in my desk, pretending to be just as shocked as the other eighth-period study hall students. Father Barnabas, Brother Timothy's substitute for the day, peered at the tan cinderblock wall speaker as if it were transmitting Swahili.

"This afternoon's meeting of the 'Rectums Anonymous Club' has been postponed," Mary Ellen informed the alert student body. "The next meeting will be held in the *rear* of the auditorium Monday after school. All eligible dingle-berries are invited to attend. B-Y-O-T. Yes, bring your own toilet."

Diablo prestige was on the rise. Our growth in popularity was at the expense of Father Malcolm, Brother Timothy, Stanley Tezeeker, and Mary Ellen Jensen. Father Malcolm was scheduled for his hospital release toward the end of January. The Diablos planned to keep the pressure on Malcolm and make the wicked sadist even more disoriented and ineffective upon his return.

Greaser school mischief often took advantage of the regularity of repeated scheduled events. The Diablos perceptively noticed that *Civil Defense* drills were routinely conducted on the fourth Monday of each marking period. The end of January had been designated as the perfect time to initiate some extensive school *turmoil,* or as Robbie put it, "A special oil the greasers are gonna' give the teachers at the end of the damned term. Term oil." The *Civil Defense* practice drill would be a case where the Ds, Ks, and Rs all united against *our* common principal enemy, school authority.

"J.W., pity this friggin' school," Carnie announced to me inside the Reagan cafeteria. "They want us to jump through their stupid hoops like we're dumb trained circus animals."

"Yeah," Robbie amiably agreed. "And if a Russian A-Bomb fell on Levittown, I don't think puttin' our heads between our legs under our desks is gonna' protect us from all those alpha and beta particles and those gamma rays Sister Margaret Frances was tellin' us about. The teachers must all think we're stupid assholes if we believe that crap!"

"Yeah," Carnie added. "And the nutcase teachers want us to give ourselves blow-jobs under our desks while the Russians are nuking our asses' right off the damned planet. And the nutty nuns expect the girls to eat themselves out under their desks, too."

"How about when we gotta' stand in the corridors facing our lockers?" I contributed.

"Yeah, J.W.," Carnie concurred. "The school brass thinks we're incompetent morons. Like the knuckleheads want us to think that the only areas of the building that's not gonna' be destroyed are the freakin' hallways and lockers."

The fourth Monday in January finally arrived. Father Malcolm was back from the hospital just in time to participate in the monthly *Civil Defense* drill. The fire alarms were sounded at 10 a.m. Brother Timothy stood in the main corridor opposite his first-floor office. The junior friar was cranking a manual siren to help the clanging bells simulate an authentic air raid. The students all filed-out of their respective rooms peacefully.

Then, Carnie, Ace, Robbie, and I yelled-out, "The Commies are here!" All mayhem broke loose. Greasers and 'tweeners threw cherry bombs and firecrackers into empty classrooms. Powerful cherry bombs were also flushed-down toilets in the boys' lavatories, and soon water gushes squirted-up from ruptured pipes and cracked toilets. Foul smoke from stench bombs further expanded the general pandemonium. Odors and fumes from heating ducts permeated the entire building. Students who were not privy to the greasers' creative (destructive) scheme scurried down the halls like frightened sewer rats evacuating big city flooding sanitation pipes.

Some gullible students actually believed that the Russians had invaded the building; were actively patrolling the school corridors, and aggressively taking hostages. At the height of the chaotic frenzy, Father Malcolm, Brother Timothy, and Father Adrian all frantically stood guard at the "Main Entrance". The triumvirate was futilely attempting to blockade the frenetic mass exodus. The turbulent scene made me think of the entire battle of *Iwo Jima* being re-enacted inside the four-story masonry structure.

Diablos, Kamikazes, Renegades, 'tweeners, jocks, eggheads, and even some girls jostled into each other shouting, "The Russians are coming! The Russians are here!"

Robbie Wilkinson was the last student to evacuate the tumultuous school. R.W. paced over to me and stated that he had to stay behind to search the edifice for a suspected "Soviet Sex Orgy".

"What on earth are ya' talkin' about!" I exclaimed.

"Well, J.W.," replied Robbie quite matter-of-factly. "Everyone was screaming their heads off, 'The Russians are coming! The Russians are coming!' I just had to stay behind to see how true it was, but I never detected any flying semen."

After *that* fourth very chaotic Monday in January, *Civil Defense* drills remained being the obeyed tradition of schools other than venerable Cardinal Reagan. The greasers were in their glory, with all the gangs participating in the unbelievable farce. It was a distinct pleasure seeing sanctimonious priests and pious nuns wildly scampering through the corridors to save their mortal lives.

"You'd think they'd hang-around longer inside the school wantin' to get to heaven sooner by dyin'," Robbie jested as we continued standing outside the ongoing fiasco in the thirty-degree cold. "What a bunch of hippo-crates!"

"I guess their immortal souls were too scared of dyin'," Carnie cleverly surmised and related. For a brief, wonderful half-hour, the faculty had become puppet actors upon the greasers' marvelous stage.

Tullytown and Edgely Fire Department trucks converged on the scene, along with a squadron of town and state police cars. Red revolving lights were seen for fifty-yards in all directions. Sirens were wailing all around the noble building.

Father Malcolm had the very embarrassing task of explaining the incredible lunacy to skeptical fire and police officials. The school disciplinarian was about to falter into a second nervous breakdown. Brother Timothy was also nearing his breaking point. The frolicking, ecstatic Diablos *were* basking in greaser heaven.

Chapter 16
"Quinn's Speech"

I'll never forget the night of February 4, 1959. Tink and I were sitting at our favorite Feed Bag table facing the Dairy DeLite. Jokes and Carnie soon arrived at 7 p.m. in Bo's green and cream Chevy. The joint got a lot louder after the two garrulous chatterboxes walked inside.

"What do ya' know ko-ko-mo," Carnie greeted, trying his darnest to be hip. "Well, if it ain't two lu-lu's from Honolulu!"

"What do ya' mean, jellybean," returned Tinker, who was even less hip than Carnie was.

"How's your dingles danglin'?" Bo inquired to both Tink and me.

"Long and narrow, straight as an arrow," I replied, completing a round of standard Diablos' salutations.

"Remember J.W.," Bo cautioned. "Your English teacher Sister Mary Barbara doesn't like lengthy participial phrases that are long and dangling."

"Don't worry, Words," Carnie mouthed his stupidity. "Sister Mary Barbara ain't gonna' give your danglin' participle any wet lip suction."

"Happy to hear that," I observed and answered.

"But your botany nun," Bo corrected. "She might wanta' do it by usin' her tulips."

That evening, Jokes Jalonec was in a very festive mood. The stud had already been accepted for the fall semester at both *Penn State* and *Rutgers,* so Bo didn't have to worry about not being admitted into a prestigious university. But what annoyed and bothered me most about Jalonec was that the stud had just two moods, happy and happier.

But Bo always had to contaminate our important conversations with his rather humorous prattle. Carnie, Tinker, and I were getting sick of his one-liners, but we couldn't understand why all the chicks always ate up his jargon as if his bull were a scrumptious banana split.

"Hey, Tink," Bo the comedian systematically bantered and baited. "What' astrological sign were ya' born under?"

"Libra," Jeremy Foster answered in his typical disgusted voice. "What sign were you born under?"

"Jalonec thought hard for a second and then said, "I think you're wrong Tink. The sign we were both born under must've read 'Operating Room'."

Angie was on duty that night and had pretended Tinker and I had been sitting in another restaurant in another universe until Bo stepped into the popular teen eatery. Jokes winked at Angie, who then made an earnest effort to hustle over to our location.

"Ya' guys ready? My pen has plenty of ink," the Italian doll said.

“So, what,” Tinker nastily answered. “My pen has plenty of dogs.”

Bo Jalonec was a little more-suave than the rest of us seated numbskulls put together. Chicks loved it even more if “lover boy” politely put them down a few pegs.

“Well Angie,” Jokes responded. “Bring’ us four servings of Salad Diablo.”

Everyone including the waitress knew quite well that no such item was printed on the Feed Bag menu. Angie begged for clarification.

“Salad Diablo? That ain’t a specialty of the house!” the bewildered waitress challenged.

“It sure is, Honey,” Bo disagreed. “Because Salad Diablo means *let us* alone.”

“Oh Blondie, you’re so clever,” the Sicilian babe observed and opined. “And I really wish I could be your honey girl. Then, I could feel ya’ all over. But I do have one question I’d like to ask ya’.”

Bo was taken back by the Sicilian beauty’s sudden sincerity. “What’s that ya’ wanna’ know, Sweetie-pie?” Jalonec nonchalantly asked, while still bathing in his overall splendor.

“Your hair is so golden blond. I got to wonderin’,” the waitress said and paused. “Does it match the patch?”

Bo was more than mildly chagrined at being outdone by the pretty Italian princess. Was it a mere coincidence? How was she privy to his joke material? Jalonec had to put it in overdrive to best her. “Look Doll, it’s the same by any other name. But you’re welcome to check the strawberries in my patch any time, if the cucumber’s not in season.”

The guys all burst out in laughter. Angie, showing solid curves galore, wiggled her way to the main counter to assist Domenick and Luigi with their monotonous routines. Jokes then addressed his companions in a more serious tone.

“Guess what guys? Carnie and me just ran into Quinn over at the *Texaco* station across the street,” Jalonec reported. “He was puttin’ some hi-test into his ‘42.”

“Listen, Bo, don’t talk to me about that friggin’ guy,” Tinker complained. “Quinn ain’t shown me no leadership since the Diablos started up. I’m seriously thinkin’ about droppin’ out of the Ds and joinin’ the Ks. At least, I could pal around with Cummings. Right now, the ugly monster ain’t got no steady woman, and I heard the hideous bastard hates cats, too.”

Carnie, Jokes, and I did our best to persuade Tinker to stay in the gang. We talked about the *Labor Day* phone booth disaster and about his head being stuck inside Dante Messina’s mailbox over in Kenwood. Then, we discussed and reviewed the exciting encounter involving Spits and Worm behind the Feed Bag. Our closing arguments must have been strong, because Tink told us he was staying in the gang to experience more impending danger.

"Tink, if ya' was half as tough as ya' say ya' are," Bo chided, "ya' woulda' knocked the Ks cold before they squeezed your dense noggin' into Dante's mail receptacle. Are ya' sure ya' don't have a postmark stamped on your trapezoid-shaped forehead?"

"Real goddamned funny, Jokes," Tinker coughed as a trace of disgusting snot shot-out of his left nostril, making the psycho snort like a wounded bull. "Real funny. Seven of em' jumped me when I was walkin' from my favorite fishin' spot at the Delaware Canal on my way to the pharmacy to buy some smokes," Tinker argued. "It took only three of em' to kidnap J.W. without a struggle. Why the hell don't ya' mention that?" Finally, Tink inelegantly reached for a napkin to wipe his runny nose.

I was really embarrassed by Tink's frank testimony. Carnie spared me from further humiliation by switching the subject back to Quinn. "Anyway, guys. Quinn's really depressed. Says he's on his way to 'the Bag' after he gases up his rod."

"Great!" I euphorically exclaimed. "I'll cheer him up with a couple of instrumentals on the juke. I'm sure 'Honky Tonk' and 'Tequila' will shift his transmission into second gear."

"J.W., you're nothin' but a freakin' brown-nosin' kiss-up," accused Tinker, who was not badmouthing Bo Jalonec in *his* captain's presence. "Quinn's prob'ly only interested in us tonight because Patty's prob'ly havin' her friggin' period."

"Havin' her bloody period as they say in England," Bo corrected. "But Tink, ya' just gave me a great idea. J.W., why don't ya' go play 'Red River Valley Rock' by Johnny and the Hurricanes fifty-times in a row on the jukebox, just to remind Quinn of his woman's delicate *minstrel* condition."

I reached into my pocket and found a shiny new quarter. I thought I'd play three instrumentals other than "Red River Valley Rock". Sometimes, Tinker and Bo together had less couth than the Marquis de Sade had demonstrated during the height of his insanity.

Before I could rise from my chair and saunter over to the juke, Quinn, rather despondently, entered the restaurant. His facial features appeared very distraught. His skin color was pallid, and his eyes bloodshot. That was the most-melancholy that I had ever seen my greaser idol. None of us could fathom the burden that his mind bore. 'Maybe our boss finally broke-up with Patty,' I guessed.

Quinn slowly approached the jukebox as if in a trance. The song "You Belong to Me" by Patience and Prudence was just finishing-up. Our Diablos' leader unexpectedly pulled the machine's plug out of the back wall socket. The instant silence captured the attention of the thirty or so customers seated inside the Bag.

The entire Feed Bag became as quiet as the moon's surface. Even several Ks and Rs present inside the joint wondered what was going on. Looking extremely distressed, Quinn stood-up on a wooden chair like an 1850s country politician "on the stump". And then, like a disconsolate minister at a dear friend's funeral, our leader, contrary to his normal reticent disposition, delivered a very stirring oration.

"Yesterday, February 3rd," Quinn began, sounding a little like Abraham Lincoln must have at Gettysburg, "a very terrible accident happened outside Clearlake, Iowa. A small airplane crashed right into a farm field during a heavy snowstorm. The plane was carryin' Buddy Holly, Ritchie Valens, and the Big Bopper. And honestly, I personally feel their loss. I would like to pay tribute to their special talents with a moment of silence. And then, I would like to honor the three dead rockers the best way I know how," our leader grimly elucidated. "I'm askin' everyone in the restaurant to stand-up for ten-minutes and listen to the music of these three artists played from the record machine. I'm sure my sadness is shared by many of you. We have all lost something wonderful forever. Please stand."

I don't think Billy Graham could have been more eloquent or sincere. Even the minor Ks and Rs in attendance showed their respect. It was as if Quinn had become Moses, consecrating a supreme covenant with everyone present, along with the souls of the three deceased entertainers. And then, towards the end of his remarkable sermon, Quinn had transformed into our Pope, and the Feed Bag suddenly became our Vatican. The Diablos were Quinn's faithful apostles; Buddy Holly, Ritchie Valens, and the Big Bopper were our instant saints; their fabulous music our gospels, and rock and roll our religion. Everyone present was deeply impacted by Quinn's *New Testament.*

The other Feed Bag patrons just stood there in awe. No one dared flex a muscle. Even Luigi and Domenick stopped flipping their pizza dough. It was as if Orpheus himself had entered the Feed Bag, and we all were enchanted and entranced by the mere mention of *his* songs.

Quinn descended from his wooden chair; again stooped-down; found the jukebox's power cord, and adroitly pushed the prongs back into the electric wall socket. After the rock and roll preacher deposited two coins down the slot, everyone in the eatery remained reverent and quiet. All in all, it amounted to a magnificent spiritual experience.

The Feed Bag patrons stood as still as statues inside a wax museum. The first song was "Chantilly Lace," a novelty number by the Big Bopper, a former Beaumont, Texas DJ named J.P. Richardson, whose unique tune was followed by "Oh Donna" and "La Bamba" performed by Ritchie Valens. The climax surged with Buddy Holly's "Peggy Sue", "Oh Boy", and "That'll be the Day". And when the lyrics to Buddy Holly's third song translated into its exact literal interpretation, the truth hit home. Almost everyone was dumbfounded and virtually in tears. "That'll be the day, when you say goodbye; that'll be the day, when you make me cry; you say you'll never leave, you know it's a lie; that'll be the day, when I die!"

'Oh my God,' I thought. 'Buddy Holly did die!' His lyrics suddenly had a macabre new meaning. The singer's life was like a candle, snuffed-out by a whim of blind winter fate. And although Buddy Holly had passed-on, I then knew that his music would be immortal.

My disturbed mind next pictured saddened Quinn as a Puritan-faced undertaker pronouncing Buddy Holly, Ritchie Valens, and the Big Bopper dead in a cold farm field outside Clearlake, Iowa. I stood there, proud to know Quinn, and coincidentally admiring his courage and will. Externally, I had always wanted to be Bo; but internally, where it really mattered, I had always wished I could be Jack Quinn. And both internally and externally, I never had any desire whatsoever to ever be mendacious Tinker.

After the six songs had been played, Quinn dropped a third quarter into the slot. The Feed Bag celebrated "School Day" by Chuck Berry. When Berry got to "Hail, hail rock and roll, long live rock and roll!" all the teens present hopped-up onto their chairs and chanted the refrain as if it were a sacred oath of loyalty. Next, Quinn played "Tequila", and at the end of the Champs' mostly instrumental number, all present lustily yelled-out "Tequila"!

Before anyone ever noticed during the in-progress euphoria, Quinn had unceremoniously left the raucous restaurant with his mission fully accomplished. The Diablos watched the enigma slide into his black '42 Ford coupe; back up slowly; put the shift into first gear, and gently ease out of the parking lot onto busy *Route 13*. The first one standing at our table to open his mouth was the most heartless Diablo.

"He didn't even come over to see us and say `hello'," Tinker complained. "He was in such a damned fog that it was like we weren't even inside the freakin' place."

"Cool it, Man," Carnie reverently advised. "Quinn had other things on his mind besides the word 'hi'. If ya' ain't bothered by what Quinn said and about the bad news ya' just heard, then Tink, I'm sorry to report that ya' ain't got no damned conscience."

"Carnie's absolutely right," I agreed, finding fault with Tinker. "I now understand why *he's* so upset. Patty had nothin' to do with it. I'm kinda' down in the dumps myself about the shocking demise of the Big

Bopper, Ritchie Valens and Buddy Holly. Where's your sense of decency? Your sense of caring?"

Before Jokes could start ruining the discussion's general integrity, the jukebox blasted out Quinn's third selection. Everyone was astounded when the lively sound of "Red River Valley Rock" filled the Feed Bag.

"Well guys," Bo said with a wide grin. "I guess Patty's not havin' her damned period after all. It's now feed the cat time once again!"

Chapter 17
"Ambushed"

Before I knew it, mid-February had come around on the 1959 calendar. The Edgely Fire Department had a recreational lounge upstairs above the fire engine garage. The "fun area" was a fringe benefit to volunteer and junior firemen to use at their leisure. Tinker and I had just completed our fourth friendly game of eight-ball on the pool table. The competition was amiable, only because Tinker was winning three games to one. After downing our refreshing *Pepsi's,* we next played a game of shuffleboard, three games of pinball, and then Tink and I shot two rounds of darts.

Carnie wanted to tag along, but was home nursing the flu, so Tink and I had the lounge all to our lonesome. The regular firemen were home with their nagging wives and bratty kids having dinner. The upstairs' "rec" would not see heavy action until around eight p.m. when Chief Bradley, Lieutenant Collins, and the others would get tired of hearing their wives complaining about paying the bills and of hearing their spoiled kids crying and whining.

Tink and I had eaten early suppers over at the Feed Bag, and all we wanted were a few hours free of parental supervision or adult hassling. My gimpy pal decided we should abandon the place at seven, because the older guys would soon be taking over the lounge.

"J.W., it's pretty cold out tonight. Why don't ya' hustle downstairs and get my car warmed up. I'll stay up here to use the hopper. My bowels ain't feelin' that great, ever since I wolfed-down those four Mexicali chiliburgers for supper. Fact is, I feel pretty fuckin' raunchy."

"Okay, Tink. I'll get on that detail right away. Just toss me your keys, and I'm off to see the wizard."

My feet quickly descended the wooden stairs, anxious to hop into Tink's black '49 Plymouth and escape the frigid-night air. When my engineer boots reached ground level, I was very surprised to be ambushed by Cummings and four other unsavory Kenwood hoodlums. Popeye, Jake Mullins, Spits, and Worm followed their nefarious mentor's aggressive lead. The contemptible creeps simultaneously pointed their opened switchblades up to my throat. My lungs gasped for more freezing air, and my legs nearly collapsed onto the asphalt from total fright.

"So, ya' gutless Punk," Cummings greeted. "Our paths cross again." My heart felt like it was sinking deep into my abdomen.

"Well, now," Popeye mercilessly added. "If it ain't the stupid jerk-off who heaved my sister and cousin into the polluted *Delaware.* Ate any knuckle sandwiches lately?"

Nefarious Spits, Worm, and Jake Mullins stood alongside their lethal, superior K officers. The intimidating trio was broadly grinning at my futile, hostage situation. The three jerks grabbed my arms and then threw me up against the firehouse's stucco wall. Cummings sarcastically told me to "keep quiet", or else I would be castrated before I could enjoy my next urination, or my first orgasm.

My ears heard an upstairs' toilet flush, and a minute later, Tinker came hurrying down the steps to the frigid parking lot. I listened to the heels of his engineer boots pounding against the varnished steps as his descent neared ground level. Tink's eyes showed surprise when four Kamikaze switchblades intercepted his exit directly under the stairway's entrance light. Popeye, Mullins and Spits grabbed and tossed Tink up against the firehouse's wall, right next to me.

"Well, well, well," Cummings acknowledged. "If it ain't Tweedle Dee and Tweedle Dumbass. Before me and my pals slash you two assholes up a bit, we're gonna' first twist your necks so hard you're gonna' think your throats was made outa' *Turkish Taffy*."

My feet were shuddering inside my cold engineer boots. The large round thermometer above the doorway entrance read 17 degrees, but most of my shaking was due to the Kamikaze danger rather than to the bitter-cold temperature. My mind reckoned that those psychopaths were out to inflict life-threatening injuries. Puffs of steam exited from my mouth as soon as my breath made contact with the chilly night air.

"And I'm gonna' kick your asses so hard," Worm predicted to Tink and me before alluding to a popular sci-fi movie, "that you're both gonna' be knocked right off *This Island Earth*."

I finally mustered-up sufficient strength and courage to speak. I had never felt so miserably frightened in all my life. "You fellas' watch too much *Science Fiction Theater,"* I boldly panted, trying to get a smile out of at least one of the five cretins. "Can't we just tolerate one another and leave each other alone?"

"Look, Punk," Worm answered. "Spits and me ain't forgot that trick you two assholes pulled behind 'the Bag'. This time you're gonna' both wish we was five wild and rabid Dobermans instead of five mean-assed Kamikazes."

I felt as if I truly had been captured in the presence of evil thugs. Death would be lurking not far behind. 'Why couldn't I have been born in prehistoric times when things were safer?' I was thinking.

"What's the matter J.W.?" Popeye laughed. "Did some faggot squirrel eat your damned nuts?"

Amazingly, Tinker had strangely remained quiet during the whole confrontation, and I wished 'Davy Crockett' would have shown some anger and had come to my defense. Up to that point, the crazy kid only seemed to be a witness to my berating. When "Mr. Fix-it" finally did say something, I wished he had kept his big mouth shut. The delinquent wearing the 3-D glasses directed his remark to Spits and Worm.

"Look here, my buddy J.W. told me you two boneheads got off too easy last time," the mentally warped mechanic commented. "Words said this time he's gonna' kick your rumps so hard you're both gonna' think your colons was semi-colons. Ain't that right, J.W.?"

My mouth had never said such a threat. Tinker was recklessly quoting Bo's rendition about *our* first encounter with Spits and Worm at the Feed Bag, and of course, Jalonec was (at *that* crucial time) parked somewhere with Susie checking-out her cat's voracious appetite. Meanwhile, the Ks had intercepted Tinker and me outside the Edgely Fire Company in the absence of recently quoted Jokes Jalonec. And as far as the abominable Ks were concerned, none of the savages knew anything about the difference between colons, semi-colons, and women's periods; nor did the *'cave boys'* care to know.

"Five against two isn't fair," I argued. "And if Spits and Worm want to get even with Tink and me, then that's the way it oughta' be. Two against two." I tried to be suave like Bo Jalonec and firm like Quinn, but I could tell that Spits and Worm were not too happy with my pertinent suggestion.

But Cummings actually considered the merits of my proposal. "Okay then, I wanna' test how good my new recruits are, so here's the damned ground rules. J.W. and Tinker Bell will fight Spits and Worm with blades. When two guys on a team lose more than a pint of blood each, then the other team wins the first round." Cummings paused a second to see if everyone understood his first imperial mandate. "If J.W. and Tinker Bell win the first round, then they gotta' battle me, Popeye, and Jake with chains." Then, Cummings pointed to my pal and me. "If ya' two turds don't like them rules, then it's five on two with blades. We know that Tinker Bell has at least one!"

Before I could open my trap and protest the terms of engagement, my not-too-swift Diablo colleague intrepidly answered, "We accept your fucked-up conditions!" I glanced over at Spits and Worm, and the recent Kenwood transplants appeared a little more concerned about dual knife combats, after Cummings had changed the odds from five on two to two on two.

Tink demanded that the Ks back off so that Mr. T could remove a pair of switchblades from his black leather jacket. Cummings motioned for his despicable comrades to honor the seemingly fair request. Tink then unzipped a pocket, reached inside, and produced two blades. My buddy handed me one, which I instantly recognized as the switchblade comb that had been used to fool Spits and Worm during our first encounter. "Just hold this!" the psycho commanded.

'Oh, great!' my brain thought. 'A switchblade comb is goin' up against switchblade knives. I'm gonna' be carved-up worse than a *Thanksgiving* turkey!' my mind imagined. I wouldn't have known how to use the weapon even if it were a real switchblade. I was facing Worm, and I nervously stared at his gleaming knife as the derelict stood underneath the upstairs entrance light. The weapon's sharp, metal tip' made my mind think about death, a subject more akin to the Ks hazardous lifestyle than to the Diablos' mischief credo. My stomach and bowels churned as my body tensed-up.

And then, much to the astonishment of everyone else there, Tinker reached into another pocket of his black leather jacket and whipped-out a small silver pistol.

"Ya' think you're a tough guy like Marlon Branflakes," stuttered an astonished Cummings with traces of fear and confusion evident in his voice. "Guns weren't in the damned rules!"

"Ya' got it right for a damned change," Tink confirmed.

"Hey, man," Popeye defensively and apologetically pleaded. "You're fuckin' crazy. You oughta' be a mental patient in *Byberry*. Cool it with the damned heater!"

Tinker informed the Ks that they'd better be wearing bulletproof vests because he was going to put two slugs into Cummings' chest, and one bullet into each of the other four's scrotum sacks.

"You're freakin' me out!" Popeye shouted, finally realizing his role had been cleverly switched from predator to prey. "You're a crazy mother-fucker!"

Tinker regarded Popeye's statement as the highest praise. The Ks had again been outsmarted by my dangerous, volatile companion. The five punks looked as scared as I had felt just moments before. Tink sensed that the pugnacious creeps had lost their thirst for combat. The five Ks held their hands above their heads to symbolize surrender.

"We was only foolin'. We're sorry if we ruffled your feathers," Cummings awkwardly apologized. "We'll do anything ya' say. Just don't pull that damned trigger."

As the Ks retreated backwards while facing us, Tinker terrorized them some more. "Okay, you low I.Q. hand-jobs," my mean-spirited pal declared. "So now, get-down on your knees and sincerely say 'the Diablos are boss' ten times. Then, I might only shoot you worthless pond scum in your ugly asses' instead of in your tickers and dicks."

The five humbled Kenwood thugs got-down on their knees like altar boys and respectfully chanted, "the Diablos are boss" ten-times in a most unpleasant-but-frightened harmony. Then, the wicked Ks were forced to say "the Kamikazes suck!" ten-times in a row while still on their knees.

"Now before I change my fickle mind," Tink convincingly advised, "put your feet to the street. I have a real twitchy index finger, and this here gun might shoot a few slugs into your asses by accident."

The five intimidated Ks were scared out of their minds. The thugs screamed some incomprehensible jargon as the fanatical creeps madly raced over to Cummings' black '52 Ford that had been parked in the rear of the Edgely Fire Company's lot. The driver gunned the engine just as the other rogues frantically jumped inside. But before Cummings could peel-out, Tink hustled-over and slashed the rear tire on the driver's side with *his* dependable switchblade. The black coupe fishtailed-out of the Edgely Fire Company's parking lot, heading west in the direction of *Route 13*.

"Tink, without a doubt, you're a mean motor scooter! You're hell on wheels!"

"Thanks, Words, but really, I owe it all to you, Man."

"I don't get it!" I replied in a confused tone of voice.

"J.W., do ya' remember that night back in '57 when ya' bought your black leather jacket at the Bristol Farmers' Market?"

"How could I ever forget? That was the proudest moment of my endangered life."

Tink's lips formed a very devious smile. "Well, while you was busy makin' your important purchase, I quietly walked-over to another stall. I bought the switchblade comb, and then traded a few greenbacks for this here metal toy gun. It's really a cool little cigarette lighter. Now, J.W., let's celebrate our little victory by lightin' up a few lethal cancer sticks."

Tinker had admirably trampled the egos of Cummings, Popeye, Mullins, Spits, and Worm with a simple cheap metal toy. The wily C-Man had, in self-defense, admirably declared war on the Ks, and had shrewdly won the second greaser battle. My all-too-proud buddy wouldn't admit it, but the Diablos now needed the services of Quinn and Bo more than ever.

Chapter 18
"More Kamikaze Aggression"

In early March of '59, I still had my paper route over in Junewood. The *Philadelphia Bulletin* delivery truck would drop-off my bundles of Sunday morning papers at the curb in front of 50 Daffodil Lane. I would get-up at four-thirty a.m., load the one-hundred-and-twenty-three papers onto my younger brother Skip's *Radio/Flyer* red wagon, and then cart my heavy cargo over to Robbie Wilkinson's house on Dogwood Drive.

On Fridays and Sundays, when the *Bulletin* was extra thick, Robbie would help me out with my route. On the other days of the week, R.W. rendered his assistance only as the spirit moved him. When Robbie felt motivated to earn a pack of smokes, my loyal pal would meet me with his kid brother's brown wood-sided wagon outside his house. Then, we would bring "yesterday's news" (Jokes called them olds-papers) to my loyal Junewood customer base.

It was dark and cold that first Sunday in March. I was disappointed that Robbie was still sleeping and not waiting for me. I knew my pal had caught the flu from Carnie, so I figured Wilkinson was in bed recovering from his winter malady.

I tugged my load across the grassy field that separated Dogwood Hollow from Junewood. My route serviced Junewood Drive, Jolly Lane, and Jester Lane. I finally got done serving Jonquil Lane, and then hastily finished-up my morning course on the remainder of Junewood Drive. It was late dawn as I cut back across the grassy meadow between Junewood and Robbie's house. Electric power towers bisected the field, bringing energy to that part of Levittown.

Three dark figures suddenly jumped-out from high weeds near one of the electric company's high-tension towers. Cummings, Popeye, and Jake Mullins grabbed me, hurled me face-up onto the *Radio/Flyer,* and then the rambunctious trio stuffed a bandanna inside my mouth. Three leather straps were used to secure me to the red wagon's frame. One belt was around my chest; the second around my abdomen, and the third around my legs. The Ks pulled and dragged the wagon and me across Dogwood Drive, down Disk Lane, and finally, onto Daffodil. The merry crew detoured onto the lawn of 66 Daffodil Lane, the impeccable domicile of Sal Palermo. The three goons positioned the red wagon (and me) directly under the Italian stallion's corner bedroom window.

I struggled to liberate myself, and my throat was grunting and gasping like a wild beast caught in a trap. As I wiggled and wriggled upon the wagon, the Kamikazes swiftly fled the scene, laughing their larynxes halfway out of their mouths. I was agitating around; the bedroom window opened, and Salvatore Palermo stuck his skull outside to investigate the noise's source. The face of Palermo's grotesque-looking wife was also very visible.

"Carmella, how come you never moan that loud like that kid outside on the wagon down there during sex," Sal lamented, peering-down at his struggling intruder. "Maybe I should start sleepin' with that little mongrel squirmin' down there, instead of with you. Oh no! That little mixed breed is that bozo kid who lives down the street. Hey freak," Palermo hollered-down. "Ya' look a little like Alfred E. Newman in *Mad Magazine.* No wonder my little angel Angie thinks you resemble the inside of a pimple."

All I could do was toss and turn atop the red wagon, mumbling and muttering muffled sounds through the bandanna that had been tickling my tonsils. Although happy to be discovered, I would have preferred being found by a more civilized barbarian.

Sal Palermo was not through with his trademark ridiculing. "Ya' must be one of those Italian ghosts," the lunatic grease-ball boomed, still peering-down and laughing at my encumbered predicament. "Do ya' know what Sicilians call an Italian ghost? Fung ghoul, you Asshole, fung ghoul!"

Sal's loud-mouthed mocking caused an early morning sensation in the neighborhood. First the Burns, who resembled Fred and Ethel Mertz, came out of their home. Soon, the remainder of the neighbors flicked on their lights and exited their warm houses to determine the origin of the commotion. Someone had actually called the Edgely Rescue Squad, and also the local police department.

Ten-minutes later, Chief Bradley pulled-up in his red and white fire patrol vehicle. A local police cruiser also skidded to a halt in front of 66 Daffodil Lane. Both men dashed-over to get a handle on the cause of the disturbance.

"Mr. Palermo," the astonished Fire Chief said. "Isn't this the same kid who got his head stuck in your mailbox? He must be an absolute glutton for punishment."

"Ya' got it right, Chief," Sal concurred. "This stupid twerp's brain musta' been squashed between the cheeks of his rectum right before the delinquent was born. I truthfully think that this dumb knucklehead needs brain surgery right away! Better notify the Proctology Department over at *Lower Bucks Hospital!"*

The temporarily befuddled policeman, who had been dispatched to look into a "disturbing the peace" violation, removed my gag and loosened the straps that had tethered me to the red wagon.

I saw Pop standing over me wearing his orange and white striped bathrobe over his gray and white plaid pajamas. "Who did this prank to you son?"

"Some kids I never saw before," I replied and fibbed as the policeman helped me to my feet.

Before Chief Bradley could ask me another question, the Edgely dispatcher's voice came over his vehicle's radio. "Chief, go directly to the Parker residence on Dewberry Lane. A male teenager is strapped-down onto a brown wagon. I repeat. Go directly to the Parker residence on Dewberry Lane."

"Roger, ten-four and out," the confused chief curtly replied.

Sal Palermo had eavesdropped on the dispatcher's official information that had been exclusively intended for the Edgely Chief and the confounded policeman. "Your kid is not the only nutcase punk in Dogwood Hollow," the mercurial Sidgy told dad. "All these Diablos are crazy, and ya' let your son be one of em'. The junior delinquents do insane asylum shit like stickin' their heads in mailboxes and tiein' each other to wagons at seven on a cold March morning. All their screwed-up friends must also be their screwed-up enemies, that's what the hell I really suspect! But I think your kid needs three psychiatrists!"

My unfortunate circumstance brought-out the Bob Hope in Chief Bradley, who hopped back into his emergency vehicle. The fire official chuckled and hollered to dad, "Your son and that other kid over on Dewberry could get on TV and make a special appearance on *Wagon Train*." Everyone laughed as the Chief, followed by the still-perplexed police cruiser, sped-off to Susie Parker's house.

The other wagon victim predictably turned out to be Robbie Wilkinson. The Kamikazes had kidnapped R.W. while he was waiting for me with his brother's brown wagon outside his place before I had begun delivering the Sunday morning papers. Just like Tink and I had been made simultaneous dupes in the twin mailbox caper, Robbie and I had been apprehended and given similar dual wagon embarrassments by the ever-vigilant Ks.

The next night, Tinker, Carnie, Bo, Robbie, and I talked it over at the Feed Bag and concurred on several conclusions.

"I think Sal Palermo might be encouragin' the Ks to beat-up on the Diablos," I claimed." No doubt, the Mafia and the Ks are in cahoots!"

"Yeah," Robbie agreed. "He's usin' Cummings and Popeye to scare you off of his daughter. J.W., why the hell would ya' want to have that crackpot Mafia group for in-laws?"

"Just your luck, J.W.," Bo added with a broad smile. "Because obviously, you're gonna' have outlaws for in-laws, no matter if ya' either marry Angie or Bubbles."

"Let's drop an A-Bomb on the Kamikazes just like the Air Force did on Hiroshima," Carnie irresponsibly demanded.

"Those rotten Italians are gonna' wish they stayed in Sicily feeding their faces lasagna, ravioli, spaghetti, and rigatoni," Tink wickedly commented.

"The Kamikazes are gonna' be sorry they had ever moved into Kenwood," Robbie lividly predicted, lusting for vengeance. Isn't my prediction, right B.J."

"Don't ever call me blowjob again," Jokes non-joked to R.W., "you pathetic reptilian weasel!"

Feeling chagrined, Bo had a minor surprise for R.W. "Susie's pop says the damage to his lawn over on Dewberry Lane was twenty-five bucks from the deep wagon grooves," Jalonec related. "Susie's not allowed to go out with any Diablo until *our* gang pays up. Her Dad appointed me principal bill collector over the telephone."

The Diablos had incurred another big debt that had been caused by the perilous Ks. We all reached deep into our pockets, and with the aid and raid of several cookie jars at home, the gang managed to come-up with the needed cash to sufficiently cover the unexpected lawn-damage/wagon expense.

Events between the D's and the Ks were becoming more frenzied. Our guys were determined to counter every Kamikaze *Pearl Harbor* with a Diablos' *Normandy Invasion,* but unless the Kenwood creeps tried something instigative with Bo and Quinn, we would never be able to defend our pride with complete unity.

I was having a minor financial crunch because of the recent Dewberry Lane lawn expenditure. And being a Diablo was also expensive because of the telephone booth door debt; the dual mailbox debts, and the regular gas and food money expenses. Although Dad was back working at the Martin and Quade Stainless Steel Company in North 'Philly, I didn't want to borrow any "new money" from his wallet, because Pop had also been strapped paying real bills while keeping the family going.

In mid-March, I negotiated a dollar an hour job over at Hal's Delicatessen in the strip mall to the left of the Feed Bag. I was lucky enough to find an industrious teen client willing to buy my flourishing paper route. An enterprising Junewood kid who Bo Jalonec knew paid me fifty-dollars for the privilege of delivering the *Philadelphia Bulletin* to make eight bucks a week profit. The kid's dad gave him the money in hopes that his son would learn to value financial responsibility and American capitalism. The boy's father also wanted to keep his son so busy participating in school academics, sports, and monotonous newspaper delivery that the encumbered kid wouldn't have time to hang-out with the Diablos.

The fifty-dollars was like new-found revenue. The cash surplus permitted me to escape the throes of adolescent poverty. I soon had additional pocket dough, but more importantly, I also had sufficient free time (when my mind was fresh) to think of some new agendas to execute against and frustrate the formidable Ks.

The following week in early March, my friends and I forgot about winter with the appearance of several warm days. Spring hadn't yet arrived on the calendar, but the guys were happy and energized by the weather change accompanying the vernal equinox's approach.

Bo Jalonec called my house and invited me on an impromptu fishing expedition. Jokes picked me up at ten on a Saturday morning, and then drove his impeccable Chevy to Tullytown. The gang jester had a favorite fishing spot next to the American Parchment Paper Company on the *Delaware River* bank. I also liked the secret location because the space was remote and isolated from the rigors and pressures of 50s civilization.

Bo parked his '57 on a side dirt road, and we trekked over a small knoll with Jalonec carrying his fishing rod and me lugging his tackle-box down a slope to the river. An old abandoned rowboat with two rotted oars was the only visible sign of past or present human activity.

"Bo, we oughta' get that guy Worm and stick this here hook through him," I declared during a mental inspiration. "But I don't think even a starvin' catfish would dig his foul taste." My plan was to first see if Jokes' opinion of Worm matched mine, and if it did, to convince Jalonec to wage war on the Ks using Worm as bait.

"Yeah, J.W.," Bo agreed. "Worm's a real bass turd."

"Ya' mean bastard?" I asked.

"Yeah, J.W. That bastard's a real bass turd," Bo clarified as the comedian contemplated decent fishing and mental relaxation. "Hey, Words. I gotta' commend you. You're really good at puttin' that bait on the line. Ya' must be a fantastic master baiter. Or maybe even a highly skilled male hooker?"

I decided that if I went along with Jalonec's stupid drivel, then the amateur comedian might get serious for a change and join Tinker, Carnie, and me in our upcoming war against the Kamikazes.

"J.W.," Bo continued his diatribe. "You're so naive that if you were walkin' by a whorehouse, and if the wind was blowin' in your direction, you'd think the whorehouse was really a well-stocked fish and bearded clam store."

"Jokes, anything ya' say, I'll swallow hook, line and sinker," I replied, hoping to establish some degree of normalcy to our extremely ludicrous conversation.

Bo and I fooled-around for a while, and I accidentally caught two small fish, which really pissed-off my friend because Jalonec was a serious fisherman, while I was simply a novice angler. I told Bo about all the problems that Tinker, Robbie, and I had been having with the Kamikazes. Although Jalonec seemed quite sympathetic, the lover-boy stated that the Ks never gave him any grief, so Bo wasn't that anxious to make enemies just because *they* happened to be my enemies.

Just as Jalonec finished his statement of neutrality, without warning, Cummings, Popeye, Mullins, Spits, Worm and four other marauding Ks came charging like maniacs over the small hill and down the slope, running directly at us. The nine demented delinquents were shouting, screaming, cursing, howling, and snarling like a wild pack of rabid, rampaging wolves.

Bo dropped his fishing line and fled down the riverbank, and I alertly followed his stellar example. Together, we pushed the old abandoned rowboat into the *Delaware,* hopped inside, and then Bo paddled it further into the murky river. The Kamikazes threw rocks and stones in our direction, and one projectile conked Jokes on the forehead, sullying his *Hollywood* profile as blood streamed down from his blond hairline. Soon, we were about four-hundred-feet out into the *Delaware,* and finally out of stone-throwing range. Cummings, Popeye, and the other Ks were still cursing and shouting insults at us from the water's edge.

I suggested that we should switch places because of Bo's injury. Jalonec acceded to my constructive request, and we carefully changed positions with me being the rower. Luckily, the weatherworn oars had still been left inside the decrepit boat.

"The next time you have a secret fishin' spot," I criticized, "don't tell or show me. Keep it to yourself!" Then, I saw the scarlet trail flowing-down from Bo's right temple, so I thought I should extend some courtesy and sympathy by listening to Bo's grievances.

"J.W., those nine boneheads are stealin' my fishin' rod and tackle," Jalonec complained, mentally sizing-up the grungy thugs who were evaluating their new-found booty.

"Yeah, Bo," I concurred. "If those primates had one more guy, those morons might have enough gray matter to build a human brain."

Bo Jalonec examined the blood inside his palms that the assault victim had wiped from his formerly perfect face. All the while, the maniacal Ks standing on shore were still gesticulating and growling like vicious Simians.

I rowed the old boat across the *Delaware's* main channel. There, the river was about sixty-foot-deep. My destination was a small island where Bo and I had rowed to, in the same discarded boat, on several occasions during more pleasant social circumstances.

Before Jokes and I could fully catch our breaths, a massive black hulk appeared rounding the bend to the north. The gigantic floating object was the familiar *Caracas,* returning south from the Fairless Hills Steel Mill. As the enormous vessel approached the rowboat's delirious occupants, the monstrous form positively dwarfed our diminutive presence in the river.

Suddenly, my comrade and I were like helpless Lilliputians. I again frightfully glanced-over at the colossal vessel. Its tremendous size was awesome. The red line from bow to stern was elevated about three-feet above the waterline, making the empty *Caracas* appear even more terrifying and threatening to our incredulous eyes.

The titanic tanker blew its ear-shattering horns at the puny obstacle lying in its nautical path. I rowed like a madman to try and escape the massive ship's wake. The Venezuelan vessel was then passing only about fifty-feet from our tiny dingy. I knew exactly how Huckleberry Finn and Jim must have felt when a *Mississippi* riverboat was about to smash their raft in half, but the *Caracas* had to be ten times as large as the biggest steam paddlewheels of the 1840s.

The ship's crew hollered and waved encouragement to Bo and me as I strenuously rowed with all the stamina I could muster. A great three-foot-high wave generated by the *Caracas* was heading directly toward us. A blast of water instantly filled the ancient rowboat, and soon the entire interior was flooded.

As Bo bailed-out water with his hands, we noticed that more water was entering from three tiny holes in the boat's inferior floor. I suspected that the conniving Ks had drilled the three small holes before Bo's fishing expedition had commenced, and before the chance appearance of the iron ore ship, causing our river misadventure an additional dilemma, resulting in being an additional bonus to the Kamikazes' clamorous shore celebration.

The heartless Ks immensely enjoyed witnessing Bo and me fighting for our lives. I still heard screams of merriment coming from the delighted Kenwood punks on shore, and cheers of support originating from the crew of the huge black vessel. The rowboat was then too full with river water, and was slowly sinking. Something had to soon give.

Bo and I were still around fifty-feet away from the little island in the center of the river. With no options left, we dove into the cold brown *Delaware,* black leather jackets, blue denim jeans, engineer boots and all. The exhausted victims awkwardly thrashed our way to the stony beach that had been geographically situated midway between Tullytown and neighboring New Jersey.

All the while throughout the difficulty, our ears could still discern the Ks taunts, a thousand or so feet to our west. Luckily, Bo and I were finally able to wade our way to land. We flopped-down on the hard sand, happy to be alive. Inhaling and exhaling air had never before seemed so necessary and appreciated as it did right then and there.

"Those jerks abused me for the last time," I panted.

"I'm with you J.W.," Bo puffed. "Tell Carnie, Tink, and Robbie I'm joinin' the crusade. Those assholes are messin' with the wrong guys. They're gonna' regret this attack for the rest of their friggin' lives."

"You're right, Bo," I gladly verified. "The Ds are gonna' cream the Ks without ever having to jerk-off our boners!"

"J.W.," Bo panted as the revenge-seeker continued his rumination. "Those Kamikazes should be ridin' on the *Caracas,* because they're *cruisin*' for a bruisin'."

Evidently, the *Caracas's* captain must have radioed the *Coast Guard* and the local authorities. At twilight, when Bo and I were shivering like naked Eskimos without the shelter of an igloo, a *Coast Guard* helicopter, dispatched all the way from Cape May, New Jersey, hovered above our location. Ten minutes later, Chief Bradley and two other Edgely volunteer rescue personnel traversed the *Delaware* in the fire company's motorized salvage boat. I immediately recognized one of the other two assisting rescuers as Lieutenant "Bingo" Collins.

Chief Bradley and Lieutenant Collins were very surprised to see one of their junior firemen desperately caught in "dire straits". I was very happy to be found, but I was equally as thrilled having Bo Jalonec as a staunch ally, now wholeheartedly dedicated to going up against the contemptuous Ks.

"Are ya' thinkin' about openin' a remote Bingo parlor out here in the middle of the river, J.W.?" Lieutenant Collins quipped.

"J.W.," Chief Bradley interrupted. "There ain't any mailboxes, telephone booths, or wandering wagon trains out here in the middle of the *Delaware,* are there?"

"Chief," Lieutenant Collins laughed. "I do believe that these stranded teens were probably waitin' for their ship to come in!"

As usual, Bo had to say and do something stupid. "I'll be good, I'll be good, I promise I'll be good!" Jokes ridiculously answered, holding his hands up high and oscillated from side to side, just like Froggie the Gremlin on the popular *Andy Devine Show*.

Even though Jokes had nearly drowned to death, the excellent swimmer still possessed a satirical spirit that magically transcended life; transcended the idea of death; transcended depression, and most of all, transcended the macabre nature of the ruthless Kamikazes.

As Chief Bradley and Lieutenant "Bingo" Collins laughed hardily at Jalonec's goofy TV antics, I thought about how Jokes would be a welcome member to Tink and Carnie's upcoming "war councils". I knew that if Jalonec could ever get-away for a night or two from gorgeous Susie Parker, then Jokes would have a lot of good schemes to contribute to our nightly Feed Bag powwows.

The amused fire department members escorted Bo and me inside their motorized boat, and we headed back to the 'Pennsy side of the river. After Jokes and I thanked the salvage men for their vital volunteer assistance, we walked over the hill to his green and cream '57 Chevy. Immediately, our pupils discerned that the windshield had been deliberately smashed. Even with the extensive damage to his wheels, Jokes still kidded-around and exhibited a blithe sense of humor concerning the obvious vandalism.

"Ya' know, Words," Jalonec articulated as the victim felt the side of his forehead with one hand and picked shards of glass from the front seat with the other. "Ya' only live a damned stone's throw away from Sal Palermo's place."

"Bo, isn't anything ever serious to you?" I objected and asked. "Ya' almost just got killed by a thrown rock; and another time by drowning, and now your former immaculate car's been all busted-up. I'd be pretty pissed-off if I was you! Isn't anything important or serious in your fantasy life?"

Bo confided to me that female love from Susie Parker was important to him, next to how my Junewood pal truly valued my friendship. Then, the zany guy offered some sage advice about dating. "Ya' know J.W., *that* Carol Zella broad over in Pinewood really likes you, but ya' waste all your vital energy goin' after Bubbles and Angie. You're really stupid, Man. You foolishly reject what ya' can have, and only want what ya' can't have!"

I didn't quite know how to answer his very perceptive observation and how to sagely counter his persuasive, erudite words. I felt dumb, incompetent, and wasted. Bo fathomed that his analysis had gotten to my super-sensitive inner being, so my loyal companion deftly changed the subject back to corny rock jokes.

"Words, I'm really glad those Kamikazes hit me in the temple with that stone." Bo exited the front seat of his damaged Chevy and stood right next to me. "J.W., being hit in the temple is a lot better than being hit in the damned synagogue." Jalonec then cupped his hands over his testicle area, which was what he meant by synagogue as a part of his anatomy, just like his injured right *temple* was. Then, Bo finished his comical speech by saying, "My divine synagogue is also my personal bird sanctuary."

A few days after Bo's exceptionally dangerous fishing expedition, Carnie and I had another encounter with Sal Palermo. My pal and I were having a friendly catch and pass session with a football on Daffodil Lane. Carnie heaved an errant spiral, which floated over my head, with the ball then bouncing all the way onto Sal Palermo's well-manicured front lawn.

"Okay ya' stupid yo-yo," Sal addressed my presence from his asphalt driveway. "How much trouble must ya' get into to finally realize you're a complete loser! Ya' ain't good enough to be a dry booger inside a dead whore's nose!"

"Sorry, Mr. Palermo," I solemnly apologized. "It was just a minor accident."

"Your suicidal parents think that *you* was a friggin' accident!" Sal shouted in my face. "You're pressin' your damned luck, punk. Why don't ya' get a job as a postage stamp and send yourself to Siberia, or to fuckin' Alcatraz! Or, you could join a school choir in Sing-Sing!"

Things were really getting out of control. Palermo's big fat Sidgy mouth was getting on my already-jangled nerves. And the Ks were about to make Victor Frankenstein look like a choirboy when compared to the Ds collective guile and awesome potential. We could only take so much of their repulsive, repetitious bullying.

First of all, the dastardly retards had almost drowned me in the green slime of the Delaware Canal. And the dual mailbox pranks could have severely cut Tink's throat and my jugular vein, and that notion led the Ds to believe that Cummings and Popeye were (according to Jalonec) merciless "cut-throats". The twin wagon capers involving Robbie and me were greatly significant when added to the Dairy DeLite phone booth embarrassment, which could have gotten several Diablos either killed or hospitalized. And now, the more recent *Caracas* close encounter involving Bo and me was another incident of ruthless Kamikaze aggression. Needless to say, things were rapidly heating-up to the boiling point.

Chapter 19
"Tinker's Tinkerin"

Carnie and Tink thought the Diablos should "beef up" our ranks, so we recruited several new members. Al Keller and Jim Amari lived over on Dawn Lane, and those two teens had been remote acquaintances of vindictive Carnie.

Bo and I needed new leather jackets. Our misadventure in the *Delaware River* had shrunk our black leather ones down two whole sizes. Jokes painstakingly re-did the artwork on the backs, and we were more than happy to sell our former apparel to Al and Jim for five-dollars each. Bo and I used the new-found revenue to help buy brand new ones at the old reliable Bristol Farmers Market, where Jokes reiterated to me his sincere promise to make the Ks pay for damaging his movie-star forehead, and for nearly drowning us during the life-threatening river dilemma. "Their *abdominal* pranks are hard to digest and really getting ugly and intolerable," Jokes maintained.

"We're gonna' have to get even," I answered.

"Only *odd* guys want to get even," Bo illogically answered in one of his characteristic convoluted riddles. "J.W., since we've always been odd, we're gonna' do some very odd things to the un-Babe Ks. Just you wait and see! I call them the un-Babe Ks because the Kenwood assholes are basically Ruth-less!"

The following Saturday night in March of '59, Tink drove Carnie, Robbie, Bo, and me into the woods near Robbie's house to drink a case of beer. After we polished-off the twenty-four bottles of *Budweiser,* we carried the empty case and bottles through the woods to Dogwood Drive, and then we quietly deposited the garbage into one of Robbie's sanctimonious neighbor's trashcans. The old, next-door neighbor happened to be a widow and a church temperance advocate, so we figured that the unsightly refuse would generate some interesting local lady gossip.

The next evening, the same five guys were out to duplicate the fun we had enjoyed the night before. We were again in Tink's crummy '49 Plymouth, on our way down Edgely Road to enter the local woods from the backside trail. Our merry contingent had another case of beer buried in the ground, because I had lent Carnie my *Treasure Island* book, and the avid reader liked the way pirates used to bury their valuable plunder. And since acquired beer was like treasure to the Diablos, we all went along with Carnie's stupid fantasy, and buried the other case of *Bud* in the woods, even if we had to later drink it warm.

Bo was complaining how Tink's black Plymouth was too old, grungy, dangerous, and obsolete to even be on the dirt trail. Tink was arguing back that Bo would never take his '57 Chevy into any woods, not even to drink beer or to get laid.

"Ya' oughta' shave your head Bo," Tinker suggested, "and after ya' get your ear pierced for a big five-pound ring, we can all call you the fucked-up title ya' deserve, *Mr. Clean*."

"Tink," Bo replied. "This tin pig piece of crap we're ridin' in makes a Chinese hog-pen look like the goddamned *Taj Mahal*."

Carnie, Robbie, and I laughed as the two arguers exchanged verbal barbs and criticisms. Two cops flagged us down for a sobriety check, just before we got to the woods to excavate our case of buried beer. I recognized the policemen as the ones that were hitting on Carnie and Tinker's moms. The cops were looking for an opportunity to speedily send the Diablos to "the clinic".

After the police searched the dirty inside of Tink's infamous vehicle, the fuzz told the junior mechanic to open the trunk for a continuation of the inspection. The inspectors detected a faint trace of beer odor, but without any direct physical evidence, the on-a-mission patrolmen couldn't take any official action.

One of the policemen asked Tink to open up his glove compartment so that the curious investigator could inspect the car's registration and my buddy's driver certificate. The nosy patrolman detected six pairs of gloves inside. The Diablos always carried along gloves. We seldom did anything illegal, but in case we had to, the gloves would conceal our fingerprints. The gloves apparently had stimulated the cop's limited imagination.

"What the hell are you kids doin' with all these gloves?" the first zealous officer asked.

"Are ya' young criminals or somethin'?" the second keeper of the peace promptly interrogated.

It was obvious to us that those two policemen had little respect for itinerant greasers. Bo Jalonec had an appropriate answer to counter the cops' inquiries.

"Officers," Jokes suavely replied. "Why do ya' think they call that box a glove compartment? To keep gloves in it, that's why! We keep all our gloves inside there, because society and our most excellent English language call that stupid enclosure a glove compartment."

If Carnie, Tinker, Robbie, or I had said the exact same words, I'm certain that we would have been detained for three-hours in 'the clinic' for being wise guys disrespecting authority. We then all got out of Tink's car to stretch our legs.

"Hey, Jake," the first cop said and chuckled. "These greaser kids are really messed-up! This has gotta' be an all time first. The imbeciles keep six sets of gloves in the glove compartment because that's what it's called. I think I'm gonna' die laughin' before I get the chance to piss my pants and die from dehydration."

"Yeah, Frank. That's gotta' be one of the best ones I've heard in my twenty-years on the force. These kids must have IQs below those of retarded chimpanzees. We could only arrest humans, Frank. We'd have to be zookeepers to take these young moronic monkeys into custody, ha, ha, ha."

While the cops delighted in harassing and berating the Diablos, I observed Tink quietly closing his trunk. Jake lit up a cigarette to further enjoy the belittling of the detained greasers. We just stood-around enduring the cops' verbal abuse. The officers tried baiting us into a contrived verbal confrontation, but we wouldn't cooperate with their unscrupulous scheme. Since we didn't act fresh or nastily answer back, the aggravated law enforcers finally decided to let us go.

"But we're still gonna' keep an eye out for you young Dogwood Hollow hoodlums," Frank warned. Officer Jake casually flicked his cigarette to the ground. Everyone was shocked to see the grass and weeds on the side of the road ignite, and then a flash of fire leaped from the grass and weeds, and traveled like a lit fuse straight to the patrolmen's car. The gas tank exploded and the police cruiser quickly burst into flames.

An Edgely fireman was driving by, stopped his car, and told us he would report the blaze to the other department members upon reaching the firehouse. Ten minutes later, Chief Bradley arrived in his special vehicle, followed by two Edgely Fire Company engines. By the time the firemen had gotten to the blaze, the police cruiser had been destroyed. Several other cop cars pulled-up to investigate the accident scene. The Diablos hopped-back into the grimy black Plymouth, and during the mayhem, Tink gingerly pulled back onto Edgely Road.

"Well," Carnie declared. "I guess we'll have to postpone that second case of beer for a few days. That had to be one of the weirdest freakin' things I've ever seen."

Tinker started laughing incessantly. Robbie asked the psycho case what was making him act so goofy. "Ya' got goose feathers under your filthy armpits?"

"Listen to this incredible bull-shit," Tink communicated. "When the cop told me to open my trunk, I obliged. Then, I kept the trunk open for the next ten-minutes. I had a large jar of gas tucked inside to use for my carburetor if I ever ran out of fuel. When nobody was lookin', I unscrewed the lid and poured the gas all the way from the cop's car to where that fuck-head Jake was standin'. Not even you guys saw me do it. I gambled that the cop would throw his lit cigarette butt down near where I had secretly poured the trail of gas, and the dumb fuck did. Then, Officer Jake humorously incinerated his own patrol car."

We all busted our guts in reaction to Tink's remarkable genius. The gimpy mechanic had cleverly obliterated the cruiser, but he had cunningly made it look like womanizer Officer Jake had performed the dirty work.

"I'm sure old Jake and Frank will be called on the carpet this time," Robbie snickered, "because they're both guilty of carelessly wasting the taxpayers' money."

I especially felt good for Carnie. Jake was the cop who had been hittin' on *his* mom. My pal hurt much more on the inside about it than Tinker did. Tink seemed not to care about vengeance for his mother's infidelity. The poor excuse for a human being had just created the demolition because he (quite pure and simple) hated cops.

"Those shit face creeps will think twice before they ever dare to stop my car again," Tink smiled and concluded. "No stupid-assed cop is gonna' make a horse's rear end outa' me."

Tinker was not one to be taken lightly. When the maniac promised he would take action against someone or something, then that person needed to call *Lloyd's of London* right away to insure himself and his property to the max.

No kid dared fool around with Tinker after he had pulverized Cardinal Reagan High quarterback Phil Jackson a week later in March behind the Feed Bag. Jackson was making fun of Tinker's Davy Crockett coonskin hat and his 3-D glasses. Tink invited Phil to "step outside", and every teen customer in the place followed the two out the door. With a flurry of six vicious punches, Tink very efficiently knocked Phil's lights out. Then, Jeremy Foster turned around and arrogantly said to his astonished audience, "I suppose that goddamned bleeding college-bound freak is gonna' have to spend more time in the weight room. Another two years of liftin'," Tink boastfully asserted, "and he might be able to go a full-thirty-seconds of combat with me."

Three days later, Phil Jackson and three of his football teammates jumped Tink while the gimpy teen had been trekking between the Feed Bag and the Dairy DeLite. Tink was eventually pushed behind the custard stand where he suffered a black eye, a bloody nose, a swollen jaw, and a wounded ego. But bruises to a Diablo were like badges of honor, similar to the ribbons and medals worn by army generals. And so, Phil Jackson and his muscle-bound offensive linemen were added to the ever-growing list of Diablos' enemies.

Tinker could destroy anything with the greatest of ease, and conversely, the kid could repair anything he wanted. On the Sunday morning following his unfortunate fight with the four brawny jocks, I was waiting to have breakfast with "Chester Goode" at the Feed Bag. Tink made his appearance wearing his signature dirty coonskin hat, and a cracked lens in his weird 3-D glasses. Big band aids also graced his left forearm and right cheek.

I had been especially aggravated that particular morning because my wristwatch, which had been a cherished *Christmas* present from my parents, had stopped working.

"Howdy, J.W.," Tink greeted. "Did ya' wash your face in vinegar or something?"

I was still in a negative mood about my prized object of sentimental value not working. My attitude was slightly irritated by my volatile pal's joviality and criticism, but then I considered the consequences of what might happen if I abruptly answered the sociopath rudely. "Why do ya' say that nonsense about vinegar on my face?"

"Because you're sportin' a sourpuss in spades," Tink giggled, despite his own recently acquired injuries. His rare humor compelled me to be a trifle more polite.

"My watch is busted," I stated and overtly lamented. "And I think the mainspring must be broken." I had always desired to live in a perfect world, and when something didn't go right or was broken, I would characteristically sulk and fret from sheer frustration.

"Let me take a look at it. I'll repair it if it's fixable!"

Tinker was usually very sloppy and careless, but when it came to mechanical devices or motors, the guy was extremely meticulous and conscientious. Mr. Fix-it laid out two paper napkins from a Feed Bag table dispenser. The pieces were carefully placed upon the plastic red and white checkerboard tablecloth. Then, my grimy pal removed a very tiny screwdriver from his leather jacket. I couldn't fathom how the mechanical wizard could see anything through his weird, broken 3-D glasses, especially with that nasty bruise and scar that decorated the top of his right eyebrow.

Tinker deftly dismantled my timepiece, very cautiously placing every dial, every miniature spring, and every tiny wheel onto the paper napkins. "Now Words, here's the easy part. Jewelers can't keep no trade secrets from me."

After making several minor adjustments, the T Man reassembled the watch just as adroitly as he had fragmented it. I sat there dumbfounded, marveling and admiring his intricate skill. In his own way, my maverick greaser pal had exhibited the patience and art of an accomplished hospital surgeon. In a jiffy, the device had been reconstructed, and much to my satisfaction, the cherished watch was again ticking like new.

"How much do I owe ya'?" I politely asked, because my parents had always taught me that all debts should be paid, and all favors should somehow be reciprocated.

"Well, J.W., my services don't come cheap, ya' know," replied Tink as coolly as the potential Delhaas High drop-out could articulate. "So that'll be fifty-cents for gas, a cheese steak with fried onions, and a half-hour blowjob. Ya' can throw in another half-buck for a porno mag', in case ya' don't wanta' do the thirty-minute blowjob. That'll definitely get ya' off the hook for compensatin' my expert services."

Chapter 20
"Angie and Bubbles"

The third weekend of March rolled around pretty speedily. I had spent most of the month scheming-up a prank to play on Angie Palermo and Bubbles Messina. I convinced Bo, Carnie, and Tinker to endorse my superb plan. Bo was having a spat with Susie Parker, so the blond hunk needed some unique diversion to keep his hyperactive mind off his high testosterone level and excessive sperm count.

The four of us finalized our plans inside the Feed Bag the night before we initiated my grand strategy. The "commandos" were sitting at our favorite table opposite the Dairy DeLite.

Carnie and I were discussing comedian Lou Costello's death that had happened three weeks before on March 3, 1959. Lou was one of our film and TV favorites, and we knew and memorized many of his absurd routines by heart.

"He was only fifty when he kicked the bucket," Carnie sorrowfully stated. "What an unfortunate tragedy!"

"We'd better pack as much fun into life as we can," I added, "or pretty soon, that Grim Reaper freak will be prowlin' our bedrooms before we know it."

"Death's okay when it happens to somebody else," Tinker philosophically pitched-in. "But when it happens to you, the whole thing really sucks."

If Tinker said something stupid, then Bo had to say something even more convoluted. "I guess Costello's partner will now have to become an *abbot* in a monastery, and go ape looking for a *monk key*," Jokes asserted with a serious face.

Sensing an argument developing, I then adroitly changed the subject to my highly anticipated prank involving Angie and Bubbles. I was surprised that the other three guys wholeheartedly supported my idea. Even Bo Jalonec, who usually only saw merit in what originated inside his own skull, surprisingly gave me his unconditional approval.

Humans are creatures of habit. The Kamikazes would keep track of the Diablos' whereabouts and schedules, and likewise, we would surreptitiously monitor and keep an eye on the Ks daily activities. Each gang had its own surveillance network to keep its members informed of news, or impending trouble.

Every Sunday afternoon, Bubbles would drive her white '55 Thunderbird to an aunt's house in Tullytown to pick-up lasagna, spaghetti, and homemade Italian bread for a family dinner. Sometimes,

Angie Palermo would accompany her cousin on the predictable, leisurely errand.

While Carnie and I were out in his Mercury on reconnaissance missions, we noticed the same pattern being repeated every Sunday afternoon. That's what gave me the inspiration to contrive my tomfoolery involving *our* association with the Edgely Fire Company, along with our general displeasure with the news that the *Howdy Doody Show* would be taken off the television airwaves because the popular program was deemed to be non-educational.

Carnie, Jokes, Tink, and I immensely enjoyed the *Howdy Doody Show*. Buffalo Bob Smith had revealed on network TV that the MC was an avid *Philadelphia Phillies'* fan, and in so doing, the narrator immediately received my viewing patronage for his major league baseball team preference.

Carnie and I enjoyed the silliness of Flub-A-Dub; Tinker liked the grouchy disposition of Mr. Bluster; Jokes would check-out Princess Summer-Fall-Winter-Spring's bust and curves, and we all dug Buffalo Bob, the show's likeable master of ceremonies.

Our favorite *Howdy Doody Show* character had to be Clarabell, a mute clown with a painted face who featured an enlarged nose. Clarabell would always squirt unsuspecting guests and invited show characters with a seltzer bottle. Consequently, the idea of full seltzer bottles inspired me to take the Diablos standard mischief to new heights. Tinker, who had access to nearly anything, obtained three "temporarily borrowed" seltzer bottles for our personal use.

The Diablos could have gotten into big trouble if the part of my plan involving the Edgely Fire Department would have been discovered. Carnie drove Bo, Tink, and me to the Edgely Fire Hall on the first Sunday in April. All the regular members were either recovering from church services, or home having Sunday dinner with their families. We then "borrowed" three sets of visor-helmets, firemen's coats, and heavy boots. After we deposited the firemen's articles into Carnie's trunk, the '49 Merc sped-off to Tullytown, a small somnolent community on the *Delaware,* two-miles north of Edgely.

A Tullytown police car passed going in the opposite direction and fortunately, Carnie had slowed-down to twenty-five miles per hour in compliance with the hamlet's strictly enforced speed limit. Precision timing was paramount for us to effectively execute the sophisticated "commando mission". After the Tullytown cop had passed by, Jokes broke the silence by yelling into my ear, "That was a close call!" as the jester made his own close call, nearly shattering my right eardrum.

Carnie stopped his black Merc' on an overpass, and we anxiously awaited the appearance of Bubbles' white T-bird convertible. At exactly 3:15, right on schedule, the expensive sports car containing Bubbles negotiated a curve, and then the driver and her passenger Angie Palermo came into full view.

Jokes, Tink and I exited the Merc' in a hurry, and after Carnie opened the trunk, we quickly removed our visor-helmets, firemen's coats, and boots. Under our left armpits we concealed full seltzer bottles, which naturally had been conveniently provided by Tinker.

Carnie guarded his car atop the overpass as his three disguised pals slid down the steep embankment to the main road in and out of Tullytown. I had brought along a cigar box to collect donations for the Edgely Fire Company from Angie and Bubbles. The fact that Bubbles had the convertible's top down made me even more excited about implementing my easy mischief.

"J.W.," Bo announced. "Get prepared to see some nice wet breast flesh." Bo then winked at me, and pointed to his hidden seltzer bottle concealed under his left armpit.

Tinker, Bo, and I hailed the approaching white sports car. Bubbles reluctantly cooperated with our signal. Naturally, our faces were hidden behind the dark helmet-visors.

"Good afternoon, young ladies," I prefaced in a very mellow voice that seemed to echo throughout my helmet. "Would you fine ladies care to contribute to our volunteer fire department?" My feigned adult baritone must have sounded official, because I really had gotten the girls' undivided attention.

The Italian dolls dug deeply into their handbags for some loose change, evaluating the firemen's presence as a mere legitimate nuisance that accompanied responsible citizenship.

"Before you make your contributions," I continued, "you'll have to tell us which famous author wrote the famous short story 'The Tell-tale Heart'?"

Bubbles Messina's addled mind searched through its literary information base, which must have contained at least two bona fide American authors.

"That Jack London guy, I think," Bubbles responded as the Sicilian chick aggressively chomped on a large wad of bubblegum while fumbling for loose change. "Yeah, I'm sure it was Jack London!"

"What country was Jack London from?" I curtly asked.

"England, I think," the doll answered with a frown as the hot chick continued her seemingly futile search for loose silver coins.

"Tell me, then," I annoyingly proceeded. "Who wrote the short story 'The Pit and the Pendulum'?"

"What's with all this literature stuff? What is this, the *64,000 Dollar Question* or somethin'?" Angie Palermo testily inquired.

"No, it's '*I've Got a Secret!"* Jokes shouted as the three of us lifted our dark visors revealing our true identities, much to the astonishment of Angie and Bubbles.

The three Diablos raised and aimed our seltzer bottles at the two stunned chicks seated inside the white T-Bird. I was unaware that Tinker had rigged my seltzer bottle so that it wouldn't work. Then, Bo and Tinker pointed their functioning seltzer bottles at me, and the force of the liquids' impact knocked my fire helmet right off my head. I was drenched pretty well by the prodigious sprays that were hitting and battering my exposed face.

Angie and Bubbles laughed hardily when the broads realized that I had become the target of a practical joke that I thought had been intended for them.

"A little squirt will never hurt!" Jalonec joyfully shouted. "And J.W., don't let another one of your wet ideas put a damper on your day!" the jokester yelled while the fluid from the seltzer bottles continued to splash against both sides of my face.

After Bo and Tink had emptied their bottles at my expense, the three of us instantly fled the scene. Our aching legs awkwardly climbed the steep embankment back toward Carnie's '49 Merc'. Dr. C greeted us with enthusiastic handshakes, nearly coughing-up his spleen in roars of laughter.

On the drive back to the Edgely Fire Company, the other three guys sang the jingle, "Take speedy *Alka-Seltzer* and feel good again!" as the dissonant chorus emphasized the word Speedy, the mascot of the '50s *Alka-Seltzer* brand product.

"Next time J.W.," Bo elaborated, "we'll use *Alka-Seltzer* in those seltzer bottles instead of water." Everyone except me laughed lustily in response to Jokes' timely wit. I simply sat mum with a sullen expression featured on my miserable face, absorbing the full brunt of *their* self-indulgent emotional abuse.

Soon, the helmets, firemen's coats, and boots were safely returned to the Edgely Fire Station. Carnie drove us back to the Feed Bag where the other three celebrated their ingenious corruption of my well-planned practical joke. I then realized from my recent misadventure that it was indeed an unpleasant experience for anyone to be on the receiving end of spontaneous Diablos' furtive mischief.

On Monday afternoon, I was working in the back room at Hal's Delicatessen when Jokes, who occasionally worked next door at Harley's Hardware, paid me a visit. I really didn't want to be bothered with his ludicrous nonsense, because I still had to peel five more pounds of spuds for potato salad, and shred seven more heads of lettuce to fill Hal's coleslaw orders.

"Guess what J.W.?" Jokes all-too-politely asked, exhibiting a mischievous grin complementing his handsome countenance.

"Too hot to guess," I answered as I turned the kitchen fan's dial to "High". But Bo's surprise visit had me curious. "What do ya' have on your mind besides brain warts? How many times have you had serious brain surgery?"

"Ya' know that hourglass neighbor of yours, Angie Palermo," Bo declared, immediately getting my attention. "Well, she came into Harley's this morning and had duplicate keys made for her daddy's house and for his spiffy ice blue '59 Caddy."

I failed to see any major significance or relevance in Bo's statement. His revelation all seemed like normal hardware store business. There had to be more explicit details to account for Jalonec's obvious excessive excitement.

"That's really nice, Bo," I automatically replied. "Did she recognize ya' from the Tullytown seltzer bottle incident? Of course, she knows your face from workin' at the Feed Bag!"

"No. Ace Roberts took care of her while I was secretly watchin' the whole transaction from the back room," Bo confidentially revealed. "Then, I called Ace over the store intercom and asked him to do the Diablos a mighty big favor."

"Okay, Bo. Ya' now you've got my attention. What did ya' ask Ace to do?" I queried. "Just give me the damned *key* details."

"I told Ace to grind-out another set of house and car keys for possible future Diablos' use", Jalonec patiently disclosed. "And so, consequently good buddy, here the are the duplicates. Don't say I never gave ya' anything!"

I stared incredulously at the duplicate keys on a chain, dangling from Bo's thumb and forefinger. I couldn't believe my eyes. Two keys to two separate Pandora's boxes. The diabolical possibilities were innumerable. Now the Diablos could clandestinely enter Sal Palermo's house and car at will.

"Those keys will only open up Sal's house and wheels," Bo expressed, "but they won't unlock the door leading to Angie's heart. If ya' mind your P's and Q's, J.W., I might give ya' a few vital lessons on successful womanizin' when I finally got time to eventually get around to it."

"Thanks a lot, Bo," I replied, somewhat confused. "But at this point, I'd be happy with just *a lock* from Angie's hair. Ace is so cool that he should someday open-up a chain of hardware stores!"

"J.W. Your last statement was two-thirds of a pun, p-u!"

I could tell that Jokes did not appreciate the idea of me successfully emulating his technique by making one of his nutty ridiculous riddles soon accompanied by a horrendous pun. "Ya' know Words, *limitation* is the most-sincere form of flattery," my linguistic idol quoted as the gang's comedian paraphrased and crucified a famous aphorism, while simultaneously and skillfully pulverizing my vulnerable ego. I knew right then-and-there that I had met my linguistic match, as I helplessly stood quiet in total defeat.

Chapter 21
"Tinker Gets Rolling"

The last Saturday in March of '59, I was riding shotgun with Tinker, who was recklessly driving his black '49 Plymouth. We were aimlessly cruising through downtown Bristol, and Tink and I were having simultaneous sugar rushes. We stopped outside a corner candy store; entered the establishment; chatted with the affable clerk, and we each bought two *Clark Bars,* a pair of *Three Musketeers,* and two *TastyKake Butterscotch Krimpets*. Our rather hungry appetites then washed-down the delectable sweets with "no deposit-no return" bottles of *Pepsi-Cola,* the official, non-alcoholic beverage of the Diablos.

As my gimpy buddy and I exited the small candy store, we were surprisingly greeted and accosted by eight malicious Kamikazes. The hostile creeps happened to be motoring through Bristol looking for fancy hubcaps to steal and to later sell on the greaser black market. After recognizing Tink's dilapidated black '49 coupe, the punks devised a quick plan, which was fairly clever for rednecks of their primitive intellectual capacity.

Cummings and Popeye led the bellicose entourage, which had surprised and surrounded Tink and me. The principal instigators were backed-up by Jake Mullins, Spits, Worm, and three other hoodlums whom I never had the displeasure of meeting.

"Well, if it ain't crotch breath and cootie face," Cummings sarcastically began his mean-spirited preamble. "What church does your lousy choir practice in?"

'These two creeps and their punk Kenwood goons are the last scum I want to see on a deserted Bristol street,' I thought. 'What kind of flowers do I want at my funeral?'

"Too bad ya' goddamned queer-gears have your bellies full with candy junk," Popeye commented. "Pretty soon you'll both be barfin' your guts out on the pavement." The cruel villain's threats were also laced with sarcasm, but in the final analysis, the threats were very real and very fearful.

"Hope you' expendable hose-noses like rock and roll," Spits facetiously added, showing some decent vocabulary mastery. "Because you're gonna' be doin' a lot of rockin' and rollin' pretty damned soon."

"No switchblades or guns are gonna' work this freakin' time," Worm emphatically declared. "Ya' two fags are gonna' be more fun than a barrel of monkeys with deadly V.D."

The insidious Ks had been mocking our pride, and the lowlife were doing a very good job at it. My psyche felt weak and demoralized. My head was thinking that Tink would ultimately come to the rescue again, so I confidently and boldly addressed our assailers.

"All you Kamikazes are a bunch of *zeroes,"* I stated, not realizing my remark's ironic-but-humorous dual meaning.

Tinker, who always had a sense of greaser street justice, demanded parity in the anticipated fight with the Ks.

"If ya' jive turkeys wanna' rumble, why don't ya' do it when the sides are even, like they were that night at the telephone booth," Tink demanded. "J.W. and me will take any two of ya'."

I really didn't want to brawl with any of the lethal Kamikazes, but since Tinker had so haughtily volunteered my services, I felt I had little recourse to do anything else but fight.

"Oh, is that right?" Popeye returned. "We don't want to fight you creeps right now. But I promise ya', you're both gonna' be in a rumble you'll never forget. Ha, ha, ha, ha!"

And with those prophetic words, the eight savages jumped Tinker and me; lifted our carcasses up into the air, and then held our arms down by our hips. The perpetrators squeezed my smelly buddy and me back-to-back and feet first into a tall metal waste barrel that had been situated outside the modest side-street candy store's entrance. The eight violent delinquents rotated the huge drum onto its side and then proceeded to merrily roll the large container (with us inside) down the center of Pine Street, which soon dipped into a steep slope.

All I could see was sky and pavement repeated over and over as the barrel barreled down the decline. Three cars nearly collided at the intersection of Pine and Bath Road as Tink and I careened on through, picking-up more speed all the way.

My unkempt pal and I were sandwiched inside the metal drum pretty tightly. I was almost glad we were rolling down the street back-to-back because (during a moment of reflection) I could only imagine what Tinker's post *Clark Bar, Three Musketeers, TastyKake Krimpets,* and *Pepsi'* breath might smell like when combined with the other miscellaneous odors filtering-out from his filthy body. Most of all, I was quite glad that my lungs didn't have to inhale Tinker's stomach acid face to face.

I could hear the idiotic Kamikazes singing, "Roll out the Barrel" somewhere from far behind our dizzying rotations, but then, a familiar clanging was discernible several-hundred-feet ahead. Flashing red lights suddenly appeared ahead. The Pine Street railroad gates were descending, and a locomotive tugging a line of freight cars was on a collision path with our spinning drum. Tink and I rumbled under the railroad gates and then zoomed across the tracks, just barely being missed by the huge whistle-blowing diesel engine.

My grungy pal and I were sick in our stomachs and unable to move an inch as we kept wildly rotating, back-to-back, down Pine Street. We were screaming, cursing, heaving, and gasping, but our exhortations were to no avail. The street curved to the right, when the huge drum hopped the curb and then slammed into an old abandoned warehouse's brick wall. After bouncing off *that* solid surface, the cylinder deflected to the left, where it smashed into a fire hydrant, and then finally, our mode of transportation came to a stop in the middle of the street.

Several civic-minded eyewitnesses tried extricating Tink and me from our uncomfortable incarceration, but their valiant endeavors proved unsuccessful. We were jammed-in so tightly that Tink and I could have passed for Siamese twins. The Kamikazes had viewed the entire travesty from their vantage point located a quarter-mile up the incline near the candy store.

Soon thereafter, sirens from several emergency vehicles could be heard. Two police patrol cars and three fire engines from the Bristol Fire Company all converged upon the hectic scene.

The Bristol Fire Chief had a visiting colleague by his side. Edgely's Chief Bradley had been visiting in town to inspect his neighboring department's shiny new fire engine. Chief B. quickly identified his two junior firemen snuggly trapped inside the enormous barrel.

"Chief Pinto," Chief Bradley laughed. "These two young daredevils inside the barrel concoct the most imaginative rescue situations I've ever seen in over forty years of service. Their brilliant stunts border on being sheer genius."

"Excuse me, Chief Bradley," the Bristol Chief answered, "but these nutcase kids appear to be two dumb simpletons trapped inside a common steel drum to me."

"Now, Lou," Chief Bradley insisted, "I've personally seen these extraordinary boys in action before. Believe you me, when I tell you all about the telephone booth affair; and about the mailboxes; and about the *Delaware River* fiasco over a couple mugs of draft beer, you're gonna' laugh so hard you might just piss your kidneys right out of your body."

Listening to the adult exchange, I really felt like a stupid moron. But when all the gossiping onlookers suspected that I actually *was* a stupid moron by virtue of tangible evidence, then my fragile ego became anchored-down by great embarrassment.

Tinker was having dry heaves inside the tight quarters while the rescue crew was preoccupied slicing-open the barrel with their specialized cutting tools. After ten-minutes of meticulous cutting, four lips were pulled and then rolled back, and Tink and I were finally liberated from the multi-functional canister.

"Come on, Lou," Chief Bradley began suggesting. "Let's go over to your station and have a few cold brewskis. Then, I'll tell you all about some of these strange lads' rather unbelievable adventures."

Tinker and I were really angry at the humiliation we had suffered at the hands of the odious Kamikazes. We traveled back to Levittown like a pair of phlegmatic zombies. The Ks had gone way too far.

Later that night, Bo Jalonec approached Tinker and me inside the Feed Bag. Bo had heard of the spectacular barrel incident through the greaser grapevine. That night Jalonec made a rather clever observation about our near-fatal freight train encounter. "J.W. and Tink," Bo gleefully communicated. "Those wicked Kamikazes really have some loco-motives."

"J.W.," Tink added, ignoring Jokes joke. "The damned Ks have gone over the edge. I promise ya', I'm gonna' give 'em some near-death experiences."

I had to do something to adequately distract Tinker from going to jail for the rest of his life while pursuing his abhorrent revenge. No Kamikaze was worth that kind of mortal sacrifice.

Bo was still on the outs with Susie, so in order to distract us from engaging in dangerous K retribution, I organized a project that required some nifty teamwork. I knew that Tink loved insects, and also woodworking. Jokes, who needed to get his mind off Susie and her furry hungry cat, assiduously helped-out with the needed artwork.

First, Bo sketched-out six diagrams. Then, with my descriptions, the talented artist provided Tink with the exact dimensions of three marching band and three sports' trophies located in the central display case inside the main Cardinal Reagan High corridor. Tinker next carefully manufactured and duplicated the half-dozen trophies right-down to the smallest minute detail.

The last Saturday of March, around midnight, Tink, Carnie, Bo, Robbie, and I broke into Cardinal Reagan High. It was really easy after Tink competently picked the lock to a janitor's entrance. Then, we climbed a short flight of stairs to the main corridor, where the bulk of the display cabinets were located. We stealthily switched the six authentic trophies with the six counterfeit ones Tinker had produced. The big deal was that Mr. Fix-it had inserted active termite and ant colonies into each of the six newly-manufactured trophies.

The Diablos clandestinely exited the school with the six original awards as souvenirs. Tink wanted to keep the stolen trophies as evidence of our illustrious secret caper. Since we wanted to get Jeremy's mind off of the Kamikaze's Bristol barrel fiasco, everyone agreed that the irrepressible "Chester Goode" should keep "the booty".

The following night inside the Feed Bag, Bo Jalonec summed-up the successful Diablos' raid. "For Father Malcolm, those planted six insect colonies could wind-up as a real catas*trophe*."

"What about the six dildos Tink got us to put inside the second display case?" fascinated Robbie Wilkinson curiously inquired. "Stanley Tezeeker and his egghead buddies can now check-out Homo *erect*us on Monday morning!"

"Not only that," Carnie chuckled and conveyed. "Those nudie decks of cards and porno' pictures we put into the third display case should also get some special notice."

Traditionally, the Cardinal Reagan student body never really paid much attention to the school banners, plaques, and myriad awards that adorned the various main corridor display cabinets. But the following Monday morning, throngs of ardent sex-scholars were intensely scrutinizing the new unique novelty items on exhibit.

Father Malcolm soon eliminated the intriguing sex displays, but the flourishing bug infestation that Tinker had coyly planted inside the cabinets went undetected, and the frisky insects soon migrated into the building's walls. Feeling vulnerable, the Franciscan head honcho put locks on the cabinets, but his action was all in vain, because Tinker could easily penetrate any security system the future thief wanted.

Bo very aptly summarized the situation that night at the Feed Bag. "Now, the Diablos really have to bug the Kamikazes," Jalonec suggested. "Hey Tink," Bo continued his verbal exposition. "Ya' should've put a colony of carpenter ants in one of those replacement trophies to repair the damage done by the damned roving ants and hungry termites."

Chapter 22
"High School Hi Jinks"

How could I ever forget April 1, 1959? A few Diablos and several Kamikazes schemed-up a neat *April Fool's Day* prank to further aggravate Father Malcolm. Carnie had persuaded Popeye and me to start a fake fight inside the school cafeteria during lunchtime. A boisterous crowd encircled Messina and me, as we wrestled our way all over the tiled cafeteria floor. Father Malcolm, Father Adrian, and Brother Timothy hustled-over to quell the pretend altercation. When the three referees arrived at the fracas area of conflict, every kid in the lunchroom yelled out, "*April Fool!*"

Father Malcolm was incensed because the fight had been contrived to make him and his pious colleagues appear "foolish". The angered Franciscan didn't like being exploited as *our* designated puppet. The head disciplinarian grabbed Popeye and me by our necks and escorted us down to the Reagan gymnasium. After Father M. briefly conferred with Coach Cocharan, the main gym instructor ambled-over to the equipment room, and in another sixty-seconds, returned with two pair of boxing gloves.

"If you two clowns wanna' fake a fight, this time you're gonna' have to wage real combat with the gloves on," Coach Cocharan grimly indicated to Popeye and me.

No sooner had the coach uttered those sagacious words that Father Malcolm made an announcement from his office over the school intercom. "There will be an assembly in the school gym in five minutes. All teachers are directed to take their classes in single file to the gymnasium immediately."

After the entire school enrollment crowded into the huge gym, Father Malcolm explained the reason for the emergency assembly. "The two students who had mocked religious authority in the cafeteria will be fighting with boxing gloves on," Malcolm informed his interested audience. "This is what happens to young anarchists who try to undermine the school administration. The bout will not conclude until either someone is knocked cold, or someone needs serious medical attention. Let the best idiot win."

During the first minute of sparring with Popeye, I felt as if I was a Roman gladiator doing battle in the *Colosseum*. We circled each other as some loud spectators in the student body shouted words of encouragement, while other more annoying personages vehemently yelled their criticisms for a lack of bloodshed. Father Malcolm got on the microphone and told the assembly to boo and jeer until something major happened.

Soon, Popeye reacted to the intense peer pressure by stopping his bobbing and weaving, and next, the junior Rocky Marciano started pummeling me with stiff punches. I felt the sting of his jabs and the fury of his left hooks. Messina's clenched fists bundled, in boxing gloves, were having an immediate devastating toll on my faltering boxing confidence.

"Hope ya' didn't eat too much spinach today," I quipped, out of the right side of my bleeding mouth.

"I've swallowed-down seven cans, ya' dumb hundred-twenty-pound weaklin'," Messina callously replied with a mean body jolt.

I was getting my lights knocked-out by flurries of right crosses, jabs, uppercuts, and body smashes. Bruno certainly was much stronger and much more skilled at boxing than I was. The devastating force of his punches resulted in sharp excruciating pain for my chest, face, and arms. Even though I was being bruised and battered, I felt I had to defend the honor of the Diablos and my own self-esteem, so I gallantly fought back.

Carnie saw the carnage unfolding and felt partially responsible for arranging the false *April Fool* fight in the cafeteria. During the mayhem, my Diablo friend slipped-out of the gym with no one noticing. The loyal C Man made his path into the hall where the clever kid quickly pulled the fire alarm. 'Thank goodness! I've been saved-by-the-bell,' I thought.

The fire drill took ten-minutes to complete, and after everyone filed back from the school parking lot and sidewalks into the gym, Father Malcolm resumed the classic boxing match.

Again, Popeye was really hammering and pummeling me something fierce. Luckily, Carnie had sneakily gone to the second-floor corridor and alertly pulled a second fire alarm. Everyone again filed-out of the gymnasium. Father Malcolm figured he'd better dismiss the student body back to their respective classes so that the over-enthusiastic students could be under direct, individual, faculty supervision. That strategy would prevent the anonymous, wily Diablo from pulling a third unauthorized alarm, thus undermining the challenged administration's reign of terror.

I certainly escaped the boxing battle less scathed than I would have if Carnie hadn't decisively interceded and alleviated my drastic pounding. That night at the Feed Bag, I personally thanked Carnie for his intrepid actions during the one-sided boxing match.

"Carnie, Father Malcolm almost got me killed today. I'm sure now that Popeye hits harder than Ingemar Johansson does."

My buddy was very sympathetic and supportive. "I know J.W. I figured it was either ambulance or hearse time for you unless I did something quick. The fire alarm was the only thing I could think of."

I really felt indebted to Carnie for his drastic fast thinking under intense fire. "Thanks for saving my life. Now, what prank can we do to repay Father Malcolm?"

"I'll talk to Tink and the guys," Carnie promised. "And we'll think of something good. Malcolm's gonna' regret ever playin' with Diablo fire. It'll be mental asylum again for the already-insane sadist."

Father Malcolm owned an old Volkswagen Beetle. The brown bomb was his pride and joy, but it soon became the target for Diablos' commando tactics. The military maneuver Carnie, Jokes, and I created would require the excellent labor of twelve Diablos. As usual, Quinn was out painting the town with Patty Van Arsdale, and the rest of the Diablo executive committee knew that our leader would never approve of our planned vendetta against a priest, even if that priest were someone as diabolical as Father Malcolm.

Jokes, Carnie, Tinker, Robbie, and I managed to recruit Ace Roberts, Slip Carson, Chuckie and Jimmy Callahan, and fledglings Gene McCann, Jim Amari, and Al Keller.

When the night of our scheduled "military maneuver" arrived, four motivated commandos traveled in separate cars belonging to Jalonec, Carnie, and Tinker. After parking in the Levittown Shop-A-Rama's expansive lot, we walked in twos at five-minute intervals across Levittown Parkway to the back door of the Franciscan rectory.

The objective of the Diablos' secret raid was to carry Father Malcolm's brown VW Beetle to a nearby woods', a distance of three-hundred-feet. After completing "Phase I" of the operation, we rolled the VW over until it was lying on its roof.

Then, the twelve of us lifted-up the tiny car, and sandwiched the foreign auto upside-down between three stout pin oak trees, which formed a rough isosceles triangle. The dozen Diablos then stood on the inverted chassis and jumped up and down to compress the small auto' between the trees, until their barks scraped off.

"Looks like this baby's ready for the old volks home," Bo aptly and germanely joked.

"I hope Malcolm's smart enough not to try drivin' this here thing outa' here upside down," Carnie giggled.

The next morning, Father Malcolm telephoned Tinker's father's gas station to dispatch an employee to come to the woods behind the Franciscan rectory to dislodge his Volkswagen from its stationary, upside-down, wedged position.

Tink pulled-up to the rectory in one of his pop's tow trucks. Jeremy told Malcolm that the job would have to entail two tow trucks because of the serious nature of the foreign car's strange entrapment.

"Son, do I know you?" Malcolm asked.

"No Padre," Tink indicated. "I went to Delhaas High, but luckily, I dropped-out. I was sixteen at the time," replied the junior mechanic. "Padre, have any kids ever dropped-out of your school?" my lame buddy devilishly asked.

Father Malcolm pretended not to hear Tinker's very profound question, so the sly priest completely ignored his inquiry. "When can you get my car free?"

"Father, just hold your frisky horses. My pop and me will be here before seven a.m. tomorrow morning to get your wheels outa' that clump of trees."

The following sunrise, Tinker and his dad showed-up at the rectory in their reliable twin tow trucks. Father Malcolm stepped outside his front door, and much to his astonishment, his brown Volkswagen was parked neatly in the asphalt parking area right next to the priests' dormitory. The twelve Diablos had returned the night before; removed the tiny auto from between the trees; hauled it to the rectory, and left the compact vehicle exactly where it had been before *we* had ever tampered with it.

"Padre, what the heck is goin' on here?" Tinker asked.

"Son, I wish I knew," Malcolm answered as the cleric shook his head in disbelief. "You yourself saw my car yesterday mashed upside-down and lodged between those oak trees in the woods over there. Some really peculiar things have been happening around here lately."

Tinker and his father (who was in on the slick trick) acted confused and annoyed. "Yes Padre, but I think you're playin' some kind of stupid mind game with us," Tink skeptically replied. "My pop and I came all the way out here to get your car out, but it's already out!"

"I really can't explain it son," confessed Malcolm, scratching his partially bald head. "It's all a giant conundrum!"

"Well, Father, I can't rightly say what kind of *drum* it's like, but even though we've witnessed some kind of weird miracle here," Tinker's dad evaluated, "that'll still be a nominal twenty-dollars service charge for two trucks to come all the way out here for absolutely nothin'."

"Yeah Padre, ya' better raid the old collection basket, or steal some bread from the Little Sisters of the Poor!" Tink bluntly contributed.

Malcolm reluctantly forked-over two ten-dollar-bills for his already retrieved vehicle. Tink and his father left the premises, pretentiously acting angry at being called-out of their Bath Road gas station on an absurd false alarm.

When the Diablos had removed the VW from its entrapment between the three oak trees the night before, Tinker had rearranged several important wires inside the targeted car's engine. The auto would not start again in the Franciscan Friars' parking lot; either inside a tree cluster; in quicksand, or in perfect weather conditions.

So, even though the foreign car was outside the rectory, Malcolm could not use it. Of course, the frustrated disciplinarian didn't discover *that* vital fact until Tinker and his pop were driving back to the family gas station on Bath Road.

On the following night, the twelve Diablos returned to reenact the first sensational upside-down stunt, and when the Cardinal Reagan disciplinarian stepped-out of his dormitory the next morning, Malcolm again observed his little brown car flipped onto its roof, and wedged between the three sturdy pin oak trees.

Upon seeing the "optical illusion," Father Malcolm slipped back into his mental depression, collapsing to the asphalt. Brother Timothy called for an ambulance, and the chief Franciscan was soon readmitted into *Lower Bucks County Hospital* for thorough bed rest, professional medical observation, and gradual convalescence.

Father Malcolm was released from his rehab' a week later to resume his administrative duties at the frenzy-oriented high school. Carnie and I deliberately played hooky that day. We met-up with Tinker in the woods in back of the rectory. The three of us desired to welcome Malcolm back to the rigors associated with his daily work regimen. Our indispensable weapons that we had in our possession were three concealed cans of whipped cream. We also carried along three small garden snakes, and two bowling balls, which were deviously cloaked inside monogrammed bags.

Tinker had jimmied the lock on Phil Jackson's white 'Vette in the "Student Parking Area" before he met Carnie and me next to the all-too-familiar three oak trees. One bowling ball and bag belonged to Jackson, and the other bowling ball and bag to Phil's Thornridge Lanes' partner, Popeye Messina. Wednesday was the school bowling league day from four to six p.m. over at the "T. Alleys", so the Diablos knew that the pair of bowling balls would be in Phil Jackson's trunk just the way they would be any other Wednesday.

Tinker had it in for Jackson ever since the beating that Phil and three of his jock buddies had administered to the gas station mechanic behind the Dairy DeLite. And I still wanted to even the score with Popeye for beating the stuffing out of me during the *April Fools Day* gymnasium assembly. Now, it was *our* turn to "even the score".

Bo was officially playing hooky from his West 'Philly Catholic High that Wednesday. According to our plan, Carnie, Tink, and I met-up with Jalonec in the third floor "Boys' Lavatory". Stanley Tezeeker, who must have been suffering from a rare and chronic bowel disorder, was taking another dump, but this time the egghead was seated in the third toilet seat stall.

"Stanley's probably spankin' his tiny baby monkey," Carnie whispered, noticing yellow and green diamond socks showing under the stall.

"Those signature socks are a sure giveaway," I observed and quietly described.

"Stanley's gonna' see so much cream flyin' he's gonna' think he's Paul Bunyan havin' a super orgasm," Bo softly snickered.

Carnie, Tink, and I monitored the stall, while Bo watched the hallway door. According to our fine design, Carnie said "Edgar", Tink said "Allan", and I yelled "Poe". The three of us then fired our whipped cream from our full cans over the top of the stall with great ferocity. Stanley was squirted and hit with a wicked white blitzkrieg he'd never forget, and when we were through with our mischief, Tezeeker must have resembled a one hundred-twenty-five-pound sundae.

"Ahhhhhhhhh! What the fudge!" the lame gutless nerd yelped four times. Those oral interjections were followed by a shrill intonation of incomprehensible egghead jargon.

Again, Stanley was made a victim of Diablos' stupidity and ridicule. After we rolled the three-empty whipped cream cans under his stall, the Diablos darted-out of the Boys Lavatory in a hurry.

Tinker had kept the three two-foot-long garden snakes in a leather pouch, which the scheming prankster wore around his waist. Without knocking, the C Man stepped into the third floor "Girls Lavatory". It was unoccupied at the time, and as Jokes, Carnie, and I impatiently stood guard outside, Tink placed a snake inside each of the three toilets. Then, the unscrupulous intruder carefully closed the flat lids to conceal his naughty tricks. Seven minutes later, we witnessed three screaming girls scurry-out of the bathroom, because the female students thought that three king cobras had snatched at their snatches.

Jokes had assigned me the duty of carrying the two bowling balls inside the pilfered monogrammed bags. Not only were the bags identified as "Phil Jackson" and "Popeye Messina", but also the bowling balls were appropriately initialed "P.J." and "P.M".

Carnie, Jokes, and I knew that every Wednesday Jackson and Messina would cut Sister Filomena's English class and hang-out in the first-floor "Boys' Lavatory". We cautiously descended two flights of steps to reach the bottom floor. The four of us spotted Father Malcolm conversing with Brother Timothy two-hundred-feet or so down the empty corridor.

"Let's get rollin'," Tink suggested.

"It takes balls to do what we're gonna' attempt," Jokes commented.

"Edgar", I hollered. "Allan", yelled Carnie. "Poe" Jokes and Tinker shrieked in unison.

Carnie and Bo rolled Popeye and Phil's bowling balls down the long shiny corridor, pretending that they were sharing the same alley over at Thornridge Lanes. Father Malcolm and Brother Timothy heard the very distinct rumbles approaching. The perplexed pair mutually became intensely petrified in their tracks.

"Light up a *Lucky Strike!*" Bo gleefully cackled.

Both hysterical clergymen leaped-up into the air. Neither was hit by rolling thunder, but the appalled Franciscans both fell to the terrazzo tile floor, and the prank victims were very slow rising to their feet after surviving their rather strange ordeal.

Father Malcolm soon did some smart-but-erroneous detective work. The mischief investigator checked the initials on the bowling balls and was sagacious enough to match-up the inscribed letters with the monogrammed bags that the Diablos had conveniently left behind at the other end of the corridor.

Phil Jackson and Bruno Messina were summoned to the "Main Office" from Sister Filomena's English class. When Malcolm discovered that the two were *AWOL* from class, the pair was suspended from school on charges of insolent behavior, cutting classes, and sacrilegious violence specifically directed toward hallowed religious personages.

Phil and Bruno were also questioned about a pornographic movie that had been partially shown in Sister Jacinta's religion class, which Tinker had switched with another film on the projector reel when the classroom had been empty.

Malcolm also blamed Messina and Jackson for the obscene dildos and nudie cards that had been found inside the Cardinal Reagan trophy display cabinets, but lacking any confessions and direct evidence, those separate prosecutions were put on hold.

Later that day, Tinker drove Carnie and me to the Edgely Fire Company. We spent the rest of the afternoon playing pool, shuffleboard, darts, and cards in the fireman's upstairs lounge. We drank at least five *Pepsi's* each, and ate an abundance of bagged popcorn and peanuts. At three-fifteen, an excited Bo Jalonec ascended the fire company's wooden steps to join our select company and make a revealing announcement.

"Guess what!" Bo chuckled, partially out of breath. "Robbie told me that after school dismissal let out, at least fifteen pest extermination trucks pulled into the Reagan parking lot. Tink's two dozen hungry termite and ant colonies are still alive and reproducing!"

Chapter 23
"Looking for UFOs"

The next Sunday in April, the Diablos wanted to experience contact with interplanetary space aliens. Jokes told the guys over the phone that Quinn was having a lover's quarrel with Patty Van Arsdale, and that our Diablos' leader would meet the rest of us at dusk in the grassy field behind Robbie's house, separating Junewood and Dogwood Hollow. The flying saucer patrol idea was just an oddball excuse for the Diablos to get together, commiserate, and shoot the bull.

Carnie picked-up Jokes, Tinker and me at Jalonec's Junewood place. Since we had about an hour to kill before our highly anticipated flying saucer surveillance, Carnie decided to take a casual ride through Bristol. The driver wanted to hear how duplicates of Angie's house and car keys had especially become the Diablos' property.

The guys then ambitiously discussed '50s flying saucer movies like *This Island Earth, War of the Worlds,* and *The Day the Earth Stood Still.* Carnie's '49 Merc' obediently braked at a Bristol traffic signal.

Jokes Jalonec was riding shotgun, and I was seated directly behind him. Bo and I glanced to our right and noticed a couple "making out" in an old green '50 Studebaker parked in front of a record shop. The two were involved in heavy petting and French kissing and were totally oblivious to our scrutiny. My big mouth had to shout some criticism out of Carnie's back window to adequately impress my equally sarcastic friends.

"Are you two weirdos crazy?" I screamed at the top of my lungs. "Ya' dingbats are daring death. Ya' might as well stick your tongues up each other's rear ends seven times," I hollered as I alluded to Bo's esoteric 'Seven Asshole Principle'. "You're both gonna' die from a wicked bacteria overdose."

The other Diablos chuckled in appreciation of my uncharacteristic audacity. I believed that I had merely caused a bit of levity.

Jokes observed that the guy's left hand was way down the girl's pedal pushers so the occasional buffoon loudly sang, "Do you know the Muffin Man, the Muffin Man, the Muffin Man?"

The totally annoyed male raised his head in our direction and yelled, "What the fuck is goin' on?" The fellow was obviously very upset at being jeered and insulted in front of his fair damsel.

The Studebaker driver then faced me and when the lover boy looked squarely at my features, my heart sank into my bowels as I realized that *he* was Cummings.

"I should've known it would be you, you pinheaded slime ball!" Cummings yelled and rankled. "Ya' didn't learn your lesson in that phone booth, or inside that garbage barrel, did ya'?"

I hadn't at first recognized the Kamikaze kingpin in his new girl's ugly green Studebaker. Cynthia Miller was a real zit-pussed skank. The hussy was perhaps the sleaziest-looking wench in all of Bucks County, and her rusty car, with its faded paint-job, looked like it recently had won first prize in a demolition derby. I never had expected to see Cummings in anything but his formidable '52 Ford. The light turned green and Carnie reflexively hit the gas pedal.

"My first two major Levittown enemies were Popeye and Sal Palermo," I reminded the guys. "And now with Cummings, that's worse than a wrestlin' triple tag-team combination of Antonio Rocca, the Butcher, and Gorgeous George."

"Ya' could throw in Dracula, too," Bo authoritatively added, "because as ya' know J.W., right now it looks like you're goin' down for the Count."

"Cummings won't mess with ya' right now," Tinker speculated and predicted. "There's four of us and only one of him, and I could beat the shit and piss out of Cummings all by myself!"

But Carnie thought that the idea of having more enemies was "super cool" and adventurous. Then, Tinker matter-of-factly agreed with Carnie's peculiar assessment.

Tinker was a violence addict of sorts. His chief drugs were fighting and danger. Jeremy needed to invent excuses to destroy property or to deliberately maim someone. The tough kid loved going to the edge with some unfortunate foe, and we all suspected that someday it would always be a prospective opponent who would mysteriously die from tumbling off a cliff, or getting killed by a bite from Tink's rabid pet raccoon.

"Don't forget the cops, too," Tink casually contributed. "They try to make jackasses out of us greasers. They're still gonna' regret hasslin' me and Carnie and pursuing our moms."

"Tink's right for once," Carnie concurred. My sensitive pal also resented cops because of *his* mother's promiscuity. "What's teen life without a few thrills and a little damned excitement?" Carnie theorized and expressed. "Who wants to sit in a rickety rockin' chair in an old age home and have nothin' excitin' to remember or talk about?"

Of course, Bo Jalonec couldn't keep his mouth shut for too long. "Until ya' freakin' jerk-weeds do something drastic to the fuzz, all your cheap talk is a *cop*out to me," concluded and jested the somewhat fascinating "Riddle Man".

Before long the guys were back in not-too-pleasant Levittown. Carnie's "James Dean Special" hopped the curb on Junewood Drive, and within seconds, we joined Quinn, who was waiting patiently, leaning against the front fender of his legendary '42 Ford.

Quinn's black coupe was parked next to Tinker's '49 Plymouth. Earlier that day Robbie Wilkinson had borrowed Tink's car to drive over to Morrisville to buy a part for Ace Roberts street-machine. When R.W. returned to Dogwood Hollow, the key Diablo discreetly left the car behind *his* house for Tink to reclaim.

"Where's Robbie?" I inquired, just to make idle conversation.

"Ace finally got his wheels goin'," Quinn somberly explained.

And then Tinker's foul mouth had to take over and totally corrupt the benign conversation. "R.W figured Ace and him would hustle a couple of sluts on cheap dates, and then check the broads' engine oil with their erect dipsticks."

Carnie noticed that Quinn was becoming aware and concerned about Tinker's foul mouth oratory. "R.W. is on a double date with Ace over at the Langhorne Drive-in. They're gonna' see the *Amazing Colossal Man* and *It Came from beneath the Sea*," the C Man clarified.

It was common Diablo practice for guys to lend each other cars when favors were needed, so it was quite understandable that Robbie had done a favor for Ace, and Tink had concurrently done one to accommodate Robbie.

All the while, Quinn remained leaning against his superb Ford's left front fender. Our head honcho was quietly puffing on a *Camel* cancer stick. I noticed Quinn's long black hair, perfectly meshed in the back, forming an enviable duck's ass, which was accentuated with Elvis' sideburns and a characteristic razor cut at the base of his neck. Quinn always kept his *Camels* in a plastic box, rolled-up in the right sleeve of his white tee shirt.

I comprehended some aspects of Quinn's mind. I surmised that our leader thought it was stupid for the Diablos to be scanning the twilight sky for flying saucers mysteriously piloted by super-superior space aliens. I reckoned *he* just wanted to spend some time with the guys to let us know he hadn't forgotten about us while he was trying to patch things up with Patty.

"Think we'll see any four-legged space visitors?" Carnie asked Quinn, who at that moment seemed to be having a supernatural premonition of something bad about to happen.

"Yeah, Quinn's lookin' at one now!" interrupted Jalonec while pointing at Carnie.

"All this flying saucer stuff is because people are afraid of atomic bombs," Quinn methodically stated. "It's really all about Americans fearing havin' a nuclear war with the Russians. *Hollywood* knows when and how to make money off of what people are afraid of."

"Quinn's right about that," I enthusiastically added. "Because all our favorite movies, *The Thing, The Beast from 20,000 Fathoms, Them, The Incredible Shrinking Man,* and *The Fly* all were about the bad side-effects of radiation. That's what this space alien fiction is all about. And because of Sputnik, it's fear that the Russians have secret weapons greater than the U.S. has."

"Don't you guys remember Roswell, New Mexico?" Carnie academically reminded us. "Those tiny, green, dead aliens were *not* any damned Russians."

"Carnie's correct," Bo insisted. "Visitin' earth is like havin' your honeymoon in a slum. Those little green men were probably so horrified by our planet, and the dumb assholes living on it, that the freaks accidentally crashed their saucer while being distracted. And the pilot was probably the best navigator on their whole friggin' planet," Jalonec eloquently concluded and shared.

Quinn puffed on his weed while Carnie, Bo, Tink, and I studied the dusky sky for signs of interplanetary spacecraft. If by chance some curious extraterrestrials were to pay us a visit, then we four Diablos were prepared to beat the toxic green urine and the radioactive purple feces out of their weak alien anatomies. On the other hand, I thought, 'Quinn would probably want to negotiate with the anemic space voyagers, because our boss would only fight as a last resort.'

The Diablos watched the sunset and enjoyed the many brilliant hues of the splendid twilight. Carnie flicked his ignition key to "Accessory", and soon WIBG's Joe Niagara announced, "There's nothin' bosser than a flying saucer. Here's Buchanan and Goodman's classic novelty number, 'Flying Saucer, Part II'."

Tinker spotted a single engine plane circling above the southern horizon. The pilot was attempting a landing at the small airport next to the *3-M* Manufacturing Plant, south on Green Lane. The tiny airport was located about a thousand-feet behind the Edgely Road woods.

No sooner had Jokes said, "I hope that pilot isn't on a crash diet," that the small plane's motor began coughing, sputtering, and droning. The craft was either running out of fuel, or the *Piper Cub* was experiencing mechanical failure. Soon, the plane's wings tilted, and the buzzing object began vacillating from side to side.

The aircraft wobbled back and forth in the air as if it were a wounded duck. Then, the flying object quickly disappeared below the tree line. No one uttered a word until we all heard a distant thud.

"That baby's crashed before it made it to the landing strip!" Tinker yelled. "Let's get there before the cops are notified!"

"Let's go see if we can help!" Quinn volunteered, flipping his *Camel* to the ground and crushing "the weed" into the dirt with his rotating engineer boot.

Quinn jumped into his Ford, and the rest of us piled in via the passenger door. My hero elected to take the shortcut through the first set of woods between Dogwood Drive and Edgely Road. Soon, we were across the paved road and speeding onto the dirt trail inside the second set of woods, which led to the small airport's perimeter.

I felt blood pulsating in my ears as we sped past trees, ferns, and bushes. Amazingly, we were at the crash site in thirty-seconds. After the '42 came to an abrupt stop, Quinn reached over, opened the glove compartment, and removed a tiny hand mirror.

Smoke was flowing-out and billowing-up from the plane's engine. The small craft had been wedged between two large evergreen trees, and the pilot's bloody head was hanging outside a jagged window. Quinn was the only one who dared approach the gruesome scene. I slowly followed in his path, wishing I could be one-tenth as courageous as he was. I'll never forget that dramatic moment, for it is permanently frozen in my memory, and its horrifying image surfaces from time-to-time as a recurring nightmare.

Our leader reached-down, scooped up a handful of dirt, and threw it onto the airplane's smoking engine. We imitated his stellar example and the fire was quickly extinguished. With the danger of an explosion being eliminated, Quinn then approached the plane's sole occupant. The pilot's left eyeball was horribly hanging out of its socket.

Quinn felt the man's jugular vein. There was no pulse. Then our Diablos' leader held his small mirror up to the pilot's nostrils. No steam appeared on its surface. Thirty-seconds later, Quinn eerily pronounced, "He's dead guys! We can't save his life or his soul!"

My stomach suddenly became queasy and I felt nauseous. A sour taste shot its way from my esophagus up to my mouth. That was the first time I had ever seen a dead body, and the unfortunate accident victim had not been cosmetically made-up by a mortician. The horror I felt and the terror I had witnessed were very real sensations. Quinn held the man's wrist for verification, but no pulse was evident.

All I could think about was Quinn telling the Feed Bag customers just two months before about Buddy Holly, Ritchie Valens, and the Big Bopper dying in that Clearlake, Iowa plane crash, and now before my very eyes, Quinn was like the county coroner, pronouncing the unfortunate pilot dead.

Sirens were heard approaching in the distance, and then two police cars and an ambulance arrived at the crash scene. The policemen ran towards the inverted plane squeezed between the evergreen trees. The rescue squad members frantically rushed-over with a stretcher.

"Ya' won't need that," Quinn suggested while pointing at the stretcher. "The man's dead."

"Get out of our way," one of the medics ordered. "We'll determine that! We might be able to revive him!"

"He's dead!" Quinn softly repeated.

"It's our job to decide *that,* not yours," the second paramedic adamantly objected. "Now, you and your greaser pals get the heck outa' here, or we'll file charges against all of ya' for obstructin' an important emergency rescue."

"There can't be any rescue if the man is dead," Quinn solemnly replied.

Our melancholy leader led us back to his black coupe. We again crammed ourselves inside, and silently watched until the rescue team officially proclaimed the pilot dead. None of us said a word as our intrepid leader carefully drove through the two patches of woods back to Dogwood Hollow.

In the stark silence, I thought about what Carnie had once told Quinn at the Feed Bag, and what Bo had said to our fearless leader on another occasion at the same place. Carnie had told Quinn, "Ya' know, you look just like Elvis with those sideburns." Quinn peevishly replied, "Elvis is Elvis, and Quinn is Quinn, and I don't pretend bein' Elvis. Next time Carnie, get it straight, and I'm not talkin' about your pecker. Think three times before ya' ever say anything weird to me again."

On another Feed Bag occasion, Bo had alluded to Quinn by referring to a sentimental afternoon TV show *Queen for a Day,* hosted by Jack Baily. A lady would be chosen from the audience to spill her heart. Jokes bellowed-out to the Diablos seated at the table, "And how would you like to be *Quinn* for a day?"

Quinn was not-too-amused with Jokes' parody of MC Jack Baily. The gang's kahuna glared at Jalonec with his penetrating steel blue eyes, and sounding a little like Edward G. Robinson, Quinn said, "Bo, the most sacred and personal thing' a person owns is his name. I never want to hear you make fun of someone's name again. Do ya' hear? If ya' ever make fun of my name again, I promise Bo, ya' won't be able to tell the difference between your teeth and your throat."

So, when Quinn was around, all the guys (especially Bo) were less loquacious, and without a doubt, more selective in our choice of words than usual. The 'boss man" always seemed to have a tranquilizing effect on the rest of us.

As Quinn's '42 entered Dogwood Drive from the woods, my tongue was parched, and it felt as if it weighed three pounds inside my mouth.

I recalled thinking just before the small plane went into its tailspin, 'What if the plane does crash? What would I do?' Well, it did crash, and I did absolutely nothing. And so, because of my inability to act in an emergency, I felt very guilty about my general incompetence and my observable cowardice. And if it hadn't been for Quinn's quick thinking, the pilot's body would have been incinerated in the fire before the man's soul ever had a chance to go to either heaven or hell.

The majestic '42 Ford arrived at the all-too-familiar meadow between Dogwood Hollow and Junewood. As we glanced over at Carnie and Tinker's cars, we all experienced another palpable shock. The two Diablos' vehicles were discovered, both resting on cinderblocks, with their tires and rims removed from their wheel mounts. Glass jars had been placed on the cars' front seats. Each of the jars contained the lug nuts for that auto's rims and tires. The jars were filled with a yellow fluid that turned-out to be Kamikaze urine. A handwritten note was found on Tinker's front seat. It read:

Dear Diablows,

Your "nuts" ain't even good enough for our piss. Your rims and tires can be recovered from the Delaware Canal next to the Windsor Pharmacy. Your eight hubcaps can be found in the first open grave as you go right after entering Heavenly Gates Cemetery.

Thanx for the fun.

The Ks

The self-centered Kamikazes were not-too-funny, even by virtue of coincidence. We had just witnessed a pilot's horrendous death, and now the Ds had to trespass into a cemetery to retrieve our missing hubcaps from a recently dug grave. There was nothing honorable or enviable about the reprehensible Ks. In our minds, the dastardly Kenwood gang members constituted the unmeritorious dregs of Levittown society, and quite frankly, everyone in the Diablos, except Quinn, didn't know exactly how to deal with the Kenwood vermin.

At their respective homes, Carnie and Tink changed into bathing suits, and then Quinn drove us to the Delaware Canal. The familiar body of water was a forty-foot-wide historic passageway that, in the 1800s, had been used to transport goods and materials between Trenton and Philadelphia. In the 1950s, the canal was a stagnant mass of water, loaded with algae from lack of use.

Quinn stood on Haines Road and held a flashlight pointed-down on the dark canal. Carnie and Tinker dove into the illuminated area. Eight-feet under, the pair found their tires and rims, and after a half-hour of arduous searching, the rubber and metal objects were finally salvaged and retrieved.

Ace Roberts and Robbie Wilkinson drove by with their dates on their way to the Langhorne Drive-in. The friends stopped, and after hearing what had happened to Tink and Carnie's hotrods, the guys put the drive-in movies on hold by volunteering to discover and repossess the eight hubcaps from the Heavenly Gates Cemetery.

After Ace and Robbie peeled-out on their relevant mission, the Diablos subsequently discussed the urgency of the Kamikaze act of war. "Those dick-headed Ks are gonna' be dead fish in the water," Tinker threatened as the gang's avenger angrily pointed to the stagnant Delaware Canal.

"J.W. started all this bull shit by makin' fun of Cummings in Bristol," Carnie, turning Benedict Arnold, accused, trying to directly indict me for *his* personal misfortune.

"Don't blame it on J.W.," Quinn candidly declared, "because everybody is responsible for his own actions. J.W. didn't make Cummings and Popeye do this to Tink and Carnie. If anything, the punks shoulda' just taken their anger out on Words, and not on you' other guys."

"First the telephone booth bullshit, and then goin' up against those scum-bag punks behind the Feed Bag and outside the firehouse," Tinker growled. "I'm gonna' make those fuck-heads shit through their dicks for this vandalism!"

Quinn was definitely the most rational-thinking member among all of us. Bo Jalonec was afraid to open his mouth with silly jargon while in Quinn's presence.

"Listen-up, guys," Quinn ordered in a firm-but-calm voice. "Instead of an ugly gang fight, the gang leaders should duke it out. I want Cummings. I want him badly. I either want to race him or fight him. Is that choice clear?"

We all stood there nodding our heads. No one dared say a word, either contrary or otherwise.

"Get the word out on the street," Quinn grimly commanded his subordinates, "because I would rather die than see J.W. or any of you other guys get killed in a stupid, needless gang war with those lowlife Kamikaze thugs."

Chapter 24
"66 Daffodil Lane"

The next Sunday afternoon in April of '59, I had just completed mowing the lawn at 50 Daffodil Lane with Pop's brand-new power mower, which was a vast improvement over the obsolete hand-pusher I had labored with since 1954. Bo drove into the driveway with Tinker and Carnie as passengers in his green and cream Chevy. I had just put the new mower into Dad's carport utility room, and I was spreading some rubbing alcohol on a bee stinger, which had penetrated deeply inside my right forearm. Ironically, Elvis was singing "I Got Stung" on the small radio I kept, blasting music inside the utility room. Upon seeing the elegant two-tone '57, I immediately sensed that my plotting friends were up to some shenanigans.

"J.W., how's it hangin'?" Carnie typically asked.

"Short as a wart," I responded, since I was exhausted from my physically challenging mowing activity.

"Well," Bo chimed-in. "We'll call the Edgely Rescue Squad. The paramedics could put *it* on a *stretcher*. Maybe then it'll get longer."

I scratched my bee sting, being thankful that I wasn't allergic to such painful skin penetrations. Seeing that I had been unfazed by his verbal stupidity, Jokes explained the purpose for the visitation. "J.W., come on and join us in a little fun," Bo proposed. "I brought along my camera to catch it all on film. What we're gonna' do is gonna' give Allen Funt a super hard-on."

I was a bit concerned about Bo's immediate motive, since I sensed that oddball Diablos' mischief was about to occur in my neighborhood. Gossip would spread like wildfire, and I didn't want to embarrass my parents' sense of Daffodil Lane modesty.

"Whatcha' got in mind?" I innocently inquired.

"Just get those two wooden soda cases over there inside your utility room and pull that stepladder off the wall," Jalonec commanded.

"We're also gonna' need your garden hose with its spray handle attached," Tinker imperatively ordered. "This job is gonna' be a fuckin' major military field operation!"

After the designated materials had been gathered, the four of us sauntered over to 62 Daffodil Lane, right next door to the Palermo residence. Jack and Stella Burns, the Fred and Ethel Mertz look-alikes on the *I Love Lucy* comedy show, were on a week's vacation to Wildwood, New Jersey. I then realized that the other three Diablos had some foolishness in mind involving 66 Daffodil Lane, on *that* exceptionally hot April day.

Bo told me that the guys intended to bother Angie and Bubbles right in Sal Palermo's back yard. Our brazen activity would send a message to the Kamikazes that the Diablos were coming out of dormancy to explicitly defy their gross intimidation; their lug nuts in a jar of urine trick, and their throwing of Diablos' tires into the Delaware Canal, along with tossing our gang's pilfered hubcaps into a recently dug cemetery grave.

Sal had constructed a seven-foot-high red cedar fence around his sanctuary's back yard. Earlier in the day, Tinker had bored two inconspicuous peepholes through the cedar wood. Jokes motioned for me to put my pupils up to the holes, and upon closer scrutiny, my eyes saw Angie and Bubbles sunbathing face-down on two large beach towels. Their' halter tops were unbuckled, and a nice amount of breast-flesh was sagging between the Italian dolls' dark bodies and their Mickey and Minnie Mouse beach towels.

Tinker had adroitly hooked-up dad's garden hose to Jack and Stella Burns's outside back wall spigot. Then, the one-man demolition team quietly dragged the utilitarian hose along the grass to Sal Palermo's red cedar fence.

Jokes motioned for me to slowly climb up pop's opened stepladder. Tink methodically handed me the garden hose as I ascended the rungs. Bo stood on one soda case holding his camera; Tink hopped-up on the second case, and Carnie peered at the two Italian princesses through the knotholes that Tink had drilled with his trusty auger.

"Bo, are ya' sure I'm not gonna' be blasted with seltzer bottles like that time over in Tullytown?" I whispered.

"J.W.," Bo very objectively whispered back. "You're holdin' the friggin' hose. *You* got control of all the water, ya' dumb Asshole."

Carnie tacitly signaled 'One, Two and Three' with his fingers, and I opened the spray attachment, which shot a jet of water onto the posteriors of the unsuspecting Sicilian honeys. Angie and Bubbles leaped-up in distress, leaving their gorgeous fronts fully exposed for our appreciative inspection.

Bo clicked-away with his *Kodak,* catching every swivel and every bounce with uncanny deftness. The gorgeous babes were so angry and so disoriented that the Sicilian dolls did not realize they had become bare-chested, and to sixteen-year-old '50s guys, the overall beauty represented heaven on earth.

"Turn that freakin' water off, you' dumb-ass stupid hose-nose!" Angie creatively-but-inadvertently screamed.

"I hope ya' get chicken pox and measles all over your body! And mumps inside your pecker!" Bubbles vehemently screamed.

Bo was inspired by the chicks' obvious public embarrassment. "This prank is only *whetting* our appetites," Jokes shouted.

"My brother is gonna' make you wish you were born in hell!" Bubbles predicted. "Get ready for some swift revenge!"

"Say it, but don't spray it!" Bo defiantly laughed and finished.

After thirty-seconds of the splendid hose treatment, Carnie, Bo, Tink, and I quickly gathered our equipment; unfastened the garden hose from the Burns's back wall spigot, and scampered like joyful kindergarten kids back to 50 Daffodil Lane. We put the borrowed materials neatly into Pop's utility room; hopped into Jalonec's '57 Chevy, and then zoomed-off in the direction of 66 Daffodil Lane.

Sal Palermo was standing in the center of the street holding a hatchet in his hands. Bo skidded to a halt to avoid slamming into the crazed lunatic.

"You Diablos' delinquents have embarrassed my daughter and my niece for the last time!" Sal shouted in a wild fit of rage.

"Grow a brain!" Tinker screamed at the delirious madman.

"I ain't gonna' take any more crap from you' dick-head dip-holes!" Sal cried-out. "You're all gonna' be dead meat!"

Jokes' right foot hit the gas pedal and we fishtailed down Daffodil Lane, leaving a very livid Sal Palermo jumping up and down, waving his hatchet in the air like it was a toy baton.

The Diablos' 1950s activities showed some carryovers from Paleolithic times when the role of primitive men was to be "the hunters". Women were prehistoric subordinates and dependents, and instead of gathering berries and watching the children inside caves, Angie and Bubbles had to be subject to the whims of '50s predatory males, whether the unlucky, contemporary cave dwellers were prowling Mafia, or Kamikazes.

The Diablos regarded teen females as being pleasure toys to be either played with, or to be exploited. Girls were regarded as "objects", while males were treated as other "people". The irony was that greasers "loved" things, so in that sense, the Diablos "loved" girls because *they* were considered pleasure "objects".

Bo readily sped-out of Dogwood Hollow, down Haines Road, and then north on *Route 13*. After passing through Morrisville, we were soon cruising around *Washington's Crossing*.

While we were relishing our recent 66 Daffodil Lane triumph, Tink had something significant to reveal. "Guys, last night I saw Quinn drivin' down Haines Road with a colored guy in his '42," the perpetual troublemaker reported.

Since no Negroes lived in Levittown, Carnie, Bo, and I believed that the reported event had to be an erroneous case of Tinker 3-D glasses' mistaken observation.

"Was it Chuck Berry or Sammy Davis, Jr.?" asked Carnie, who always put a degree of credence in anything Tinker imagined and said.

"Neither," Jeremy Foster insisted. "I got eyes like a hawk. I'm sure of what the hell I saw."

"Tink, your optometrist must be Ray Charles," laughed Jokes, who seldom missed an opportunity to make the rest of us giddy.

As Bo drove around the historic Washington Crossing site, Tink (in rare form) giddily retold the story of how Cummings and the Kamikazes had hung two black kids from the Edgely and from the Trenton/Morrisville train bridges. The Ks were avowed racists, who would declare war on the Diablos should the ruffians find-out that Quinn was buddying-around with a trespassing black kid.

"I don't like darkies, either," Tink claimed. "And I should really join the Ks, 'specially if our leader is kissin' up to black butt."

On the way back to Levittown, Bo thought that he would change the subject to a more humorous mode. Since we had just briefly toured *Washington's Crossing,* Jokes slid into his *Revolutionary War* repertoire. I regretted I was part of his captive audience, which had been mercilessly trapped riding inside his magnificent wheels.

"Hey Words," Jokes began his narrative. "Did ya' know what General George W. said to one of his cowardly soldiers at *Washington's Crossing* before the big *Battle of Trenton?"*

"No, Bo, I haven't the slightest clue," I disgustedly replied.

"Well, J.W. Old George W. said, 'Chicken, catch a Tory'!" Bo pathetically chuckled.

And after relating *that* particular bit of trivial dumbness, Bo told us how the British had all of the *Revolutionary War* Tories on their side, except one, a guy by the name of Vic Tory. And then inimitable Jalonec elucidated on how Mollie Pitcher never hurled on the mound for the *Phillies,* because she had "gone to the well" once too often with her fastball. And after receiving no positive response from his disgusted listeners, Jokes reminded us that Patrick Henry once said, "Give me liberty or give me *Lipton's Tea"*. And next, Jokes informed us that John "Handcock" was not the big jerk-off that the British thought he was, even though *he* ate a lot of "beef jerky", and how the *Constitution* was a funny-looking ship that was shaped somewhat like the *Declaration of Independence*. Still not receiving any laudatory reaction, Bo told us how George W. had a huge horse named Vernon, and how difficult it was for Washington to *"Mount Vernon"*.

When we finally entered Dogwood Hollow from Haines Road, Jalonec said that Colonel William Prescott, a former ship's chef, yelled to his militiamen at Bunker Hill, "Don't fire until you see the whites of their eggs." After I was finally left off at 50 Daffodil Lane, I was never so happy to see my family and my bedroom.

That night I met Bo, Carnie, and Tinker at the Feed Bag. I was disenchanted with the idea that my traveling companions weren't quite through with aggravating Sal Palermo.

"Cool it guys?" I pleaded. "Let's keep vandalism in and around Dogwood Hollow down to a minimum!"

"J.W. Where are your miniature balls?" Tinker chided. "In that friggin' pinball machine over there?"

"We're tired of hearin' Palermo's trashy mouth. Now we're gonna' give him some trash right back," Bo insisted.

"Words," Carnie addressed me. "Hand over the keys to Sal's car and his house. We're gonna' have some legitimate fun. If ya' don't want to participate in the glorious caper, just sit back and watch, ya' wimpy faggot!"

My beleaguered mind was extremely concerned about causing additional trouble in my normally placid neighborhood. I didn't want to see Sal Palermo and Dad getting into a serious fight over juvenile Diablos' mischief. I begged the guys to do something drastic in one of *their* own neighborhoods. "Aren't you guys afraid of the damned Mafia?" I worriedly asked.

"J.W.," Tinker laughed. "The Mafia ain't gonna' fool around with greaser street punks like the Diablos. Are you fucked-up or what? Sal will appoint the Ks to get even with us."

"But Tink, won't the police get after us?"

"No, Words. The Mafia' don't report their problems to the cops. It's sorta' like Quinn will only fight Cummings. Mafia goons only fight other Mafia goons."

I reluctantly handed-over the forged keys to Carnie. Before I could utter "Stop this craziness!", Tinker was driving us over to Dogwood Hollow. Palermo was out with his wife and daughter visiting the Messina's over in Kenwood. First, Tinker weed-sprayed Palermo's coveted front lawn. "It'll all be dead within a week," the incessant avenger guaranteed.

Then, the guys (quickly acting like fanatics) gathered twenty-five full garbage cans from around the neighborhood and fanatically strew the accumulated trash all over Sal Palermo's lawn to take care of the "trash mouth". We then quietly returned the empty rubbish cans to their respective owners' properties.

Herman, Tinker's prized twelve-foot-long boa constrictor, had died three years before in 1956. Tinker had kept the boa constrictor's body frozen solid in his mom's utility room freezer. Using the duplicate keys that Bo and Ace had manufactured at Harley's Hardware, the Diablos stealthily entered the Palermo home at 66 Daffodil Lane. Tinker paced to the bathroom and removed Herman's frozen body from a burlap bag, and planted the grotesque-looking snake inside the pink bathtub.

I entered Sal's utility room where I unexpectantly caught Bo taking a whiz into Palermo's lawnmower's gas tank.

"J.W., whatever you do, don't *leak* this confidential information to the Mafia!"

"Why are ya' doin' that?" I curiously asked.

"You'll know the next time you're followin' *your innate* drives," Bo cryptically answered. "Say J.W., I'll bet you didn't know that someone named a town up in New England after good old Sal Palermo. The damned place is called Marblehead, Massachusetts."

While Carnie smeared butter on all the "dork knobs" (door-knobs), Tink entered Palermo's home office and looked-around. Then, Dr. Destructo stepped to the front door and dropped three-dozen marbles that the rogue/rascal had taken along on the mission, placing the round items inside the home's foyer. We quietly exited the violated house and locked the front door. The four of us walked-over to Tinker's driveway, where we impatiently waited inside his car. Palermo's driveway was visible, looking through two lawns from Tink's unkempt property on nearby Dewberry Lane.

Everyone sat mum for a half-hour until ten o'clock, when Sal's ice blue Caddy entered his cement driveway at 66 Daffodil Lane. Sal suddenly got some butter on the palm of his right hand as the notorious bully grabbed the front doorknob. Then, after entering his violated residence, we saw Palermo flip up into the air, and land squarely on his back after Angie's father had stepped on Tinker's discarded marbles. A minute later, Angie and Carmella let out dual loud screams as Herman's frozen body was finally detected, placed inside the family's pink bathtub.

"Sal's bathtub drain must have been clogged," Bo observed and chuckled.

"I don't get it!" I naively responded.

"Well. Words," Bo aptly elaborated. "*Roto-Rooter* uses a snake to clean-out clogged drainpipes."

Chapter 25
"The Horserace Game"

The last night of April '59, the Diablos were congregated inside the friendly "neutral" confines of the Feed Bag. Tink and Carnie were discussing the recent bad-luck-skein experienced by Sal Palermo, when Bo changed the subject to the upcoming drag-race between Quinn and Cummings. Although the exact date of the contest had not yet been established, Tink, Carnie, and Robbie had negotiated the general rules with Popeye, Jake Mullins, and Worm. The event would definitely take place on Haines Road. It would be a winner-take-all arrangement, with the loser surrendering his car and its ownership documents to the victor. Speculation between the Ks and the Ds was thick and heavy. The guys were making merry as we gossiped and sipped our standard *Pepsi's*.

"Hey there, Jokes," Carnie casually mentioned. "I know where you're gonna' attend college, and it's not *Penn State* or *Rutgers*."

"Where?" Jalonec impulsively asked his emulator.

"What's A Matter U," Carnie laughed, as the immature fool waved his closed hand back and forth like a hyperactive Sicilian with severe dual cases of arthritis and rheumatism.

"Ya' know, Tuna-breath," Bo angrily replied. "I've been studyin' American History real hard to ace the course, and I figure and conclude that you' pecker-heads would've made great Minutemen during the *Revolutionary War*."

"Thanks Bo, but I don't follow you," I verbally reacted, showing a dash of naivete.

"Because you silly warped jerk-offs always have premature ejaculations," ejaculated Jokes un-empathetically. "That's why you'd all make good minutemen, 'cause none of ya' could hold back your discharge for more than sixty seconds."

Carnie was angered at being again outdone by Bo, so the depressed loser stood-up to hit the head and drain his full radiator. Tinker wobbled-out to his grungy '49 Plymouth to obtain his homemade, hand-held horse-race game. Tink wanted to provide the fellas' with a little casual entertainment to relax our torqued-up minds.

Jokes asked Carnie his destination to help set-up Mr. Merc' for a surprise punch line.

"To take a healthy piss," the C Man snorted-back over his shoulder.

"Ya' could've played for the 1950 *Phillies* and been one of the *whiz kids*," Jokes jested.

"I've heard that one before," Carnie lividly criticized.

"Well then," Jokes persisted. "Don't sit in the urinal. Ya' might get pissed-out, which is even worse than bein' pissed-on, or pissed-off!"

Tinker re-entered the Bag with his nifty horse-race track. Carnie was returning from his call of nature and Jenny, the Feed Bag's platinum blonde waitress, whose brown eyebrows didn't exactly match her hair color, gingerly approached our corner table.

"Well, if it isn't Manny, Moe, and Jack!" the waitress exclaimed as she spotted Jokes, Tinker and me.

"Ya' must've attended one of our recent *pep* rallies," Bo smartly answered. "It sounds like you're ready for a jiffy lube!"

And then Jenny spotted Carnie returning from the latrine. "Well, if it isn't Captain Kangaroo, too!"

"You're right, Jenny," Bo verified. "Carnie's really jumpy tonight because someone put some lit firecrackers in his pouch. He's even thinkin' about changin' his name to *Joey*."

Carnie, feeling perceptive, sensed Jenny's negative disposition and asked her why she was in such a rotten mood.

"Because Angie lent me six bucks, a fin and a *George Washington*. I think I lost the fin," the saddened waitress lamented. "I've searched high and low, but it ain't nowhere."

"Maybe some wounded card *shark* stole your fin," Jokes laughed. "Or maybe it was *Superman*, man of *steal*."

Jenny's sadness was soon somewhat alleviated. Tinker gave the disappointed platinum blonde hope of gaining a five-dollar Diablos' bonus. "Well, Jenny, Carnie will surely win five-dollars for ya' in a little horse-race game," Tink slyly indicated. "It'll only cost Carnie a buck to enter a bet. We'll get Robbie and Ace over there to join us. There'll be six horses entered. The winnin' horse will get Carnie's original bet back, and a profit of five bananas to boot."

"Sounds mighty temptin'," said Carnie, who thought he could earn an easy date with Jenny by winning her the five-dollars to replace the five bucks she had lost or misplaced.

Tinker's race-track was a foot-long miniature "Kentucky Derby" with six parallel lanes. Tiny jockeys were attached to six numbered horses, and the track model was slightly inclined at the starting line and a trifle lower at the finish pole.

Tinker wound-up the knob that tightened-up a set of springs. The six lanes then rattled and shimmied back and forth once the operator fully released the spring tension. The half-dozen horses would then shuffle slowly down the straight track toward the finish line. Bo then called Robbie and Ace over to join our illustrious company.

"Now, Luigi has agreed to hold our six bets to show that this is gonna' be a fair race," Tink ethically declared.

Luigi collected a dollar from each of the six enthralled gamblers.

"Before we begin the contest," Jeremy announced, "each horse must have a proper name."

"I'll be Number One," Jokes boldly stated. "Citation, ridden by Willie Shoemaker."

"And I'll be Number Two, Bold Ruler, piloted by Eddie Arcaro," Ace confidently declared.

"I'll be Number Six," Robbie contributed. "Dark Star, with Henry Moreno as the jockey."

"I'll be Gallant Man, ridden by Johnny Adams, sittin' atop Number 5," I commented.

"Give me Number 4. I'll have Bill Hartack in the saddle ridin' High Gun," Tink indicated.

"I don't know the name of any other horses or jockeys!" confessed Carnie, with a trace of guilt being apparent on his confused-looking countenance.

"Don't feel bad," Jokes replied very helpfully. "Ya' could be Will Harmatz ridin' Number 3, Nads. And if Nads wins," Bo said to Carnie, "then Jenny will get her five bucks reward and be indebted to you."

Tinker completed his assiduous winding of the starting knob, and Jokes counted: "One, two, three," but there was a false start. The horses had to be reassembled at the imaginary gate position for a proper start. Then, Bo chanted, "Ready, Set, Go."

The tiny track lanes swiveled back and forth, as all of us, Luigi and Jenny included, were totally absorbed in the intense competition.

"Come on Dark Star," Robbie yelled.

"Come on High Gun," Tink shouted.

"Come on Nads," Jenny wailed.

"Let's go Citation," Bo echoed.

"Let's go Bold Ruler," Ace hollered.

"Let's go Nads," Carnie cried out.

"Go Gallant Man," I shrieked.

And as the six horses came down the home stretch, the cheering gamblers became even more rabid and enthusiastic. Even Domenick ceased twirling and flipping his pizza to view the final suspenseful outcome. Citation was in the lead, and Dark Star and Carnie's "Nads" were vying neck and neck for second, only trailing Bo's horse by an inch.

"Go High Gun," Tink screeched.

"Go Gallant Man," I loudly yelled.

"Go Dark Star," Robbie bellowed.

"Go Citation," Jokes roared out.

"Go Bold Ruler," Ace cried out.

"Go Nads," Carnie cheered.

And then Bo put his hands over Jenny's lips so that she couldn't root for Carnie's horse any more, and the five Diablo' conspirators became absolutely mum. All that the thirty or so Feed Bag patrons could hear and see was Carnie jumping up and down like a fanatic, blaring out repeatedly at the top of his lungs, "Go Nads, Go Nads, gonads, gonads, gonads!" nine boisterous times in a row.

When Carnie finally realized his bizarre indiscretion, the entire Feed Bag audience burst-out in tremendous whoops of approval. The fact that Bo Jalonec's Citation with Willie Shoemaker aboard had won the race was immaterial to the well-designed joke that had been expertly played on Carnie. Jenny suddenly slapped Carnie across the face for his gross public indiscretion.

"What was that for?" the totally disgruntled C Man asked.

"For losin' the freakin' horserace, you dumb dip!"

Much to our delight, Jenny then unscrewed the cap off of a salt-shaker, pulled Carnie's dungarees outward from the belt buckle, and proceeded to pour the shaker's entire contents inside his blue jeans.

"Now Carnie can make gunpowder out of his saltpeter," Jokes sarcastically laughed.

The guys again all burst-out in another demeaning roar. Feeling largely insulted and humiliated, Carnie left the Feed Bag in a hurry. The obsessed guy with the defeated ego paced-over to the Dairy DeLite, where the mortified victim ordered a Polar Sundae to cool off from his most recent embarrassment.

"Sir, do you want your nuts dry or wet?" asked the pretty blonde attendant, whose eyebrows, incidentally, matched her hair.

"I haven't gotten laid in over two months," Carnie moaned and lied, "so what do ya' think?"

"You definitely need wet nuts!" the tanned honey answered very professionally.

While Carnie was brooding over his Polar Sundae featuring wet nuts, Bo Jalonec gave Tink, Robbie, Ace, and me a scholarly dissertation on the art of dating females.

"Ya' guys getting' any?" Bo asked.

Tink, Ace, Robbie, and I all simply shook our heads negatively.

"What's your secret?" I submissively inquired.

"The trouble with you slime balls is that you're all too vegetarian. To get a hot broad, ya' havta' be carnivorous like me," Bo boasted.

I figured that Jokes was again being facetious, as was his general nature. His presentation always seemed like that of a cheap used car salesman, and we were always willfully buying his junky highway puddle jumpers.

"What's this vegetarian and carnivorous crap supposed to mean?" Robbie challenged. We were all showing more than mild distaste for Bo's highly ultra-sophisticated lexicon.

"There are different types of chicks," Bo clarified. "Ugly, skanky ones with zits and pus all over their faces are like chopped liver. Grotesque wide-bodies that look like heifers or Holsteins are like hamburger meat. Average lookin' females with mediocre bods' are like roast beef. Tough looking broads are like prime rib. And totally succulent *Miss America* types like Susie Parker are like lobster tail," Jalonec solemnly pontificated.

I imagined that I should visit a food chain supermarket's meat and seafood department to find the right woman to suit my needs. "So, what am I to do?" I wondered and asked. "Use a butcher's chart for me to locate the right female?"

"No Pecker-head," Bo admonished. "I've explained this scenario to you dumb-shits once before. Ya' gotta' settle for what you can get. That's your basic problem. You want lobster tail when ya' oughta' be happy with roast beef. J.W., you want Angie and Bubbles when ya' could have Carol Zella any time ya' damned want. Once ya' have lobster tail like I do, you'll always get lobster tail any time ya' want," Bo sternly and sanctimoniously lectured. "But until you get lobster tail, ya' oughta' settle for all of the chopped liver and hamburger meat ya' can get."

I then thought that the ocean floor would be the best place to find the ideal lady companion. 'My mermaid will be hiding in a coral reef, or near the shore of a tropical island,' I imagined.

"Now, I think I see," Robbie interrupted. "So first, I havta' grind my salami into some chopped liver, and then systematically go through hamburger and roast beef as I screw my way up the meat chain. I've been spinning my wheels all these years tryin' to hustle lobster tail in vain," Robbie realized and confessed.

And then Jenny finally ambled-out of the kitchen with six large *Pepsi's* on her tray. The encumbered broad was heading to our familiar table facing the Dairy DeLite.

"Hey, Jenny," Bo softly mentioned. "Here's your' dollar back plus an *Abe Lincoln* blue-sealed fin. The tip is for your time and trouble during the exciting horse-race game."

"Gee, thank you so very much," Jenny ecstatically returned. "You're a doll with a capital D. It's too bad you have that knockout blonde girlfriend. I'd like to do a little humpty-dump with you!" Jenny massaged the cheeks of her rear end to emphasize her splendid point before the *experienced* waitress made her way back into the restaurant's greasy kitchen.

"See, guys," Bo summarized. "Lobster tail beats prime rib every time. That's why I only now eat seafood, when I'm not busy feedin' the cat some pork!"

I glanced-over at the Dairy DeLite, and poor Carnie was still consuming his Polar Sundae with wet nuts. Tinker took the opportunity to inform Bo, Robbie, Ace, and me of a great discovery the avid instigator had made. The four of us listened intently to Tink's sparkling gem of knowledge.

"Bo, do ya' remember the other night when we broke into Sal Palermo's place on Daffodil Lane?"

"Sure do. It was marbleous, simply marbleous!" Jokes laughed. "We didn't even need the services of that highly skilled friend of yours, Jimmy De Locke."

"Well, anyway, while I was explorin' the house, I entered the third bedroom, which Palermo uses as his private office. I used one of my special entry keys that spring all locks to gain access. It'll open any door in Levittown, or just about anywhere else."

"I'll bet it doesn't open Loch Ness?" Bo drolly answered. "Did you buy the skeleton key from a desperate undertaker?"

"Stop bein' such a goddamned wise-ass and get serious for a change," Tinker cautioned. "I found this here business card in a stack of 'em lying on Sal's cluttered desk."

Tink showed us a card that revealed Sal and Dante's place of business in Bristol: Specialty Enterprises, 3647 Cedar Street. "Carnie and I checked it out last night," Mr. Fix-it divulged. "It's an office connected to a medium-sized warehouse. Only trouble is, there's a mean-assed Doberman guardin' the front door."

Dr. Destructo then announced that he and Carnie were going to return to Specialty Enterprises later that night. "Robbie, you gonna' lend us Queenie? I wanna' see what kind of business those Sidgees' are really into. You guys all want to come on the expedition?"

"Sure," Bo and I said, almost simultaneously.

"I gotta' get up early tomorrow mornin' for work. I've pulled Harley's early shift," Ace complained. "I'll havta' take a rain check."

"I'll bring my lady Doberman," Robbie promised. "And I gotta' tell ya'. It's just about mating season for Queenie."

Ace walked back over to the pinball area to play a few games. My eyes were focused on Carnie as the despondent kid ambled back to the Dairy DeLite counter window and ordered a large *Pepsi* to wash-down his extra-large Polar Sundae.

"How were your nuts?" asked the really cute blonde featuring the terrific tan.

"Very wet," Carnie answered. "Just the way I like 'em!"

"Well, Idiot King," the pretty girl yelled. "The next time ya' talk to me like you had, your nuts are gonna' be crushed, you understand, ya' demented corn-holer!"

Carnie was so shocked and so pissed-off that the defeated Diablo trudged-over to the Dairy DeLite phone booth on the Feed Bag side of the custard stand. He inserted a coin and dialed the appropriate number. Mr. C had not heard Bo's pertinent lecture about chopped liver, hamburger, roast beef, prime rib, and lobster tail. In fact, Carnie thought that the only way to fascinate a girl was to talk fresh over the telephone while imitating inimitable Bo Jalonec. Mr. Merc' tried a ploy that Bo had successfully enacted at least a dozen times. After three telephone rings at the Feed Bag's main counter, Jenny responded to the intended crank call.

"Ya' say you'd like to order a medium pizza to go with pepperoni and extra cheese. What's your name? Richard who? How do you spell your last name? H-E-R-T-Z," Jenny repeated as the ditzy airhead wrote the essential data on her check pad.

"That's correct," Carnie replied to fill a void in the conversation.

"You're Dick Hertz?" Jenny incredulously asked.

"Yes, I am," Carnie lied. "How many times I gotta' tell ya'?"

"Well," Jenny returned. "If your dick hurts, why don't ya' just do what Popeye does?"

"What does Popeye do?" Carnie seemed puzzled by the odd riddle.

"He sticks it in Olive Oyl!" Click.

Jenny rubbed her hands together as if she had accomplished something major, and essentially, she had. Carnie mashed-down the Dairy DeLite phone onto its vertical holder, and the thirty or so very amused Feed Bag patrons again all broke-out in a loud roar. Then, the appreciative Diablos gave Jenny a standing round of applause for her splendid guile and sagacity. The platinum blonde waitress had made the transition from goat to heroine in a matter of seconds, simply by knowing her TV cartoon characters, and then cleverly using a pair of English grammar homophones to ingeniously dismantle Carnie's failed attempted ruse.

Chapter 26
"The Diablo Raid"

Carnie returned to the Feed Bag after his failed episode over at the popular Dairy DeLite phone booth. We tried consoling our melancholy friend, and Jenny even agreed to date Carnie should he ever be able to fool her with a fake name and pizza order. The Diablos reluctantly paid for our *Pepsi* and food orders. Jenny brought our money over to the cash register. Jokes just had to antagonize Carnie some more.

"Carnie," Bo deliberately busted. "Jenny never even said, 'Who's Dick Hertz'?"

"I guess I'm just a pathetic born loser," Carnie admitted. "I'd rather be lost in deep space around Mars rather than lost in Levittown."

"Too bad your mother didn't have you inside a transcontinental airplane," Jokes told Carnie. "Then, you'd be an *airborne* loser." Jalonec then continued to batter the C Man's faltering pride. "I heard ya' made that *pretty* blonde over at the Dairy DeLite *pretty* mad."

I thought I'd change the subject to something more edifying to Carnie, so I invited the Merc' Man to drive us over to Bristol to investigate Sal Palermo and Dante Messina's Specialty Enterprises. Feeling more energized, Carnie agreed to be the commandos' chauffeur. Bo, Tink, Robbie, and I all hopped into our friend's black '49 Merc', after we promised the C-Man that none of us would pester him about his recent bad luck streak.

Our first stop was Robbie Wilkinson's place where affable R.W. momentarily exited the car, and two minutes later returned with Queenie, his four-year-old pedigree Doberman. Queenie sat on my lap in the back seat and affectionately licked my chin. As we pulled-out of Dogwood Hollow onto Haines Road, I asked Tinker about the chance of accidentally springing the building's burglar alarm system.

"Don't worry, J.W. That alarm the bozos have will only be activated if a window or door is smashed in a boner-fide breakin' and enterin' situation," Tinker clarified. "I've fuckin' got everything under control with my skeleton keys!"

"Boner-fide skeleton key?" Bo indulgently and *humerusly* asked. "That must be *hard-on* the window or door!"

Everyone ignored Jokes' petty nonsense because we were on a critical raid being conducted into foreign enemy territory.

I then asked Tinker about the possibility of a police hookup alarm system. I didn't know if any even existed anywhere, but the general thought intrigued me.

"J.W., leave everything to me," Tink recommended. "When I turn the master lock with this here master key, the type of alarm Sal and Dante have will automatically be neutralized. The only real thing we havta' fear is Sal's fierce Doberman."

Queenie then licked all of the minute Feed Bag crumbs off my face and lips, and everybody laughed with that tension-breaking activity.

"Words," Robbie giggled. "That's exactly why we brought your lady friend Queenie along. It's doggie-heat season, and Queenie oughta' keep Pasta interested long enough until we finish our snoopin' around. Either that, or your lousy after shave lotion must smell like dog food based on the way Queenie is lickin' your chops!"

I was inspired and compelled to say something involving American literature. "Usin' Queenie is sorta' like Edgar Allan Poe usin' people to cause a diversion in a short story, just like the author had done in 'The Purloined Letter'," I academically indicated.

"Very good analogy," Bo replied and commended. "And if we uncover any damagin' evidence inside Specialty Enterprises, Sal and Dante will wind-up in the *Poehouse* before either of them ever will know what the hell hit them," Jokes uttered *pun*intentionally.

It was perfectly evident to the Diablos that Sal Palermo, Dante Messina, Popeye, and Cummings were loose cannons, and the only thing that loose cannons feared were looser cannons, and that was exactly what the Diablos aspired to become that evening.

Bo then reviewed the details of our covert operation. Tinker, Robbie and Queenie would enter the building first. Queenie would be used to distract and amuse Pasta, Sal's vicious Doberman watchdog. Carnie would stay in his "James Dean Special" in case we had to make an emergency quick getaway. Jokes would remain in the Merc' with Carnie and act as our alert scout. If we had to exit the building in a hurry, Bo would give us the word.

I would enter the premises next in case my assistance would be needed. As usual, the Diablos all wore gloves to avoid leaving fingerprints behind. Robbie and I had flashlights to be used once we encroached into the warehouse section of Specialty Enterprises.

Carnie parked his Mercury in an alley next to the Sidgees' illicit place of business. We all suspected that the fancy title "Specialty Enterprises" represented an elegant generic cover for some form of illegal commerce. Tinker, Robbie, and Queenie got out of the car. The two Diablos stealthily approached the dark building. I exited the passenger side slowly, and momentarily stood next to the black '49.

Sure enough, Tinker's key deactivated the alarm system, and sure enough, Pasta barked wildly as the beast ran to the front door. The ferocious canine bared his fangs and showed his gums, sensing unwarranted intrusion. But as soon as the wicked beast laid eyes on Queenie, Pasta began whimpering like an eager-but-harmless puppy. Robbie's Doberman must have been lobster tail in the mutt world, because after she led us inside on her leash, Pasta wanted to first rub noses and then share other more vital external organs with his new-found playmate.

I arrived inside the building just in time to see the two animals excitedly sniffing each other's genitalia. Tinker noticed Pasta's infatuation with Queenie's crotch and remarked, "I thought only cats had pussies." Robbie attached Queenie's leash to one of the coat hooks, which was nailed to a wooden wall panel inside the main office.

A dim stream of light filtered through the glass front door and penetrated through the window's semi-shut Venetian blinds. Further inspection of our alien environment showed that the illumination originated from a streetlight across Cedar Street. I was nervous; I wished we would get the heck out of there as quickly as possible, without being detected, arrested, or killed.

Tinker led Robbie and me into the warehouse area where Robbie and I flicked on our trusty flashlights. A quick recognition of some unique products and supplies immediately captured our attention. Pornographic books and decks of nudie cards were piled high on numerous shelves and racks. A shelf directly before my eyes had a variety of dildos, porn films, and lewd open-beaver photos.

Tink quickly grabbed various magazines and other obscene merchandise from the shelves, and the sex addict haphazardly stacked his obtained contraband into Robbie's arms, and then the remainder into my hands. Thanks to Tinker's propensity for crime, I instantly became an immoral goods thief.

"Dig it J.W.," Tinker proudly proclaimed. "it's Marilyn Monroe before her platinum blonde *Playboy* centerfold days! That's what Jenny really looks like under her Feed Bag waitress uniform. Check-out the fluffy brown bush!"

"Wow!" Robbie agreed. "The bitch must use brown shoe polish on her snatcheroo. And when Jokes sees those blimps and nice pubic fur, I'll bet the dumb-ass will say he wants to move to Africa to become an accomplished Bushman."

Tinker then led Robbie and me into the rear section of the well-stocked warehouse. Our flashlights revealed a number of small marijuana bags, neatly arranged on separate shelves. Tink confiscated samples from the inventory and stashed myriad bags into his black leather jacket's pockets. Next, the accomplished robber zipped-up the pilfered goods, keeping the acquired dope safely stored inside his various jacket compartments. "This is almost like the movie 'Bounty on the Mutiny,' Tink told us.

"Ya' got the title backwards," Robbie corrected.

"Now I know where the Ks got the marijuana that Jokes put into Brother Timothy's cigarette," I realized and shared.

"And where the Ks obtained the dildos, nudie cards, and porn pictures to distribute to the Renegades to sell to Tink, so the Ds could ultimately put the items inside the Reagan display cabinets," Robbie intelligently added.

"I suspected *this* illegal bullshit right along," Tink bragged. "I'm glad you' *dopes' drug* me in here to steal the dope!"

After Tinker stuffed more marijuana bags into the pockets of Robbie's black leather jacket and blue denim jeans, the petty larcenist led us back to the office. Robbie and I flicked-off our flashlights to avoid scrutiny from passing night vehicles on Cedar Street.

"Okay, Queenie, no time for sweet afterglow," Robbie ordered. R.W. then politely tugged the obedient bitch away from her now docile suitor. Tink and I quietly and swiftly exited the front door, and then we watched Robbie gently nudge his female pet outside the building.

Tink handed me his souvenir Marilyn Monroe porno calendar that the crafty delinquent had exclusively pilfered for his own visual enjoyment, and the main heister then locked-up Palermo and Messina's formerly secret business tight as a drum.

The three junior pirates and Queenie scurried to Carnie's sleek '49 automobile. We clumsily piled inside; shut the doors, and in a matter of ten seconds, the 'black Merc' was heading toward Radcliffe Street. In transit we eagerly divulged the essence of our adventure to Jokes and to the neurotic driver.

"Won't Sal report his stolen property to the cops?" I asked.

"No J.W., not a friggin' chance," Tink answered with impressive certainty. "Because any true Mafia guy who doesn't control the fuzz by payoffs or extortion will wanna' keep a low-profile. To Sal, our surprise heist is just a little thorn in his big fat butt."

Carnie's '49 Merc' eventually arrived at Robbie's Dogwood Drive house. R.W. yanked his dog's leash and chain, signaling to the happy Doberman that it was time to exit.

"Queenie must think I'm Pasta," I quipped as I noticed the dog's reluctance to leave my company. "Robbie's mutt must think I'm a real stud!"

"Yeah," Jokes agreed, "and your stench-breath smells about the same as Pasta's does."

At last, Queenie was coaxed from my warm lap. I almost vomited right there and then when I saw and felt half of Pasta's ejaculation smeared all over my formerly clean dungarees.

Everyone got ample laughs from my sticky situation. "This is gonna' be a great X-rated *Lassie* movie based on its *coming* attractions," Jokes cackled. "Or maybe we can get *Lassie* and *Rin-Tin-Tin* in a homo' dog bitch and bastard flick! On second thought, Words, maybe ya' should open-up a sex clinic for impotent and sterile canines!"

The following day, Tinker and Carnie collaborated on a new project. The schemers had obtained Bo Jalonec's negatives from the bare-breasted pictures that Jokes had taken of Angie and Bubbles in Sal's sacred back yard. The two tricksters then paid a photographer to enlarge the revealing photos' to poster size.

The T Man and the C Man then naughtily taped three posters each to their bedroom walls. So, whenever I wanted to visit "My Blue Heaven" without Fats Domino, I would simply trek over to either of their houses and admire the gorgeous Sicilian dolls blown-up, and fully exposed, stapled on the guys' bedroom walls.

Chapter 27
"The Two Fires"

In '50s Levittown, wives were mostly dependent on their husbands' incomes, and the women generally stayed home and took care of the kids. Parents stuck it out together and sacrificed egos for the sake of maintaining family unity. Mom was content watching her favorite soap operas on TV, and vicariously lived the various melodramas portrayed on *Search for Tomorrow*, *The Guiding Light*, *Love of Life,* and *As the World Turns*.

Pop was so fatigued from commuting to North 'Philly to put in a hard day's labor being a welder that he scarcely had time to read the daily newspaper before taking his nap. In early May of '59, Dad announced his intention of moving the family back to Hammonton, New Jersey. He broke the news at the dinner table.

"Levittown is too violent a place to raise a family," Pop began his justification. "And that gang over in Kenwood is a bunch of young hoodlums, and the Diablos aren't too far behind. J.W., I want you to stay clear of those reckless Kenwood hooligans. The only decent friend you have is Bo Jalonec. He has direction. He has goals. I hear he's been accepted at *Penn State*. The rest of your' loser buddies aren't worth a pot to pee in."

Dad had a great business opportunity to buy a retail fruit and vegetable farm market and was quite excited about the prospect of becoming an independent Hammonton area produce merchant. And with Sal Palermo and "the Mafia" living in our Dogwood Hollow neighborhood, Dad believed that Daffodil Lane was indeed a dangerous place to reside. Pop contacted a real estate agency, and a "For Sale" sign appeared on the front lawn in early May. Coincidentally, another "For Sale" sign was placed on the front lawn of 66 Daffodil Lane about a week later. I then realized that Levittown would be a transient place for in-and-out upwardly mobile white American families.

I was sitting on Carnie's bed the first Friday night in May, admiring the three bare-breasted, enlarged posters of cousins Angie and Bubbles adorning the wall over my buddy's bureau.

"Ya' ain't gonna' have stuff like this over in Jersey," Carnie insisted, pointing at the wonderful blown-up pictures. "Jersey girls have smaller tits than 'Pennsy chicks do!"

"Don't remind me," I agreed with regret. "I wanna' be with the Diablos forever. I don't wanna' move back across the river."

Carnie drove me over to the Feed Bag where we were to meet Bo for a common seminar. Jokes greeted us enthusiastically, and after we sat-down at the Diablos' favorite table, the notorious jester initiated one of his standard lectures. This one had as its principal treatise the various stratifications of feces, which we had heard being delivered several times before.

"Ya' see guys," Bo prefaced, "there are different levels of shit. Unimportant facts and details are basically chicken shit, which is everyday crap not even worth thinkin' twice about. Then, there are the academic ideas that ya' learn in school that have no meaning in the real world. That crap is called horseshit," Bo elaborated. "Above horseshit, ya' have bullshit, which every television and radio commentator and every newspaper lays on you to make us believe that ya' really need to know what they're sayin' or printin'. And at the top of the dung world is serious shit. Serious shit is real and dangerous, and it could even kill ya', like the heavy feces goin' on between the Diablos and the Ks. Ya' got that into your thick skulls, you' yo-yos?"

"Well, Bo, what about Alaska becomin' the forty-ninth state?" I asked. "That's been makin' newspaper headlines almost daily."

"Juneau that Carnie?" Jokes said with a smirk.

"If I want to know more," Carnie angrily said, "*I'll ask a* expert instead of you!" Carnie had once gotten A's in sixth-grade geography over at St. Mark School in Bristol, and his abundant knowledge was showing and irking the heck out of Jalonec.

"Don't forget Hawaii," I added. "It'll probably become the fiftieth state in late August."

"And how do ya' say 'hello' in Hawaiian?" Jokes asked.

"That's easy. Aloha," I answered.

"And how do ya' say 'goodbye'?" Jokes continued.

"Aloha again," Carnie replied.

"That clearly proves," Bo maintained, "that the damned Hawaiians don't know whether they're comin' or goin'." Bo seemed very pleased with his verbal punishment of Carnie, and *his* smiling visage sported a prodigious grin.

"Real hilarious," Carnie criticized. "But what kind of shit would you describe all this retarded news about the two new states?"

"Definitely bullshit," Bo insisted, "because the press wants ya' to believe that Alaska and Hawaii are important enough to make ya' think about them all the time."

"Well," I muttered. "What about the Navy sayin' in the papers there's three-hundred more percent radiation in the air than before the A and the H-Bombs were invented? That stuff could get us killed!" I still needed further clarification about Bo's unique system of fecal hierarchal classification.

"J.W., that news is simply horseshit propaganda," Bo confidently responded. "It's the same type of immaterial academic crap they feed us in school textbooks. It's all designed to distract us from serious shit like girls, sex, Polar Sundaes with wet nuts, big tits, hairy pussies, and the screwed-up Kamikazes." Bo seemed rather confident on advancing those particular points.

"Well," snapped back Carnie. "What about the *Boston Celtics* beating the *Minneapolis Lakers* in the pro basketball championships?" Carnie was a little peeved at Bo's Polar Sundae with wet nuts remark, while the jealous kid was still showing a mild interest in Jokes' novel hierarchy of fecal matter.

"Who really cares?" Jalonec challenged. "That's bullshit right now, but forty-years from now, it'll just be irrelevant chicken-shit!"

"Well, Bo, what about getting laid?" Carnie directly interrogated, wondering where sex would fit into the J Man's complex theory.

"If ya' just think or talk about sex, it's equal to something between chicken-shit and horseshit," Bo claimed. "But if ya' actually act to do it, then it's serious shit. Get it amigos?"

I then asked Bo what kind of feces would represent the American government bureaucracy. Jalonec pondered my salient question for a few seconds and then aptly responded.

"J.W.," Bo expounded, "could President Eisenhower protect you from the Kamikazes? No, he can't," Jalonec' argued while answering his own rhetorical question. "The U.S. government is not real to the average teenager. It is irreverent and immaterial to our daily lives. In fact, I plan to write an important-*feces* on the subject when I go out to start college at *Penn State*."

Angie Palermo was working the floor that night and reluctantly shuffled-over to our table. Angie's glum face reflected her true displeasure with our illustrious presence. But when the doll caught a glimpse of Bo's charismatic smile, her sneer was immediately shattered, and the doll's obstinate opposition quickly melted-down to feigned courtesy.

"Do ya' fellas' want to order anything?"

"Does a bear shit in the woods?" Carnie remarked, trying to enchant Angie with a typical crude reference.

"Wait a minute, Daddio!" Jokes laughed. "I didn't discuss anything about bear shit. If ya' remember, I just talked about chicken-shit, horseshit, bullshit, and serious shit!"

I figured I would change the subject because I was beginning to see some merit in Bo's absurd hypothesis, and also in his stupid logic and facetious nomenclature.

"Angie, who are ya' goin' to the Reagan Prom with?" I asked my mind's perfect dream girl.

"J.W., does your face hurt?" Angie surprisingly asked.

"No," I instantly and self-consciously replied.

"Well, it's killin' me," Angie indicated. "But if ya' really wanta' know the truth, I'm goin' to the prom with Phil Jackson, the biggest hunk over at Reagan."

A large degree of spite suddenly rose up inside me. "But Angie," I neurotically challenged. "Phil's biceps are so exaggerated that they're abnormal and actually look artificial. Don't ya' prefer a Tarzan-like body like, let's say, like mine, to a *Mr. America* Joe Weider body like Jackson's?"

"J.W. Did ya' have your left testicle amputated?"

I couldn't figure out why the Italian babe was interested in the loss of any of my personal equipment. "No, why?" I suspiciously inquired.

"Because you're half-nuts, that's why!" Angie answered.

"Angie, do ya' know Ben?" Bo asked.

"Ben who?"

"Ben Dover," answered Bo, "because I wanna' check your map of Australia to see how things are down under in the bush country."

"Oh, Blondie! You're the ginchiest!" the Sicilian chick replied. "If all guys were cute like you, I'd go absolutely crazy tryin' to pick the best one."

Carnie and I were extraordinarily peeved because Bo could get away with sexual allusions and with sexual expletives, where *we* would flounder and never stand a ghost's chance at achieving success.

At that moment, Jokes had one of his patented allergy attacks, with his lily-white hands quickly grabbing several napkins from the table dispenser and rapidly sneezing into them. The jester's eyes produced big tears, and if Bo had one principal defect, it was his hyperactive nasal sinuses.

"Bless you!" Angie exclaimed, as 'Blondie', who never ate any Dagwood Sandwiches, blasted a barrage of snot and germs into the already contaminated Feed Bag atmosphere.

"Angie, if ya' think my nose is runnin', well it'*s not!"* Bo coughed-out. "This wouldn't happen to me if I had a hose-nose like Carnie!"

"Oh, Golden Boy, ya' have what your friends lack. I'd love to play strip poker with you," Angie deliberately declared, just to make Carnie and me jealous and feeling inferior.

"Well, Angie, I already have twelve wonderful photos' of you and Bubbles naked from the waist up, so I don't really havta' play strip poker to study your vital equipment," Carnie laughed, much to the approval of everyone within hearing distance, except our waitress.

Angie recalled the 66 Daffodil Lane back-yard camera/hose debacle; turned very red in the face, and swiftly left our table in a rage without ever taking any of our food orders.

The three of us discussed the upcoming Reagan Prom, scheduled to go-off at the end of May. The theme was "Wonderland by Night", and Father Malcolm had appointed Stanley Tezeeker as Chairman of the Decorating Committee.

Bo had recently made-up with Susie Parker, who would be his prom date who had invited him. I was taking Carol Zella, whose twin sister Barbara had accompanied me to the Eighth-Grade Cotillion over at St. Michelle's School. Carnie would be going with Jackie Harrelson, who, like Carol Zella, was sirloin steak in the female flesh hierarchy.

Jokes then confided that tension was rising between the jocks and the greasers, and that Tinker planned to get more revenge against Phil Jackson at the late May Cardinal Reagan Prom, and also at the early June *Amusements of America* carnival.

The following week cruised by without any major incidents. High School was really becoming a major drag, and Carnie and I desperately needed a holiday.

Finally, *Ascension Thursday,* a Holy Day of Obligation, arrived at Cardinal Reagan High. Everyone in the school attended Mass after fourth-period, and the students had the remainder of the day off to reflect on the importance of faith being a crucial element of emotional survival on planet Earth.

At noon, Carnie drove me over to Tink's place to pick up Mr. Fix-It. The '49 Mercury then took off for the forest trail situated between Edgely Road and the *3-M* Manufacturing Plant on Green Lane.

"Where's Bo?" Tinker asked.

"He's workin' on a secret prank he's plannin' to use against the Ks," I revealed. "And it involves some nifty artwork. Jokes will tell us all about it when he's all done the confidential project."

"Oh yeah, well-now," Tinker interrupted. "I'm workin' on my own secret Kamikaze project, too." Carnie drove Tink and me to the scene of the late April small airplane crash. Being curious, we wanted to see if any plane fragments were still lying-around, but to our disappointment, all of the debris had been gathered-up by the various investigating authorities.

The three of us, being bored, wasted a little time lighting matches to several caterpillar cocoons that were prevalent on some of the nearby tree branches. This activity suddenly inspired Tinker to get psyched about a more major destructive idea.

"Have any of you guys ever been to a real fire?" Tink asked. "I mean, we belong to a fire company, but we don't fight fires. All we do is work stupid dumb-ass Bingo games."

Carnie and I were also bored with the lack of firefighting in our limited fire department membership.

"Yeah, you're right about that," Carnie concurred. "And we haven't even gone to a training session yet. It's about time we attend our first inferno. But if we start a major fire right now, someone might see us frantically leavin' the scene."

I didn't like the way the conversation was going and didn't want any part of committing arson. I tried changing the discussion to Bo Jalonec. "If Jokes were here, he'd probably say we would be fired from the fire department," I added. My attempt at humorous diversion was a failure that fell upon deaf ears. I felt big trouble closing-in from all directions. 'If only Quinn were around,' I thought. 'Then crazy stuff would never happen.'

"Who gives a damn about Bo Jalonec?" Carnie demanded. "The Junewood phony is as fake as they come! And as far as Quinn is concerned, the guy might as well be livin' in Limbo for as much as we ever see him!"

Before I could say anything else, Tinker reached into his black leather jacket and removed a small magnifying glass. "Listen, guys. I have a neat idea," Tink stated. "I'll angle this here lens toward the sun, and in about an hour, the sun's rays will focus through the glass right on these here dry leaves," Tink predicted, kneeling-down on one knee. "Then, this here magnifyin' glass oughta' start a pretty-neat fire. We'll be upstairs at the Edgely Fire House havin' snacks and drinkin' *Pepsi's.* When the fire alarm goes off, we'll hop on the trucks and go to our first blaze."

"Great idea," Carnie agreed before I had any chance to render an objecting opinion. "Fightin' a roaring fire is the next best thing to fightin' the Ks inside an active volcano!"

Tinker prevailed because Carnie was too weak to resist his wickedness. I didn't have the gumption to challenge the psycho because I feared the idea of being on his "hit list". In an earlier life, Tinker must have been a savage cannibal, or a lethal Neanderthal Man, since his ideas were both deadly and primitive. And Carnie must have been an obedient soldier of Genghis Khan, or a faithful Spartan at Thermopylae, since the weak-minded kid dutifully followed almost any command from another Diablo. And I must have been a reincarnated wimp throughout history, because I was always afraid of speaking my mind during times of crisis. At that moment, I had the backbone of a clam.

Tinker carefully situated his magnifying glass near the dry leaves, slanted the lens to the desired position, and promised Carnie and me that the fire would ignite "in about an hour".

Carnie drove his black '49 machine to the Edgely Fire Company, where we scooted upstairs to the recreational lounge. Three regular firemen were present to corroborate our innocence. We watched *The Edge of Night* soap opera on TV, played a game of rotation pool, and casually mingled with the adult volunteer firemen in our company.

At exactly 1:15, the phone rang, and the siren on top of the building sounded. The six of us that were in the recreational lounge raced down the steps. We all entered into boots, coats, and hats. One of the regular firemen answered the call and wrote on the chalkboard, "Woods fire: Near *3M* Plant, Green Lane."

Chief Bradley arrived to coordinate the overall operation and insisted that his three junior prodigies go along on their first firefighting adventure, so that ironically, we could experience our "Baptism of Fire".

"But Chief Bradley, we don't have any formal training!" I observed and verbalized. "What do we havta' do?" I was stunned by the distinguished senior citizen's peculiar answer.

"Don't you worry, J.W. It's all as easy as sex'. When ya' get your two pieces of hose, just stick the male end into the female end, and start screwin' like crazy," Chief Bradley replied.

The two fire engines zoomed-out of the firehouse's opened doors and then sped west down Edgely Road and across *Route 13*. In less than five-minutes, we were into the woods, and three-minutes later, we were squirting gallons of water at burning grass, leaves, and trees. The raging blaze was extinguished in another ten-minutes, and by then, only a few smoldering limbs on charred trees remained. We shot streams of water for an additional fifteen-minutes to make certain that all sparks and embers had been eliminated. Then, the entourage neatly rolled-up the hoses and returned the equipment onto the trucks.

"I'll bet some punk juvenile delinquents with nothin' better to do started this fire," the Chief theorized and stated. "There's too many screwed-up arsonists and pyromaniacs around now-a-days. If all kids were as service-minded as you three boys are, then we'd have a much better society, yes, we would," the Chief emphasized and praised. "You boys know the value of community. It's lads like you that give the older generation hope for the future."

The three Diablos thanked Chief Bradley for his strong vote of confidence. Carnie, Tink, and I boarded our fire engine, and the driver headed-back to the stationhouse. No sooner had we entered the driveway that the alarm again blasted. Chief Bradley answered the call, scribbled his message on the chalkboard, and without any further delay, we were again back onto the trucks, ready for our second exciting mission of the afternoon.

"What in *blazes* is happening?" asked Carnie while trying to imitate Bo's dynamic wit.

"I'm still recoverin' from the thrill of my first fire. Where we headin'?" I asked.

"To Delhaas High School," Chief Bradley replied. "Some crazy kid started a fire in the auditorium. The police have him in custody right now. Too bad all kids aren't as decent as you three fellas'."

"The moron's name is probably Charlie Brown!" I jested.

It was a thrilling fire truck ride to Delhaas High School. The sirens were blaring loudly; the red lights were flashing, and the sheer speed of the large red vehicles was very exhilarating. Cars, buses, and tractor-trailers veered-out of our paths. The three volunteer Diablos were standing and riding on the first truck's back platform , and our frozen hands were firmly clinging onto the shoulder-high metal holding bar.The trucks sped south on *Route 13,* turned right, and in another three-minutes, we were on the scene of dire emergency. Other fire companies already had the conflagration under control, and the two Edgely Fire Company engines were utilized as backup units.

Chief Lou Pinto of the Bristol Fire Department had been first on the scene and had been supervising the fleet of trucks from other companies that had responded to the call.

Extensive smoke damage was evident inside the auditorium section of the massive high school. Water was ankle-deep in the main corridor. Carnie, Tinker, and I were assigned to perform clean-up duty. We swept waves of water out of the school's main entrance using "thick-bristled brooms". The job was tedious and laborious, but we stubbornly persevered. A fire hose was left lying nearby on the tiled floor in case smoke or flames would be emitted from one of the walls or ceiling. We toiled for about forty-five minutes, until the hallway flood had been pushed outside the building.

Fooling around, I picked-up the fire hose and pretended that I was going to shoot a jet of spray at Carnie, who then pointed in my direction and shouted, "Behind you, J.W. Look behind you!"

I swirled-around and was immensely surprised to recognize Angie Palermo and Bubbles Messina, both Delhaas High School students. The cousins had sneaked into the school to see if any personal belongings in their lockers had been damaged.

Before I could get over my initial shock, the girls yanked the hose's nozzle from my grasp. Soon, I thought I was under *Niagara Falls* as the spray's force splashed against my chest, knocking me into Carnie and Tinker. The three of us smashed up against the metal hall lockers. After being blasted and drenched for thirty-seconds or so, the girls turned off the wild water jet.

"That was for what ya' creeps did to me in *Pomeroy's!"* Bubbles assertively yelled.

"And that was for the hose incident you creeps did in my back yard!" Angie hollered. "Not to mention the embarrassin' *Delaware River* shoving fiasco!"

"Now ya' three horny perverts can go home and start jerkin' your gherkins," Bubbles angrily added.

The revenge-oriented girls dropped the fire hose, and then hurriedly exited the building in a huff. Chief Bradley entered the main corridor thirty-seconds later.

"What's wrong with you dunce-headed guys?" our firehouse superior incredulously asked. "This corridor should've been swept clean ten-minutes ago. "I oughta' find three giant, wet paper bags to see if ya' lackadaisical clowns could fight your way out of them."

Chapter 28
"Tinker's Tactics"

A week after the two fires, Tinker was driving me around Dogwood Drive in his '49 black jalopy. We spotted Quinn working on his '42 coupe, so Tink pulled into the driveway of Chuckie and Jimmy Callahan's house. Quinn and a companion were making vital adjustments to the flat-head engine's three gleaming two-barrel carburetors in preparation for the planned, big Haines Road drag-race against barbarous Cummings.

My mechanic friend and I were very surprised to discover that Quinn's friend was a Negro, for no "colored people" lived in any section of Levittown, Pennsylvania in May of '59.

"Getting' ready for Cummings?" I asked.

"Ya' got it right, J.W.," Quinn answered. "That viper has a super-fast machine, and my Ford has to purr like a kitten to be lucky enough to beat his '52."

I then asked Quinn who his friend was, who had been skillfully using his rachet wrench, and our Diablo leader introduced me to Marcus "Sugar Ray" Spellman. I shook Marcus's greasy hand, but Tink ignored the black kid's presence while pretending to be examining the car's magnificent chrome motor.

Quinn told us that "Sugar Ray" was a boxing wizard, who could virtually knock-out anybody in a fair fight. I was very impressed with learning that specific information. Since Tinker was evidently unsociable to *our* new acquaintance, I asked Marcus where he lived.

"In Yardley, over near Morrisville," Sugar Ray replied with a smile. "Quinnie would always bring his '42 Ford to the shop where I work, and soon, we became good friends."

It was a strange sight to see a black kid in Dogwood Hollow, and I didn't quite know how to react to the novel experience. Tinker still pretended that Marcus wasn't even there in our presence.

"We don't see many colored kids around here," I admitted. "But any friend of Quinn's is a friend of ours."

"Don't feel bad, J.W.," Marcus answered. "Because we don't see too many albinos or wanderin' pecker-woods in my all-black Yardley neighborhood, either."

"Well," Tink uttered to Quinn in an effort to gain control of the dialogue, while also indirectly discrediting Marcus. "That race between you and Cummings is gonna' be pretty excitin' stuff."

"That's right, guys. And when I win, and since Sugar Ray here will be a big part of it, I want to make him an honorary Diablo."

Tink and I left the two mechanics to their important responsibilities, and then my spiteful chauffeur drove around Dogwood Hollow. My mechanic amigo didn't like the idea of having a Negro in the gang, let alone having Marcus Spellman anywhere in Dogwood Hollow.

"That's all that the fuckin' Ks have to hear or see," Tink argued. "Cummings, Popeye, Mullins, and the rest will make us the laughin' stock of Levittown."

"You've got it right there, Tink. The Ks are racists," I agreed. "And they're gonna' start big trouble."

"They ain't gonna' beat me to the punch," Tink vitriolically predicted. "And I certainly don't need goddamned Quinn around to tell me what the hell to do, or when to take a piss, or how to wipe my ass!"

"What do ya' have against Quinn?"

"Damn it, J.W. I know all about cars, more than anybody else around here, and our fearless leader has got to get a goddamned nigger to fix his engine. Why didn't the bastard ask me?"

"Marcus is probably a certified mechanic," I countered.

"I've forgotten more about motors than that black son-of-a-bitch will ever know or learn," Tink negatively replied. "That prick Quinn has betrayed my friendship!"

I felt like telling Tinker that Bo Jalonec thought that *he* was a "nigger rigger" when it came to fixing cars, but I figured I would keep my trap shut and live to see another day to eat pizza, and another night to dream about Angie Palermo and Bubbles Messina.

After Tink and I discussed the impending issue a bit more, I temporarily convinced the mercurial nut-job that Quinn was *our* leader, and if Quinn wanted Sugar Ray admitted into the Diablos, then Marcus must be a good guy. We would have to accept Spellman for *his* loyalty and integrity, and not automatically reject him because of his skin's dark pigmentation.

"Ya' can bullshit all ya' want, J.W.," Tinker argued. "But the only reason I might say 'yes' to a nigger in the Diablos is because I want us to stay together, so that we can have a real dangerous war with the fucked-up Kamikazes."

"Tink, what if the Ks hang Sugar Ray from a bridge, or tie him up in a freight train headed for Texas? Would ya' fight for Marcus?" I bluntly asked.

"J.W., I only fight for fightin's sake, and because I like doin' it. I enjoy hurtin' people, and if the gutless Ks did those things ya' mentioned to the rug-head, then I'd fight, but not because of him," Tinker insisted. "I would do battle for the glory of it, and for the Diablos' area reputation!"

"The ends justify the means," I philosophically replied.

"Talk regular fuckin' English, or I'll kick your butt so good ya' won't be able to shit anymore," the antagonized driver threatened. "I'll even shove a two-foot-long cork up your' rear-end, just in case ya' have diarrhea! Then, you'll wish ya' never had an asshole in the first place. And with the damned giant cork up your ass," Tink elaborated, "when I finally beat the shit out of you, it'll really mean somethin' with crap coming out of your mouth!"

Before I gladly exited Tink's grimy Plymouth, the amateur boxer informed me that I had to contribute three-dollars to a just cause. I reluctantly surrendered half the cash in my wallet. Tink then told me he was planning a creative plot against the Ks, and that I should keep that privileged knowledge a secret, or else I would have to face severe consequences.

"Ya' oughta' be more than glad ya' donated to my project," Tink maintained. "If ya' make me your enemy, ya' won't live to have any other enemies." The hostile teen was the most vindictive individual I had ever known, and I would rather give *him* extortion money to keep him happy than be maimed, lynched, or decapitated while waiting for the fuzz, the Army, or President Eisenhower to protect me.

I got out of the filthy car, scratching my head, because I had also given Bo Jalonec three-dollars for *his* secret project the week before my contribution to Tinker, and I suddenly realized that being a Diablo was becoming a very expensive proposition.

'What are Jokes and Tink up to? Is it a joint venture, or two separate schemes? Quinn doesn't charge us dues to belong to the Ds,' I thought as I entered the family house.

It was a late Saturday afternoon in mid-May. I had just finished making a batch of potato salad at my deli job. I handed my apron to Hal Irving, and told my boss I'd see him Tuesday night.

Tinker was waiting to pick me up outside the back door to the delicatessen. "How ya' doin', Albino?"

"It's great finally bein' outa' there, Pecker-wood!" I answered, as we both used some new vernacular learned from Sugar Ray Spellman. "Let's take a nice ride in the country." Then, I asked Tink what was on his mind. "What's up?" I inquired as Tink (alias Jeremy Foster) peeled-out from the Haines Road light onto *Route 13*.

"Tink, are you a *foster* child?" I jested.

"Stop breakin' my balls, J.W. Or else, I'll see to it that you won't have any nuggets left at all!" Jeremy then partially fibbed and told me that Ace Roberts had borrowed Carnie's '49 Mercury for a "blind date with a Bristol girl without any eyes. His next statement was back on track. "Ace's '55 Olds is in the shop again for repairs. That friggin' car's a damned lemon with too much freakin' sour juice."

Jeremy Foster drove his black bomb north on *Route 13,* and then cut into Tullytown. We talked about Sugar Ray being a skilled boxer, and we discussed the possibility of a fight between him and one of the Kamikazes as soon as the K made a racial insult.

Tink proceeded along the road that paralleled the *Delaware River* until we came to a very familiar quarry. "The pits" was where the L-Town greasers often drank beer and made-out with girls. The quarry was an acclaimed area remote teen hangout. The Kamikazes and the Renegades frequented "the pits", too, so like the Feed Bag and the Dairy DeLite, the place was neutral turf shared by local gangs.

"Now, J.W., there's two parts to my special prank," Jeremy Foster declared. "Phase one involves Carnie, and phase two involves Popeye Messina, so don't let this confidential bullshit I'm tellin' ya' phase (faze) ya'!"

No sooner had Tinker revealed his secret information that I spotted Carnie's black '49 Mercury resting nose-down in twelve-foot-deep quarry water. The Merc's rear end was floating above the water's surface, and I further noticed that its hubcaps had been removed from the back wheels, and that its back license plate was missing.

The partially submerged auto glistened in the late afternoon sunlight. At that moment, I felt as if I was attending a funeral, for I had loved Carnie's "James Dean Special" as if it were a family member or friend, and I reckoned that I would never again illegally navigate it through the hills and dales of Bucks County.

"What the heck is goin' on here?" I gasped. "Is this what I spent a whole three-dollars for?" I definitely felt like crying.

"You'll understand everything in a few minutes, so don't get fuckin' diarrhea or start vomiting piss."

Several minutes had elapsed when Quinn pulled into the quarry with his '42 Ford, and Marcus Spellman and Carnie were seated inside. Carnie's open mouth revealed his total astonishment at seeing his '49 Merc' tilted downward inside the pond. After slowly getting out of Quinn's polished coupe, the C Man stared blankly at the apparent catastrophe. Soon, the unstable greaser began bawling like a baby. Marcus, Quinn, and I tried consoling him.

"Ace's Olds is in the shop getting fine-tuned," Tink began explaining as Carnie and I listened. "Ace had a hot date tonight with some roast beef, so Carnie lent him *his* wheels."

"That's right," Carnie sobbed and acknowledged. "I liked my Mercury more than I like my dick!"

"Ace drove-out to the quarry to buy a case of beer from a guy who works in a liquor store over in Jersey," Tinker added. "When the money was being exchanged, Carnie's car slid down the embankment and landed in the quarry."

"What happened to the girl?" I asked.

"Luckily, she jumped-out before the Merc' slid all the way down. You're right J.W.," Tink attested. "This coulda' been a homicide case if the chick drowned."

Carnie and I were in mourning, but the other Diablos in attendance didn't appear to be quite so depressed.

"That's the last time I'm ever gonna' trust anyone with any of my personal property," Carnie vowed. "But when I get my hands on Ace, I'll wring his skinny throat, the pencil-neck fink!"

Just after Carnie uttered those negative words, another strange event occurred. Ace Roberts drove Carnie's authentic black '49 Merc' into the quarry area. Robbie Wilkinson was riding shotgun with Slip Carson and Chuckie Callahan in the back seat. Ace's '55 Olds then followed Carnie's sleek Mercury into the formerly deserted quarry. Al Keller was driving Ace's car. Gene McCann, Gabby Spencer, and a new Diablo, Jim Amari, were passengers.

"What the frig' is goin' on here?" Carnie wondered and asked in total disbelief. "Is this a twisted hallucination, or what?"

Everyone else was busting a gut except Carnie and me, because we lacked the specifics of Tinker's marvelous grand deception.

As it turned out, Tinker had collected three-dollars from twenty-one Diablos or, from everyone except Carnie. Quinn had approved Tinker's tactics because our leader wanted to take some action against the Ks for what the junior criminals had done to Tink and Carnie's wheels after the small airplane had crashed in the woods.

"Chester Goode" had purchased a wreck that was almost identical to Carnie's '49 Merc'. The wreck's front grill, hood, and fenders were seriously mangled, but from the doors to the taillights, the car looked like an exact duplicate of Carnie's boss street machine. The quarry's azure water concealed the wreck's true front damage.

And so, Carnie was the dupe of a very cunning-but-costly prank. The practical joke had worked perfectly, judging from the pale expression that had ornamented Carnie's face, when his pupils had first perceived the water-logged vehicle floating in the lake.

"Now for *phase* two of my plan, which will really *faze* the Ks," Tink insisted. "J.W., you come with me. We'll meet the rest of you feather-brained turkeys at the Feed Bag at eight p.m. sharp. If everything goes according to Hoyle, Popeye will be even more surprised than Carnie was."

Tinker drove out of the quarry leaving a cloud of dust. We talked about the neat trick Jeremy Foster had masterminded on the way back to Tullytown. Being hungry, we then stopped at a luncheonette and ordered burgers, fries, and *Pepsi's*. Quinn, Carnie, and Ace drove by with the other Diablos who had traveled to the quarry to enjoy the nifty joke's perfect execution. Their enterprise made me wonder what kind of oddball secretive scheme Jokes had been organizing against the despicable Kamikazes.

"Tink, ya' gotta' tell me phase two," I begged.

"You'll find-out soon enough," Tinker mysteriously promised. "All that I can tell ya' is that Carnie's hidden Merc' is gonna' lay low in a safe place for a couple of weeks, while that impostor Merc' stays in the quarry."

Tinker then drove his rickety Plymouth to his father's old, grimy gas station, over on Bath Road. I thought in my mind that Jeremy, his dad, and his dad's gas station all needed a bath on Bath Road, but I discreetly bit my tongue before I ever released that verbal gem. The sky had turned to dusk, and the descent of darkness added a degree of mystery to phase two's riddle. We hopped-out of the '49, and Tink motioned for me to climb into the cab of one of Tink's dad's old Ford tow trucks. My partially lame pal wouldn't answer any of my delving questions all the way from Bath Road to the Levittown Towne Theater, located to the left of the giant shopping center, across the parkway from Cardinal Reagan High.

A double feature was playing that evening. The early film was *Gigi,* and the later show was *Ben-Hur,* starring Charlton Heston and Stephen Boyd. Tink casually drove around the theater's expansive parking lot until his eyes spotted a familiar auto'. The license plate number revealed the identity of the car, Popeye Messina's black '52 Ford. Tink backed-up his tow truck with expert precision. He put a chain under Popeye's front bumper, elevated the Ford's front wheels, and then instructed me to hop back into the cab. Soon, the tow truck and Popeye's '52 were heading in the direction of Tullytown.

"What in the world are ya' doin'?" I yelled. I was too timid and meek to curse at my psychopathic companion. I was afraid of Tinker's violent, volatile temper, when someone would oppose or question his warped will.

"You'll find out very *shortly*," Tink cryptically affirmed. "So, ya' don't have to stoop-down, like you're takin' a shit!"

Tinker drove through Tullytown and motored onward to the familiar quarry. By then, twilight had nearly ended. My crazy pal towed the black Ford through some soft sand, and we nearly got stuck. The obsessed loon stopped about twenty-feet from where the look-alike Mercury was stationary, pointing nose-down in the water.

"Now we get out and push," Jeremy commanded. I obeyed the imperative instruction, preferring to be Tinker's live slave than a dead free man. I believed all along that my fanatical and possessed companion was more frightening than Cummings, Popeye, Spits, Worm, and Mullins all added together.

My conscience feared that I was an instant accomplice to a crime. Tink and I pushed the black Ford directly above a steep slope, and upon reciting "Edgar Allan Poe", the car began sliding downward. Soon, the Ford rolled-down and splashed into the quarry water below. After an initial big plunge, the automobile drifted forward for around fifteen-feet, and then the car gently nudged the '49 Merc'. The black cars soon were resting there, side by side.

I stared-down at the two black, stationary objects in the quarry. 'Black is the color of choice for the jackets, boots, and cars of the Ds, Ks and Rs,' I thought. 'Black must be a power color,' I imagined. 'Marcus Spellman must also be cool because he's black, too!' I speculated. "Where'd ya' ever get this crazy idea?" I stammered. "It's a major felony we've just enacted!"

"If I told ya', you'd never believe me," Tink confided. "And J.W.," the future felon continued, "next time your toe falls off, just call a tow truck," Tinker laughed like an insane juvenile delinquent as the insane kid repeated a joke Bo once told him.

At eight p.m. sharp, the Diablos found Cummings and some of the other obnoxious Ks who were hanging-out inside the Feed Bag. Quinn approached Cummings and *his* chameleon lieutenants, so I figured our scheme would appear to have a believable degree of validity.

"Where's Popeye?" Quinn inquired.

"At the movies with a date," Cummings nastily answered.

"Well, you'd better go and get him right now. His car's been stolen, and so has Carnie's. Their wheels have been dropped into the quarry above Tullytown."

"What the hell is goin' on?" Jake Mullins asked.

"I don't rightly know," Carnie answered. "But whoever's done it is gonna' have to answer to two gangs!" my *mercurial* friend finished.

Just then, Robbie Wilkinson and Ace Roberts came storming into the Feed Bag. The excited pair ran-over to the (crucial summit meeting) circle of Ds and Ks.

"Guess what?" Robbie anxiously panted. "Ace and me were just at the quarry to drink some brew. Carnie's car and a black '52 Ford have been mysteriously dumped into the water."

"It's unbelievable, actually incredible," Ace confirmed, "And I never saw anything like that before in my life!"

"We heard all about it already," Quinn stated. "Good thing you guys aren't newspaper reporters, or you'd get fired for givin' us old stale news."

"This better not be a fuckin' trick," Cummings sneered. "I'll go to the movie house and fetch Popeye. The Ks will meet you freaks at the freakin' quarry in twenty-minutes."

"How ironic!" Mullins exclaimed. "Popeye's watchin' *Ben Hur* while *his* black chariot is in the goddamned quarry!"

Four carloads of Diablos and three Kamikaze hotrods zipped-out of the Feed Bag's parking lot, and fishtailed north up *Route 13*. Cummings veered his '52 Ford onto Levittown Parkway en route to the theater to find Popeye. The rest of us arrived at the quarry fifteen-minutes later, and we waited for Cummings to make the scene with his victimized first lieutenant.

Soon, Cummings' car showed-up; Popeye leaped-out, appearing greatly distressed, and next, the psychopath quickly dashed-over to join the assembled greasers standing above the man-made lake.

"Who do ya' think pulled this happy horseshit?" Popeye asked in a rare, jittery voice.

"Don't know," Quinn responded. "But it looks like Carnie's loss is as great as yours."

"Whoever did this is gonna' pay through the nose for a hundred-years!" Carnie pledged, as if he were vying for an *Academy Awards*' nomination.

Noticing something, Tinker reached-down to the gravel road. "What's this?" my perverted mechanic pal asked as if he had discovered gold.

"It's an empty pack of *Chesterfield Kings*," Carnie excitedly stated. "There's only one greaser guy who smokes that foul brand. All the rest of us smoke *Camel*s and *Lucky Strikes*."

"Yeah, you're right for once in your goddamned life," Popeye theorized and chided. "Langford, leader of the Renegades, smokes that foul crap."

"And look here," Quinn observantly added. "Here's an empty bottle of blackberry brandy. There's only one greaser who comes here often that drinks this lousy brand of blackberry brandy."

"Yeah, Langford," Popeye repeated.

"But we can't be sure," Quinn objected, "because I think we need more direct evidence."

"We'll keep Langford under suspicion," Cummings vowed. "He's fucked-up enough to do this vandalism, whether or not the demented asshole's drunk or sober!"

The black Merc' and the black Ford remained in the quarry for several months. Carnie would then claim he had time to buy another '49 Mercury, when actually, his original black car would come out of hiding from the closed-in junkyard behind Tinker's dad's garage.

I traveled back to Levittown with Tinker. As demented Jeremy Foster wildly drove around a series of bends and curves, I couldn't exactly express the many internal concerns which my worried mind had been contemplating.

"J.W., that quarry trick was done for *you*, and that one was also for when Popeye nearly expired your ass in the Reagan gym with the boxin' gloves on."

I tried pacifying Tink before he might *accidentally* turn his car over, recklessly speeding around a series of treacherous S-shaped curves. "And what about our heads stuck in those mailboxes, and your tires and rims chucked into the Delaware Canal?" I fearfully added.

"And J.W., don't forget you being strapped to that red wagon, and having to hear Sal and his ugly wife having sex, soundin' like two wounded elephants in heat," Tink inaccurately cited, completely distorting the story.

I really felt badly for Popeye and his lost Ford, but I had to placate "Mr. Break-it" to avoid shaking hands with telephone poles and peripheral quarries along the winding way south back to Levittown.

"You're right again. Tink," I compatibly agreed and conceded. "Popeye has deserved *this* punishment for a long time. You're as sharp as a tack on a railroad track," I verbally concluded.

"Truer words was never spoken," Tink succinctly stated as his heavy right foot forcefully mashed-down on the accelerator.

Chapter 29
"Bo's Project"

Bo Jalonec was not associated with Tinker's brilliant twin Mercury quarry scheme. Jokes was quite preoccupied devising a clever project of his own. Whenever Jalonec became inspired, the fanatic would enter into his private shell as if he were a turtle, and the other guys might not hear from or see thr rascal for weeks, until the schemer had successfully polished his secret idea to the point of implementation.

Three nights after Tinker's auto' destruction tactics, Carnie, Jeremy Foster, and I were seated at our favorite Feed Bag table. Jokes pulled in with his boss green and cream Chevy, and we were all glad to see him because of his extended absence from the gang.

"Jokes," I greeted. "Where ya' been hidin'?"

"Under Susie's dress. It's really damned ironic that a pretty pussy like her wears a damned poodle skirt."

"What's ya' been doin' with that three-bucks we all gave ya'?" frugal Carnie insisted on knowing. "I gotta' protect and monitor my generous investment, ya' know!"

"Don't worry, champion dipsticks," Bo cavalierly replied. "Those Kamikazes are gonna' pay royally for cuttin' my head with that stone and shatterin' my windshield down by the river."

"And I'm still gonna' get even for that fucked-up barrel roll over in Bristol!" Tinker vowed. "I'm still dizzy from that fucked-up downhill rollin' ride!"

Carnie pointed-out and testified that Cummings had left his '52 Ford in the rear of the building; got into Spits' black '53 Pontiac, and the two spiteful Ks took-off south in the direction of 'Philly.

"That's just the good news I was waitin' for," Jokes announced. "Now we can put my fantastic strategy into action." Jalonec then disclosed his creative plan, and we listened intently to the details.

"That's a really terrific scheme," Carnie jealously complimented.

"It might even top my idea," Tink confessed. "Let's get it done right now. Thanks Bo, for givin' me a call and tellin' me what ya' need." Chester Goode only showed and expressed gratitude because the scoundrel realized that he had a chance to again be destructive at the dreaded Ks expense.

Tinker and I stepped-out of the Feed Bag and walked around back. In a matter of ten-seconds, my companion deftly jimmied his way through Cummings' door lock. Mr. Fix-it then hobbled-over to his Plymouth; opened the trunk; found some random equipment usable in Bo's project; closed his rear compartment, and then slyly carried his materials to Cummings' '52 Ford. By the time Jokes and Carnie had paid our food bill and reached the back of the Feed Bag, Tink had already tossed his indispensable paraphernalia onto the targeted Ford's back seat.

"Chester Goode" next hot-wired Cummings' wheels, and in less than a minute, the most dangerous Diablo was driving us over to Bo's house in Cummings' all-too-familiar hotrod. After reaching Jalonec's driveway on Jonquil Lane, Jokes quickly exited. A minute later, Bo returned with three black leather jackets that the artist had recently purchased at the Bristol Farmers' Market. The gang's Michelangelo had spent two weeks meticulously painting the Kamikaze's name and insignia onto the backs. The Diablos were going to wear the Ks' jackets and cause some major havoc around Levittown.

Bo, Carnie, and I quickly exited our Diablos' jackets and entered the fake Kamikaze' apparel. "Diablos' brains will defeat Kamikaze brawn as sure as there's curly hair around my salami, and no sweat on my gonads," Jokes predicted.

Tink drove us south to Silver Lake, just off *Route 13*. Langford, leader of the Renegades, would often park with his woman on Snake Road, situated behind the lake. Bo had placed three skeleton masks inside each of the three black leather jackets. It was dark out when we pulled into the target zone, and Jokes, Carnie, and then I furtively exited Cummings' '52 Ford. We slithered over to Langford's old green Buick puddle jumper, where the Renegade honcho was making-out with Candy Miller, his on-again-off-again special lady.

Tinker carried over a lengthy, rolled-up cable. My buddy stealthily slid under Langford's car and expertly connected the cable hook to the rear axle. Jeremy then crawled to the opposite side of Snake Road and attached the cable's other hook to the rear end of a red and white '58 Edsel. Since both Langford's Buick and the '58 Edsel were tuned-in to WIBG Radio 99, Dr. Destructo's secret maneuvers were very effectively drowned-out by the cars' dual radios.

After Tink hopped back into the driver's seat of Cummings' Ford, Jokes, Carnie, and I approached Langford's parked auto'. The sudden sight of our skeleton masks must have initially been frightening.

"Hey, how you guys 'making out'?" Carnie loudly asked the startled occupants through his skull mask.

"Hey, Jerk-off!" Jokes vociferated. "How far is the Old Log Inn?" Bo disguised his voice like a ventriloquist's dummy's high-pitched, staccato, spoken through his skeleton mask.

"What did ya' say?" Langford returned in a confused state of mind.

Candy Miller let-out three ear-shattering screams that made the hair on the back of my neck stick straight out.

"Listen, Asshole," Jokes again addressed *our* rattled victim. "How far's the old log in? Ya' oughta' calibrate your stupid dick in inches!"

"What the fuck?" Langford vehemently shouted. "I'm gonna' kill you sons of bitches once I find out who' the hell ya' are!"

The three Diablos scampered-back to Cummings' car. But then, Carnie dashed-over to the red and white Edsel, lit a cherry bomb, and next threw the explosive through the opened back window as if it was a hand grenade. Mr. Merc' was the last one to return and jump into Cummings' borrowed Ford.

Tink drove-away from the popular passion pit in a cloud of dust. The Diablos heard the cherry bomb explode, scaring the crap out of the Edsel's two romantic occupants, and also out of all the other Snake Road lovers parked nearby. We were all certain that Langford caught a good glimpse of the three Kamikaze jackets and of the Kamikaze leader's black '52 Ford.

Jeremy stopped about three-hundred-feet down Snake Road. We all turned-around to witness Langford fire-up his Buick's engine; shift his standard transmission into reverse; spin twenty-pounds of dirt into the air with his rear tires, and then wildly tug his gearshift into first. The incensed maniac's Buick sped forward like a vulture flying out of volcanic Hades.

Soon, Tinker's cable reached maximum length, and Langford's auto' yanked the '58 Edsel out of its Lover's Lane parking spot. In his reckless rage, Langford's Buick dragged the Edsel a hundred-feet down Snake Road until the dunce finally realized there was a major problem. After the head Renegade applied his brakes, the Edsel smashed into the trunk of the chief Renegade's jalopy, creating a tremendous dent of major magnitude. The Edsel's owner emerged from the driver's side, traded a litany of insults with Langford, and then a really good fistfight ensued.

"Ha, ha, ha," laughed Tinker as the black Ford skidded-out of Snake Road onto solid asphalt. "Jokes, thanks for callin' and tellin' me to bring along the cable and my other tools," Tink, out of character, congratulated. "And I'm enjoyin' myself so much I think I gotta' shit my ass off! This gettin' even crap is definitely more fun than jerkin' off with both hands!"

"Don't get your stenchy bowels in an uproar!" Jokes jested. "Think nothin' of it. The next time, we'll send Langford a letter instead of a *cable,"* Jalonec continued with his singular banter. "And Tink, if ya' crap your pants, we won't know anyway, 'cause that's the way ya' always smell every damned day."

"Did you guys see Langford's face?" I asked, not wanting to see or hear a needless argument develop between Tinker and Bo. "The scumbag looked like he saw three ghosts!"

"But Carnie," Jokes interrupted. "Why'd ya' throw that cherry bomb into the red and white Edsel? Some innocent people could've been hurt, or had their eardrums punctured!"

"I figured we could kill two buzzards with one stone," the C Man claimed. "The guy in the Edsel was the cop who's been puttin' the make on my mom. He's also been flirtin' with Jackie Harrelson, my prom date."

Carnie said he had spotted the Edsel's license plate and instantly recognized the identity of its owner. After peering inside, the bomb tosser threw the explosive into the back seat.

"That scare oughta' be a signal for that cop to lay-off my mom and to stop tryin' to pick-up my prom date at the coffee shop where she works," Carnie declared.

Carnie's revealing statement made me shudder. In some respects, "Mr. Merc" was almost as crazy as Tinker was. But Tink never showed any emotion about his calculated insanity. Carnie's bizarre behavior came straight from his heart. Tink's mom also was having an affair with the amorous cop, but the sly desperado would act the same all the time, like he didn't care. Even if "Chester Goode" found-out that his mother was sleeping with the whole police force, the delinquent still would be cold and calculating, instead of being visibly emotionally upset like Carnie was.

"Say guys, Cummings' car is pretty damn fast," Tink admitted. "And old Quinn's gonna' have a hard time beatin' this baby."

"Why don't ya' loosen a wire or rig it so that Cummings couldn't win?" Carnie asked the gang's mechanic. "How about some creative sabotage while you're at it?"

"Because Quinn has to beat Cummings fair and square, that's friggin' why!" the driver angrily answered, showing evidence of strong greaser morality. "I might fool around with you' asshole punks; and I might destroy an enemy's property; and I might send some jerk-off to the hospital or to the morgue, but I never cheat without good reason. Cheatin' is plain dishonest. A car race is like a good fight; it has to be even, and it has to be son-of-a-bitchin' fair, or the contest ain't no goddamned good."

I knew that Tinker felt stronger about cheating in a drag-race than about his mother cheating on his father, or about his father cheating on his mother to get even with her cheating on him. The only real emotions Tink ever showed were negative ones like fury, jealousy, revenge, and animosity.

Tinker stopped the borrowed Ford at a traffic light, and when the signal changed to green, the speeder wound-out first and second gears. The loud dual exhausts hummed like a sweet greaser Doo-Wop melody. The WIBG DJ's voice came on the radio and proclaimed, "If you will, here's David Seville, and ya' can't go wrong with this novelty song, *Witch Doctor.*" The Diablos were in a festive mood after the parallel Snake Road encounters with Langford and the philandering cop. Bo, Carnie, and I sang the lyrics to the "Witch Doctor" tune while still wearing our macabre-looking skeleton masks and accompanying Kamikaze jackets.

Mr. T stopped at another red light at the intersection of Mill Creek Parkway and Green Lane. An elderly couple in a red '56 Buick had also stopped in the lane to our right. The insane driver blasted the radio; rolled-down the window, and then the three masked skulls all unharmoniously sang-out loudly, "Ooooh, eeeee, ooh-ha-ha, ting-tang walla-walla-bing-bang."

The intersection was quite illuminated, and the stunned senior citizens had expressions of appalled consternation upon their visible faces. The intimidated old gent zipped-off on the amber light. The Diablos laughed rather lustily at our most recent accomplishment.

"What scared them more?" I asked. "Was it our masks or our terrible singin'?"

"Definitely our singin'," Carnie answered. "It frightened the shit out of the old farts, who have no more gas left in their asses."

"I'm sure they'll have some fine opinions of the younger generation to share with their fossil-faced friends," I giggled.

"J.W.," Bo added to the dialogue. "Those two old farts are so ancient that their best friends are Methuselah, Noah, Adam and Eve. If the elderly fossils live to tell about their recent thrilling experience, their old coot friends will think they're off their' friggin' rockers."

"That old codger should see a friggin' doctor before he has a heart attack," Tink chuckled, still wearing his skeleton mask.

"Which doctor?" Carnie asked.

"The Witch Doctor!" the passengers all shouted in unison.

"If the Old Fart goes to a Mexican restaurant," Jokes remarked, "then the Elderly Coot could have a heart a-taco!"

"We're gonna' have to hurry," Tink stressed. "We've had this car out for about a half-hour. We gotta' get it parked back at the Feed Bag pretty damned soon."

I was becoming a minor criminal just going along for the joyride, but the excitement of the ongoing adventure definitely had my heart racing. I was concerned that Quinn had not participated in Bo's majestic plan. I brought-up the matter in casual conversation.

"Don't worry," Carnie claimed. "Quinn's already gotten involved in Tinker's caper."

"That's right," Tink reluctantly concurred. "And he's gonna' race Cummings, or he might even duke it out with the King K."

"And J.W.," Bo chimed-in. "I'll bet a fin and a bottle of gin that Quinn will win," the jokester inanely rhymed.

The second stage of Bo's plan had quickly gotten the endorsement of Carnie and Tinker, who both hated the local cops. The Diablos were going to conduct a surprise raid on the area police station while wearing our morbid-looking skeleton masks, along with sporting our counterfeit Kamikaze leather jackets.

"Make sure the fuzz see the Japanese Zero and the Rising Sun on the jackets," Tink reminded us of our responsibilities.

"We'll even play chopsticks on the cops' piano, if they have one," Jokes whimsically replied. "I love breakin' cops' chops!"

The police never expected such daring, and such magnificent audacity. Three cars were parked outside the station. Two were police patrol cruisers, and the third belonged to an apprehended motorist who had been hauled into "the clinic" for a recent major traffic violation.

Our first task was to disable the police cruisers to prevent "the fuzz" from chasing us. Carnie and Jokes poured a three-pound mixture of sand and sugar into the first patrol car's gas tank. The ingredients flowed through a large funnel, which was part of the equipment Jokes had prescribed for Tink to bring-along on the crucial mission. Tinker then crawled underneath the second cop vehicle and used a small wrench to unscrew the cap nut, draining all the oil from the cruiser's powerful eight-cylinder engine.

Tink then turned the '52 Ford in the opposite direction to facilitate a swift getaway. Jokes led Carnie and me into the police station. I imagined that I was an audacious crusader from my medieval history textbook, about to raid the main camp of the Muslims during the *Holy Wars*. But the Diablos were far from being medieval assassins; we were prime disrupters of '50s culture, intentionally preying on jocks, eggheads, rival greasers, and in *this* particular case, the vulnerable police, cleverly dressed in the guise of a rival greaser gang wearing grotesque-looking skeleton masks.

The desk sergeant was preoccupied explaining a multiple traffic citation to an impatient motorist. Two other patrolmen were sipping coffee and munching on doughnuts. Our skull masks took the officers completely by surprise. We were lucky that none of us got shot.

"What do they make old pennies out of?" Jokes shouted through his Grim Reaper mask. "Dirty copper!" Bo promptly answered his own rhetorical question.

"The only good *fuzz* is on my balls!" Carnie loudly screamed.

"You jerk-weeds should've been vacuum cleaners because you really suck!" Jokes howled.

'What the heck have I gotten myself into?' I regretfully thought.

The shocked officers on duty were startled by our extreme boldness. The distressed motorist reacted to our buffoonery by giving us a mock round of applause. We dashed-out of the police station, doing a bee-line directly to Cummings' black '52. The three of us nearly knocked over an elderly couple about to enter the stone building. The owner of a red '56 Buick had driven to police headquarters to report the Mill Creek Parkway "skull mask/Witch Doctor" incident to the appropriate authorities. Their new problem was that the appropriate authorities were now also being wonderfully pestered and besieged by the wily Diablos disguised as Kamikazes.

"That's them, Martha. That's them!" the old codger futilely yelled as the aged coot experienced his greatest sensation in the last thirty-years or so.

"Come back here you brazen Kamikaze punks!" shouted one of the pursuing keepers of the peace.

"You'll never get away with this prank!" hollered a second officer.

The three of us leaped into the "borrowed" '52 Ford'. We were certain the cops got a good glimpse of our Kamikaze jackets and of Cummings' super bad street machine. Tinker ripped-out of the parking lot, leaving a patch of rubber twenty-feet-long. The initial cop in pursuit jumped into his patrol car, but the engine didn't favorably respond to the sand and sugar formula. The spark plugs failed to fire.

The first cop quickly joined his partner inside the second cruiser with the oil-less engine. The vehicle sped-out of "the clinic's" main entrance with flashing lights and shrill sirens blasting. The powerful cruiser was catching-up to us in a hurry. Tink stepped hard on the accelerator to increase our already high speed. As our heads turned and our eyes looked back, we noticed a puff of dense smoke wafting-up from the patrol car's hood. The engine had burned-up from a deficiency of premium motor oil. The perplexed patrolman had to pull-over to the road's shoulder.

"Did ya' hear that cop yell out 'Kamikazes' at the station?" I asked.

"Yeah," Tink growled with satisfaction. "Let's go over to the Edgely Firehouse. We might be called to come and put out the flames."

"Too chancy, too risky," Carnie prudently replied. "We'll plant Cummings' wheels back at the Feed Bag. Then, we'll get lost and lie low for the rest of the damned evening."

"Carnie's as *right* as a German Fascist," Jokes concurred. "Come over to my place. We'll watch a little of *Your Hit Parade* with Snookie

Lanson and Giselle McKenzie. Also, there's a preview of an upcomin' show about Prohibition-era Chicago gangsters I wanna' watch. I think it's called *The Untouchables."*

I didn't know what to think. I was too paralyzed from our most recent ordeals to even say or do anything. I was beginning to suspect that all my friends were crazy, and that all of a sudden, the nutcases were weirdly attempting to out-crazy each other.

Tinker pulled into the Feed Bag, as if nothing irregular had ever happened. After parking the '52 Ford exactly where we had found it, we all quickly hopped-out. Tink was able to pop the trunk open and to my surprise, he unzipped his leather jacket and threw several bags of Specialty Enterprises' marijuana, along with several porno' pictures inside. Tink's last act was to remove a hacksaw that the delinquent had placed inside Cummings' Ford. "Dr. Destructo" crawled under the car and expertly sawed-off the header pipes that extended from the sides of the engine. We then strolled-over to our Diablos' vehicles and drove from the Feed Bag over to Bo's place for an evening of well-deserved, calm, television relaxation.

The next night, Bo, Carnie, Tink and I walked on Haines Road behind the Windsor Pharmacy. We removed the cesspool lid and threw our counterfeit Kamikaze jackets inside the septic cesspool. Carnie and Tink then slid the lid back on, and the group ventured-over to the Feed Bag in Jokes' Chevy.

Robbie Wilkinson was inside our favorite hangout with Ace Roberts, feeding coins into the jukebox. Seeing our entrance, the two Diablos raced-over to tell us something significant.

"Last night around ten o'clock, Spits pulled-up to *the Bag* with Cummings inside as his passenger," Robbie anxiously stated. "The two Ks hopped-out; came into the restaurant; then the creeps walked over to the pinball machines, and played for about fifteen-minutes."

"Soon, the fuzz showed-up," Ace interrupted, "and Cummings had to walk-out to his Ford that was parked near the back."

"Let me finish the story," Robbie quibbled with his best buddy. "Then, the cops made Cummings fire-off his engine, and the loud noise from his exhaust system gained their undivided attention."

R.W. and Ace thoroughly told us that the suspicious police next searched the '52's trunk and discovered bags of marijuana and several obscene photos'. There happened to be four Kamikazes in the Feed Bag when the cops had originally entered the restaurant. So, Cummings, Popeye, Jake Mullins, and Spits were hauled into "the clinic" to answer to a wide range of charges including: harassing law officers, obstruction of justice, speeding, loud exhaust pipes, possession of illegal drugs, possession of vulgar materials, disturbing the peace, and terrorizing senior citizens.

Langford never reported his negative Snake Road experience to the police. It was his policy, just like that of the Diablos, to settle disputes with other greaser gangs without any third-party intervention.

Cummings and his henchmen were flustered and befuddled by the maelstrom of charges that had been unexpectedly levied against them. The K's had been assaulted by the Diablos' fury, and their dense heads were spinning-around so fast that the punks couldn't distinguish right from wrong, up from down, or yes from no.

The plagued Kamikazes were fit to be tied, but the proud Diablos weren't exactly through with tormenting the repugnant pond scum. And thanks to Specialty Enterprises, the Ds were able to dunk the "Special Ks" into hot water with the on-the-warpath Renegades, and also with the local fuzz.

I had to bite my tongue at the supper table the next night. Dad read aloud a front-page *Levittown Times* article describing how the Kamikazes had raided a local police station and had destroyed two police cruisers. "We're getting out of this place as soon as possible," Pop adamantly declared. "I can't live around thugs like those unpatriotic Americans from Kenwood. It's much too dangerous!"

Later that night, I encountered Tinker and Bo at the Feed Bag. I asked the pair where the plotters had gotten their ingenious ideas to victimize the Kamikazes. I was stunned to learn the exact source of their creativity.

"From Stanley Tezeeker," both Bo Jalonec and Tinker Foster laughed simultaneously.

"Fact is, the brainy egghead hates the Ks even more than we do," Jokes giggled.

Thanks to the studious, school library bookworm, Cummings and Popeye had suffered vast punishment at the hands of the intrepid Diablos. The funny part about the whole scenario was that Stanley had lent Bo and Tinker his valuable expertise, and *his* stellar contributions had allowed the dual Diablo "commando operations" to be fully and successfully implemented.

Chapter 30
"The Reagan Prom"

The Cardinal Reagan Junior-Senior Prom was held on the last Friday night in May. Jokes and I double-dated Susie Parker and Carol Zella. We went in style in Bo's classy Chevy Bel Air. On the way to the high school gym, all I could think about as I glanced back and forth between Carol and Susie was 'surf and turf' and 'lobster tail and filet mignon.'

"What are you mumbling?" Carol asked me in the back seat. "We're going to the Reagan Prom and not to a fancy restaurant!"

"Nothin'," I tersely replied. "I'm just hungry for some expensive menu food."

"When J.W. is hungry," Jokes stupidly commented, 'he's not Austria or Poland!"

In the promenade line the four of us joined-up with Carnie and Jackie Harrelson. Carnie had double-dated with Robbie Wilkinson, who had escorted Candy Davis. Robbie had taken his dad's '56 Pontiac because Carnie's black Merc' was still hidden in the junkyard behind Tink's father's Bath Road gas station. After the couples showed-off our smiling formal appearances to our adoring parents, relatives and friends, we strolled inside and walked-around the gym to inspect Stanley Tezeeker's colorful crepe paper and *Kleenex* decorations.

After we found our assigned tables, the attendees were entertained by a live area band, "The Fabulons," a black Doo-Wop group that performed many slow-dance classics. Every half-hour, there was a fifteen-minute break, and during that brief interval, a local DJ spun popular rock and roll songs.

While everyone was acting cordial inside the gymnasium, devilish things were occurring in the high school parking lot after dark. Tinker led Gene McCann, Al Keller, and Jim Amari on their essential Diablos' initiation rites. The four scoundrels were causing some big future problems for the Kamikazes and the school jocks, who were behaving normally inside the building, attending the sophisticated prom.

As the DJ played Marty Robbins' "A White Sport Coat and a Pink Carnation", Susie, Carol, and Jackie departed to the Girls Room to powder their noses. I casually strolled over to the "Picture Bridge" and struck-up a brief conversation with Angie Palermo.

"How ya' doin' Angie?" I flirtatiously asked. "If this were a *pink car nation*, every automobile would look so similar and borin'!"

"You'd better beat it pronto before my cousin and Phil see ya' buggin' the hell outa' me," the swarthy-skinned doll replied. "And I hear you're plenty good at *beatin' it*," Angie laughed and mocked.

"I was only tryin' to be civilized," I maintained.

"Why don't ya' have a sex change and become a lesbian nun, or somethin' like that!" Miss Angela Palermo ridiculed.

I wished right then and there that my dream girl would at least show a casual politeness towards my eminent existence. "I was only tryin' to be friendly," I enunciated a little too sincerely, while seeking some genuine compassion.

"Ya' know, J.W. I think ya' should first get sterilized, and then get castrated," Angie critically answered. "I've decided the planet would be much safer without you and your future children tearin' up the whole damned place."

"Wouldn't simple basic sterilization without the castration part be enough?" I curiously asked.

Just then, Phil Jackson came ambling-over to the Picture Bridge. I could tell by the quarterback's swagger and facial snarl that the muscular athlete wasn't too pleased with me casually talking with his gorgeous date.

"Watch your step, Creep," Phil threatened, "or I'm gonna' make mince-meat out of your limp salami."

I courteously excused myself and headed to the "Boys Room" to drain my radiator. As I was zipping-up my black tuxedo trousers, Popeye Messina and Phil Jackson aggressively entered the lavatory. Within three-seconds, Phil had my head in a full-nelson, and Popeye addressed me with an arrogant barrage of nasty words.

"Well, Asshole. I think you're behind a lot of the shit that's been happenin' to the Kamikazes," Popeye alleged. "Do ya' own any land?"

I remembered Jokes and Carnie smashing Mortimer Ralston's groin on the escalator at *Pomeroy's Department Store,* after making *their* similar real estate statement. "Er, yeah, I already own two acres!" I worriedly gasped.

"Well Dip-shit, ya' now own *a lot* of pain!" Popeye yelled as the petulant K gave me such a jolt to my testicles that I thought my gonads had married my pancreas.

"And J.W.'s favorite *Christmas* play is probably *The Nutcracker!"* Jackson cackled as the jock used my scrotum sac as his punching bag.

The two bullies laughed their buttocks off, and finally Jackson released his submission hold from around my abused neck. The abominable friends dashed-out of the "Boys Room" yelling "Wub, wub, wub!", just like Curly of the Three Stooges. I circled-around on the tile floor, writhing in agony, just like the pathetic egghead had done inside *Pomeroy's*. I fully realized that it was no fun being the victim of greaser and jock physical abuse.

Three eggheads entered the lavatory a minute later. Stanley Tezeeker, Mortimer Ralston, and Melvin Speigleman saw me lying and anguishing on the floor, and the humanitarians benignly helped me to my feet. "Should I get Father Malcolm, Sister Jacinta, or Brother Timothy?" Stanley asked.

"No thanks," I answered with a grimace on my facial features. "That kind of assistance will only lead to more trouble." I was still wincing with pain, but the guilt in my conscience seemed to hurt even more. "Stanley, I wanna' apologize for all the grief I've caused ya', especially pouring the whole ink bottle down your clean white shirt in eighth-grade."

"That's okay, J.W. I understand that some of your buddies dared you to do it," Stanley formally and politely responded. "If you hadn't done it, your uncivilized buds would've tortured the heck out of you."

Stanley and his effeminate companions politely accepted my sincere offer of friendship. Tezeeker shook my hand, and I was surprised that his grip was a lot stronger than I had thought it would be. After I thanked the other two accommodating eggheads, the lavatory door again opened, and Bo and Carnie walked in.

"Well, Stanley, have ya' read any good books lately?" Bo was expecting the egghead to say something like *Silas Marner* and *The Scarlet Letter*, but Tezeeker fooled all of us with his witty answer.

"Well, Bo, if you really want to know," Stanley declared, "I just finished reading *Cellophane Bathing Suit* by Seymour Hair, *The Cat's Revenge* by Claude Balls, and *Old Age Sex* by Jerry Attricks."

Bo was both impressed and amused with Stanley's literary acumen, but Carnie still had massive animosity for the smartest kids in the entire high school.

"Let's de-pants these faggots," Carnie insisted. "And then we'll take off their white jackets and black trousers and see if they're wearin' chastity belts or Mollie rags underneath."

I then realized that it was time for me to take a moral stand. "No, Carnie," I objected. "Before ya' lay a hand on Stanley, you'll have to go through me first. I'll fight ya' to the death if I have to, even with only one healthy gonad." I then rubbed my tender crotch. Bo finally noticed my severe anguish and agony.

"What the hell happened to you?" Jalonec asked.

"Popeye and Phil Jackson just molested me good," I answered. "And then Stanley and his pals came in like the U.S. Cavalry and helped me out."

The eggheads immediately verified and confirmed my testimony. Stanley precisely summarized *their* shared sentiments. "Jackson and Popeye threatened to beat me and my friends up for wearing yellow on

Thursday," Tezeeker revealed. "The baboons said that only un-cool school queers wear that shameful color on Thursdays."

Jokes saw the possibility of a truce between the Diablos and the eggheads. We could ally to oppose the Kamikazes and the jocks. "Don't worry, Stanley," Bo consoled. "We'll take good care of those punks for you, and ya' won't even have to be directly involved in the conflict. Just sit back and enjoy the Diablos' spectacular fireworks."

The eggheads were glad that at least some greasers wouldn't be tormenting them anymore. "Gee thanks," Mortimer expressed with a sigh of relief. "We want to graduate high school before we die."

The Diablos shook hands with the appreciative eggheads, sealing our effective truce. Carnie showed reluctance, but the obstinate kid finally cooperated, because Mr. C Man feared that Bo and I would ostracize him from our company.

While Bo was negotiating a strategic alliance with the eggheads inside the building, Tinker and the three new Diablos were kicking serious butt outside in the school parking lot. In fact, their high jinks were the high jinxes for many of the Diablos' adversaries on that wonderful, gala night. In short, it was also a "Wonderland by Night" *outside* the Cardinal Reagan High Prom.

First of all, Tink and his novice associates had stolen Pennsylvania license plates and bolted and switched the items onto six jocks' cars. About an hour later, an anonymous phone call to the local police station aroused the fuzz's attention about possible illicit activity occurring in the Cardinal Reagan parking lot after the prom. Upon exiting the parking lot, all student vehicles were halted for routine license and registration checks.

Phil and Popeye had gone to the big event with Angie Palermo and Wendy Meyers in Jackson's dad's luxurious tan '59 Lincoln. After checking the stolen tags on the Lincoln, along with the actual registration, the cops demanded that Phil open the trunk. Inside, the fuzz found marijuana bags and pornographic literature, thanks to Specialty Enterprises via the Diablos' sensational intercession. Tinker had maliciously planted the drug and smut treasures, in addition to the six original sports trophies that had been deftly pilfered from the Cardinal Reagan display cases.

"Whose car is this?" a grim-faced policeman asked.

"My dad's," Jackson honestly replied, his mind being in a quandary about the fraudulent license plates and about the contraband that had been discovered inside the Lincoln's trunk.

"You kids better come on down to the station and answer some tough questions," a second concerned officer demanded.

Phil Jackson and Popeye were the victims of a classic Diablos' frame-up. Jokes, Carnie, and our dates watched *our* enemies being harassed (as a result of "Tinker's Diablo initiation bandits") by Carnie's personal enemy, the police.

When Bo drove his '57 to the parking lot checkpoint, the cops gave the Chevy a thorough examination, and after no illegal pot or immoral porn had been found, one patrolman made a stellar remark. "At least there is some future hope left for society, Here is a car-full of kids out to have a good time, without drugs, alcohol, or smut to get them goin'. Have a great time, kids. You're model citizens."

The following Monday, Father Malcolm charged Popeye and Jackson with "conspiracy to sabotage the prom and undermine the school's chaste reputation," and the two studs were judiciously suspended for three days. A comprehensive police investigation was conducted, and the overall disgrace made Jackson ashamed of the prevailing gossip and scandal, which blemished his elite family's prestigious name. Tinker had finally gotten some satisfaction from punishing Phil Jackson, but the most lethal Diablo was not yet through with annoying Bruno Messina, or *his* bitter Cardinal Reagan High athlete-enemy.

Chapter 31
"Carnie Never Learns"

The first Sunday afternoon in June of '59, Tinker drove Carnie and me to the Langhorne Speedway up on *Route 1*. Tink was in his glory because the main event was a hundred-mile-long motorcycle race. Whenever I thought of 'Langhorne', the name reminded me of Samuel Langhorne Clemens, more affectionately known as American author Mark Twain. Immediately, I thought that it would be great if the Diablos could use an idea from one of Twain's outstanding novels to further frustrate the already-frustrated Kamikazes.

After the three of us paid our one-dollar grandstand admissions, we joined several thousand screaming fans in the bleachers, cheering on the fifty-seven determined biker contestants. Tink and Carnie seemed fascinated by the grueling event, but I became bored watching bearded guys on *Harleys* speeding around in monotonous circles.

It was so hot that afternoon that we had to take off our leather jackets at the race's culmination. Tink raised his arm and made Carnie smell his pits' foul odor, and I didn't believe that Carnie enjoyed Chester Goode's despicable sense of humor one bit, especially when Tink emphasized, "It's now time for your pit stop!" Carnie and I both knew that Tink possessed the most horrible, stenchy underarms, even in the height of winter when *he* wasn't egregiously perspiring.

"How about those daring capers you pulled on the jocks and the Ks in the Reagan parking lot?" I asked Tink. "Do ya' think they'll catch on and suspect the D's ruining their prom night?"

"J.W., did ya' graduate from Idiot University or from Cretin College?" Tink cynically replied. "Of course, they're gonna' think it was us. Now who do ya' think they're gonna' accuse: A) the Red Cross; B) the Salvation Army; C) the Amos and Andy Fan Club, or D), the fuckin' Diablos?"

"Well, Tink. I gotta' give ya' credit because I don't got any more cash," Carnie cynically congratulated and joked. "Ya' busted Popeye and Jackson's chops really good this last time. Now, the next move is up to the Kenwood killers!"

"Not if I have anything to do with it," Tink insisted. "I'll always be ten freakin' steps ahead of those little-dicked jerk-offs!"

After the monotonous motorcycle competition, Carnie and I wanted to go to Chummy's Burger Paradise, a fast-food restaurant over in Middletown. The modern teen joint featured California-style carhop service with pretty girls hustling around on roller skates, but naturally, Tink was driving, and Jeremy had the final say.

"Let's go where we know the place and where the waitresses know us," I logically suggested. "And the Feed Bag's my first choice."

"Naw, I wanta' try somethin' different," Mr. T insisted. "So, I'm callin' the shots and takin' ya' turkeys to the Carousel Grille over in Bensalem. Bo tells me the waitresses are easy to torment, and easier to hit on over there."

The Carousel Grille had a similar menu to the Feed Bag, so I stopped objecting and enjoyed the lazy ride to Bensalem. After an exotic-looking, auburn-haired, pert hostess seated us, a dark-skinned waitress approached our booth. I guessed that the chick was of Italian descent because her complexion was comparable to Angie Palermo's.

For once I wished that we could act dignified and sophisticated. Whenever Bo Jalonec was not around, Carnie would imitate Jokes to try and impress some hostess or waitress, but his frivolous antics and semantics would always negatively backfire.

"I honestly wish I was a Moslem (Muslim)," Carnie told the swarthy doll, who apparently was a Muslim.

"Why is that?" the attractive, dark-skinned waitress curiously asked with a contrived smile.

"Because, Baby Doll, meanwhile, back at the oasis, all the AAAA-rabs are eatin' their dates."

"If you want to eat dates," the insulted dark-skinned waitress yelled, "then go chew on a calendar! Now, what could I get you?"

I was hoping that Carnie would curtail his juvenile stupidity, but before I could tell the dolt to "zip it", the extremely irritated waitress had something else of relevancy to say.

"You Levittown gang punks are totally disgusting. We get your kind in here all the time. You're absolutely disrespectful and repulsive!" the stunning young Arab babe exclaimed. "I wish you'd take your crummy business somewhere else!"

"Well, Doll," Carnie answered while trying to act cool like James Dean. "Why don't ya' pull down your panties and shit on my face!" In his haste the dumb-ass blockhead accidentally inserted a consonant blend while attempting to mimic Jokes Jalonec saying the word "sit".

"You detestable creeps are worse than white trash!" the infuriated waitress shouted. "You're white scum with a capital S. Do you realize I'm a Libyan and my boyfriend is an Egyptian? You're so insensitive and abominable! We're both Arabs!"

Something told me that Carnie had really overstepped the bounds. I was so shocked that I didn't even realize that the Muslim doll had classified me with Carnie, and that the princess was also criticizing me, even though I hadn't yet said a word.

"That's just great!" Carnie egotistically exclaimed. "And I'll bet your Egyptian boyfriend would walk a mile for a *Camel* during a nicotine fit. I don't know why people smoke camels? They taste worse than goddamned giraffes do!"

Carnie, Tink, and I were unprepared for exactly what followed. The waitress screamed some foreign words and then yelled, "Mohammed! Mohammed! Come out this instant and avenge my honor!" the swarthy babe exhorted.

The restaurant's kitchen doors flew-open, and a giant, dark figure resembling Aladdin's lamp genie appeared. A turban adorned the Goliath's enormous head, and the brute wielded two sharp butcher knives in his huge hands. "Infidels! Satans! You have insulted my virgin fiancee's good name!" Mohammed shrieked.

"Well yes, sort of!" Carnie gulped.

"All three of you fools, right now, get-down on your knees and beg Allah for forgiveness!" the crazed Arab brandishing the sharp knives demanded. "Ask Allah for forgiveness ten times! You must say 'Allah forgive us, Allah be praised' ten times, or I will cook your heads in the three greasiest pots I can find in the kitchen!"

The three of us, being at a distinct disadvantage, got-down on our knees and repeated the catchy chant ten times, much to the amusement of the applauding adult diners inside the Carousel Grille. And then, regaining our feet, we hastily sprinted-out of the establishment like true cowards. But before craven Carnie fully exited, the stooge remembered a stupid Bo Jalonec' joke. "Mohammed, do you know any good *Cairo*-practors in Egypt?"

The Arab fanatic hustled-out of the Carousel Grille and frantically raced after us. Thank goodness Tinker never locked his filthy car, because I was certain we would have been decapitated if incensed Mohammed had ever caught-up with us during our hectic evacuation.

Fortunately, Tink's reliable machine started up on the first try. The daredevil put the gear shift in first; popped the clutch, and we squealed out of the crowded parking lot, thankful that benevolent Allah had mercifully spared our asses.

Carnie was really pissed-off at failing to make any time with the Libyan broad, for we all knew damned-right-well that if Bo Jalonec had uttered the exact same phrases, everything would have turned-out just fine. Revenge instead of regret dominated Carnie's insecure personality. The wimpy fool told Tinker to pull-over to the side of the highway next to a pay phone. Carnie desired to get the last word in on the vociferous Arab chick. After fumbling through the yellow pages for a full two-minutes, Mr. C decided it would be easier to dial the information operator. Finally, the searcher obtained the business number for the Carousel Grille.

"Hello, is this the Carousel Grille?" Carnie inquired. "I'd like to speak to the Libyan waitress."

"I am the only Libyan waitress here. May I help you?" the still-angry Muslim chick politely answered.

"Do you have any crabs?" Carnie was so upset and disoriented that he didn't realize he was initiating another bizarre self-satire.

"Yes," the desirable Arab waitress sincerely replied.

"Well, if ya' have crabs," said Carnie, "shouldn't ya' be takin' some strong vaginal medication?"

"What did you say?" The Libyan waitress finally recognized the carry-out caller as her former feckless tormentor, who should have been beheaded by Mohammed.

"Er. I mean," then stuttered Carnie. "I would rather order a large pepperoni pizza with extra cheese to go. How long will it take?"

"About twenty-minutes," the swarthy-skin beauty replied. "What is your name?"

"Richard Hertz." Carnie was still somewhat-confident that his guile would be effective and would ultimately prevail.

"How do you spell your last name?" the perturbed-but-un-rattled veteran restaurant chick asked.

"H-E-R-T-Z," Carnie recited very deliberately. "Just like in the car rental company!"

"You're Dick Hertz?" the waitress asked.

"Yes," Carnie admitted with fake certainty.

"Well, if your dick hurts, you should do what Bluto does."

Carnie was confused because he knew what Popeye did, but he had no idea what Bluto did. "What does Bluto do?"

"He sticks it in Olive Oyl when Popeye's not around!" Click.

Tinker and I split our guts laughing as Carnie despondently returned to the '49 Plymouth. "Pray to Allah for forgiveness!" we chanted ten-times in waves of splendid jocularity.

Bo met the three of us later that afternoon inside the Feed Bag. Jokes chastised his derelict audience for being preoccupied with sex all the time. Jalonec was one-hundred-percent right about our addicted obsession. His degenerate apostles weren't following his rather simple instructions.

"You freakin' jive morons don't know hormones from whore-moans," Bo effectively chided. "Ya' spend all friggin' day thinkin' about sex, but ya' never do it. All your time and energy each and every day is wasted over worryin' about a stupid ten-minute biological process. If ya' would just do it and get it out of the friggin' way,"

Jalonec garrulously emphasized, "then your lackluster minds would be clear, and ya' could get normal stuff done just like normal people do that are smart enough to get laid or masturbate first damned thing in the morning."

Carnie completely ignored Bo's fantastic prattle because the constant failure was still smarting from his recent phone booth escapade with the shrewd Libyan honey.

"Well, Bo," said Tinker. "That's easy for you to say! Carnie won't ever get laid until he gets buried and put into the ground."

"Carnie," Bo lectured. "Someday you'll be unhappily married to some frigid dominant hag, and you'll wish you never had friggin' sex at all and had become a sterile Buddhist priest instead!"

Carnie's ego plummeted to an all-time low. Bo insisted on hearing the entire Carousel Grille tale "from stem to stern". After Jokes heard the entire bizarre misadventure, the jester boisterously laughed and exclaimed, "You cootie biters oughta' be glad that the crazy Egyptian from the kitchen didn't 'a-*nile*-alate' your scrotum sacs!"

But that was the way Bo Jalonec always was. If the waitress's boyfriend had been British, Jokes would have said he had seen the confrontation on the "English Channel"; or if the pretty young lady had been from Italy, Jokes would have asked if her name was "Florence" and if she would "Rome" around the restaurant for him. If the waitress had been from Brazil, she would have been an "Amazon". Or if she were from Russia, Jokes would have asked us if we saw her "Ma's cow". If the waitress liked African horses, she would have worn a massive "Z-bra", or if she liked birds, the joker would want to know if she ever got *hammered* by drinking "*Wild Turkey* with non-union carpenters at the *Crow Bar".*

If the lunatic boyfriend had been from France, then the hunchback, who played fullback at Notre Dame, would have obviously been "in-Seine". But that's the way Jalonec's personality presented itself. Bo found all language malleable, and virtually any word could be contortioned into an idiotic pun, or into what the gang's comedian often described as "two thirds of a pisser pun, pee-u."

And even Bo's "chicken-shit" often sounded like "bullshit" incidentally ascending above common "horseshit", because one time inside the Feed Bag Jalonec told me that the flush toilet had been developed by an obscure British inventor named Thomas Crapper. And after I had done extensive research in the Levittown Library, I found Jokes' remarkable "chicken-shit" to be true. So, Bo's "chicken-shit" that always sounded like "bullshit" actually often turned out to be "serious shit", important enough to research and to remember. Bo concluded his berating of Carnie by specifically saying, "That screwed-up Egyptian with the *flighty* personality must've had a jet engine in his freakin' *turban!"*

Carnie, Tinker, and I just sat there with our mouths agape, trying to keep our jaws attached to our sagging maws.

But Jalonec was not through with his verbal assault. "Carnie," Bo deviously continued his perpetual verbal assault. "I suppose that *that* Carousel Grille place over in Bensalem is not exactly a *Mecca* for Catholic or for Protestant Levittown greasers."

Chapter 32
"The June Carnival"

During the second sweltering week of June, a large traveling carnival, *Amusements of America,* annually visited Levittown. It was erected on the asphalt parking lot that served both Cardinal Reagan High and St. Michelle's School. Its appearance was definitely a major highlight of the warmer seasonal months. The glittering night-lights and exciting atmosphere attracted area greasers, bikers, jocks, and wimpy eggheads.

On Thursday evening, Jokes had taken Susie Parker to the fair and Quinn had escorted Patty Van Arsdale. But Quinn had designated Friday evening as being "boys' night out". Jalonec picked me up in his boss wheels and immediately suffered a severe allergy attack.

Bo reached over, opened the glove compartment, and then removed some napkins the chronic sneezer had taken and accumulated from Feed Bag table dispensers. After sneezing profusely seven times, Jokes profoundly uttered, "It's a good thing these damned napkins are sanitary."

"Yeah," I answered. "They'll really look authentic if ya' sneezed any more blood into 'em."

Whenever Jokes felt that someone was challenging his humor dominance, the gang's Bob Hope would assault his rival with violent verbal ferocity. With bloodshot eyes, Bo deftly changed the subject, which was another admirable verbal skill which the jester had mastered to confuse his perceived rival. "J.W.," Jalonec addressed me after lustily blowing his perfect-looking nose. "I once had a girlfriend in North 'Philly named Barbara Wire, but I dumped her because Barb was always cuttin' me up and getting under my damned skin."

Before I could respond to his absurd *barb,* Bo masturbated his throat; coughed-up some heavy phlegm, and spit the green glob out of the driver's side window, simulating an oral ejaculation. "J.W., if the Trojans had only won that freakin' war that the rubber-heads fought against the ancient Greeks," Bo wheezed, "then there wouldn't be such a shortage of rubbers in this world. We have all this disgustin' venereal disease because those stupid pecker-head Trojans lost that friggin' Homer homo war." Next, Jalonec told me all about Al Tuna, Charlie Tuna's younger brother.

And then Bo spit a huge green lunger out the window that would have annihilated a Martian. "Words," Jalonec continued, "some people think I'm *Flemish,* but actually, my national origin is German."

Bo and I met-up with Carnie and Tinker in the Levittown Shopping Center's parking lot, right in front of Tinker's familiar dirty '49 Plymouth. Carnie looked totally wasted and bewildered.

"What's wrong with you?" I asked Mr. Merc'.

"I'm tired," my psychotic, neurotic, paranoid pal returned.

"Ya' say you're tired!" Bo yelled with his nose running like an open faucet. "I could have sworn your name was Carnie."

"Jokes," agitated Tinker countered. "Besides stupid funnies, what else are ya' up to?"

"I'm up to six-foot-tall," Jalonec preposterously replied. "But I haven't grown an inch since kindergarten."

"Very funny," Dr. Destructo replied with obvious disdain. "That probably goes for *your* tiny fadorkenbender, too! Tell me, is it still on tonight with the Kamikazes and the Renegades?"

I sensed that Tinker wanted even more revenge on Phil Jackson and his tough jock friends for giving Senor T a massive beating behind the Dairy DeLite.

"You know it," Jokes answered. "And those jock straps are goin' to have more than athlete's feet and jock itch when we get done with 'em. They'll never again be *broad* jumpers or long-distance lappers once we neuter their dingles."

In our hearts, the Diablos knew that we were more akin to the Ks and Rs than we were to the jocks and eggheads. That year's June carnival presented the ideal opportunity for greasers to temporarily forget their prime differences and unite against common enemies. After Tinker's thrashing, several other brawls had occurred around Levittown between greasers and brawny jocks.

The asphalt fairground was the stage where the greasers were going to contrive a rumble with the jocks, and in the process, aggravate the cops, too. Tink and Carnie figured the fuzz had it too easy, constantly issuing traffic tickets and random parking citations to good American citizens. The two chronic schemers figured that the police needed a change of pace to supplement their ordinary ticket-issuing duties.

Carnie's dad had signed on with *Amusements of America,* and the itinerant barker owned several popcorn, candy-apple, and cotton candy concessions situated on the carnival's midway. Carnie had a rather peculiar relationship with his pop. When they were separated, which was the bulk of the time, Carnie never mentioned his father at all. But when the pair were together, they interacted caringly. It was as if Carnie had a melodramatic split personality that alternately featured denial and acceptance.

The greasers started the preplanned conflict with the jocks on the bumping car ride. Some Kamikazes and Diablos teamed-up on several football linemen, double and triple ramming them and *their* dates whenever the aggressors could accelerate.

And later Jokes, Tinker, Carnie, and I had some fun under the Haunted House's metal grate. Tink surreptitiously located a lever that controlled a pair of air hoses, and when a jock and his cute girlfriend walked above the grate, the Diablos administered such an air blast that the chick's ruffled dress (or poodle skirt) would fly-up above her head. Several of the dolls weren't wearing underwear, and *that* majestic splendor made our activity even more enjoyable, much to the chagrin of *their* enraged jock boyfriends.

Jokes then found a furry gorilla costume inside an obscure Haunted House storage room. The ludicrous joker came-out wearing the hairy disguise while pounding his chest and going completely ape. King Kong's first victims were four burly bikers, who after initially being frightened, regained their courage and proceeded to smash the living crap out of their Simian impersonator. The quartet of Barbarians twisted Jalonec's ape mask backwards, nearly dislocating his very human jaw. Fortunately, Bo fell through an opening between two wobbling barrels where Tink, Carnie, and I managed to drag his battered butt to safety.

"That's the last time I'm ever gonna' engage in *gorilla* warfare for you' petunias, or should I say pansies," Jalonec vowed.

Four police departments patrolled Levittown, because the city had been built within four already-existing governmental jurisdictions. The Tullytown Police Department was in charge of the area around Cardinal Reagan High and the Levittown Shop-A-Rama. Other police units at the fair were from Bristol Township, Falls Township, and Middletown Township.

The cop who had been hitting on Carnie and Tink's moms was also there, wandering-around. When C-Man and T-Man noticed the amorous patrolman watching the Levittown Fire Department's cherry picker plucking marooned passengers out of the lower compartments of the carnival's stalled Ferris Wheel, Carnie, his dad, Tink, Bo and I got even with the meddling officer. We filled the interior of his police cruiser with seventy servings of sticky cotton candy obtained from Carnie's pop.

The Don Juan soon returned to his shiny new patrol car and couldn't believe that anyone would have the audacity to commit such a contemptuous and defiant act of vandalism. What a gooey mess!

The cop fraternity on-duty was too preoccupied with the cotton candy embarrassment to notice that Tinker had shoved a pair of baseball bat handles into the exhaust pipes of another police cruiser. When *that* officer fired-off his engine to leave the grounds to answer a dispatcher's call, the inserted bats caused loud backfires. Everyone in the vicinity thought that a major gunfight was in progress.

The greasers and jocks were emotionally keyed-up for a major rumble. After the Ferris Wheel problem was finally corrected, Phil Jackson and Angie Palermo were rescued and safely emerged from the disabled ride. Jackson believed that Tinker had caused the wheel to stop rotating by sabotaging the ride's generator, or its engine, so the incensed quarterback and a jock contingent accosted Carnie, Tink, Jokes, and me. In support of greaserdom', Robbie Wilkinson, Ace Roberts, Al Keller, Jim Amari, Slip Carson, and several Renegades and Kamikazes lined-up behind us in a massive show of support. Battle lines were quickly drawn, and much to the Diablos' satisfaction, four Barbarians and three War Lords aligned with the assembled greasers, because the bikers thought themselves to be more like us than like the clean-cut jocks.

Coach Cocharan saw the about-to-happen melee developing. The Reagan Athletic Director scrambled through the three rows of letterman's sweaters to warn Phil Jackson and company of the potential consequences of *their* impetuous actions.

"Guys, don't get involved with this greaser rabble!" the anxious coach pleaded. "Think of your futures, your scholarships, your careers. These greasers are going nowhere fast! If ya' get criminal records, it could affect all you've worked for these past four years." Coach Cocharan paused to make the rest of his speech even more dramatic. "Don't jeopardize all your hard work to fight some losers in leather jackets. It's just not worth it! Father Malcolm will suspend all of you; you might not graduate next week, and you'll even be riskin' expulsion from school! Back off, I beg you. Back off!"

True to form, the jocks did disperse, muttering epithets and uttering random threats. The greasers and the bikers' let-out boisterous jeering waves of protest that belittled the obedient jocks', who' were subserviently conforming to arbitrary school authority. The mock "rumble" had been a psychological triumph for the greasers, and the Kamikazes, Renegades, and Diablos all shared celebrating *that* cherished moment in time.

Sunday was the carnival's last day in Levittown. The Diablos decided to visit the midway in the afternoon when less police surveillance would be present. That Sunday afternoon's activities even surpassed those of the evening before.

Quinn was there with Patty, and my hero won his sweetheart two jumbo stuffed animals and a kewpie doll at various side-game concessions. Langford was in attendance and challenged Quinn to a muscleman's ring-the-bell contest. The keen competition ended in a draw. Each participant hit a plate with a wooden mallet, sending a metal bar up a twenty-five-foot-high wire to ring a gong.

While the Diablo and Renegade chieftains were engaging in their friendly contest, Carnie, Tinker, Bo, and I organized some other devilish carnival projects. Our enterprises were specifically designed to aggravate Angie Palermo, Bubbles Messina, and Phil Jackson.

Angie and Bubbles were operating the Delhaas High School kissing booth. Each girl would accept a smooch from white Levittown high school males to benefit the school's nebulous "General Activities Fund". Their service was consistent with the American spirit of volunteerism, and being attractive, well-endowed females, the dolls lured many prospective high school contributors to their stall.

Public affection was contrary to the James Dean greaser image, but everyone was aware that it was acceptable for a greaser to go against *that* conduct code if the kiss were exaggerated or extended indefinitely, violating the norms of appropriate behavior. So, when I appeared at the counter with a hard-earned five-dollar bill, Angie and Bubbles opted to take a long intermission. Both girls suspected that my moist tongue was about to tickle their tonsils for undesirable, prolonged periods.

"I remember when you used to think ya' was a superstar baseball player for Meenan Oil," Bubbles ambitiously chided. "Why don't ya' try knockin' us into the Delhaas High water-tanks, instead."

"Yeah," Angie readily added. "And if you and Carnie can do that to us, we might just call you guys on the phone and ask for dates."

Bubbles and Angie had good reason to come-up with such a seemingly delicious proposition. The odds were certainly in their favor, and the prospect of Carnie and me failing to dump them into the dual water tanks appeared much more propitious to them than me getting my five-dollars-worth, at fifty-cents a shot, by sticking my wet, wriggling tongue down both of their alluring throats.

The object of the water tank challenge was to heave baseballs at protruding discs attached to metal arms. If a hurled baseball hit a bulls-eye in the center of the metal disc, then the taunter seated upon the wooden chair above that water tank would plunge into the wetness below. Out of the last fifty-tosses, only one had hit the mark.

"J.W.," Bo yelled from afar. "Don't throw your balls at their curves. Throw your curveballs at the discs. Just think that you're back pitching for Meenan Oil." All of the spectators, including Quinn, laughed hardily at Jalonec's inane monologue.

As mentioned, two seats were mounted atop trapdoors situated above two six-foot-deep water tanks. Angie and Bubbles confidently climbed-up the ladders to their separate wooden thrones, and the Italian princesses dared Carnie and me to waste five-dollars each attempting to send them falling into the water chambers below. Within seven minutes, Carnie and I foolishly wasted ten-dollars, and the assembled jocks laughed at our apparent and embarrassing incompetence the whole time, making our accumulated frustration virtually unbearable.

The crowd was mocking Carnie and me so badly that we believed we had to do something drastic. Angie then foolishly yelled a distinct insult in our direction.

"My cousin and me can throw better than you two bozos, and left-handed, too, if we had to," the Palermo chick ridiculed. The crowd let out a boisterous roar of approval.

"Oh yeah!" Carnie screamed. "You' both probably throw like girls." Naturally, the almost-hostile crowd heckled, booed, and jeered my pal and me even more than before.

"We dare ya' to switch places with us!" Bubbles screamed at the top of her beautiful lungs.

"Gladly!" Carnie replied before I could even think of anything relevant to holler back.

Bo volunteered to hold our Diablos' leather jackets as the girls descended the two ladders to ground level. Carnie and I reluctantly climbed-up the rungs leading to the platforms that held the wooden chairs. Then, we sat up there, thinking that the girls would be just as ineffective at throwing at the small metal targets as we had been.

Next door to the water tank game was a concession that featured shooting basketballs through hoops. Before Carnie and I knew what was happening, Phil Jackson picked-up several basketballs and started throwing the round masses at the bulls-eyes on the protruding discs. With two amazingly accurate tosses, first Carnie and then I plummeted into the cold water below. Two carnival attendants were gracious enough to rescue our butts from our aquatic enclosures. The two-hundred or so gleeful eyewitnesses sent-out very loud cheers, mockingly celebrating our obvious defeat.

Carnie had swallowed a mouthful of water during our horrible semi-nautical ordeal. My co-victim felt nauseous in his stomach. Before the aborted Kissing Booth episode, C Man had eaten a big bowl of spicy chili. Bo and I escorted Carnie to the woods behind the Franciscan rectory where my sick friend up-chucked his entire meal. As Bo led his soggy' associates back to the noisy carnival grounds, the zany jester had the audacity to call Mr. C's disgusting regurgitation *chile-con-Carnie*. Despite my heightened aggravation, I even had to indulgently laugh at hearing *that* absurd punch line.

Bo decided to treat Carnie and me to some food because we had lost a total of ten-dollars each futilely trying to sink the Sicilian honeys into the giant water tanks. Jokes believed that I had a small appetite and that Carnie would not consume anything because the silly ignoramus had felt sick and had recently vomited. We surprised Bo by each ordering three slices of pizza, two hamburgers, three large *Pepsi's*, two corn-on-the-cob delights, and then Carnie bravely ate another bowl of hot chili. Frugal Jalonec was visibly irritated because the parsimonious guy's generosity had cost the tightwad about the same amount of dough that *we* had recently lost in the water tank fiasco.

Carnie, Bo, and I were much more in our element at the carnival than we were at the Reagan Prom. Despite the ninety-degree heat, we still proudly wore our black leather Diablos jackets, and we habitually combed our greasy hair whenever annoyed, or whenever we felt insecure, or whenever we just felt like self-consciously doing something radical in public.

Jokes soon lost his miserable mood and exactly described the way we all felt. "Ya' know guys," the gang's self-appointed professor remarked. "Give me my Diablo jacket, engineer boots, and denim jeans any time, instead of white tuxedo coats, curly bowties, and those really stupid prom' cucumber-buns (cummerbunds)." Despite the fact that Carnie and I were still wringing wet, we mutually felt the joy of true camaraderie, honestly believing that our mediocre existence was the envy of everyone we passed at the fair grounds. The greaser facade was much more compatible with the carnival scene than with the formal and artificial "Wonderland by Night" experience.

Our prime target that Sunday afternoon suddenly became Phil Jackson. Carnie and I resented Jackson about half as much as Tinker did. Bo told us that it was "okay" to do something to Jackson after the aquatic disaster the jock had done to Carnie and me at the water tank farce. "Quinn had said, 'As long as nobody gets hurt or killed'," Jalonec accurately quoted our fearless leader, "then it's okay."

Robbie Wilkinson spotted Phil Jackson strolling between the *Tilt-A-Whirl* and *Octopus* rides. The star athlete was in search of the nearest *Port-a-Potty* relief facility. Five Diablos quickly surrounded the muscular quarterback. Jackson made an attempt to break our gang's perimeter, but Robbie, Ace, Al Keller, and Jim Amari nabbed and subdued their prey. The Reagan quarterback was taken hostage, and put-up a major struggle, until Tinker joined-in and helped drag the resisting athlete's body under a canvass drape hanging beneath the miniature Roller Coaster Ride.

Carnie had been impatiently stationed there with a wooden chair the idiot had borrowed from one of his dad's junk food concessions. Tinker had a set of handcuffs he had stolen from the police cruiser before the patrol car had been filled with cotton candy. The Diablos applied the derbies onto Jackson's left wrist and onto the roller coaster's metal frame, with our strategic location being near the bottom of the first hill. Using short ropes, Tinker then tied Phil's ankles to the front legs of the chair, rendering *his* feet and knees immobile.

"You guys aren't goin' to hurt me bad, are ya'?" the frightened athlete pleaded. "I ain't got no grudges with any of ya'! That's the plain honest truth!"

"You're gonna' pay good' for what you and your friends did to me behind the Dairy Delite," Tinker lividly promised his principal foe.

"And for what you did to J.W. and me with the basketballs," added Carnie with genuine rancor. "Our memories ain't as short as your miniature dick!"

"You' Diablos really hold grudges, don't ya'!" Phil accused.

"Not only that," observed and hollered Jokes, "but we're also gonna' make ya' curse your brains out of your half-empty head!"

"Go to hell, all of ya' dirty pricks," our irate captive yelled back. "I only curse when I wanna' curse!"

"We'll see about that shit you're speakin', you simple-assed fuck!" Tinker nastily challenged.

The small roller coaster had been activated to accommodate afternoon young thrill seekers. We all heard the ride's chain pulling the train of cars up the first incline. As I yelled out "Edgar Allan Poe", the Diablos hoisted Phil Jackson's chair up into the air. Tinker aimed the jock's noggin through two parallel slats inside the overhead tracks. The roller coaster rapidly descended the first hill, approaching the quarterback's exposed head and neck. "What the fuck!" the wholly incapacitated letterman imprisoned upon the wooden chair exclaimed. Just as the first car was about to decapitate Jackson, we lowered the wooden seat before the coaster whizzed by overhead.

"Next time you'll be able to star as the Headless Horseman in *The Legend of Sleepy Hollow* play," I laughed as I recalled Washington Irving's classic tale.

"If ya' see a naked girl next time, Action Jackson," Jokes ridiculed, "don't lose your head over a stupid piece of ass! Or Angie Palermo might have to sever her convenient relationship with you!"

"If ya' don't curse louder this next time," Tinker indicated and predicted, "we'll keep you up there a little longer to see what happens when the first car rips your throat from your neck!"

The next entourage of youthful thrill seekers entered the coaster's cars, and a minute later, we could hear the train again chugging up the initial hill. Soon, the mini-roller coaster was zipping down the slope heading directly towards Jackson's vulnerable Adam's apple, which was almost protruding through the parallel tracks. Phil was so terrified that I heard and smelled a loud, horrendous, noxious fart rip through his white, summer, cotton pants.

"Ohhhhh fuccccckkkkkk!" the wise-ass jock shrieked, cursed, and shouted very distinctly.

The Diablos again lowered the chair just in the nick of time. We were very satisfied that we had successfully completed our prime objective, breaking Jackson's will and spirit by making our avowed enemy frightfully bellow a series of expletives. We merrily freed the encumbered athlete from his arm and leg constraints. Bo then threatened that the next time the Diablos captured Phil we would re-circumcise his penis, and then attach the new skin to his eyelids. "Then, you'll be *cock*eyed for the rest of your damned life!" Bo firmly claimed and exclaimed. Feeling that our imaginative prank had been accomplished, we finally and officially released the traumatized quarterback from our non-benevolent custody.

One final incident occurred at the June '59 *Amusements of America* carnival that's worthy of mention. Popeye and the Kamikazes arranged the sudden disappearance of Father Malcolm's brown Volkswagen. Bruno Messina wanted to get even with the Cardinal Reagan disciplinarian for suspending him from school for the Diablos' creative bowling ball episode, and again for the possession of marijuana bags and porn' pictures inside the trunk of Phil Jackson's dad's tan Lincoln.

A tractor-trailer had backed-up behind a food concession stand to unload essential carnival supplies. After making his scheduled delivery, the driver stepped-around front and bought a hotdog and a *Coke* from Carnie's pop's concession. The Kamikazes picked-up Malcolm's little brown driving machine, rolled it up two long planks that served as a ramp, and then deposited the tiny vehicle into the trailer. After applying the VW's emergency brake, the pranking Ks closed the rig's back panels.

Several minutes later, the driver returned to his rig, and as a result, the trucker drove the eighteen-wheeler all the way to Chicago, over a thousand-miles away. In Illinois, the incredulous operator reported the German vehicle problem to the *Windy City* police. Father Malcolm had to pay a hefty return freight bill, which actually amounted to more than the priest's precious wheels were worth.

Chapter 33
"Tink Pours It On"

After the June carnival had left town, Bo Jalonec was back with Susie, and Quinn was back romancing with Patty, so that meant I was back commiserating with Carnie and Tinker. The following Saturday night in June, Quinn and Bo double-dated their girls to see a double feature of musicals in the Mayfair section of North 'Philly, *Carousel* and *South Pacific*. Carnie still remembered Phil Jackson's private phone number from when *we* had done some very profitable engine work on the jock's white '55 Corvette.

Phil Jackson was the only kid I knew back in '59 who had his own private phone inside his room. Carnie, Tink, and I walked-over from the Feed Bag to the Dairy Delite's all-too-familiar phone booth. Mr. Merc' had memorized the script that Bo Jalonec had diligently prepared, and my insecure pal was absolutely determined to finally achieve some satisfaction using a convenient telephone. Jackson answered Mr. C's anonymous call after only two rings.

"Hello, is Phil there?" Carnie asked with a handkerchief draped over the bottom part of the phone.

"Yeah, this is me speakin'. Who's callin'? Popeye?"

"Phil," continued Carnie. "I wanna' tell ya'all about my pet collie. The dog's name is Gil."

"Who the hell is this?" Jackson demanded in a very perturbed tone of voice. "Is this a friggin' crank call? How'd ya' ever get my private number?"

"Phil," Carnie proceeded while staying focused on reading his script. "My dog is Irish. In fact, it even has an Irish last name, but it's a collie and not a setter."

"Who gives a flyin' shit about your friggin' dog? "You gutless Worm! Who the hell is this?"

"Now, Phil, when I call my pooch by its full name, I say 'Gil O'Tine, Gil O'Tine, Gil O'Tine'!"

"Now I catch-on to your bull-shit, you' anonymous jerk-off!" Jackson defiantly bellowed. "You're one of those Diablo' assholes, who nearly chopped my head off at the carnival, aren't ya'! Well, Jerkenheimer, I'm gonna'..." Click.

The three of us enjoyed a good half-hour of laughs over Phil's general emotional aggravation. Then, Carnie drove Tink and me to the Levittown "Towne Theatre" where we viewed *The Girl Can't Help It* starring Jayne Mansfield, because we liked the way big breasts looked even bigger up on a big screen.

Soon, it was late June, and the doldrums of summer had begun, following the arrival of the Summer Solstice. Tinker still felt a compulsive need to torment Phil Jackson. Carnie, Mr. T, and I talked it over at our favorite Feed Bag table. "Tink, lay off man," I insisted. "Phil's suffered enough pain from the roller coaster episode and from Carnie's pesterin' phone call."

"I think J.W.'s right," Carnie agreed. "Because I believe that Jackson's already paid big time for dunkin' us two young salts into the water tanks with the basketballs."

"Look, you dumb-ass fuckheads," vile Tinker contemptuously answered our objections. "Jackson and his chums threw me into a bramble bush behind the Dairy DeLite. I felt *pain* all over my damned body and didn't like it one bit. I had gotten over fifty nasty cuts all over my face, arms, ass, dick, and legs."

"But you've already gotten more than even," I argued.

"No way, J.W.," Tink stubbornly retorted. "I'm gonna' keep an eye on that bastard's activities, and when the time is right, I'm gonna' drive the bastard fuckin' absolutely crazy."

Phil Jackson didn't realize it, but Tinker was one of the most dangerous teenagers in all of Pennsylvania. The last Saturday in June, Phil met up with Graham Meyers, another rich kid living along the historic Delaware. Phil innocently left his mint-condition '55 `Vette along the Feed Bag side of the Dairy DeLite and hopped into Meyers's white '56 Thunderbird. The unsuspecting pair went cruising south on *Route 13* in quest of loose female companionship.

It soon was lunchtime, and I was working the nine-to-five shift in the kitchen at Hal's Delicatessen when all of a sudden, Tink's squeaky Ford tow-truck appeared at the rear entrance.

"Hey J.W., are ya' on your lunch break?"

"Yeah. What's up?" I asked. I was at that moment feeling despair from the monotony of peeling twenty-pounds of Idaho potatoes.

"Come take a little ride with me. It'll only require about twenty-minutes of your time. What do *ya' say?"*

The T Man's temptation was all too alluring. I was being overwhelmed with the rigors of adult work reality and needed a temporary diversion to catch my juvenile breath. "I usually *say* words," I smartly replied. Sure," I replied through the back-entrance screen door. "Hal's busy up front and will never know I'm gone."

Tinker had imagined the most outrageous plan, but the conniver furtively kept each part secret until I would experience each phase separately. At that moment, I was skeptical of his sinister motives, but deep-down inside, I feared the consequences of having Tink for an enemy, so honoring my ascending fear, I went-along with his whim to demonstrate my basic moral support.

Tink drove-over to the side of the Dairy DeLite facing the Feed Bag. The obsessed vandal hopped-out of his escape vehicle, hot-wired Phil Jackson's '55 'Vette, and next told me to jump inside the sports car and follow his dirty greasy tow truck. I did as commanded and trailed Tinker over to Edgely Road, where we stopped alongside the Edgely Fire Company. Construction workers had been pouring cement for new sidewalk installation, but the tradesmen were taking their lunch break and had gone somewhere for a bite to eat. Since no one was around to detect *his* shenanigans, Tink decided to enact part two of his fanatical reprisal.

"Dr. Destructo" was a skilled expert when it came to the repair or operation of any kind of machinery. The nefarious fiend instructed me to position the beautiful 'Vette parallel to a cement mixing truck. I then exited the white sports car, and before I could say a word, Tink had deftly angled the cement chute (which reminded me of a water flume) directly into the open interior of Phil Jackson's precious and immaculate white Corvette convertible.

With masterful precision, my wicked and devious friend turned several switches, pulled a couple of levers, and soon, cement was flowing down the chute and falling directly upon the car's red rugs and matching upholstery. Tinker skillfully maneuvered the trough so that the mixture distributed smoothly throughout the white 'Vette's open front and back-seat interior. In three short minutes, the demolition job had been satisfactorily completed.

The semi-lame criminal then stepped-over to the tow truck, reached behind the front seat, and removed an old shabby bed quilt, which he used to cover the immense destruction. Tink directed me to get inside the tow-truck while attaching his chain, and soon adroitly hoisted the Corvette's front wheels off the ground. Next, the crazed psycho was back, sitting behind the tow truck's steering wheel.

"Are you a Kamikaze?" I objected. "That's the kind of malice that those thugs do!"

"Sorry J.W.," Tink matter-of-factly answered. "But I just gotta' do what I gotta' do." No trace of guilt, remorse, or regret had been evident in his unemotional tone of voice.

"What if we get caught?" I nervously asked. "I'm involved in a major crime here! I'm what's called on TV news being an accessory!"

"That'll never happen, because most guys don't know if their fly is down unless you tell 'em it is. Most women don't know that their tits are hangin' out of their bra or bathin' suit unless ya' stare at 'em for fifteen-minutes with your goddamned tongue hangin' out. And when they're finally payin' attention, people don't want to notice other people's problems and get involved."

"But you just destroyed an expensive sports car," I pleaded. "It'll take us centuries to pay for it." My conscience was definitely bothering me, and I definitely realized that I had been a real-life accomplice to a very serious crime.

"That's why they got insurance, J.W. That's why they got insurance," Tinker repeated like a stupid, low I.Q. parrot. "The 'Vette will be covered by Jackson's auto' policy," my demented companion replied all-too-calmly. "I think when the cement dries, it'll match the white exterior pretty good, don't you?"

I told Tink on the ride back to Hal's Deli in the old tow-truck that I didn't want to spend the rest of my life confined inside a jail. I was afraid I would crack under the pressure of intense police interrogation. My heinous friend had a counter argument for anything I said, suggesting that I should tell the cops that I didn't own a driver's license, and that I didn't know how to drive cars. Therefore, according to *his* suspect logic, I couldn't have possibly driven the white 'Vette over to the Edgely Fire Company.

"Do ya' have a Pennsylvania driver's license?"

"No. Only a fishin' license," I confessed.

"Ya' see, J.W. I believed ya' all along. That's why I would let ya' drive my Plymouth around Bucks County. Ya' fooled me and ya' could fool the cunt-lappin' cops just as easy. Tell the same shit with a straight face to them, and the fucked-up fuzz will believe it, too." There was little doubt in my mind that Tinker was really the Devil in disguise.

My mad companion towed the '55 'Vette back to the Dairy DeLite, and then adroitly manipulated the crank and lowered the white sports car to ground level. The insane teen then straightened-out the old tarnished bedquilt that covered the damage, and before I could register any protest, the warped Diablo hopped back into his tow truck.

"But Tink, this time you're goin' too far," I insisted, "because you're wreckin' fancy cars with cement and plunkin' other ones into deep quarries." I was almost delirious, trembling with a rare sense of shame. I felt that my conscience couldn't live with the mounting guilt, even if I intensely disliked jocks and Kamikazes in general, and Phil Jackson and Popeye Messina in particular.

"That's why they have insurance, J.W.," Tinker predictably replied. "That's why they' have fuckin' insurance," the junior felon reiterated, showing no evident remorse or guilt.

Tink bypassed Hal's Delicatessen and drove me down Haines Road past the James Buchanan School over to Dogwood Hollow. I didn't say a word as I worriedly sat frozen on the passenger side of the stench-laden tow-truck. My unwanted chauffeur pulled into the driveway at 50 Daffodil Lane to abruptly turn around. The young vandal pointed over to Sal Palermo's front yard, where a landscaping crew was sowing a new lawn to replace the one that the young crook had maliciously weed-sprayed and killed.

"That's why they have insurance J.W.," the teen thug snickered. "That's why the hell they have fuckin' insurance. J.W., do ya' want to get-out and make a confession to Sal's wife or Angie, and after you apologize, then help those minimum wage flunkies toilin' over there, the sweating assholes re-seeding Palermo's lawn?"

"No, Tink," I answered. "Just please drive me back to Hal's Deli, before I lose my job."

On the way back to my safe workplace, Mr. T told me that he wasn't through with Phil Jackson and articulated that the demolition expert also wanted more vengeance performed on Popeye Messina. "With all the treacherous shit those toxic guys have pulled on you and me, Words, I ain't through with either of 'em by a long shot."

"But you've already drowned Popeye's Ford in the quarry and destroyed Phil's 'Vette with cement! Isn't that more than enough needed revenge?"

"Hell no, J.W., hell no!"

My mind was certain that Tinker was an evil madman, a wanton criminal, far worse than any vile Kamikaze. The over-qualified mental hospital patient desperately required advanced psychiatric help. The demonic fiend was a member in the wrong gang, and I believed that demented Jeremy Foster should have lived in Kenwood instead of in Dogwood Hollow.

"But how long can ya' get away with stuff like this?" I emotionally asked. "How do ya' know we won't get caught and wind-up in prison?"

"J.W., listen to me very carefully. If ya' ever cross or squeal on me, I'll burn your fuckin' house down with you and your' damned family sleepin' in it. That's why I really brought you to 50 Daffodil Lane to turn-around, so that I could tell you *that* reality. Of course, I might do it when ya' ain't sleepin', so that it's only arson, and not murder."

The insane Diablo finally crossed *Route 13* on Haines Road and pulled into the rear of Hal's Delicatessen. I was quite relieved to be getting back to my tedious work.

"J.W. If ya' ever rat on me, you're a cemetery resident for certain after I burn-down your folks' quaint little house. You'll be pushin' up daisies and growin' weeds, do ya' read me?"

"You've got no heart or conscience," I nervously accused. "And you should've been a Kamikaze."

“J.W. If I was a Kamikaze, there wouldn’t be any Diablos alive to fuckin’ bother me. So be thankful I’m still a goddamned angry D.”

I falsely thanked Tink for his inglorious companionship, exiting and slamming his tow truck’s passenger door tight. Mr. T took off as if nothing irregular had ever happened. As I turned to view the field behind the Feed Bag, my eyes saw Phil Jackson’s Corvette still over beside the Dairy DeLite, its form covered with the tarnished bedquilt, camouflaging the reprehensible vandalism underneath.

I opened the deli’s back screen door and shuffled my feet inside. My hands then locked the door with its hook-and-eye fastener. I still felt rather dumbfounded while I sauntered like a robot into the main part of the store where Hal was quite busy conducting his thriving noontime business.

“J.W., glad to see you,” Mr. Irving declared. “I’ve been so occupied with retail customers up front here that I haven’t had a chance to sit down in over two-hours. Business has really been brisk, I’m glad to say. Sorry I wasn’t able to go back to the kitchen and chat with you. Did ya’ take a lunch break and go over to the Dairy DeLite?”

“Sure did, Mr. Irving. Sure did,” I reiterated. “Life is really kinda’ dull around these parts. I wish something excitin’ would happen once in a while to break the monotony.”

“I know what you mean, J.W.,” my cheerful employer confirmed. “I know exactly what you mean.”

That late June night, Bo Jalonec approached me inside the Feed Bag. My friend had a wide grin appearing on his handsome visage. Tinker had been bragging to Jokes about the fate of Phil Jackson’s formerly magnificent ‘Vette. My guilt was still affecting my mental stability, and so at that moment, I had little tolerance for any of Jalonec’s annoying quips.

“Well, Words. By now the cops oughta’ have enough *concrete* evidence to have a *solid* case against Tink and you.”

“Bo, right now I need you like I need a second appendix,” I angrily and contemptuously answered.

Chapter 34
"A Full Moon"

Before any other convoluted June events could materialize, July 1st had rolled-around. Robbie Wilkinson had gotten the word from Jake Mullins that the big drag-race between Quinn and Cummings had been postponed to August 3. Cummings had encountered some unexpected difficulties with the law in regard to loud exhaust pipes, marijuana, pornography possession, disturbing the peace, and indiscriminately harassing senior citizens on Mill Creek Parkway. Cummings was just as perplexed as Popeye Messina had been about the police allegations and the subsequent expensive court convictions. Bruno had also experienced a disheartening automobile problem when his black '52 Ford' had been found mysteriously floating in the Tullytown quarry.

I was really anticipating a big summer rumble between the Ds and the "Special Ks". Psychological warfare and general friction were evident wherever and whenever members of the two gangs shared common space. The dual animosities were ascending to a zenith; suspicion was rampant, and I feared that some Diablos might wind-up in jail, in the hospital, or in the cemetery. Early July mornings found me standing bare-chested in front of the bathroom mirror, emulating contemporary muscleman Charles Atlas, straining my biceps and doing repeated poses of "dynamic tension".

Despite the prospect of imminent gang violence, I still found time to help the Diablos engage in assorted mischief. On a very torrid early July night, I was riding shotgun in Jokes' '57 Chevy. Mr. T and C-Man were passengers in the back seat. Tinker, Carnie and I had been planning a cute trick for several weeks, and finally we convinced Bo to go along with it, as long as his immaculate automobile would not be ruined, damaged, or pulverized. Tink (according to his destructive nature) secretly kept the contents we needed hidden inside a brown paper bag, and it would be just a matter of time before *our* Diablo contingent stirred-up some major pandemonium on *Route 13*.

"Mooning" was a popular-yet-harmless tradition of '50s teenagers. The practice was a rather simple exercise in zaniness. A car of teens would pull alongside another vehicle usually loaded with teens of the opposite sex. The passenger in the front seat and a rider in the back would pull=down their blue jeans and underwear, exposing "full moons" out of open windows. The remaining occupants seated inside the mooning vehicle would make a ruckus to draw attention to the exhibited "moons", and after the fascinating deed had been satisfactorily performed, the "mooning car" would accelerate and speed-off in triumph.

That evening, Jokes pulled behind the unsuspecting female occupants of a brand-new, red '59 Chrysler. Bo then entered the passing lane as we straddled the expensive "adult-mobile". Carnie and I lowered our dungarees and jockey shorts and exposed our butts out of our open windows. Bo turned the radio-up to maximum decibels and shrieked along with Tinker in order to add to the general mayhem. The four females inside the boss red Chrysler simply sat there', stunned and shocked by our unexpected reckless abandonment.

"Ten bucks gets you one greenback that they'll try to do the same thing to us at the next light," Jokes predicted. We just had to believe Bo, because we professed that the Don Juan knew the female psyche better than the rest of us knew the alphabet.

"Bo, did ya' see who was sittin' in the front seat?"

"No, Words," the blond wonder boy answered. "I didn't even recognize the *driver.* Of course, I have the same damned problem every time I have to tee-off and hit a damned golf ball."

"Angie was ridin' shotgun and Bubbles was drivin'," I stammered. I certainly didn't anticipate encountering my two Sicilian dream-girls on my first official mooning expedition. "Dante must've just gotten a new red car!"

Bo motored-over to the right-hand lane and slowed-down. Blondie advised us that the red Chrysler would catch-up to us at the Edgely Road traffic light. Jalonec was positive the girls would attempt to moon us back before the babes got to the area of the Dairy DeLite and the Feed Bag. Since the narcissistic blond Adonis was the premier authority on all matters involving luscious chicks, Carnie, Tink, and I completely trusted Jokes' impeccable judgment. Besides myself, the C Man also had heartthrobs for the two Italian princesses, and the concerned novice asked Jalonec if the honeys had recognized *us.*

"Probably not," Bo authoritatively declared. "But I'm sure that the dolls identified my car. And they probably think it's me out cruisin' with some guys other than you perverted idiots. Truthfully, Angie and Bubbles think I'm too cool to be hangin' around with you three freaks all the time," Jalonec typically needled his horny passengers. "The broads in that red bomb only know that they want to go on record sayin' they got even with my boss '57. Then, the chatty babes could go and brag the exciting news to all their buddiacos."

I was deeply impressed with Bo's extensive knowledge of mature women. Jokes knew more about the female sex than I knew about myself, or about my own skinny bare chest, reflected in my medicine cabinet's mirror. At that moment, I was so enamored with Jalonec's wonderful wisdom that I couldn't think either straight or crooked.

"But how can you be so damned sure they'll even waste their time bothering with us?" asked befuddled Tinker, who was always pessimistic and had a poor self-image when it came to wooing and conquering heavenly chicks.

Bo Jalonec always had an explanation for anything. "For two reasons," the know-it-all confidently lectured. "Number one, it's human nature to want to get even with someone who has just made a complete fool out of you. Number two, mooning' is just like yawning. Once ya' see someone do it, it's contagious. It plants a seed inside your delicate brain, one so powerful that it won't go away until ya' wind-up makin' a visible *ass* out of yourself."

Bo Jalonec's logic sounded both plausible and infallible. The Edgely Road and *Route 13* traffic signal turned to amber. The bright headlights from the red '59 Chrysler refracted through the '57 Chevy's back window. And sure enough, the red vehicle halted in the passing lane parallel to us. We were all happily awaiting being moonstruck.

Angie and an anonymous honey in the back seat stuck their magnificent buttocks out of their respective windows. Bo immediately told us he wanted to become a proctologist, since firm fannies like those had never been spotted on the lunar surface with even the most powerful optical devices. Because if the beautiful visions we were witnessing were visible on the moon, every normal male over the age of ten would have a powerful telescope pointing-out of his bedroom window, every cloudless night.

Tinker then removed two leak-proof water pistols that had been concealed inside his brown paper bag. The chronic avenger had filled the guns with jet-black ink, so that when he and Carnie took aim from just behind the driver's seat, Angie's and the other girl's marvelous "moons" suddenly turned into total lunar eclipses.

"Ahhhhhhhhh!" the two curvaceous babes screamed in response to the sensation of instant wetness hitting their gorgeous femininities.

"I haven't seen beauty like that in many moons!" Bo boomed-out at the red Chrysler's occupants. The famous '57 Chevy sped-off before the girls could ever regroup and formulate a plan of retribution.

After my family's supper the following evening, Salvatore Palermo and Dante Messina showed-up at 50 Daffodil Lane. As the Diablos had theorized and suspected, the red Chrysler that Carnie and Tink had squirted black ink into belonged to none other than Mafia Don, Dante Messina.

The surly, burly Sidgees looked like hostile, hairy gorillas that had recently escaped from their zoo cages. An abundance of thick black fur jutted-out from under their sleeveless, white, wife-beater undershirts.

My parents were extremely alarmed by the unsolicited guest appearance from the local "Cosa Nostra". Pop believed the two vociferous Italians to be official card-carrying members of *that* ignominious crime organization. I braced myself against the kitchen wall, fearful of hearing a litany of vituperations from our visitors.

"Your juvenile delinquent punk kid trashed my brother-in-law's new red Chrysler last night," Sal accused. "Wordsworth here squirted at least a gallon of black ink into the brand-new Chrysler. All the upholstery, rugs, seats, and dashboard are ruined."

Dad feared that there might be an element of truth in Sal Palermo's blunt accusation. "Son, did you squirt black ink into this man's car?"

I sorted-out the exact facts I wanted to use before offering my explanation. "No, Pop," I replied, withholding several vital facts. "I haven't touched any black ink since eighth-grade over at St. Michelle's School. If you recall, I had specifically promised that I'd never use ink again, ever since I had that big problem with Stanley Tezeeker."

"Your half-assed kid is messin' around with the wrong people," Dante Messina quickly asserted. "Him and those other delinquent *Amerrygans* he hangs around with are big trouble and bad news. They're all penitentiary candidates!"

Although Sal's sarcastic remark was intended to belittle Dad, the fact-of-the-matter was that my father was only making eighty-five dollars a week in 1959, and when Sal Palermo ridiculed my father by saying *he* only made a "Ben Franklin" a week, then that offensive comment constituted a double insult.

"I believe my son," Pop maintained. "He would never squirt black ink into your car. Until you two men can prove beyond a shadow of a doubt that J.W. had committed the act, I stick with my kid. I'm gonna' call the cops if you two gentlemen don't leave my property right now."

The irate Sicilians realized that the accusers didn't have adequate direct evidence to substantiate their claim.

"We'll cool it for now," Palermo conceded. "But your sneaky kid is not the little angel ya' think he is. He was the one who pushed our daughters into the *Delaware Rive*r."

The truth was that Carnie and Tinker were the actual culprits who had squirted the ink-filled water guns at Angie and the anonymous back-seat broad. Thanks to fate or bad luck, I happened to be riding shotgun in the front that night. I could not have participated in the terrific frolic, although I must confess, I was very proud to be a vital part of the Diablos' legendary "full moon" caper.

Chapter 35
"The Windsor Pharmacy Debacle"

The second Tuesday evening in July of '59, Tinker drove me to the Windsor Pharmacy on Haines Road to buy a couple packs of smokes. I had to patiently wait over five-minutes because four fastidious female customers were standing in line ahead of me. I browsed-around the checkout counter and picked-up a pack of *Juicy Fruit* chewing gum and two *Three Musketeers* candy bars. I had selected that candy brand because I was thinking about using some idea from the famous novel *The Three Musketeers* against the "Special Ks", as well as some stellar plot constructions borrowed from *Robin Hood* and *The Prince and the Pauper*. Finally, I advanced to the cash register and also purchased two packs of *Camel* cancer sticks, the Diablos' choice of weed.

My eyes noticed that it was just about dark outside, and when I stepped out the pharmacy's front door and casually walked around the building's sidewalk, I was unexpectedly greeted by Cummings, Popeye, Jake Mullins, Spits, Worm, Dave Evans, and two other newly recruited Kamikazes. Evans had arms like tree-trunks, and the giant punk nearly ripped my skull off my neck while administering a wicked headlock.

"Where's Tinker?" I asked, gasping for air.

"Oh, your good buddy has abandoned you and is playin' pool right now," Cummings answered. The puzzling, sarcastic remark seemed rather illogical.

"Pool?" I panted and gasped while I futilely struggled and squirmed. "Lightning's Billiards Parlor is fifteen-minutes away from here over in Fairless Hills!"

"Stop complainin', Punk," Popeye commanded in a very haughty tone of voice. "Because you and Tinker Bell are both gonna' be behind the eight ball mighty soon."

The Kamikazes all laughed in response to Popeye's "pool" allusion. I still needed more accurate information to accurately figure-out exactly what was going on. "Where's Tinker's Plymouth?" I demanded from beneath Dave Evans' muscular forearm.

"No sweat, Creep," Cummings snickered. "It's flooded."

I still could not crack the encryption behind the Kamikazes' strange language, mostly because the dumbbells seldom spoke figuratively. All eight of the Ks were laughing hysterically.

"If it was flooded it couldn't start," I panted-out and gasped. "How come it's flooded and not sittin' in the parkin' lot?" I only wanted some straight answer from the surrounding Neanderthal class of local sub-human vermin.

"Because we pushed his junker into the Delaware Canal," Popeye finally clarified, "so that's why it's freakin' flooded!"

The other Kenwood nutcases found Messina's revealing answer rather amusing. Then, the bellicose thugs dragged my carcass about thirty-feet behind the Windsor Pharmacy to the same cesspool where the Diablos had previously disposed of the three imitation Kamikaze jackets, just after successfully consummating Bo's extraordinary commando project.

"The manager of the pharmacy called me after he had a septic service truck pump-out his cesspool," Cummings informed me. "And then Popeye and me put two and two together and figured-out all the friggin' trouble we had with the law. All signs and clues then pointed to you and the Diablos!"

"And I figured," Bruno Messina added, "that your filthy bullshitin' lame buddy with the bad case of B.O. had something to do with my Ford being drowned in the quarry."

Before I knew anything else, Cummings, Popeye, and the rest had a thick rope tied-around my waist. I was swiftly lifted-up and then deposited into the throat of the lidless cesspool, suspended above the stinking muck by the rope wrapped around my midriff. I was then un-gently dropped into the putrid stench below. The Ks then threw the remainder of the rope into the hellish septic container. I soon discovered that Tinker was my involuntary companion also incarcerated inside the foul-smelling receptacle. The overall odor was quite nauseous as we clumsily stood in chest-deep fecal matter.

"I told ya' J.W. that you was goin' to play some pool," Cummings cackled-down from above. The Kamikaze kingpin appeared rather proud of his foul, dastardly deed. "Cesspool!"

"This is the kind of crap you get when ya' give the Ks any of your stupid shit!" Popeye's voice shouted-down, his huge ape hands forming a megaphone over his mouth.

And then Cummings and Popeye Messina poured quart bottles of Kamikaze urine down on Tinker's head and mine, as if it was some sort of culminating K sacrilegious rite similar to church Baptism.

"Ya' two pinpricks aren't even good enough for our piss!" hollered-down Cummings. "Just like your friggin' lug nuts!"

At last, the intolerable humanoids made their jolly way to their separate vehicles. Ten seconds later, I heard the Ks' cars peel-out of the Windsor Pharmacy's side parking lot.

Tinker and I were sick in our stomachs. In the horrendous close quarters, being face-to-face, my raunchy pal started vomiting in my face, and I began barfing on him, and even our terrible sour breaths and disgusting heaves were less desirable than the chest-deep slime and scum below and around us.

"This is all that asshole Jalonec's fault!" Tinker blamed. "It was *his* fucked-up idea to paint those three leather jackets and then terrorize the police station disguised as Kamikazes!"

"But Tink," I said before coughing and choking. "It was your idea to throw the three jackets into this here foul cesspool."

I begged Mr. T to climb-up on my shoulders so that I could elevate his body to a height where the human spider might be able to clamber out of the sordid, bacteria basin. However, Jeremy's engineer boots couldn't get any decent traction on the slippery walls, and Tink toppled-over, wildly splashing into the effluence, and momentarily disappearing below the mucky surface. The human arachnid soon came-up for air, and spit-out about a half-pound of liquid waste directly into my face.

"We can't panic!" I deliriously yelled.

"We're gonna' die like rats down here J.W., I just fuckin' know it!" my co-victim predicted. "Those shit-head hoodlums don't care if they kill us accidentally or on purpose!" panted my brown-coated companion, who quite frankly, never smelled so repugnant as he did at that particular moment. Then, my brain got a sudden inspiration.

"Tink, we got just one chance for survival," I mentioned while sucking-in air. "Ya' always carry a screw-driver in your leather jacket. Ya' could somehow make a spike in the wall and use it like a ladder rung to climb outa' here."

"That's it, J.W." Then, once I'm outa' here, ya' could toss up the rope, and I'll tug ya' out of this goddamned hellhole!"

Tink managed to unzip a side-pocket of his leather jacket. "J.W., the screw diver's right here in my hand. This Diablo jacket must be waterproof!" Tink exclaimed.

"Shit-proof, too!" I spewed-out in temporary relief.

I bent-down under the muck, and next I felt Tink climbing onto my shoulders. I somehow gained the required strength to desperately hoist him up above my filthy head. The beleaguered prisoner then managed to awkwardly stand on my shoulders and attempted to pound the screwdriver with his right closed-fist between two bricks to make a secure rung. I could hear Tink's deep, rhythmic breaths as the motivated kid incessantly hammered with his clenched fist. And then Jeremy lost his balance, and awkwardly flipped backwards from my grasp, again plunging into the waist-deep stench.

I feared that the deep cesspool would become *our* dark death chamber. I knew I didn't want to die at that particular time in that particular place. I began praying out loud for forgiveness and for divine deliverance. Tinker joined me in the recitation of the "Our Father", even though the atheist never went to church in his life; never had been baptized, and could never make it to heaven under Catholic rules. As our hearts and souls sank deeper in despair, a familiar high-pitched, anxious voice called down to us.

"Who's down there? Should we call the police?" the very squeaky human tone asked.

I glanced-up and was never so happy to see Stanley Tezeeker's skinny face half-illuminated by a nearby streetlight. The egghead was peering-down along with Waldo Hunsburger, Melvin Speigleman, and Mortimer Ralston, the foursome forming an irregular circle.

"Stanley," Tink hollered-up. "When I throw this here smelly rope up to you, just grab it. Then, try pullin' me the hell outa' here. And don't be afraid to get your lily-white hands dirty with globs of shit! Hope you've fuckin' eaten your *Wheaties* this morning!"

Tezeeker understood the unique request, even without the aid of a slide-rule or a complicated logarithm table. After four failed attempts, Tink had the wherewithal to successfully toss the rope above the cesspool's mouth. The four academic geniuses got their clean hands smelled-up, and soon tugged the brazen mechanic out of the stinking quagmire. After taking ten deep inhalations, rejuvenated Jeremy Foster assisted the four eggheads in getting me tugged back to ground level, where we gratefully thanked our improbable rescuers. My gimpy friend then told Mortimer to drive Stanley's Nash over to the Feed Bag to tell some Diablos about our near-death experience.

"Stanley," I gasped out of breath. "I really can't thank ya' enough," I praised. "Ya' saved our lives," I added as I wiped some of the excess sludge off of my black leather jacket and blue dungarees.

"J.W., I know you'd do the same for me. You're basically a humanitarian type of guy, just like me and my buds!"

I thought about the egghead's profound statement for a second. I looked over at Tinker and realized that the ungrateful ingrate never thanked anybody for anything. Then, regaining enough strength, I felt compelled to speak. "I don't know if I would've done the same for you before tonight," I confessed, "but I certainly would do it now."

Stanley informed Tink and me that the eggheads had been driving past the Windsor Pharmacy on their way to the Dairy DeLite. Their keen eyes detected the Kamikazes dragging someone around the side of the building. The brainiacs then carefully and vigilantly "cruised" the area until the Ks cars had left the premises. The four curious library hounds had sufficient curiosity to then investigate the open cesspool.

"How would you guys like to become honorary Diablos?" I offered.

"Yeah," Tinker added. "And we even now have a goddamned nigger in our gang. Why not admit a few, asshole, crossword-puzzle solvers, too? Let's also bravely go for a couple of faggots and lesbians while we're at it!"

Stanley Tezeeker politely ignored Tinker's blatant prejudice. "Thanks, but no thanks," the egghead diplomatically answered. "We live in Stonybrook and Pinewood, and I don't think the Sabers and the Pythons would like us being Diablos too much!"

Then, Tinker injected a more appropriate observation. "Not to mention the lousy Kamikazes, who would hunt your asses down, and leave you bookworms in this cesspool with the lid on!"

I was glad that the eggheads despised the Kenwood ruffians ten times as much as they loathed the Diablos.

"You said it," Stanley agreed. "At the teen dance last weekend at the Brooke Swimming Pool, Popeye and his buddies made me stuff a sixteen-inch salami down my pants," Stanley regretfully disclosed. "And then the Ks made me walk-around in circles so that all the girls present would laugh and mock me."

I really felt sorry for Stanley and his perpetually exploited friends. My heart finally sympathized with all of the physical agony and mental torture the four academic scholars had endured at the hands of predatory greasers. "Are ya' sure you don't wanna' join the Diablos?" I repeated. "After this cesspool saga, you're quite welcome!"

"It's entirely too dangerous," Stanley claimed. "We want to live so we could go to college, graduate, and get filthy rich."

"Well anyway," I humbly consented. "I'm filthy without being rich. "Thanks for givin' Bo the jacket idea and Tink the quarry idea. We used both of 'em against the Ks, and the two plans really worked."

"Anytime I can help, I will," Stanley congenially replied.

Mortimer pulled into the Windsor Pharmacy parking lot in Stanley's diminutive yellow and white Nash Rambler. Ace Roberts soon pulled into the drugstore's asphalt area, driving his often-broken '55 blue and white Olds, with Robbie Wilkinson riding shotgun. Ace was followed by Quinn's black '42 machine, which also had always-been-absent-when-needed, with Bo Jalonec seated inside.

"What happened?" Quinn demanded.

After we retold the whole story, our Diablos' leader had something vital to say. "You guys sometimes think I don't care about ya', but in my heart, I really do. The Ks have gone too far this time with this near-death experience crap. I officially declare war on the Kamikazes!"

"It's about time!" Tinker seconded. "What's General MacArthur's phone number? We'll bring the courageous war hero out of fuckin' retirement, too!"

After the humanitarian and altruistic eggheads departed the cesspool scene, Tink and I removed our outer garments and threw them into Ace's trunk to be later taken to a nearby all-night laundromat. Then, Ace drove Tink and me to Robbie's house because R.W.'s parents were out wining and dining for the evening.

After the two cars reached Robbie's place, R.W. doused Tink and me down pretty hard with his powerful garden hose. When "Mr. Un-Clean" and I had been upgraded to rinsing condition, we stepped into the bathtub, grimy and bare-assed naked, and stood under the showerhead for fifteen-minutes. Our hands vigorously washed our disgusting heads four times each with different shampoos, and we scrubbed each other's backs until we had almost scraped our epidermises off. And after our thorough scourings were complete, Tinker looked and smelled more tolerable than he ever had before our bodies experienced our very harrowing cesspool debacle.

Carnie found-out later that night about our perfidious Windsor Pharmacy adventure over at the Feed Bag, and the sub-human hustled-over to Robbie's place on Dogwood Drive because his '49 Merc' was still parked in the junkyard behind Tinker's dad's garage. The T Man was actually happy to see Jeremy Foster and me still alive.

Robbie was generous enough to donate some fresh underwear and clothes, and for once, Tinker didn't look like a visually-impaired Davy Crockett, wearing broken 3-D glasses.

"Those bastards ruined my coonskin hat," Tink finally realized. "And my 3-D' specs, too. They're drowned in the damned cesspool; all my most prized possessions."

"Be happy you didn't also lose your life!" Quinn preached with moral clarity. "Things can always be replaced!"

"I had no idea so many people used the two toilets inside the pharmacy," Carnie added. "The owners and the customers must all have very serious shit-related problems."

"I think J.W. and Tinker should stop acting like a couple of *sewer*-heads," Jokes cackled. "Ya' two turds really had a very shitty experience studyin' the effects of colons and semi-colons!"

The Diablos all piled into the '42 Ford and the '55 Oldsmobile, and we drove out to Tink's dad's gas station on Bath Road. Tink commissioned and commandeered one of his pop's tow trucks; Carnie reclaimed his '49 Merc', and then we all zoomed off to Haines Road and the Delaware Canal. I rode to our prime destination with Carnie.

"How come ya' want your Merc' back right now?" I asked.

"The Ks are wise to us, J.W.," Carnie neurotically answered. "And I predict there's gonna' be a gang war, and the Kenwood killers no longer trust anything the Diablos do or say."

Carnie's Merc' pulled into the Windsor Pharmacy's parking area. We then walked-over to the Delaware Canal and viewed Tink's ramshackle, rusty '49 Plymouth planted in five-foot-deep water. Tinker used a winch from the back of his tow truck to pull the totaled black junker out of the shallow canal. The Diablos wanted to accomplish the task before the disaster (vandalism) would be reported to the township police. Even though the Ds despised what the Ks had done to Tinker, to his car, and to me, we strongly desired to square matters away with the Kenwood brutes without any assistance from the local cops.

The Diablos would resolve our arduous struggle with the brutal bullies "Our way". Within a week, Jeremy's dad had gotten him some new wheels at a 'Philly auto auction.

Tink proudly drove his dark blue '49 Plymouth into the driveway at 50 Daffodil Lane. I came running out of the house to inspect the menace's new acquisition.

"J.W., Tink announced rather proudly. "Check-out my new set of wheels! How do ya' dig my sloppy jalopy?"

"Tink, it just looks like ya' painted your black Plymouth blue," I accurately answered. "I sure hope this rusty puddle-jumper can pass motor vehicle inspection!"

Chapter 36
"Ring-a-Ding-Ding"

The Kamikaze cesspool fiasco was the catalyst for the reciprocating *Three Musketeers* incident, which the Diablos initiated in mid-July. I was in a rare vengeful mood, with my animosity for the heinous Ks almost rivaling Tinker's. My mind, heart, and soul wanted to instigate, agitate, and aggravate the Kamikazes more than ever.

I had been leafing through a copy of Alexandre Dumas's *The Three Musketeers* while I was lying on my bed. D'Artagnon, a musketeer wannabe', individually challenged each of the *Three Musketeers* to a duel in three separate incidents with Athos, Porthos, and Aramis. None of the trio was aware of the identity of the other's supposed adversary, even though each Musketeer knew that the other two would be having a saber fight with someone. Certainly, a brash upstart had insulted all three members of the French king's royal guard. The novel's hero D'Artagnon showed-up for his triple duels behind the designated setting, the Carmelite Convent. The brash challenger was immediately identified as the exclusive opponent of each of the *Three Musketeers*, two of whom had arrived as seconds.

My scheme was a variation of D'Artagnon's wonderful ruse. Instead of tricking Athos, Porthos, and Aramis, the Diablos were going to instigate conflict between Popeye Messina and Langford, leader of the Renegades. Carnie, Tinker, Bo, and I talked over my proposed trick inside the Feed Bag.

"J.W.," Carnie commended. "That's a great idea. Popeye's gonna' pay for wreckin' Tink's car in the canal and almost drownin' you and Chester Goode in the serious-shit-hole."

"That's right," Jokes agreed. "But next time ya' two guys go swimmin' inside a cesspool, smear some antiseptic on before ya' decide playin' a game of craps. I'm in favor of most everything, but I'm really anti-septic, especially anti-septic tanks!"

"Bo," fully disgusted Jeremy Foster sneered. "Sometimes you're somewhere between a mean-ass drag and a piss-ant bummer. We're talkin' serious shit here, so cut your dumb-ass chicken-shit!"

"Anyway," Bo diplomatically interrupted Tink's diatribe. "Carnie did such a great job with Phil Jackson speakin' over the horn, I figured 'ring-a-ding-ding'. The C Man could get callin' on the phone again, and fool Langford and Popeye, too."

"Now wait a minute," Carnie objected. "Bo, you're the unrivaled expert when it comes to the Dairy DeLite phone booth. You' oughta' do the damned callin'. Not me!"

"Look Carnie," Tinker again sneered. "I've been wantin' to beat the shit out of ya' for a long time. If ya' don't do what Jokes here says, I'll make ya' my private punchin' bag and pretend you're all the Kamikazes' faces showin' at the same time."

"In that case, what do I havta' do and when do I havta' do it?"

Jokes authored a plausible script for Carnie to memorize and read over the phone. Carnie practiced his assignment for two whole nights, even rehearsing with a handkerchief to shroud his normal voice.

On the following evening, the four of us strolled-over to the landmark Dairy DeLite phone booth. Carnie nervously dropped a coin into the slot and dialed the Renegade leader's number.

"Hello, Langford?" Carnie asked.

"Yeah, who the hell is this?" the Renegade kahuna miserably sounded, his voice being just as arrogant as his counterpart Cummings.

"How's that big dent comin' along on the back of your car?" Carnie inquired. "Have ya' been to Snake Road lately?"

"Who the hell is this?" the recipient of the huge dent asked. Apparently, Langford had a fuse shorter than his little finger.

"Tell me Langy, old boy, how far is the damned Old Log Inn?" Carnie persisted under fear of persecution from his listening buddies.

"What did ya' say?" the enraged Renegade asked.

"I said," Carnie assertively responded. "How far is the old log in, you dumb stupid bastard!"

Langford lost his very limited patience with the anonymous caller. "Look Dick-head, I'm gonna' kick your ass good once I find out who the hell ya' are! If ya' had any guts in your stomach, any nuts below your *dick,* or any hair on your balls, you'd tell me!"

There was a brief pause as Carnie formulated and finally delivered the correct written response. "Oh really! Well, my name's not Richard Head," Carnie enviably adlibbed. "And I want ya' to know this Kamikaze ain't backin' down to any rank Renegade fungus like you. Dip-shit, ya' wanna' fight me?"

"Damn straight!" Langford shouted like a livid barbarian.

"Terrific," Carnie calmly replied. "There's a phone booth right near the battle zone. This way the Renegades could call the rescue squad right away to cart your ass over to the hospital emergency room. You're gonna' need expert medical care in a hurry!"

"Look, you mangy Fuck-head, get to the time and place!" Langford wildly screamed.

"Behind the Dairy DeLite, Thursday night, eight p.m. sharp. And bring along your gang of scrotums so that the weaklings can see ya' embarrassed in public. Be there or be square." Click.

Carnie took ten deep breaths, and after Tinker made a threatening fist toward his comrade's fragile jaw, my nervous friend dialed Popeye Messina. Carnie asked Popeye if he had been eating his daily regimen of spinach, and if he stuck his reproductive organ in Olive Oyl whenever it became sore.

"Who the hell is this?" Messina asked. "I ain't expectin' no calls from anybody!"

"Popeye," Carnie stated under duress. "Do ya' remember the empty *Chesterfield's* pack and the empty blackberry brandy bottle left at the quarry? Well, I'm the Renegade who dumped your crappy Ford into the swamp. Ya' got any objections to that shit?"

"I thought the Diablos were the ones that pushed my Ford into the quarry!" Popeye claimed.

"Not a chance at a raffle, Asshole," Carnie firmly replied. "The Renegades was the ones who also threw those three Kamikaze jackets down the cesspool behind the pharmacy. How ya' like them apples?"

Carnie had really twisted Popeye's horns pretty well. The Diablo stealth was working perfectly, and brains were triumphing over biceps. It did not take Messina long to reply.

"I'm gonna' give ya' the beatin' of your life!" Popeye exclaimed. "Just give me the time and place!"

"Behind the Dairy DeLite, Thursday night at eight p.m. sharp. And bring your gang of scrotums along so that they can see your ass get embarrassed in public. Be there or be square." Click.

Thursday night arrived, and the Diablos had "ring-a-ding-ding" seats at their corner Feed Bag table facing the Dairy DeLite. The Kamikazes and the Renegades congregated in a circle around Popeye and Langford. Ironically, the setting was the exact same spot where Tinker had gotten his clock cleaned and had been thrown into the sticker bush by Phil Jackson and his muscular offensive linemen.

First, Popeye accused Lang*ford* of ditching his Ford in the quarry, and Langford denied it, calling Popeye a liar. And then Langford accused Messina of wrecking-up his car with a cable at Snake Road, and Messina emphatically denied that action, calling Langford a liar. Then, the verbal exchange heated-up to pushing; pushing soon became shoving; shoving converted into punching, and punching evolved into brawling, bloodshed, and fiercely thrashing around on the asphalt.

The Diablos derived great satisfaction from viewing the fantastic altercation. The gladiators rolled over and over into the thorny giant sticker bush that had lacerated Tinker in fifty places. The Dairy DeLite manager panicked and notified the fuzz. The cops quickly arrived in four squad cars to quell the escalating scuffle. The Diablos had cunningly created bad blood between the Ks and the Rs, and the entire confrontation could be attributed to a new slant to the fictitious Frenchman D'Artagnon's guile, savvy, and trickery.

Meanwhile, the high-stakes poker game between the Diablos and the Kamikazes had developed into a dangerous crapshoot. Quinn got the word out that there was "safety in numbers", so the Diablos were advised not to travel alone at night.

Carnie and I were very nervous on the inside, while externally, we feigned a "cool as a cucumber" facade. Jokes and Tinker remained their normal selves, but Quinn was under pressure because Patty Van Arsdale threatened to break-off with him for good should my idol lead a combative Diablos' campaign against the Ks.

The following night, Carnie picked up Jokes, Tink, and me in his resurrected '49 Merc', and naturally, we wound-up at the Feed Bag. It seemed that when we were inside the place, the Ks didn't enter, and when the Kenwood creeps were inside the restaurant, we would drive around until they finally had left the new "Alamo".

After we sat-down at our standard table, the four of us entered into a contest to determine who would buy a round of *Pepsi's*. Tinker took a fast unexpected swat at Carnie's jaw and if Carnie had "flinched", Tink would say, "I made ya' flinch!" Then, Carnie would have to purchase a round of soft drinks. But Carnie did not budge or move one iota, and no one had the guts to demand that Tinker buy the round of sodas for not being able to make Carnie move his 'glass jaw'.

And then Jokes and I participated in a game of trivial facts. Usually, we chose subjects like television shows, popular westerns, or baseball minutia. The J Man said the topic for the evening would be nifty songs from the past, and the loser would have to treat the other three guys to large *Pepsi's*.

"Who played drums in 'Topsy, Parts I and II'?" Jokes asked.

"That's easy," I answered. "Cozy Cole."

"Who sang 'Short Shorts'?" I challenged.

"Get to the damned hard ones, J.W. The Royal Teens, of course. But if their short shorts were too tight, they must've been the royal pain in the ass teens!"

When it came to '50s music, Bo and I were so knowledgeable that the competition was destined to end in a stalemate. Bubbles Messina came-over and interrupted our intense dialogue. The Sicilian doll seemed rather reluctant to intrude upon our familiar table. Bubbles was subbing for her cousin that night, because Angie was out on a date with Phil Jackson. As soon as the doll saw Bo grin in her direction, her snarl instantaneously transformed into an amiable smile.

"Hi, Bubbles," Jokes facetiously greeted. "Could ya' tell me what kind of bees give milk on *Halloween?"*

"I haven't the slightest notion," Popeye's well-stacked sister answered, batting her intrigued eyelids at Bo without even realizing what he was saying, or what she was doing.

"Boobees," Bo laughed as the gang's clown feigned grabbing Bubbles's alluring knockers. "Look, Honey. I lust for your bust!"

"Ya' know, Blondie, even though ya' might have a *hollow wienie,* I still would love to take a tumble in the weeds with you. Unlike your butthead friends, ya' sure have class and charm. And ya' don't have nasty cooties or zits, either."

"Now, Bubbles, we could make a western porno' flick and be a couple of tumbleweeds stuck together," Bo amusingly answered.

"How do ya' think of that cute stuff so quick?" the chick asked.

Instead of replying to Bubbles's question, Bo flattered the Italian babe by calling her an "Earth Angel", a popular early '50s slow song by the Penguins.

"I don't know what heaven ever does without you," Bubbles complimented. "You're so unlike your *mid-evil* friends sittin' here. They don't know whether they're coming or goin'."

Carnie didn't like being insulted by Bubbles' rhetoric, so naturally, the insecure flake had to ruin the entire conversation with his foul mouth. "Oh, I know the difference between comin' and goin'," Carnie interrupted. "When I'm comin', the fluid is white, and when I'm goin' the stream is yellow."

Nobody laughed, but we all knew that if Bo had said the exact same words, which he had once done to a waitress in Carnie's company, everybody would have found the lingo thoroughly amusing.

The Diablos ordered our customary sodas and steak sandwiches. Bubbles, still under the influence of Bo's magic spell, scooted into the kitchen to give our orders to Domenick.

Jokes then rose from his chair. "Ya' know guys, you' motley jerk-offs oughta' become builders," the gang's jester declared in one of his typical riddles. "If ya' learn how to construct a lot of houses, then ya' moron hand-jobs can have all the erections ya' want!"

And with *that* borderline crazy remark, Bo sauntered out the restaurant's front doors and ambled over to the infamous phone booth adjacent to the Dairy DeLite.

Jokes dialed the Feed Bag, and since it was a slow interval for "carry out", Bubbles exited the kitchen and answered the contrived "ring-a-ding-ding". Jalonec disguised his voice very cleverly, and the substitute waitress appeared quite mesmerized by his baritone's mellow quality.

My keen pupils observed that Bubbles was toying with her goddess-like hair whenever Bo (or Bo's sexy telephone voice) was speaking.

Jalonec had always instructed Carnie, Tink, and me that whenever a girl subconsciously fondles her tresses while talking to a guy, either on or off the phone, the broad is actually fantasizing, in a Freudian way, having a very deep and serious "male beef injection".

"Hello," Bo began like a true gentleman. "I want to order a medium pepperoni pizza to go. And please put on extra cheese."

"What is your name, please?" infatuated Bubbles requested.

"Michael Lit," Jokes replied.

"Your pizza will be ready in fifteen-minutes," Bubbles finished in true business-like fashion.

Five glorious minutes later, Bo returned from his most recent "communications' mission". His brief absence was hardly noticed by anyone because two girls had entered the restaurant while Bubbles was busy taking a pizza carryout order from Michael Lit. One of the young ladies had big breasts, while the other female was not so well-endowed. Some of the Cardinal Reagan jock jerks on the pinball machine side of the Feed Bag hollered a chorus of *Good and Plenty, Milk Duds, Juicy Fruit,* and *Milky Way* to the point where their chorus made most of the other males in the restaurant snicker and wish they had butterfingers.

After the seated Diablos were served our redundant junk food meals and predictable *Pepsi's,* our astute members nervously awaited the announcement that Michael Lit's large pepperoni pizza with extra cheese was ready. Still being under Bo's magic spell, Bubbles made a low, sexy resonant declaration.

"I have a large pepperoni pizza with extra cheese for Michael Lit. Where are ya' Michael?"

After obtaining no favorable response, hot-to-trot Bubbles repeated her entreaty a little bit louder. "Pizza for Michael Lit? Where are ya' Mike?"

Still no acknowledgement or claim had been advanced by any of the restaurant's patrons. The Diablos began chuckling with our heads down. Poor Bubbles was becoming especially irritated.

"Pizza for Michael Lit," Bubbles yelled and reiterated. "Does anybody here know where Mike Lit is?"

"Sure Bubbles!" Carnie hollered. "Look between your legs in the middle of your fuzzy bush!"

Everyone in the place broke-out in a boisterous roar. The hysteria lasted for a full minute. Even Luigi, who seldom cracked a smile, laughed lustily after his tossed pizza came down upon his face when the distracted proprietor forgot about flinging the flattened dough high up into the Feed Bag's rafters, as was his skilled habit.

Bubbles dashed into the kitchen to recompose her sanity and to reorganize her mental stability. Jokes stared at Carnie with a very disappointed expression on his face.

"Carnie, ya' seem to succeed with guys over the phone, but fail miserably with chicks both over the horn and in person," Bo judiciously criticized. "Maybe you're a genuine homo', and don't yet even know which sex you prefer."

Chapter 37
"Tinker Goes Bonkers"

The following night, Bo, Carnie, and I were again seated at our favorite Feed Bag table. I felt sorry for Mr. Merc' because Jalonec's caustic remarks had virtually destroyed my Dogwood Hollow pal's frail, sensitive ego. I figured I would talk about baseball, since it was a venue in which Carnie had some fundamental knowledge and felt some self-confidence in discussing.

"It's in all the papers," I discreetly began. "The *Phillies* are thinkin' about tradin' Richie Ashburn within the next year."

Carnie agreed that Ashburn had been the heart and soul of the *Fightin' Phils* throughout the '50s. "J.W.," Carnie impulsively reacted. "Do ya' think Ashburn will ever make it to Cooperstown? I know he's been your favorite player since we were in *Little League*."

"He's only a left-handed singles' hitter," I regretfully replied.

"Does he hang out at singles' bars?" Jokes stupidly bantered.

I ignored Bo's annoying jive talk and tried to remain serious with Carnie. "Sluggers who hit for average get first preference to the *Hall of Fame,"* I authoritatively replied. "And if Ashburn's lucky, Whitey might get to the *Hall* by a quirk of fate before the year two-thousand. But the players would have to vote him in, because besides us, they're the only ones who really know how great he is."

"Did ya' guys know that the ancient Greek Homer invented the four-bagger'?" Jokes facetiously inquired.

"You oughta' be glad that your ass is not grass! Now then Bo, is a four-bagger a new revolutionary lawnmower attachment?" Carnie countered, attempting to rival Bo's wit.

"No," Jokes answered. "It's when four old women alcoholics drink too much whiskey. Then the four bags are loaded, and soon some lucky wino first baseman magically hits one into the bleachers, where everybody peroxides their damned hair."

"But Carnie," I butted-in, ignoring Bo's preposterous drivel. "I've seen Ashburn deliberately foul-off a dozen pitches until he either walks or gets the one pitch that the bat wizard wants to slap for a single. That's a real important baseball skill often overlooked by the narrow-minded sportswriters. They're just interested in writing about home runs and no-hitters."

"I know a couple of guys who are switch-hitters!" Bo disruptively interrupted. "The fags even date each other!"

"Bo, why don't ya' go pound the electrical fuse box in your utility room," Carnie snapped. "Then *you* could be a friggin' switch-hitter too!"

"I get it," volleyed back Bo. "You guys are talkin' about the Major League Circuit! Ya' don't havta' work for the electric company to realize that ya' could really get electrocuted there, if ya' can execute without ever employin' the use of electric chairs!"

"What do ya' think about sportswriters?" I asked Carnie, mostly to avoid more escalating conflict between Bo and my dialogue partner.

"They don't know shit about shit!" Carnie haughtily replied.

Just then Robbie Wilkinson briskly entered the Feed Bag. After spotting us, R.W. swiftly paced-over to our table and told the guys that Tinker had a surprise for us, and that we should immediately drive over to Heavenly Gates Cemetery.

'Oh no! Don't tell me! Tink has killed somebody, and now the murderer wants us to bury the victim for him!' I quickly guessed.

"Now, J.W.," Robbie began elaborating. "You know Tink would never bury a person in a cemetery. The frugal bastard thinks that graveyards are wasted real estate."

"Hasn't Tink gotten us into too many *grave* situations already?" Bo asked. "Next thing ya' know, we'll all be *coffin* our Adams' apples out of our throats!"

The four of us paid our bills, quickly hopped into Carnie's Merc', and soon we were on our way to the remote cemetery. Robbie refused to reveal any more essential details about our secret escapade, but somehow, we all equated our trip to getting some sort of revenge for the Kamikazes' dastardly "Windsor Pharmacy cesspool incident".

Robbie instructed Carnie to make two quick rights inside the cemetery, and to stop at the first fresh grave. We were happy to see Tink standing by his new, dull, blue, rusty '49 Plymouth. Ace Roberts had transported a carload of Diablos to the scene in his unreliable '55 Olds, and Fritz Feldcamp had borrowed his pop's old Dodge and had brought along some other Dogwood Hollow guys.

Tink called us all over and we stood around him like we were a high school football team listening to their sagacious coach.

"Now guys," began Tink. "I had Robbie go over to Popeye in the Feed Bag and show him one of the pictures Bo had taken of luscious Angie and of Bruno Messina's curvaceous sister. The girls were naked from the waist up."

"Let's call in the Pope," Jokes injected. "He's an expert on breasts because he's the titular head of the church!"

"That's right," Carnie confirmed, ignoring Jalonec while answering Tinker. "You and I got some glorious posters hangin' on our bedroom walls. But now we have to get the Sicilian chicks on film, naked from the waist down!"

"Not only that," Tink added, ignoring Carnie's obnoxious frivolity. "We also got the negatives. Robbie told Popeye the Diablos would sell him all the negatives for twenty-bucks. If ya' remember, twenty-bucks is what the Ks had stolen from the Diablos during that ugly *Labor Day* Dairy DeLite phone booth trick. When Popeye said he might not go for the deal, I told Bruno *we* knew a girlie magazine editor who was willin' to publish the photos of his sister and cousin."

Tink finished his interesting story, saying that Popeye had stepped behind the Feed Bag to pay Tink's twenty-dollar extortion price, but somehow, Messina began debating the terms and conditions, and then the exploratory negotiations fell through.

"So, guys, here's the result of the failed deal!" Tinker surprisingly announced. The most deranged Diablo slowly opened his car's trunk. We were all astonished to see Popeye Messina lying inside in a fetal position. Tinker and Robbie had captured and kidnapped Bruno and then transported him to Heavenly Gates Cemetery.

"Ya' don't need a photographic mind with a negative attitude to get the picture!" Jokes exclaimed. "Popeye's not much of a *hood* if he's lyin' there inside your trunk!"

"Did the bully put up a struggle?" I asked.

"No," Jeremy answered. "All I did was point my tiny metal pistol at his head and I threatened to make him more *holey* than a religious sponge. Bruno reckoned that I wasn't *toying* around. Ha, ha, ha."

Even though my name wasn't Douglas, I looked-down into the newly dug gravesite. A vault had not yet been inserted; the pit was simply a fresh, dark, seven-foot-deep rectangular hole that had been excavated in a very scary place. I felt sorry for Popeye, but then I considered that Cummings' Lieutenant had been one of the chief instigators who had thrown Tink and me into the Windsor Pharmacy cesspool, and who had totaled Tink's black Plymouth after spitefully depositing the bomb into the Delaware Canal.

Tink, Robbie, Ace, and Slip grabbed Messina; lifted his screaming body out of the trunk; carried the K to the recently dug hollow, and then roughly flung the *pit*iful Kamikaze down into the hole. Fear was in the Sidgee kid's eyes. Popeye was too frightened to even utter a short syllable.

Tinker limped-over to his car and removed a roll of cyclone fence from his back seat. Robbie, Tink, Slip, and Ace unrolled the metal fence and laid it directly above the open grave. Tink went back to his blue Plymouth and returned with ten giant metal staples, which to me looked like croquet wickets. Using a mallet, the obsessed Diablo quickly and expertly hammered the ten dual-pegged staples through the edges of the fence and into the hard ground, securely anchoring the grate over the open grave. My lame pal then removed his toy cigarette lighter from his black leather jacket, handed it to me, and spoke loudly enough for Popeye to hear.

"J.W., if that scumbag down there moves a cunt hair, shoot a slug into him!" Next, Tinker yelled down to Popeye. "Just remember, Fuck-head. Ya' came outa' a damned hole when ya' was born, and you'll be put back inside a damned hole when ya' die!"

Ace Roberts flipped *his* car's trunk open, and we all were delighted to see two full cases of *Ballantine Beer*. The generous host distributed four bottles to each Diablo, which was enough to keep us entertained for at least an hour. Three guys had to serve as "chickie guard" duty if the fuzz was to accidentally invade our temporary sanctuary. Tink nominated newcomers Gene McCann, Jim Amari, and Al Keller for that all-important detail, and the three fledglings walked to the cemetery's main entrance to drink beer and to pretend being alert sentinels. If the lookouts should sense anything suspicious, the sentries were to whistle like birds, and if the cops were spotted, the three guards were instructed by Tinker to howl like wolves.

"So, Popeye," Carnie taunted while peering-down into the cavity. "That's exactly where ya' belong, because your dear pappy is an underground figure."

"Yeah," Jalonec concurred. "The entire Mafia is loaded with underground figures. Now you're one of 'em Bruno, just like your daddy and your uncle."

"Ya' dirty mother-fuckers are gonna' regret this prank a hundred-times!" Popeye yelled-up in a loud tense voice. "Make *that* promise a thousand-times!"

"Ya' want J.W. to put two slugs in ya' instead of only one?" Tink arrogantly asked his personal enemy.

Popeye suddenly became silent. I saw our incarcerated enemy quivering and breathing heavily while staring-up at his captors.

As far as thuggish Jeremy Foster was concerned, the festivities were just beginning. The lunatic again ambled-over to his car's back seat and returned with a wooden box containing six opened cans of spinach. Tink, Robbie, Bo, Carnie, Ace, and Slip each poured their vegetable contents onto Popeye's head. I saw Popeye panting and gasping for air as I pointed the silver toy gun through the grate directly at his face.

After we each drank two beers, Tinker drove his blue Plymouth over the horizontal cyclone fence. Ace got down on his knees and used a wrench to unscrew the cap nut. Five quarts of dirty motor oil cascaded down into the hollow. The same technique was soon used with Carnie's '49 Merc', Ace's '55 Oldsmobile, and Fritz Feldcamp's archaic Dodge. Popeye stood ankle-deep in twenty-quarts of "greaser motor oil". Mr. T next threatened to throw a match into the pit should Popeye cry-out or yell too loudly.

While the Diablos worked on our third and fourth beers, Tink and Robbie distributed twenty-quarts of fresh motor oil from Ace's trunk, and we all took turns adding quarts of petrol to the engines of the four utilitarian cars.

I noticed Popeye squirming and shaking down below, and even if our hostage dared to scream, his voice wouldn't have had a ghost of a chance to be heard by any Kamikaze miles away.

"You Kamikaze jerk-offs will have to wake-up *oily* in the morning to outsmart the Ds," Jokes insultingly shouted-down to our persecuted and terrorized captive. "Oil's well that ends well!" Jalonec then quite imaginatively quoted Shakespeare.

"If ya' roll-around in that oil," Tink chided, "you'll soon look like a real greaser, just like me."

Popeye, on the verge of melting-down, became desperate as our hostage began wildly rattling the improvised, flat cyclone fence in an effort to escape being cruelly persecuted inside the pit. I honestly felt some sympathy for Bruno's ongoing trepidation.

"Okay, you warped Asshole!" Tinker yelled-down into the hollow. "You asked for it! J.W., shoot a fuckin' slug into the no-good punk!"

I aimed the toy gun at Popeye's chest and pulled the trigger as commanded. A loud blast was heard, and a bullet ricocheted off a link in the metal fence. I dropped the gun in sheer panic. All of the other Diablos were awed by the occurrence, everyone except Tinker. The betrayer slowly bent-down and picked-up what I thought had been a novelty cigarette lighter.

As I recovered from my shock, Ace flicked on his flashlight and sent a beam down into the grave. Popeye's eyes were bulging-out of their sockets, as his exasperated lungs sucked-in all the oxygen that his chest organs could gather.

"Now, I know why they call ya' Pop-eye," Jokes scoffed and laughed, peering-down. "Your peepers are poppin' out of your skull!"

"Just remember, Scum-face," Tinker yelled at the wholly petrified K. "Ya' came from a hole when ya' was born, and when you're fuckin' dead, ya' stay in a goddamned hole forever!"

Tink had one last evil inspiration to enact. The obsessed fanatic found a garden hose attached to a nearby cemetery spigot that serviced the grass around several nearby grave plots. The future San Quentin inmate stretched the hose over to Popeye's pit; turned the valve, and then methodically filled the hole with several hundred gallons of water. Soon, the water level reached Popeye's chin as the scared-to-death K stood on his toes to avoid drowning. When the Diablos walked back to our cars, we could hear Messina futilely bellowing and cursing. Ace picked-up Al Keller in his vehicle and Fritz Feldcamp stopped for Jim Amari and Gene McCann. The amused Diablos zipped-out of the cemetery, and then the car caravan journeyed back into the normal conventions of Bucks County civilization.

Most of the Diablos possessed more couth and conscience than the Kamikazes did. Jokes made an anonymous phone call to Cummings' house from the Dairy DeLite booth. Being intrigued, Cummings took his henchmen Evans and Mullins over to Heavenly Gates to investigate Mr. J's reliable report. The search party was successful in rescuing their lost comrade from his eerie "solitary confinement".

Much to my dismay, Tinker was not quite finished with Popeye Messina. In late July, Jeremy was driving Carnie and me to an outdoor basketball court located just off Mill Creek Parkway. We were cruising along merrily, reviewing the particulars of the bizarre cemetery frolic.

"Tink," I remarked. "Ya' told me that silver gun was a toy, a novelty cigarette lighter. I almost killed Popeye by accident. All because of your unreal insanity!"

"You're right on that count, J.W." the brash juvenile delinquent answered. "And this here cigarette lighter in my black leather jacket happens to look a lot like the real gun ya' nearly blew Popeye's head off with!"

Tinker reached over while going eighty-miles-per-hour; banged the glove compartment open, and exposed an object that was either the toy cigarette lighter or the real gun I had fired. The reckless driver then lifted the object out of the compartment; flicked the flint, and a bright flame shot-up. "Ya' see, Words," the punk scoundrel prefaced. "This here is the cigarette lighter. What I got in my leather jacket is a functional gun that looks just like this here lighter."

After Tink made that rather astounding revelation, the Bedlam candidate suddenly hit the brakes so hard that my head nearly smashed into the windshield. The demented driver then rotated the steering wheel and turned his Plymouth into the parking lot of the breakfast-luncheonette place where Carnie's occasional girlfriend, Jackie Harrelson, worked as a waitress.

I noticed that a police cruiser and a red and black '56 Ford Crown Victoria were parked next to the side of the restaurant. I immediately observed that there weren't any of the eatery's side windows facing the parking area, so our presence was hidden and undetected from any patrons seated inside.

"The cop is probably havin' doughnuts and coffee," I speculated and stated. "That's the fuzz's standard diet! The hungry gluttons even eat the holes in the center of the doughnuts!"

"Isn't that black and red Ford Popeye's new car? I heard Dante had bought the wheels for his kid!" Tinker assumed and related.

"Yeah," Carnie answered and confirmed. "But I heard at the Bag that the rich punk bought it with the insurance money he got for his drowned '52 in the quarry. The rest was paid for by Daddy Dante."

Tink was sharp enough to notice a septic tank truck parked next to the restaurant's cesspool cover. "The driver's probably inside eatin' bacon and eggs after he had drained the place's cesspool," Tink said as the gang's principal vandal maliciously contemplated using the all-too-convenient "honey wagon" against Popeye.

"Tink, I only came along to play a little friendly game of basketball," I protested. "Haven't ya' caused enough trouble already?"

"J.W., if ya' wanna' continue livin', then shut the hell up!" jittery Jeremy indignantly threatened.

The most dysfunctional Diablo hopped-out of his jalopy, and in ten-seconds, "Dr. Destructo" managed to stealthily open the driver's side lock on the red and black Ford. The possessed avenger then used a hammer to puncture a hole in the driver-side window, leaving a foot-long opening. And to my utter astonishment, Tink next limped-over to the loaded septic tank truck and unraveled a length of thick hose. The nutcase tugged the nozzle to the red and black car's window; shoved the head inside; limped back to the "honey wagon"; turned-on a few accessible valves and switches; pulled several levers, and proceeded to fill the '56 Ford's interior with raw sewage.

I sat petrified in the front seat of Tinker's blue Plymouth with my mouth agape. I watched dark brown stenchy fluid seep-out and then flow from the car's door frame.

Before I could say a word, demonic Foster pulled the hose from the red and black Ford's window; moved over to the nearby police car, and then duplicated his astonishing vandalism. Two minutes later, the furtive marauder quickly put the hose back onto the "honey wagon", scampered back to his blue Plymouth, and soon escaped the premises, heading south on busy Mill Creek Parkway.

"You've gone bonkers, gone right off the deep end!" I accused my warped-minded companion. "Tink, you destroyed Popeye's new Ford. It had a fine pair of dual exhausts, too!"

"You're absolutely right," Tinker guiltlessly agreed. "A jalopy with only one exhaust pipe is like a girl with only one goddamned tit."

"But that could've been someone else's Ford," I continued. "And ya' might've accidentally ruined an innocent stranger's spanking-new car by mistake!"

"Cool down, J.W.," Carnie advised. "I heard that Popeye had said to Luigi and Domenick that he ain't gonna' take any more crap from the Diablos. Now he's taken a friggin' carload of crap!"

My throat gulped as my disturbed brain thought about the dual vehicle disasters that my disbelieving eyes had just witnessed. My mind pictured a dingy jail cell with me being its sole occupant. I had been an unwilling accomplice to twin felonies, while simply going on a pleasant ride to play basketball. 'Should I report my guilty greaser friend to the police?' I seriously considered. 'Are these two barbarians seated on either side of me really my friends?'

"But Carnie, where's your conscience?" I morally argued. "You sat and watched Tink trash both the red and black Ford and the black and white cop car. Killed them! Why?"

"Because that dirty son-of-a-bitch cop has been hittin' on my mom," Carnie snarled-out. "And now the bastard's sittin' in the doughnut shop tryin' to hit on Jackie!"

"Well, J.W., Popeye now is aware that the Diablos really know *our* shit!" Jeremy-the-Jerk exclaimed in a rare accidental display of humor.

I had to marvel at Tinker's unremorseful audacity. The junior felon didn't even care one iota about the amorous cop also hitting on *his* mom, or if he did, the psycho was either too ashamed or too "cool" to show it. The most antagonistic Diablo had transferred all of the years of accumulated hatred welled-up inside his black heart into pure high-test animosity for Popeye Messina and for Phil Jackson.

As Tinker drove us around Levittown to let off steam, all I could think of was crap seeping out of car doors. At a traffic light, Tink interrupted my concentration by showing Carnie and me two sets of handcuffs he had pilfered from the parked patrol car before competently "honey-wagoning it".

But in the final analysis, pouring wet cement into a Corvette convertible seemed much more civilized than desecrating a decent set of wheels with disgusting human waste. I sat between the two 'possessed Diablos', whom I believed had both 'gone asylum'. I honestly wished that my parents would be moving out of Dogwood Hollow the next day so that I could start a new life back in Jersey.

Tinker had become a psychopathic maniac who needed a qualified exorcist, a certified psychiatrist, and a lengthy bath in that order. Carnie was going through traumatic teenage rebellion against adult authority, and Mr. T's disciple had been easily conforming to negative peer pressure. After Tink's blue '49 Plymouth dropped me off at 50 Daffodil Lane, I needed to swallow-down three aspirins, along with a tall glass of water containing two fizzing *Alka-Seltzer* tablets.

Chapter 38
"Letting-off Steam"

Believe it or not, some of the Diablos had to let-off some more steam. Friction was on the rise between the Ds and the Ks, but most of us didn't want a gang fight to interfere with the scheduled August 3rd Haines Road drag-race between Quinn and Cummings. I thought that it would be better to hang-around with Bo and Robbie, because I believed that Tinker was obsessed, possessed, and insane, and I theorized that Carnie would imitate any and all of those fundamentally flawed negative qualities exhibited by *his* heinous mentor.

A lot of Kamikazes were gathered and conferring outside the Dairy DeLite, so Jokes drove Robbie and me into the Feed Bag parking lot. Bo chose a slot with us sitting right in front of our favorite table, so that we could keep our eyes directly focused on his precious set of wheels from our vantage point.

"Are you and Susie back together?" I asked Bo inside the legendary Levittown restaurant.

"Our relationship is on again and off again," Bo admitted. "When Susie's not havin' her period, I'm on her bod' again, and when she is, I hop off and listen to 1920s rag time music. I've objectively concluded that her periods happen too damned periodically."

"It's a good thing they do," Robbie replied. "Otherwise, she'd be pregnant all the damned time."

"I can't understand this period stuff," Bo answered, "because as I've often told you guys, every day in school, I have eight periods, and I don't get cranky or miserable. Girls have trouble handling one period a month, and I experience eight periods every single school day without any trouble like a bloody nose, whatsoever."

Bo then facetiously announced to Robbie and me that he might drop Susie for good and join the Four F Club. Robbie asked Jalonec what *that* letter designation represented.

"Find 'em, feel 'em, F 'em and forget 'em," Jokes disclosed. "That really simplifies the male-female relationship down to the very basics."

Bo, Robbie, and I then discussed how Tinker and Carnie had also gotten even with the honey wagon operator outside the Mill Creek Parkway breakfast-luncheonette where Jackie Harrelson worked. The fellow happened to be the same septic truck operator who had found the planted counterfeit Kamikaze jackets laying inside the Windsor Pharmacy's cesspool, and then the honey-wagon operator had reported his discovery to the store's manager, who innocently informed the Kamikazes. Now, the unfortunate septic tank driver had to account for the extensive damage done to two ruined cars, caused by his parked-truck outside the Mill Creek Parkway eatery.

"Isn't that about the fifth cop car those two guys have destroyed?" Robbie asked. "Pretty soon, we're gonna' need a fancy calculator just to keep tabs."

"Yeah," I confirmed. "Because Carnie and Tinker won't quit until the local Visigoths get the whole police force fired. Tink also thinks that Sal Palermo and Dante Messina are payin' off the cops to keep 'em quiet. The T Man thinks that if the cops come after the Diablos," I opined, "Specialty Enterprises will be exposed, and a lot of cops will surely lose their jobs when the Feds' do a complete investigation and clean-up the major area mess."

Since no waitress had approached our table, and because we did not want our private conversation about the Mafia/Kamikazes/cops connection overheard, Jokes wisely suggested we should continue our suspended music trivia contest from the other night, before we would eventually discuss the fantastic Heavenly Gates Cemetery caper.

"Who sang 'Treasure of Love'?" Bo asked.

"That's nursery school stuff," I evaluated and shared. "Clyde McPhatter."

"If Clyde went on a diet," Jokes speculated and verbalized, "the singer could change his name to Clyde McSkinnier."

"Very funny," I declaratively returned. "But who sang 'A Rose and a Baby Ruth'?"

"George Hamilton the IV," Jokes replied with a determined expression on his face. "J.W., how about that number 'Deck of Cards'?" Bo aggressively challenged. "Who recorded it?"

"That's a piece of cake. Wink Martindale."

Before I could get to "Black Slacks" by Joe Bennett and the Sparkletones and "Happy, Happy Birthday Baby" by the Tune Weavers, our waitress finally stepped-over to our table. Maggie was subbing for the ever-absent Angie. After what the Palermo girl had been gossiping to her friends about the Diablos, Maggie frowned at us like we were three of the Four Horsemen of the Apocalypse.

Before anyone could order anything, Carnie and Tinker pulled-up in the '49 Merc', and in a matter of thirty-seconds, the new arrivals were occupying chairs at our table. I could tell from their body language that Robbie and Bo didn't want to be in *their* inglorious company any more than I did.

"Okay, now that the *Peanut Gallery* is all here, what can I get you?" Maggie asked.

"I'm not that hungry," answered Carnie. "So, what do ya' have for D, meaning dessert?"

Maggie knew that Carnie had memorized the Feed Bag's menu by heart and that he was simply pulling her chain. "If ya' want something for D, then why don't ya' look on the M?" the waitress snapped.

"Do ya' have any crabs?" Carnie asked, obviously trying to imitate one of Bo's famous sexual allusions.

"We don't serve crabs here," Maggie replied. "We kick them the hell out if any customers act grumpy." It was evident that Maggie was showing hostility toward the Diablos in general, and toward immature Carnie in particular.

"Well then, Bitch," Tinker chimed-in. "Why don't ya' bring your car over to my garage. I could have *you* up on the lift, check your oil, and give ya' a nice lube job in no time."

Maggie couldn't take any more of Carnie and Tinker's unnecessary, mindless vulgarity. The tough cookie was entirely fed-up with their adolescent and callous behavior. "You two dingbats couldn't get sex if ya' were sperm whales!"

I blushed, Bo bit his tongue, Robbie smirked, and Carnie sat there, mortified and humiliated. But unfazed Tinker sat mum in his chair and pretended that everything was business as usual.

"Do ya' see that van out there?" Maggie asked Carnie.

"Sure do," Carnie alertly replied. "That vehicle belongs to old Mr. Johnson, the electrician. I think he's doin' some special work in the kitchen for Luigi and Domenick."

There was a brief pause, and then Maggie continued her brutal verbal assault on the C-Man. "Well, Carnie. Why don't ya' go outside, rip-off the antenna, stick it up your' rear-end, and get a bad case of *van-aerial* disease!"

Even though her joke was an old one, everyone in the Feed Bag who had heard the rather loquacious utterance cheered Maggie and simultaneously jeered Carnie.

Mr. Merc' was so angry that the guy rose and walked toward the nearest side exit, slamming the door on his way out. The rest of us ordered bags of pretzels and large *Pepsi's*. After Maggie went into the kitchen the four seated Diablos watched through the large slanted pane-glass window as Carnie marched like a disgruntled, wounded warrior over to the often used and abused Dairy DeLite phone booth. After fumbling for a coin to insert, the ignoramus dialed the Feed Bag. Maggie loyally answered the call.

"I'd like to order a large pepperoni pizza with extra cheese," Carnie's disguised voice requested.

"Ya' say your name is Michael Lit. Are ya' sure that's your real name?"

"Sure, I'm sure," Carnie defensively answered. "It's printed on my two birth certificates."

"Well, Jerk-weed!" Maggie exclaimed. "I don't believe in havin' kinky phone sex with a little tin-horned perverted toad like you. Ya' say your name is Mike Lit?"

"That's right!" Carnie stated and verified.

"Well, then, ya' sound more like your asshole than *my clit!"* Click.

Carnie was so excessively pissed-off at his own ineptitude that the phone call loser slammed and pounded the pay phone's receiver hook. The outsmarted kid sat fuming inside the Dairy Delite booth, while all of the Feed Bag's thoroughly entertained patrons gave Maggie a standing round of applause for her remarkable craftiness.

When Carnie finally trudged back to our favorite hangout with his head crestfallen, Bo and I pretended we were ignorant of his frustration by feigning a continuation of our music trivia game.

"Who sang 'Bony Maronie'?" I began.

"That's elementary school stuff," Bo replied. "Larry Williams. What about 'La Dee Dah'?"

"Even Sherlock Houses would know that one," I comically replied. "Shirley and Lee. What about 'Teenage Crush'?"

"Hey, Worm-brain," Bo admonished me and my question. "Tommy Sands."

"Hey, Carnie," I commented as our thwarted amigo stood like a zombie alongside our table. "Do ya' remember who sang 'Singing the Blues'? Was it Guy Mitchell?"

"No, Knucklehead!" Carnie nastily exclaimed. "It should be me who sang that damned song! Now please stop disintegratin' my swollen testicles into sex powder!"

Carnie's ego needed healing. I thought I would spare him any further embarrassment by changing the subject.

"Say, Tink. Do ya' think Popeye is gonna' come after us for destroyin' his new red and black Ford?"

"No, Words. I hear Bruno still believes that Langford had committed the Mill Creek vandalism because of what the Renegade bossman thinks Messina and the Ks had done with the cable at Snake Road, and because of the fight Popeye and *him* had behind the Dairy DeLite."

I was really worried. My mind was in a swirling quandary. I had too many doubts and fears about recent events to ever believe anything that Tinker or Carnie would have to say. "Tink, won't the cops be hot on our tails for turnin' their newest patrol car into a septic tank?"

"No, J.W. "If *that* cop comes after Carnie and me, we'll spill the beans about him hittin' on our moms. He's too afraid of losin' his good reputation, his pension, and his career. And if we can accuse the bully of bein' involved with smut and marijuana by takin' payoffs from Sal Palermo," Jeremy Foster elaborated, "the guy will be in the slammer way before either Carnie or me ever get to see the insides of one."

"That's right," Carnie reflexively agreed and echoed. "And I won't be happy until I bust that daffy womanizer down from a lieutenant to a puny *Cub Scout!"*

"Tink and Carnie may be absolutely correct," Jokes declared. "The public disgrace and scandal will ruin the cop's life, his marriage, his career, and his testosterone level!"

By the end of July, my conscience was really tormenting my rational thinking. The guilt I felt about all the wild vandalism was making me very restless and extremely nervous. I had trouble sleeping at night, and dark circles were appearing under my eyes. I woke-up in the middle of a nightmare where Tinker was a vampire that had bitten Carnie and me, and then I wanted Popeye Messina's blood as much as *he* did. "Dr. Destructo" wanted to have Popeye again kidnapped and tortured, and according to my dismal bad dream, so did Carnie and me.

Despite my psychological dishevelment, I considered using some ploy on the Kamikazes from the *Adventures of Robin Hood* novel I had been reading. Another idea from my high school literature class that was swimming-around inside my muddled head was the ancient Greece stage production idea, "the machine of the gods".

Dad sensed that something burdensome had been bothering me and suggested that my flagging spirit would be improved by attending an advertised religious retreat sponsored by Cardinal Reagan High School. The event would be held August 1st to August 4th at Malvern, on the west side of 'Philly, near *Villanova University*. The assigned dates conflicted with the highly anticipated August 3rd showdown between Quinn and Cummings.

I thought over Dad's constructive proposition and concluded that I did not wish to be removed from adventurous real-world sensations in order to practice far-fetched moral abstractions like abstinence, sacrifice, and penance at Malvern. I promised dad I would attend the next retreat during the *Christmas* holidays.

August 3rd was only a few days away. The upcoming drag-race dominated the Diablos' thinking and conversations. No one could put its intriguing hype on the back burner. The contest would not only be a winner-take-all automobile race; the event would actually be a supremacy test between the Dogwood Ds and the Kenwood Ks.

Chapter 39
"The Drag Race"

On August 1st, I was just getting ready to go to work at Hal's Deli when Carnie paid a visit to 50 Daffodil Lane. I was not too happy to see his lackluster appearance. Tinker had cruelly influenced and had wickedly corrupted Carnie's fragile, vulnerable mind. And the most delinquent Diablo was so crazy that I imagined that my gimpy acquaintance would probably chase the Devil around hell for all eternity while brandishing his small silver pistol and a switchblade.

"Hi, J.W.," Carnie greeted. "What are ya' doin'?"

I pointed to a novel and an encyclopedia laying on my bedspread. "I was readin' about *Robin Hood,* and this here is an illustration of the 'machine of the gods' that had been used by the ancient Greek playwrights during their brilliant stage productions."

"Did Robin Hood use any cool methods?" Carnie asked. "Didn't the glorified archer take his craps in a little john, and hang-out with a faggot freak named Friar Fuck?"

I told my rude visitor how Robin Hood would set-up the Sheriff of Nottingham's henchmen by taunting the guards, and then having the riled-up deputies' chase his rear-end into Sherwood Forest. Soon, Robin's band of green-clad merry men surrounded the bungling sheriff's constables; captured the pathetic clowns, and held the surprised prisoners for ransom.

"Hey, that's pretty neat!" Carnie admitted. "I'll havta' study your book after I learn how to read."

"Very funny," I answered. "You're just as brainy as I am. The trouble is you're totally lazy and unmotivated."

"Well, J.W., what's this here machine of the gods all about? Tell me so I don't have to waste my valuable time readin' about it."

I informed Carnie that I had read about the "theos ek mechanes" in Brother Timothy's Ancient History class. "Carnie, the machine of the gods was a really cool crane that would lower ancient Greek actors onto a stage. Here's a drawing of one," I revealed and showed my paranoid friend. I then explained that the ancient Greek actors were playing the roles of Mt. Olympus gods like Hermes and Ares in front of large amphitheater audiences. The performers were attached to ropes that made them appear as if the players were superhuman gods, descending to and ascending from earth.

"That's super-neat, J.W.," Carnie commended. "So, what time ya' start workin' at Hal's?"

"I gotta' run. I'm due at work in twenty-minutes. I've got some big orders to fill."

I decided to stay home the night of August 2nd. I felt that I shouldn't get involved in any lunacy created by Tinker or Carnie that might sabotage the important drag-race slated between Quinn and Cummings. Mr. C and Mr. T both craved more power in the Diablos, and Tinker was jealous of Quinn, and Carnie was especially envious of Bo. That night I received an unexpected phone call from Jalonec.

"Words, dig this," Bo began his lecture. "Quinn and me don't like the crap Tink and Carnie are pullin' with Popeye and the cops. We don't trust those two guys any more. I'm askin' ya' to keep a watch on those traitors during the big drag-race, so nothin' crazy happens to make Quinn look stupid."

"Okay, Bo, I understand," I acceded. "I'll definitely side with you and Quinn rather than associate with those two dismal imbeciles."

"Good," Bo ecstatically replied. "So, stick with those two freaks like a fly on shit every minute, right especially after noontime tomorrow. Quinn and me are countin' on ya'."

August 3rd finally arrived. I tried to act nonchalant at family lunch, pretending it was just another hot summer day on the August calendar. The Burns' and the Kalens had told Pop about the April break-in over at Sal Palermo's house, and about the twelve-foot-long dead snake found deposited inside the pink bathtub. My parents inquired if I knew anything about the gossip, or about the front lawn at 66 Daffodil Lane, promptly dying from an excess of weed spray.

I answered that it was probably "gang related" and that possibly other rival factions of the Mafia were involved with the incident. "Mr. Palermo has a lot of enemies," I pointed-out. "It looks a little like the mob violence I saw on the *Untouchables* T.V. preview over at Bo Jalonec's house way back in April."

"J.W., one reason we moved to Levittown was to escape the social problems connected with wild city criminal life," pop sermonized. "We wanted you, Annie, and Skip to grow-up in a safe place. There's too much of a criminal element existing around these parts. There're too many rebellious greaser gangs, too. I believe that your sinister Diablos' friends are also a very bad influence on you."

I felt blood surging in my throat, ears, and brain. I could almost taste the thrill of competition my mind was imagining. Quinn wanted Cummings, and Cummings wanted Quinn, and Tinker wanted Popeye, and Popeye wanted me, and the Ds and Ks all wanted each other. But the tenseness all hinged on the upcoming Haines Road drag-race which Quinn, Cummings and their gang ambassadors had spent weeks diligently preparing for.

At precisely four p.m. Carnie and Tink picked me up in the '49 Merc'. Carnie had gotten the word out that he had bought a similar' black Mercury to the one he had lost in the Tullytown quarry, but even if the Kamikazes had accepted *his* gaudy lie, I believed that with their propensity for violence, the ruthless thugs would still destroy Diablos' property at random, or at whim.

Every summer day, Monday through Friday, Popeye and Jake Mullins drove to Radcliffe Street in Bristol to pick-up Dave Evans from work. Evans was employed at the *Kaiser Aluminum Plant* in the fabrication department. Dave Evans, like Mullins and Cummings, had quit school at age sixteen.

I sat in the middle of Carnie's James Dean Special, listening to the driver and Tinker talk about how the pair liked to keep the Kamikazes under watch during secret reconnaissance missions. I agreed that I saw some merit in their quiet spying activities. We observed Evans enter Mullins' black and white '57 De Soto, and then we tailed them at a distance leaving Bristol.

Suddenly, Carnie stepped on the accelerator and pulled alongside the dumfounded and surprised Kamikazes at a traffic light to berate our unscrupulous enemies.

"Hey Popeye!" Tinker yelled. "How's your new red and black Ford doin'?"

"Visited any area cemeteries lately?" Carnie hollered-over.

"Today you die!" Popeye screamed back. "All three of ya' mangy Piss-ants are gonna' bite the big one!"

I was in total shock at Carnie and Tinker's overt arrogance. It was hard for me to tell at that moment which loon was the greater psychopath. And now, Popeye was equating me with my two demented traveling comrades.

"You're both mentally ill, going on retarded!" I exclaimed to my pals. "Do ya' wanna' get us killed?"

Carnie then loudly recited a limerick for the already incensed Kamikazes, specifically directed at Dave Evans.

"There was a man named Dave,
Who kept a dead whore in his cave
You must admit, it smelled like shit
But look at the money Dave saved!"

Dave Evans could easily break Carnie's spine in two with one lethal punch. The three Ks in the black and white De Soto did not value Carnie's poetry one iota.

The light turned to green, and Carnie floored his black Merc', which was no slouch in the automotive kingdom. Mullins put his pedal to the metal and fishtailed right after us. Our car dangerously sped through two red lights, and the pursuing De Soto did also. Both rods squealed through a yellow light at the intersection of Bath Road and *Route 13,* and I felt as if I was a frightened cheetah being hunted at full speed by three angry lions.

"You guys said nothin' about pullin' this insane stuff!" I criticized. "I was never consulted! We were just supposed to kill some time before the big drag-race!"

"Just sit back and enjoy the ride," Tink calmly replied. "Things will get interestin' pretty soon!"

Carnie made an illegal left turn across two lanes onto Haines Road, and we flew by the Windsor Pharmacy and next the James Buchanan School. Despite our reckless velocity, the De Soto was gaining on us. Mr. Merc' made a very desperate left onto Junewood Drive, nearly sideswiping a little old lady in an old blue Hudson. A thousand-feet down Junewood Drive, our Merc' hopped the curb, and as Carnie sped into the grassy field between Junewood and Robbie Wilkinson's house, the '49 hotrod kicked-up enough dust to shroud all visibility within two-hundred-feet.

Carnie's sleek auto came to an abrupt halt, and the three of us exited in a hurry. Our butts darted as fast as our legs would carry us to the trail leading into the woods that led to Edgely Road. If the Ks were a little more intelligent, the doltish pursuers would have stopped to destroy Carnie's Mercury, but the rabid chasers were so torqued-up that the dupes trailed us on foot into the woods.

I was just as surprised as the three Ks were when sixteen Diablos leaped-out of the thickets and ambushed the thickheaded rogues. Tinker commanded the other Diablos to wrestle the three Ks to the ground, and then after accomplishing that difficult task, the Dogwood Hollow boys chained the trio of nincompoops to three separate oak trees. Popeye, Mullins, and Evans cursed and seethed, but their strong physical resistance had already been overwhelmed.

"Whose crazy idea was this?" I demanded to Tinker.

"Yours," Carnie frankly answered for *his* new best buddy. "And I told Tink all about how Robin Hood would capture the sheriff's guards inside Sherwood Forest. He liked the idea so much that we decided to try it on the brain-dead Kamikazes. And J.W., the son-of-a-bitchin' plan really worked!"

"Quinn's not gonna' like this!" I challenged.

"Who gives a crap what he and Bo think!" Tinker spitefully replied in a peeved tone of voice. "After tonight, I'm takin' over the Diablos. Carnie's gonna' be my lieutenant."

Tinker and Carnie treated the three Kamikazes as if the Ks were wild rabid beasts. The crude pair poured three jars of live ants down the necks of the chained hostages. Popeye, Evans, and Mullins squirmed, itched and screamed myriad profanities, but to no avail. Tinker then told me that psychological torture was much more effective than mere physical punishment, or even death, because pain will go away, but fear will always rise from the subconscious, as long as a tortured person was still alive.

"Have some mercy," I ineffectively pleaded. "And isn't wreckin' two of Messina's cars enough retaliation?"

"No, that only made Popeye angry," Tinker balked. "But fear is a much greater weapon than revenge. That's where these itchy ants become a big factor."

Carnie seemed to be enjoying the impromptu torture session very much. "How come ya' three jerks have so many ants and not too many uncles?" my former best pal asked in a sophomoric attempt at impersonating Bo Jalonec.

"Look Tink," I declared. "I gotta' go home for supper or my parents will call the cops and report me missin'."

"Okay, you go home J.W., and Carnie and me will pick ya' up at eight o'clock sharp," Tinker ordered. "Better be friggin' ready, or I'll treat ya' worse than these three asshole Ks!"

As I walked home from the woods, I thought about the ugly mutiny that was going-on within the Diablos. Quinn and Bo had trusted me to monitor Tinker and Carnie, and it now appeared that I had either betrayed *their* confidence, or had failed my assigned responsibility. Now, Mr. T was leading a conspiracy against Quinn, probably wanting him to lose the race so that a new Diablos' leader could surface. I also believed that Carnie was aspiring to replace Bo as first lieutenant.

Maniac one and maniac two picked me up at eight sharp in the blue '49 Plymouth. We zipped-down Dahlia Lane to Dogwood Drive, and then we hightailed it over to Haines Road. Tinker pulled-over to the shoulder, and then parked his wheels next to several tall evergreen bushes. We got out of the car, and I was quite amazed when "Dr. Destructo" popped the trunk. Inside was Popeye Messina, handcuffed and gagged. Tinker's two pet skunks, Perfume and Cologne, were scratching their sharp claws inside a cage, right next to Popeye's face. The skunks were a part of Tink's cruel campaign of psychological warfare, then being quite brutally implemented against Bruno Messina.

"What are ya' doin'?" I worried and insisted. "You're more insane than insanity!"

"You'll see soon enough," Tinker predicted. "And I owe my thanks to you, J.W. It was all your terrific idea, and after that nigger-lover Quinn loses the drag-race, and after I scare the shit out of Messina, then you'll be rewarded by being given a high office in the new Diablos high-ark-key."

Tinker adroitly shinnied up a telephone pole that had a street-lamp illuminating a small stretch of Haines Road. Carnie threw up to him a length of rope. Mr. T must have had ancient ancestors who were part nimble chimpanzees, because the adept climber reached the neck of the street-lamp in a hurry. Exhibiting great dexterity, the ape-man flung the rope over the extended frame. The mentally unstable mechanic then reached into his leather jacket, removed his small pistol, and then shot-out the overhead lamp bulb.

The *mad,* mentally-warped Diablo then deftly clambered-down the telephone pole. With exactly four-minutes to go until race time, Tink advanced to his car and removed a harness from the back seat. Carnie and his co-conspirator then pulled Messina from the trunk. The loyal assistant held Tinker's small metal pistol to Bruno's head as Mr. T. loosened Messina's handcuffs, lifted his arms, and attached a sturdy harness around Popeye's chest. Strong metal hooks had been secured to four different sections of the harness. Tinker threaded the rope through each of the four buckles, making a tight sailor's knot to finalize his inspired deviltry. Popeye had now been very competently tethered to the harness.

Carnie and Tinker then tugged the other end of the rope that had been hurled over the lamppost, and because of cause and effect, Popeye was soon suspended three-feet above Haines Road. Seeing that their practice run had been successful, the two fanatics allowed their stringed puppet to drop to the asphalt. Tink then removed Popeye's gag from inside his mouth.

"You crazy sons-of-bitches are insane!" Bruno shouted. "You're all fuckin' hospital mental cases!"

Off to the distant west, we could hear the racing of engines. Most of the Ks and Ds were at the start and finish lines, and a few were assigned traffic duty blocking-off entrances onto Haines Road from Dogwood Hollow, Farmbrook, Kenwood, and Junewood sections both before and during the race. The roar of the powerful motors sounded like distant peals of thunder as the '42 and '52 Fords skidded from their due west starting positions. Quinn was in the left Haines Road' lane, and Cummings in the right lane, unknowingly bearing-down in the darkness on *his* apprehended lieutenant, Popeye Messina.

The two hotrods topped-out first gear, racing neck and neck. The cars back tires screeched when each machine shifted into second, and the whining and the bellowing of the two powerful engines greatly increased my anxiety. Popeye was screaming a litany of obscenities, but his shouts amidst all the excitement were as if the suspended-in-air puppet had been starring in a silent movie. Tinker and Carnie violently yanked the rope, and their prisoner was quickly hoisted another foot above Haines Road. Messina was hanging from the unlit lamp-post like a spider dangling from its web.

Soon, the two racers shifted their marvelous machines into third, heading towards the main entrance to James Buchanan School, the designated finish line. Cummings's visibility had been obscured by the incapacitated streetlight, and soon the chief Ks car was within fifty-feet of his dangling lieutenant. The sudden shock of seeing his best buddy about to become road kill sent Cummings into a panic. As Carnie and Tinker again pulled the taut rope, the chief K spontaneously hit the brakes. Popeye (like a manikin/marionette) was then quickly elevated twelve-feet above Haines Road. Cummings's speedy machine shot by and skidded right underneath the delirious hanging Kamikaze. Bruno Messina was screaming like a hysterical mental ward patient, and Cummings was also shrieking as the '52 Ford' veered off the road.

Tinker and Carnie hastily dropped the rope, fleeing the area like intimidated matadors sprinting from a raging bull. Cummings' screeching car just missed the accomplices, and the next thing I knew, my eyes saw Popeye plummeting ten-feet onto Haines Road. Cummings' car tore two long grooves through grass and community landscaping, winding-up in a cluster of holly bushes and red maple trees behind several Farmbrook residences.

Quinn maintained his composure and kept his shiny Ford speeding toward the finish line. My hero would win the race, but my Diablo champion would be unhappy about not being victorious on his terms, the contest being fair and square.

I glanced-up at the rope still suspended from the lamp-post and then looked-down at Popeye, who was shouting explicit expletives on his knees while trying to get himself out of his handcuffs and cumbersome harness.

Then, it all came to me in a sudden brainstorm. Tinker had improvised a version of the "theos ek mechanes," a brilliant 1959' "machine of the gods," which Carnie had thoroughly described to him, along with the entrapment methods utilized by Robin Hood. And by Zeus, Carnie's pilfering of the literary ideas that I had inadvertently provided Merc' Man had almost dissolved the Diablos for good.

Chapter 40
"The Quarry Fight"

Feeling guilty about what had occurred, I dashed-over to Popeye and evaluated that Bruno was pretty dazed and disoriented. After helping the groggy K to his feet, I curled his arm around my shoulder and dragged him to the side of Haines Road. I dropped his body gently to the ground, where Messina would be temporarily safe from oncoming traffic. Tinker and Carnie were yelling for me to hop into the '49 Plymouth. After I clumsily clambered inside, Tink turned-around and took-off, cutting through Dogwood Hollow, and next sped west to Mill Creek Parkway, and soon making a left onto Edgely Road, Finally, the intent villain turned left onto *Route 13* en route to the Feed Bag.

"What was all *that* hangman craziness about?" I abruptly asked with a bewildered voice.

"I guessed wrong," Tinker admitted in a rare display of honesty. "I thought that Quinn would've been in the left-hand lane bearin' down on hanging Popeye. Then, Cummings would've won the damned race instead of undependable Quinn."

"That was real race interference!" I squawked and objected. "Now, Quinn's gonna' blame me for what happened because you two jerks got the Robin Hood woods' ambush idea and 'the machine of the gods' idea from me. Sometimes, it just doesn't pay to be too intellectual, just like what happens to always-abused Stanley Tezeeker."

"Take it easy, J.W.," Carnie suggested. "Either Quinn is gonna' get on the stick and lead the Diablos against the Ks, or we're gonna' have to have a new leader callin' the shots."

"You're both loony bin material," I loudly replied. "What was supposed to be a simple drag-race is gonna' end up evolvin' into a bloody gang fight. And it's all because you two bozos are jealous of Quinn and Bo makin' decisions and bein' in the limelight all the time."

Tinker was inspired by my use of the word "bozos". "I'm not *afraid* of either of those two clowns!" Jeremy retorted.

"Who's talkin' about fear," I answered. "I'm talkin' about other positive abstract qualities like respect, honor, and leadership!"

Tinker had taken the roundabout route to the Feed Bag just to avoid driving past all the confusion that must have existed at the Haines Road finish line, which was the James Buchanan School. Neither Tinker nor Carnie said another word as we slowly exited the blue Plymouth and then entered the bustling fast-food restaurant. It seemed that I had allowed the other two depraved Diablos to be destructive during a greaser sacred rite, an honest drag-race. I had allowed Mr. T and Mr.

C to interfere with and manipulate the outcome of the thrilling contest, and in the process, had let both Quinn and Bo down.

I also knew that Tinker and Carnie's coup d' etat against Quinn and Bo had failed, and also, that neither of the insurgents could be trusted in good faith. The dual scoundrels were essentially crass pirates with pipe dreams of being navy admirals.

I wished I hadn't been associated with Tinker and Carnie's dimwitted lamp-post experiment. The pair of despicable traitors had committed inexcusable treason, and now I was waiting for *Judgment Day* with *them* being on trial. Maybe the Greek playwrights could pull off the "machine of the gods", but Tinker and Carnie were self-centered, incompetent imbeciles. By making Popeye Messina into a suspended marionette, the ambitious idiots might have destroyed the Diablos' camaraderie for good. If those imbeciles ever took over the gang's helm, I knew I absolutely wanted to quit, and instead, pal-around with Stanley Tezeeker and Mortimer Ralston.

Bo Jalonec, Susie Parker, and Patty Van Arsdale entered the Feed Bag. The trio reluctantly sat-down at our table, looking at the three of us as if we were confirmed lepers. Bo slowly explained how he had started the race by dropping his heavy Diablos' jacket onto Haines Road. Jalonec also told us that Quinn had invited Marcus Spellman to attend the contest, since Sugar Ray had faithfully worked on the '42 Ford's engine for two whole weeks.

After Cummings had *mysteriously* veered off Haines Road, his wheels became embedded in sand and mud. Quinn had turned around without even crossing the finish line. The head D drove to the Farmbrook lamp-post, attached a chain to the '52 Ford's under-frame, and played the *Good Samaritan* role by yanking Cummings' car out of its quagmire.

"Quinn's thinkin' about resignin' from the Diablos," Bo revealed. "He says that he no longer wants to be connected with dunces and ignoramuses who act like prehistoric sub-morons."

I noticed Tinker giving Carnie a quick eye-wink, indicating that he could easily bypass Bo and become the new Diablos' chieftain should Quinn retire. I felt weak as if I had been suffering from iron deficiency anemia, and I imagined that five bottles of *Geritol* wouldn't have cured my "tired blood" condition. My conscience also felt guilty for indirectly masterminding Popeye's near-fatal "theos ek mechanes" misadventure. I feared that Quinn would accuse Tinker, Carnie, and me of being three Judas apostles that had traduced the reputation of *my* master by turning *his* finest moment into a terrible travesty. My heart nearly tumbled into my stomach when I noticed Quinn and Marcus

Spellman stepping through the Feed Bag's main doors and then hastily approaching the two D betrayers and me.

"Who thought-up that insane street-light stunt involvin' Popeye and Cummings?" Quinn demanded.

"What ya' three cats did wasn't too cool!" Marcus Spellman exclaimed. "In my section of Yardley, the brothers in the 'hood would hit ya' three nitwits ten-times upside your heads, and that ain't no jive-talkin', either! Man, ya' three cats is serious traitors!"

Before Sugar Ray could continue his scathing indictment, our Diablos' leader admonished the three of us "dunces" some more. "Didn't you dummies realize how important that race was to me and to the Diablos' reputation?" Quinn directly questioned his suspected conspirators. "It was my goal to beat Cummings fair and square. When word gets out to the Renegades about the hangman stunt, the Diablos will be the laughin' stock of Levittown. Doesn't pride and honor mean anything to you three loons?"

I felt real shame while I was sure that Tinker and Carnie felt nothing but blind ambition. Guilt, regret, and remorse dominated my spirit, but *they* had desire, power, and tyranny prevailing and possessing their narrow minds.

Sugar Ray Spellman bombarded us with even more valid criticism. "Quinny's layin' it on ya' straight," Marcus chastised. "The last time ya' three jiven' turkeys got your wigs blasted, the barber must've cut inside your skulls, instead of outside."

Just as Tinker was about to say *he* wanted to fight Quinn for leadership of the Diablos, Robbie Wilkinson came running into the Feed Bag like a contemporary Paul Revere. "The Kamikazes are coming! The Kamikazes are coming!" R. W. announced.

If it had not been for the chance presence of Marcus Spellman, and if it had not been for Cummings' despicable racial prejudice, Quinn would have definitely dropped-out of the Diablos that eventful night. But because of a strange twist of fate, the head D remained our leader; Tinker and Carnie's betrayal was never thoroughly exposed, and hostility between the Ks and the Ds was almost instantly re-ignited.

Quinn was about to apologize to the Kamikazes for Popeye's rather outrageous, imitation crane/lever caper, when Cummings' gross bigotry changed the direction, along with the complexion, of the entire conversation.

"Ya' three dirt-bags almost got me killed tonight!" Cummings accused, while pointing at Tinker, Carnie, and me.

"And me, too!" Popeye echoed. "There ain't no mental hospital big enough to hold you three psychos."

"And I think ya' three creeps have somethin' to do with our cars being fucked with!" Cummings alleged.

"And with the porn' and the marijuana planted in our trunks after the Reagan Prom," Popeye accused.

Feeling afraid and threatened, Carnie handed-over the handcuff keys to Cummings, who quickly freed Bruno from the derbies.

Quinn was aware of the earlier pranks that had been initiated by his aberrant disciples, so "the boss man" deftly changed (and limited) the subject to that evening's events to avoid defending un-defendable acts. "I'm really sorry for what happened tonight," Quinn graciously apologized to the incensed Ks. "And I promise to race ya' again fair and square without any outside interference."

Cummings finally recognized the presence of Marcus Spellman, and matters got very ugly in a hurry. "Say, what are the Ds doin' hangin' around with a nigger-baby for? Don't ya' know that the only good nigger is a dead nigger!" Cummings ridiculed. The King K's anger had suddenly converted into bitter racial hatred.

"Sugar Ray here is my friend," Quinn replied. "He's a good man that also works on my car. I've got great respect for him!"

But Cummings did not know when to stop with his grotesque condescension. The all-too-biased Kamikaze leader was as diplomatic as a sociopathic anarchist. "What happened to ya' boy?" the King K nastily derided Marcus. "Did they tar and feather ya' with all the feathers painted black?"

"Look here, Cummings," Quinn retorted. "If ya' insult my friend, ya' also insult me. Is that perfectly clear? And besides, Sugar Ray is a skilled boxer who could teach *you* a thing or two."

"I can't learn nothin' from a damn nigger!" Cummings rudely answered. The chief K then argued that he was a skilled street fighter, and that he wasn't afraid of a boxer, because boxing was not the same thing as fighting. "In a brawl," Cummings maintained, "a greaser could also wrestle, bite, kick, claw, and use lethal weapons besides punching the shit out of somebody."

"Can't we just forget everything, have peace, and pretend nothin' has happened?" Marcus suggested.

"We don't want no niggers livin' or hangin' out in Levittown!" Popeye maliciously chimed-in.

"Marcus doesn't live in Levittown. He lives in Yardley," Quinn astutely clarified.

Cummings was becoming more irate and more volatile with each heated verbal volley. "Well then, Trench-mouth. We don't want no white trash hangin' around with niggers in the Feed Bag."

Somehow, I summoned the courage to enter the debate. I felt loyalty to Quinn and pity for Marcus. "Listen up Cummings," I stated. "The *Civil War* ended almost a hundred-years-ago. Black people are no longer slaves."

Even Bo Jalonec argued in defense of Marcus Spellman's right to human dignity. "Yeah, don't ya' thick-headed rednecks see that times are changin'," Bo argued to the toxic Ks. "On TV, the public schools in Little Rock, Arkansas are even integratin'. Black people are Americans, just the same as you and me."

Cummings was not through with his very blatant discrimination. His remarks made me ashamed that both he and me were bona fide American Caucasians.

"The Diablos ain't nothin' more than a bunch of goddamned nigger lovers," Cummings concluded and asserted. "And no nigger's worth his weight in either cow manure or chicken-shit!"

I knew that the Kamikazes would often travel around Bucks County and North 'Philly looking for black kids to kidnap or beat-up, and I was afraid Sugar Ray was going to be *their* next selected victim.

Marcus Spellman could not bite his tongue any longer. "What do ya' mean?" Sugar Ray challenged. "The blood under my skin is just as red as yours. I'm not scared of you! I'll fight ya' anywhere, if that's what ya' want!"

"I mean to say," Cummings continued his horrendous diatribe. "You're black as coal, and ya' eat lots of watermelons and grits, and stink to high heaven, even without doin' any sweatin'. That's why the Kamikazes hang coloreds from railroad bridges."

"So, you're the guys who nearly killed my brother Harris and my cousin Ellis!" Marcus realized and articulated. "The boys just came over to the Feed Bag a couple of months ago on their way to deliverin' a part for Quinn's car."

"That does it!" Quinn shouted. "Cummings, I was gonna' offer ya' a new race, but your brain is poisoned with hate, and your mouth needs tightenin'. Looks like we're gonna' have to duke it out, David and Goliath style, one on one."

The tension inside the Bag was extreme as everyone seated and standing became silent. I was anxiously waiting for Cummings' reply. I looked at Tinker and Carnie, and I instinctively knew exactly what the Benedict Arnolds were thinking. Each wanted to see Cummings defeat Quinn in combat. That embarrassment would automatically trigger a reorganization of the Diablos leadership. The charlatans wanted to achieve power by default.

"Okay, with me," Cummings indicated. "Give the Ks the exact time and place."

"Words," Quinn sternly commanded. "Tell us when and where."

I was caught totally off-guard. My frazzled mind was in full disarray. My ideas were dizzily spiraling-around in a mental maelstrom, and my memory was caught in terrible emotional turmoil. "Er, ah, the Tullytown quarry, at ten tonight. Rules, left hands handcuffed and no holds barred."

After demonstrating my ability to function under extreme duress, I breathed a deep sigh of relief.

Cummings then continued with vociferating his cocky tirade. "Fine with me. Only an asshole would fight for a pathetic rug-head. See you Ds at the quarry at ten. And oh, yeah, bring along Gorilla-lips, too!"

"One other thing," Popeye stipulated. "You turkeys gotta' give us the keys for the chains and locks for Mullins and Evans. They're still tied to trees in the woods behind Dogwood Hollow."

"I don't know what you're talkin' about!" Quinn questioned.

"You'd better learn what's goin' on inside *your* damned gang!" Popeye angrily stated. "Those three lyin' jerks sittin' with ya' know all about it!" Messina yelled as the infuriated K Lieutenant pointed at the three Ds sitting at the table in real 'Three D'.

My pupils looked at Carnie and we both looked at Tinker, who then unzipped a compartment of his leather jacket and threw Popeye a set of keys. Cummings and his Kamikazes confiscated the items and stridently stormed-out of the Feed Bag to rescue their abandoned buddies still trapped and tethered to trees inside the woods.

Quinn, Bo, and their girls sat there in a stupor, trying to figure-out why and how Jake Mullins and Dave Evans had been chained to trees. The worried babes were also probably wondering why and how Popeye Messina had been tied to a rope and had been dangling from the neck of a Haines Road street-light that was not illuminating.

If it hadn't been for Marcus Spellman's presence in the Feed Bag, I am certain that Quinn and Bo would have interrogated Tinker, and Tinker would have blown his stack, and a fight would have resulted between the chief Diablo and his jealous, power-hungry subordinate.

The Diablos rapidly exited the Feed Bag. I rode to the quarry with Tinker and Carnie; Bo drove Susie in his green and cream '57, and Quinn rode with Patty and Marcus in his '42.

I thought about Marcus Spellman saving the Diablos without him even knowing it. I felt sorry for Marcus, being black in a white man's world. Everything about the 1950s seemed black and white, including our televisions, our newspapers, our music, our photo' film, our sneakers, and our social values. Racial prejudice was an ugly mask of the hypocritical "Happy Days". In the not-so-fabulous '50s, things were either right or wrong; were either good or bad; were either smart or stupid; were either funny or serious, or were either black or white. Few gray areas of interpretation existed, and according to the era's method of classification, Marcus Spellman was supposed to know his abysmal place in the well-defined social universe.

As Tinker drove north on *Route 13* toward Tullytown, the more I thought about Cummings' abuse of Marcus, the more I related to the black kid's social dilemma. I recalled Phil Jackson's snobbish mother and her sanctimonious attitude in her conversation with her son about Carnie and me. She had made us feel like scumbag indigents, just because we lived in Levittown, and her *cultural* prejudice was very similar to how, using *racial* prejudice, Cummings had brutally belittled and labeled Sugar Ray, simply because of the pigmentation of his skin.

While Tinker and Carnie talked about the upcoming fight between Quinn and Cummings, I thought about how my father had gone to war against Hitler's regime to defend the freedoms of people like Mr. and Mrs. Jackson, Cummings, Popeye, and Sal Palermo. Dad had fought for both freedom and discrimination without much awareness or consideration of the latter. The Jacksons were class-prejudiced in a similar manner as Cummings and Popeye were race-prejudiced, and those truths meant that Marcus Spellman had been born with the double whammy of being black, and being lower middle-class.

The only redeeming aspect to the '50s era, I thought, was the existence of fine decent men like Luigi, Domenick, and Hal Irving, a Jew who believed enough in a Polish/Italian/Catholic kid to trust him with the back room of his delicatessen. Hal Irving showed faith in a boy who wasn't of his "faith". And then, I admired Quinn even more, because I finally realized that my Diablos' hero, unlike Tinker and Carnie, was more of a social reformer than even my deli boss was. My introspection was cut short by one of Tinker's trashy, unsavory comments. I listened to the driver's pathetic rhetoric.

"I hope Quinn gets his ass kicked good!" Jeremy Foster wished and articulated. "Cummings is right. No white guy oughta' be fightin' for any goddamned nigger. If Quinn is lucky enough to win, then I'm joinin' the friggin' Kamikazes, and then I'll be able to pulverize the misguided Shit-head without hearin' any cornball bullshit from you, Mr. Words."

"Me, too," Carnie parroted. "I mean I'll join the Ks, too!"

I was afraid of committing myself to such a preposterous idea. "I'll think about it," I remarked in utter disgust.

As Tinker motored through Tullytown, I wondered if Quinn and Bo had suspected the extent of the conspiracy being waged internally against them. Were Robbie, Ace, Slip, and the others really backing Tink and Carnie's in-progress coup d'etat? And had the two devious betrayers riding on my opposite sides lied by telling the other Diablos that the Robin Hood and the lamp-post schemes really had originated from me, and not from Bo or Quinn?

The remainder of the tension-filled drive to the remote quarry was very suspenseful. The anticipation of savage conflict had my heart beating rapidly. Cummings had those massive biceps protruding-out of his black tee-shirt and popping-out of his cut-off leather jacket. His arms featured hideous red and blue tattoos, which reminded me of the coloration of poisonous snakes, warning imperiled intruders to keep their distance.

Then, I thought of Quinn, the greaser's greaser, who was a complete gentleman of good character. Quinn was of a different fabric than Tinker was. He was generally courteous, polite, and honorable. And on the night of August 3rd, *my* leader proudly wore his white tee-shirt, showing his Diablos that he was a very determined *rebel with a cause,* defending his special singular version of greaser truth, justice, and the American way.

An excavation company had left the quarry abandoned for several years. The firm had found a more favorable site several miles north towards Morrisville. The fast-moving procession of Diablos and Kamikaze' cars entered the restricted area, and then wound its way along the serpentine gravel road. Soon, Tinker passed by Popeye's partially submerged '52 Ford and the counterfeit '49 Merc', both still bobbing up and down inside the small, man-made lake.

Fifteen vehicles had made the journey north from Levittown. The cars were parked in a horseshoe formation, with the open-end leading to a diagonal grade that sloped-down to the water's edge. Headlights were left on (with motors running) to illuminate the makeshift combat arena. Everyone was tense as Quinn and Cummings faced each other. I was very concerned that their one-on-one fight would proliferate into a full-scale greaser rumble.

Tinker attached a pair of handcuffs to each combatant's left wrist. Excitement reigned supreme. The ideas of fists and blood, the fundamentals of battle passed-down from our primitive ancestors, caused the eyewitnesses' hearts to pound much faster than usual. The learned laws and rules of culture no longer governed our thinking.

The two '50s gladiators slowly rotated in a circle, tugging and pulling with their manacled left hands, each attempting to gain a subtle advantage. And then, Cummings tallied a right cross to Quinn's chin, but shortly thereafter, the Kamikaze King was the recipient of two forceful uppercuts to the chest that made the villain wince with pain. The swinging became more violent and more accurate, as each gang leader landed powerful blows to the other's face and shoulders, causing crimson to trickle from Cummings' mouth and from Quinn's nose.

Quinn and Cummings tangled in a clinch, wrestled to the ground, and then rolled intensely down the stony slope, sliding into waist deep quarry water. We all scurried to the hill's brink to get a better view of the ongoing clash. Quinn had Cummings lifted into the air, but soon lost his footing. The two flipped backward, momentarily submerging beneath the water's surface. As both combatants rose-up and gasped for air, Cummings had Quinn in a headlock, but soon, the Kamikaze giant lost his balance and both noble adversaries fell below the surface. Just as Quinn was gaining the upper hand in the violent struggle, a loud overhead flapping noise was heard. A police helicopter with huge propeller blades was whipping across the night sky, several-hundred-feet above our heads.

The giant chopper had detected the horseshoe headlight pattern from a distance, and had zoomed-down to investigate. The two dauntless warriors suddenly terminated their altercation. A voice from an overhead bullhorn was very audible.

"Cease and desist immediately! This is the police! Rescue personnel are on their way! Do not evacuate! Stay right where you are!" a monotone voice originating from the now-stationary helicopter imperatively commanded.

Right! Tinker, Ace, Popeye, Phil Jackson, Spits, and Worm climbed down the mini-cliff and assiduously dragged the two exhausted gladiators out of the lake, where Tinker unlocked the handcuffs. Members of the two gangs helped Quinn and Cummings up the steep grade. Popeye, Phil Jackson, Jake Mullins, and Dave Evans had another matter on their scheming minds. The four renegades grabbed Tinker, lifted his body up, and hurled his despicable form into the quarry.

"Help! I can't swim!" Jeremy cried-out as the insidious bigot frantically thrashed and splashed about in the man-made lake.

Quinn, who was already fatigued from brawling, dashed-down the incline, dove into the water, swam-out to Tinker, and after two-minutes of intense effort, managed to get Jeremy to where Carnie and I could pull the ruthless subordinate's wet frame out of the quarry.

The police helicopter futilely repeated its unheeded commands. The greasers' cars recklessly fishtailed-out of the police detected battle zone. A very wet and chagrined Tinker drove Carnie and me back to the safety of Levittown.

"Quinn saved your ass from drownin'," I reminded Tinker. "That was the first time I ever saw ya' scared, besides maybe when we were trapped down in the Windsor Pharmacy cesspool."

No one answered my indictive statement until Carnie tried to relieve Tinker's loss of pride. "Nobody won the damned fight," Carnie regretfully noted. "Everything's still the same as it was before. We're back to square one!"

"How did the cops know about the fight?" I asked.

"They didn't," ungrateful Tinker insisted. "I'll bet it was by accident. The fuzz prob'ly saw the two cars sittin' in the quarry and thought the drivers was still trapped inside. That's why they talked about callin' rescue personnel. That's how friggin' stupid mother-fuckin' cops are!"

"Well, Popeye, Jackson, Mullins, and Evans really got even with you," I added. "You got really soaked!"

"Nobody ever gets even with me," Tinker bristled. "Don't worry! Those shit-faced pricks are gonna' get rewarded by me personally."

I knew that Quinn would never seek revenge, since Cummings had bloodied his nose, and then I realized exactly how juvenile Tinker's vengeance policy was. I could never support *his* ambitious desire to become the Diablos' leader. The power-hungry dreg had no discretion, no couth, and no regard for the welfare of others.

A *Philadelphia Inquirer* newspaper article reported the next morning that the city's Police Commissioner had been flying in a helicopter from New York back to the *Quaker City*. The Diablos put two and two together and theorized (just as Tinker had suspected) that the police had incidentally stumbled across the quarry fight scene while traveling airborne between the two cities.

The following night at the Feed Bag, Bo Jalonec referred to the police helicopter sighting of the two cars partially submerged in the Tullytown quarry. "J.W., the fuzz *auto* know better than to mess with treacherous greaser gangs."

Somehow, Jokes' remark seemed petty, hollow, and shallow. Bo had unknowingly escaped a serious Diablos' internal rebellion, and there he was, still pretending that life was one big happy bowl of delicious cherries.

Chapter 41
"A Little Huckstering"

Two days after the unforgettable quarry fight, my conscience was really bothering me. I decided to take a walk over to Chuckie and Jimmy Callahan's where Quinn lived with his good-natured cousins. I wanted to tell my fearless leader about Tinker and Carnie's conspiracy against his Diablos' leadership, even though such behavior would be a violation of the greaser ethics' code to never squeal on another teen.

When I knocked on the door at 318 Dogwood Drive, I found Quinn holding an ice bag to his head. The Boss Man cordially invited me inside, and we sat-down and chatted at the breakfast table.

"Where are Chuckie and Jimmy?" I asked. "Are they in church makin' solemn confessions to Father Malcolm?"

"They're out with Uncle Charlie looking for some fruit to buy for his new hucksterin' route," Quinn explained.

"Look," I nervously commented to my idol. "I'm sorry about what happened during the drag-race. There's a couple of things I have to tell ya'," I disclosed while alluding to the potential gang mutiny that had incredibly been averted.

"J.W., you're the Diablo I trust the most. Forget the past. It's all water over the dam. Actually, I find some of the crazy stuff that you, Tink, and Carnie come-up with as bein' pretty creative, in a rather strange sort of way."

"Ya' do?" I skeptically asked in disbelief.

"As sure as sunshine. So now, J.W., get the word out. I wanna' race Cummings again without any advantages or interference. I'm assignin' you the duty of findin' a first-class location for a planned rematch drag-race. I think that you're the best qualified to do that service."

Quinn went on, explaining how the area cops were increasing their patrols of Dogwood Hollow and Kenwood, and how his mercy was completely forgiving Carnie, Tink, and me for irritating and chaining Jake Mullins and Dave Evans to the oak trees in the woods. "J.W., congratulations," Quinn continued. "That fancy trick with Popeye usin' the street-light and rope as a liftin' device was one of the most imaginative pranks I've ever seen or heard of!"

How could I rat on Tink and Carnie when Quinn had already forgiven (and praised) the mutineers for chaining Mullins and Evans to the trees, and for making Popeye bounce-around in the air in *suspended* animation. The only thing that Quinn didn't seem to know about was that Popeye had also been temporarily harnessed to a separate tree in the woods behind Robbie's house, too, before being freed to reside in Tinker's trunk, and soon dangled from the Haines Road' derrick light-post.

"I talked with Robbie and Ace," Quinn confidentially added, "and the guys told me that Tinker and Carnie had said you and Bo gave the approval for the Popeye incident, and also the Mullins and Evans idea after ya' had spoken to me. Now I know that *we* never talked about those incidents," Quinn emphasized, "but since the Diablos did those things to three fanatical Ks, I'll have to defend the fact that my gang was inspired to do the deeds. If I didn't, it would look like I don't know what's actually goin' on inside the Diablos."

Chuckie and Jimmy returned with Quinn's Uncle Charlie, so I couldn't talk in private any more with my revered Diablos' mentor. Jimmy mentioned to his dad that I knew a little about fruit and produce, and Mr. Callahan told me he wanted to make some spare "vacation money" starting a weekend summer huckstering route around our part of Levittown.

"My mom's father owns Square Deal Farm Market on *Route 30* over in Jersey," I proudly stated. "Grampa' Tony used to take me all over South Jersey, and I know every farm and what they grow within a fifteen-mile radius of Hammonton."

I gladly shared my agricultural knowledge with Mr. Callahan, mostly because I liked his jovial personality, and partly because the man was an interested adult, asking a kid like me for assistance. His confidence in what I had related made me feel important. I wholeheartedly agreed to take Quinn's uncle for a *Garden State* fruit and vegetable excursion.

I believed that Carnie needed mental rehabilitation and had to escape from the demented "Dr. Destructo". Tinker was a bad influence on his new best pal, and if I could detach Carnie from the evil plotter's negative control for a day or two, I figured that then perhaps my former close buddy would return to his senses and become the ordinary kid I had remembered ever since sixth-grade. I called Carnie that night on the phone and was happy that the mimicker was receptive to the suggestion of going along with Mr. Callahan and me over to New Jersey to buy wholesale produce the next morning.

That night I dreamed about my grandfather who had come to America from Sicily via *Ellis Island*. Gramps had started in business by pushing a fruit and vegetable cart down Philadelphia's Ninth Street, eventually earning enough money to invest in five-acres of land in New Jersey, where he quickly pioneered the farm market trade between 'Philly and Atlantic City. Gramps couldn't read or write, and would often ask me what certain signs and billboards read along the highway as we traveled about to buy wholesale produce. He only knew how to scribble two letters, his initials "A.G.", which Grandpa Tony used to certify a purchase on a sales slip.

I dreamed about how I used to travel with Gramps up *Route 206* beyond Atsion Lake to Indian Mills where he would daily buy two-thousand ears of freshly pulled corn. Then, I would bury myself up to my chest with ears in a back corner of his pick-up truck and would wave to motorists passing us heading south on *206*. Thanks to Gramps, I had sufficient constructive background that would give Mr. Callahan a terrific lesson in South Jersey agricultural geography.

In my surreal dream, I had looked over to the other corner of the pick-up truck, and to my amazement, Tinker was also anchored beneath green husks while pointing a gun at me that at first looked like an innocent ear of corn. Then, I promptly woke-up from my nightmare in a cold sweat.

After breakfast, with Mom, Annie, and Skip, I strolled-over to Carnie's house. My *former* close friend drove me over to the Callahan's Dogwood Drive residence, and soon, the three of us were on our way into the South Jersey hinterlands. I introduced Quinn's uncle to a corn farmer in Indian Mills; to a peach farmer in Hammonton; to a cucumber farmer in Winslow; to a cantaloupe farmer in Nesco; to a tomato farmer in Folsom; to a string bean farmer in Vineland, and to a pepper and zucchini squash farmer in Weymouth. Our last stop was the Atlantic Blueberry Company plantation on *Route 322* in Mays Landing. Carnie and I surveyed the huge six-hundred-acre-farm as Mr. Callahan was busy purchasing ten-flats of the luscious blue fruit.

"This is it!" I exultantly exclaimed. "Carnie, here it is!"

Sometimes, Carnie had trouble deciphering and fathoming my language and my symbolisms. "This is what?"

"This giant blueberry farm," I replied. "It's the perfect place for a rematch drag race between Quinn and Cummings. Now, don't you agree?"

"You're right J.W. You are beyond-question, an absolute genius when it comes to connecting ideas!" my seemingly rehabilitated chum complimented.

I chuckled at my companion's loose choice of words. "No, Carnie," I maintained. "I'm not a genius. I'm just a clever asshole who can associate two unrelated ideas."

Before Mr. Callahan drove us back to Levittown, we stopped at Royale Crown Custard on the White Horse Pike in Hammonton, a business very similar to the *Route 13* Dairy DeLite. I was surprised to be reunited with a couple of old friends from St. Joseph School. I introduced Carnie to Warren Watson, Joel Salvo, and Mark Benedetto, who all belonged to a feared local greaser gang, "the Ramrodders". My two old acquaintances also wore black leather jackets with insignias on the back. It struck me that greasers were popping-up all over the map, even in remote farming communities like Hammonton.

When we finally returned to Dogwood Hollow, Mr. Callahan's green '51 Ford pick-up was loaded to the max' with farm-fresh Jersey produce. Carnie and I manned the tailgate and did most of the selling through Dogwood Hollow, Farmbrook, Junewood, and Greenbrook. The next section on the itinerary was Kenwood, formidable Kamikaze territory. Throughout the hot afternoon, I practiced some one-liners Jokes had suggested I should use along the huckstering route.

"Young Man, how much are the cantaloupes?" a fastidious woman asked in a formal summer dress.

"Thirty-five cents each, three for a dollar, m'am," I quoted.

"I'm on a very tight budget. Can't they be reduced?" the frugal woman inquired.

"Well, Lady, certainly, if ya' keep on squeezin' them the way you're doin', they will be reduced!" I flippantly replied.

The lady wiggled her nose and stuck-out her tongue at me to show her dissatisfaction and disdain before the customer wound-up selecting three of our finest cantaloupes.

"Young Man, are these freestone peaches?" a matronly woman with a cane asked.

"They s are, M'am," I confirmed. "And if ya' buy the peaches, the stones are free!"

"Sir, do you have any Jersey tomatoes?" a young, attractive, married woman innocently inquired.

"No, Lady. All my girlfriends live in Pennsylvania!" The female customer laughed at my silliness. I was glad to notice that at least one person in Kenwood had a decent sense of humor. But I valiantly persisted in pressing my luck.

"My mom wants to know if you have any berries," a young boy curiously requested.

"Sure, Kid, but no dingle-berries. I took a bath last night and wiped my' rear-end pretty good with the washcloth," I sarcastically quipped. The impressed youngster bought two pints of blueberries and merrily scampered back to his mother, proudly exhibiting his new-found prized acquisitions.

"Sir, do you have any apples?" a man asked at another Kenwood huckster stop.

"Sorry Mister, but you'll have to drive out to *Appalachia* to buy some," I responded.

"Is this corn fresh?" an elderly gray-haired grand-mom courteously asked.

"Yes M'am," I verified. "It just arrived from a military base, and if ya' hold one up to *your ear,* you can still hear the *colonels* cursing!" I laughed. After the grumpy old lady purchased a dozen ears, she told me I should stick my "nasty tongue" inside an active beehive.

"I'll take a pound of green peppers," ordered a distinguished looking mustached gentleman. "Do you have any fryers?"

"No, Sir," I tersely answered. "I think you'll havta' get some *friars* at the nearest monastery." The appreciative guy gave me a fifty-cent tip for my ludicrous wittiness.

"Hey Kid!" a man yelled at our next strategic stop. "Do ya' have any onions?"

"Yes, I do," I replied. "But I can't sell 'em to you because they're attached to the middle of my body."

I could tell that Carnie was getting jealous because Jokes' puns that I was using were working pretty well on our customers, while Mr. Merc' could hardly think of anything original to say. Too much contact with Tinker had systematically destroyed what little individuality and what diminishing sense of humor Carnie had left.

Most of the Levittown citizens we had encountered appreciated my good humor, and I wasn't even selling ice cream, but merely distributing wholesome fresh fruits and vegetables. A few grimaced, several sneered, and one elderly granny gave me the royal middle finger. But without exaggeration, the highlight of the retail produce venture was our stop in front of the Messina abode on Kenwood Drive.

Angie Palermo was visiting her cousin, and the two broads casually strolled-over to Mr. Callahan's huckstering truck. Each beauty was wearing Bermuda shorts and a tight-fitting tee shirt. When the Sicilian dolls saw Carnie and me standing in the back, the swarthy-skinned dolls were hesitant to advance any closer to Quinn's uncle's fruit and produce wagon.

"Oh no, Angie," Bubbles regretted. "It's those two little horny Dogwood Hollow squirts again!"

"Hi Angie," Carnie pathetically greeted. "So how would ya' like to go to bed with J.W.?"

"I'd rather sleep with King Kong or Mighty Joe Young," Angie negatively answered. "You ain't got no secret camera hidden in any of these tomatoes, do ya?" the Palermo honey asked as she examined several of the finest ones inside a crate.

"Hey Bubbles, how ya' doin'?" Carnie flirtatiously asked.

"Call me by my real name, Toilet-bowl!" Bubbles replied.

"Well, all right then, Toilet-bowl. How are ya' doin?" Carnie immaturely persisted.

Bubbles felt rather compelled to overreact to Carnie's juvenile impertinence. "Look, Twerp! Stop actin' like a stupid ten-year-old jerk-off!" Popeye's sister yelled. "Grow some damned freckles and dimples and look ten-years more mature than ya' do now!"

"Okay Josephine, how are ya' doin'?" Carnie asked, still believing he could make some significant headway, despite all of the abundant evidence to the contrary.

"For your information, my first name's Antoinette," Bubbles insisted. "Stop insultin' my high intelligence!"

"All right Antoinette, all kiddin' aside," Carnie promised. "I'll bet your panties get damp every time ya' lay your eyes on me." Carnie was just like petroleum. Sometimes, the idiot was refined, but most of the time, he was crude.

"What!" the Sicilian babe screamed. "You must be having a serious birdbrain hemorrhage, or something!"

"Really, Antoinette," the relentless Merc' Man repugnantly repeated. "Your panties must get damp every time ya' see me."

I was really getting annoyed with Carnie's total disrespect for the opposite sex. I didn't think that the offended girls appreciated him any more at that particular moment than I did. Right there and then, I was actually ashamed to be a Diablo.

"Ya' stupid shit!" Bubbles hollered. "Every time I see you, it's my chest that gets wet, not my damned panties!"

My sex-crazy companion raised two large ripe cantaloupes out of a carton. "Look here girls," Carnie explained. "These two plump melons are almost as big as the ones bouncin' around on your bosoms."

And with those foolish and preposterous words, Carnie lifted the lid off of a bushel, and four specially prepared water-balloons were concealed inside. The Italian broads were completely taken by surprise. Carnie threw the full spheres directly into their magnificent chests. The two "Spaghetti Chicks" screamed and yelled a litany of derogatory remarks as Mr. Callahan hit the gas pedal, speeding-off to Stonybrook for more fruit and vegetable sales.

That night, Carnie and I met Jokes inside the Feed Bag. Jalonec told us that when girls freak-out on guys like Angie and Bubbles often did on Carnie and me, then their wild reactions meant that we had skillfully gotten to their "inner beings". Even though the Sicilian dolls' outward behavior appeared hostile, internally, where it really mattered, Bo explained that Angie and Antoinette actually loved our presence. And now, Carnie had aggravated the pair to the point where the indignant broads wanted to kill us, so according to Bo Jalonec's sterling theory, the knockout beauties were waiting (and indirectly requesting) for us to ask them out.

"Jokes, when it comes to dating hot women," I cited with sheer admiration, "you're the ultimate expert."

"Yeah J.W.," Carnie agreed. "If Bo's logic is right, I wouldn't be surprised if Angie and Bubbles called us up for dates real soon."

"Keep on dreamin' and schemin'," I laughed.

"You two guys will get perfect blow-jobs from *Playboy* centerfolds before Angie or Bubbles will ever call either of you silly shits for anything on the phone!" Bo finished.

Chapter 42
"The Andalusia Drive-in"

I had to find a way to keep Carnie away from Tinker's evil tentacles. The day after the early August huckstering adventure, I was cleaning-up the dishes after family supper, and was getting ready to watch the *Pinky Lee Show* and *To Bet Your Life* starring Groucho Marx on the living room TV.

In the late '50s, few teenagers had phones in their rooms, so the Diablos' did as little-talking as possible while we were speaking on their family line. The phone rang and Dad answered it.

"Hey J.W.," Pop said. "There's some sexy-soundin' girl who wants to talk with you. Remember what I told you about too much whorin' around. It could only get you into big trouble."

I held the phone to my ear and was astonished to hear the very identifiable, exotic voice of Angie Palermo.

"Hi J.W. How ya' doin' big boy!" the Sicilian doll oddly began.

Blood rushed to my head. I had no suspicion I might have been targeted for becoming a victimized fool. "Er, fine, I guess," I replied while attempting to discreetly clear my throat.

"My cousin Ant' and I were discussin' how cool you and Carnie are," the Italian chick declared in a sexy tone of voice. "I mean, no other guys on the planet have the guts to do what you two have done to Ant' and me. Bubbles, er, I mean cousin Ant' and I tingle all over just thinkin' about you and Carnie wantin' to feel our wet breasts, ya' know what I mean? It's such a real sensual feeling."

No female had ever spoken to me in that kind of enticing manner, and hearing the inspirational language coming from my Sicilian dream-girl's lips, *that* sensational auditory reality had my mind swimming in sweet euphoria. "Er, golly, yes indeed," I stuttered as I almost creamed my pants in a premature ejaculation. But I didn't want my folks to know the nature of the private conversation, so I kept my replies as terse as possible.

"How would you and Carnie like to double-date tomorrow night?" Angie softly asked. "I'm sorry for the short notice, and all that jazz, but it was just a wonderful spur of the moment idea that Ant' had."

I had no inkling that Angie was exploiting the pleasurable male fantasies that my flimsy mind was then enjoying. I was still trying to reassemble my emotional composure. "Terrific. Where would ya' like to go?" I asked, while still searching for my lost poise.

"To the Andalusia Drive-in down on *Route 13* near 'Philly," the sexy caller requested. Angie stated that the drive-in was having an Audie Murphy triple-feature at a dollar a carload. "I figure we'd do a little makin' out before we get down to more advanced romantic business," Angie suggested.

I could feel warm pulses throbbing all over my body. The crazy conversation was just like experiencing heaven on earth. "That's fine, but isn't there an Elvis triple-feature over at the Langhorne Drive-in on *Route 1?"* I asked.

"Yeah, but Ant' and I have seen those movies already," Angie declared. "I really dig Audie Murphy. He's handsome, courageous, and strong, just like *you* are. And I'll bet my C bra and pink panties that you can ride in the saddle all night. I can't wait because I'm so hot and horny for your stud bod'. I know your stamina won't disappoint me, Killer."

I gasped as I almost inhaled the bottom part of the telephone. "Oh no, don't worry about that," I nervously answered. "Whose car?"

"Ya' can drive in style Daddy's '59 ice blue Caddy," Angie volunteered. "It's a gas-guzzler, but that don't matter. Are ya' ready to show me what you've got?"

The entire conversation was unbelievable. It was as if my deepest desire was coming true while simultaneously giving me a massive four-aspirin headache.

"Your father doesn't mind you goin' out with me?" I nearly whispered.

"Don't be silly," Angie maintained. "Because my Daddy really has learned to respect ya'. He was only testin' your general toughness all along. Daddy says ya' got more balls than the Thornridge Bowling Alley does!"

I was in sheer ecstasy. I told Angie to meet me at Carnie's house only two blocks away on Darkleaf Lane. "Ya' can't miss it. His black Mercury will be sittin' in the driveway," I said. I pinched my rear-end to convince myself that the verbal exchange with my fantasy girl was actually happening.

"Fantastic, Lover Boy," Angie returned. "Did you say Dingleberry Lane? Just kidding! So, we'll pick ya' two studs up at six-thirty. And J.W., I just know you're gonna' bring out the woman in me." Click.

After I hung up the phone, I thought of how Bo Jalonec really knew his stuff about the opposite sex. I remembered Jokes instructing Carnie and me that when a girl was horny for a guy, then her emotion transcended her ability to reason straight. Angie and Bubbles had all the reason in the world to hate Carnie and me, yet their hearts dominated their logic, and consequently, the Sicilian broads had no alternative other than to succumb to our abundant masculine charms. We obviously greatly appealed to their biologically-driven, animal-based instincts.

My biggest fear was whether or not I had the endurance and the staying power to satisfy my ideal female. Later that night, I ambled over to Carnie's house and announced the good tidings. Merc' Man was equally as thrilled as I was. We each praised the universal wisdom of Bo Jalonec for its impeccable validity.

The following evening, Angie and Bubbles arrived at Carnie's place at precisely six-thirty in *her* daddy's luxurious ice blue Caddy. Each doll was wearing a tight skirt with a matching form-fitting tee shirt, and one glance in their direction gave Carnie and me instant stiffies. But then, I recalled Bo Jalonec once saying that when a guy gets an erection, a lot of blood leaves his brain and flows down to his fadorkenbender, and soon the aroused teen begins thinking with his wrong noodle, and then an hour-long boner might result in having massive cerebral damage to the weakened medulla oblongata.

"What three Audie Murphy films are playin'?" I asked as I assumed the driver's seat without any operator's license.

"Oh, there's a cowboy feature, *Destry*, about a gunfighter who helps a drunken sheriff," Angie aptly replied. "And then there's *To Hell and Back* where Audie plays himself in *World War II*. And finally, I can't wait to see the movie star in *Ride a Crooked Trail*. That one is only a year-old flick," Angie impressively informed.

I was trying to act suave to disguise my intense insecurity as I cautiously backed-out of Carnie's driveway. "Are ya' sure you want to go to Andalusia?" I asked after smoothly shifting the blue Caddy's transmission into "Drive". "Elvis will be great in *Love Me Tender, Loving You,* and *King Creole* over at the Langhorne. It's much closer than Andalusia is," I mildly argued.

"Look, Lover Boy," Angie chastised. "Treat me like a lady and you'll eventually get whatever the hell ya' want!"

We arrived at the Andalusia Drive-in at around seven. After paying the special admission fee of one dollar for a carload, I found a cozy slot to the left of the concession stand to park the expensive Caddy. Angie and I made some small talk about popular television programs, and I was somewhat-stunned to learn that the Sicilian chicks enjoyed watching *the Red Skelton Show* and *the Colgate Comedy Hour*, especially when the program headlined Jimmy Durante.

In casual conversation, Bubbles Messina found the strange humor of Ernie Kovacs entertaining, particularly when the TV comedian portrayed the intoxicated poet, Percy Dovetonsils. Antoinette also dug school theme shows like *Our Miss Brooks* starring Eve Arden, and *Mr. Peepers* with Wally Cox.

The four of us seemed to be hitting it off pretty well. Smack dab in the middle of *Destry,* Angie and I were necking, and when she began rubbing the zipper area of my dungarees, I had to tug her hand away to avoid an urgent sticky predicament.

After the first Audie Murphy feature expired, there was a brief intermission. The two Italian babes begged to be excused to freshen-up a bit, and the voluptuous honeys promised that they would hit the concession stand and come back with some popcorn and sodas. Carnie and I slouched-down in the fancy Cadillac, compared notes, discussed the possibility of Snake Road behind Silver Lake later-on, and appreciatively philosophized about the unparalleled, splendid wisdom of Bo Jalonec.

I should have gotten the approaching omen correct when the WIBG radio DJ played "You Cheated, You Lied" by the Shields. My casual relaxed existence was quickly and rudely interrupted when the swarthy-skinned girls rushed back in alarm to the Caddy.

"Oh no guys, you're gonna' want to kill us!" Bubbles began her feigned apprehension. "My cruel brother Popeye is here with the Kamikazes. Angie and I thought they were goin' over to the Langhorne Drive-in tonight, but instead, they showed-up here!" Bubbles apologized. "They'll cause lots of trouble if they ever find-out we're here on dates with two of the most feared Diablos!"

All of a sudden terror replaced love as the dominant emotion dominating my mind. "That's really great, Angie!" I exclaimed. "What a dilemma! What should we do? Do we have to defend our honor and fight 'em?" I asked, still baffled by the heavy bad news that the chicks had relayed.

"No, there's over twenty of 'em and ya' wouldn't stand a chance," Angie explained. "They don't know you and Carnie are here. Why don't ya' two brave guys hop into the trunk until the Ks disappear back to their cars. When they leave our vicinity, we can go park at Snake Road and have some real hot and heavy action. Quick," Angie advised. "Climb into the trunk so my cousin won't know you're here."

What could Carnie and I do? The Italian girls were madly in love with us, and naturally, the olive-skinned beauties didn't want us to mutilate or maul the Kamikazes in public. Since the dolls were hot for our sexy bodies, Carnie and I opted for the non-violence route. We were certain that the immediate crisis would quickly pass, and that soon, we would again be masters of the female universe.

Without thinking twice, Mr. C and I hopped into the Caddy's spacious trunk. Angie gently closed the lid, and at that moment, I recalled Jokes once telling me that most girls preferred Tarzan-like muscles to *Mr. America* type biceps. "I'm sure glad I do 'dynamic tension' like Charles Atlas instead of powerliftin' like Joe Weider does," I softly told Carnie about competing magazine ads.

"I know exactly what ya' mean," Carnie whispered. "The girls are hypnotized by our strong slender bodies, no doubt about it."

No sooner had we been stashed and hidden inside the dark enclosure that the external lock turned. The trunk was opened a crack, and a second later, Popeye Messina, Jake Mullins, and Dave Evans were peeping inside and staring-down at their duped cargo.

"Well, if it ain't the dumb ass hernia twins," Popeye greeted. "Done anything stupid lately?" The three Ks smiled and giggled, apparently very elated at the capture of two prized enemy warriors.

"You didn't possibly think Angie and I ever thought you two silly tiddly-winkers were sexually attractive, did ya'?" Bubbles effectively reprimanded the trunk's astonished occupants.

"Ya' stupid jerks are dumber than retarded!" Angie acrimoniously asserted. "You're both less smart than a box of rocks!"

"Ya' two imbeciles are gonna' suffer for leavin' Evans and me chained to those trees!" Mullins predicted. "Get ready for our version of 'Unchained Melody'."

Popeye also enjoyed holding a grudge. "And don't forget my red and black Ford bein' flooded with crap, and the freakin' street-light suspension caper during the drag-race!" Messina added. "You fucked-up punks might not live to see the sun rise tomorrow."

Carnie and I both felt betrayed by Cupid, by Bo Jalonec, by Angie and Bubbles, and by Tinker in *that* particular order. We desperately tried pushing-up the trunk's lid, but the Kamikazes had leverage and easily smashed the cover closed, nearly severing the fingers off of my right hand.

My trunk companion and I shared some personal thoughts on the dark, bumpy ride north up *Route 13* toward Levittown. I told the C Man how I had faithfully sat in the Cardinal Reagan library, looking up the island of Sicily in an atlas. I explained how I had located the cities of Messina and Palermo on a map, and how Bubbles Messina had stated earlier that evening at the Andalusia Drive-in how her parents were from Palermo, and how Angie Palermo had told Carnie and me that her folks had originated from Messina.

"This entire love puzzle scene is very geographically confusin'," I mentioned to my warped-minded buddy bouncing-around inside the dark trunk. "I mean, Carnie. The illustrated map showed that there were dire straights between Sicily and the Italian boot!"

Carnie and I then cursed everything we could think of that represented love. I cursed Aphrodite, and Carnie cursed Venus. We both cursed Cupid, and while we were on the topic of ancient Greek mythology, we both cursed the famous "theos ek mechanes". Then,

Carnie cursed *Valentine's Day,* and finally, we both woefully cursed our incompetent love adviser, Bo Jalonec.

"Jokes made us put our guards down," Carnie vehemently complained. "And then he had us believin' Angie and Bubbles had gone goo-goo over us, wanting to show us their hairy woo-woos. Jalonec made us both vulnerable to *this* downright stinkin' trick!"

"I think Tinker is more to blame than Bo is," I argued without satisfaction. "He's more toxic than arsenic or hemlock!"

The Caddy hit several big bumps on *Route 13* in what I suspected was Croydon, and Carnie's head and my skull bounced-off the top part of the expensive car's huge trunk.

"Tink's the one who should be punished by Popeye, Mullins, and Evans. Not us!" I insisted as I held my aching head inside the dark confinement.

"J.W.," Carnie softly beckoned. "Something tells me that the three monsters that have captured our asses are gonna' make you and me pay for everybody's damned sins, either mortal or venial. That's gotta' be the name of the game!"

Chapter 43
"Mr. Sandman Turns Pyromaniac"

Carnie and I became very angry when our ears heard the Cadillac full of jollied Kamikazes laughing jubilantly at our frustrating situation inside the car's trunk. "To me, the boisterous jerks sounded like Robin Hood and his *merry* men celebrating *our* inglorious capture.

"Those double-crossin' broads!" Carnie sadly lamented. "We should never trust women with tantalizin' tits bigger than oranges," the Merc' Man grieved. Up until the Andalusia Drive-in disaster, Carnie and I had always had a fascination with big female chests. But because of recent circumstances, our perception of the opposite gender's anatomy had suddenly and radically changed.

"Yeah," I granted and grunted. "And never trust a chick with breasts smaller than watermelons," I expressed as I again cracked my head against the top of the trunk when the Caddy hit another large pothole.

"Honeys with big boobs really know how to bust on you!" my pal ironically concluded and shared.

Mr. C and I knew all of the roads in the vicinity like the alphabet, and we mentally traced our highway itinerary to Tullytown near the *Delaware River*. The '59 Caddy abruptly halted, and after a few outbursts of merriment, the Kamikazes got-out and soon opened the cargo trunk. Carnie and I were removed and roughly escorted to a sandy beach bordering the historic river.

My bleary eyes observed that various multi-colored lanterns were lighting-up the beach area. Three five-foot-deep holes had already been dug into the sand, and Carnie and I were un-gently planted into the hard white soil. The third pit was presently occupied by my biggest Dogwood Hollow nemesis. Tinker had been kidnapped by a Kamikaze patrol when the most dangerous Diablo had responded to a false dead battery call over in Farmbrook.

Cummings led Popeye, Jake Mullins, and Dave Evans over, and I noticed that the four Kenwood ruffians were carrying shovels. The landscapers-none-landscapers pushed sand and dirt into the two unfilled hollows, making it impossible for occupants Carnie and me to move an inch. Eight other Kamikazes were standing along the riverbank being thoroughly amused. I recognized Pete Atkins, who had played *Babe Ruth League* baseball with me on *our* last place Window Mart team. My squinting pupils noticed that beer bottles and picnic baskets were strewn-about the remote beach, and the already intoxicated Kamikazes were about to celebrate a festive victory party.

I was thinking of how I had been trying to isolate Carnie from Tinker, and ironically, we were now all imprisoned and anguishing in the same miserable buried situation. My concentration was broken by Popeye Messina's gruff voice.

"Now for a little Italian fun, boys!" Bruno joyously proclaimed. "Let's have an enjoyable game of boccie ball!" Popeye declared, lifting a soccer ball from the wet sand near the river's edge.

My eyes were only six-inches above ground level, and from my perspective, Cummings, Popeye Mullins, Dave Evans, and the other punk Kamikazes looked quite gruesome and invincible.

My dismal spirit was terrified more than ever. The Kamikazes were awesome opponents, even without having a definite advantage. I also felt stupid and naïve for being so easily *hood*winked by a car trunk. 'How gullible!' I thought. 'Being *sneaked out* of a drive-in theater in a car trunk when the greaser tradition was always taking pride in being *sneaked into* such a cool place inside a car trunk.' The "stupid" part of my recollection had to do with *only* traveling with chronic loser, Diablo Carnie. That dumb act violated the "safety in numbers" principle that had been clearly outlined and advocated by Quinn. And I really felt like a pusillanimous, wet-behind-the-ears adolescent when I recollected how I had let Angie charm me into a treacherous Kamikaze trap. I reckoned that the two Italian broads must have been descendants of infamous Lucretia Borgia.

The beach pits were teeming with sand fleas and other pestering river bugs. I felt small creatures crawling all over my sunken body. High tide would be arriving in two-hours, and if we weren't excavated soon, the rising *Delaware River* would be splashing waves into our faces. 'Cummings and his band of thugs might leave us here to starve, or be pecked to death by hungry scavengers,' I worriedly thought.

The boccie ball game was a horrendous experience for the three helpless Diablos, buried-up to our necks. But somehow, we managed to suffer through the painful ordeal.

"Hey Diablos!" Cummings bellowed. "Did ya' ever eat shit on a stick?"

"No," we replied in unison.

"I see," Cummings chuckled. "You corn-holers don't like the taste of sticks! Ha, ha, ha!" The entire contingent of inebriated tormentors derived ample pleasure from our unenviable predicament. The acerbic Ks favorite hobbies must have been sadism and crucifixions.

"Remember, Assholes," Popeye firmly contributed. "The next time those three holes dug for you creeps will be three-feet-deeper, and then covered-up with cow manure on top!"

"You three dipsticks will be *bury* unhappy," Mullins laughed as the vile vampire strained his mental dynamics to their limit. "What gang do you' dingles belong to, the dipshit Dogwood Dunces or the dumb-ass Dogwood Dolts?"

"Hey, J.W.," Popeye addressed. "Did ya' ever get caught jerkin' off in the closet?"

"No," I stammered from my obvious position of weakness.

"Great hidin' place, ain't it! Ha, ha, ha, ha," Messina finished and then loudly belched.

The greatest embarrassment was our being displayed as idiots and failures in front of Angie and Bubbles. The exotic females seemed to be immensely appreciating the nasty ridiculing of the three Diablos.

The boccie ball game was about to commence. Popeye had Jake Mullins pour a gallon of Italian olive oil over the soccer ball's surface. Then, Messina reviewed the simple rules. Tinker was positioned nearest to the Kamikazes, and if the rolled or kicked ball hit him in the face, then one point would be awarded. Carnie and I were buried behind and three-feet distant on either side of Tinker. If the kicked or rolled ball directly hit Carnie or me, then two points would be credited. But if either of us were hit by a deflection off of Tinker's face or head, then three points would be earned for the "combination shot".

The horrible event went-on for over thirty-minutes, and the oil-smeared, rolling soccer ball, and its spinning sand, effectively dirtied-up our abused faces. Each impact really hurt, too. Fortunately, we each had a few inches leeway for head mobility to luckily avoid broken noses, black eyes, smashed teeth, and painful jaws.

Spits and Worm had brought along on leashes Angie's two fierce Dobermans, Pasta and Caesar. The ferocious hounds whizzed on Carnie and Tinker's heads, apparently mistaking their exposed skulls for fire hydrants. Jeremy Foster was fuming because his newly purchased Davy Crockett coonskin hat had been adequately perfumed by Pasta. And then came the Kamikaze egg-tossing contest, originating from a range of twenty-feet away. Soon, our foreheads and faces were splattered with yolks', shells, and egg whites that slowly dripped down our cheeks and chins onto the surrounding sand.

That inhumane humiliation was followed by an unexpected event. A covey of seagulls flying up the *Delaware* from the *Atlantic* bombarded Tinker, Carnie, and me with putrid bird crap, and our merciless, mixed audience, including Angie and Bubbles, nearly coughed their balls and nipples off, laughing at our bonus humiliation.

I remember thinking that I never wanted to have any enemies in Levittown, but with loser idiots like Tinker and Carnie for friends, belligerent foes were certainly in ample supply. I still honestly believed at that moment that Carnie was still morally salvageable, but I was certain that Tinker's black soul was doomed for volcanic hell.

The lanterns and beer bottles were finally gathered-up, and Cummings and Popeye led the demented revellers back to their cars. The rising river washed some of the bird feces and egg residue from *our* affected faces and heads.

If it had not been for Pete Atkins's sense of mercy, the three of us would have probably drowned. Pete had enough compassion to call Robbie Wilkinson about our terrible travail, and R.W. and Quinn arrived with shovels in what seemed an eternal half-hour. The three rescued survivors were dug-out of our triple pits about fifteen-minutes before our lungs would have been filled with murky river water.

All of the craziness between the Diablos and the Kamikazes would have ceased if someone had had the humility to go to the police for help. The two gangs were too proud to ever seek or ask for assistance; in fact, so proud that we were arrogant, and so arrogant that we preferred taking the law into our own hands while practicing vigilante-style justice on each other. We risked our lives and jeopardized our futures trying to perfect the art of getting even, and whichever gang had the last laugh would ultimately win the bitter rivalry.

The next morning, I called Carnie's house to see if Merc' Man wanted to have breakfast at the Feed Bag. He picked me up about nine. Maggie was on duty, and before she approached our table, Bo Jalonec sauntered into the hangout. Jokes's shift over at Harley's Hardware wasn't going to start until nine-thirty, so Susie Parker's Beau decided to join and deliberately antagonize us for a while. Then, much to my disappointment, the dishonorable Jersey Foster coincidentally pulled into the parking lot in his blue Plymouth.

Jokes played "Red River Valley Rock" on the jukebox because the antagonist hypothesized that Maggie was again having her period by the way she looked and by the way she acted. After the fifth redundant playing, the melancholy waitress finally got the message and hid in the kitchen, since we all knew her monthly "secret".

Bo told us his ears had heard of the disastrous drive-in fiasco, and of the boccie ball beach tournament earlier that morning from Robbie and Quinn. Before Jokes left for work next door, the ball-buster played "Mr. Sandman" by the Chordettes. After the repetitious song resonated for the eighth-time in a row, we finally realized Jalonec was satirically "bustin" on our sand burials via the jukebox, the same way the music perpetrator had been busting on Maggie's period.

"You dumb turkeys weren't *hood*winked in the Caddy!" Jalonec laughed at Carnie and me. "You two dingles were trunk-winked! And Tink, how come ya' only got a freakin' tan on your zit face and nowhere else!" Then, Bo expeditiously evacuated the premises and paced over to Harley's Hardware before the three of us took our collective animosity out on his thin hide.

The insulted T Man was so angry at being mocked that J.F. told Carnie and me we had to do something drastic to degrade the Ks.

"Haven't we done enough damage already?" I asked. "Thank goodness you don't have access to the Atomic Bomb!"

"No," Tinker adamantly replied. "The weak never wins wars!"

Mr. T led us to the rear of his car where the persistent conniver had creatively attached a frame to the rear bumper. The metal square was big enough to hold several five-gallon cans of gasoline. The madman had also provided Robbie Wilkinson and Ace Roberts with identical five-gallon cans of fuel. And with a mere twenty-gallons of high-octane fuel, Tink planned on destroying Popeye's new '57 Ford, Jake Mullins' '57 De Soto, and Dave Evans' red and white '58 Dodge.

Around eleven o'clock each morning, several Kamikazes would have a football catch in the field situated next to the James Buchanan School, which bordered Kenwood. The Ks had collectively purchased an old barn several hundred-feet-away, and the red wooden structure was being utilized as the gang's clubhouse.

Tinker drove Carnie and me to the back of the James Buchanan School. The incorrigible nut-job opened the blue car's trunk and removed his two full five-gallon gas cans. "Dr. Destructo" instantly placed the dual cans tilted-upside-down inside the steel frame. J.F. unscrewed the gas cans' caps and then drove his decrepit-looking wheels from behind the elementary school. The mad mechanic deftly criss-crossed the grassy field where the Kamikazes soon would have their game of catch, leaving two trails of invisible leaked gas behind. After the pair of slanted five-gallon cans had been drained, the most psychologically disturbed Diablo returned to the parking area behind the school. Dr. T stopped his Plymouth, walked to the rear of the vehicle, lifted the empty gas cans, and put the two empty containers back inside his grimy trunk.

"What the heck are ya' doin' now?" I anxiously protested.

"Fightin' dirt and sand with fire," Tinker symbolically replied.

"The Spanish have a distinct word to describe you, and *that* special word is loco."

"Muchas *grass ass*," Tinker answered as the smart-ass delinquent remembered and conveyed a Bo Jalonec' bilingual one-liner.

Tinker, Carnie, and I awaited the arrival of our unaware foes from our lookout position behind the school. 'The Ks could've killed us last night,' I thought, 'but the thugs didn't.' But malignant Tinker was more ruthless than all of the "Killer Ks" put together. His pathetic pranks were often lethal death traps in disguise. We nervously smoked four *Camel* cigarettes each before the unsuspecting drivers of three Kamikaze autos' innocently pulled into the grassy field for their regular football-tossing exercise.

Jake Mullins had the misfortune of parking his newly acquired '57 De Soto precisely near where Tinker's invisible gasoline trail had ended. Jake-the-Snake and Pete Atkins got-out of the polished car to greet the occupants of Popeye's recently obtained '57 Ford and Dave Evans' '58 Dodge.

Tinker flicked his and my lit cigarettes onto the beginning of the flammable highway, which soon ignited into dual five-foot-high moving fire fences. The flames shot like bolts of lightning around the rear of the school, made right angle turns, and then headed straight toward the petrified Kamikazes. The startled victims fled in all directions from the oncoming red-hot walls, and when the path of the flames reached the '57 De Soto, Mullins' car burst into a fireball. The gas tank loudly exploded, and debris and shrapnel went flying-up into the air as if the James Buchanan field had become a military war zone.

Tinker's malice had another level of destruction to achieve. The arsonist instructed Carnie and me to hop into his filthy car, and we hypnotically and fearfully obeyed his austere command. I became very stressed when the uncivilized culprit drove at full speed directly toward the very rattled Kamikazes. The pyromaniac abruptly stopped, rolled-down his window and yelled, "Hey Pud-pullers! Any of ya' have a goddamned match?"

Immediately, the Ks realized their antagonists' true identity. The Kenwood creeps leaped and hustled through the criss-crossing walls of fire to their two remaining automobiles, where the incensed morons jumped into their cars and speedily pursued Tinker's blue Plymouth out of the school's empty faculty parking lot. The Ks were livid obsessed butchers, chasing us at eighty-miles per hour down Haines Road in the direction of Dogwood Hollow. I turned-around and recognized that the '58 Dodge and the '57 Ford were very quickly closing the gap between them and us.

Robbie Wilkinson and Ace Roberts were pretending to be hitchhiking on Haines Road in the opposite direction. When Tinker passed the duo going west, Robbie and Ace threw lit cigarettes down onto the highway, precisely where the accomplices had just poured five-gallons each of gasoline minutes before. Instantly, a tremendous wall of flames shot-up and sped across the two-lane road.

Dave Evans, inside his '58 Dodge, slammed on his brakes and skidded sideways in a vain attempt to avoid entering the enormous blaze. Then, Popeye's new '57 Ford' duplicated Evans' evasive maneuver. Both cars skidded through the inferno and collided on the opposite side of the raging wall of fire. The eight frightened occupants leaped-out and sprinted in all directions for cover. Several loud explosions occurred ten-seconds later.

Robbie Wilkinson and Ace Roberts had hightailed it through several backyards where Tinker finally picked-up the out-of-breath co-cpnspirators on Dogwood Drive. An alert and concerned resident had summoned the Edgely Fire Department, which dispatched one truck to the Haines Road accident scene, and a second tanker to the grass field next to the James Buchanan School, to thoroughly extinguish another mysterious inferno.

The Kamikazes were scared to death from their extraordinary, separate pyrotechnic confrontations, but the crazies stubbornly refused to press charges against Tinker, electing to honor the code of silence that bonded the area greaser gangs. The Kenwood Ks were becoming very apprehensive and wary of "Professor Demento's" excessive fury and dreadful wrath. The barbarians feared that their principal enemy was even more deranged than the maniacs had ever aspired to be.

Cummings was very frightened of Quinn, and all of the Ks were quite terrified of demonic Tinker, who was the most warped and deranged desperado, who the rival gang, or I, had ever encountered.

Chapter 44
"Quinn Gets Involved"

Bo Jalonec was absent and not involved with Tinker's triple Kamikaze automobile pyromania. "Beau" was too busy trying to patch-up a lovers' quarrel with gorgeous and sweet Susie Parker. Quinn was also experiencing a similar romantic dispute with Patty Van Arsdale, all over male allegiance to the Diablos.

The crux of the problem was this: Susie and Patty were jealous because their boyfriends were having more fun and excitement with the Diablos than the girls' hungry cats could provide on a double-date with Jokes and Quinn. Love and sex could never compete with tantalizing greaser thrill after thrill. And so, Jalonec and Quinn were now in with the Diablos, and out with their' envious ladies, and the Kamikazes were in for a new series of novel calamities.

Since events were rapidly spiraling-out of control, it was essential that Jokes and Quinn abandon their primitive courting and mating rituals and return to the necessity of escalating greaser business. I felt that I urgently needed Bo and Quinn's guidance if miraculous divine intervention was not available.

Carnie and I were sitting in the Feed Bag two nights after Tinker's sensational three-car fire rampage. I had still wanted Merc' Man to be my best friend because Tinker was too psychopathic; Jokes was too insincere; Robbie was a manic depressant, and Quinn was too aloof and oblivious to Jeremy Foster's constant plotting against his imperial authority. I admired Quinn too much to have to hurt my idol with the truth about a Brutus and a Benedict Arnold mutually conniving inside his disheveled gang. Carnie was the one Diablo who was similar to me in temperament; that was, when the extremely vulnerable target wasn't under Tinker's reprehensible influence.

"Carnie," I mentioned. "Do ya' remember the first big prank we played on the Kamikazes last November?"

"Sure do, Words.," Merc' Man recalled. "Cummings, Popeye, and three other Ks were sittin' on their side of the Feed Bag right over there near the pinball machines. Tink, Jokes, you, and me dropped a black twelve-by-twelve tarpaulin from the roof right over that slanted pane window," Carnie recalled as the kid pointed to the giant glass window on the opposite side of the "greasy spoon".

"Yeah," I interrupted. "And the tarp was painted with red letters that read 'Kamikazes Suck'. Jokes spent three whole days doing the fancy lettering in cursive. Sometimes I wish that he wasn't such a meticulous perfectionist."

"The four of us then quickly jumped off the roof," Carnie recollected and added. "And you almost broke your ankle."

"Yeah," I pensively recalled. "But simple fun pranks have led to car destructions; us near-drownin' in cesspools and inside beach holes, and cemetery baths in greasy water."

"The bastard Kamikazes still suck, just like the pricks did last friggin' November," Carnie concluded and opined.

"Like pregnant vacuum cleaners," I finished.

I was constantly worried about Carnie being negatively influenced by future penitentiary felon, Jeremy Foster. The C Man was becoming recalcitrant while being a robotic disciple of Tinker, whom I had assessed as being incorrigible, and would ultimately be destined for a criminal career as a chronic practitioner of habitual recidivism.

I was almost happy to see Bo pull-up to the Feed Bag to sabotage our mediocre conversation. A minute later, Quinn entered the parking area in his '42 with Marcus Spellman. Sugar Ray was wearing an old Diablos' leather jacket that was the "Q Man's" first D apparel from the summer of '57. Some of the more snobbish Feed Bag patrons stared at Spellman as if he was a ruthless child molester. Quinn told us he had called and invited Tinker along for the conference, because the gang had to act as a unit rather than as individual fragments. Soon, "Fearless Foster" pulled into the parking lot and joined our illustrious company.

When everyone was finally seated at our favorite corner table, I wondered if Marcus knew how much Tinker hated blacks. I also wondered if Quinn had been aware that the most dangerous Diablo was still aggressively scheming against *his* dominance, even though our leader had humanely saved Tinker from drowning at the quarry.

Cummings pulled off *Route 13* toward the Feed Bag, but when his passenger Popeye Messina spied us sitting inside, the Ks peeled-out of the establishment's asphalt lot in a hurry.

"I think they're intimidated by our presence," Quinn observed with a grin. "There's finally something that those slime-ball culprits are scared of!"

"They looked exhausted, just like their tailpipes," Jokes laughed. "And Tink, first ya' got Popeye suspended twice from school, and then ya' got him suspended from the telephone pole on Haines Road. Now, you're keeping *us* in suspense about your next strategic move!"

Everyone laughed at Jokes's witty remark. The jokester possessed the unique ability to be able to alleviate anxiety whenever the rest of us felt overwhelming stressed.

"I never thought I'd see the day when the Ks would retreat from anything, including the awesome Ds," Carnie very perceptively commented.

"The bastards stunk-up my new coonskin hat on the isolated beach with their Dobermans' smelly piss," Tinker graphically complained. "The bitchin' greaser war ain't over by a long shot!"

The fact that the Diablos had achieved a definite psychological advantage over the relentless Ks gave us tremendous satisfaction. We had made their main combatants feel inferior, and even Quinn smiled at the mention of the "Kenwood Killers" overall trepidation.

Since "Duke Diablo" was now again one of the boys, Quinn wanted to invent a "safe trick" to play on our diabolical foes. The daring scheme would impress Patty and make her want to get back with her gallant boyfriend even more. Jokes found himself' entangled in a similar heartthrob situation, and the genial jester wanted Susie to realize how much colossal fun our lieutenant was having with the Ds, just to make her jealous ascend some more.

Carnie strolled-over to the jukebox and pressed the corresponding keys for "Tequila" by the Champs, "Good Golly Miss Molly" by Little Richard, and "School Day" by "the merry Mr. Chuck Berry".

"I'm glad the buffoon didn't play 'Red River Valley Rock'," Jokes commented. "I can't take that song more than once a month!"

"Or 'Mr. Sandman'," Tinker contemptibly sneered in regard to *his* recent negative beach episode. "Now, I hate that friggin' lesbian' song more than ever! Those goddamned Chordettes oughta' suffocate crowded inside a tiny fart chamber!"

About twenty other teenagers were congregated inside the Bag, and we all sang-out "Tequila" at the end of that upbeat instrumental song, and "Hail, hail rock and roll, long live rock and roll!" at the termination of the aforementioned Chuck Berry teen classic.

Sugar Ray Spellman was deeply impressed with our excellent camaraderie and good spirit. "Hey Diablo Dudes, give me some skin!" Marcus howled in appreciation of our antics and gesticulations. "Ya' cats dig music almost as much as us cool black folks do."

Everyone gave Sugar Ray some skin except Tinker, who pretended he was looking over at the Dairy DeLite.

"There are some good white singers, too," Carnie stubbornly argued in defense of Caucasian entertainment.

"Yeah, like who, Man?" Marcus challenged. Tinker tried coming to Carnie's defense and the defense of assumed white supremacy.

"Well, like Elvis, for instance."

"Let me tell you white-stray-cats somethin'," Marcus explained. "Elvis is good only because he sounds black. The guy's a talented white cat with a black dude's voice. Elvis sings blues like a Southern Negro. If Elvis was black, why man, he'd be no-where!"

"I don't get it?" I questioned Marcus Spellman's bold statement, which seemed to defy reason and required more clarity for it to appear logical in my mind.

"Ya' fellas' remember that song 'Shhh-Boom'," Sugar Ray cited as an example. "The tune was cut by two groups, the Chords and the Crewcuts."

"On most sailin' ships," Jokes injected, "the *crew cuts* the cords."

Everyone ignored Bo's weak and irrelevant attempt at providing polysemantic word humor. The topic of discussion took precedence over anything Jalonec's sick mind could manufacture, unless of course, the subject of girls' beaver beavior was being reviewed.

"I certainly do remember the song and also the two groups, even though the records weren't instrumentals," Quinn stated.

Everyone at the table agreed that "Shhhh-Boom" was a major step in the direction of rock and roll's musical birth.

Then, Sugar Ray elaborated on his original remarks. "Well, which group sounded better? The Chords or the Crew Cuts?"

"Definitely, the Chords," Carnie determined. Quinn, and I nodded our heads in tacit agreement, with racist Tinker abstaining.

"Don't ya' blancos get it?" Marcus continued his pertinent dissertation. "The Chords was black, and the Crew Cuts was white. But the Crew Cuts sold four times as many records doin' the same song that was first done by the Chords. The white cover group stole 'Shhhh-Boom' from the Chords, who actually sounded four times better."

Then, it all began to make perfect sense. "I think I understand," I admitted. "It's just like Pat Boone toyin' around with Little Richard's 'Tutti-Frutti' and Fats Domino's 'Ain't That a Shame'. Pat Boone's recordings of those songs can't hold a candle to the better Negro versions, but the white cover records sold more copies in the stores. That's definitely not fair!"

Marcus Spellman was teaching the Diablos some new insights about rock and roll music that we had never really thought about before *that* relevant discussion. We all seemed eager to learn more except Tinker, who was a white supremacist in addition to being a Diablos' greaser supremacist. While Marcus howled, Tinker scowled.

"J.W., you're now jivin'!" "Hershey" praised and exclaimed. "Now ya' comprende, Amigo."

"Oddy Oats," Jokes spoke with a Spanish accent, "and *Esso* gas es bueno. Hasta Luigi-board," the gang's mentally sick comic added as the punster exhausted his favorite Spanish fun lines.

"Elvis is white but sounds black," Marcus summarized. "Pat Boone is white and sounds white. But the kids groove on whites like Elvis that sound black. Ya' all dig?"

I thought that I had always understood rock and roll, but I then realized that I had been blind to the truth behind the new music that parents absolutely abhorred.

"That's as cool as a ghoul in a swimmin' pool," Carnie rhymed from memory as originally stated by *B.J.,* whom the C-Man often nicknamed *B*low-*J*ob when Jalonec was not around!

"It's so cool that it's colder than an Eskimo's tits, who keeps her bra together with e-glue!" Jokes drolly concurred.

"There's more shit at this table than up a fat elephant's ass," Tinker objected. "Ya' guys all sound like graduates of the famous Dingleberry Farting Institute!"

I then described to Quinn, Jokes, Tinker, and Sugar Ray exactly how Carnie and I had been victimized at the Andalusia Drive-in and also at the near disastrous *Delaware River* boccie ball debacle.

Jokes couldn't resist a boisterous laugh when his ears heard about the olive oil that Popeye had smeared on the soccer ball. "I told ya' guys a hundred-times that Bruno Messina and his relatives are nothin' more than a bunch of grease balls," Bo pontificated, slapping his knee in glee. "I'm surprised that the 'Sandmen' didn't put the Ks to sleep before the three Ds were beach-buried in 3-D. Right Tink? Who rescued ya' anyway? The friggin' Chordettes?"

And when Bo heard about Pasta and Caesar urinating on Tinker and Carnie's heads, the sit-down comedian jested, "Popeye had to stay-up into the *wee-wee* hours of the mornin' to brainstorm that prank!"

We all sat there and shook our heads in total disbelief. At that meeting, Jalonec was about as funny as a submarine with screen doors, or a telephone book without names and numbers during an emergency.

"Sugar Ray," Quinn addressed our honorary recruit in a more serious tone. "These toxic Kamikazes are bad news. Do ya' have any ideas how we can deal with and neutralize them?"

"Well, my Uncle Clyde is a fisherman and has a small seafood store over near the Jersey shore," Marcus informed. "Fish can cause a lot of grief if ya' use 'em right."

Quinn looked in my direction. "J.W., how can we use fish against the Kamikazes?"

All I could think of was 'Edgar Allan Poe". My brain quickly searched through a list of the author's stories, and after twenty-seconds of rapid mental sifting, it all suddenly came to me: *the Murders in the Rue Morgue*. 'A lady had been stuffed *up* a chimney after being killed by an orangutan. Why couldn't objects like fish be stuffed *down* chimneys?' I rationally considered.

I revealed my marvelous and innovative "fish story plot" to my intrigued colleagues. Quinn recommended that the rest of his assembled war council unanimously support its future implementation. All that was required was a vacant Kamikaze clubhouse chimney, and the rest would be Levittown greaser history.

Gerri, a new brunette waitress at the Feed Bag, had become close friends with Angie Palermo. Sal Palermo, wanting to unload and launder some cash, had purchased a vacation chalet up in the Pocono Mountains, and Gerri had recently visited there as Angie's invited guest. The space-cadet waitress cooperated fully when Jokes elected to indirectly interrogate her.

"Gerri," Bo began. "Aren't Angie and her folks goin' up to the Poconos *Labor Day* weekend?"

"No, Blondie. They're goin' up this comin' Friday night. They're stayin' in the mountains until Sunday afternoon," Gerri revealed. "Angie's dad will be away on business with Mr. Messina. I think they're goin' down to Mexico."

"Who else is goin' to the Poconos besides Angie?" Bo asked.

"Her cousins Ant' and Popeye, and her boyfriend, Phil Jackson," Gerri disclosed. "Her mom Carmella's gonna' do the chaperonin'."

There was a ten-second delay as Bo decided exactly how the amateur private detective should phrase his next question. "Doesn't Angie's dad have his place in East Stroudsburg?"

"Wrong, Cutie," airheaded Gerri contended. "It's in Bushkill." The ditsy waitress had no idea that she had been divulging very useful strategic information to the all-too-perceptive, listening Diablos.

"If my memory serves me correctly," Jokes amiably stated, "the house is on Silver Fox Trail?"

"Ya' have it all wrong, Sugar," Angie's scatter-brain friend declared. "It's on Purple Marten Court."

Jokes could have earned an *Academy Awards' Oscar* if his acting had been captured on film. "Oh yeah, Gerri," Jalonec aptly responded. "I now remember the address. It's Number 39 Purple Marten Court."

"Darlin', ya' really got a poor memory," Gerri criticized with a cute smile. "It's Number 87."

Bo Jalonec was the only one among us who could have pulled that incredible reconnaissance caper off. Gerri was so infatuated with his magical charm that the scatter-brain answered all his inquiries as if she were a mechanical robot answering questions on the witness stand. The wifty broad had no knowledge that she had been involuntarily contributing to the demise of her girlfriend's invited weekend companions.

After Gerri stepped into the back room to fulfill our orders, the Diablos finalized our fish story plans. Quinn wanted to commandeer the imminent "clubhouse fishin' mission". Our leader was certain that the Kamikazes were the subordinate members of the Specialty Enterprises' drug and smut distribution network, and that kind of immoral/illicit activity was repugnant to *his* austere value system.

Over the next two days, Quinn and Bo had gone around and collected fifty-dollars from the other Diablos. Since the gang never had to contribute dues for daily operating expenses, that type of money-pledging often took its place.

The following August afternoon, three Diablos' cars crossed the *Burlington-Bristol Bridge* into Jersey. Quinn drove the lead squad with Sugar Ray Spellman providing the directions to his Uncle Clyde's place in Manahawkin. Tinker and Robbie Wilkinson were in the blue '49 Plymouth, and Jokes and I rode with Carnie in his black Merc'. Bo was too fastidious to take his immaculate '57 Chevy, being afraid of getting its trunk contaminated with dead seafood odors.

The Diablos had several hours to kill while we were pretty much enjoying each other's gregarious company, with the exception of Tinker. We journeyed to Seaside Heights, played some boardwalk games of chance, and Quinn and Bo won two large stuffed elephants at wheel spins to make amends with their broken-hearted girlfriends.

The Diablos left Seaside Heights with our prize booty and swung over to nearby Manahawkin. Sugar Ray's Uncle Clyde had a modest wholesale seafood business on *Route 9*. Marcus negotiated a terrific fish bargain with his relative (for the Diablos). We were able to purchase fifty plastic buckets of day-old shad for a dollar a pail, and Jokes described the deal as "no fluke because we didn't flounder around. Now, we can go *nuclear fishin'* against the *naughty-cal* Ks!"

The buckets of stinking fish were divvied-up and carefully stashed in the three Diablos' cars' trunks. Just like George Washington had crossed the *Delaware* to surprise the British and Hessians at Trenton, the Diablos were crossing the *Delaware* in the opposite direction to shock the unprepared Kamikazes in Levittown. Our vehicles arrived back in Dogwood Hollow at around ten that night, and the guys partied in the woods near Robbie's house, drinking a case of beer until two in the morning, when Marcus decided to drive back to Yardley. At three-thirty, the rest of us swung into action.

The commando raid's objective was the Kamikaze clubhouse, located on Haines Road next to the James Buchanan School between Farmbrook and Kenwood. The Ks had converted an old red barn into four partitioned rooms. The clubhouse contained old den furniture, a refrigerator, and several cheap beds for shacking-up with chicks. A functional old stone fireplace had been added for warmth during the cold winter months. The Diablos had to act swiftly with surgical precision before the Ks would realize what Jokes appropriately described as "somethin' fishy goin' on".

Tinker trekked two blocks to his house and brought back an expandable and collapsible ladder to facilitate our daring surprise operation. The three gang cars entered the school parking lot, and then each driver turned-off his headlights. The Ks headquarters had been vacated, much to our elation. We furtively exited our vehicles and formed a makeshift "bucket brigade". Quinn, Bo, Carnie, and Tink climbed-up the expandable ladder onto the clubhouse's roof to drop the fifty pails of dead fish down the stone chimney.

"This is for usin' Angie and Bubbles to betray J.W. and me," Carnie venomously proclaimed as Mr. Merc' poured the first bucket of fish into the chimney.

"Holy mackerel there, Kingfish!" Jokes gushed, dumping the second stenchy load.

"Hope you Ks like the smell of three-day old shad," Quinn said.

"This is for all the grief ya' damned dirty Ks have caused me," Tinker added while depositing another bucket of rotting fish.

Bo Jalonec thought about what was going on. "The U.S. *Sturgeon* General is gonna' condemn this here clubhouse."

Quinn had a serious question to ask. "What will Popeye say when he smells this mess a few days from now?"

"He'll prob'ly say that Cummings' girlfriend forgot to douche!" Bo imaginatively answered. "He'll also think that the Ks red barn has been converted into a national skunk whorehouse."

Carnie and Tinker, who both envied Bo's handsome looks and wit, were so peeved and spiteful at his charm that the jealous jerks each shoved a smelly fish between Jalonec's neck and jacket. Jokes was so surprised and upset that when the wet shad recipient reached to the back of his Diablos' black leather jacket, B.J. *floundered,* lost his balance, and stumbled to his knees. Then, being confused, Jalonec rolled-down the roof's shingles, and plunged ten-feet to the ground.

Quinn, Carnie, and I climbed-down the ladder to see if Jalonec had injured himself. Tinker, who disliked Bo almost as much as he resented Quinn, stayed on the roof and dumped the last few buckets of fish down the old red barn's chimney.

"Bo, are ya' all right?" I asked, as Quinn and I helped the dedicated jester to his feet.

Bo reached between his undershirt and his jacket and pulled out the two slimy fish. The irrepressible joker then held the right side of his chest with his left hand and his back with his right appendage. It was actually a shock to see the perfect male hurting all over. "Now guys, I know exactly how Humpty Dumpty musta' felt."

"You'll have to travel to Egypt and see your *Cairo*practor," Carnie cracked as my neurotic friend repeated a Bo Jalonec line that *he* had told the crazy Arab with the butcher knives inside the Carousel Grille.

Bo looked at the two smelly fish that had caused him massive trouble. "I hope I don't get *salmon*-ella or some serious *back*terial infection," Jokes humorously remarked. "And maybe now, ya' guys can take me over to the Feed Bag and treat me to some spare ribs. I could really use 'em!"

Carnie tossed the remaining two shad fish up to Tinker, and the accomplished raider then generously deposited the decaying seafood inside the almost-full chimney. I helped Jokes back to Carnie's car, and finally, the Diablos called it a night. I remember thinking, 'I can't wait until dad sells our Daffodil Lane house, and I can get back to living a more peaceful and safer existence in good old Hammonton, New Jersey.'

Chapter 45
"The Pocono Mountains Foray"

Two nights later in August of '59, Dad was reading the daily edition of the *Levittown Times*. A front-page article reported that a Kenwood greaser gang's clubhouse had been vandalized with around five-hundred pounds of dead, rotting fish poured-down the building's stone chimney. I was deeply fearful that 50 Daffodil Lane would soon be targeted for a Kamikaze arson crime before my family had a chance to ever move out of Dogwood Hollow.

"J.W.," Dad began his evening lecture. "It states here in the paper that a number of masons will be needed to replace the old chimney."

"Yeah, Pop, but I think Mr. Messina is gonna' pay for the new chimney. At least that's the rumor I heard over at Hal's Deli."

"It even says in the paper that the Kenwood gang is not cooperating with the police investigation. I wonder why?"

"All I know is Bo Jalonec told me that if somebody lit a match with all those fish in the chimney," I related, "Jokes said the Kamikazes could own a *smeltery*."

"Hang around with that Bo fella'," Dad suggested and advised, "because he's the only pal you got who has any kind of bright future."

Pop then went-off on a tangent and insisted that the Kenwood gang must be connected with the Mafia, particularly associated with nefarious Sal Palermo and Dante Messina.

"Dad, Mafia 'Dons' don't live in little ten-thousand-dollar Levittown houses," I maintained. "Those wealthy dudes can afford exotic mansions and mountain chalets."

"Jack and Stella Burns told me that Palermo just purchased waterfront property on the *Delaware* not far from the Jackson estate," Pop affirmed. "He plans to relocate his family there in early 1960. 66 Daffodil Lane is just *his* temporary residence until his other plans reach fruition."

That week, Sal Palermo and Dante Messina were still in Mexico on an important business excursion. I wondered if Angie and Bubbles knew that their fathers were engaged in illegal drug commerce, or if the two volatile Sidgees just kept their daughters busy working all over Levittown to keep the dolls insulated from the truth. 'Maybe Angie and Bubbles are in denial,' I thought. 'Jokes would say that the Sicilian broads are in *the Nile!'*

Angie, Bubbles, Popeye, and Phil Jackson were finally off to their one-week hiatus up to Bushkill in the fabulous Pocono Mountains. Carmella Palermo was their designated chaperone, and thanks to Gerri over at the Feed Bag, the Diablos knew that their next destination was 87 Purple Marten Court, Bushkill, Pennsylvania.

The Diablo Pocono Mountain foray details had been discussed thoroughly the night before near the phone booth outside the Dairy DeLite. Quinn, who was still having spats with Patty Van Arsdale over his Diablos' involvement, drove his '42 the following morning with Sugar Ray Spellman and Bo Jalonec as his passengers. Carnie took his reliable Merc' and very punctually picked-up Tinker, Robbie, and me. The Kamikazes never suspected that the Diablos would make a key offensive strike a hundred-miles north of Levittown.

I felt more secure having Quinn and Bo along leading the gang raid. Their maturity would neutralize any stupidity that might be instigated by either rambunctious Tinker or mimicking Carnie. Quinn and Bo would give the Diablos stability, even if the main officers were only going up to the mountains to spite Patty and Susie.

Carnie trailed Quinn's boss '42. Our Diablos' leader took scenic highways all the way north. At the *Delaware Water Gap,* we stopped at a picturesque overlook just south of East Stroudsburg. Underneath his stellar greaser façade, Quinn must have been a naturalist who immensely enjoyed viewing the majesty of God's green Earth.

"Ya' know every highway the way ya' know the back of your hand," Bo complimented Quinn as the rest of us admired the lush, tree-covered mountains. Whenever Jalonec addressed his chieftain, Jokes was always less facetious than when he spoke to the rest of the Diablos.

"One of my hobbies is studyin' maps," Quinn sternly replied. "And I always like to know where and how I'm goin' before I get there."

Carnie then contributed to the dialogue stating that he also knew the area well because he had several relatives that lived in the Poconos.

"Look, Carnie. If ya' go to *Oxford University*," Bo emphasized, "ya' could study maps and be a *roads scholar*. Say J.W.," Jokes continued. "How would ya' like to have a punch in the face?"

"Er, no thanks," I stammered. I did not wish to be embarrassed by frivolous Jalonec in front of the other guys.

"Well, then, here's a poke-in-nose." Jalonec pushed my snout with the palm of his right hand. I felt like taking a wild swing at Jokes' jaw, but I resisted the urge. I realized that the former West Catholic wrestler could kick my butt anywhere, including in the scenic Poconos.

"This sight is beautiful," I seriously admitted, "but have any of you guys ever been up the *Hudson River* and seen the Catskill Mountains?"

"I've never seen the cats kill mountains," Bo replied, "but I've seen the 'cats kill' mice."

All the guys slapped their foreheads in sheer disbelief. I pitied Bo's prospective *Penn State* dorm' roommate, for a two-hour trip with

Jalonec was one thing, but perpetual play-on-words for an entire year in a college dormitory was another, and quite candidly, I really didn't know how the verbalist did his prolific witticisms. In the three-years that I had known Jalonec, I seldom heard the same joke twice. Bo was a wellspring of continuous new material. But Jokes often was so relentless to the point where his nauseating routine became obnoxious.

B.J. next told the guys at the scenic overlook that before his family moved to Levittown and he then met Susie Parker, Jokes had dated two girls in 'West Philly named Anna Conda and Mandy Lifeboats. Bo claimed that Anna Conda would always squeeze him half to death, and then Bo dumped Mandy Lifeboats, because the chick started dating a muscular lifeguard named Ty Tannic.

"Say, Words," Jokes continued his exposition. "Did ya' know that Pinocchio had a woodpecker?" And then frugal Bo told us that he planned to drive all the way to Little Rock, Arkansas to buy Susie's engagement ring. That's when we all knew it was time to re-enter our cars and resume the trip up to Bushkill, where Jalonec claimed that no straight men in the town ever got laid because a gay pyromaniac had, out of spite, set all the town's female bushes on fire.

I had brought a smelly bag along from Hal's Delicatessen, and before Carnie got behind the wheel, he requested that I place *my* two pounds of Limburger cheese in the Merc's trunk. Tinker never objected to the Limburger cheese's aroma, because the weirdo claimed that he really liked the horrendous "perfume smell".

After making it to Bushkill up *Route 209,* Quinn and Carnie cruised-around until we finally located 87 Purple Marten Court, Salvatore Palermo's country chalet.

Sal's '59 ice blue Cadillac was parked in the stone driveway of the rustic brown home. Popeye and Phil Jackson had driven-up to the Poconos in Dante Messina's reconditioned red Chrysler, while the three females had ridden the distance to Pocono Mountain Lake Estates in the blue Caddy. The chalet was unoccupied at that moment, and the neighboring homes were either vacated or under construction, so those factors made the Diablos' raid all the more-easier. Everything that we planned to do was efficiently performed in a mere fifteen-minutes. Presumably, the girls had gone out to eat in the red Chrysler with Carmella, Popeye and Phil Jackson.

Tinker deftly opened the Caddy's hood and trunk. Quinn supervised the logistics of the operation, reminding us that the Q Man didn't want "anyone to get hurt, us or them". All-too-stealthy Jeremy threw marijuana bags and pornographic literature left over from Specialty Enterprises expedition into the parked Cadillac's trunk, and then slammed the lid shut.

Sugar Ray, Carnie, and I smeared the pungent Limburger cheese all over the engine heads of the blue luxury sedan, so that the car would "stink like Skunksville" when the motor would become hot. Jokes preferred to keep guard, refusing to get any of the smelly substance on his soft, clean, lily-white hands.

Robbie removed the Caddy's hubcaps, and he and Tinker loosened the lug nuts on each wheel, which would make the tires shimmy, wobble, and then eventually fall off during a high-speed chase.

Tinker used a "secret device" to unscrew a fire hydrant's cap next to Sal Palermo's mountain-retreat. His tool's use caused a torrent of water to immediately flood the property's front lawn and driveway. It was then time for the Diablos to speedily evacuate the driveway.

The gang then staked-out the area, using Tinker's new set of walkie-talkies to facilitate communications between Quinn's Ford and Carnie's James Dean Special. The cars were parked about a thousand-feet apart in separate wooded areas. Mink Trail's access to Purple Marten Court was highly visible to both cars' occupants.

A half-hour later, the red Chrysler carrying its rollicking vacationers turned off Mink Trail onto Purple Marten Court. The vehicle soon stopped in front of the handsome, newly-constructed mountain chalet. The driver and four passengers immediately exited to survey the extensive water damage that was still wildly gushing from the hydrant onto Sal Palermo's newly-seeded lawn and driveway.

Popeye Messina splashed through ankle-deep flooding and quickly climbed into the tampered-with '59 Caddy; fired-up the ignition, and then drove the ice-blue sedan backwards to the street. Bruno quickly hopped-out, and he and Phil Jackson tried tightening the fire hydrant's loose nut with their bare hands. Jets of water shot into their angry faces, wetting their cotton shirts, and saturating their dungarees.

As Popeye and Phil participated in their comical folly, Carnie drove his '49 Merc' down Purple Marten Court. "Hey Popeye!" Tinker yelled out the passenger-side window. "Are there any Diablo' punks livin' up here in these goddamned hillbilly mountains?"

Popeye and Jackson instantly put two and two together and recognized the identity of their chief nemesis. Bruno and Phil jumped into Sal's tampered-with Caddy, and Popeye was beyond nuts as Messina crazily chased Carnie's Merc' up and down area hills, around bends and ridges, and through dangerous mountain intersections.

Quinn tailed the altered blue Caddy and clocked its speed up to fifty-miles an hour around several treacherous mountain curves. All the while, Carnie, Tinker, and I knew exactly how an antelope felt when the animal was being hunted and chased by a pack of fierce leopards. I was really frightened during the frenetic pursuit, but I tried concealing my anxiety from Tinker and Carnie, who always thought that their hearts were much braver than mine.

The mountain turns were very precarious. and several innocent motorists suddenly found themselves accidentally involved in the high-speed mania. The Caddy zoomed-around another difficult curve, and its front wheels suddenly released several loose tires. Sparks flew everywhere as the luxury sedan's bare wheels screeched and grinded against the asphalt road.

Popeye lost control of the impaired auto'. The Cadillac slid-down a ravine and soon shot across the fairway of an exclusive private golf course, where two petrified duffers were about to tee off. The Caddy kept on its erratic route, going through the center of a sand trap, across a rough ruff, and the tireless wheels next ripped-up the ninth green's thick, rich grass.

Finally, the ice blue Cadillac came to a stop after it crushed the ninth' hole's flag. Popeye and Phil Jackson leaped-out, wondering what had become of their front tires. Soon, the terrible stench from the hot engine's Limburger cheese smelled-up the entire vicinity.

Messina and Jackson apologized to several golfers for the prodigious property damage. The golf course management contacted the local police, and Popeye was given a citation for reckless driving and another ticket or endangering the lives of two of the exclusive golf course's prestigious club members.

The local authorities conducted a comprehensive search of the disabled Cadillac, and upon opening the trunk, the police discovered plenty of pornography and bags of Mexican Red. After doing a routine check on Popeye and Phil Jackson, the Bushkill cops came across a similar charge of illicit porn' and marijuana possession by the boys, which had been shrewdly planted after the May Cardinal Reagan Prom. The two teen violators were taken into custody to tour the local "clinic" for further interrogation.

On the way back to Levittown, the Diablos stopped at a hamburger joint in Morrisville. Bo Jalonec told us that the golf course incident must have really *teed-off* Popeye and Phil Jackson. "Those guys must enjoy playing golf as much as the dick-heads enjoy practicing bowling," Bo concluded his nifty oratory.

"Jokes," I sai., "Have you ever played golf?"

"Well, yes," Bo chuckled. "But when I do, I always wear two pair of pants in case I get a hole in one! And I usually shoot in the low 80s. If it gets any damned warmer, I refuse to play!"

After the Diablos victoriously returned to our familiar haunts, Bo Jalonec summed it all up at the popular Feed Bag. "Ya' know guys, between the fish stench in the barn chimney and the Limburger cheese odor from the Caddy's engine, Popeye is wishin' he was born without any damned taste buds in his mouth and nose. Even his spinach must smell like a cheap, horny prostitute's raunchy VD crotch."

"I sat disgusted inside our favorite hangout, listening to the gang's happiness at destroying enemy property and getting the Ks into mammoth legal trouble. In my heart, I really wished that the tribal warfare would stop, so that I could finally lead a calm, ordinary, peaceful, high school life.

Chapter 46
"In the Spotlight"

In late August of '59, Carnie, Tinker and I were waiting for Bo Jalonec at our favorite Feed Bag corner table. Gerri was on duty, and it was obvious that the airhead employee sympathized with Angie and the Ks, and by her frowning facial expression, I also could tell that the substitute waitress regretted accidentally giving the Diablos Sal Palermo's confidential Bushkill Pocono Mountain address.

Domenick insisted that Gerri wait on our table, which ironically seated the Feed Bag's most frequent, if not best customers. Angie's girlfriend appeared to be feeling guilty about revealing the very confidential town, street, and house number to Mr. Bo. The other Diablos felt little remorse about causing the destruction of Sal Palermo's expensive ice blue Cadillac, but I had some second thoughts about the successful escapade.

"Well, if it isn't Scum, Scummier, and Scummiest," Gerri greeted as the no-nonsense broad referred to Carnie, Tinker and me, in regard to *our* blatant betrayal of her confidence.

Just then Bo entered our official hangout, and the appearance of his handsome face and meticulously combed long blond hair knocked Gerri into a more courteous mood. The wift immediately curtailed her overt hostility in favor of standard public politeness.

"Hi there, Gerri," Bo graciously greeted. "Ya' know, I think I need a new epididymis. Do ya' know where I could get one?"

"Yes, my knight in shining *amour,*" Gerri un-amorously replied. "Try the local junkyard. I'll bet Davy Crockett over here could get ya' one cheap."

"That's cool, Doll! Really cool!" Bo praised. "Now tell me, what do ya' have that's hot, pink, and wet?" Bo was a master at delivering sexual allusion as if it were casual, pedestrian, English vernacular.

"Oh Blondie, I have something wonderful that'll send you to the moon and back. Just give me your precious phone number," Gerri gladly suggested.

Carnie, Tinker, and I were extremely annoyed, especially since we knew we couldn't get to first base with Gerri, but as usual, Bo was skillfully hitting a grand slam home run from the dugout.

Jokes borrowed Gerri's pencil and quickly jotted-down some false numbers on a table napkin. Jalonec handed Gerri the napkin with the fraudulent phone number, and the thrilled waitress possessively tucked the phony info' inside her bra for safekeeping. Then, the infatuated hussy bent-down and softly whispered some sweet words into his ear.

After taking our orders, Gerri moved into the kitchen to provide Domenick with our dining preferences.

"Bo, what did Gerri whisper in your ear?" Carnie demanded to know. My insecure friend was aggressive on the issue because no girl ever softly uttered even a "sour nothing" into *his* ear.

"Hair pie," Jalonec answered very calmly. "So that's what I presume she'd give me, some of her hair pie to lick."

I nearly swallowed my epiglottis, which is nowhere near my epididymis. Then, B.J. broke the good news that the Adonis was to share, but since Jeremy Foster positively hated dancing, the envious saboteur refused to participate. Carnie and I readily accepted Bo's very exciting invitation.

"Guess what guys?" Jokes cheerfully introduced his special announcement. "I've got four special admission cards to *American Bandstand.* Some of my old pals in West 'Philly can't make tomorrow's show, so here they are. Who wants to join me for a national TV appearance?"

"I freakin' hate dancin'," Tinker indignantly indicated. "This here lame leg is a lousy curse." The most savage Diablo tilted his newly-stolen Davy Crockett coonskin hat above his forehead, and then pointed to his shorter leg.

Carnie and I were exhilarated at accepting the offer. We both had always wanted to go on the nationally televised hit teen dance show.

"That's okay, Tink," Bo answered, feigning sympathy. "But I had forgotten all about that minor detail that ya' once got polio. I'll invite Susie as my second choice. And what about you two ball-busters?"

"Tough as nails!" I jubilantly exclaimed.

"Neat as a concrete toilet seat!" Carnie proclaimed.

"That's just great, guys! Because tomorrow we roll. I've made up again with Susie, and I'll pick you dudes up at one. We'll cruise into 'Philly, and show the Dick Clark regulars how to cut a rug."

I was happy to again be able to isolate Carnie from Tinker. I believed that with a few more positive social experiences, the Merc' Man would finally return to his normal, amiable good-hearted self.

The following day at one o'clock sharp, Bo and Susie arrived at 50 Daffodil Lane. Mom was so psyched about the prospect of seeing me on national television that she promised to abstain from watching her sentimental afternoon soap operas, just to get a brief glimpse of her cherished son jitterbugging on the living room picture tube. Carnie soon made the scene, and then the '57 green and *cream* (as Bo insisted the car's colors had always been, and definitely not green and *white*) Chevy backed-out of the asphalt driveway.

As Bo motored south on *Route 13,* the four of us discussed how big *American Bandstand* had become, ever since Dick Clark had taken the teen show over from a Levittown DJ, Bob Horn.

When Bo passed the Andalusia Drive-in, a thought popped into my head. "Jokes, don't Angie Palermo and Bubbles Messina go to *American Bandstand* sometimes?" I still couldn't get the Italian girls out of my mind, in spite of all the Diablo and Kamikaze conflicts that had been transpiring.

"Yeah, and I've seen both of 'em on the show five or six times. Maybe you and C Man will be selected by the Sicilian chicks to dance to a Ladies' Choice slow song. Glad to see that you jerks are wearin' some formal threads for a change."

I weighed Bo's absurd suggestion about Angie and Bubbles slow dancing with Carnie and me, and then I did a serious reality check. "Fat chance," I ruefully disagreed. "I think the chesty broads would rather dance with Rootie Kazootie and Mortimer Snerd than with us."

"Prob'ly also with Stanley Tezeeker and Mortimer Ralston, too," Carnie added to my zany metaphor. "But to tell you the truth, I feel naked in public without my black leather jacket and blue denim jeans!"

"Thank goodness ya' only feel naked and don't look naked!" Jokes laughed, staring at my face in his rear-view mirror. "I've already pissed myself' once today!"

Bo's fantastic blonde girlfriend was a little more diplomatic than he was. "Ya' know, guys, Carol Zella and Jackie Harrelson are good friends of mine, and J.W., they really like *you* and Carnie," the Miss Bucks County contestant disclosed. "Forget about Angie and Bubbles, and go for those *good* girls who really think you're both hot stuff."

Carnie and I knew that Susie was one-hundred-percent correct, but forgetting about Angie and Bubbles was like suddenly forgetting about oxygen, food, pinball, cars, music, sports, the Diablos, and sex. We just couldn't do it, no matter how hard we tried.

Bo Jalonec had lived in 'West Philly before moving into Junewood and knew the myriad city streets and avenues like he knew the shape of his pearly white teeth, which thr Casanova would admire in his bathroom's medicine-cabinet mirror for at least five-minutes each time the egotist inspected his fangs.

Susie Parker didn't say too much the remainder of the trip. Bo traveled down Roosevelt Boulevard and then maneuvered through city traffic until we cut over to Broad Street. As I quietly sat in the back seat with Carnie, I became aware that beauty often speaks for itself. Bo was the envy of every guy who would see Susie, and she was the envy of every chick that would spot her with Jalonec. It was as if Carnie and I were in the company of two perfect-looking Mt. Olympus deities.

Bo w's Chevy went half-way around *City Hall,* which featured a statue of William Penn perched at its summit, and then we headed west on Market Street. The major traffic artery featured the famous 'Philly El-train tracks overhead. We all knew we were close to our very special destination, the *WFIL* studios. *American Bandstand* was produced by *that* 'Philly *ABC* affiliate.

B.J. parked his wheels in a lot on 47th Street and then we anxiously paced a block to the television studio. We patiently waited in line with the other visitors standing behind "the regulars", who were the kids who appeared on the show almost daily. Slowly, the line advanced, and the four of us were very concerned that it would stop moving. Thank goodness that we were among the last lucky ones admitted inside.

My wandering eyes scanned the *American Bandstand* bleachers, and I became quite thrilled when I saw Angie and Bubbles seated, incessantly blabbing with each other. When my keen scrutiny caught their attention, the swarthy cousins shriveled-up like a pair of dried prunes, apparently disgusted with my surprise presence. I felt a trifle guilty, and I could almost identify with the dolls' detestation of Carnie and me, after all the wicked destruction that the Diablos had wrought upon the Kamikazes over that past four months.

Dick Clark and the show's director gave the live television audience some basic instructions. We carefully and silently listened to the repertoire, not wanting to embarrass ourselves on national TV. Soon, the lively introductory Bandstand Theme was played; the cameras were activated, and the regulars were jitterbugging on the dance floor.

Carnie and I discussed how we once had the pleasure of seeing DJ Dick Clark doing a record hop at *Clementon Lake Amusement Park* over in South Jersey, and the popular television personality was just as gracious and sincere in person as the genial host had always appeared on TV. Dick Clark was simply a nice guy, who always portrayed himself as having a great interest in other people.

Carnie and I conversed with a few girls in the bleachers, who had also gone to *Bandstand* as singles. The babes were from Willow Grove, a Philly' suburb, which also had a famous area amusement park having the radio slogan, "Life is a lark at *Willow Grove Park"*.

After talking for about ten-minutes, the indomitable C-Man and I danced several fast numbers with the Willow Grove girls, much to the dissatisfaction of Angie and Bubbles, whose day evidently had been spoiled by our surprise *Bandstand* attendance. Mr. C and I must have seemed like adult satanic devils, instead of as adolescent Diablos to the beleaguered Sicilian cousins.

The highlight of the afternoon for me proved to be Angie's low point. One segment of the show featured a "Roll Call", where teens announced their names, high schools, and towns to the national audience. I was the last one in the single file line, and I thought that Dick Clark would never get to me.

When I finally approached the microphone, I gave a standard salutation. "Hi, I'm J.W.," I proudly proclaimed. "And I go to Cardinal Reagan High in Levittown, Pennsylvania."

"J.W.," the show's M.C. said, "how would you like leading-off our Spotlight Dance? Is there a particular girl you'd like to choose to lead-off the slow number?"

At first, I was going to say, "Carol from Willow Grove" and select the song "Oh! Carol" by Neil Sedaka, but then my brain had a sudden irresistible, brilliant flash.

"Yes. I'd like to dance with Angie Palermo, my neighbor from 66 Daffodil Lane in Levittown."

"That's great, J.W. And what song would you like to dance to?" the popular *Bandstand* M.C. asked.

I thought deeply for a second. Then, I put my mouth where my heart was. "I would like to dance with Angie to 'My Prayer' by the Platters," I requested, while speaking directly into the host's microphone.

"Terrific choice," Dick Clark complimented. "Angie, why don't you come-over to J.W. and start off our 'Spotlight Number'."

How could Angie refuse? She would be a conceited fool on national television if the doll declined my gracious offer. As the studio lights dimmed, Angie Palermo stepped hesitantly towards me. My Daffodil Lane neighbor had a fake smile on her face that camouflaged her true indignation. After several bars of the Platters' love song, I struck-up a trite conversation with the olive-skinned, Italian beauty.

"How's it goin' Angie?" I coyly asked. "I haven't seen ya' since the Poconos." I realized I had made a very stupid remark, but I was so nervous slow-dancing with my dream girl on national television that I could not think of anything more constructive to express.

"Do ya' have a tiny comb stuck in your pocket?" Angie inquired.

"No! Why?" I could not at first interpret Angie's true intent.

"Well, what about half of a pretzel rod?"

"Er, no." I finally determined that Angie was deliberately busting-on and insulting my masculinity on national television.

"Did ya' eat only half of a celery stick and put the other half in your pocket?" Angie asked, pretending to be smiling to the enthralled kids out in Fresno, California and Miami, Florida.

I couldn't believe it. I was being turned-on by being put-down. "Look Angie," I imperatively answered. "Stop bustin' my *como se llamas* on national TV." I gave a cursory wave to everyone viewing our slow dancing out there in TV-land. I had spoken to the Sicilian goddess through closed teeth, so that no attentive viewer could read my fixed lips.

"Wow!" Como se llamas! That's almost Italian. It really turns me on," Angie uttered in amazement as the popular slow song and I reached dual climaxes.

When Bo Jalonec left me off at 50 Daffodil Lane later that afternoon, I immediately noticed that Sal Palermo's television set was sitting on the curb with a smashed-in picture tube. I entered the house and asked Mom what had happened to the Palermo's damaged mass media device.

"Jack and Stella Burns called around two hours ago," Mom reported. "Mr. Palermo had just returned from Mexico last night. When our upset neighbor saw you dancing with his pretty daughter on TV, her father became so mad that he punctured the picture tube with his left foot. His wife had to drive Mr. Palermo to *Lower Bucks County Hospital*. I understand from gossiping with Stella that his big right toe needed five stitches."

September was close at hand. Robbie Wilkinson and Ace Roberts had had several Feed Bag conferences with Jake Mullins and Dave Evans about organizing the details for the New Jersey blueberry farm rematch drag-race between Quinn and Cummings. The scheduled contest was set to happen on *Labor Day*.

Chapter 47
"The Atlantic City Boardwalk"

Seven p.m. on *Labor Day,* 1959, had been confirmed as the time for the rematch drag-race between Quinn and Cummings. I dictated to Jokes the layout of the Atlantic Blueberry Company plantation on *Route 322* in Mays Landing, New Jersey. Bo adroitly drew-up several sketches of the contest's course for Cummings and Quinn to study.

The race's distance would be about five-miles in length. A half-mile-long asphalt road stretched from the 600-hundred-acre farm's main gate to its central packinghouse. Equal dirt roads branched-out to the left and right in two identical semi-circles, forming forward and backward figure nines. The ends of the figure nines ended back at the asphalt road where the drivers would switch lanes and speed back to the packinghouse. Then, each driver would follow the opposite figure nine until the charioteers reached the asphalt road again. Finally, Quinn and Cummings would again alternate lanes and go full throttle straight toward the finish line a hundred-feet in front of the packing facility.

The asphalt main road and dirt roads were elevated twelve-feet above canals, which served as the farm's irrigation ditches. The race would end at a flag erected one-hundred-feet before the packinghouse. Since blueberry season had ended in the middle of August, the farm owners and workers would not be present on *Labor Day* weekend. The drag race on the farm's treacherous dirt and hard-topped causeways could and should go off without any outside interference.

The morning after *Labor Day,* I knew that Bo Jalonec would be driving-up to *Penn State*. B.J. opted not to motor-over to the blueberry farm drag race because the spoiled "only child" insisted that his '57 Chevy was packed with clothes and personal belongings, which the freshman would be taking along to college.

Susie Parker and her close friend Patty Van Arsdale were planning to make the trip to Jersey in Susie's '55 Ford Crown Victoria, so Quinn and Bo were free to have plenty of time before the seven' p.m. race to review last minute strategy. The basic rule was that the winner (in an undisputed victory) would receive the loser's car title.

Quinn traveled into Jersey with his chief mechanic Marcus Spellman, with Robbie, and also with the Diablos' leader's cousins Chuckie and Jimmy Callahan. I had made the jaunt in Carnie's '49 Mercury. His two other passengers were Bo and Tinker.

On that September morning, the '42 Ford' and '49 Merc' stopped at an *Esso* station on *Route 13*. Since the Diablos were all gas-asses, the notion of a blueberry farm drag-race fifty-miles away seemed an appropriate change of environment. The Levittown cops on patrol were becoming entirely too interested in local greaser gang affairs, and a new venue was desirable to both the Diablos and the Kamikazes.

As the gas station attendant filled the Merc's tank, I just knew that Bo would have something profound to say. "Quit *fueling* around," Jalonec jested to the gas garage's grease monkey. "Can't ya' tell we're on an important business trip to nowhere."

And after the annoyed service station employee checked the Merc's engine oil supply, Jokes aptly noted that it was a hazy summer morning, and *that* fact soon inspired him. "Hurry-up, Dip-stick. It's a little hazy this mornin', so we're anxious to get the *fog* outa' here!"

Ace Roberts was bringing a carload of Diablos to the event later that afternoon, and other Dogwood Hollow chums were cleaning-up their street machines to also make the eventful Jersey trip. Everyone was told via the Feed Bag grapevine to assemble at the main gate of Atlantic Blueberry Company, *Route 322,* Mays Landing at exactly ten minutes before seven p.m.

Quinn and Carnie stopped for breakfast at a *Route 130* diner over in Jersey about two-miles south of the *Burlington-Bristol Bridge*. When the Diablos entered the diner, most of the patrons stared at us as if we were criminals, and after the customers spotted Marcus Spellman in our company, I could just tell that some of the 'regulars' felt uncomfortable and had prejudice in their hearts for colored people.

The Diablos, with the exception of Tinker, were more flexible about race than most '50s white citizens, and if Quinn wanted the attitudes of society bent to accommodate Marcus, then we would skew them, regardless of what the public (or Tinker) thought. Our contingent must have looked a little devastating to our audience of fellow diners, because no one made a catcall or gave a derogatory Bronx cheer. A daring blonde waitress scurried-over to take our orders.

Everything went rather normally until Carnie had to imitate some of Bo Jalonec's favorite lines. Apparently, we had gotten a veteran waitress skilled at dealing with obnoxious, egocentric greasers.

"What do ya' have that's pink, wet, and hot?" Carnie repulsively asked while poorly impersonating Bo Jalonec.

"Tomato soup!" the luscious blonde curtly replied, much to our appreciation and to Carnie's frustration.

Being somewhat insulted, Carnie attempted to establish his male dominance in defense of his fragile ego. "Listen, Honey. I think I need a new epididymis."

"Stand up!" the waitress commanded.

"What?" Carnie incredulously asked.

"You heard me Dip-head, I said 'stand up'!" the tough female imperatively ordered.

Carnie rose to his feet, and the young lady must have had some paramilitary training in self-defense. Instantly, the broad gave Carnie a swift knee to the scrotum as if she had been a certified *Parris Island* drill instructor. Our humiliated buddy bent-over in excruciating pain.

"Well, not only do you need a new epididymis," the aggravated waitress persisted, "but now goof-ball, you also need a new set of testicles, too!"

The other Diablos broke-out in a spontaneous wave of laughter. The diner's patrons that had witnessed the encounter joined in the merriment, and the only somber person at our table was poor Carnie. After our general silliness subsided, Quinn made Carnie apologize to the young honey, and my unstable friend finally realized that only Bo Jalonec could be Bo Jalonec.

The Diablos all ate comprehensive breakfasts of eggs, bacon, and pancakes, and in another half-hour, we were on the road again. Quinn and Carnie took *Route 130* south to *Route 73,* and then headed east toward *Route 30*, the *White Horse Pike*.

All the distance from the *130 Diner* on the way to Hammonton, Jokes was working on Carnie about his bad experience with the pretty blonde waitress. "Carnie, maybe ya' can buy a new scrotum at *sacks* Fifth Avenue in Manhattan." And that zinger was followed by, "Or maybe you're Balls Hertz, Dick Hertz's younger brother." And when Jokes elaborated, "I'm surprised the waitress didn't have the courtesy to ask if ya' owned any land before she smashed your nuts into a double hernia," Carnie turned the car radio up to maximum decibels, nearly shattering our vulnerable eardrums. Tinker and I negotiated a truce between the warring factions, and soon tranquility had been restored.

Somewhere between Hammonton's crowded Bellevue Avenue and somnolent Weymouth Road, Jokes had the notion that we should all sing the lyrics to Fats Domino's "Blueberry Hill" until Carnie could find *that* song playing on his Merc's radio. Thank heaven he did, on *W-ABC* out of New York, because the melody we had sung for twenty-minutes was extremely horrendous, making the Almighty sorry that sound had ever been created.

Sometimes, Bo Jalonec could be more nauseous than an extremely long and rocky deep-sea fishing expedition. Carnie turned right off of Weymouth Road, and drove past the historic chimney of the Weymouth Iron Works that Jalonec erroneously thought dated back to the *Revolutionary War* era. Jokes prematurely declared, "George Washington needed big balls to shoot off his cannon in order to win the war, and here's where *they* came from!"

"Jokes, that chimney belonged to a foundry that made munitions during *World War I*, not the *Revolutionary War!"* I historically clarified and knew, since I had previously lived in the general area.

"I sometimes get my wars and my whores mixed-up!" Jalonec specified. "I could've sworn that *that* chimney once belonged to a disreputable house of prostitution frequented by John *Hand*cock and Davy Crotch-it."

Soon, we were heading east on the Black Horse Pike (*Route 322*) to pass and view the Mays Landing Division of the Atlantic Blueberry Company. The enormous plantation must have been a mile long, and as we zipped past, I pointed-out the layout of the fields. "The farm has forty-five fields," I remembered and stated from my past. "These fifteen are in the W section; the next fifteen are in the C section, and the last fifteen are in the E section."

When Bo heard C-section, the gang's comedian had something irrelevant and inane to discuss. "My mom had a C-section when I was born, but then she went into convulsions, and almost suffered a Julius Seizure."

I ignored Jalonec's idiotic drivel, which at times could be very annoying. I concentrated my mind on clarifying my serious blueberry farm description. "W stands for west fields; C for center ones, and E for east sections." I couldn't believe Bo's permanent attitude toward life. Our quixotic friend had never been serious about anything, not even his own birth.

After we passed the middle length of the farm, Carnie's Merc' was on its final leg to Atlantic City. Bo Jalonec's mouth formed a scoundrel smile. "Wow guys! I haven't seen so many bushes since a hundred-thousand naked girls chased me through *Independence Square* because they wanted to rip my birthday suit off my bod'!"

All of us burst out into a roar of laughter, since we knew that a birthday suit was non-existent and could not be torn off anyone. And if Jalonec could cause so much commotion with 'Philly females when fully clad, then maybe, quite possibly, his nude torso could really generate a wild pursuit of a hundred-thousand horny, Philadelphia eager-beaver chicks.

Bo interpreted our reaction as being just cause to continue his characteristic insanity. I was fully aware that the remaining twelve-miles to Atlantic City would probably seem like an eternity. Mr. C and Mr. Fix-it thought Jokes' mediocre funnies as being humorous, but I valued his ridiculous statements as being grossly absurd and contrived.

Bo Jalonec's arduous Black Horse Pike monologue included how George Washington's wife once owned a winery on a large island off the coast of Massachusetts, and how *Lincoln's Gettysburg Address* was

14 Maple Street. Jokes also told us how President Franklin Pierce had finally found a good use for the earring, and how John *Adams* was the true discoverer of nuclear energy. When Bo informed his captive audience' that New Jersey had gotten its name from the need to replace a torn football shirt, Tinker and Carnie screamed with delight, while I remained somewhat somber an irritated.

I had wished that a thorny cactus had been available to shove-down Bo's trachea, and when Jokes asked us why more Americans were not born on *Labor Day,* I thought that the thorny cactus shoved-down his throat should be replaced by a giant saguaro. I gave a sigh of relief when Carnie's dependable Merc' finally entered the outskirts of tourist-oriented Atlantic City.

Quinn and Carnie parked their hotrods in a Virginia Avenue lot. While Quinn and Marcus Spellman worked final adjustments on the '42 Ford's carburetor linkage, the rest of us walked the world-famous boardwalk, the full-mile from the *Steel Pier* down to the *Million Dollar Pier* on Missouri Avenue.

We played some wheel games of chance without much luck; had lunch at a pizza parlor; bought a large box of salt-water taffy, and then trekked the mile north back to the *Steel Pier*.

The renowned pier's marquee featured South 'Philly's Fabian, who was appearing on stage to sing his latest hit "Turn Me Loose". Fabian's brand of music was labeled "bubble gum", a hybrid of the dreaded Pat Boone' sound, so the Diablos boycotted the sanitized rendition of original black rhythm and blues, which we keenly preferred.

A teen dance television show similar to *American Bandstand* was in progress on the pier. It was hosted by Wilmington, Delaware Channel 12' DJs Joe Grady and Ed Hurst, but the Diablos were denied admission because we were wearing black leather jackets, blue denim jeans, and engineer boots. Those trademark greaser articles of apparel were violations of the show's inflexible dress code.

The Diablos passed the rest of *Labor Day* afternoon playing arcade games, getting our photos taken at an old-time picture stall, and smoking *Camel* cigarettes. Several Kamikazes were also on the boardwalk checking-out the *Steel Pier* attractions, simply to burn some time before the big race, but we avoided the Ks, and the hoodlums reciprocated by staying away from us.

I was experiencing stomach pains from eating too much pizza and salt-water taffy, and without cessation, Bo Jalonec kept on peppering my tolerance with stupid verbalizations. At first, I politely listened to his pestering litany, but as the afternoon advanced, and as my intestinal fortitude fought-off cramps and excessive gas, Bo's zaniness pushed my spirit to the brink of insanity. It was a torrid, late-summer day, and the sultry weather only added a degree of emotional disenchantment to my physical misery.

"Say, Words", Bo began his idiotic monologue. "Do ya' know how Tinker learned to open locks?"

"No, I don't, Jokes. And I don't particularly care, either." I innocently and semi-politely answered. "Enlighten me, even though I'm not a damned table lamp."

"Tink took a correspondence course from *Yale University,"* Bo prevaricated. "Not only can the criminal genius open Yale locks, he can also jimmy any Master lock as well." Bo was a wordsmith at associating two unrelated ideas, and for some remote reason, Carnie, Tinker and I were always captivated by his peculiar language trickery.

"Maybe Tinker received *his* Master's Degree at *Yale University*," Carnie theorized and conveyed.

Bo resented when Carnie tried challenging his humor dominance. "Say, Carnie," Bo countered. "Did ya' hear about the stick-up on the *Ben Franklin Bridge?"*

"No Jokes, I didn't," Carnie gullibly confessed.

"Some moronic kid threw one up there!" Bo volleyed. I then hoped that the next thirty-minutes would pass by quickly, because a half-hour with Jalonec could be equivalent to a full-month burning in hell.

"Say, Tink," Bo habitually continued his lackluster repertoire. "If the Kamikazes lived in ancient times, the sadists would've persecuted the Christians worse than the Romans did. The Ks would've put the Christians on the Rotary; would've hurled the disciples to the Lions, and if those methods didn't effectively work, the Kamikazes would've thrown the Christians to the damned Kiwanis."

I didn't know whether it was the intense heat, the anticipation of the rematch drag-race, the thrill of trekking the world-famous Atlantic City Boardwalk, or my apprehension about Bo Jalonec leaving for *Penn State* that was causing my unsavory, disconsolate disposition. Jokes' conversation was getting under my skin like a twenty-pound, foot-long hypodermic needle. Carnie said that my face was rapidly changing from pale green to deep purple. As we strolled by a crowded boardwalk seafood restaurant, Jalonec persisted in his repulsive verbal rambling.

"Ya' know, J.W. You often say ya' wanna' have a Tarzan-type body with smooth muscle tone. Ya' see those dead sea-creatures in the window?" the ingrate rhetorically asked. "They're called mussels. If ya' eat six of 'em a day, you'll soon develop a Tarzan physique. But ya' gotta' be especially careful. If ya' eat a dozen a day, you'll develop a Joe Weider *Mr. America*-type body, and that's just what ya' don't want, too many damned mussels."

At that moment, I wished that Bo would get a very severe laryngitis attack. Just the thought of eating a half-dozen of those squiggly mussels on top of four slices of pizza and a half-box of already devoured salt-water taffy made a sour taste squirt-up to my mouth from my queasy stomach. And when Jalonec further pursued his sickening lingo, my eyes began rolling, and I started to audibly hiccup and burp.

"Say, Carnie," Jokes addressed his chief admirer. "Did ya' know that Queen Elizabeth cut a hit record over there in England?"

"Er, no Jokes, I didn't," Carnie stuttered. The unbearable heat, my excessive junk food diet, and the silly, stupid jokes were making me feel dizzy and ready to regurgitate.

"That's right, she did," Bo insisted and persisted. "But Queen Elizabeth couldn't collect any royalties, because she was already blue-blooded nobility."

I was about to puke, but I held my head back while walking with my hand over my mouth, and my throat kept redundantly belching and hiccupping.

"Ya' know, Tink," Bo garrulously bantered. "They call this here giant platform a boardwalk because if ya' spot a good-lookin' chick, ya' just *lumber* over and introduce yourself."

I thought I would either die from brain damage listening to Jalonec or from drowning in my own barf when my vomiting abdomen couldn't deal with any more of his relentless aggravation. Fortunately, I only remembered a fraction of the crap that Bo Jalonec laid upon us that *Labor Day* as we ambled-around the plethora of exhibits and games on Atlantic City's biggest and most famous pier. Throughout it all, I prudently bit my tongue and tried swallowing and breathing in a relaxed manner to settle my urge to throw-up, because to a bona fide '50s greaser, puking in public was tantamount to crying or kissing in public. It was considered a taboo to the Diablos' rigid value system.

But finally, after three-hours of B.J.'s irritating oratory, my cesspool was about to overflow. I felt I couldn't handle any more of his chicken-shit, horseshit, and bullshit, which the amateur orator deftly packaged and merchandised as serious shit. And when Bo suggested that we ride a miniature roller coaster and then go down to the ocean's bottom in the *Steel Pier's* "Diving Bell", I blew my cork.

"Ya' know, J.W.," Jokes said, "I betcha' a..."

"Bo, do me a big favor and shut the hell up!" I uncharitably snapped. "Shut your trap even though you ain't no damned bear or rabbit hunter!"

"Excuse me?" Jokes asked as he cupped his outer ear with his left hand in an exaggerated manner. "I do hunt beaver!"

"I said 'shut the hell up'!" I emphatically reiterated.

Finally, Carnie, Tinker, Bo, and I made it back to the Virginia Avenue parking lot. I glanced at my watch and noticed that it was almost six p.m. Quinn and Sugar Ray Spellman had completed their final engine tune-up preparations. I admired the chrome shining on Quinn's beautiful flathead engine, right before Marcus closed the black '42s' hood.

When Bo Jalonec's presence caught his commander's keen attention, Jokes suddenly turned solemn and asked our fearless leader an intelligent, sane question. "You're up against stiff competition. Ya' ready to kick ass?"

"Sure am, Bo," Quinn confidently stated. "I'm not exactly racin' Oscar Mayer in his Wienermobile, ya' know. Cummings is gonna' be hard to beat."

"Well, *good luck!"* Carnie wished and stated as the wimpy coward shook Quinn's strong right hand.

"Well, Carnie," Quinn replied with a firm grin. "When you're *good,* ya' don't need *luck.*"

Chapter 48
"The Blueberry Farm Rematch"

The '42 Ford and the '49 Merc' smoothly exited the Virginia Avenue parking lot. When Carnie's James Dean Special slowly passed Pacific Avenue, Bo spotted several hookers standing on the corner and startled the streetwalkers by yelling-out, "I'm a visitin' District Attorney. Could ya' tell me where the local *prostitutor's* office is?"

Quinn, followed by Carnie, turned left onto Atlantic Avenue, and after around twenty traffic lights, the cars reached *Route 322,* the *Black Horse Pike.*

I figured I'd try to hold a decent conversation without Jalonec contributing his very disturbing prattle. "Things have really changed since last *Labor Day,"* I soberly recalled and said. "Because a year ago, the Ds were afraid of the Ks. Now it's hard to tell which gang is the protagonist, and which gang is the antagonist."

"You said it," Carnie concurred. "Cummings fooled us good with that friggin' telephone booth scam last *Labor Day."*

"The Kamikazes are still dangerous fucks," Tinker concluded and stated. "And if you' totally weak assholes didn't have me on your side, you'd have lost the greaser war ten-months ago."

"Carnie's right," Bo declared, ignoring Tinker's conceited opinion. "Those Kamikazes made all ya' jerks stuff yourselves into the Dairy DeLite phone booth, just to see exactly how the Ds would stack-up against the Ks, who never did stack-up!"

As Carnie motored past Pleasantville on our way to Mays Landing, anxiety and suspense were peaking in our hearts and minds. Bo came through with a goofy one-liner as a meat delivery truck sped by us in the passing lane. "Now, that's what I really call fast-food."

We all laughed at Jalonec's witty observation, mostly because a giant void existed where nothing was being said, and any language would have aided in filling-in the vacuum.

B. J. then told us about some of his former acquaintances over in West 'Philly named Monty Zuma, Vic Trolla, Cliff Dweller, Luke Warm, Hans Zoff, Philip Yertanc, and Buster Cherry. I had to open the back window on the passenger side to get more ventilation. So much perspiration was rolling-down my forehead that I thought it needed a windshield wiper.

I complained to Jalonec that his sick humor was giving me a terrible headache at the base of my neck, and Jokes even had a dumb remark for *that* spoken grievance. "Well, Words. Why don't ya' visit a doctor and have your *Medusa* oblongata checked?" And before I could adequately respond, Bo editorialized, "J.W. If ya' don't have a family physician, I know a barkin' veterinarian, ya' sick pup, that'll take ya' in as a new patient."

Carnie was laughing so wildly that I thought the craven fool might get his head stuck inside his car's steering wheel. Mercifully, the '49 Mercury finally reached its destination, and soon the rod was inside the entrance parking lot of the enormous blueberry farm.

Carnie followed Quinn down the entrance road as it snaked around several bends, and in half a minute, we were obscured behind tall pine trees, our presence being hidden from anyone who was driving behind us along the busy highway. Seven cars were already waiting at the Atlantic Blueberry Company's main gate. I was happy to see Ace Roberts's '55 Oldsmobile, and I noticed that Slim Jennings had borrowed Tinker's blue '49 Plymouth. Looking around, I also observed Jim Amari, Al Keller, Gene McCann, Fritz Feldcamp, and Slip Carson proudly standing-around the various Diablos familiar street machines.

Three Kamikaze hotrods were already there, too, present to give Cummings representation and support, and my eyes fearfully glanced-over at Jake Mullins, Popeye Messina, Dave Evans, Spits, and Worm, leaning against the Ks all-too-formidable black machines.

Soon, Susie Parker and Patty Van Arsdale showed-up on the property in the classy powder blue and cream '55 Ford Crown Victoria, and a minute later, Bubbles Messina's white Ford Thunderbird pulled into the front gate area with Angie Palermo as her passenger.

Tinker swiftly moved to the blueberry plantation's gate, and in ten-seconds, the future safecracker uncorked the lock. Carnie and I pushed open the cantilever entrance gate on its rollers. "The farm's ours!" Robbie proclaimed, for it was a custom of both the Diablos and the Kamikazes to temporarily use private property in order to serve *our* own selfish needs.

Cummings designated Popeye Messina as "the official flagger", since Bo Jalonec had been the starter at the first drag-race, occurring August 3rd on Haines Road.

'This is how it should all be settled, just like Quinn had declared it should be,' I thought. 'Instead of two gangs fighting-out a solution with greasers getting maimed and hospitalized, the leaders of both factions should compete, winner take all, title for title.' But could the Kamikazes be trusted, if Quinn were to win the contest fair and square?

Carnie, Tinker, Jokes, and I briskly hustled-down the blacktop road to our appointed observation station. The asphalt strip was barely wide enough to accommodate two automobiles side by side. The four of us stood over a dirt ramp that sloped-down from the paved main road, which was really a causeway built above parallel canals lying twelve feet below on either side. Everyone stood nervously at their assigned posts, awaiting the competing cars to be positioned at the starting line.

Susie Parker and Bubbles Messina cautiously drove their autos the half-mile distance, down to the expansive plantation's packinghouse. Ace, Robbie, Mullins, and Evans were selected to stand at the finish line next to the two girls' location to determine the true victor, should the contest's outcome be too close for comfort.

All in all, twenty-three Diablos and twenty-four Kamikazes showed-up for the dramatic race. Even Langford had heard about the event, and the Royal Renegade brought a carload over to Jersey to view the impending contest. About fifteen other curious Levittown chicks had also driven over from Pennsylvania to excitedly witness the highly-anticipated event.

I was so nervous I could feel the pizza, salt-water taffy, and the imaginary six mussels churning-around in my very sensitive gut. Only a two-foot-wide tolerance would separate the speeding steel frames, and any minor error or deviation could easily knock both vehicles off the narrow asphalt road and plummeting-down into the parallel canals.

The cars were evenly matched in terms of gear ratios, engine performance, horsepower, and speed. The race's conclusion hinged on the skill and the courage of each driver. Neither Quinn nor Cummings had ever lost a fair and square drag-race.

On the count of three, Popeye flicked on his flashlight, and the two black chariots' back wheels loudly squealed, and the hotrods instantly sped down the straight, long, perilous blacktop road. Both cars wound-out first gear, and then almost simultaneously, their rear wheels screeched when second had been achieved. As the souped-up engines whined, third gears were entered at around seventy-miles per hour.

The avid racers had to be extremely vigilant. Soon, sharp right and left turns had to be made onto the farm's dual airstrips, where during the harvest season, crop-dusting planes took-off and landed to spray the thousands of rowed blueberry bushes. The '42 and '52 Fords kicked-up clouds of dust as the hotrods rounded their respective turns and speedily entering onto the respective twin airstrips, which led to identical narrow dirt causeways that were also elevated twelve-foot-high above treacherous canals.

Quinn and Cummings appeared dead even as their rods sped ahead on similar elevated dirt and gravel roads on opposite sides of the enormous farm. Suddenly, a police siren was heard originating from near the guard's trailer, located at the race's starting line.

A few seconds later, a New Jersey State Trooper drove his cruiser through the open entrance gate and onto the center asphalt road. Soon, the state cop was in desperate pursuit of the two greaser chieftains. His car was going at least eighty-miles per hour on the narrow, elevated blacktop road, and as the patrolman zoomed by me, the officer seemed focused on his objectives and quite oblivious to the presence of greaser' bystanders. When the state cop arrived at the airstrip fork, he decided to chase the car that had originally started in the left-hand lane, which happened to be Quinn's black '42 coupe.

The racing Fords entered their' respective elevated, dirt, figure-nine causeways. Their speeds had not diminished one iota. The trooper's vehicle that had been chasing Quinn looked like a cloud of dust in pursuit of another cloud of dust. The elevated twin causeways were actually dangerous serpentine dirt roads, winding through the twin eastern and western sections of the massive plantation, and a single mental lapse by either Quinn or Cummings would result in either serious injury or even death.

The speeding cars soon reached the elevated blacktop road again, completing their forward figure nines. Upon re-entering the smooth asphalt surface, the howling vehicles switched lanes, and then again sped-off toward the two opposite side airstrips. The police car's siren wailed as the determined cop took a shortcut, and now his cruiser was only a thousand-feet behind Quinn's Ford, but with the honor and prestige of the Diablos on the line, there was no way that *our* leader was going to stop for any stubborn state trooper. Dust and dirt billowed-up from the three speeding cars, wafting into the twilight sky, and all three drivers still appeared very obstinate about completing their individual missions.

The sixty or so spectators gathered at the finish line began leaping up and down', wildly cheering in sheer excitement, and the fuzz's diligent presence added a new dimension of sensationalism to the nerve-racking spectacle. The dirt causeways' second laps again led back to the blacktop road, and the drivers would have to safely and swiftly negotiate their turns; switch lanes, and then accelerate across the airstrip to the finish line located in front of the packinghouse. The victor's gang would earn honor and bragging rights at every Levittown teen hangout. The Diablos and the Kamikazes both knew that our gangs' reputations were on the line.

Cummings and Quinn simultaneously reached the asphalt road from opposite directions, in what constituted a classic game of "chicken". Quinn expertly rotated his steering wheel, and Cummings, anticipating a head-on collision, panicked and applied his brakes. The Diablo leader successfully (and miraculously) skidded back onto the paved road, and then, Cummings' '52 Ford spun-around and crashed into the trailing police cruiser's left front fender. The impacted cars caromed off one another, each auto flipped-over three times into separate irrigation ditches, falling twelve-foot-below. Completely unfazed, Quinn continued onward toward the established finish line.

The terrible accident momentarily stunned us all. The ricochet of the powerful metallic objects and their subsequent tumbling-down the opposite slopes into parallel canals froze everyone in their tracks. When the closest spectators finally sprinted to the collision scene, the onlookers found that the trooper was in far worse shape than Cummings. The cop's car had landed roof-down in the shallow canal.

The trooper's head was partially submerged under murky, brown canal water. Tinker and Carnie slid-down the steep embankment, hopped up onto the inverted chassis, and then the lame Diabo leaped into the irrigation ditch's waist-deep water. Tink managed to partially pry open the cruiser's door on the driver's side.

Reaching inside the patrol car, Tink and a wet Carnie grabbed the trooper's blue jacket and leather holster strap, and the pair managed to pull the cop's head above water. Robbie and Ace rendered their assistance, and the four Diablos tugged the trooper out of the smashed-up, inverted vehicle. The officer was laid on his back on top of the upside-down chassis.

Tinker, who had been performing some primitive artificial respiration on the cop's chest, soon was able to revive the gasping trooper. The cop coughed-out three gushes of swamp water before finally opening and blinking his eyelids.

Meanwhile, Marcus Spellman, Dave Evans, Jake Mullins, Bo, and I ran toward Cummings's '52 Ford, which had been tilted face-down inside the opposite canal. Cummings obviously was in shock. Cuts, bruises, and lacerations were evident all over his pallid face. Blood was dripping from his forehead, mouth, and nose.

Sugar Ray compromised his own safety in order to rescue Cummings. Spellman and Mullins had splashed and waded through the mushy canal; reached the '52 Ford on the opposite bank, and after several desperate attempts, the pair successfully yanked the Kamikaze King from the wrecked vehicle.

Before Cummings went unconscious, his dark eyes stared blankly at Marcus Spellman's chocolate-brown face. The racist K leader took a deep breath, and then lapsed-off into insensibility.

After Cummings had been extricated from his doomed car, the '52 Ford gradually slid, at its steep angle, sideways down the remaining seven-feet of the soft, muddy embankment. The driver's door was soon submerged beneath lily pads in five-foot-deep brackish canal water. The state trooper and Cummings would have drowned if alert and courageous greasers had not descended the twin trenches and salvaged the two very lucky accident victims.

Quinn raced back to the accident scene in his victorious '42 Ford. "We havta' get Cummings and the trooper to a hospital quick!" the Diablo leader insisted.

Fortunately, a second state trooper arrived on the scene and radioed for emergency vehicles to render assistance. Two ambulances, one from Hammonton, and the other from Hamilton Township, arrived on the blueberry farm fifteen-minutes later. The dazed survivors were transported to Atlantic City Hospital for treatment and observation. Police citations were written-up by the second trooper, and a New Jersey court appearance was scheduled for the evening of October 6th.

Quinn had won the second drag-race fair and square, no doubt about it. But since Cummings's '52 Ford had been totaled in the impact with the trooper's car, the auto's title was valueless. Quinn's satisfaction came from the honor and prestige that my valiant hero had earned from honestly defeating his awesome arch-rival. That's what I really admired most about Quinn. Abstractions and virtues meant more to him than either money or mere material property.

Chapter 49
"Bo Goes to College"

The morning after Quinn's spectacular *Labor Day* drag-race victory, Carnie, Tinker, and I had a farewell breakfast for Bo Jalonec at the Feed Bag. Mr. C and I were taking leaks in the "Men's Room" urinals, and Tinker was eating a chocolate doughnut while taking his morning dump into a toilet bowl inside a bathroom stall. The Diablos had to feign cheerfulness to camouflage genuine sorrow being felt. In our provincial group judgment, grief always had to be brief.

Jokes unceremoniously banged open the lavatory door. Although it was a melancholy occasion, Bo felt he should first be jolly, and then believed he should share his inane folly with his Diablos' comrades. I had never seen Bo sad since I had met him back in the spring of '57. Not even a smashed windshield, or a rock-damaged forehead would keep him in a negative mood for long. Even after the fanatical motorcycle gang had battered Bo in the carnival's Haunted House, the *Peen State* bound freshman never allowed that embarrassment to dampen his spirit.

B.J. immediately spotted Carnie and me in the awkward social situation of taking dual whizzes. "Hey!" Bo exclaimed. "I always said that you two guys know how to hold your own!" And then, Jalonec noticed Tinker's familiar grimy engineer boots along with large doughnut crumbs showing beneath the toilet's stall. "Who ya' datin' now Tink, Hedda *Hopper?* Why don't ya' show some couth, get your grimy ass off the old crapola, and formally honor my upcoming departure from Levittown?"

I wanted to evade more of Jokes' embarrassing, critical, scathing remarks. "Hey, Bo," I interrupted to avoid unnecessary trouble between Tinker and him. "Is it still drizzlin' outside?"

"The weather's just mist-ifying J.W. Simply mist-defying!"

"Did ya' get to say goodbye to Quinn this morning?" Carnie asked.

"Yeah," Bo replied, without expressing extreme emotion. "And our fearless leader told me not to have any meals in the college cafeterias. Quinn said I should eat-out more often, and also advised that once I get past the fur, I'd have the damned problem licked."

I knew perfectly well that Quinn would have never said *that* immoral statement, which Jalonec was falsely attributing to him. Bo was again fabricating fantasy, creating a wild scenario that was a figment of his deranged-but-fertile imagination. Jalonec knew that if he said something outrageous, his example probably would get a decent audience reaction to his ludicrous commentary. It was his preposterous way of getting attention and approval.

I would not fall for his devious baiting. "Are ya' gonna' study business at *Penn State?"* I inquired, as I quickly zipped-up my blue jeans' fly. "And please don't tell me that it's your business, whether or not you're goin' to study business!"

"Maybe, or maybe not," Bo cryptically answered. "Or I might transfer to a Russian college, and in four years, be either a Stalin*grad* or a Lenin*grad*." As usual, any extended conversation with B. J. made the listening Diablos experience instant vertigo, because the dialogue always went-around in upside-down circles, and the developing whirlpool took us along for the ride.

"The natives drink an awful lot of vodka in Russia, don't they?" Carnie inquired as Bo's jealous protege zipped-up his blue jeans. Although Carnie envied and sometimes hated Bo, the annoying brat also valued *his* stupid sense of humor and *his* zany commentaries.

"You're finally right about something, Carnie," Jalonec replied in his standard tone of voice. "And I probably would never last there on vodka alone. Sometimes, I'm a gin rummy. I also have a wry (rye) personality. And ya' cheap guys won't go for salt. You're too scotch to go-down to New Orleans and have a good time on Bourbon Street."

I felt like telling Bo to stop acting like a 'BOzo' and to again 'shut the hell up!' just as I had done on the Atlantic City Boardwalk. Sometimes, I wished that B.J. would just vaporize into some unknown dimension and get permanently lost there. But I felt miserably disconsolate about *his* departure for the *Nittany Mountains,* and none of his condolences could ever possibly alleviate my sadness. I didn't want to steal or destroy any of his thunder on his last 1959 Levittown summer morning. I remained reticent out of respect for the occasion.

Carnie was finally finished using the urinal. Jokes felt compelled to acknowledge the event. "Carnie, it's a good thing ya' didn't flinch when I busted open the bathroom door, or ya' would've been playin' pee-knuckle with yourself." Before Carnie could say or argue anything ridiculous, Bo continued, "Don't shake your wiener more than five times, or it might grow into a frankfurter, and then that midget faggot Oscar Mayer will have the hots for ya'."

"Let's get the fog outa' here," I uttered, remembering a clever Bo Jalonec witticism.

"Flattery is the sincerest form of imitation, and it'll get you everywhere," Bo replied in one of his typical twisted quotation reversals. "And besides that factual axiom, flattery will get ya' anywhere ya' want to go, until you finally put air in your tires."

The Diablos exited the Feed Bag's "Men's Room" and then sat down at our familiar table facing the venerable Dairy DeLite. Babs, a terrific looking auburn-haired morning waitress, took care of us. We ordered an extravagant breakfast worthy for kings, and Luigi prepared the bacon, eggs, pancakes, home fries, ham, and toast to our exact culinary specifications.

"Hey guys," Bo addressed his non-listeners with bland enthusiasm. "Don't let the despicable Kamikazes give ya' the royal salami just because I'll be away at college for a while. Too much salami could make your *liver worse.*"

"Don't worry about that," Tinker jealously promised. "We'll kick 'em in the A-double-scribble if we have to. Stay absent from Dogwood Hollow all ya' want!"

"Do the Ks have any cars left to go gallivantin' around in?" Bo laughed, ignoring Tinker's lack of compassion, while intelligently alluding to the recent demise of Cummings' '52 Ford at the Jersey Mays Landing blueberry farm.

"Probably not," Carnie thoughtfully answered. "After it slid sideways down the slope, it planted itself into that murky canal with all the jagged roots and lily pads."

"It sure did," Bo instantly verified. "And that weird blueberry farm had more damned root canals than the *American Dental Society* does."

I shook my head in disbelief. I knew I would be missing Bo and his harmless jesting an awful lot. Jalonec was the most popular and most extroverted Diablo. Carnie, Tinker, and I often attempted duplicating his suavity, but none of us ever achieved his wonderful results with the hot ladies. His quick-wittedness was inimitable.

As I sat there staring at Bo's flawless countenance, I recalled when he and I were recreating up at Thornridge Alleys in the spring of '58. Jalonec had very demonstrably hoisted two bowling balls up over his shoulders. Then, the incredible guy simultaneously rolled the two spheres down separate alleys, amazingly obtaining two strikes.

"Wow!" I marveled. "Where did ya' learn to do that?"

Without batting an eyelash or missing a heartbeat, the quick-witted humorist succinctly replied, "Two-Lane University!"

And as I continued reflecting on Bo's bizarre and complicated personality, I recalled another time in the summer of '58 when Jalonec claimed he had recently gone to a circus in North 'Philly with Susie Parker. Bo had told me that a barker had ballied them into a tent along with several 'midway circus shills'. The man with the straw hat, bowtie, and black cane was soliciting and yelling, "See the man-eating crabs," and according to Jalonec's testimony, he and Susie entered the tent after paying a dollar each and witnessed a corpulent man sitting at a table eating crabs. Right to the end on that damp September morning, Bo Jalonec's absurd remarks were totally unbearable, and his verbal veracity truly was more than suspect.

The Kamikazes would soon get new wheels, and within a short time, the human vermin would be mobile, agile, and hostile again. Bo, Tink, Carnie, and I conjectured all along that the nefarious Ks were the hood surrogates of Sal Palermo and Dante Messina's drug and porn' distribution network. We also theorized that Popeye and Cummings were the main links in the repugnant local hoodlum chain. As we sat and discussed the Kamikazes and their obedient women, our comments were laced with both humor and sarcasm, because those two elements were the defining characteristics of the Dogwood Hollow greasers.

"Hey, Tink," Bo remarked to his greedy and envious acquaintance. "Did ya' know that beer is good for ya'?"

"No," the most sadistic Diablo bluntly answered.

"It certainly is," Bo maintained. "It made Bud wiser." But Bo was not finished with his silly and ludicrous jargon. "Hey Carnie," Jalonec said, changing his audience focus. "Did ya' hear any gossip about the idiotic Kamikaze who swallowed his trousers?"

"No Bo, I didn't," Carnie confessed.

"Well, the stupid asshole' shit his pants!"

I thought I would soon be ready for admission to a mental institution if Jokes wouldn't shut the hell up before departing for Happy Valley. As we were finishing our elaborate breakfasts, Bo Jalonec intimated to us that the blond stud had once taken Susie Parker to an exclusive restaurant over in *Princeton* before he and she toured the prestigious Ivy League *University*. The waitress was in a rush and forgot to serve Susie her vegetable. So, Bo asked the harried waitress, "Do ya' have her peas?" The appalled waitress replied, "Don't ask such personal questions. But for your information, I don't have *herpes!"* Now, *that* particular story was so bizarre and so off the charts that the tale was borderline insanity, and even Tinker laughed hardily at its unique quality.

Finally, our breakfast banquet had ended, and with full stomachs and heavy hearts, it was time to say "bon voyage" to our golden-haired colleague. We each shook hands with Bo; slapped him on the shoulders, and to cover up our sadness, pretended that we were all grandly enjoying ourselves.

Bo's green and white Chevy was stuffed to the gills with clothes and personal belongings. Before Jalonec entered his crammed regal vehicle, *my* friend pointed to his chrome-covered tailpipe extensions. "Boys, my next car is not gonna' have *dual* exhaust pipes. They're a royal pain in the ass because they're always fightin' with each other."

Regardless of how jealous Tinker and Carnie felt, I was holding back tears and clearing my throat as Bo finished his nonsensical-but-imaginative oration. "Ya' know, guys," Jokes continued while kicking his left front tire. "I think I might change my major from business to something more interestin' at *Penn State*. I hear there are a lot of *openings* in gynecology. Proctology is something else I oughta' look into. I mean to say, after knowin' you three guys, I've already become a foremost authority on assholes!"

As Bo wheeled his '57 out of the Feed Bag parking lot, I felt unhappiness welling-up inside my chest. On one hand, I was glad to be getting rid of Bo Jalonec's annoying comedy routines. But I also knew I was losing the company of a true pal who, despite his extraordinary propensity to speak perpetual bull, amounted to one remarkable friend I'll always remember.

Chapter 50
"Tinkermania"

By mid-September, Carnie and I were already bored with school academics. Tink was still talking about getting even with Phil Jackson for helping Popeye, Mullins, and Evans throw him into the quarry after the abbreviated fistfight between Quinn and Cummings. Unlike Bo Jalonec, Phil Jackson had not gone off to college. The talented high school athlete had suffered a minor mental breakdown toward the end of August. Phil's parents suggested that he start at *Notre Dame* the second semester to avoid the initial pressure of freshman academic accountability. The planned delay would give Jackson sufficient time to fully recover from his emotional depression, and to ease more gracefully into the sophisticated and demanding college scene.

A number of factors had contributed to Phil Jackson's "mental breakdown". The haughty quarterback had experienced several major setbacks that were damaging to his reputation, self-esteem, confidence, and ego. Phil had gotten suspended at Cardinal Reagan for being accused by Father Malcolm of being a co-conspirator with Popeye Messina in the infamous main corridor bowling ball episode. And having his white '55 Corvette convertible cemented by Tinker didn't help Phil's emotional health, either. And then there was the indignity of being identified by Malcolm as one of the felons who had stolen the six sacred trophies from the Cardinal Reagan display case. Adding to Jackson's plight, the missing band and sports awards were found several months later after the junior-senior prom inside the trunk of his dad's Lincoln. Smutty porn and marijuana were also discovered in the luxury auto's trunk, and finally, several Levittown and Bushkill police investigations into Jackson's biography caused the talented jock further loss of pride.

The Cardinal Reagan star quarterback felt compelled to retreat from a fight with Tinker and the other greasers at the June carnival, and everyone knew that Phil had been beaten-up fair and square by Tinker between the Feed Bag and the Dairy DeLite. After Mr. T and the Diablos had nearly decapitated Jackson by hoisting-up his body on a chair with his head protruding through roller coaster tracks, the petrified athlete was scared out of his wits. The Bushkill Pocono Mountain chase in the blue Caddy didn't help Jackson's fragmented nerves, either. One additional mid-September nightmare proved to be the straw that finally broke the dromedary's spinal cord.

Materialism was usually the solution to life's travails to Phil Jackson and his pompous, rich parents. After Phil's cherished 'Vette had been ruined by Tinker's "cement treatment", the rich kid's folks acquired a new expensive driving machine for *their* only doted-on offspring. The second Corvette was a virtual twin to the one that had been "tinkerized". Phil became very attached to the second sports car, as if it were the reincarnation of his beloved first vehicle.

The athlete had spent mid-September forgetting his plenteous problems. The distraught Cardinal Reagan graduate occupied himself on late summer afternoons navigating his speedboat on the Jersey side of the *Delaware*. The Notre Dame-bound quarterback had met some gorgeous chicks over in Burlington, and Phil arranged a triple date with two jock pals still in high school, offensive linemen Graham Meyers and Trent Dixon. The three rich kids took Phil's speedboat across the channel; docked at the girl's father's boat wharf, and then had a lavish picnic on a Jersey-side lawn overlooking the historic river.

It was a scorching hot Saturday, and feeling lonesome, Carnie had visited me at noon in the back room of Hal's Delicatessen. We played some two-handed poker to pass-away my lunch hour. My former close buddy and I were munching on some dill pickle spears when Tinker knocked on the deli's back screen door. If Quinn or Bo had been around, then nothing out of the ordinary would have ever happened. But Carnie and I were very vulnerable to Jeremy Foster's propensity for demented schemes and impulses, occurring during *their* absence.

"Hi, Tink. What's up?" I asked.

"Quick, you' junior jerk-offs. Come with me!" the unscrupulous villain demanded without providing any explanation.

Mystery and adventure had always intrigued Carnie and me, regardless of the source. We chewed and gulped-down the rest of our sour pickle spears and followed our lame amigo out the deli's back screen door.

"Let's take my Plymouth so that Carnie's Merc' avoids suspicion," Tink suggested without any further details.

"Dr. Destructo" took Haines Road east over the Edgely Railroad Bridge, and next headed south on River Drive along the tranquil *Delaware* in the direction of Bristol. Phil Jackson and Graham Meyers lived along that stretch in splendid mansions situated on beautifully landscaped properties. Tinker stopped his blue '49 in front of the Meyers' castle. "Carnie," Tink ordered. "I wants ya' to drive my Plymouth and follow me into Bristol after I get this here idle T-bird started."

"What for?" my neurotic pal asked.

"For revenge!" Tinker tersely replied. "Ask me any more fuckin' dumb questions and I'll rip your dick off!"

"What do ya' got against Graham Meyers?" I asked my mechanic colleague while covering-up for Carnie's inquisitive nature. "I think he's a pretty decent guy!"

"He's Jackson's scumbag friend, that's what!" Tinker ranted. "He's one of the asshole jocks that jumped my fanny between the Feed Bag and the Dairy DeLite!"

Tinker wasted little time in getting Graham Meyers' white '56 Thunderbird hot-wired and running. The insane loon drove the expensive sports car in reverse out of the wide asphalt driveway, and then Carnie and I (like a pair of programmed robots) trailed the maniac into Bristol in the less-than-mediocre blue Plymouth.

"What's he up to?" I asked.

"No good, that's for damned sure!" Carnie answered, shaking his puzzled head.

"Why we followin' him?" I asked the equall-perplexed driver.

"Because right or wrong, he's a Diablo," Carnie loyally returned. "And that happens to be even better and more important than bein' prison blood brothers, or college fraternity members at *Penn State.*"

Tinker led us down Radcliffe Street where we passed St. Mark School. A quick right hand turn had us within sight of one of Phil Jackson's dad's grocery stores. Tink flew into the parking lot at about thirty-miles an hour, and before Carnie and I could grasp his bizarre motivation, the craziest Diablo crashed Graham Meyers' white T-bird into the front of Phil Jackson's new white 'Vette. The fancy sports car sustained substantial damage, but Jackson's second Corvette had been totaled from the impact. At that moment, my conscience recalled a quote from Bo Jalonec that stuck inside my worried mind. "I'm goin' to college at *Penn State,* but Tinker's goin' directly to State Pen!"

"Mr. Break-it" leaped-out of the wrecked T-bird and quickly hopped into the passenger side of the blue Plymouth. Carnie peeled-out of the premises, heading toward Bath Road. In another four-minutes, we were hightailing it north on *Route 13,* and three-minutes later, we were at the back screen door of Hal's Delicatessen.

"Let's get out," commanded Tink. "And I wants ya' both to act like nothin' ever happened. Just pretend ya' both have bad cases of magnesia (amnesia)!"

My conscience was really bothering me. I was sick and tired of being a helpless accomplice to Tinker's obsession to destroy an enemy's property. I felt I had to take a strong stand. "I don't care if ya' beat the crap out of me or not," I obstinately balked. "But this crazy bull has got to stop!"

Carnie took a deep breath, awaiting Tinker's acerbic response to my strenuous objection. "Look, J.W.," Jeremy calmly warned. "Who said anything about beatin' ya' up? If ya' go against me, I won't waste my time merely kickin' your ass. I'll just fuckin' kill you. I won't *murder* ya', like you was a person. I'll simply kill ya' like you was a diseased animal. Is that absolutely clear now, *you* freakin' degenerate?"

Carnie opened the back screen door to Hal's Deli, and he and I entered the kitchen. Tinker jumped into his Plymouth and took-off as if nothing out of the ordinary had ever happened.

Twenty-five minutes later, Phil Jackson's enraged rich old man showed-up at the deli with two uniformed policemen. Fearing being interrogated, my legs were trembling and my knees were knocking together. Phil Jackson was a jock, and jocks would squeal on other kids, especially on hard luck middle-class greasers.

"My son told me about a kid called J.W. and his Levittown punk buddies," Mr. Jackson said to Hal Irving. "He thinks they're the ones that put cement inside his first Corvette."

The two police officers tried to be more objective and less indictive than Mr. Jackson had demonstrated. "Where have you two boys been the last hour or so?" the first patrolman asked, pointing directly to Carnie and me.

"Right here in the back room seriously playin' two-handed poker," Carnie lied, conveniently holding-up a deck of cards. "Care to join us?"

"I can vouch for these boys," Mr. Irving claimed, "because they've been back here the last hour just like they've said." My deli boss obviously valued loyalty over basic truth.

"Let me check that car out back," the second keeper of the peace insisted. We all stepped outside to witness the officer's cursory investigation. "Is that your black Mercury parked out back?"

"Yes, Officer," Carnie courteously verified.

We all listened and watched near the rear screen door as the police carefully checked Carnie's James Dean Special. Phil Jackson's livid, wealthy, snobbish father still appeared peeved at Carnie's deceptive confidence and at my convincing denial.

"The tires aren't hot, and the engine isn't warm," the first policeman observed and reported. Then, the curious cop pointed at me. "Son, do ya' have a car?"

"No," I politely answered, "because my dad won't let me get a driver's license."

"Sorry for the sudden inconvenience, Mr. Irving," the second cop apologized. "Mr. Jackson, I believe it was some other kids that wrecked those two sports' cars over in Bristol."

After the fair-minded cops and vindictive Mr. Jackson left the back parking lot, Hal Irving pulled Carnie and me aside. "Listen boys," my boss confidentially said. "I know you fellas' left the store for a half-hour because I stepped back into the kitchen to check on my soda bottle supply. And I know ya' two probably did something bad to Jackson's kid's car, but since I like you boys, and since Jackson is tryin' to control the whole food distribution in the area," my employer qualified, "I swore to our investigating visitors that you boys had been in the kitchen all along."

"Why do ya' dislike Mr. Jackson so much?" I asked Mr. Irving.

"Mr. Jackson and Sal Palermo are both swindlers in different ways," my exploited boss explained. "Their big difference is that Mr. Jackson does it legally."

Chapter 51
"The Pomeroy's Affair"

I couldn't believe that a whole week had passed by without any major conflicts with brawny jocks or with the ruthless Kamikazes. By late September, Carnie and I happened to be extremely bored with the strict regimentation of the Cardinal Reagan academic curriculum. And truthfully, I really missed Bo Jalonec and his idiotic ramblings. Mr. Merc' and I were discussing *that* ironic fact in the school cafeteria.

"J.W.," Carnie began his cynical criticism. "The next time ya' call Jokes up at *Penn State,* pretend that he's *Broadway,* and give the son-of-a-bitch my regards."

"Beau*regards?"* I asked and jested to my fellow classmate.

"Right, Dorkenheimer," Carnie nastily replied. "Why don't ya' get Stanley Tezeeker to find the square root of your dick using one of his freakin' logarithms or abstract slide-rules?"

"Leave Stanley alone," I insisted. "He's not a bad guy once ya' give him a chance to prove himself."

"Why the hell should I leave that jerk-off *a loan?"* Carnie joked and bristled. "I wouldn't even lend *you* a damned quarter I had stolen!"

Mr. C and I were sitting in the Feed Bag the last Saturday night in September, discussing everything from how Vice-President Richard M. Nixon had crucified Nikita S. Khrushchev in the famous kitchen debate at the American exhibit in Moscow, to the intense Jersey blueberry farm drag-race won by Quinn. Our contemporary discussion also rehashed Phil Jackson not attending *Notre Dame,* and then our wandering conversation reviewed the star athlete's tragic loss of his replacement Corvette.

"Forget Jackson," Carnie suggested, sounding apathetic, very much like Tinker. "Let's have a game of cowboy trivia."

"Okay, big shot," I consented. "Loser gets to take a twelve-hour bath with Tinker."

"You're just sayin' that shit because *he's* not here to tan your hide," Carnie noted. "Tink's often told me he wants to shove an oversized pineapple up your butt hole!"

"Ya' got several points accurate there," I agreed and joshed. "But it's too bad your points are on top of your rock-hard skull."

"All right, wise ass," Carnie quipped. "Who played Palladin in *Have Gun, Will Travel?"*

"Even the most stupid, retarded Kamikaze would know that one," I maintained. "Richard Boone. Which hotel in what city was featured on Palladin's calling card?"

"That's easier than landin' a cheap Hong Kong hooker," Carnie stated. "Hotel Carlton, San Francisco."

The TV cowboy contest went on for a good twenty-minutes until our brains had become scrambled into serious, dual mental meltdowns. We both knew about Hugh O'Brien as *Wyatt Earp,* Rory Calhoun as *The Texan,* Gene Barry as *Bat Masterson,* William Boyd as *Hopalong Cassidy,* and Will Hutchins as *Sugarfoot.* We finally realized that a draw was not only feasible, but also inevitable. Our discussion then focused on our stellar fellow Diablo, the missing Beauregard Jalonec.

"How does Jokes like it up at *Penn State?"* Carnie curiously asked about his missing gang nemesis.

"I was talkin' about it with him on the phone," I mentioned. "Jokes repeated his simpleton one-liner, stating that *Penn State* was better than the *state pen.*"

"What else did rgw bullshitter say?" Carnie demanded knowing.

"Jokes told me he had learned from one of his professors that the history books we've been studyin' are all wrong," I answered. "Bo said that George Washington and his troops had crossed the *Delaware River* twice and not once as reported in all the textbook accounts."

"Why twice?" Carnie inquired, showing more than a mild interest in my baffling comment.

"Because, according to Jokes, Washington wanted to double-cross the British and the Hessians at Trenton!" I explained with a wry smile.

"Speakin' of double-crossing," Carnie remarked, "I'm still smartin' from that time those two Italian dames double-crossed us at the Andalusia Drive-in. Got any brainy ideas?"

For several months, I had been feeling intellectually challenged and threatened by Stanley Tezeeker's mental prowess. The egghead had adapted and used his cerebral dynamics outside of traditional school academics, where the brainiac had given the Diablos several valuable ideas to implement against the Kamikazes. Since I was supposed to be "the brains" of the Diablos, I felt I had to come-up with something even better than Tezeeker's two brilliant past plans in order to satisfactorily preserve *my* gang image and reputation.

I determined that I had to respond to Carnie's oral challenge, since my reputation for creativity was at stake. My cerebrum pondered seriously for a moment, trying to invent an appropriate ruse. Immediately, Jokes' comic allusion to George Washington "double-crossing" the British came to mind.

After Quinn had convincingly vanquished Cummings in the second drag-race, Patty Van Arsdale and Susie Parker told me that the chicks would like to get in on the Diablos' dramatic excitement against the reprehensible Kamikazes. Quinn would have never gone for the idea under normal circumstances, but since Patty wanted in on the action, Dr. Q said to me one September night at the Feed Bag, "Okay, J.W., as long as no one gets injured or killed. I can have it both ways; Patty *and* the Diablos."

All I had to do was persuade Bo of the merits of my plan, and Susie and Patty would automatically take care of the rest. Bo's special woman agreed to participate in my creative scheme, when I encountered her outside the Dairy DeLite. Susie confided that Quinn and Cummings' two drag-races were the two most thrilling events of her sheltered, all-too-perfect life. Bo gave his immediate telephone approval to my idea involving Susie and Patty, which was actually a blatant plagiarism of what Angie Palermo and Bubbles Messina had done to Carnie and me at the drive-in movies.

My strategy began with a telephone conversation initiated by Susie from the Dairy DeLite booth. The call was directed to Popeye Messina.

"Hello, is Bruno there?" Susie inquired, possessing a very sexy phone voice, featuring a very impressive demeanor.

"Speakin'. Who's this?" Popeye inquired.

"My name is Susie Parker. I used to date one of the Diablos, you know, that jerk in the green and cream '57 Chevy."

"The *Penn State* creep?" At least Bruno knew the identity of *one* of his principal enemies.

"Yeah, him. We broke-up about a week ago," Susie prevaricated in a feigned, depressed tone.

"Wow! Now I know who you are!" Popeye realized and exclaimed. "You're that vivacious blonde broad with the terrific ponytail. How ya' doin', Gorgeous?"

"Just great!" Susie answered in a deliberately-stated heightened tone of voice. "Bruno, I want ya' to know that I quiver whenever I think of your huge biceps."

"Yeah," Popeye agreed. "And they're really my pride and joy."

"And Bruno, I want you to know that my panties get real moist whenever I think about how big and strong you must be in all the right places," Susie exaggerated, contrary to her normal shy, lady-like personality.

"Er, thanks Doll," Popeye acknowledged in response to the unsolicited flattery. "Most girls are afraid to show their appreciation of my strength and power. You must need a new beau!"

"Very funny!" Bo's true girlfriend replied. "But I wanna' tell ya' I'm really horny and lonely. How would ya' like to take me out on a special date?"

Popeye seemed stunned at being propositioned by beautiful and exotic Susie Parker. "Er, tremendous. Where to? When should we meet?" the special K nervously stammered while nearly inhaling the phone's receiver.

The pretty blonde then told Popeye that she had a close girlfriend named Patty Van Arsdale who was disgusted with Quinn, and who was dying to meet Jake Mullins. Bo's gal convincingly explained that Quinn had recently dumped Patty, and Susie wanted to arrange a double-date with two Kamikazes to make Bo and Quinn jealous. Bruno quickly agreed to Susie's romantic request, and then Bo's true girl suggested that the four romantics should meet at the indented area midway up the dirt trail that paralleled the Delaware Canal between Haines Road and the Levittown Shop-A-Rama.

"See ya' about eight-thirty, just after dark," Susie promised with a sexy voice. "And don't forget to bring Jake along, or my girlfriend Patty will be very disappointed. Ya' got your rear in gear?"

Bruno Messina couldn't believe what his magical ears were hearing. "We'll split up into two cars after Jake and me get there, right?" Popeye proposed.

Susie was anxious to bring quick closure to the distasteful, unconventional conversation. "Exactly. Then, we could rock and roll like there's no tomorrow. I wanna' see your face at that place."

"Sure thing, Hon," Popeye stated. "See ya' then, Sweets." Click.

Susie Parker and Patty Van Arsdale had set-up Popeye Messina and Jake Mullins just like Angie and Bubbles had double-crossed Carnie and me at the drive-in movies. It was a good thing that Popeye's blood had drained from his cerebrum to some other part of his anatomy, because under normal thinking conditions, the suspicious K would have recognized that my plan was merely a Kamikaze ruse in reverse. When that late September Friday night arrived, all facets of the Diablos' strategic military operation were carried-out to perfection.

Right after Popeye and Jake Mullins arrived at the prescribed Delaware Canal location in a borrowed red and cream '56 Chevy, the bruisers met-up with Susie and Patty, and the Kamikazes were as civil and convivial as could be. As soon as everyone introduced became acquainted, the four daters split-up into pairs. Susie and Popeye walked to her powder blue and white '55 Crown Victoria, and Patty and Jake strolled holding hands to the red and cream Chevy.

As soon as the couples reached their respective cars, twenty Diablos leaped-out of the brush in what constituted a most magnificent ambush. We overpowered and wrestled the astonished Kamikazes to the ground, and then Tinker employed two sets of pilfered police handcuffs to further subdue our feisty foes. I didn't think Popeye was too fond of my very effective, reverse double-cross scheme.

"Ya' dirty mother-fuckers!" Messina futilely shouted. "I shoulda' smelled a dirty rat in the woodpile!"

"Ya' was just smellin' your own lousy asshole!" Tinker insisted.

"Haven't you guys done enough fucked-up mischief already?" Mullins pleaded. "It's about time you Dogwood dregs said 'Bye-bye' to Byberry!"

"Forget the 'Philly insane asylum! This trick is payback time for the Andalusia Drive-in kidnappin'!" Carnie yelled.

"And the boccie ball sand burials!" Tinker added his footnote.

The Diablos tied each hostage's legs and feet together; shoved used snot-filled handkerchiefs into their mouths, and then threw our two captives into Susie's Ford's trunk to be immediately transported to a prescribed destination.

Quinn was at the canal but refused to get involved in the brief scuffle, saying that gang leaders only fought gang leaders. Since Cummings was not present, Quinn was only a spectator and a passive accomplice to the glorious prank.

Within three-minutes, a commando team of six Diablos was heading north in Susie's Crown Victoria (on the dirt road in the direction of the Levittown Shop-A-Rama) to initiate "Phase Two" of our dynamic canard.

Quinn drove the impeccable '55 Ford, with his destination being *Pomeroy's Department Store*. With no police cars in sight, Tinker got out; limped-over to the store's service entrance, and deftly picked the lock. Then. he, Robbie, Carnie, Ace and I dragged Popeye and Mullins inside the closed-for-business department store.

Tinker had brought along Perfume and Cologne to accompany handcuffed and gagged Popeye and Mullins inside Susie's formerly pristine trunk. Robbie and Carnie ran-inside to the first-floor and moved a huge soda machine in front of the elevator doors. The trespassing pranksters would soon repeat the pattern on the second-floor with another similar vending machine, so that when the elevator's doors would open, a passenger exit would be impossible.

Tinker then handcuffed Popeye's left wrist to Mullins' right wrist. Next the two were turned back-to-back, and the process was repeated with the opposite hands. Then, the Kamikazes' legs were again tied together, so that the hostages would have to hop in coordination back-to-back in order to jointly maneuver anywhere. Tinker intentionally released his treasured skunks Perfume and Cologne into the elevator enclosure, as Popeye and Mullins shrieked muffled expletives through their already-used mouth gags.

Standing at the elevator's door, Tink quickly hit the "close" button and jumped-out from the shutting doors' jaws. We next moved a third large vending machine to adequately block the basement elevator exit. Popeye could manage to get the elevator's doors to open by pressing his nose against the correct control button, but his bold effort would be frustrated when his eyes would see the massive soda machine obstacle obstructing his path. The same pattern would be repeated on the first and second floors of the eerily quiet department store.

Pomeroy's night security guard was a friend of Tinker's, who owed the Diablo a favor for towing his car out of a ditch. As long as it was only an elementary gang prank, and as long as there would be no insurance liability claim, the jovial guard played along with *my* plan.

The following morning, the cooperating security guard told store management that he had discovered the Kenwood "nitwits" in the elevator with two skunks at about four in the morning, and that *they* were probably involved in enforcing the "Kamikaze gang's initiation rites. The store's executives didn't want any negative newspaper publicity, so the managers logically declined pressing charges, as long as no store property had been damaged.

When I called Jokes over at *Penn State* about the scam's excellent success, Bo was quite ecstatic. "How did Susie and Patty do?"

"Terrific," I revealed. "And the chicks were even more deceiving than Angie and Bubbles had been at the drive-in."

"I'm glad ya' used the elevators," Bo cryptically declared. "That must've been an uplifting experience for Popeye and Mullins." There was a second's pause in Jalonec's standard delivery. "And J.W., the Kamikazes have every right to raise a big stink after Tinker used his two pet skunks inside the elevator."

I detected a trace of disappointment in Bo's tenor for not being in Levittown to participate in the adventurous *Pomeroy's* caper. My ears detected that B.J. really wished he had been part of the thrilling action. "Jokes, the skunks really were sensational," I added, "because Susie and Patty couldn't have freaked Popeye and Jake out more if the animals were hissin' cobras instead."

"Then, the prank shoulda' happened at Snake Road and not at *Pomeroy's*," Bo humorously declared.

I could tell by the inflection of Jalonec's voice that he was a trifle jealous that I could function within the gang fairly-well without his benevolent guidance.

"Where did Tinker get the skunks?" Bo asked.

"In the woods, near the Ole' Factory. Tink skillfully trapped them," I specifically stated.

"What Old Factory?" Bo asked in a puzzled tone.

"The Ole' Factory," I reiterated. "You're now a big-shot college guy. Look-up the definition in a good dictionary." Click.

Fifteen-minutes went by. I waited patiently by the family phone for Jalonec to complete his academic research. Bo had to locate either a dictionary or encyclopedia; analyze the topic, and then call me back to tell me the result of his vocabulary expedition. B.J. might even have to consult the glossary of a biology reference book for verification. The phone rang, and I told my parents I was expecting a return call from Bo at *Penn State*. My folks smiled, being glad that I was still associating with a high-caliber college student.

"Hey Words," Bo began. "Olfactory means 'sense of smell". That's pretty good! Hey J.W., Carnie called earlier and told me ya' got a little bush last night."

I instinctively sensed that Bo had to have the last word as he usually did whenever someone tried rivaling his phenomenal cleverness. "Jokes, what the heck are ya' talkin' about?"

"I heard that it was Angie's birthday, and you took advantage of the opportunity and bought her a small azalea!" Click.

Bo Jalonec often was annoyingly relentless. Five-minutes later, the phone again rang. My mind was still eddying from the ridiculous azalea comment. Jokes called to tell me about a recurring dream he was having. A *Civil War* Union officer was in love with a young southern girl, who looked just like Susie Parker, but her name wasn't Susie Parker.

"J.W., guess what her name was in the dream?"

"Gee, I don't know. How about Anita Truce?" I answered. I braced myself before Jalonec delivered his cute-but-stunning reply.

"No, Wick-dick! The friggin' girl's full name was Frieda Slaves!" Click.

I was a little perturbed at Bo, who would often say anything to anybody just to make a stupid joke without any consideration of its repercussions or impact. Sometimes, the joker had little regard for his audience's sensitivities. The mirthful guy would have even presented the "slavery joke" to Marcus "Hershey" Spellman, and Sugar Ray probably would have wildly laughed aloud, simply because the punch line had been delivered by inimitable Bo Jalonec.

Chapter 52
"Carnie's Blarney"

The first October Sunday of '59, I wanted to go to the Levittown Towne Theater to see Sandra Dee and John Saxon in *The Restless Years,* but Carnie and Tinker preferred driving over to the Langhorne Speedway to see a boring hundred-mile stock-car race. As usual, I was in the minority and outvoted two to one.

The stock-car race was a little more exciting than the previous motorcycle contest we had seen at the speedway earlier in '59. While my non-illuminating greaser companions were analyzing in detail the monotonous laps, my active mind again pondered "Langhorne", which steered me to thinking about Samuel Langhorne Clemens.

I was still reading Mark Twain's novel *The Prince and the Pauper*. In the book, a sixteenth-century prince, Edward VI, traded places with a poor look-alike lad, Tom Canty. I thought about the story's main plot while Carnie and Tinker were enthralled and enamored with the grueling stock-car race. If the jocks or the Kamikazes were to do something drastic to the Diablos, I wanted to be ready with a good counter-measure scheme borrowed from some literature plot. I figured I would soon have a well-conceived strategy if Quinn were to instantly demand one to be implemented.

After the stock-car race, Carnie, as usual, said that he was hungry and immediately invoked the privilege known as "driver's choice". We discussed the possibility of the Carousel Grille, but then we decided to avoid the dangerous place with the crazy Arab chef along with the vicious Libyan waitress.

"I don't want to be decapitated by some loony Muslim who happens to hate cool greasers," Tinker complained. "When I'm old and ready to die, we'll go back to that dump!"

"Let's go to some place safe and familiar, like the Feed Bag," I suggested.

"Look guys, I'm drivin'!" Carnie stated while tyrannically pulling rank. "And that means we're goin' to that new Palace Diner over in Trevose."

Like most of Carnie's twisted ideas, this new one also proved to be a colossal mistake. The three of us entered the respectable restaurant without incident. After a beautiful red-haired hostess showed us to our booth, we sat-down and scanned our extensive menus. Carnie initiated a Levittown current events' conversation.

"Ya' know, J.W. If Tink keeps up his rampage, the only Levittown greasers that are gonna' have cars to drive around are the Diablos."

I was the only one seated at our booth who had any misgivings about the recent mass destruction of Kamikaze, jock, and cop automobiles. I remained laconic, hoping that the flow of chatter would take another more fortuitous course.

"If it weren't for me," Tinker arrogantly and redundantly boasted, "the Ks would've easily won the greaser war against the Ds six months ago." Jeremy was determined to keep repeating that statement until there was evidence that someone had heard it.

"Yeah, Tink," Carnie acknowledged. "But how did ya' manage not getting hurt when ya' crashed Graham Meyers's T-bird into Phil Jackson's new 'Vette over in Bristol?"

"All I did was pretend I was drunk," Jeremy F. replied before snickering. "Alcoholics hardly ever get hurt in car accidents. Their reflexes are too goddamned slow, so the drunks get blasted around the upholstery like an eight ball on a pool table hittin' off the side cushions. Boozers never get a shittin' scratch!"

Tink was sincere in his explanation, even though his logic was more than a trifle warped. I wanted to talk about television shows or sports, instead of hearing Foster bragging about his tremendous success at destruction and violence.

"I heard that Jackson screamed like a wounded warthog when the jock found-out the bad news about his second 'Vette," Carnie added, while indirectly praising his new idol. "He must be a *vet* at losin' his 'Vette," Mr. C said in a lackluster imitation of the missing Mr. J.

I still was a listener and not a contributor to the inferior conversation. I actually felt some compassion toward Jackson's loss, but my fear of Tinker, peer pressure, and loyalty to the Diablos made me hide my empathy.

"Yeah, and after his second 'Vette was mysteriously cracked-up," Tinker continued boasting, "I heard Jackson cracked-up, too! The jerk snapped like a friggin' weak twig!"

Our Palace Diner waitress approached our booth, so I figured I would be the first to order something. My mind was a little confused and my common sense altered to a degree. I committed a grave error in judgment when I tried being cute with the busy, veteran, red-haired, big-breasted woman.

"Give me a 'roast beast' sandwich," I snidely ordered. "And while you're at it, I'll have a Michigan to drink," I related as I casually implemented a familiar Bo Jalonec word pattern.

"Pray tell, what is a Michigan?" the hefty, middle-age waitress curiously inquired.

"Well then, I equivocated, "if ya' don't have a Michigan, then give me a *mini-soda,* and please make it a *Pepsi.*"

Naturally, when the other two clowns heard me quote a special Bo Jalonec restaurant order, like brainless chimpanzees, the mimickers had to imitate Jokes, too. The inherent difficulty was that Bo was absent, and the other two Diablos in my company encountered negative consequences whenever those incompetent knuckleheads attempted to mimic *his* stellar vernacular.

If Bo or Quinn were present that afternoon at the Palace Diner in Trevose, the worst-case scenario would have been Carnie receiving a swift knee to the testicles from the no-nonsense waitress. The punishment would have been similar to the inflicted pain Merc' Man had encountered inside the *Route 130* Diner over in Jersey, and then *he* would talk like a soprano for five-minutes, before we could finally eat our meals in peace. Carnie's contrived macho demeanor was about to put the three of us in serious physical jeopardy.

"Do ya' have chicken breasts?" Carnie asked the tough-looking, experienced waitress. I could tell that my impulsive pal was up to no good, and so could she. The middle-aged wench grimaced when her ears heard Carnie's asinine remark.

"What did you say?" the confrontational, stocky hussy asked.

"I asked ya' plain and simple if ya' had chicken breasts?" Carnie brazenly reiterated.

Apparently, the waitress had been experienced at handling rude greaser patrons. "No, I don't have chicken breasts. I happen to have dinosaur tits," the angry lady caustically answered. "Can't you tell by my huge D cups?"

"How do ya' know that's what Carnie meant!" Tinker interrupted in defense of his fellow idiot. "Is your daddy Dick Holmes, or is he Sherlock Tracy?"

Before the aggravated diner employee could reply to Tinker's impertinence, Carnie double-teamed her. "How come you middle-aged waitresses all act like you're livin' in the damned *Middle Ages!"*

"Look, you puny, dirtball Levittown greasers," the insulted waitress replied in an accusative tone of voice. "I've read plenty in the papers about you uncouth slobs! And I wish I had read about you on the obituary page, instead!" The irate waitress's outburst had then gotten the attention of the other Palace Diner clientele.

"Well, Lady," Carnie persisted in pursuing his immaturity. "If ya' don't have chicken breasts, then maybe ya' got elephant thighs! Have ya' ever sung solo at the end of one of those German operas? Do ya' ever wear Viking horns on your big fat head?"

"Why don't you horny little faggots go somewhere else!" the chagrined waitress insisted. "You can start by visiting Hell's volcanic basement!"

“Ya’ know, Lady,” Carnie idiotically proceeded. “Ya’ should move to Holland. They have a lot of *dikes* over there, and ya’ would fit in perfectly. I pity the poor little Dutch boy who has to put his finger in *you* to plug-up your tremendous hole!”

“Now come on guys, cool it!” I unsuccessfully implored. “We’re just here to eat and not to argue!”

“Okay, J.W., I’ll simmer down!” Carnie falsely agreed. “Lady, *les be in* a better frame of mind. Then, we could really be close friends, all right! What do ya’ say?”

“Look, Creep!” the waitress indignantly shouted. “I dare you to stand up straight! Then, I’ll show you how the spicers officially squeeze nutmeg!”

“No thanks, you’ woolly mastodon,” Carnie responded. “I think I already know how the spicers do that!”

“Bernice, Gladys!” the red-hair, corpulent server loudly yelled. “I have another group of punk greaser wiseasses. Code two-drill! I repeat, Code two!”

Before one could say “condiment” three times, two other enormous Amazons charged-out of the diner’s kitchen doors, carrying squeeze containers of ketchup, relish, and mustard. And before I could claim my innocence and my independence from Carnie and Tinker, the three nasty beasts were squirting multi-colored fluids into our shocked faces, and all over our hair and scalps.

Our original, savage waitress/wildebeest was the first one to speak-out during the unanticipated assault. “Well, you scummy Levittown Lice. I have to *catch-up* on some unfinished business!” the old hag screamed as she unmercifully half-emptied her container.

“Relish this, you pathetic Dingle-berries!” the second water buffalo hollered.

“This yellow liquid matches the color of your putrid guts!” the third crazed tigress shouted as the sicko mustered-up the right words.

It seemed that the bizarre diner adventure was a complete disaster, and that the same thorough disaster was also an unprecedented life-or-death adventure. Somehow, the assaulted victims managed to rise to our feet during all the commotion, and as the three of us fled through the front doors to the safety of the Palace Diner parking lot, Tinker turned and yelled, “Ya’ three pachyderms oughta’ come to my auto repair shop. You hippos could use a little bodywork, because no guy in his right mind would want to lube any of ya’!”

The three enraged, middle-aged, immense females chased us all the way to Carnie’s car, where we quickly entered and locked the doors. The frantic female dragons were wildly spraying their condiments onto the windows and windshield, as my neurotic pal turned on his faithful ignition; hit the gas pedal, and squealed-out of the diner's crowded parking lot. Around thirty customers had left their seats and rushed outside to cheer the three hideous waitresses, who had forced us to evacuate the premises in defeat and dishonor.

That night I telephoned Bo up at *Penn State,* who lustily laughed when I described *our* hasty but very necessary retreat from the Palace Diner gladiator arena.

"Words, that's a really outrageous story," Bo merrily admitted and commended. "I guess the three ugly beasts of burden didn't want to get kinky with you three horny little perverts. You're lucky that the incensed witches didn't make you swallow and choke on incense!"

"Guess you're right on that count," I guiltily acceded.

"I'll have to go and check-out that diner over in Trevose when I get back to Levittown," Bo casually jested. "I'll bet they serve a great 'condimental' breakfast!"

At the start of October, I thought that the major craziness between the Diablos, Kamikazes, and jocks was finally over. Several unforgettable incidents occurred later that month. Those outstanding events were indeed the most memorable of all the Diablos' '50s adventures and misadventures.

Chapter 53
"Tragedy"

On the evening of October 6th, Carnie, Tinker, and I attended Quinn's New Jersey Court appearance. Quinn and Cummings were chastised by the presiding Hamilton Township judge for trespassing onto the blueberry farm, for reckless driving, and for endangering human life.

On the positive side of his analysis, the judge commended the Diablos and the Kamikazes for "valuing life over property and self" in our heroic rescues of Cummings and the New Jersey State Trooper. We were also praised for not fleeing the scene of near-tragedy, and the magistrate spoke very favorably on how we had administered first aid to the unconscious victims, until trained paramedics arrived in their ambulances to take the injured drivers to Atlantic City Hospital.

Quinn and Cummings received fifty-dollar fines for reckless driving on private property, and the speeders each had to pay one-hundred-dollars in additional fees for the other charges presented by the township's prosecutor. Langford had also driven to the Hamilton Township courthouse, and incredibly, the Renegades volunteered to chip in fifty-dollars to help defray the total court expenses.

On the way back to Levittown in Carnie's Merc', I asked Jeremy a personal question. "Tink, are ya' still thinkin' about challengin' Quinn for leadership of the Diablos?"

"Not right now, J.W. I gotta' admit, Quinn did alright at the quarry fight, and also in the blueberry farm drag-race. I also liked the way Mr. Q supervised the cool raid that put handcuffed Popeye and Mullins into the *Pomeroy's* elevator."

I was glad to hear that Mr. T had pulled-in his horns. Quinn was a true leader who would only fight as a last resort. Tinker liked to fight simply for the sake of mauling and hurting another human being. But Quinn was probably aware of Tink's below-the-surface conspiracy, because Mr. Q suddenly became more active in the struggle for dominance between the Ds and the Ks.

Meanwhile, Phil Jackson had really gone off the deep end, authoring a suicide note, despite his rich parents' overindulgence and pampering. Jackson mysteriously disappeared out of Bucks County civilization, and his hasty departure made big headlines in area papers. Phil's parents offered a generous ten-thousand-dollar reward for information leading to the whereabouts of their bewildered and confused son.

Tinker's destruction of the second 'Vette had caused the athlete to cross the bridge between acting crazy and being crazy. It worried and distressed me that Tinker never knew when enough was enough. The human demon believed that if the psychopath destroyed most of an enemy's property, then the chosen adversary would eventually destroy himself.

I had to return my overdue copy of Mark Twain's *The Prince and the Pauper* to the Levittown Library. Carnie showed-up the next morning to drive me to that peaceful destination, but I was not-too-thrilled when Tinker also appeared as a tag-along at my side door.

On the way to the library, Carnie discussed how his alert ears had heard at the Feed Bag about Phil Jackson "needin' a straight-jacket". The cunning driver then reminded me that I had promised to divulge my Diablos' strategy involving the main plot to the Mark Twain novel I had just finished reading.

"You'd better keep your' fuckin' promise to Carnie," Tinker threatened, snapping-open his switchblade and holding the point an inch from my throat. "I haven't killed anybody yet this month!"

"Tink, if the Diablos don't learn to live in peace, pretty soon we're gonna' rest in peace. Put the damned knife away! If we hit a bump or a pothole, you'll accidentally slit my throat!"

"Don't worry, J.W. I'll make ya' suffer plenty before I finally decide to kill ya, but it won't be by goddamned accident!"

"I'm no longer afraid of you, and I'm not afraid to die!" I loudly and foolishly answered in a moment of fake courage, without ever daring to move my neck a mere centimeter.

Carnie was amused by our friction-oriented exchange of words. I couldn't believe that my two companions were so callous and cruel. Neither felt any guilt or remorse at causing Phil Jackson to go completely bonkers. It was as if Tinker and Carnie were animals, devoid of consciences, values, hearts, and souls.

Carnie's Merc' entered the library's parking lot from the Mill Creek Parkway side. As I got out, Tinker had something didactical to say.

"J.W., are ya' afraid to die?" the psycho weirdly asked. "Tell me the goddamned truth!"

"Yes!" I replied without thinking twice.

"Well, the only ones afraid of dyin' are those fucked-up assholes that are afraid of livin'. It's better to have a short excitin' life than live a long borin' one. J.W., your new plan against the Ks better involve death, or you're gonna' visit the fucked-up Grim Reaper before the dreaded death stalker ever thinks about visitin' you!"

I exited the Mercury and worriedly entered the library, wishing that my family had never moved from Hammonton to Dogwood Hollow. Under self-imposed duress, I quickly paid the library clerk my fifty-cent fine and returned my borrowed Mark Twain novel. I returned to Carnie's automobile, and under extreme peer pressure, divulged to my two comrades my inspired "double prince caper". Being impressed with my vivid description, Carnie and Tinker endorsed my creative idea right away. "J.W.," Tinker blandly mentioned. "I'll let ya' live for now, ya' wimpy bastard, until ya' have to come-up with another even better scheme."

Quinn had again broken-up with Patty Van Arsdale, so I was not too surprised when our fearless leader fully endorsed my "double switching" plan inside the Feed Bag, "As long as no one gets hurt or killed". Bo Jalonec was returning home for the *Columbus Day* weekend, so over the phone, I invited Jokes to collaborate on the Diablos' new project. Susie Parker was anxious to collaborate and get active in another exciting Diablos' adventure. The knockout blonde promised Jalonec she would enlist the assistance of Patty Van Arsdale in order to patch-up things again between Quinn and his pretty lady friend.

On Saturday night, Dr. Q and Mr. Bo entered the Feed Bag with a wrinkled copy of the *Levittown Times*. The two instigators approached Cummings, Popeye Messina, Dave Evans, Spits, and Worm, who were all seated next to the pinball machines on the Hal's Delicatessen side of the teen hangout.

Carnie, Tinker, Robbie, and I stepped over to the Kamikaze side of the restaurant to give our leader and his lieutenant moral support. Quinn brought attention to the front-page article about Phil Jackson's suicide note, just like Cummings had brought to my interest the *Life Magazine* story about happy-go-lucky college students (like Bo Jalonec) piling themselves into telephone booths.

"Check-out these headlines," Quinn indicated to his chief rival. "Phil Jackson's disappeared out of sight!"

"We know all about it," Cummings muttered. "That's old news."

Quinn and Jalonec had fully expected the Ks to react in *that* predictable, nonchalant manner. The gang officers knew that a big sum of money might stimulate Cummings' curiosity.

"There's a ten-thousand-dollar reward for any information," Quinn positively stated. "We're talkin' big bucks here!"

The Kamikazes still tried acting stoical about the dismal local news. Our adversaries didn't want the Diablos to think that a rival gang could get any emotional reaction from the "cool" Kenwood thugs.

"Ya' goons ain't tellin' us anything new," Worm opined. "And the money factor has even been on 'Philly TV news several times."

"One of our Dogwood guys, playing detective, found Jackson," Bo matter-of-factly declared. "Phil's dead. Been stone-cold-dead for maybe a day or so."

"Is that so? Who found him?" asked Popeye Messina, who was the only Kamikaze who cared anything at all about Phil Jackson's welfare.

The bait had been set. It was time for our Diablos' leader to give the opposing gang the hook. Carnie, Robbie, Bo, Quinn, and I only wanted to entice the Ks with a little tantalizing taste of reward money.

"That's not important," Quinn continued. "But we're willin' to split the reward money fifty-fifty with the Kamikazes. All the Ks havta' do is come-out to Croydon with us to claim the body."

Naturally, the other gang was skeptical of our motives. "After what you' dipshit creeps did to Popeye and Jake inside *Pomeroy's,"* Cummings angrily maintained, "I can't trust any of ya' as far as I can throw an adult male elephant!" I noticed that the "King K" still had a band-aid on his forehead from his blueberry-farm ditch accident.

"That's right," Popeye injected into the conference. "Why the hell should we believe you jerks? Why wouldn't ya' punks just keep the ten-grand for yourselves?"

Bo had a rational explanation that remarkably got through to the hostile Ks. "Because we wanna' bury the hatchet. We wanna' stop the craziness before someone else gets killed besides Jackson," Jalonec persuasively answered.

Quinn nodded his head convincingly. I knew that our boss simply wanted to have a little more fun toying with the Kenwood gang; get Patty back; show Tinker that *he* was still the Ds' "head honcho", and in the end, enhance the reputation of the Dogwood Hollow dudes. "That's right!" Quinn readily agreed. "We wanna' have a truce. After you were almost killed at the blueberry farm," my hero explained to Cummings, "we figured things had to stop. The best way would be a dual expedition between the Ds and the Ks. We get five G's. You get five *thou'*. Everyone's happy with five *grand* each. There's then peace in the valley."

"What could we lose boys? Let's give it a try," Cummings suggested to his suddenly interested subordinates.

Bo Jalonec drove his Chevy with Quinn, Robbie, Carnie, Tink, and me as his reliable bodyguards. The green and cream '57 led the way out of the Feed Bag parking lot. Worm drove his father's '58 blue and white Edsel, and Cummings, Popeye, Evans, Mullins, and Spits were his fearsome passengers.

The Kamikazes entourage followed Bo south on *Route 13* to Croydon, where we traveled a main county highway, and then motored on three separate country roads until we arrived at a dark farm trail. We stopped and got-out of our vehicles, and continued the expedition on foot until we approached a forest. Then, we paused our advance and waited for further directions from Bo and Quinn.

The sky was pitch black on that overcast Indian summer night. Hardly any stars or constellations were visible. The only discernible sounds were the hooting of an owl in a remote tree, and the croaking of frogs in a distant creek.

"If frogs are always croakin'," Bo speculated and commented, "you'd think they'd all be damned dead by now!"

"Get serious for a change," Quinn effectively reprimanded his second-in-command. "Not even that owl up there gives a hoot about *your* stupid verbal bull-crap!"

Cummings and Popeye smiled in reaction to Quinn's compelling admonishment of Bo. The reprimand coincidentally added credibility to Quinn's story about Phil Jackson's body.

Tinker and Robbie flicked on flashlights, and Cummings and Jake Mullins followed suit. Every breath taken was very discernible to the assembled greasers, all standing in a circle. Quinn told his audience that Phil Jackson's corpse would be found about three-hundred-feet down the dirt trail, lying inside a wooded area.

"How did your friend find the body way out here?" Popeye skeptically asked Quinn without using a curse word. Messina was indeed the only K more concerned about Phil Jackson than in gaining *his* share of the reward money.

"One of our guys dates a girl from Croydon," Quinn attested. "The couple always neck up here near her uncle's bungalow. They went into the woods with their blanket and then accidentally discovered Jackson's body."

"How did Jackson get here?" Evans asked as we entered the trail leading into the secluded woods.

"Don't rightly know," Quinn said without much eloquence. "But we think he was murdered. The motive was probably robbery. The rich kid's wallet is missin'."

The contingent of greasers rounded a bend, and the four flashlights fell upon a motionless human form, lying between clustered briers and ferns. Everyone gasped and then gulped. It was a rather macabre, gruesome sight.

Quinn stooped-down, put his fingers to Phil's neck, and held the limp right wrist with his left hand. Then, the chief Diablo removed his small mirror from his black leather jacket. Our leader held the image reflector up to Phil Jackson's nostrils for a full-thirty-seconds, but no steam appeared upon the surface. With a grim expression on his face, Quinn pronounced Phil Jackson dead. Everyone stared-down at the stiff form in total disbelief, as the four flashlights still beamed on the limp body.

"That bloodstain from his scalp down to his chin is prob'ly from a bullet wound," Quinn observed and articulated. "I don't want anybody touchin' it because of fingerprints."

"I hate the thought of death, but I'm fuckin' glad it's not me. Who do ya' suppose did it?" Worm asked.

"Don't rightly know," Quinn responded. "That's a job for the cops to decide. Cummings and me will report our finding to the local fuzz. All you other guys stick by the edge of the woods until we return. Make sure no one enters this dirt trail."

All of us began walking back towards the green and cream Chevy and the blue and white Edsel. We trekked a hundred or so feet down the dirt trail when we heard a horrendous scream that sent chills shooting up and down our spines. Tinker and Robbie beamed their flashlights to the right, and there stood Phil Jackson, or Phil Jackson's ghost, hissing and snarling at our intrusion.

The two Diablos then turned their flashlights back to where the body had been lying, but it was no longer there. The ghastly specter to our immediate right then raised its morbid hands above its haunting head. Crimson was seeping down from its scalp and forehead, and the horrible apparition gave forth a most hideous howl as the anomaly slowly advanced in our direction with outstretched palms.

All of the Diablos let-out boisterous screams, and the Kamikazes followed our emotional example. The greasers made mad dashes to our respective cars; leaped into the vehicles as if our very lives depended on it, and the two autos skidded very hectically out of there. No one wanted any further contact with the supernatural.

That is what the Kamikazes thought had occurred, but this is what the Diablos knew what had actually happened. Al Keller, the newest kid in Dogwood Hollow, looked a little like and was built similarly to Phil Jackson. Al had a cousin in Croydon named Rick Amos, who could have passed for Jackson's twin brother. Jokes, Susie, Patty, and Lori Amos (Rick's sister) served on the Diablos' makeup committee. The four artists had applied cosmetics to Al and to Rick, making the twin impostors appear like bloodstained cadavers, ready for coroner autopsies.

Using my "Mark Twain double prince" identity-switching method, Al Keller was the Phil Jackson temporarily lying dead on the ground, and Rick Amos was the Phil Jackson who acted as the aggressive zombie. Before the entourage of visiting greasers had sprinted back to their cars, Al stood-up off the ground and then hid in a thicket of bushes and trees. When Tinker and Robbie beamed their' flashlights to where the original body had formerly been lying, Rick had already staggered-out of the woods to haunt and scare the unsuspecting Kamikazes.

Instead of switching one prince for one pauper, the Diablos had surreptitiously substituted two ghouls for one missing Phil Jackson. And I owed the entire ruse all to Mark Twain's incomparable genius.

The vehicle holding the panic-stricken Kamikazes fishtailed east toward *Route 13*. The blue and white Edsel could be heard screeching around sharp curves, almost a full half-mile ahead.

The Diablos laughed rather hardily at the pathetic state of our bitter rivals, who were convinced that we were equally as intimidated by Phil Jackson's supernatural ghost as the Ks were. As Bo drove his Chevy within the forty-mile per hour speed limit, we giddily conversed about the success of our most recent imaginative prank. Even Quinn was mirthful about "the K' con", as the '57 Chevy slowly followed the escape route of the speeding '58 Edsel.

"Words," Quinn congratulated me with a smile. "Ya' sure come-up with some dandy ideas."

"Tremendous cosmetic work, Jokes!" I wholeheartedly praised. "Tell Susie, Patty, and Lori Amos the beauticians did a great job on Al and Rick!"

"Now that the four of us used plenty of makeup on Al and Rick, I think it's time for Quinn and Patty to officially *make-up,"* Bo joked.

We six occupants inside the '57 Chevy were immensely enjoying our new-found camaraderie. The six of us felt proud that we had decisively outsmarted the barbarian Kenwood clan.

"All for one," Carnie began.

"One for all!" the remainder of the BelAir's merry occupants enthusiastically chanted and laughed.

Quinn then brought to our attention several distant flares appearing ahead on the road. Jalonec slowed-down, and as we cautiously advanced toward the warning lights, everyone immediately recognized that a terrible auto mishap had occurred at a very dangerous intersection.

"It's Worm's car!" Quinn exclaimed.

The '58 Edsel had run a stop sign, and a tractor-trailer had folded-up the car's front as if it were an accordion. The Diablos were among the first spectators on the scene.

Quinn was always cool during a crisis and very deliberately dragged Spits from the front passenger side. The victim's limp body was gingerly placed on the side of the county road. Another motorist who had stopped covered Spits with a blanket. Quinn then quickly moved to the Edsel's driver's side and managed to pull Worm from the wreckage. Our leader took-out his small hand-mirror and placed it up to Worm's pale nostrils. In thirty-seconds, Quinn pronounced the Kamikaze "dead".

Popeye appeared to be unconscious in the front seat, and Cummings, Mullins, and Evans were moaning in the Edsel's rear. The collision had collapsed the '58's roof, and we had to wait fifteen-minutes for the local rescue team to arrive, and then cut the trapped occupants from their terrible confinement.

Worm's death in the horrible tragedy was a definite experience in maturation for the shocked Diablos. As I stood alongside the dark county road, all my thoughts were bundled in deep personal guilt. 'If my Mark Twain scam had not scared the *dickens* out of the Kamikazes, then Worm would still be alive,' I remorsefully thought.

The next day, the Diablos found-out at the Feed Bag that Spits had been severely paralyzed and that Cummings and Mullins required hospitalization because of broken bones and internal bleeding. Popeye Messina had suffered a concussion, and Dave Evans survived the accident with only superficial lacerations and bruises.

"That's the second time Cummings has been hospitalized in two months," I reminded Carnie and Tinker.

"Your prank really backfired," Carnie stated.

"Too bad it didn't kill all six of the bastards," Tinker evilly added. "The goddamned Edsel shoulda' be goin' at least 100 instead of only 70!"

"One death is one too many," I regretfully answered.

Three nights later, a viewing was held in a Penndel funeral home for Worm, whose real birth name was Harold Baxter. Quinn demanded that the Diablos all attend the wake out of respect for the deceased, so twenty-three of us showed-up wearing suits and ties. Bo Jalonec had gone back to *Penn State* so Jokes was the only absent member.

The Diablos sat in the third and fourth rows of the silent funeral home. We remained mum, totally mesmerized by the stiff, pale, lifeless figure positioned horizontally before us.

Harold Baxter's family sat mourning in the first row couch. Strong emotions and their expressions of grief were difficult gestures for the Diablos to endure. Sobbing, crying, kissing, hugging, and sorrow were not our forte. But my gang persevered by witnessing the very sad spectacle for over an hour to show our tribute to a fallen foe.

My mind kept re-creating strange suppositions while I was sitting inside the Penndel funeral home. 'Why did Worm have to die? Were the Diablos responsible? Was I the main perpetrator to be held accountable by Heaven?' I guiltily considered.

'Worm had deliberately attempted murdering me on several occasions, and I now had murdered him by accident. Why was Harold Baxter lying there instead of me?' I weighed and reflected as my guilty mind examined my conscience. 'I had almost perished under ice in the

Delaware Canal; in sixty-foot-deep cold *Delaware River* water, and in five-foot-deep human feces inside the Windsor Pharmacy cesspool. Why hadn't I been killed in the barrel wildly rotating down a Bristol street; in the sandy beach at Tullytown; in the Dairy DeLite phone booth, or in other bizarre situations devised by the Kamikazes?' I apprehensively wondered.

And by some quirky chain of miracles, I was still alive after all of those wild adversities. Harold Baxter had checked into the Eternity Hotel, where only the spirits of restless souls leave for brief intervals to occasionally visit our world of breath, blood, flesh, and heartbeats, yet, I still breathed, and my young heart still beat.

The next day, Carnie, Robbie, Ace, and I skipped school to attend the dearly-departed's funeral services. St. Mark Church on Bristol's Radcliffe Street was one-third full as Harold Baxter's oak casket was wheeled-down the center aisle.

I looked around at all of the church's religious statues. '50s teens could more easily understand the saints' moral messages if only the statues wore black leather jackets with blue denim jeans,' I thought. 'The ancient garb worn two-thousand-years-ago has nothing to do with letterman's sweaters, *Camel* cigarettes, blue denim jeans, and engineer boots,' I concluded. 'If only the statues could wear penny loafers instead of sandals; pegged pants instead of tunics and robes, and greasy hair instead of halos, then the entire church scene would make more sense to the Diablos and to the Kamikazes,' I meditated.

The reality of Worm's violent death kept occupying my mind. I had interacted with Worm on numerous, dangerous occasions, and if mathematical probability had any direct correlation with death, then I, and not Harold Baxter, should have been the everlasting tenant of the oak coffin positioned before the St. Mark altar.

I'll never forget Harold Baxter's burial. The Kamikaze was laid to rest (Tinker meanly remarked that Worm was now an Earth-Worm) in Heavenly Gates Cemetery, directly across from the former hollowed-out grave where Bruno Messina had been imprisoned under the horizontal cyclone fence, where Tinker had cruelly changed the oil to the Diablos' cars.

And again, I felt extremely guilty standing there in the cemetery. The first dug grave had been used to humiliate Popeye Messina, and the second one had now been dug to contain Worm's body. Ironically, I had been involved in the use of both gravesites. I never conveyed my true feelings about the two burial sites to Carnie, Bo, Robbie, or Quinn, but *the dual graves* proximity to each other was too powerful of a pain for my frail conscience to endure.

Quinn had volunteered to be a pallbearer, and as Harold Baxter's remains were lowered into the cold stone vault, I asked myself, 'Why him? Why not me? Why anybody?' Worm's death along with Spits's paralysis had virtually anesthetized the perilous rivalry between the Diablos and the Kamikazes. The morbid funeral was a very sobering experience for all of us to suffer.

Cummings and Mullins were still hospitalized, and the duo was unable to attend Worm's Mass and cemetery services. Spits, whose real name was Byron Talbert, had been crippled from the waist-down from the terrible collision, and his rehabilitation would require years of physical therapy.

As it turned-out, Phil Jackson was not dead like Harold Baxter. The young aristocrat had run-away from confronting the great social embarrassment that he had caused his WASPish' parents. Jackson had hitchhiked cross-country to San Francisco. A wealthy cousin provided Phil sanctuary until the addled athlete was able to fly back east and enter a Pennsylvania sanitarium for much-needed psychological counseling and rehabilitation.

Bo Jalonec would not be coming home again to Levittown until *Thanksgiving* vacation. Although Jokes and I communicated by phone once a week, our close friendship was beginning to fade. Up until mid-October of '59, I never fully realized exactly how much I truly valued his supportive companionship.

Chapter 54
"43 Deepgreen Lane"

In late October of '59, a noteworthy event happened right down the street from 50 Daffodil Lane. Marcus Spellman's six-member family moved into the center of Dogwood Hollow at 43 Deepgreen Lane, directly across from Salvatore Palermo's up-for-sale residence at 66 Daffodil Lane.

Just like Jackie Robinson had broken the color barrier in major league baseball, and just like Chuck Berry, Little Richard, and Fats Domino had swayed '50s teenagers away from pure "white country and western music" to "black rhythm and blues", Sugar Ray Spellman and his family had integrated Levittown. A firestorm of white backlash erupted. and the opposition grew into a protest of massive proportions.

The Spellmans had done the unthinkable. Marcus's family had crossed the imaginary "racial demarcation taboo line" of "separate but equal". The black family had moved from their formerly restricted sector of Yardley into a forbidden white zone on the '50s latticed sociological grid.

The Spellmans were telling Levittown's "White America" that they had equal rights to affordable housing, a full five-years before Congress enacted the *Civil Rights Act*. My parents, who were normally docile, were even deeply disturbed by the Spellmans' audacity. The black family's decision to move into Dogwood Hollow coincided with dad's desire to move-out.

"No sooner do I put a 'For Sale' sign on the front lawn that a black family wants to move into the neighborhood," Pop negatively lamented. "Seventeen-thousand homes in Levittown, and this debacle has to happen right down the street from us."

I dared not reveal to my folks that I knew and liked Marcus Spellman, because I could tell that it would cause a major controversy within the family. But I could fully understand Dad's economic perspective on the issue.

The Levittown citizens were fearful that big city strife and crime were beginning to invade the middle class's sacred suburban turf, and that rural house values were certain to depreciate. What the residents had labored a lifetime to save and achieve would be economically threatened, and *that* apprehension was exactly what most of the local citizens thought and felt.

Word of the Spellmans' arrival into Dogwood Hollow spread as if it were wildfire. Soon, crowds of curiosity seekers milled-around Daffodil Lane to get a better glimpse of the cultural aberration in progress at 43 Deepgreen Lane.

Within days, newspaper reporters, national television camera crews, and major magazines gave extensive coverage to Levittown's first racial integration. *Look Magazine* chronicled the Spellmans' arrival with a three-page pictorial depicting the massive white resistance and the general pandemonium that surrounded the iconoclastic event. White supremacy groups were also attracted to the hotbed of social unrest, and formerly serene and placid Dogwood Hollow quickly became the focal point of international notoriety.

In the '50s, blacks and whites feared and distrusted living near one another. Whites were convinced that crime rates would rise and that home values would decrease with the appearance of blacks in Levittown. Many whites came from other sections of the suburban city to protest the sudden existence of the Spellmans in Dogwood Hollow.

Sugar Ray only wanted to be closer to his new friends, Quinn and most of the Diablos. I had mixed feelings about the evolving situation, because Pop told me the real estate agency had lowered the sale price of our home from twelve-thousand-dollars down to ten, a substantial decrease of almost twenty-percent.

Blacks were highly defined by racial stereotypes in the '50s. The race was often perceived as being lazy, listless, watermelon-eaters, who also consumed grits, fatbacks and greens, and chitlins. Beulah was a domestic servant on a popular radio program; Rochester was Jack Benny's obedient chauffeur; Aunt Jemima was a post *Civil War* cook and baker, and Uncle Ben had a secret formula that gave the white population "converted rice".

A highly volatile and potentially explosive atmosphere enveloped 43 Deepgreen Lane in late October of '59. The new ethnic danger was intensifying daily.

"J.W., what do ya' think of Sugar Ray movin' into Dogwood Hollow?" Carnie asked me at the Feed Bag.

"He's done a lot for the Diablos," I diplomatically answered. "Marcus is Quinn's buddy, so maybe we oughta' just judge him like we would any white kid."

"Leave all of the lousy niggers rotting-away in the shitty city," Tinker discriminated and objected. "Isn't that why I moved outa' the goddamned Bronx? To get away from the damned spear-chuckers, but now, the nigger spear-chuckers are knockin' on our doors. Soon, the whole fuckin' place is gonna' be swamped with wall-to-wall shines!"

"Our white ancestors like the Romans, the Greeks, and the barbarian tribes were spear-chuckers too," I academically replied as I confidently quoted something significant that I had learned in Brother Timothy's Ancient History class.

Every evening, Sal Palermo and Dante Messina led a contingent of white demonstrators up and down Daffodil Lane. Loud raucous crowds assembled, chanting nasty slogans and offensive epithets. Around seven-hundred angry protesters would nightly congregate outside Marcus Spellman's new residence.

Many racists, anarchists, and atheists were drawn to the general mayhem to try popularizing their fanatical beliefs, and simultaneously, inadvertently polarizing all opposing views. The entire spectacle did not bode well for Marcus and his family. The outraged demonstrators performed three basic chants.

"Two, four six, eight
We don't want to integrate."

A second nasty rhyme was also practiced and repeated like a mantra. "You're no damned good for the neighborhood."

Two groups of well-organized antagonists on either side of the Spellman residence alternated shouting some other impolite language.

"One, two, three
Don't live near me.
Four, five, six
Whites and blacks don't mix.
Seven, eight, nine
Don't dare cross the line!"

Caucasian anger was seeking a decisive objective, and I feared that Sugar Ray and his family would soon be in physical jeopardy. The Pennsylvania State Police were on patrol to keep the peace, but tempers were flaring, and many whites sought physical removal of the Spellmans for audaciously and brazenly violating the strict unwritten racial compartmentalization that was the essential material comprising the 1950s social fabric. When protest was evolving and culminating into actual fury, a most startling thing happened.

Marcus Spellman emerged from the safety of 43 Deepgreen Lane amid the taunts and cackles of the hostile white mob. Quinn's friend held his hands in the air for silence and remarkably, the crowd's clamor reduced to whispers. A dramatic hush soon prevailed within the electrified social atmosphere. Sugar Ray bravely addressed scorners and sympathizers alike.

"Now, I know you folks are upset about me and my family movin' in here," Sugar Ray nervously began his speech. "We never thought we would cause all this commotion. We don't mean to cause anyone harm. And we don't want livin' where we ain't welcome," Marcus emphasized. "So, if there's anybody out there that doesn't mind us livin' here, they're now invited to step onto this lawn. If no one wants us around, then stay where ya' are. We'll be outa' here first thing in the mornin'."

There was a thirty-second tense and uneasy pause. No one moved a muscle. And then Quinn, the iconoclast, the maverick, the introvert, the lone wolf', stepped onto the lawn at 43 Deepgreen Lane. His stride advanced toward Marcus Spellman; his right-hand shook Sugar Ray's right palm, and then his head slowly turned, facing his stunned Caucasian audience. And then amazingly, Cummings, fresh out of the hospital, stepped onto the lawn and hobbled over to Quinn and Sugar Ray. Cummings admired his former foe, the Diablos' laconic leader, and the head K was indebted to Marcus for courageously saving his life at the Jersey blueberry farm.

And then Carnie and I joined those intrepid souls standing stationary on the front lawn. Surprisingly, feeling alienated, Tinker quickly mimicked our bold action. The vindictive mechanic had temporarily set-aside his racist views and decided to conform to doing what was basically right. The Dogwood Hollow guys had set foot on the lawn in support of Diablos' unity. Jake Mullins, Dave Evans, and then Popeye Messina joined our company. It was plainly evident that Bruno was rebelling against his father's very obvious prejudices. And then, Langford stepped from the sidewalk onto the grass, and soon, the remainder of the Diablos, Kamikazes, and Renegades did likewise to signify greaser unity on the complex issue.

And next, Susie Parker, Patty Van Arsdale, Angie Palermo, and Bubbles Messina demonstrated courage and followed suit. And to everyone's amazement, Stanley Tezeeker was loyally followed by fellow eggheads Waldo Hunsburger, Melvin Speigleman, and Mortimer Ralston.

Even motorcycle gang members of the Barbarians and the War Lords joined our ranks, and next some local Dogwood Hollow residents showed compassion by crossing the boundary that had been established and defined by Marcus. Soon, there were as many people on the lawn as off, and more citizens wanted to enlist in our company.

The fair-minded humans standing upon the lawn let-out a tremendous cheer, much to the chagrin of Sal Palermo, Dante Messina, and their irate disciples. As I turned to my left, I was very happy to see Mom and Dad standing there, for my parents also realized that human dignity was on a higher moral plateau than was mere money. Marcus

Spellman had admirably survived his 1959 invasion of Caucasian persuasion.

I called Jokes later that night up at *Penn State* to report the 43 Deepgreen Lane phenomenon. All Jalonec could think of was to critically refer to Angie's father's enormous paunch. "J.W., I always knew that Sal Palermo was a *big gut*," Jokes quipped. "But now I know that he has *discriminating* taste, too!"

Although I usually and thoroughly appreciated Bo's effervescent and congenial personality, my mind finally realized that everything in life was not a joke. The blueberry farm race; the Phil Jackson affair; Worm's sudden death, and Sugar Ray's steadfast courage had all been valuable "coming of age" experiences that defined and supported my eventual passage into adulthood.

Chapter 55
"California Dreamin"

The Diablos had reveled in more '50s high adventure than the average person experiences in a lifetime. I've had some joys, successes, and triumphant moments since then, but the '50s battles between the Ds and the Ks still stand-out as some of the most extraordinary events in my life. My mind was now geared to reuniting with Quinn, Bo, Carnie, Tinker, and Robbie after forty-one years of separation.

On December 27, 2000, I boarded a *Continental Airlines* jet at *Philadelphia International Airport*. The first leg of my flight to Houston went smoothly, and after an hour stopover in Texas, I was soon on another 737 en route to San Diego. All through my much-anticipated excursion, I wondered how many of the other Diablos would honor the commitment that the six members had made in the Feed Bag on December 28, 1959.

I fondly recalled how innocent and naïve Carnie and I had been back in 1954. We were content playing stickball, and sometimes half-ball, and spent hours tossing baseball cards against our bedroom walls to try and obtain "leaners", and playing hand-tennis while using two of the sidewalk's rectangles as front and backcourts. The Kamikazes, Tinker, and Phil Jackson soon entered our carefree lives, and before we knew it, Carnie and I had become mischievous greasers. Next, we became pranksters, and later connivers, and finally, we found ourselves accomplices to an assortment of Levittown greaser crimes and shenanigans.

I thought about my life after moving back to Jersey on December 29, 1959. Since then, I had graduated from *Edgewood Regional High School* in 1960, and from *Glassboro State College* in '65. I believe I had entered American education to redeem the troubles and headaches I had caused my perplexed teachers back in the "fabulous '50s". My present students often wonder how I know when they're trying to pull-off some misbehavior in my English classes and my stock reply is, "I was once a student, and I know all of the subtle tricks from both ends."

I had finally settled-down, married an Italian Hammonton girl, and we have three sons. Joe, the oldest, and Steve, the youngest, are graduates of *Rutgers University*. J.T. attended *Rowan University* (formerly *Glassboro State),* and is pursuing an acting and writing career.

By coincidence, Steve was living in San Diego, "finding himself", as my wife Joanne claimed. Our youngest son had become an avid surfer and was enjoying living the *West Coast* lifestyle of *Espresso,* bagels, sea gulls, and gorgeous *Pacific Ocean* sunsets.

As my mind daydreamed on the second western plane flight about California and other subjects, my mind recalled how I had been an English teacher for thirty-four years in a New Jersey public school. I had co-owned summer businesses on the Atlantic City, Ocean City, Maryland and Rehoboth Beach, Delaware boardwalks, and I've made some money dabbling in the stock market. I own my house and have made and saved enough cash to educate my three sons. As my second flight descended onto a runway at *Charles Lindbergh Airport,* my hope was that the rest of my Levittown Diablo' chums had, over the years, encountered similar or better good fortune.

Steve met me at the airport terminal's baggage claim area. After I retrieved my two suitcases, my youngest son drove me over to the nearby *Avis* building where I rented a red *Buick Skylark.* I followed my son's ghastly '84 blue Pontiac station wagon up *Interstate 5* to La Jolla Village Drive, which led to my lodging for the next three days, a luxurious *Marriott.*

After I checked into the fine hotel, Steve and I got caught-up on the latest family gossip. We had a late lunch, and then made plans for my second day in subtropical southern California.

The following morning, Steve met me in the hotel lobby. I insisted that we should travel in my rented red Buick, fearing that my life might be in danger in dense freeway traffic while riding in the California surfer's shoddy '84 wagon. We had breakfast at a La Jolla *Denny's* just off of Torrey Pines Road, and after consuming our pancakes and eggs, our first challenge was locating Quinn's San Diego residence, which was in the Mission Hills section of the beautiful city. I suggested that Steve should drive the red Buick so that I could take in the sights, observe some prominent area landmarks, and write-down specific directions.

My son was familiar with all of the main areas of San Diego. Steve motored south on *I-5* past the *Sea World* exit. The surfer took the off-ramp to Washington Street, bore left at the first light, and then crossed State and India Streets. Next, my personal chauffeur drove up a ridge on Washington, and then veered onto University Avenue. All the while, I jotted-down the in-progress directions as the "Beach Boy" babbled-on about "hangin' ten" and "shootin' the curl".

A right turn at the first light put us on Goldfinch, and another right had us on Sutter Street. As Steve talked about great surfing beaches along the coast, I scribbled-down "four blocks-right on Kite Street". A left-hand turn put my *Buick Skylark* on Brookes Avenue. Three blocks down, just before the canyon, my eyes spotted a cul-de-sac. Quinn's San Diego residence was situated right before the aforementioned canyon. I eagerly read the number 1028 below the house's mailbox. No cars were in the driveway of the handsome, white, stucco home.

My surfer son then gave me directions to the Corvette Diner, a couple of blocks off of University Avenue. Obtaining the exact directions to Quinn's residence, we had the morning to leisurely burn, so after finding Laurel Street, heading toward Balboa Park, and then, a left turn onto Park Boulevard, our journey led us to the internationally famous *San Diego Zoo,* where we toured the fabulously landscaped exhibits. The flamingoes looked magnificent in their re-created environment, which meticulously simulated the birds' natural habitat. The gorillas, reptiles, tigers, and giraffes were equally as fascinating.

After our relaxing four-hour zoo visit, Steve drove back to La Jolla, where we spent a half-hour checking-out *Pacific Ocean* seals basking on large beach rocks along Coast Boulevard. Then, we walked the pavement on Prospect Street and examined expensive merchandise in the storefront windows of ritzy emporiums.

I gladly treated Steve to a sumptuous steak at the Chart House Restaurant, and after enjoying some pleasant table conversation, we returned to the *Marriott,* chatted for a while, and I finally retired to my quarters to take a nap. I was still feeling a little jet-lag, and I wanted to be well-rested for the scheduled Diablos' Corvette Diner reunion.

Later that day, I drove my rented car from La Jolla into downtown San Diego. The anticipated seven p.m. meeting was merely an hour away. Next to Mission Hills was Hillcrest. The city section was lit-up in large red lights that were arched over University Avenue. A San Diego oldies radio station was playing the Dovells popular tune "Bristol Stomp", and that lively number immediately set my mind to recollecting '50s record hops in Bristol where I would often see Angie Palermo, Bubbles Messina, and Carol Zella trying-out their new, sophisticated dance steps.

I parked my rented car in a lot and ambled a block to the Corvette Diner. A slight drizzle was coming-down from an overcast sky, but that mild precipitation neither affected my anticipation nor thwarted my enthusiasm. As I entered the '50s theme establishment, I instantly recognized the melody to Chuck Berry's "Rock and Roll Music". A black DJ wearing a fluffy wig was humorously impersonating '50s zany recording artist Little Richard.

Displays of fifties merchandise and food products were stacked along the right-side wall in neat piles. Baseball cards, enlarged *Bazooka* bubblegum boxes (with the standard *joke* and cartoon) were offered for sale, and *that* particular recognition made me fondly remember Bo Jalonec. Enlarged, colorful *CrackerJack* display boxes advertising the characteristic prizes inside were also on exhibit.

Various '50s soap and candy items had also been offered for retail sale. The products were packaged exactly as I had remembered during my memorable Levittown teen years.

A white '55 Corvette was situated on a stage directly behind the diner's retail vending area. The resplendent automobile was being flaunted anf highlighted on a slow revolving platform. I marveled at the lustrous sports car, an authentic facsimile of the ones owned by Phil Jackson, until Tinker had methodically destroyed the dream machines. The magnificent 'Vette was identical to Jackson's two cherished possessions, right-down to the plush red interiors and matching rugs. As I studied the treasured white sports car slowly revolving before me, a crisp familiar voice broke my concentration.

"Hey J.W. How the hell are ya'?"

I turned and stared at a gaunt figure wearing a Davy Crockett coonskin hat and accompanying 3-D plastic glasses. I couldn't believe my pupils.

"Why Tinker! You're a sight for sore-eye-asis!" I exclaimed as I immediately resorted to a classic Bo Jalonec salutation.

"Quinn just told me it never rains in sunny southern California," Tinker complained. "It's gonna' shower the whole goddamned night of our reunion."

"Have no fear, Tink," I answered, feigning sincerity. "As Jokes always used to say, Queen Elizabeth has been *reigning* in England since 1954."

"Well, Words," Tinker reminisced with a serious expression on his face. "I'll bet you had trouble recognizin' this 'Vette without s ton of cement poured into it, or without a T-bird wrapped around its grille."

"Damn straight," I amenably replied, wondering why Jeremy was speaking appropriate English and not obnoxiously cursing. "Any of the other guys here?"

"Sure," Tinker almost phlegmatically informed me. "Actually, the other Diablos are anxious to see ya'."

Chapter 56
"The Corvette Diner"

Tinker and I entered the main dining room of the Corvette Diner. We sauntered by and hastily wove our way through a crowd of '50s wannabes'. The short walk led us to a rather large circular table. The two gentlemen seated there turned out to be Carnie and Robbie Wilkinson. Each rose, smiled, and warmly shook my hand. Feeling sentimental, I was momentarily overwhelmed. I readily perceived that both Carnie and Robbie were quite eager to reminisce past shared experiences.

"Hey Words, is that really you?" Carnie asked. "How's your Aunt Chovy?" My eyes noticed that Carnie was fat and bald, and his appearance looked nothing like the skinny kid I remembered from 1959 Levittown.

My memory instantly recalled the patented Bo Jalonec answer to Carnie's droll salutation. "Well, Carnie," I chuckled. "Ever since her husband died, my Aunt Chovy has been livin' with my Aunt Arctica!"

"J.W.," Robbie interrupted. "Do ya' got an *Internet* web page?"

I figured that Robbie was trying to show me he was up on the latest technological advances. "Yes, I do," I amiably replied. "I actually put some spiders in my computer terminal screen to successfully form my own website."

"Make sure ya' don't get a terminal illness," Carnie cracked as my old friend attempted showing me that 'the mimicker' still retained a degree of Bo Jalonec's amazing wit.

"As Shakespeare once said, 'Clean-up your act and don't make a scene', I chanted, remembering another of Bo Jalonec's classic lines.

I studied Carnie's appearance and then something suddenly registered in my mind. "Hey Carnie, you're the guy I had bumped into last July 1st on the steps of the Bristol Post Office. Do ya' remember *that* mild collision?"

"Well, I'll be damned!" Carnie exclaimed in sheer amazement. "We never even recognized each other!"

"Where's Quinn hidin'?" I inquired.

"Over there," Mr. C answered and indicated, nodding his head. The former Merc' Man pointed to the black DJ's more permanent announcing booth, located against a sidewall inside the classic restaurant's second main dining room.

Quinn had just finished making a trilogy of oldies requests for the black disc jockey, who later-turned out to be none other than Marcus Spellman. As I soon found-out, Quinn and Spellman had joined the

Army and served together in Vietnam. After the war, the two friends settled-down in San Diego, where Sugar Ray had several relatives.

I was shocked to see Quinn using a cane as 'my hero' walked-over to warmly greet me. His dependence on the object contradicted my memory of him as being virile, formidable, fearless, and omnipotent. I shook Quinn's right hand, and by his body's reaction, I noticed that his left arm and leg were partially paralyzed.

"How are ya' doin', old Buddy?"

"Really great," I humbly replied. "But what on earth happened to you?"

"Shrapnel injuries from a Viet Cong mine outside Da Nang. Almost died back in '68," Quinn explained. "J.W., I want ya' to know you were the heart and soul of the Diablos. Ya' might not have realized it at the time, but you were the glue that kept the gang together. '58 and '59 were the glory years of my life. I owe it all to you! Since then, though, it's been all downhill for me."

"What ever happened to Patty Van Arsdale?"

Quinn described that he and Patty had gotten married in '63. "Then, the war started," my former '50s hero lamented. "After I became seriously wounded, Patty had trouble adjusting to my disabilities. We separated, but now she wants to get back together again, so there's still some hope for our relationship to rekindle." Quinn reiterated that fate had been really cruel to him since the Diablos had last met at the Feed Bag on December 28, 1959.

"I want ya' to know that in my mind, you'll always be the greatest!" I sincerely replied. "If it weren't for you, I would've drowned while buried in the sand next to the *Delaware River*."

"J.W., don't be silly!" Quinn insisted. "Robbie's the one that really saved you. All I did was help out at the end."

"A lot went-down between the Ds and the Ks, especially in '59," I said. "What do ya' recall most from that turbulent year?"

Quinn pondered for a moment. "Everybody thinks that Fidel Castro takin' over Cuba was the biggest negative event of '59, but it wasn't," Quinn related and insisted. "The worst catastrophe of '59 was that damned plane crash outside Clearlake, Iowa. Buddy Holly's death was the biggest tragedy of that lousy year. Those freakin' politicians and newspapers always get everything ass-backwards."

Quinn went on to say that Marcus Spellman moving into Dogwood Hollow, along with Worm dying in the tragic Croydon auto accident, were the two Bucks County events he remembered most from *that* rather incredible year.

I then recalled some terrific things about Quinn that had stuck in my mind over the past four decades. "I'll never forget that early

February Buddy Holly speech you made inside the Feed Bag," I admitted. At that moment, I had never been so honest in all my life. My heart truly believed that Quinn had been the major positive influence on my future character development.

"Thanks, Words," Jack Quinn graciously acknowledged. "And coming from you, that's a tremendous compliment."

I was happy to note that my hero had not, over the years, lost his integrity, and still was a very special person, despite his very apparent physical handicaps.

"Hey, J.W.," Carnie interrupted, getting my attention. "So, do ya' remember pouring those friggin' buckets of fish down the Kamikaze clubhouse's chimney?"

Over four decades later, I was hardly proud of *that* particular activity, but I recalled something that Bo Jalonec had said about the bizarre incident. "Sure, do Carnie," I answered. "And Jokes claimed he didn't want to stay on the clubhouse roof for too long because...."

"Because he was afraid of contracting a bad case of shingles," Carnie, Quinn, Tinker, and Robbie all replied in chorus.

The five of us returned to our circular table. After sitting down, we listened to the three songs that Quinn had requested Sugar Ray to spin, which were Feed Bag favorites: "The Wayward Wind" by Gogi Grant; "Tequila" by the Champs, and the very excellent classic "School Day" by Chuck Berry.

The five former Diablos sang the fantastic lyrics to "School Day" rather robustly, and two tables of Japanese tourists were so impressed with our enthusiasm that the courteous U.S. visitors requested a repeat performance, which we readily agreed on doing.

As my eyes casually glanced around the dining room, I evaluated caricature drawings of '50s icons. There were depictions of Elvis, Buddy Holly, Jerry Lee Lewis, Fats Domino, Chuck Berry, Bill Haley, Little Richard, Frank Sinatra, James Dean, Natalie Wood, and Marilyn Monroe, which were tastefully portrayed all over the room's nostalgic interior. Colorful neon signs on the Corvette Diner's walls advertised the popular brand names of the '50s. *Coca-Cola, Pepsi-Cola, Dr. Pepper*, *Seven-Up, Good N' Plenty*, *Lucky Strike* and *Camel* cigarettes, along with *Edsel* automobiles were all represented in neon.

Then, a lucid observation flashed through my sentimental mind. Most of those other people seated inside the Corvette Diner, including the two tables of Japanese tourists, were merely '50s wannabes'. The Oriental diners also longed for the excitement and the adventure of yesteryear, which the Diablos had actually lived and exploited in real life to the hilt. To the other customers, the Corvette Diner was an intense vicarious experience, but to the five former Diablos, it was simply a modern-day re-creation of a typical '50s hangout like the incomparable Feed Bag.

And when the five of us screamed-out "Tequila!" and "Hail, hail rock and roll, long live rock and roll!", we stood (except Quinn) on our wooden chairs and vigorously waved our arms in the air, just like we had done in the Feed Bag over forty-years before. The other captivated Corvette Diner patrons amazingly copied our stellar example, fully realizing that we were legitimate former '50s teenagers.

A pretty well-built brunette waitress came-over to our table to take our orders. Carnie stared at her lengthy ponytail.

"Are you guys the Five Keys about to sing 'Ling Ting Tong'?" the cute doll cordially asked.

"Do ya' have chicken breasts or frog legs?" asked Carnie, who was either trying to again become his teenaged self, or who had never really evolved out of his primitive, adolescent stage of development.

"No," the young waitress answered. "And I don't have elephant thighs, either!"

"Well then, do ya' have crabs?" asked Tinker, who thought that modern civilization hadn't happened yet.

"D.D.T.," the good-looking young doll curtly replied.

"Drop dead twice?" Carnie asked, remembering a popular '50s slang response.

"No, Silly," the pert waitress corrected. "D.D.T. in my book stands for 'Don't do that!' But I really like 'drop dead twice' better. I'll have to put that one on file."

"Before we order I just have to know something," Carnie demanded of the very patient waitress. "Do ya' own any pet owls?"

"Pet owls? Why no! Why do you ask something so improbable?" the young lady curiously inquired.

"Because ya' have a nice set of hooters there!" Carnie answered.

I whispered to Carnie that we were having our Diablos' reunion to celebrate the '50s, and not to realistically relive them. Carnie and Tinker both frowned and stared at me as if the adult knuckleheads resented that I had evolved into a sensitive, fairly-educated, ethical human being.

The five of us ordered an eclectic array of foods as if we were supping at the glorious Feed Bag again. All the while, I wished that Carnie wouldn't try any more juvenile indiscretions until Bo Jalonec had arrived, but being a dumb creature of habit, my neurotic friend couldn't resist getting risque again with the very tolerant and attractive Corvette Diner brunette.

"Hey, where did you get that awesome Davy Crockett coonskin hat?" the hot babe unfortunately asked Tinker, while neglecting to mention his trademark plastic 3-D glasses.

Before reformed Jeremy Foster could muster a viable response, Carnie was ready to hammer the girl with some inane sexual allusion that *he* remembered from the Feed Bag. "Look Hon. All ya' gotta' do is shave your beaver every six months or so, and after five or six years, you'll have enough material to make your own damned coonskin hat!"

"You're a dirty old man, ya' know that!" the mortified waitress yelled. "Who knows what kind of screwed-up childhood you had?"

"That's right, Doll," Carnie agreed. "And when I was your age back in the '50s, I was a dirty young man!"

I was so embarrassed that I felt like sinking my entire body under the huge table. Right then and there, I wished that I had boycotted the reunion, but being reconnected with my boyhood idol Quinn made me reconsider my initial inclination.

The aggravated waitress became so flustered and peeved at Carnie that she quickly stepped over to the *Bazooka* bubblegum bowl, next to the cash register, and started hurling small hard pieces of wrapped gum at the C Man's disgusting presence. Other waitresses joined in the impromptu assault, and soon, even the other alert customers were pelting us with little tokens, souvenirs, and memorabilia being tossed from their respective tables.

Sugar Ray Spellman sped-over to our location, held his hands up into the air attempting to avoid further havoc, and told the crowd that *we* were "street-smart, wild greasers from the fifties", and that we should be respected because we were living models of what "Corvette's Diner is all about".

The amused mob toned-down their aggression and honored Sugar Ray's request for calm. Marcus Spellman then announced that before dinner would be served, everyone in the crowded place had to participate in special leg-stomping and foot-tapping renditions of "The Chicken Dance", "The Stroll", "The Hand Jive", and "The Jitterbug".

In the middle of "At the Hop" by Danny and the Juniors, I practiced my former jitterbug routine, showing a pretty Japanese girl some of my *American Bandstand* moves. The Tokyo teen told me that her great-grandfather had been a Japanese Kamikaze pilot that had died in *World War II*. I told her that my father had fought in Europe against her great-grandfather's German allies in the same war, and how it was so ironic that we were dancing and co-mingling inside the Corvette Diner in San Diego, USA, as if nothing disastrous had ever happened in 1941.

And then the Japanese girl became completely befuddled when I informed her (without sufficient background information) that I had "shot down" plenty of Kamikazes in Levittown, Pennsylvania in the 1950s. The Tokyo girl asked me if I had "ever visited a psychiatrist" because *World War II* had ended in 1945. After the jitterbug dance, being thoroughly amused, I rejoined my old Diablo pals for more memorable reminiscence.

"J.W." said Carnie. "Do ya' remember when Tink here started that woods fire with his magnifyin' glass?"

"F-in A," Tinker crudely recalled, forgetting that he was an adult.

"Yeah," I verbally returned. "When Bo had heard the story, Jokes called Tinker a real trailblazer!"

Then, I fondly recalled our frequent expeditions into the *City of Brotherly Love*. "Hey, Carnie. Do' ya' still try to pick up *chicks* on *Broad* Street in Philly'?"

"No, Words. I've finally graduated to old hens and expensive filthy slut prostitutes on Pacific Avenue in Atlantic City," Carnie snickered. "J.W., did ya' ever get to stick a lit pack of weeds up Stanley Tezeeker's rear end?"

"You got a short memory," I objected. "Stanley was a great guy once we gave him a decent chance. If you remember, we used a couple of his ideas against the Kamikazes, and the egghead once saved Tink and me from dying in the deep cesspool behind the pharmacy."

I began to think of Bo Jalonec. "Say Tink, have ya' seen any maps of Australia lately?" I asked.

"Sure have, J.W.," Jeremy Foster replied. "Like Bo used to say, I always like the way things looked down under in the outback bush country. Carnie and I have even caught a few horny bushwhackers in the act of massaging their clit buttons!"

It was truly amazing. Bo Jalonec's warped mind had infected all of our thinking in one way or another, even over the past four decades. My eyes evaluated the other four men seated at the table. Quinn's personality had hardly changed; Robbie and I had matured into bona fide adults, and Carnie and Tinker were still 1950s' deadbeat Diablos.

Before our conversation could degenerate any further than it already had, Marcus Spellman came-over to greet me. I was very surprised that Quinn's friend vividly remembered me because I barely had known him back in the late '50s. But from what I had seen of Marcus, I liked his style, his courage, and his determination. Sugar Ray shook my right hand very energetically.

"You're J.W., aren't ya!" Sugar Ray exclaimed. "I remember ya' from the trip to Uncle Clydes' in Manahawkin, and from the big fight between Quinn and Cummings at the quarry. Quinny's told me all about ya' many times. Everything from the head in the mailbox; the boccie ball game; the *Bandstand* gig; the phone booth thing; the cesspool incident; the Bristol barrel roll, well, everything! Man, you're a damned livin' legend!"

I couldn't get over how the other guys had held me in such high esteem. All throughout my Levittown teen years, I had felt insecure, immature, and indecisive. And now, over four decades later and three thousand-miles away from remote Dogwood Hollow, the other Diablos remembered me as a leader, a dynamic, powerful force in all our relationships, and also in all of *our* extraordinary exploits. I was deeply flattered contemplating it all.

"What can I get you nasty greasers in the line of refreshments?" Marcus asked. "And please don't request five finger-lickin' good, wet, juicy snatcheroos!"

The five Diablos ordered a round of large *Pepsi's* "for old times' sake". Carnie challenged the guys to a game of "Cowboy Trivia" to determine who would defray the all-important beverage part of the bill. Quinn decided that Carnie should go first.

"Who played Hopalong Cassidy?" the short, fat baldheaded Mr. C asked his old buddies.

"That's as easy as apple pie," Tinker declared, "William Boyd. "Who starred in the roles of the Lone Ranger and Tonto?"

"Clayton Moore and Jay Silverheels," I answered, since I was next in turn. "What does `Kemo Sabay' mean?"

"I know that one," said Quinn. "It means 'Trusted Scout'. What was the Lone Ranger's horse's name?"

"Silver," Robbie authoritatively replied. "What was Gene Autrey's horse's name?"

"Champion," Carnie snapped. "What about the name of Dale Evans' horse?"

"Buttercup," Tinker quickly answered from memory. "What was the jeep that Pat Buttram rode around in?"

"Nellie Belle," I proudly stated. "Who played Zorro?"

"That's pretty tough, but I believe it was Guy Williams," Quinn answered with an element of doubt. "Who played the roles of the Cisco Kid and his sidekick Pancho?"

"Wow, I remember now," Robbie' stated. "It was Duncan Rinaldo and Leo Carillo. Carnie, what singin' group backed up Roy Rogers?"

"Glad ya' asked," Carnie cockily replied. "The Sons of the Pioneers. Say Tink, what was the name of the Cisco Kid's horse?"

The correct answer seemed to evade Jeremy Foster's recollection. After a full-minute of suspense, Mr. T admitted that he couldn't extract the appropriate data from his mental memory banks.

"DIABLO!" we all shouted and laughed in a roar. Ironically, Tinker had failed to recall the one vital '50s word that connected the five men seated at the Corvette Diner table.

"J.W.," Quinn addressed me. "Why didn't ya' come back to Levittown after ya' moved to Jersey? Did ya' get pregnant with triplets or something?"

The truth was that I had made many new friends over in Jersey, and I also never wanted to see Tinker again, but I didn't want to disclose those two relevant facts to the curious guys. "I did go to a couple of Cardinal Reagan basketball games in February of '60," I recalled and related. "I saw Carnie at a March party given by Carol Zella. But then I cracked the engine block on pop's '55 Chevy on the way home, so I wasn't allowed to take the car out of Hammonton for a full year. And you guys know how greasers hated talkin' over the phone in front of parents." Then, feeling a bit uncomfortable about lying, I decided to hit the ball into *their* side of the court.

"How come you fellas' didn't visit me over in Jersey?" I coyly asked. "I would've shown you guys around Hammonton."

"It just wasn't the same after ya' moved away," Quinn confessed. "Carnie's mom and him moved-out to Ohio; Robbie moved to New York State, and then I entered the *Army.*"

"And then almost everybody else moved away, too," Tinker remembered and told us. "I was the only one among the main Diablos that was still left in Dogwood Hollow."

I had known the other men at the table for six wonderful '50s years, but then it occurred to me that we all had to become reacquainted all over again.

"Quinn and Carnie are right," Robbie affirmed. "Nothin' we could've done after you flew the coop back to Jersey could've matched what went-down between the Diablos and the Kamikazes. After Cummings and the other Ks supported Sugar Ray's movin' into Dogwood Hollow, the gangs didn't mess too much with each other. Then the Ds and the Ks slowly disbanded."

There was so much to talk about that I hardly had time to sort-out all the details. Finally, names began to surface, and naturally, I wanted to know what had become of Sal Palermo and Dante Messina.

Tinker whipped-out an old newspaper article dated March 21, 1960. A massive fire had destroyed Specialty Enterprises on Cedar Street in Bristol. Local and Pennsylvania State Police had discovered a large quantity of pornographic literature and marijuana among the building's salvaged remains. The two tyrannical Sicilians were arrested on felony charges, and convicted of federal mail violations, along with the illicit use of interstate commerce. The repugnant pair had spent twenty-years in an Illinois penitentiary.

"Did ya' start the Bristol' fire described in the newspaper article?" I asked Tinker.

"I admit it," Tinker disclosed. "I still had a grudge with Popeye, so I got back at his criminal family. The Ks nearly killed me' and you a couple of times. I gambled that Palermo and Messina would go to jail if caught with the discovered goods being legal evidence."

"Didn't ya' worry about getting caught yourself?" I asked.

"I thought and gambled that the cops would discontinue their search for the fire's cause after comin' across the warehouse's illegal contents," Tinker stated. "And once the drugs and smut evidence were found, the insurance claim would not be allowed, and there would be no need for the cops to do an investigation into the fire's cause. I just happened to guess right, as usual."

"Tink, you've always had a weakness for fires, even though you never had any *old flames* back in Levittown," I added and chuckled. "I know what your parents probably say about you."

"What's that?" Tink wondered and asked.

"That's *our son*, the pyromaniac!" I yelled.

Tinker proceeded to give me the middle finger to demonstrate his displeasure with my stellar Bo Jalonec imitation.

"What about Angie and Bubbles?" I asked.

"We don't really know," Robbie replied with a weak grin on his face. "After the big Bristol fire, the dolls moved-out of state to live with relatives. It was almost as if the chicks never had lived in Levittown. Then, my folks moved to Syracuse after my dad's job was again transferred, and I haven't seen any of you guys since."

One final very essential question remained to be answered. A lump formed in my throat. I feared I might not be pleased with learning the truth. I braced myself before asking what my mind had been wondering since the very second that I had entered the Corvette Diner. I had known that Bo Jalonec's family had moved from Levittown to Pittsburgh shortly after my Dad had relocated back to Hammonton.

"Where's Bo Jalonec?" my throat coughed-out.

No one at the table said a word. I was hoping that Bo was late for the reunion the way he had always been for Diablos' meetings back at the Feed Bag. Finally, Quinn summoned the courage to clue me in. "Sorry to say, J.W.," his voice began in almost a whimper. "But Bo died of leukemia in the late summer of '94. After Jokes graduated from *Penn State,* our old friend became a prominent shopping center developer and invested his money wisely. In ten-years' time, the entrepreneur became a multi-millionaire."

"What good is bein' the richest man in the cemetery?" I sorrowfully replied. "Perhaps Bo's career was influenced by the Levittown Shop-A-Rama!" My eyes met Quinn's, begging for more background.

"Patty and Susie kept in touch over the years," Quinn added. "In fact, Susie was a runner-up in the Miss Pennsylvania Beauty Pageant. A few years later, she and Bo married, and now she's one of those rich socialites ya' read about in the big city newspapers. The couple had two beautiful blonde-hair daughters, and that's about all I can tell you about Bo's history since Levittown."

I felt like crying, but somehow, I fought back the tears and the sobs. I took three very deep breaths. "That's got to be the saddest news I've heard in a long time," I softly expressed. "Please, is there anything else *you* could tell me about him?"

Quinn cleared his throat. The other three men remained silent out of respect for Bo. "Only one major thing right now," Quinn replied. "Look over on that back wall. You'll see two large neon signs saying 'The Feed Bag' and 'The Dairy DeLite'. The two artistic arrangements were dropped-off Special Delivery at my home about a month ago. Bo had stipulated in his will that the pair of neon signs be donated to and hung inside the Corvette Diner in honor of the Diablos' reunion. Those signs hangin' over there are Bo's testament to the Diablos."

I turned and glanced at the wall mirror behind me and noticed several tears glistening in my eyes. As I wiped-away the drops, I turned and stared at the bright red and green Feed Bag and red and blue Dairy DeLite neon signs, both positioned on the Corvette Diner sidewall, directly above where the Japanese tourists were seated.

I felt like choking because my windpipe was constricting, but I still managed to say something genuine. "Bo may be gone, but a large part of him is still alive in all of us," I said, straight from my heart. "And I thank God I've had the privilege and the pleasure of knowing him."

"Truer words were never spoken," Carnie appropriately agreed.

"As sure as super-shit in a bull pit," Tinker vulgarly added.

Marcus Spellman was meandering-around on his DJ break. During the intermission, I sauntered-over to the jukebox. Chuck Berry's "Sweet Little Sixteen" was just finishing-up, but I wanted to escape to a decade other than the '50s to adequately express my mixed feelings.

The songs I selected were still "oldies" by definition, but the tunes had originated from a more recent decade. I felt so melancholy and so disconsolate that I wanted and needed recorded music to do my talking for me. Those bittersweet melodies I had selected best expressed my depressed, dismal mental state.

Before dinner was served, the five former Diablos sadly sang to the jukebox's presentations of Ben E. King's "Stand by Me"; James

Taylor's "You've Got a Friend", and Bill Withers bittersweet rendition of "Lean on Me". We turned all three numbers into solemn dirges, and to our utter astonishment, all of the Corvette Diner's clientele, including the very impressed Japanese delegation, willingly joined-in on our formal Bo Jalonec' tribute.

After dinner, the five of us decided to get "ripped" at a nearby bar. We used to refer to ourselves as "Alcoholics Synonymous" back in Levittown, and San Diego was a great placid setting to rekindle our past association. After two hours of *Southern Comforts* on the rocks and "double screwdrivers" as "chasers", we were becoming a tad rowdy at a popular University Avenue bar, so we retired to 1028 Brookes Avenue to continue our nostalgic celebration of the past. Fortunately, I was still sober enough to drive my rented car over to Quinn's cozy residence.

Adrenaline must have been liberally flowing within our veins, because we all seemed to be enjoying great stamina. I showed the other guys the scar above my right wrist where the Dogwood Drive cop's mutt had bitten me. I had a second scar on my left ankle from the time Tinker and I were rolled-down the Bristol Street inside the rumbling trash barrel. Tinker showed everyone a scar the ruffian had received on his right elbow from when the bully tried scaling the slippery wall inside the Windsor Pharmacy's putrid cesspool. Quinn brought to our attention a big scar on his right shoulder that had been inflicted by Cummings during the memorable quarry fight. And Robbie showed a scar he had received when R.W. tried freeing himself from his Kamikaze bondage, upon his younger brother's brown wagon.

It was as if we all had to prove who we were to each other, and our various scars were our individual badges of honor, valid proof that we had survived myriad deadly encounters with the dreaded Kamikazes.

Even in my half-inebriated state of mind, I still observed that Quinn had retained his James Dean/Elvis sideburns and his neatly-groomed '50s greaser haircut. The other four of us looked like aging Norman Rockwell characters, exhibiting gray-hair and receding widows' peaks. Robbie, Carnie, and I had grown double chins and well-developed paunches, but Tinker had transformed into a veritable, contemporary-looking Ichabod Crane.

The five of us revellers talked all about people we had known back in '50s Levittown. We mentioned and discussed Hal Irving, Luigi, Domenick, Ace Roberts, Gene McCann, Slip Carson, Al Keller, and Jim Amari. We discussed Teddy, the *O'Doyle's* ice cream vendor, and Edgely Fire Chief Bradley, Father Malcolm, Brother Timothy, Coach Cocharan, Bristol Fire Chief Lou Pinto, Mr. Callahan, Chuckie and

Jimmy, Jake Mullins, Spits and Worm, Dave Evans, and finally Cummings and Bruno "Popeye" Messina.

Nostalgia and sentimentality dominated our hearts and minds. We were celebrating our disreputable past, and it seemed that Quinn's three extra bottles of "*Southern Comfort*" obtained from his liquor cabinet made us remember even more Levittown minutia.

And then later into our partying, we thoroughly discussed all of the places we had known along with the fantastic adventures that had occurred at each location. We fondly prattled about the Bingo games at the Edgely Fire Hall, the Dairy DeLite phone booth, the Carousel Grille, the Tullytown bridge overpass, and we even remembered the elevators and escalators at *Pomeroy's Department Store*.

After that lengthy conference had transpired, the former Diablos recalled how we had punished the hell out of Stanley Tezeeker and his brainiac egghead friends, and how we had triumphantly gotten more than even with Father Malcolm and with Brother Timothy over their disciplinary inquisitions at Cardinal Reagan High.

Next, the self-appointed Dogwood Hollow Levittown historians recollected the Kamikazes and reviewed what the "Killer Ks" had done to us at the Delaware Canal, at the *Delaware River,* at the Windsor Pharmacy, and at the Andalusia Drive-in.

Then, we laughed about how Susie and Patty had professionally double-crossed Popeye and Mullins at the Delaware Canal dirt road ambush, and we merrily talked about the Haines Road "machine of the gods" thrilling drag-race; about the blueberry farm rematch race, and about the Atlantic City Boardwalk.

And then finally, the buoyant reunion delegation focused on reviewing the Phil Jackson double-switch murder scam, and we verbally shared how Tinker had efficiently destroyed the whole fleet of Kamikaze cars after they Ks had rolled his filthy black '49 Plymouth into the murky Delaware Canal. And last but not least, the five of us conversed about Worm's tragic death, and about intrepid Sugar Ray Spellman's racial integration into Levittown.

But every time Bo Jalonec or the Feed Bag entered into our discussion, *their* distinctive names were held in great honor. Bo was edified with praise as if he was the Pope, and the Feed Bag was revered as if it was the sacred *Vatican.*

Chapter 57
"Several Final Surprises"

Seven in the morning chimed on Quinn's grandfather clock, and the five Diablo alumni were still reviewing the not-so-illustrious past. Quinn had scheduled an important luncheon for "one p.m." at the magnificent Hotel Del Coronado. We finally "shacked-out" on various available chairs, sofas, and beds. Only short four-hours of shuteye remained until we had to shower and shave for our aforementioned hotel lunch appointment.

Fortunately, I had brought-along a change of clothing in my rented red *Buick Skylark*. After waking, I washed, shaved, and changed into the summer suit that I had brought along.

Quinn drove us over to Coronado in his black '96 *Ford Taurus*. The driver explained that when Bo had heard of *his* disabilities, Jalonec had generously set-up a trust fund for Quinn' as part of *his* will. That wonderful revelation about Quinn's additional 'personal social security' payment made me reflect on what a truly benevolent individual Bo had been furtively concealing under his cute, facetious, frivolous facade.

As the *Taurus* was about to leave the Mission Hills section of San Diego, a carload of city punks pulled-up next to us at a traffic light. The young hooligans first stared and then began heckling us, probably thinking that we were a collection of middle-aged, defenseless wimps. The inner-city hoods were traveling in an old, green, rusty *Mustang* convertible. The modern-day 'greasers" seriously misinterpreted our senior citizen appearances (riding inside the black *Taurus*) as being easy prey.

"Hey old, dudes," the kid on the front passenger side yelled. "Bros', check out the nursin' home on wheels right next to us. Is there a doctor in the house to check your weak pulses?"

Obviously, the street punks had no idea what the idiots were initiating, or exactly whom they were messing with. Tinker and Carnie peered menacingly at their vile antagonists and were ready to play hardball offense.

"Are ya' old fogies or are ya' old farts?" hollered-over a second wise-ass kid sitting in the convertible's back seat.

"Ya' old jerks think you're bad, ridin' alongside us rappers," the driver mockingly bellowed-over. "You old creeps ain't got no cribs in the 'hood and are trespassin' into our turf!"

I studied the faces of the four wise guys and noticed that the toxic thugs had earrings and metal pieces pierced all over their all-too-visible features. I couldn't help thinking that the uncivilized urban hecklers were nothing more than modern Kamikazes on patrol, out to antagonize anyone and everyone they could abuse and aggravate. Their verbal challenges and taunts had effectively juiced-up Tinker and Carnie so much that Quinn's back seat passengers shot-out several nasty salvos of their own. The city punks looked startled that a group of old bucks would offer any resistance to their uncouth insolence.

"What's ya' old shits lookin' at?" the front passenger-side youth screamed in our direction.

"Nothin' much, Creep!" Carnie fired back. "If ya' jerk-weeds had two brains each, you'd all be twice as dumb as ya' are now!"

"Say what!" the totally-confused young freak shouted-back.

"My pal said ya' couldn't find your fuckin' anuses with a dozen telescopes, and ya' punks couldn't find your dicks with the same amount of microscopes!" Tinker exclaimed as Jeremy remembered an old Bo Jalonec punch line, but added a few derogatory expletives. "Have ya' snot-nosed junior jerk-offs been assholes all your mother fuckin' lives, or has it only happened recently?"

Tinker and Carnie were all motivated and ready to do physical battle if necessary. The occupants of the green rusty *Mustang* convertible looked shocked and baffled by their elderly critics' defiant audacity.

"Go suck a few wet ones!" Carnie screamed at our contemporary gang' adversaries, and obvious Kamikaze substitutes.

Tinker then quickly lit and hurled two cherry bombs into the open *Mustang* convertible. In an intense panic, the four baggy-pants' harassers leaped-out of their car, all shouting a flurry of exclamatory obscenities. The small bombs sizzled and exploded, but before the boys from the 'hood could hop back into their dilapidated auto', their beloved *Mustang,* which had been left in "Drive", began coasting forward down a hill.

The unmanned, rusty, green convertible drifted through a second crowded University Avenue intersection amidst honking horns, and then the runaway vehicle gained momentum as the auto rolled faster down the dip. The four urban idiots chased-after their wheels, but much to their horror, the car crashed through a guardrail and then careened down a steep embankment. After the *Mustang* tumbled into the deep canyon, it instantaneously burst into flames.

As Quinn drove slowly by the mortified and astonished quartet, Carnie told the *Taurus* driver to repeatedly blow his horn. "That's what ya' get for messin' around with a bunch of honkies!" the former Merc' Man yelled. "Next time, show more goddamned respect to your elders, especially if they're awesome crackers like us!"

Quinn sped-off in his black Ford as if University Avenue was Haines Road or Dogwood Drive. "Just like old times," the bodacious driver laughed. "Don't mess with the Diablos!"

"The cops will never believe that a group of decrepit senior citizens would ever do such a malicious thing to dangerous street punks," Tinker laughed. "It was fun teachin' those dumb barbarian fuck-heads a lesson in respect!"

I showed my skepticism for *their* actions by challenging Tinker and Carnie to apologize for their unbridled aggression. I claimed that the San Diego visitors should have just ignored the wise guy kids and should have set a good public example by quietly dismissing the name-calling and disrespect.

Tinker became very obstinate and upset with my liberal reasoning. "J.W., haven't ya' learned anything fuckin' important ever since Levittown? Those young assholes are just like the Kamikazes used to be. First, the urban punks abuse ya' verbally, and if ya' don't take a stand and defend yourself, next they'll kick your ass, and if ya' don't stop the shit-face bastards mouth spewin' then and there, they'll fuckin' kill ya' on the spot!"

I thought to myself that Tinker and Carnie were still practicing social Darwinism, where survival of the fittest and survival of the smartest prevailed. I decided to resurrect the past, rather than to argue the present. On the way to Coronado Island, I brought-up the subject of Phil Jackson, and *that* pertinent topic again got everyone talking on the same wavelength.

While the guys discussed the former Cardinal Reagan quarterback all the way to the San Diego waterfront, I thought about what each of my former companions had evolved into. Quinn had answered the call to military service; had honorably defended his country's principles in a dishonorable war, and his unjust fate was to be partially paralyzed for life. Carnie had become a slick talking auto' tools salesman, traveling with his briefcase of catalogs from town to town like a contemporary Professor Harold Hill, usually with a cigarette in his mouth. Robbie Wilkinson had become a dentist and had done quite well for himself. Tinker had gone into the scrap iron business, and was in his own right, a blue-collar millionaire.

Jeremy was the only member of the former Diablos' brain trust that had remained in Bucks County. According to his boastful statements, J. F. operated his very profitable business out of Doylestown. Since Carnie's letter, besides mine, was the only one remaining in Quinn's Bristol Post Office box on July 1, I had presumed that something might have happened to *him* and not to Bo Jalonec. I had figured at the time that Jokes had already been to Bristol and had gotten *his* reunion confirmation letter. But since Bo had passed-away from leukemia in the summer of '94, Quinn had never written him a July 1st letter. officially announcing and confirming the San Diego celebration.

On the remaining way to Coronado, we had time to stop at *Seaport Village* along the panoramic San Diego waterfront. We strolled in and out of various souvenir shops, working up appetites for our highly anticipated feast at the *Hotel Del Coronado.* Even though we were still suffering from mild hangovers, the former Diablos still managed to fill-in some missing pieces to our ignoble Levittown pasts.

"Tink," I said to my backseat riding companion. "I'm glad that you and Bo both got into lucrative business niches."

"There's only one fuckin' difference," Tinker austerely and crassly replied. "I'm alive to enjoy my goddamned money. And if ya' was half as smart as me, J.W., ya' woulda' never became a stupid public-school teacher. If ya' hadn't done that shit-brain job all those wasted years, ya' would be a multi-millionaire today, just like me."

At that particular moment, I wished that Bo was still alive, and that Tinker had been the one buried six-feet-under. 'Why should the good be the first to push up daisies?' I thought. 'In many respects, fate is very cruel and unfair!'

Precisely at high noon, Quinn drove his shiny black *Ford Taurus* out of the *Seaport Village* parking area. Soon, we were ascending the spectacular, curved *Coronado Bridge.* Being from the East Coast, I was surprised that only cars with a driver (and no passengers) had to pay a crossing toll. The intelligent practice obviously encouraged car-pooling. I astutely fathomed that California was a trend-setting state, keeping a full decade ahead of its East Coast counterparts.

I had to marvel at the stately *Hotel Del Coronado*, a splendid piece of Victorian architecture. The quite elegant structure featured very impressive red-roofed towers and spires. The awesome building was a tribute to a bygone age of cultural refinement, that complemented elaborate craftsmanship.

Quinn pulled into the opulent-looking edifice's parking area, where a courteous valet took the car keys. After touring-around the magnificent mahogany-paneled main lobby of the century-old palace, we entered a buffet line inside the luxurious hotel's grand dining room. While waiting to be served, the five of us talked about Cummings, about the pernicious Kamikazes, about the wild and crazy Renegades, and about the mischievous Diablos. I hadn't relished such terrific camaraderie since the old and glorious '50s Feed Bag days.

After we forced-down some delectable baked Alaska for dessert, Quinn announced that he had "a final surprise" to show us. We stepped out of a side entrance of the very impressive Victorian castle, and there, right before our eyes were mint-condition replicas of the Diablos' former street machines. There was a black '42 Ford coupe; a black '49 Mercury James Dean Special; a black '49 Plymouth; a green and cream '57 Chevy BelAir, and a blue and white '55 Olds 88.

"Guys," Quinn declared like an honest politician. "These cars are gifts given to us by Bo in his will. J.W., the green and cream '57 Chevy is all yours!"

Emotion surged from my heart directly up to my throat and eyes. I was overwhelmed that Bo Jalonec would still remember me after all those years of separation. The other Diablos, including Tinker, were equally as choked-up as I was. Inside each car was a black leather jacket with "Diablos" attractively painted on the back, along with authentic pairs of accompanying denim' blue jeans and engineer boots. In Bo's final days on this wonderful earth, he too had recalled the unbelievable events and the fond friendships we had shared from 1957 to '59. Those exquisite tokens in the form of Diablos' automobiles were *his* final wish and testament to his '50s friends.

A letter was addressed to me on the front seat of the '57 Chevy. I hastily opened the envelope. The message inside read:

Words,

Please remember always, *Black Leather and Blue Denim*. May God bless everything you attempt and do. And J.W., I'll see ya' in Heaven! Good bye, good buddy!

Your Diablo friend forever,
Bo Jalonec
July 1, 1994

I will always cherish my very special '57 Chevy; my black leather jacket; my blue denim jeans, and my new engineer boots for the rest of my life, just like I will treasure the memory of Bo's companionship deep in my heart. The others had received similar letters and gifts, and all I could say was, "God bless and rest his good soul!" Robbie, who was given the '55 Olds, which was just like the one driven by Ace Roberts, echoed my sincere sentiments. Needless to verbally express, we were all deeply moved by Bo's exceptional generosity. Feeling uncomfortable with the excessive emotion he was feeling, Quinn commanded, "Let's split!"

The '42 Ford coupe led a caravan of antique cars eastward over the *Coronado Bridge,* back towards downtown San Diego. Two things greatly disturbed me as I drove along, with my new-found green and cream '57 Chevy being second in the cavalcade. The two thoughts were Bo's death and Quinn's walking cane. Both ideas contradicted the vitality and strength each true friend had exhibited back in the '50s.

I glanced into my rear-view mirror and admired Carnie in his replica James Dean Special; and Tinker seated in his *clean* and shiny black '49 Plymouth, and Robbie in the blue and white '55 Oldsmobile 88, all forming a very nifty chain of wonderful vintage vehicles.

Quinn unexpectedly stopped his '42 Ford at the crown of the *Coronado Bridge* and motioned for me to do likewise. He and I quickly exited our classic cars, when our host pointed at a familiar object drifting in the channel under the bridge's superstructure.

My eyes focused to receive and distinguish more accurate visual information. My pupils immediately recognized the Venezuelan ship *Caracas,* which unlike me and the other Diablos, appeared to be not a minute older than it had looked when it had first been passing by Bristol in 1954. Then, I smiled, recalling Angie and Bubbles having their unexpected rendezvous with the *Delaware River.*

Soon, Carnie, Tinker, and Robbie also exited their superb machines and joined Quinn and me. I offered Quinn my assistance, but he refused, preferring to make it to the bridge's railing on his own with his reliable cane.

A massive traffic snarl soon formed atop the bridge in both directions. Some upset drivers were angrily honking their horns, but we paid the annoyed, inconvenienced motorists little heed. I knew from 1954 newspaper accounts that the *Caracas* had been fabricated in the early '30s. Bo Jalonec had first seen the noble ship on the *Delaware* after the Kamikazes had chased us to the rowboat that *he* had taken-out into the river during our disastrous fishing expedition. Later, on that early-March day in '59, Bo applied a word he had learned from a West Catholic High School English class vocabulary list. "J.W.," Jalonec had casually told me. "That ship is archaic." And then I recalled Jokes immediately stating, "We can't have *our cake* and eat it, too!" 'How true and prophetic those memorable words were and still are,' I appreciatively thought. 'Especially with Bo then being a deceased multi-millionaire.'

The five of us gazed over the *Coronado Bridge's* sturdy railing as we shockingly peered-down at that final link with our Diablos' ignominious past. The only things I could think of was the time when the *Caracas* had nearly killed and drowned Bo and me in the rowboat incident on the *Delaware,* and the fact that now Bo was dead and could not share *that* wonderful moment on the *Coronado Bridge* with his former 1950s Diablos' buddies.

When the *Caracas* finally and majestically sailed under the span, traffic had become gridlocked a full mile in both directions. Soon, a plethora of California motorists copied our fine example. The curious spectators observed the *Caracas* below, viewing the spectacle from the *Coronado Bridge,* exactly like the *East Coast* travelers had done six-months-earlier on July 1st from the narrow, two-lane *Burlington-Bristol* span.

When the noble ship had completed its slow passage into port, everyone standing and watching broke-out into a spontaneous cheer. The native Californians thought that they had merely been applauding a grand old vessel passing under the landmark *Coronado Bridge*. The five former Dogwood Hollow gang members knew otherwise. We were paying a sentimental salute to Bo Jalonec, and in the process, also enacting a nostalgic tribute to our remarkable, unforgettable, '50s Diablos' adventures.

About the Author

Jay Dubya is the pen name for John Wiessner and also his initials (J.W.). John is a retired New Jersey public school English teacher, having taught the subject for thirty-four years. John lives in Hammonton, New Jersey with wife Joanne and the couple has three grown sons.

Jay Dubya has written other adult fiction besides *Black Leather and Blue Denim, A '50s Novel* and its sister book *The Great Teen Fruit War, A 1960 Novel. Frat' Brats, A '60s Novel* completes the "coming of age" action/adventure trilogy. *Pieces of Eight, Pieces of Eight, Part II, Pieces of Eight, Part III and Pieces of Eight, Part IV* are four collections of eight novellas each that are available in e-book formats. *Nine New Novellas, Nine New Novellas, Part II, Nine New Novellas, Part III* and *Nine New Novellas, Part IV* are also sci-fi/paranormal stories written in the spirit of the *Pieces of Eight* series. And *Ron Coyote, Man of La Mangia* is an adult-oriented satire/parody on Miguel Cervantes' *Don Quixote.*

The Wholly Book of Genesis and *The Wholly Book of Exodus* are adult satirical rewrites of the first two book of the *Bible*. The four books of the *Thirteen Sick Tasteless Classics* series are satirical/parody rewrites of famous short/story/novella literature. *Mauled Maimed Mangled Mutilated Mythology* and *Fractured Frazzled Folk Fables and Fairy Farces (Parts I and II)* are also adult rewrites of famous legends and children's stories.

Jay Dubya also has written a trilogy of young adult fantasy novels, *Pot of Gold, Enchanta* and *Space Bugs, Earth Invasion.* All three books are available in e-formats and hardcover/paperback versions. *The Eighteen Story Gingerbread House* is a collection of eighteen imaginative children's stories. *So Ya' Wanna' Be A Teacher* is a humorous but informative autobiographical account of Jay Dubya's thirty-four-year teaching career.

Jay Dubya likes '50s music and he also enjoys pop songs by the Beatles, the Beach Boys, Fleetwood Mac, *ELO*, the Eagles, the Rolling Stones, John Mellencamp, and John Fogarty. When not listening to pop' music Jay Dubya likes watching *76ers* basketball and *Phillies* and *Yankees* television baseball games.

Author Biography

Born in Hammonton, NJ in 1942, John Wiessner had attended St. Joseph School up to and including Grade 5. After his family moved from Hammonton to Levittown, Pa in 1954, John attended St. Mark School in Bristol, Pa. for Grade 6, St. Michael the Archangel School in Levittown for Grades 7 and 8 and then Immaculate Conception School, Levittown, Pa. for Grade 9. Bishop Egan High School, Levittown PA. was John's educational base for Grades 10 and 11, and later in 1960, the aspiring author graduated from Edgewood Regional High, Tansboro, NJ. John then next attended Glassboro State College, where he was an announcer for the school's baseball games and also read the nightly news and sports over WGLS, GSC's radio station.

John Wiessner had been primarily an English teacher in the Hammonton Public School System for 34 years, specializing in the instruction of middle school language arts. Mr. Wiessner was quite active in the Hammonton Education Association, loyally serving in the capacities of Vice-President, then building representative, and finally, teachers' head negotiator for a period of 7 years. During his lengthy teaching career, John had been nominated into "Who's Who among American Teachers" three times. He also was quite active giving professional workshops at schools around South Jersey on the subjects of creative writing and the use of movie videos to motivate students to organize their classroom theme compositions.

In addition, John Wiessner was very active in community service, being a past President of the Hammonton Lions Club, where he also functioned for many years as the club's Tail-Twister, Vice-President and Liontamer. John had been named Hammonton Lion of the Year in 1979 and in 2009 received the prestigious Melvin Jones Fellow Award, the highest honor a Lion can receive.

John also was a successful businessman, starting with being a Philadelphia Bulletin newspaper delivery boy for two-years in the late 1950s in Levittown, Pennsylvania. After his family moved back to New Jersey in 1959, John worked at his grandparents and his parents' farm markets, Square Deal Farm (now Ron's Gardens in Hammonton) and Pete's Farm Market in Elm, respectively. He later managed his wife's parents' farm market, White Horse Farms in Elm for three summers.

Also in a business capacity, for 16 summers starting in 1967 John Wiessner had co-owned Dealers Choice Amusement Arcade on the Ocean City, Maryland boardwalk and also co-owned the New Horizon Tee-Shirt Store for eight summers (1973-'81) on the Rehoboth Beach, Delaware boardwalk. In addition, "Jay Dubya" was a co-owner of

Wheel and Deal Amusement Arcade, Missouri Avenue and Boardwalk, Atlantic City. And then, for 18 summers beginning in 1986, John had been the Field Manager in charge of crew-leaders for Atlantic Blueberry Company (the world's largest cultivated blueberry farm), both the Weymouth and Mays Landing Divisions.

After retiring from teaching in 1999, writing under the pen name Jay Dubya (his initials), John Wiessner became the author of 75 books in the genre Action/Adventure Novels, Sci-Fi/Paranormal Story Collections, Adult Satire, Young Adult Fantasy Novels and also Non-Fiction Books. His books exist in hardcover, in paperback and in popular Kindle and Nook e-book formats.

In January of 2022, John Wiessner (Jay Dubya) was nominated into Marquis Who's Who in America, and in April of that same year, was one of nine distinguished Who's Who in America members honored with receiving Lifetime Achievement Awards, all nine sharing a news article of recognition appearing in the Wall Street Journal.

Google: Jay Dubya books
Google: Walmart, Jay Dubya

www.ingramcontent.com/pod-product-compliance
Lightning Source LLC
Chambersburg PA
CBHW020556310726
48979CB00008B/1237/J

* 9 7 8 1 9 3 1 9 2 1 7 6 3 *